MW00757788

PRAISE FOR THE NOVELS OF SIMON R. GREEN

Blue Moon Rising

"This fantasy adventure is one readers will savor and enjoy for a long time to come."
—Rave Reviews

"Delightful."
—*New York Daily News*

"Easily my favorite of Simon Green's fantasy novels."
—Chronicles

Beyond the Blue Moon
Chosen as One of the Year's Best Books by Chronicles

"I was completely caught up in their adventure and read it intently and impatiently until they finally achieved their destiny. If they're making fantasy adventure much better than this, I don't know about it."
—Chronicles

"Fans of Hawk & Fisher will particularly enjoy the revelations about the deadly duo's background, and, as always, Green provides plenty of spectacular violence and some spectacular wonders. Solving the mystery is almost incidental, but that doesn't really matter in this engrossing adventure."
—*Locus*

"Continuing the adventures of a pair of charmingly roguish and intensely honorable heroes, this fast-moving, wisecracking sequel to *Blue Moon Rising* belongs in most fantasy collections."
—*Library Journal*

"Very satisfying."
—*Wiltshire Times* (UK)

"One of the best fantasy books I've read all year . . . a truly enjoyable and fulfilling sequel. . . . I can't recommend the book highly enough."
—The Green Man Review

continued . . .

DON'T MISS THE ADVENTURES OF
HAWK & FISHER

SIX ACTION-PACKED NOVELS IN
TWO OMNIBUS EDITIONS

Swords of Haven
and
Guards of Haven

In the dark city of Haven, where everything's for sale, City Guard cops Hawk & Fisher cannot be bought. A husband-and-wife team with fast blades and even faster mouths who dare to cleanse Haven's corrupted soul. Together, they are the perfect crime busters . . . with a touch of magic.

The war against crime is forever.

"I think what charmed me about it is the absolutely unabashed manner in which Green has copied the style of almost any current cop/detective/sleuth TV show. . . . The situations and dialogue are straight off your current screen."
—*Asimov's Science Fiction*

"Green's very different approach to writing fantasy adventure—bearing a strong resemblance to the private eye novel—works surprisingly well."   —Chronicles

"Simon R. Green's books are fun books that grab you, suck you in, and don't let you go. They are always fun, and the Hawk & Fisher books are no exception. Hawk and Fisher are a couple of honest, straight-talking, tough-as-nails guards who use steel as often as wits to keep themselves out of trouble. They bully their way through situations, often just letting their reputations work their magic. The plots are straightforward, with just enough of a twist to keep you guessing until the end. If you've read and enjoyed Green's other books, you don't want to miss these books. If you haven't read Green before, *Swords of Haven* is a good way to get a taste of his style of writing."   —SF Site

"Green has a marvelous gift of leavening grim situations with wicked wit, and the intrigues are intricative enough to leave even the most practiced mystery solver puzzling. A stormer of a series. Fine stuff."   —Prism UK

Also by

Simon R. Green

ONCE
IN A
BLUE
MOON

SIMON R. GREEN

A ROC BOOK

ROC
Published by the Penguin Group
Penguin Group (USA) LLC, 375 Hudson Street,
New York, New York 10014

USA | Canada | UK | Ireland | Australia | New Zealand | India | South Africa | China
penguin.com
A Penguin Random House Company

First published by Roc, an imprint of New American Library,
a division of Penguin Group (USA) LLC

First Printing, January 2014

Copyright © Simon R. Green, 2014
Penguin supports copyright. Copyright fuels creativity, encourages diverse voices, promotes free
speech, and creates a vibrant culture. Thank you for buying an authorized edition of this book and
for complying with copyright laws by not reproducing, scanning, or distributing any part of it in any
form without permission. You are supporting writers and allowing Penguin to continue to publish
books for every reader.

 REGISTERED TRADEMARK—MARCA REGISTRADA

LIBRARY OF CONGRESS CATALOGING-IN-PUBLICATION DATA:

Green, Simon R.
  Once in a blue moon/Simon R. Green.
    pages cm
  ISBN 978-0-451-41466-3 (pbk.)
  I. Title.
  PR6107.R44O53 2014
  823'.92—dc23   2013021844

Printed in the United States of America
10 9 8 7 6 5 4 3 2 1

Set in Adobe Garamond
Designed by Spring Hoteling

PUBLISHER'S NOTE
This is a work of fiction. Names, characters, places, and incidents either are the product of the
author's imagination or are used fictitiously, and any resemblance to actual persons, living or dead,
business establishments, events, or locales is entirely coincidental.

ONCE
IN A
BLUE MOON

ONCE IN A BLUE MOON, SOMETHING MAGICAL HAPPENS…

It's been a hundred years since the Demon War. Since Prince Rupert and Princess Julia of legend rode into the Darkwood to defeat the terrible Demon Prince and banished him from the world of men. A hundred years since the Blue Moon shed its awful Wild Magic over the Forest Kingdom.

Many things have changed, and many have not. But we all know: fate does so love an anniversary.

ONE

NO ONE EVER ESCAPES THE PAST

The Dutchy of Lancre's greatest pride, problem, and most profitable tourist attraction is the Hawk and Fisher Memorial Academy. Also known, less formally, as the Hero Academy. Founded some seventy-five years ago by Captains Hawk and Fisher, late of the City Guard in some less than salubrious city port down in the depths of the Southern Kingdoms. There are many stories about Hawk and Fisher, apparently the only honest guards in that city; all of the stories are of a resolutely heroic nature, though not always particularly nice, or suitable for mixed company. But apparently these two venerable warriors reached an age where they preferred teaching to doing, and so—the Academy.

Hawk and Fisher spent many happy and informative years teaching young men and women how to be warriors, got everything up and running, and then they moved on and were never seen again. Presumably they went back to being heroes, and died alone and bloody in some far-off place, fighting for some cause they believed in. Because that's what usually happens to heroes. The Hero Academy kept their names, and many of the traditions they established, including that all the married warriors who came in to run the place took the names Hawk and Fisher for as long as they stayed. Out of respect for the original founders, or possibly to simplify merchandising rights. Either way, there have been a great many Hawks and Fishers through the years.

For decades, hopeful parents have sent their more troublesome sons and daughters to the Hawk and Fisher Memorial Academy, from all sorts of countries, cities, and stations in life. To learn how to be heroes. For a great many reasons—fame and fortune, of course, duty and honour . . . and sometimes just because the hopeful applicants feel they have something to prove to their parents. Of the many who feel called, only a few are chosen every year; but it doesn't stop them from coming, by the hundreds and sometimes thousands. Some are hopeful; some are hopeless. The Academy holds regular Auditions at the beginning of each term to sort out the wheat from the chaff, in a similarly destructive process. The Auditions are bloody hard, and often very bloody, and no one gets to moan about the decisions. Even if the applicants leave with less dignity or fewer limbs than they arrived with. Because the Hero Academy believes that if you can be dissuaded or frightened off, it's better to find that out right at the beginning. The Academy's tutors are strict but fair . . . but strict.

The Hawk and Fisher Memorial Academy teaches people how to fight, and what to fight for, and how to stay alive while doing it. The Academy provides classes in weaponry, magic, lateral thinking, and really dirty tricks, and every year it turns out a whole bunch of highly motivated young people determined to go forth in the world and make it a better place. The world shows its appreciation every year by sending assassins to kill the current Hawk and Fisher and their staff, and if at all possible burn down the entire Academy and salt the earth around it.

But that's politics for you.

On a day that at first seemed much like any other day, Hawk and Fisher were out taking an early-morning constitutional, strolling unhurriedly across the great open plain that surrounded the Academy. Most of it was dry, dusty ground, studded with just enough awkwardly protruding rocks that you had to keep your eyes open and your wits about you, and punctuated here and there with optimistic outbursts of grey-green shrub. Thick woodland marked the western horizon, and the DragonsBack mountain ridges the eastern. Not much to look at, and even less to do, out on the plain, which helped concentrate the minds of the students wonderfully.

On that particular morning the sun was barely up, the sky was an overcast grey, and the air was so still that even the smallest sound seemed to carry forever. Hawk and Fisher wandered along, side by side, their movements so familiar to each other they were practically synchronised. They looked like they had a long history together, most of it concerned with organised violence. They looked like they belonged together, and always would be.

Hawk was well into middle age, a short and stocky man with a broad face, thinning grey hair, and a spreading bald patch he was growing increasingly touchy about. He wore a simple soldier's tunic over smooth leather leggings, and rough, functional boots. His cool grey eyes were calm and steady, and gave the strong impression that they missed nothing. He limped slightly, as though favouring an old wound, but given that the limp had a tendency to transfer itself from one leg to the other and back again without warning, no one took it particularly seriously. He carried a great axe at his side instead of a sword, by long tradition. He studied the world with a thoughtful, watchful gaze to make sure it wouldn't try to jump out and surprise him. Everything in the way he moved and held himself suggested he'd been a soldier or mercenary in his previous life, but he never spoke of it. Tradition demanded that all the Hawks and Fishers leave their pasts behind, along with their original names, when they took over control of the Hero Academy.

Fisher was also advancing into middle age, and with even less enthusiasm than her husband. She was of barely average height and more than average weight, with short-cropped grey hair, a jutting beak of a nose, and a brief, flashing smile. She wore the same simple tunic and leggings as Hawk, and carried a long sword in a rune-carved scabbard down her back. She studied the world with fierce green eyes, in a way that suggested the world had better not give her any trouble if it knew what was good for it. A potential student who claimed to be a Bladesmaster, and therefore unbeatable with a sword in his hand, once told Fisher to her face that a woman's place was in the home, and especially the kitchen. Fisher laughed herself sick, and then duelled him up the hall and back down again, beat the sword out of his hand, kicked him in the nuts, and rabbit-punched him before he hit the ground. And then sent him home strapped to a mule, riding backwards.

No one messed with Hawk and Fisher.

Stumbling along behind them, grumbling constantly under his breath, was the Administrator. He was not a morning person, and didn't give a damn who knew it. Normally at this very early hour of the day, he would have been sitting alone at a table in the kitchens, holding on to a mug of mulled wine with both hands, as though that was all that was holding him up, and giving the sudden-death glare to anyone who tried to talk to him. But it was the first day of the new autumn term, the Auditions were to be held at midday, and Hawk and Fisher had been very insistent that they wanted to talk to him somewhere extremely private; so here he was. Taking an early-morning stroll that was undoubtedly good for him, and hating every moment of it. Birds were singing happily in the sky above, and every now and again the Administrator would raise his weary head and look at them with simple and uncomplicated loathing.

If the Administrator had ever been blessed with anything as common as a real name and a proper background, no one knew about it. He'd arrived at the Academy some forty years earlier as just another student, bluffed and bullied his way onto the staff, and lost no time in proving himself invaluable at taking care of all the dull, soul-destroying but unfortunately wholly necessary administrative work that no one else wanted to do. All he had to do was threaten to leave, and he was immediately awarded a substantial pay increase and a straightforward assurance that no one gave a damn what his real name might be or where he'd come from.

The Administrator was tall but heavily stooped, and tended to stride through the Academy corridors as though he personally bore all the cares of the world on his narrow shoulders. And wanted everyone to know it. He wore stark black and white formal clothes, comfortable shoes, and an old floppy hat that didn't suit him. Though given the appalling state of the thing, it would be hard to name anyone it would have suited. He was a long and stretched-out gangly sort, all knees and elbows. His face was grim and bony, he frowned as though it were a competitive sport, and on the few occasions when he was seen to smile, everyone knew it meant someone somewhere was in really big trouble.

He basically ran the Hero Academy, from top to bottom, and had done so under many Hawks and Fishers.

He raised the volume of his grumbling, just to let Hawk and Fisher know he hadn't forgiven them, kicked noisily at the dusty ground before him, and scowled around at the world as though daring any of it to get too close. Hawk and Fisher finally came to a halt, at the top of a long ridge giving an uninterrupted view out across the plain. The Administrator crashed to a halt beside them, and let out a loud groan that might have been either simple relief or a plea for sympathy. He put both hands on the small of his back and straightened up slowly, while his spine made loud protesting noises. Hawk and Fisher exchanged amused glances. They made a lot of allowances for the Administrator. They had to; it was either that or run like fun every time they saw him approaching. The Administrator rotated his shoulders, slowly and individually, and they made ominous creaking noises.

"All right," said Hawk. "You're just showing off now."

"You know nothing about backs! Nothing!" snarled the Administrator. "They should give you a handbook, the moment you hit forty, warning you of all the terrible things that are going to go wrong with your body as you head into middle age. It should be full of useful diagrams and helpful advice, and detailed notes on which drugs are the best and have the least embarrassing side effects. I'm a martyr to my spine." He sniffed loudly, and looked coldly out across the open plain. "Why are we out here, at this indecently early hour of the morning? God created hours like these specifically to break the spirits of people dumb enough to get out of bed before they were meant to. Everybody knows that."

"There are things we need to discuss, you miserable old scrote," Hawk said cheerfully. "Important things."

"The kinds of things best discussed where there's absolutely no one around to overhear," said Fisher.

"You haven't killed anyone important again, have you?" said the Administrator, wincing. "You know how much extra paperwork that means."

"We've been good," said Hawk. "Mostly."

"Right," said Fisher, scowling. "It's been ages since I got into a decent scrap. I must be getting old. Or civilised. Don't know which of the two disturbs me more."

"Then what is so important I had to be hauled from my nice warm bed and thoroughly disgusting dream?" snapped the Administrator.

"What brought you here, originally?" said Hawk. And there was something in the way he said it that made the Administrator give the question more than usual attention.

"My parents thought I had the makings of a master swordsman," he said gruffly, "because I had a habit of getting into trouble and then cutting my way out of it. They thought I might be Bladesmaster material. I knew better. I knew I wasn't a warrior, let alone a hero—just a man with a short temper and no real sense of self-preservation. I said so, loudly, but no one listened. My father put me on a horse, handed me a bag of silver, and sent me out into the world to find my place. Maybe he did understand about me, after all.

"I came here after I'd tried everywhere else. The previous Administrator had let things get into a real mess, so I pushed him down some stairs, several times, and took over. The Hawk and Fisher back then knew exactly what I'd done, but they gave me a chance. Told me I had six months to prove myself, or they'd have the Magic Tutor turn me into a small green hopping thing. Took me less than three. Now, some forty years later, I'm still here, and I'll be here till they carry me out feet first."

"Are you happy here?" said Fisher.

The Administrator looked at her for a while, as though he didn't quite understand the question. "I never wanted anything else. I'm part of a legend, and that will do me."

"Did you never want marriage, family, children—things like that?" said Hawk.

"Marriage isn't for everyone," the Administrator said firmly. "People just get in the way when I've got important lounging around to be getting on with. My fellow staff are all the family I ever needed, or wanted." He looked at Hawk and Fisher thoughtfully. "You've been here, what, ten years now? As Hawk and Fisher? And you never once showed any interest in my personal life before. So why now?"

"Because it's time for a change," said Hawk. He looked out across the plain. "Look at the Tree. Isn't it magnificent?"

The Administrator felt like saying a great many things, but the conversation seemed important enough that he played along. For the moment. They all looked out across the open plain, at the one thing of importance it contained: the ancient and mighty Millennium Oak. The biggest tree in the world; a thousand feet tall and probably more, with a trunk very nearly half as wide, and massive layers of branches reaching out a lot farther than was naturally possible. Just one of many clues, if its sheer size wasn't enough, that the Millennium Oak was a magical thing. Its cracked and crinkled bark glowed a dull golden, and so did its massive bristling foliage. The Tree dominated the landscape, as though its overpowering presence had sucked most of the life out of the dry and dusty plain. It rose up and up into the sky, its topmost branches disappearing into the clouds. There were climbers of renown who'd tackled every mountain in the world but who wouldn't dare attempt an assault on the Millennium Oak. And not just because of its height. The Tree had a presence, and perhaps even a personality, and it didn't want to be climbed.

You could tell.

All around the Millennium Oak, the plain swept away for miles and miles, alone and deserted and untouched. If you travelled far enough to the west, you reached the wild woods. Perfectly ordinary trees, packed closely together, all the natural shades of brown and green, slamming right up against the edge of the plain as though the trees had met an invisible fence. All kinds of wildlife roamed the wild woods, but none of them ever ventured out onto the plain. They knew it wouldn't be healthy.

To the east, even more miles away, stretched the DragonsBack mountain ridge, tall and brutally ragged, marking the border between the Dutchy of Lancre and the Forest Kingdom. There were a great many stories about these mountains. Once, it was said, dragons made their homes in caves up and down the long ridge. Long and long ago. The caves were still there, unnaturally large and worryingly dark, but no one had seen a dragon in ages.

"The first Hawk and Fisher made a point of checking out the caves," said the Administrator. "They didn't find any dragons. Looked rather disappointed, or so I'm told. Long before my time, of course. There are songs and stories from the Demon War that say Princess Julia rode a dragon into battle against the demon hordes. The last sighting of a dragon in the world of men."

"You can't trust minstrels," said Hawk. "Never was a bard who wouldn't sacrifice the facts for a better rhyme."

"There are a hell of a lot of stories concerning the origins of the Millennium Oak," said Fisher. "Some of them so old and so strange they might even have some truth in them. When the wind moves between the branches, the leaves seem to move with a life of their own, and sometimes it sounds like voices. Something the Tree heard, long ago. But the words are from a language no one speaks anymore, or even recognises. A language of a people who no longer exist. So no one now can understand what it is the Tree is remembering. The Tree is *old* . . ."

"And birds of every species come here from all over the world," said Hawk. "Every shape and size, and all the colours you can think of, including some specimens long thought extinct . . . just to perch on the golden branches and sing to the Tree. They sing a thousand different songs, yet somehow they're always in harmony."

"Though you never see a woodpecker," said Fisher. "I think they sense they're not welcome."

"None of them are, when they're sounding off outside my bedroom window first thing in the morning," growled the Administrator. "Bloody dawn chorus. I've had to move my bedroom three times. I swear the bloody things are following me." He glared at Hawk. "Have we indulged in enough whimsy yet? Can I just say *I don't give a damn about any of this* in a loud and carrying voice, so we can finally get to the damned point?"

"The Millennium Oak is a wonder and a miracle," Hawk said firmly. "Haven't you ever wondered who it was that originally hollowed out the Tree's interior, to make hundreds of rooms and halls and interconnecting corridors, so long ago that no one now remembers who or why? Seventy-five years the Tree has been home to the Academy, and we still haven't occupied half the available rooms. A Tree with a city inside it. Who would have thought?"

"Not forgetting the city of tents that surrounds it," said Fisher. "All the student population, set out in ranks and circles round the trunk. I can see a dozen different flags from here, from countries near and far, flapping proudly in the breeze . . . Though I'm glad to see everyone is following tradition, and no one flag is set any higher than any other. I'd hate to have to go down there and punch someone. I really would."

"I did enjoy it when you set fire to the last flag that tried to flout tradition," said Hawk solemnly. "And the way you set fire to the flag's owner when he objected. In the end they had to wrap him in his own tent and roll him back and forth in the mud to put the flames out. He cried real tears."

"The Millennium Oak has never flown a flag," said Fisher. "The Tree is in the Dutchy, but not of it."

"Go back a couple of hundred years," said Hawk, "and there is the story of one Duke who tried to occupy the Tree. To make a point, over who was really in charge here. The Duke led his army of some three hundred heavily armed men inside the Tree; and none of them ever came out. We've never even found a trace of the bodies. The Tree's roots dig deep, and no one has ever sought to discover how deep, or what nourishes them."

"I think we should take a tour through the tent city on the way back," said Fisher. "Show the students we take an interest. I mean, yes, they're expected to provide for and look after themselves; that's the whole point of not letting them take it easy inside the Tree. Self-sufficiency starts at home, and all that. But it wouldn't hurt to remind the students we're still keeping an eye on them."

"Someone's started a still again, haven't they?" said Hawk. "What's the matter? You not getting your fair share?"

"It's the principle of the thing," said Fisher.

"Won't be long now before the Auditions begin," said Hawk. "Look at the shadow."

The thousand-foot Millennium Oak cast one hell of a long shadow, and the tents that lay within it were always markedly cooler than those without. So the older and more experienced students struck their tents inside the shadow during the hot summer months, and outside it during the winter. All the newer students thus had no choice but to do the exact opposite, and dream of better times to come as they sweated through the summer and shivered through the winter. And of course once a year there was a mass migration and re-setting of tents, as the two sides swopped places to follow the shifting seasons. This usually involved a certain amount of armed skirmishing, as certain individuals disagreed as to which side they were properly a part of. It was all very good-natured, and usually ended at first blood. Because students who couldn't or wouldn't follow the rules and traditions of the Hawk and Fisher Memorial Academy didn't last long. Hawk and Fisher saw to that.

It had to be said: the students didn't seem to mind living in the tent city. It was all very communal, with lots of eating and drinking and singing, and giggling under canvas. There were the wild woods to hunt in, several streams in which to fish and wash and perform necessary functions (and woe betide anyone who didn't keep those uses strictly separate), and several towns beyond the woods, for more sophisticated fare. Often at dirt-cheap prices—the merchants indulged the students because they attracted the tourists. Who were, of course, quite properly soaked for every penny they had. That was what they were for.

No tourists ever approached the Tree, or even the tent city. The Tree didn't allow such over-familiarity.

The Administrator sighed deeply, and massaged his lower back with both hands. It was clear that whatever Hawk and Fisher had brought him all the way out here to discuss, they were determined to take their own sweet time about getting to the point. So he gritted his teeth, plotted future revenges, and played along.

"I have often wondered why the original Hawk and Fisher came to the Dutchy of Lancre," he said, "to set up their Academy. We're not exactly a big or famous country, after all."

"I think that was probably the point," said Hawk. "The DragonsBack ridge does a very good job of separating Lancre from the Forest Kingdom, and there's only an ocean on the other side."

"Far from everyone else, and protected by perfect natural defences," said Fisher. "They couldn't have picked a better bolt-hole if they'd tried."

And that was when they both stopped and looked directly at the Administrator, who felt a sudden chill run through him as he found himself the target of their cool, thoughtful gaze. The Administrator decided that whatever it was they wanted to tell him, he almost certainly wouldn't be better off for knowing.

"It's time," said Fisher.

"Time we were moving on," said Hawk.

The Administrator nodded slowly. "Of course. That's what this has all been about. Looking at things for the last time, and saying goodbye."

"It's the first day of the new term," said Hawk. "Which means the biggest Auditions of the year. Our last before we move on, to make way for the next Hawk and Fisher."

"Will you miss us?" said Fisher.

The Administrator did them the courtesy of considering the question. "I suppose so. You've been here longer than most, almost ten years now. You've done good work. I was starting to think . . . Do you have to leave?"

"Yes," said Hawk. "People are starting to get too used to us."

"A new Hawk and Fisher will shake things up," said Fisher.

"All these years we've worked together," the Administrator said slowly, "and I can't say I know either of you any better than the day you arrived here to take over from the previous Hawk and Fisher. Of course, I can't say I really knew any of your predecessors any better. You always keep yourselves to yourselves."

"All part of being Hawk and Fisher," Hawk said easily. "We're here to be role models, not friends or family. It would undermine the legend and authority of the names if people could see just how ordinary we really are."

"And we did come here, after all, to leave our pasts behind," said Fisher.

"Except . . . you never really do escape your past," said Hawk. "It has a nasty habit of sneaking up on you from behind, when you least expect it."

Fisher looked at him. "You feeling your age?"

Hawk was looking out over the plain, his gaze far away. "It's cold early, this autumn."

Fisher moved in close beside him. "Are you . . . feeling something?"

"I don't know," said Hawk. "Maybe."

Fisher waited until she was sure he had nothing more to say, and then turned back to the Administrator, her face artificially cheery. "So, are you going to miss us?"

"Not if I aim properly," growled the Administrator. "I've seen Hawks and Fishers come, and I've seen them go. And all that matters is that they leave me alone, to get on with the work that really matters. Running the Academy efficiently. I will say . . . you have been less of a nuisance than most."

Fisher surprised him then, with a sudden bark of genuine laughter. "You soppy sentimental old thing, you. We know you do all the real work. And don't think we're not grateful. We'll authorise another raise for you before we go. Throw you a party, with a barrel of ale and a whole bunch of loose women. What do you say?"

The Administrator shuddered. "No. Thank you. Really. And if I want a raise, I'll just fix the books again."

"We've already arranged for our replacements," said Hawk. "They're on their way. Fisher and I will be leaving at the end of the week. We wanted to break the news to you first, so you can set the necessary procedures and protections in place, before the news spreads all over the Tree."

"Once the Auditions are over, we can start setting our affairs in order," said Fisher. "And then we'll be off. No point in hanging around. I hate long, drawn-out goodbyes."

"We've been here too long," said Hawk. "People are . . . getting used to us."

"I trust you'll make our replacements welcome?" said Fisher.

"Of course," said the Administrator, back on his dignity. "I always do. Got a special speech prepared, and everything. Mostly about staying out of my way, and what forms they have to fill in whenever they find it necessary to kill someone. I pride myself on having a good working relationship with every Hawk and Fisher. Do you . . . know where you're going?"

"We're still working on that," said Fisher. "But it's time for a change. You're right, Hawk. It is cold, for this early in the autumn. I can feel it in my bones."

Hawk and Fisher looked at each other, for a long moment. The Administrator could sense something moving between them that he wasn't a part of.

"I have this feeling," said Hawk, "that something bad is coming."

"Yes," said Fisher. "Something really bad."

"Well, yes," said the Administrator. "New students."

14

He didn't normally do jokes, but he felt a sudden need to change the mood.

They all managed a quiet laugh. Only to break off abruptly as a whole flock of dead birds fell out of the sky, plummeting to the ground all around them. The soft, flat sounds of small dead bodies hitting the ground was like a round of heartless applause. The Administrator almost jumped out of his skin as he realised what was happening, and then his heart lurched again as Hawk and Fisher drew their weapons with almost inhuman speed and moved to stand back-to-back, weapons held out before them, at the ready. But there was no attack, no obvious enemy. Just dead birds, dropping out of a calm and empty sky for no obvious reason. And then that stopped and all was still and quiet.

The Administrator realised he was wringing his hands. He could feel his heart beating painfully fast. Hawk and Fisher looked carefully around them, and only when they were sure there wasn't an enemy anywhere in sight did they relax, just a little, and put away their weapons. The Administrator got down on one knee, painfully slowly, ignoring the harsh creaking sounds from his joints. He was careful not to look at Hawk and Fisher. He tended to forget, until it became necessary for them to demonstrate, just how fast and dangerous they could be. That they were, in fact, highly experienced trained killers. He made himself concentrate on the bodies of the dead birds before him. He sniffed the air carefully but couldn't detect any scents out of the ordinary. He leaned forward and looked the small bodies over as thoroughly as he could, while being very careful not to touch anything. Their eyes were open, dark and unseeing, not a breath of movement anywhere, not a mark of violence on any of them.

"Not predators," said Hawk.

"Not natural predators, anyway," said Fisher.

"It's almost like someone's gone out of their way to give us a sign," said Hawk.

"They didn't have to shout," said Fisher.

"I'll send some of the witches out here to take a look," said the Administrator, straightening up again with a minimum of fuss. Exaggerating his various infirmities seemed small-minded in the face of so much casual death. As though some force or power had reached out and slapped the birds out of the air. Just because it could. He looked out across the plain, at the city of tents grouped around the Tree. "It could be one of the students, I suppose, showing off, but . . ."

"Yes," said Hawk. "But."

"Let some of the more advanced magic students investigate," said Fisher. "Be good practice for them. If nothing else."

The Administrator looked around him, at all the dead bodies scattered across the stony ridge. Dozens of the things. And then he looked sharply at Hawk and Fisher.

"Is there any chance this could be connected with your decision to leave so suddenly?"

"I don't see how," said Hawk. Which wasn't really an answer, and they all knew it.

"Some old enemy, caught up with you at last?" said the Administrator.

"Unlikely," said Fisher.

The Administrator glared at both of them. "There's something you're not telling me, isn't there?"

Hawk grinned broadly, a sudden but very real moment of affection. "More than you ever dreamed of, old friend."

"I think we should get back to the Millennium Oak," Fisher said briskly. "We have to prepare for the Auditions. Get ready to sort out the potential heroes and warriors from the deluded and the wannabes. One last time."

They turned away from the dead birds and made their way back down the stone ridge and onto the dry and dusty plain. The mystery of the dead birds would have to wait until after the Auditions. Because some things just couldn't wait. But it was silently understood among the three of them that this . . . matter wasn't over yet. The Administrator never let go of a problem once he'd sunk his teeth into it. Particularly if it posed any kind of threat to his beloved Academy.

"You don't always produce heroes," he said roughly. "Even the best students can let you down. The Black Prince of Land's End—he was one of yours, wasn't he?"

"Unfortunately, yes," said Fisher. "Hawk and I had to go all the way down there to sort him out personally."

"I know," said the Administrator, just a bit pointedly. "You were supposed to bring back an erring student, not a collection of bits in a box!
We're still getting dunning letters from the Land's End Council, demanding we pay for all the damage you caused, taking the Black Prince down!"

"You're not actually planning on paying them, are you?" said Fisher.

"Of course not! I'm just making the point that your problems don't
always stop just because you've killed your enemy."

"Exactly," said Hawk.

The Administrator decided he really didn't like the way Hawk said
that.

Hawk and Fisher made a point of walking back through the middle of
the tent city surrounding the Millennium Oak, instead of sticking
to the main paths, so they could talk with the students one last time. The
Administrator would have preferred to hurry back to the Tree so he could
make his report on the dead birds and set wheels in motion. But he made
himself slow his pace to that of Hawk and Fisher's because he wanted to
hear what they had to say. It wasn't that he suddenly distrusted them after
so many years of working together; it was more that the Administrator
didn't trust anyone.

The tents came in all sizes and all colours, like a ragged rainbow lying
scattered around the base of the Tree. There were small cooking fires all
over the place, and the delightful smells of a dozen different cuisines wafted
through the early-morning air. Heavily laden washing lines flapped between the tents, displaying more kinds of underwear than the mind could
comfortably cope with so early in the morning. Students ran back and
forth, laughing and chasing, or sat in small circles lacing up each other's
armour, or ran through exercise routines of exhausting thoroughness. No
one ever missed first class in the Millennium Oak. They'd all worked too
hard to earn their place.

Hawk and Fisher moved easily among the students, greeting a surprisingly large number by name, inquiring how they were doing and seeming
genuinely interested in the answers. The Administrator didn't join in.
Partly because his people skills were strictly limited, as he'd be the first to
admit, but mostly because he didn't give a damn. He cared about the

Academy's successes only after they'd left and were off doing suitably heroic things at a distance and were no longer his responsibility. He had been heard to say, quite loudly and in all apparent sincerity, that the Academy would be a lot easier to run if it weren't for all the damned students getting in the way.

Hawk and Fisher could feel his brooding presence at their backs but refused to be hurried. They kept moving, never actually stopping, because they knew if they did, a crowd would soon gather and they'd never get through. A large number of the newer students saw their presence as an opportunity to show off their various skills. An archer casually shot an apple off the head of a trusting friend, only to be immediately upstaged as another archer targeted an apple set between the thighs of an extremely trusting friend. The look in that particular young man's eyes was frankly terrified, but give him his due—he didn't flinch. Possibly because he didn't dare to. The archer made his shot successfully, and the friend left the apple pinned to the tree and walked quickly away. Probably to have a nice lie-down. Hawk and Fisher made a point of congratulating him as well as the archer.

They did pause briefly to observe an exhibition bout between two top-rank swordsmen, who courteously stopped at regular intervals to explain to the watching crowd exactly what they were doing, and how.

A young sorcerer, barely into his mid-teens, sat alone at a table, staring fixedly at the single piece of fruit set out on a platter before him. He concentrated, scowling till his eyebrows met and beads of sweat popped out on his forehead, and the apple before him changed into a lemon. And then into a pear. The piece of fruit transformed itself over and over again, but the student was clearly making hard work of it. Though basic transformations were always impressive, they often took more effort than they were worth. Practice does make perfect, however. Eventually. Hawk paid the young sorcerer a vague compliment, whereupon the sorcerer blushed happily, lost his concentration, and the apple exploded. Messily. All over him. Hawk and Fisher moved quickly on.

It seemed like everyone had some speciality they just had to show off. Students hovered uncertainly in midair, or juggled balls of flame, and one young witch danced a decorous waltz with an animated scarecrow. Hawk and Fisher smiled and nodded, and kept moving. They passed one young man struggling to set up his tent but making a real dog's breakfast of it. He finally lost patience with the whole flapping mess, stood back, and snapped his fingers sharply. The tent immediately set itself up: canvas stretched taut, wooden pegs digging deep into the ground, ropes twanging into place. Hawk nodded to Fisher.

"He shows potential . . ."

The tent burst into flames. The student burst into tears.

"Or perhaps not," said Fisher.

And that was when a cocky young bravo pushed his way through the crowd to stand before Hawk, blocking his way. The newcomer was a big, muscular sort, wearing chain mail that had been polished to within an inch of its life, and hefting a massive double-headed battleaxe. He struck an arrogant pose and looked Hawk up and down, his gaze openly contemptuous. Clearly he'd heard all the stories about Hawk and decided they were far too good to be true. He wanted to make an impression in a hurry.

"Time to show what you can really do, Hawk," he said loudly. "I am Graham Steel, of the Forest Kingdom, warrior from a long line of warriors. I don't need to hide behind the legend of another man's name. You want me to Audition for you? Well, I say let's do it right here, right now, where everyone can see."

Hawk looked at him thoughtfully. People were already starting to back away, if only to make sure they wouldn't get any blood on them. Hawk glanced at Fisher.

"There's always one, isn't there?"

"Make it quick," said Fisher. "You don't have time to play with him."

Steel raised his axe and started to say something provoking, and Hawk lunged forward so quickly he was just a blur. His axe was suddenly in his hand, and he was upon his opponent before the young man could do more than lift his axe up before him. Hawk's axe rose, came flashing down, and sheared right through the other axe's wooden shaft. Steel's hands were jarred open by the sheer force of the blow, and the two pieces of his axe fell from his hands and dropped to the ground. Hawk set the edge of his axe against Steel's throat. Steel stood very still, his empty hands twitching, as though they couldn't believe they were empty. His face was slick with sweat, and he would have liked to swallow, but he didn't dare, not with the axe at his throat. He'd never seen anyone move so fast . . . He tried to meet Hawk's eyes, so close to his, but couldn't. Hawk stepped back, put his axe away, and moved on, without saying anything. Steel flushed angrily at being so coldly dismissed. He whipped a slender dagger from a concealed sheath in his sleeve and went for Hawk's turned back. Fisher clubbed him down from behind with one blow from her sword's hilt. Steel crashed to the ground, and didn't move again, and Fisher walked right over him to catch up with Hawk. Who hadn't even glanced back. The Administrator hurried after them, shaking his head.

"Show-offs . . ."

They went back into the Millennium Oak through the main entrance, a massive arch carved deep into the golden trunk. Centuries' worth of intricate carving and decoration covered the inner walls, from a dozen countries and even more cultures, transforming the whole entrance hall into a magnificent piece of art. Other, less decorated arches and corridors led off to rooms and halls and storerooms. The walls, the floor, and the ceiling were all the same pear-coloured wood. No stone or metal had been used in the Tree's interior. Like a single gigantic piece of intricate scrimshaw. Though in fact there was no indication of human workmanship anywhere—no signs of tools, no markings. The only human contributions were the carvings and decorations, and a few examples of human ingenuity. Like the single elevator that carried people from the base of the Tree to the very top, for when there just wasn't time to take the curving wooden stairway that wound round and round the interior walls of the Tree. The elevator was just a flat wooden slab that rose and fell according to an intricate system of counterweights. No one had ever been able to find them. The Tree liked to hold some of its mysteries close to its chest.

The Administrator stomped off to his very private office, to rest his feet and his aching back, and prepare for the new term. He grumbled loudly about his workload every year, and didn't fool anyone. Everyone knew he lived for his paperwork.

"You know," said Hawk, heading straight for the elevator, "given that we will be leaving soon, I think it is incumbent on us to do one final tour of the various departments. Make sure all the tutors are up to the mark, all the students are working hard, and . . ."

"And just generally put the wind up everybody, one last time?" said Fisher. "Sounds good to me."

So up the elevator shaft they went, standing right in the centre of the wooden slab because there weren't any handrails. To discourage people from using the thing if they didn't have to. Hawk and Fisher were looking forward to seeing how the many and various departments of the Academy were doing. The Hero Academy didn't teach just the basics of soldiering— sword and axe and bow . . . There were also serious studies in magic, High and Wild, and all sorts of classes in such useful skills as infiltration, espionage, politics, information gathering, sneaking up on people, and general underhandedness. As Hawk was fond of saying, *A properly prepared warrior has already won the fight before he's even turned up.* And as Fisher liked to say, *When in doubt, cheat.*

Hawk and Fisher started their casual and entirely informal inspection with the main training hall, on the second floor. A huge open area, with light falling heavily through the many circular windows. There was no glass in any of the Tree's windows, just openings in the wood. But somehow the Tree was always cool in the summer and comfortably warm in the winter. Which was just as well, because no one was ever going to be stupid enough to start a fire inside the Millennium Oak. Except for the kitchens, on the ground floor. Where the cooks were often heard to murmur that they always felt like someone was watching them. When it got dark, foxfire moss lamps shed safe silver light.

Roland the Headless Axeman was in charge of Weapons Training. A tall man, originally, presumably; it was hard to be sure now that he didn't have a head anymore. His neck had been neatly trimmed, just above the shoulders, and the tunic he wore had no hole for where the neck should have been. Roland was a large and blocky sort, with muscles on his muscles, and arms so heavily corded that he could crack walnuts in his elbows (for other people; he had no use for the things himself). He wore steelstudded leather armour that had been beaten into a suppleness smooth as cloth, over functional leggings, and battered old boots with steel toe caps. He had large hands, a soldier's stance, and was so impressively imposing that he all but sweated masculinity. He had a deep, booming, authoritative voice. No one was too sure exactly where it came from, though people had come up with some very disturbing and even unsavoury possibilities. Roland may not have had a head, but he saw all and heard all, and absolutely nothing got by him. Unbeatable with his massive war axe in his hand, Roland was a patient and demanding and very dangerous tutor who never failed to get the best out of his students. Whatever it took.

Some say he cut his own head off . . .

Many sorcerers and witches had run extensive, though carefully unobtrusive, tests on Roland the Headless Axeman down through the years. From what they hoped was a safe distance. They were sure he wasn't a ghost, or a lich, or an homunculus, or any of a dozen other unlikely things. But as to who or what he really was? No one had a clue. Not even Hawk and Fisher; or if they did, they weren't talking. An awful lot of people had asked Roland, right to where his face should have been . . . but no one ever got the same answer twice. Roland always made a point of telling these people exactly what they didn't want to hear, so they'd go away and stop bothering him. The Administrator made a point of asking each new Hawk and Fisher to get rid of Roland, because he wouldn't take orders from the Administrator, and had been known to do very painful and destructive things to students who disappointed him. Usually for having the wrong attitude . . . The Administrator kept pointing out that Roland the Headless Axeman scared the crap out of the students, and most of the Academy staff; and every Hawk and Fisher in turn said the same thing: that this was the best possible reason for keeping Roland around.

Because if the students could face him, they could face anyone.

And it had to be said: Roland did turn out first-class warriors. All just packed full of the right heroic attitude.

Hawk and Fisher stood at the back of the practice hall just long enough to make sure all the students were giving it their best shot, and then they nodded to Roland. He made a brief movement of his shoulders that suggested he might be nodding back. (Hawk had once let his hand drift casually through the space above Roland's shoulders, where his head should have been, just to assure himself that there really was nothing there. Roland let him do it, and then said, *Never do that again*. All the hairs stood up on the back of Hawk's neck, and he decided right then and there that he had no more curiosity in the matter.) The students duelled up and down the hall in pairs, stamping their feet hard on the wooden floor, thrusting and parrying in perfect form. The clash of steel on steel was oddly muffled, as though the wood of the Millennium Oak absorbed some of the sound, to show its disapproval of so much steel inside the Tree.

Hawk and Fisher were heading unhurriedly down the long, curving corridor that led to the Alchemist's laboratory, when there was a sudden and very loud explosion. The floor shook ever so lightly beneath their feet, and the door to the laboratory was blown clean off its hinges, flying across the corridor to slam up against the far wall, while black smoke billowed out through the open doorway. Followed by howls, screams, and quite a lot of really bad language. The Alchemist didn't take failure well. The black smoke smelled really bad, and dark cinders bobbed and floated on the air. Hawk breathed in a lungful of the smoke before he could stop himself, and for a moment wee-winged bright pink fairies went flying round and round his head, singing in high-pitched voices a very suggestive song about someone called Singapore Nell. Hawk shook his head firmly, and the pink fairies disappeared, one by one. The last one winked, and blew him a kiss.

The fairies might actually have been there, temporarily. The Alchemist could do amazing things with unstable compounds.

"I see our Alchemist is still hard at work," Fisher said solemnly, batting at the black smoke with one hand as it curled slowly on the air, before being quickly sucked out the open corridor window. The Tree could look after itself, though the Alchemist tried its patience more than most. "Is he still trying to turn lead into gold? I keep telling him, if gold becomes as common as lead, it won't be worth anymore than lead; but he won't listen to me. I think it's all about the thrill of the chase, myself."

"A surprisingly good cook, though," said Hawk. "I suppose all that messing about with potions gives you a feeling for combining the right ingredients . . . Is he still banned from the Tree's kitchens?"

"Damn right he is," said Fisher. "That macaroni pie of his had me trapped in the jakes for hours."

"It was very tasty," said Hawk.

"Strangely, that didn't make me feel any better," said Fisher.

"It cured your hiccups."

"Only because I was scared to."

Hawk sniffed deeply at the last evaporating swirls of black smoke. "I smell . . . brimstone, mandrake, and . . . is that cardamom? That mean anything to you?"

"It means we're going to have to have another hard word with him," said Fisher. "I don't mind him blowing his lab up, because the Tree always absorbs the damage, and clears up after him, and the Alchemist always bounces back . . . but it does take a lot out of the students."

"He doesn't blow things up nearly as much as he used to," said Hawk. "And it does do wonders for the students' reflexes. They can duck and cover and jump out a window faster than anyone else in the Academy."

"But when he does go wrong, it all goes very wrong," Fisher said sternly. "And parents really don't take kindly to having their loved ones sent home in a closed casket because we couldn't find all the pieces."

"You're exaggerating now," said Hawk.

"Only just!"

"All right, all right. We'll pop in just long enough to put the hard word on him. But only because I hate having to write letters of apology to students' next of kin."

The Alchemist wasn't in any mood to be lectured. So Hawk knocked him down and sat on him, while Fisher lectured him very sternly until he agreed that they were right and he was wrong, and would they please let him up now as he still had some fires to put out.

Hawk and Fisher walked on through the long, curving wooden corridors, going up and down stairs as the mood took them, peering into any room that attracted their attention, and even a few that were trying really hard not to. All the Tree's ceilings were marvellously smooth and polished, even though no one ever polished or waxed them. The Tree looked after itself. Whoever originally carved out the interior of the Millennium Oak had done an excellent job. Current scientific theory was that the Tree allowed it to happen, and probably even cooperated in the process, on the grounds that it was hard to conceive of anyone powerful enough to enforce their will upon the Millennium Oak. Various sorcerers had tried, in very small ways, because some sorcerers just couldn't resist a challenge, and usually ended up with headaches that lasted for days. One had been heard to wail plaintively, *Dammit, the Tree's realer than we are!* Before someone led him away for a nice lie-down with a damp cloth over his eyes. The latest thinking was that the Tree had allowed its hollowing-out because it was lonely and wanted to be occupied, for the company. A theory that was really disturbing only if you thought about it too much, so most people tried very hard not to.

Many people had lived inside the Millennium Oak, and used it for many purposes, down through the years. The Tree didn't discriminate. The original Hawk and Fisher found the Tree deserted and abandoned, and just moved in. The Tree must have approved of them, because nobody stays for long inside the Tree if it doesn't approve of them. They either depart at great speed, or they don't leave at all and no one ever sees them again. The one thing that everyone agrees on is that the Tree is quite definitely awake and aware, in its own ancient woody way. A few deeply mystical types have claimed to be able to talk with the Tree, but only after ingesting truly heroic portions of the local mushrooms.

The original Hawk and Fisher founded their Hero Academy with a cellar full of treasure they'd brought with them from the Forest Kingdom. Presumably stolen. There was still more than enough left to keep the Academy going, even after all these years, added to by very generous donations from grateful alumni. Presumably tribute. The original Hawk always said it was vital that the students got everything they needed to help them develop their various talents, irregardless of their previous backgrounds. The original Fisher said he only said that so he could use the word *irregardless*.

The warrior students looked down on the magic students, who looked down on the alchemy students, who looked down on the political students, who looked down on everyone else. All the Hawks and Fishers encouraged healthy rivalry, whilst at the same time coming down hard on anyone who descended into bullying. Which very thought was enough to add a certain preoccupation to their step as they approached a particular sword-practice hall. They'd been hearing reports about the secondary Bladesmaster, Anton la Vern, for some time. And not the kind of reports you wanted to hear about a man entrusted with the teaching of impressionable young souls. Hawk and Fisher had listened carefully, watched even more carefully, given Anton la Vern a lot of room and as much benefit of the doubt as they reasonably could . . . because he was a Bladesmaster, after all. Supposedly unbeatable with a sword in his hand. Such people were rare, and even harder to acquire as tutors of the Hero Academy. They brought prestige to the Academy, and helped attract the very best kind of student.

And la Vern was a good tutor—everybody said so—turning out many great young swordsmen and -women. But there comes a point when you just have to stop making excuses for someone. Because, as Hawk quite rightly pointed out, the only thing lower than a bully was a worm's belly.

They stopped in the open doorway of the training hall and watched silently as dozens of grimly determined students went head-to-head with steel in their hands. The air was full of the clash of blade on blade, heavy breathing and harsh grunting, and the stamp of booted feet on the wooden floor. No practice blades here, and no protective armour. Real danger, and the occasional spurt of blood, speeded up the learning process wonderfully, and helped weed out those students who weren't really committed, or suited, to the warrior's way. It did help that there was always a medical sorcerer at hand to heal wounds, stick severed fingers back on, and deal with everything short of mortal wounds or the more severe forms of decapitation.

Hawk and Fisher watched from the doorway, so still and silent that no one even noticed they were there. And all too soon they saw what they were looking for. La Vern moved back and forth across the hall, watching all the fighters closely, dropping a word of commendation here, a sharp reprimand there, but always moving on, looking for something in particular . . . the one thing he really couldn't stand. He watched two young men duel each other up and down the hall, lunging and parrying, leaping back and forth and attacking each other with dizzying speed. And then la Vern moved in and stopped the fight, and called for everyone else to stop. The hall fell suddenly still and silent. Dozens of young men and women stepped away from each other and lowered their swords, sweating hard and breathing heavily, to watch Anton la Vern shout and sneer at the better of the two swordsmen before him, mocking and humiliating him in front of everyone. Doing his best to destroy the young man's confidence and break his spirit—because that was the one thing Anton la Vern couldn't bear. That someone in his class might become as good as he was. La Vern had to be the best, whatever the cost. He quickly worked himself into a spiteful fury, shouting at the white-faced student before him so loudly he didn't even hear Hawk and Fisher enter the practice hall.

He realised something was wrong only when he looked around and found no one was listening to him anymore. No one was even looking at him. Every student in the hall was looking past him, and when he turned to find out why, his face went suddenly pale, as he saw Hawk and Fisher heading straight for him. He didn't need to ask why; he saw the answer in their faces. Knew from the way they looked at him that he hadn't covered his tracks as well as he'd thought he had. For a long moment he couldn't find anything to say. He could have defended himself, could have sought to justify his behaviour . . . but he had only to look in their eyes to see there was no point. So he just drew himself up, looked them both square in the face, and silently defied them. Hawk and Fisher crashed to a halt before him, and something in the way they looked and something in the way they held themselves had the watching students decide this was a good time to start backing away. Because whatever was about to happen, they really didn't want to be a part of it.

"Anton," said Hawk, "I didn't want to believe it. I had no idea you were so . . . insecure."

"I had no idea you were such a small-minded, mean-spirited little prick," said Fisher.

"You'll have to go, Anton," said Hawk.

"I'm not going anywhere," said la Vern. His voice was flat and firm, his gaze unwavering. "I'm not going, because you can't make me. I'm a Bladesmaster. You know what that means. Unbeatable with a sword in my hand. I'm a master of steel, while you're just two burned-out mercenaries hiding behind the reputation of someone else's names."

Hawk kicked him really hard in the groin. Anton made a low, shocked noise, and then his eyes squeezed shut. Tears streamed down his cheeks.

He tried to suck in a new breath, and found he couldn't. He dropped to his knees. One hand scrabbled numbly for the sword at his side. Fisher leaned over and rabbit-punched him with vicious force on the back of his exposed neck, and Anton la Vern crumpled unconscious to the floor.

"Unbeatable, yes. But only with a sword actually in your hand," said Hawk. "You really think you're the first Bladesmaster I've had to deal with?" He gestured to the two nearest students. "Pick that piece of crap up and haul him out of here. Hand him over to security, and tell them to take away his sword, strap him onto a mule facing backwards, and then send him on his way."

The students moved quickly forward, and gathered up the unconscious Bladesmaster. One of them looked uncertainly at Hawk.

"What if he comes back?"

"If he's dumb enough to show his face here again, we'll let the sorcery students practice on him," said Fisher. "There's a reason we keep that big lily pond of frogs down on the basement level."

Hawk and Fisher wandered on through the gleaming wooden corridors, not headed anywhere in particular, thinking their own individual thoughts. Hawk had approved la Vern's position as tutor, and he hated to be wrong about people. Fisher was thinking about what was for dinner. She'd never been much of a one for self-recrimination. People passed them by in the corridors, nearly always with a nod and a smile. The current Hawk and Fisher were popular, respected heads of the Hero Academy, though they would both have been surprised to hear it. They liked to think of themselves as cool and distant governors.

"How long have we been here?" Fisher said finally.

"Longer than I ever expected," said Hawk. "What's the matter? You getting tired of all this?"

"You know I'm not," said Fisher. "I like it here—doing good work, changing the world for the better, one hero at a time."

"It was either this or retire and run a tavern somewhere," said Hawk. "And that always seemed far too much like hard work to me. This . . . suits me better."

They paused by a large open window to watch a line of rather nervous-looking students file uncertainly out along a broad branch of the Tree.

They took their time getting into position, checked that they were an arm's length apart, and then looked glumly down at the long drop below. A gusting wind tousled their hair and plucked at their clothes with a rough hand. To a man and a woman, the students all looked like they'd much rather be somewhere else. Anywhere else. A few were quietly praying, a few were quietly whimpering, and several had their eyes squeezed firmly shut. Their tutor, the Witch in Residence, Lily Peck, walked along the branch behind them and briskly pushed them off, one by one. They plummeted swiftly out of sight, leaving only their screams behind.

"It's the only way to teach them to fly," said Hawk. "Ask them to jump, and they'd still be there at dinnertime."

Fisher sniffed. "If we really wanted to motivate them, we should take away the safety nets."

They moved on. Some time later, they paused before a very firmly closed, locked, and bolted door. Various sounds of an extreme nature drifted past the heavy wooden door, which bore the sign *Exams Under Way.*

"I see the magical tantric sex classes are still very popular," said Hawk.

"For those who survive them, yes," said Fisher.

They lingered for a while outside the door. They had no business there, but still . . . Sudden raised voices from the base of the Tree travelled up the open elevator shaft behind them and caught their attention, and they reluctantly decided that they'd better check them out. They shot down the shaft on the flat wooden slab, just a little more quickly than they were comfortable with, and made their way to the entrance of the Millennium Oak, where a Famous Name had turned up, demanding entrance.

The Tree's security guards were blocking the newcomer's way, politely but very firmly, with closed ranks and drawn swords; but Warren Wulfshead wasn't the kind to be easily impressed or intimidated. He just stood there, his fists planted solidly on his hips, glaring right into the guards' faces, loudly demanding to be allowed to enter. Demanding that he had a right to enter the Academy, because of who and what he was, and that he had every intention of tutoring all the students, teaching them everything he knew and recruiting the best of them for his own purposes.

Everyone had heard of the Wulfshead, of course, though for many this was the first chance they'd had to see the outlaw legend in the flesh. He was tall and darkly handsome, lithely muscled, and even standing still he burned with barely suppressed nervous energy. He looked like he'd much rather be killing a whole bunch of people, and only basic politeness was holding him back. He looked down his prominent nose at everyone present, his mouth set in a flat, determined line. He had a high, bony forehead, a receding hairline, and cold, cold eyes. It was hard to believe he could have done all the heroically violent things he was supposed to have done, and still appear to be only in his early thirties. Just looking at him, you got the impression he was quite prepared to walk through and over absolutely anyone who got in his way. You could also tell that he quite clearly saw himself as a Born Leader. Such men are dangerous. Especially to those they lead.

Warren Wulfshead, legendary bandit and brigand of Redhart, wore clothes of green and brown, for camouflage, so he could blend into the scenery and shoot his enemies in the back, from ambush. And then run away. Though that was rarely mentioned in the many widely circulating stories and songs based on his exploits. Warren Wulfshead was a professional outlaw, a renegade by choice, and if the rumours were to believed . . . he was also the author of most of the stories and songs about him.

Hawk and Fisher had heard of him. They didn't approve of him at all.

They shouldered their way through the crowd that had gathered in the entrance hall, eager for a look at a living legend and maybe even an autograph, and then they eased their way through the ranks of security guards, to finally stand before the Wulfshead. Who looked Hawk and Fisher up and down, curled his lip briefly to show how unimpressed he was, and then went for the bluff and hearty approach. He gave them both a quick, manly smile, nicely calculated to demonstrate that he was officially pleased to meet the current heads of the Hero Academy but that they weren't on his level and so shouldn't use the opportunity to take advantage. The Wulfshead was always the hero of the story, wherever he happened to be, and no matter whom he was speaking to. But before he could say anything, Hawk got in first. Because he was never impressed by anybody.

"Yes, we know who you are, and no, we don't care," he said bluntly. "You're not welcome here."

"We don't approve of you," said Fisher.

"Whyever not?" said the Wulfshead, honestly taken aback.

"Because we've talked with people who've actually met you," said Hawk.

He took a careful, deliberate step forward, so he could plant himself directly in front of the Wulfshead and block his entrance to the Tree. The Wulfshead didn't budge an inch, and the two men faced off. The Wulfshead made a point of playing to the eagerly watching crowd. He was famous, or perhaps more properly infamous, for leading a pack of political outlaws that liked to be called the Werewolves, in the darker and more primitive woods of Redhart. The country was ruled by King William, who was, in turn, very strictly advised by the elected Parliament. But the Wulfshead saw growing democracy as too slow a process. There was a certain amount of support for his cause, but not for his methods. Which tended to be brutal, murderous, and self-serving. You were either on the Wulfshead's side or you were dead. The Wulfshead had never actually said who or what should replace the King, but no one would have been at all surprised if Warren's name turned out to be at the top of the list. He was, after all, a Born Leader.

"We'd heard you'd been doing badly," said Hawk. "That your vicious activities had undermined your cause and turned most of Redhart's population against you."

"Lies, spread by my enemies," said the Wulfshead, still playing to the crowd.

"Most of your followers have been killed, arrested, or just deserted," said Fisher. "Because you treat your people worse than the King does."

"And because you don't know a thing about strategy," said Hawk. "Hiding in the deep woods, attacking from ambush and then disappearing, is all you know. Last I heard, you'd been chased right out of Redhart, with your few remaining followers. You tried to set up business in the Forest Kingdom, but since that's mostly a democracy these days, with just a constitutional monarchy, your brand of outlaw politics never stood a chance. The Forest army kicked you out before you'd even had time to write a song about being there. And now here you are; with a mere seven followers, none too impressive, I might add, demanding the right to tutor my students in your own brand of extreme politics, so you can carry them off to be battle fodder in your own private war. Like I'm going to let that happen."

"I need a new base, and a new army," the Wulfshead said calmly. "And I have found them both here. You can't stand against me. I have destiny on my side. They're not your people anymore. They're mine."

"Over my dead body," said Hawk.

The Wulfshead smiled happily. "That's the idea, yes. A ship can't have two Captains." He looked at Fisher. "I'm here for him. The man in charge. You don't get to interfere."

"Wouldn't dream of it," said Fisher. "My Hawk may not be as young as he used to be, but there will never be a day when he needs my help to take out a jumped-up little turd like you."

The Wulfshead gestured imperiously to his followers. "Seize her!"

Fisher stepped forward and glared right into the faces of the seven Werewolves. They backed away despite themselves, huddled together and shifted their feet uncertainly, and didn't make a single move to go for their weapons. They didn't know what to do with people who weren't scared of them. Fisher let loose with a harsh bark of laughter and set herself firmly between the Werewolves and their leader. She nodded briskly to Hawk, who looked thoughtfully at the Wulfshead for a moment before drawing his axe and hefting it meaningfully. In a simple, straightforward way that showed it was something he did every day. Something he was very good at.

The Wulfshead stepped back, looked quickly about him, and realised he'd lost the attention of the crowd. He pulled open the front of his brown and green tunic to reveal a preserved wolf's paw hanging on a silver chain over his very hairy chest. Some people in the crowd made impressed noises, but not many. They'd all seen stranger things, studying at the Hero Academy. The Wulfshead drew his long sword, making a real production of it. He swept the blade back and forth before him, the burnished steel shining bright and sharp in the golden ambience of the entrance hall. He smiled mockingly at Hawk, who hadn't moved an inch.

"See the wolf's paw, little man? I cut it off a werewolf I killed in Redhart, when I was just starting out. Hacked the paw right off and had it made into this useful charm, so I can share the wolf's strength and speed.

No one gets in my way and gets away with it. I have a destiny to fulfil! I'm going to carve you up and cut you into little pieces, little man."

Hawk said nothing. Just stood where he was, in his experienced fighter's crouch, axe at the ready, looking like the solid, skilled warrior he was. Students were running into the hall from all directions—not to interfere, but to watch and learn. News of the two clashing legends had spread quickly through the Millennium Oak, and now students and tutors alike were pressing forward to watch the fight. Because some lessons are best observed firsthand. Hawk didn't move, or even look around, but he did smile briefly at the Wulfshead.

"Don't mind them," he said easily. "They just like to watch me work."

The Wulfshead laughed theatrically, and swept his blade back and forth. He shifted his weight from foot to foot, flexed his muscles ostentatiously, and sneered at Hawk. "Pay attention, everyone!" he said loudly. "And I will show you how it's done. And when it's over, Fisher, you can take me on a guided tour of my new home."

He surged forward while he was still speaking, an old trick, and Hawk went forward to meet him. The Wulfshead stamped and danced around Hawk, darting this way and that, moving almost too quickly for the human eye to follow. He laughed at Hawk, taunting him, darting in and out, his sword seemingly everywhere at once . . . without actually committing himself to anything, trying to provoke Hawk into making the first attack. But Hawk just held his fighter's crouch, shuffling slowly round so he was always facing the Wulfshead, no matter how quickly the outlaw tried to catch him off balance. For all the much younger man's speed and fury, somehow Hawk was always in the right place at the right time.

Finally the Wulfshead realised he was getting short of breath to no purpose. He roared deafeningly and hurled himself forward, his sword flashing in for the kill . . . and there was Hawk, waiting for him. His axe lashed out in one simple, brutal movement and buried itself in the Wulfshead's chest. There was a loud cracking sound, as the heavy steel axe head slammed right through the silver chain holding the wolf's paw, through the outlaw's breastbone, and deep into his heart. Blood coursed down from the terrible wound, and the Wulfshead stood very still. His hand slowly opened, and the sword dropped from his numb fingers. The blade made a loud noise as it hit the floor, but neither Hawk nor the Wulfshead looked down. They only had eyes for each other.

The outlaw's mouth moved. Blood came out of it, and spilled down over his chin. "How . . . ?"

"The High Warlock made this axe, for the original Hawk," said Hawk. "It can cut through anything, including magical defences. Like the disguised charm hidden inside a wolf's paw. This axe was handed down to me through all the other Hawks, just so I could deal with dangerous little shits like you."

"Oh," said the Wulfshead.

Hawk jerked the axe head out of the outlaw's chest, in a flurry of blood, and the Wulfshead collapsed and fell to the floor, as though that had been all that was holding him up. Hawk looked down at him, and then raised his axe and brought it swinging sharply down again, to cut off the Wulfshead's head. Just in case. There was a great burst of applause, and not a little cheering, from all those watching in the entrance hall, from students and tutors alike. Some money changed hands here and there, but not a lot; most people had more sense than to bet against Hawk.

"Nice work," said Fisher, moving forward to stand beside Hawk. "I knew you could take him."

"But you would have cut him down from behind, if it looked like I was losing?" said Hawk.

"Of course," said Fisher. And they shared a quiet grin. Then they turned unhurriedly to look at the Wulfshead's seven followers, standing very close together and doing their best to appear completely unthreatening.

"All right," said Hawk. "There's a place for you here, if you want it. Stay here as students, learn how to be real fighters, and how to atone for all the things you did before you got here. Or you can leave. Now. Your choice."

"We'd like to stay," said one of the former Werewolves, and the others nodded quickly in agreement. Fisher signalled the security guards, who moved forward and disarmed the outlaws.

"See they get a good meal," growled Fisher. "They look half-starved."

The guards led the ex-outlaws away. A student in the watching crowd held up his hand to ask a question, as though he was still in class.

"Excuse me, sir Hawk," he said diffidently, "but according to all the old songs and stories we heard in the Forest Kingdom, the original Hawk's axe, the one made specially for him by the High Warlock, was lost during Hawk and Fisher's visit to the otherworldly realm of Reverie, home to the Blue Moon, where they finally confronted and destroyed the Demon Prince."

Hawk waited a moment, to be sure the student had finished, and then nodded briskly. "Even that couldn't keep the axe from its rightful owner." He paused for a moment, to clean the last of the blood from his axe head with a piece of cloth, then tucked the cloth back into his sleeve and put the axe back at his side. He realised the student was still looking at him. "The axe turned up again, when it was needed. As such things have a habit of doing."

"It just goes to show," Fisher said cheerfully, turning her back on the dead body lying on the floor, "never believe everything you read in a story or hear in a song."

"And never trust a minstrel," said Hawk.

The Auditions started at noon, but long before then the massive Audition Hall at the heart of the great Millennium Oak was packed from wall to wall with willing hopefuls, heroes-in-waiting, and desperate last-chancers. They came from far and wide, from every country and background, and some from cities and cultures no one had ever heard of. There were no entrance fees and no conditions. By long tradition, if you could find your way to the Hero Academy, you would get your chance to show what you could do and demonstrate your worthiness to be accepted. There wasn't even a limit to the number of students admitted to the Academy every year; if you could prove you had what it takes, the Academy would make room for you. Of course, every potential student had to show their stuff right there, when called on, in front of everyone, and tough luck if you froze. The Audition process wasn't for the faint of heart, but that was part of the challenge. If you couldn't deliver in front of an audience, what use would you be in a battle?

Hawk and Fisher got there early. They always liked to make a point of that, taking their seats on the dais at the rear of the Audition Hall, so they could watch the place filling up. Long experience had taught them that if they didn't, potential students would look in, see the empty chairs, and go away again. Because if Hawk and Fisher weren't there, it meant the Auditions weren't anywhere near getting started, so there was no point in showing their faces. Besides, Hawk and Fisher liked to sit back and watch the students gather, study their hopeful faces, and make quiet side bets on which ones would faint or wet themselves, or have a fit of the vapours, the moment they were called on to perform.

Some tutors turned up to watch and some didn't. Because some were people persons and some most definitely weren't. Some weren't even people, strictly speaking. You didn't get on staff at the Hawk and Fisher Memorial Academy by having a pleasant manner; you secured your place by demonstrating extraordinary skills and sheer force of will. Roland the Headless Axeman turned up for every Audition, standing beside Hawk, disdaining anything as soft and comfortable as a chair. He stood unnaturally still, his back perfectly straight, seeming to observe absolutely everything. Even though he didn't have any eyes. Or ears.

He doesn't miss anything, Hawk said once.

Oh, he must do, said Fisher. It was a very old joke, even then.

I heard that, said Roland. *I'm not deaf.*

Then what are you? said Hawk.

Complicated, said Roland.

Fisher then said something extremely rude, and everyone present pretended not to have heard.

The Alchemist would slouch in whenever he felt like it, glaring around at everyone else as though they'd kept him waiting. He wore a grubby white lab robe, with many colourful stains and scorch marks. He'd been wearing it for years, and on bad days you could smell it coming long before you ever saw the Alchemist. He could have had it cleaned, or even bought a nice new one, but apparently he considered the various signs of hard use as battle scars or marks of honour. It made a statement, he liked to say, though of what exactly, no one was too sure. Survival against the odds, probably. And it did help to put his students into a suitably cautious state of mind.

The Alchemist himself was painfully thin, jumpy, and a decidedly testy sort, with a number of nervous twitches that chased one another round his body. He had an ascetic scholar's face, with a haunted, preoccupied look. There were always a great many bets among his students as to whether he'd actually make it to the end of term. But somehow he always did. Even if his laboratory sometimes didn't. There was no doubt he knew his stuff, and a whole bunch of other stuff that nobody else knew; and he was an excellent teacher, as long as you paid careful attention, and hit the floor when he told you to. He might not be able to turn lead into gold, yet, but he could blow shit up with great skill and never-ending enthusiasm. Many a battle had been won with one of the Alchemist's little helpers. It was just that his extensive knowledge was accompanied by a wide-ranging curiosity and a complete lack of self-preservation instincts. At all of his lectures, there was always a scuffle between those who were going to sit up close, where they could see everything, and those who just wanted to stay safely at the back, near the door. And it was standard practice that if the Alchemist should say "Oops," it was every student for himself.

Jonas Crane the Bladesmaster, head tutor in all the soldiering skills, sauntered into the hall at the very last moment and stood at parade rest next to Fisher. He was the Academy's only Bladesmaster, now that Anton la Vern was gone. He didn't say anything, as he stood glaring out over the Audition hopefuls; he didn't have to. His whole stance, wrapped in gleaming chain mail armour, spoke volumes. Fisher sighed, heavily.

"You're not happy, are you, Jonas? I say this on the grounds that your stance is disapproving so loudly it's giving me a headache."

"La Vern was a Bladesmaster," said Crane, in his harsh soldier's voice. "We don't grow on trees. Even if some of us teach in them." That might or might not have been a joke. Crane wasn't exactly famous for his sense of humour. In fact, some said that if he did smile, it meant it was going to rain for forty days.

"We'll get you another assistant Bladesmaster as soon as we can," said Hawk.

"I want a raise," said Jonas Crane.

"It's nice to want things," said Fisher. "Now stop moaning, or I will slap you one, and it will hurt."

Crane snorted loudly but had nothing more to say. For the moment.

In Hawk and Fisher's experience, Crane was never short of things to say, in his own good time. He also had a tendency to loom, in a meaningful sort of way. Crane was a large and blocky man in his late forties, as ugly as a cow's arse, and strangely proud of his great barbarian's mane of long blonde hair. He dyed it, and only thought no one else knew. He had a certain kind of animal magnetism, which attracted a certain kind of student, and his bed was rarely empty. If any of his conquests started getting too possessive, Crane would let them fight it out in a public duel.

Lily Peck, the Academy's Witch in Residence, was always the last to arrive. A gifted and highly experienced adept at every kind of magic you could name, and some best not discussed in front of the easily shocked, Lily was short and dumpy, defiantly middle-aged, in a sweet and cosy way, who turned people into small, smelly snot creatures only when they really annoyed her. She was always ready to lend an ear, because she loved gossip, and she could brew a lust philtre that would blow the top of your head off. This sometimes led to complaints, particularly when she drank the stuff herself, and then there would be loud recriminations, and tears before bedtime, and before you knew it . . . it was small-hopping-thing time again.

Lily Peck preferred to stand at the very back of the dais, half-hidden behind the other tutors. Not because she was shy, but because she didn't believe in making a target of herself. You don't get to be a really powerful witch without making many enemies, among the living and the dead. She always carried a dead cat balanced on her shoulder, which hunched and spat at everyone and observed the world through malevolent fused-over eyes. Hawk winced as Lily took up her usual position, just behind his chair.

"I do wish you'd get yourself a new familiar, Lily. That cat is getting decidedly whiffy."

"You're just prejudiced against the mortally challenged," said Lily. "Spot's a good cat."

"He is not mortally challenged, he is dead," Hawk said firmly. "And he stinks! I know he's dead because my dog keeps trying to roll on him, and I can tell he's decaying because my eyes start to water every time you bring him anywhere near me. Why couldn't you settle for a parrot on your shoulder, like most people?"

"Because I am not like most people!" said Lily. "And I am not a pirate! I'm a witch, and some traditions you just don't mess with. I'll get a new familiar when this one falls apart, and not before. That is one of the traditional tests for how your familiar's doing; if he nods his head and it falls off, it's time to upgrade."

"I remember Cook talking to me once," said Fisher, "about how you can tell when a game bird is ready to eat."

Hawk looked at her suspiciously. "What?"

"You hang it up by the head, and when the neck rots through and the body falls to the floor, that's when it's ready to eat," said Fisher. "And she also told me that when she had to deal with game meat, she was always careful to grease her arms up to the elbows, so that when the maggots came crawling out of the meat, they couldn't get up her arms."

"I am never eating game meat again," said Hawk.

"You are so unadventurous," said Fisher.

By now the massive Audition Hall was packed with row upon row of hopeful prospects, squeezed so tightly together they could hardly breathe. The only space left open was the demonstration area, before the dais. It was marked out with white chalk lines on the floor, with guards standing by to enforce them, the guards were hardly ever needed. No one was stupid enough to risk being thrown out before they'd even had a chance to show what they could do.

The crowd didn't contain just hopeful young things; unfortunately, there were parents too. There to be supportive, or protective; to cheer or cry or pick arguments with the judges, as necessary. There were always some parents determined to live out their dreams through their children, to make them the heroes and warriors they'd always known they could have been . . . if only they could have found the time. And some parents (usually but not always mothers of a certain age) were there to fight to the death over any decision that didn't favour their particular offspring. The heavily armed security guards drew lots in advance to see who got this duty, because the hazard pay was never enough to justify what they had to go through.

When it finally became clear that you couldn't cram one more Auditioner into the hall, even if you greased them from head to foot and used a crowbar, Hawk and Fisher rose to their feet and the whole hall fell silent.

The crowd was hushed, wrapped in an almost unbearable tension. Hawk and Fisher gave their usual brief speech of welcome and warning (Give it your best shot, but don't waste our time) and then sat down again and gestured for the Auditions to begin. They kept the speech short because they knew everyone there was so on edge, and so caught up in themselves, that they could have announced the imminent end of the world and no one would have noticed.

The Administrator appeared, apparently out of nowhere, and jabbed his blackthorn staff at the first petitioner, and just like that, the Hero Auditions began.

First up was a really impressive performance from a would-be sorcerer. He was still in his late teens, though the black robes and white face paint made him look older as he produced clouds of billowing black smoke, shot flames from his hands, and pulled a dead rabbit out of his hat. Given his reaction to the rabbit being dead, and the speed with which he stuffed it back into the hat, presumably the dead part hadn't been intentional. He got some applause, and bobbed his head quickly in all directions, until Lily Peck stepped forward and fixed him with a cold glare.

"Nice try," she said, "but that's not sorcery. Those were all tricks and illusions. The quickness of the hand deceives the mind, and all that. Come back when you've learned some real magic, and not before."

The young man disappeared back into the crowd before she'd even finished talking. *Bunny-killer,* murmured some sections of the crowd.

An archer was the next to step forward, longbow in hand. He then made a long and tearful speech about what an honour it was to be there, and how much this would have meant to his poor dear dead granny, who had always believed in him . . . and how he was doing this for her . . . Until Hawk leant forward and shut the archer up with a cold look.

"Sorry," said Hawk, "but we don't do sentiment here. There's a target off to your right. Hit the bull's-eye or piss off."

"Right," said Fisher. "What are you going to do in the middle of a battle, make the other side cry so hard they can't see to shoot straight?"

The archer swallowed hard, took careful aim, and hit the stuffed target every time. Unfortunately, nowhere near the bull's-eye. The archer glared at Hawk and Fisher.

"You put me off! You made me nervous! I demand a second chance!"

"We don't do demands, either," said Hawk.

The archer slunk back into the crowd, close to tears again. No one paid him any attention. Partly because everyone there knew it was all about the performance, but mainly because they were all too wrapped up in their own moment of truth. None of them would allow themselves to be put off, or need a second chance. They were the stuff of heroes and warriors, and they were here to prove it.

Next up was a bright-eyed young swordsman wrapped in flashing silks. He nodded and grinned at the judges, and put on an extraordinary solo performance, dancing and stamping and thrusting, his sword whipping back and forth in flashes of gleaming steel. He was fast and graceful, and undeniably skilled, and when he finally crashed to a halt and saluted the judges with his sword, breathing hard, his face covered with sweat, there was a grudging but real ripple of applause from the crowd. Hawk nodded slowly.

"Impressive. Bladesmaster Crane, if you would . . ."

The Bladesmaster stepped down from the dais, his long sword already in his hand, and launched a vicious attack on the young swordsman. Crane didn't say a word, just cut and hacked with brutal skill. The swordsman almost fell over himself backing away, and had to use all his strength and speed just to fend off the attacks. The Bladesmaster beat the sword out of the young man's hand and set the point of his sword at his opponent's throat. The young swordsman stood very still but wouldn't back away. The Bladesmaster nodded briefly to him, turned away, and sheathed his sword, then resumed his place on the dais. He wasn't even breathing hard. Hawk looked sympathetically at the wide-eyed young swordsman.

"Nice skills. Very practiced. But playing with yourself won't get you anywhere. Go away and learn some duelling skills, fighting real people. And come back again next year, when you're ready. You've got potential, but sword-fighting isn't about the thrust and parry; it's about killing the other man before he kills you."

The young swordsman nodded, just a bit shakily, and put a hand to his throat where the Bladesmaster's sword point had cut the skin. He looked at the blood on his fingers, picked up his sword from the floor and sheathed it, and marched out of the Audition Hall with his head held high. Several other swordsmen went quietly with him.

The next would-be warrior was an axe-man. Tall and blocky, heavily muscled, wearing well-used leather armour, he strode forward and planted himself firmly before Hawk. He brandished his axe fiercely and demanded in a loud and carrying voice that he be given the opportunity to demonstrate his skills by going head-to-head with Hawk. Roland started to step forward, but Hawk stopped him with a raised hand.

"There's always one, at every Audition. Someone always wants to take me on, to see if I'm worthy to teach here. Best to get it out of the way now. Everyone got a good view? Then let's do it."

He came down from the dais with his axe in his hand, and it seemed like everyone drew in a sudden shocked breath. Hawk was smiling a cold and disturbing smile, and he didn't look like a stocky middle-aged man anymore. He looked every bit the fighter and warrior everyone knew he must have been before coming to the Millennium Oak to be Hawk. The young axeman suddenly looked a great deal less sure of himself, but to his credit he stood his ground as Hawk advanced on him. They surged forward at the same time, going head-to-head and toe-to-toe, swinging their great axes with vicious strength and speed, throwing everything they had at each other. They stamped and grunted loudly, slamming their axes together, crying out with the impact of each blow, beads of sweat flying from their faces. Hawk never stopped grinning for a moment.

The young axeman was good, but in the end his skills came from practice and his knowledge was mostly theoretical. Hawk had experience. He fought the young axeman to a standstill, his axe seeming to swing in from every direction at once, until finally the axeman disengaged, and fell back several steps. He was gasping for breath, and soaked in sweat, and hardly had enough strength left to raise his axe. He still had some fight left in him—everyone could see that—but he knew he was outclassed. He lowered his axe, and bowed his head to Hawk, who bowed briefly in return. He was breathing hard too, but he hadn't lost that disturbing grin.

"You'll do," said Hawk. He put his axe away and resumed his seat on the dais. Fisher smiled at him fondly.

"Show-off."

"They get faster every year," murmured Hawk. "Nearly got me, several times. But I've still got the moves."

Guards led the young axeman away, to begin his new life as a student of the Academy. He was smiling dazedly, as though he couldn't quite believe it. He got a round of good-natured applause from the crowd.

A quite ordinary-looking teenage girl shuffled forward next, and professed herself a witch, in a quiet, mumbly voice. No one even suspected she was a Seductress, until she mouthed a few words and suddenly every man in the hall was in lust with her. And not a few women. The smell of musk was heavy on the close air, and everyone's eyes were fixed unblinkingly on the still very ordinary-looking young woman, as though she was the most splendid thing they'd ever seen. She laughed happily, turned to Hawk, and hit him with everything she had.

"Aren't I lovely?" she said breathily. "I think I belong here, in this silly little school, don't you? In fact, I think I should be running it. Don't you?"

She was quite taken aback when Hawk laughed at her, not unkindly. And just like that the spell was broken, and all the spectators in the hall shook their heads in bewilderment, as though they'd just had a bucket of cold water thrown in their faces. They looked at the ordinary teenager and wondered what they'd ever seen in her. There were a few angry murmurs, cut off when Hawk glared at the crowd before giving his full attention to the Seductress.

"You've certainly got one hell of a gift," he said cheerfully. "And there is a place here for you, if you want it. But listen to me, young lady, and be warned: you ever pull that trick again, outside of your supervised classes, and you will be expelled."

"And we'll cut your tongue out before we let you go," Fisher said flatly. "Lily, if you would . . ."

"She is a one, isn't she?" said Lily, stepping down from the dais. "But I think she's more Richard and Jane's sort. You come with me, dear, and I'll escort you to the tantric people. Sink or swim, that's what I always say."

She led the Seductress away, while the young girl was still trying to make up her mind as to whether she'd got what she wanted.

A young man stepped out of the crowd, at the Administrator's instruction, and stood diffidently before the dais. He too looked pretty ordinary.

He wore rough peasant clothes, he didn't carry a sword, and he didn't have the look of magic about him.

"I'm a shape-shifter," he said quietly, his eyes downcast. "I'm Christopher Scott, of the Forest Kingdom. I . . . change shape."

"You're a werewolf?" said Hawk.

"Not a werewolf, sir, no," said Scott, still not raising his eyes from the floor. "I'm a were demon. You must have heard, sir, that back in the day, during the Demon War, when demons broke out of the Darkwood and roamed the Forest Land, they didn't always kill their victims. Some of them were human enough that they . . . wanted human women. Raped them. That was what happened to my grandmother, when she was still just a girl. I am descended from a demon. I can . . . change, back and forth. And when the moon is full, I change whether I want to or not."

Hawk and Fisher looked at each other for a long moment. Hawk looked suddenly older. "No," he said finally. "I hadn't heard."

"Show us," said Fisher.

Scott bobbed his head quickly. He looked around him, to make sure he had plenty of room, and smiled briefly, understandingly, as he saw the front rows of the crowd already backing away from him. He didn't seem to concentrate, or make any kind of effort; but just like that he was gone, and in his place stood something that was in no way human.

It was a good eight feet tall, covered in night-dark scales, while a long barbed tail lashed eagerly back and forth behind it. It had fangs and claws and cloven hooves, and a horrid fright mask for a face. Just looking at it made you want to kill it. The demon was not a natural thing, and its very wrongness raised the hackles on everyone's necks. It wanted to break loose, to tear and kill and do horrible things, and everyone could feel that.

The demon put back its hateful face and howled gleefully, a vile sound that reverberated in the Great Hall and sickened everyone who heard it. Hawk and Fisher were on their feet, axe and sword in hand, ready to throw themselves at the demon . . . But it just stood where it was, and made no move to attack. It wanted to kill men and women and glory in their slaughter; but something held it back. Just standing there, it was the most dangerous and deadly thing in the hall, and you could tell that the thoughts that moved in its misshapen head, and the emotions that stirred in its demon heart, had nothing of humanity in them . . . and yet, still, something held it where it was.

It changed again, as easily as a man might shrug off a cloak, and Christopher Scott was back, standing before the dais. His face was white and drawn, and he looked sick, and shaken. He hugged himself tightly, as though afraid that what was inside him might come out again. Hawk made himself resume his seat, and after a moment Fisher did too.

"Impressive," said Hawk, in a surprisingly steady voice. He looked out across the unhappy crowd, many of whom were still shocked and disturbed. He didn't know how long they would stay quiet, so he hurried on. "A were demon. Well. You see something new every year. How much control do you have over your . . . other self, Christopher Scott?"

"Not as much as I would wish," Scott said steadily. "I can feel it inside me, straining against the bars of the cage that holds it. Growing stronger every day. That's why I came here, sir. Because I just can't do this anymore. Not on my own. Please, sir Hawk. Tell me you can help me."

"You've come to the right place," said Hawk. "We have tutors for everything. We'll find someone who can help you."

"But," said Fisher, "we reserve the right to chain you up in a cellar every full moon."

"Thank you," said Scott. "Oh, thank you." He was still saying that when the guards led him away.

Next up was a dark magician. He made no bones about what he was; in fact, he gloried in it. Emboldened by the rapt attention he was getting from the crowd, he struck a practiced pose before Hawk and Fisher, all the better to show off his dark robes, swirling night-dark cape, and the many kinds of demonic amulets hanging from chains over his chest. He'd even cultivated a nicely trimmed goatee and added some subtle dark makeup around his eyes.

"All the dark arts are mine to command!" he said grandly. "I can summon up spirits from the vasty deeps, strike down the living and command the dead. All the powers of the night bow down before me . . ."

"Oh, get on with it," said Hawk. "We haven't got all day."

"Right," said Fisher. "Amateur dramatics are auditioning next door."

And somehow, in the face of their entirely unimpressed attention and the fixed gaze of the crowd, it turned out the master of dark forces couldn't do a damned thing. He tried to chant and curse, but the words just wouldn't come, and his hands shook too much to manage the scary gestures. He grabbed at one of his demonic amulets, but it came off in his hand and he dropped it onto the floor, where it shattered into a hundred pieces. He finally stamped his foot, said a few baby swear words, and strode out of the hall without looking back.

"Try again next year," Hawk called after him. "Only next time, leave the nerves at home."

"Nice speech, though," said Fisher.

"I've heard worse," said Hawk.

The next Auditioner claimed to be able to fly, but when pressed, could only hover a few feet off the floor.

"Is that it?" said Hawk.

"That's why I'm here!" said the young witch, dropping heavily back to the floor. "I need training!"

"Come back when you can touch the ceiling," said Fisher ruthlessly.

The young witch had barely moved out of the way when a mature woman of a certain age and bearing, wearing a gown of so many gaudy colours that they were practically fighting it out for domination, strode forward; dragging a resentful young man along with her. She scowled at Hawk and Fisher, sniffed loudly at the other tutors, and pushed her tall, skinny son forward.

"Show them what you can do, Sidney!"

"Oh, Mum!" said Sidney, staring at his feet. "I don't want to. Leave me alone! You're embarrassing me!"

"Don't be silly, Sidney! This is your big chance. Now show them your miracles!"

"Don't want to go to the Hero Academy," muttered Sidney, still stubbornly staring at the floor. "Don't want to be a hero. I told you. I want to be a tailor, and do interesting things with fabrics."

"Where's the money in that?" said his mother, grabbing his arm and giving him a good shake. "Where's the fame and glory? If your father was still alive he'd be very upset with you. Now show them your miracles, or there'll be trouble!"

Sidney heaved a very put-upon sigh, and pebbles fell from the ceiling like a hard rain, appearing out of nowhere. There were various shouts and curses from the crowd, packed too closely together to dodge out of the way, but none of the pebbles were large enough to hurt anyone or do any damage. The hard rain stopped abruptly, and Sidney made it rain properly. Though it was more like a drizzle, and didn't last long enough for anyone to get wet. He made people's clothes change colour, temporarily, cured a few headaches, grew hair on a bald man's head, and made it feel as though it might thunder, if you just waited long enough. He then folded his arms tightly across his sunken chest, sniffed moistly, and glared firmly at the ground.

"Is that it?" said Hawk, quite politely under the circumstances. Because even the smallest of miracles was, after all, a miracle.

"Don't you speak to my Sidney like that!" snapped his mother. "He's going to be a great man one day, whether he likes it or not! He can do anything, if he just puts his mind to it."

"You've already done one great thing, haven't you, Sidney?" said Lily Peck, recently returned to the hall. Something in her voice made Sidney raise his head and look at her, and she smiled kindly on him. "Tell me, Sidney, how long ago did your mother die?"

"It's been four months now," said Sidney. "I missed her so much, being on my own, so I brought her back. Except it isn't really her. Just her body, raised up, saying all the things I remember her saying. And now I can't get rid of her. Can't make her lie down again and leave me alone. That's why I finally let her bully me into coming here. Because I hoped someone here would be able to teach me what I need to know; to make her dead again."

"Sidney!" snapped the dead woman. "That's no way to speak about your mother!"

"Allow me," said Lily Peck. She snapped her fingers, and Sidney's mother crumpled to the floor and lay still. Sidney looked down at his dead mother, prodded the body with his boot, just to be sure, and finally let out a long sigh of relief. And then he started to cry. Lily leaned in close beside Hawk.

"He really does have a great power. You should see his aura. Better let me keep him here, under training, where we can keep a watchful eye on him. And take measures, if necessary."

"Agreed," said Hawk. He raised his voice to address Sidney. "All right; you're in. But no more raising the dead without expert supervision."

"Of course," said Sidney. He stopped crying, and blew his nose loudly on a spotted handkerchief. "Trust me—some mistakes you only have to make once." He looked down at the dead body again. "My mother wasn't like that. When she was alive. Not really."

He went quietly with the guards. It took four more guards to carry out the body.

That was the last of the excitement. After that, it was just ordinary fighters, pedestrian magic-users, and a whole bunch of wannabes. Hawk dealt with the fighters by saying they'd have to duel with Roland the Headless Axeman before they could be allowed access to the Academy. Which was more than enough to scare off the insufficiently dedicated. Some departed so fast they left skid marks on the floor. And even after everything they'd seen, a lot of the potential students failed some quite basic tests when they finally got their turn. A potentially very skilled swordsman duelled Roland to a standstill, and then annoyed all the judges by looking down his nose at them. So Hawk said, "Bring in the goat." Everyone looked on, in a puzzled sort of way, as a guard brought in a very scruffy-looking black goat on a strong leash. The goat looked around, entirely unfazed by the crowd, obviously used to people. Probably some sort of pet, or mascot, murmured the crowd.

Hawk looked at the snooty swordsman. "All right. Go ahead."

"What?" said the swordsman, looking from Hawk to the goat and back again. "I don't understand."

"Yes, you do," said Hawk. "Kill it. Kill the goat. Now."

The young swordsman looked at the goat again. The goat looked back, in a quite amiable way. And the swordsman lowered his sword.

"I can't," he said almost pleadingly. "I can't just . . . kill it. Not just like that. Not in cold blood!"

"You can't turn to your commanding officer in the field and say you can't kill the enemy because you're not in the mood," Hawk said sternly. "Now kill the goat."

But the swordsman couldn't. He tried several times to nerve himself to the sticking point, but he couldn't even look the goat in the eye.

"It's all right," Hawk said finally. "You'd be surprised how many people just don't have the killing instinct. Even when it's only an animal. They're just not killers. It's a useful thing to find out about yourself in a peaceful setting rather than on a battlefield."

The surprise came at the very end of the Auditions, at the end of a very long day. The hall was almost empty, pretty much everyone who wanted to be seen had been seen, and judged, and Hawk and Fisher and the other tutors were just sitting it out through the last stubborn few and getting ready to call it a day, when a striking young man strode forward and bowed gracefully before Hawk and Fisher. Tired as they were, there was something about this one that made them both sit up straight and pay attention. He smiled easily at Hawk and Fisher, calmly confident, and there was just something about him . . . He had that easy charisma, that not-quite-cocky charm, and the assured stance of the experienced fighter. He was tall and elegant, handsomely blonde and blue-eyed, and he wore his chain mail with the ease of long familiarity. He carried a sword at his side, and looked like he knew how to use it. In fact, he looked a hell of a lot more like a hero than anyone else they'd seen that day. Hawk immediately decided he didn't trust him, just on general principles. No one had any right to look that impressive at that young an age.

"I have travelled a long way to be here, my most noble Lord and Lady, Hawk and Fisher," he said, in a crisp, commanding voice. "All the way from the Forest Castle, and the Court of King Rufus, of the Forest Land. I was raised there, and have spent much of my life studying the Castle records of what happened during the legendary Demon War. I think I can safely say I know all there is to know about the heroic Prince Rupert and Princess Julia, and their glorious exploits in that time."

"Really?" said Hawk. "Bet you don't. You do know you can't trust everything you read in official reports?"

"But I have been allowed access to more than just the public accounts, sir Hawk," the young man said smoothly. "Because I am the grandson of Allen Chance, once Questor to Queen Felicity of the Forest Land, and his wife, the witch Tiffany. I am Patrick Chance."

Hawk and Fisher looked at each other, and then back at the young Chance.

"They were good people," said Hawk.

"According to all the stories," said Fisher.

"Their names assure you of our full attention," said Hawk. "So make sure that whatever you've got to say is worth hearing."

"You're a bit late for the Auditions," said Fisher.

"Oh, I didn't come here for that," said Chance. He smiled briefly but dismissively at the few remaining Auditioners, and then turned his back on them. He didn't look at the tutors, either. His gaze was for only Hawk and Fisher. "I am here to speak privately with you, Lord and Lady. I bear grave and important tidings, from King Rufus himself. And my words are for your ears only."

Hawk and Fisher looked at each other again, and a silent communication passed between them. And then they both stood up and looked thoughtfully down at Patrick Chance. Hawk glanced at Roland the Headless Axeman. "You take care of the last few hopefuls. We'll abide by your judgement."

"I should bloody well hope so, after all these years," said Roland. "You wander off and have a nice chat with young snotty boots here, and I'll finish off the real work."

"Graceful as ever, Roland," said Fisher.

"It's been a long day," said Roland. "My head aches."

Hawk beckoned to Patrick Chance to follow him and Fisher, and they led the way out of the Audition Hall, down a few corridors, and into a quiet side room. Hawk sat down at the only table and gestured for Chance to take the seat opposite him, while Fisher firmly closed the door. Chance politely declined the offered chair, and wandered round the room, looking it over. Fisher came back to stand beside Hawk. Chance turned abruptly, to smile briefly at the two of them. He didn't look charming any longer. He looked cold and focused, as though he had a necessary but unpleasant duty he was determined to perform.

"Time," he said. "So much time . . . Did you really think you could escape your past, just by running away to another land, to become someone else? Did you really think you could ever be forgiven for what you did? No. It's time . . . for you to die."

He didn't go for the sword at his side. He raised both his hands in the stance of summoning, and an ancient and awful Word of Power issued from his distorted mouth. A change spell manifested on the air around Hawk and Fisher, spitting and crackling, designed to reshape their bodies, their flesh and bone, and remake them into something entirely incapable of surviving. A slow and nasty way to die. Except . . . the spell couldn't reach Hawk and Fisher. It howled and coruscated on the air around them, unable to get a hold on them or affect them in any way at all. Strange lights flickered and flared, strange energies beat frustrated in the room, and none of them worked. The spell fell apart and dissipated harmlessly and was gone, leaving Patrick Chance to look stupidly at the unchanged Hawk and Fisher before him.

"That's not possible," he said numbly. "The charm of unmaking is one of the oldest there is; nothing in this world can withstand a change spell of that magnitude!"

"It was a nice try," said Hawk. "But change spells are no use against us."

"Not after everything we've been through," said Fisher.

"The lesser magics can't touch us," said Hawk. "We have been touched by the Wild Magic, and we will always be . . . what we are."

"Damn right," said Fisher.

Hawk rose unhurriedly to his feet and looked coldly at Patrick Chance. "So. You're not really the Questor's grandson, are you? Who sent you?"

"Who is there who still knows who we really are?" said Fisher.

Chance drew himself up and sneered at them both. "You'll never know. You can't make me talk."

"Oh, I think you'll find we can," said Hawk.

"No," said Chance. "You can't. This moment was prepared for, before I left. The price of failure was made very clear to me."

His back arched suddenly, his face contorted by an awful agony. He fell to the floor and lay there convulsing, trying to force a scream through clenched teeth. Hawk and Fisher hurried towards him, and then stopped abruptly as what had been Patrick Chance changed its shape into something not in any way human. It was a demon. Not the huge and dark-scaled thing they'd seen in the Audition Hall earlier, though; this was just a squat, distorted shape, with needle teeth and scarlet eyes and jagged claws. It kicked a few times, lashed out at them once, for spite's sake, and then it died. The flesh melted quickly from its bones, which dissolved in their turn, until there was nothing left but a dark stain on the wooden floor and an unpleasant smell on the air. Hawk and Fisher moved over to the open window and breathed deeply.

"Well," said Hawk. "That was . . . interesting."

"Interesting, hell!" said Fisher. "Someone knows who we really are!"

"It had to happen eventually," said Hawk. He turned to look back at the dark stain on the floor, already being absorbed by the wood. "A hundred years since the Demon War . . . and we encounter two demons in one day. If I didn't know better, I'd say someone was trying to tell us something."

"Not forgetting the flock of dead birds that landed on our heads first thing this morning," said Fisher. "What was that? A threat, or a warning?"

"It's late," said Hawk. "And I'm tired. Let's go to bed."

It was late evening and already dark outside by the time they finally got to bed. They hadn't realised how long the Auditions had dragged on. They sat side by side in a large four-poster bed, on a goose-feather mattress they could sink right down into. Their backs were currently supported by a padded headboard, and a warm golden light glowed from the walls. The Tree looked after its own. Hawk had a nice mug of steaming hot chocolate. Fisher had a large glass of brandy. With a paper umbrella in it. Both of them warming the inner self in their own ways.

They were both wearing long white nightshirts, complete with their initials picked out tastefully on the left breast. They never used to wear anything to bed when they were younger, but they'd reluctantly agreed to wear the things because otherwise it shocked the students when they went to the jakes in the early hours of the morning. And besides, the winters were a lot colder these days. Their room was comfortable, even cosy, though, and absolutely nobody bothered them.

Hawk and Fisher sat slumped together, the bedclothes pulled up round their waists, quietly discussing the day's events. At the foot of the four-poster, on a pile of really smelly blankets, their really smelly old dog lay curled up, snoring loudly. He was a great, long-legged, high-shouldered brute of an animal, of no particular breed, old now, as they were old, but still active enough to get into his own fair share of trouble. His fur was grey, and white around the muzzle. He twitched restlessly, chasing rabbits in his dreams. He farted loudly.

Hawk shook his head slowly. "He's getting past it."

"Aren't we all," said Fisher.

"At least I don't lick my privates in public," said Hawk.

"You would if you could," said Fisher. "Actually, I think I'd pay good money to see that."

The dog let loose with a quick series of bubbling farts, like a miniature rumbling volcano and almost as explosive. Hawk and Fisher both winced.

"I'll have the Alchemist whip up some more of those little blue pills," said Hawk.

"It's either that or a bung," said Fisher.

"Are we really not going to talk about the demons?" said Hawk, putting his empty mug down on the bedside table.

Fisher emptied her brandy glass and tossed it casually into a cushioned chair. "What is there to say? It's just a coincidence. Has to be. There's no one left alive who knows what we did. Who we used to be."

"Someone must have sent that demon assassin, pretending to be Patrick Chance," Hawk said stubbornly. "They knew just the right name to get past our defences. Someone wants us dead!"

"What can we do?" said Fisher. "Run? I don't think so. No one chases me out of my own home."

"We were planning on leaving anyway," Hawk said carefully. "Perhaps our mysterious enemy wouldn't go after the new Hawk and Fisher. Our replacements."

"I don't know what to believe anymore," said Fisher. "I thought we were safe here. I thought . . . all that was over."

"The past is never over," said Hawk.

And then they both sat up sharply and looked around them. Something was wrong. They could feel it. Something bad was coming, coming right at them, from a direction they could sense but not identify. Something forcing its way into the world, from Outside. And then suddenly there he was, standing right in the middle of the room, grinning nastily at them from the foot of their bed.

The Demon Prince.

He looked something like a man, close enough to human to mock and discredit humanity with the comparison. He was unnaturally tall, and slender to the point of emaciation. His pale flesh had a lambent pearly gleam, unhealthy as leprosy, and he dressed in rags and tatters of purest black, as though he'd wrapped himself in snatches torn from the night itself. He wore a battered, broad-brimmed hat, pulled down low over his fiery crimson eyes; and from what could be seen, his features were blurred, uncertain, as though they could never settle on just the one face. He held his pale hands up before him, as though in mocking prayer or entreaty, and his long delicate fingers ended in vicious claws, from which dark, clotted blood dripped constantly. There was nothing human in his stance, in the way he held himself. He looked like a man because it amused him to do so. Once, he had looked like something else, and might again, but for now he lived in the world of men and shaped himself accordingly. If the word *lived* could ever be properly applied to something that had never been born.

The Demon Prince, lord of all the demons in the Darkwood. Who had tried to wipe out all humanity in the Demon War and rewrite the living world in his own awful image.

His presence seemed to bruise the air, and stain the light, to foul the room just by being in it. Slow creakings moved through the wood of the room, as though the old Tree was disturbed by the Demon Prince's very existence. His feet burned through the rugs on the floor, and scorched the wood beneath. The Demon Prince smiled slowly at Hawk and Fisher, showing pointed teeth, and when he spoke, his voice was the one you hear in your very worst nightmares.

"Well, well . . . hello again, my sweets. It's been such a long time, hasn't it? Did you like my little assassin, my calling card?"

"How did you get in here, past all the Tree's defences?" said Hawk. His voice wasn't quite as steady as he would have liked.

"You invited me in," said the Demon Prince. In a voice like babies crying, like children dying, like a scream in the night. "You let me in, with your precious applicants for the Auditions, and no one saw me. I live inside people now. You saw to that. You'll never find me, and I'll be long gone anyway. Aren't you glad to see me again, my most treasured enemies, my dearest rivals? You're as much a legend as me now, Rupert. Julia."

"What do you want?" said Fisher.

"Your grandchildren are in danger," said the Demon Prince sweetly. "They will die, slowly and horribly, unless you return to the Forest Kingdom to save them. A war is coming. Country against country, army against army . . . Farms and towns and cities burning in the night, blood and slaughter in the woods, terror on the march. The darkness is rising, the Blue Moon is coming back, and you and I will play the game of Fate and Destiny one last time. And I will finally have my revenge . . . when the Wild Magic is loosed in the world of men forever. Stop me, my dear ones, if you can."

He vanished, gone in a moment. Nothing left to show he had ever been there, except for the scorch marks his feet had left on the floor. The old dog at the foot of the bed raised his great grey head.

"Oh, bloody hell. Not again."

"Hush, Chappie," said Hawk.

TWO

A Marriage Is Arranged

On a perfect early-autumn day, under a perfect sky, Princess Catherine of the Kingdom of Redhart went running happily through the huge cultivated gardens outside Castle Midnight, along with her lifetime friend and one true love, the King's Champion, Malcolm Barrett. She was tall and blonde and beautiful, and he was tall and dark and handsome, and they were so much in love that sometimes they would look into each other's eyes and find it hard to breathe. They ran back and forth across the great sprawling gardens, chasing and being chased, laughing happily as they revelled and sported across the wide lawns. They ran round and round the artfully piled-up rockeries with their tumbling, bubbling streams, raced round and round the massive flower beds that blazed with brilliant colours, and finally in and out of the neat rows of poplar trees, where squirrels chattered angrily at them from the high branches.

Two young people, so happy in love, on a bright autumnal day. Not a cloud in the sky to warn them that a storm was coming.

Princess Catherine had hair so blonde it all but glowed, bouncing halfway down her back in heavy curls. She had eyes as blue as the sky, lips like heart's blood, and without even trying she was as cool and refreshing as a drink of clear water straight from the well. Her face was high-boned but not harsh, with a merry gaze that could flash with fire in an instant, and a smile that sometimes seemed to go on forever. She was always happy, always laughing—except for when she lost her temper. And then wise men would flee for the horizon, or at the very least hide behind the furniture until she stopped throwing things. Catherine was always very sorry afterwards, and would even help clean up the mess. As the King's only daughter, she had been thoroughly indulged, and to her credit, she knew that. Anyone who thought they could use her to get to the King, through gifts and flatteries and blatant insincerities, was in for a rude awakening. And quite possibly a good kick in the arse. Catherine had few real friends, by her own choice, and she was fiercely protective of all of them.

Today, as most other days, Catherine was wearing rough boy's clothes, consisting of a simple tunic and trousers and boots, because she was always off doing something she knew she wasn't supposed to be doing, like riding, hunting, exploring, and generally getting into trouble. When cautioned, or even scolded, by her father or others, she would just say that expensive robes and dresses and formal clothes weren't practical. As though that was the answer to everything. If anyone was ever stupid enough to press the point, she would lose her temper. So most people didn't press the point. The King had long ago given up trying to make her behave like a Princess.

The King's Champion, Malcolm Barrett, was tall and wide, with a barrel chest and broad shoulders, and surprisingly graceful for his size, thanks to a lifetime of military training. He was Champion because his father had been Champion before him, and it had honestly never occurred to Malcolm that he should want to be anything else. He was slow and thoughtful, never allowing himself to be hurried into anything; except on the battlefield. No one could move faster than Malcolm Barrett when steel clashed on steel and fire roared in his blood.

Malcolm and Catherine had been close friends since they were children, and in love since they were old enough to understand what that meant. To his credit, Malcolm still couldn't believe he'd been lucky enough to win Catherine's favour. He would have died for her, lived for her, conquered a country for her. She was everything he'd ever wanted, everything he'd ever dreamed of.

On this particular autumn day, he was wearing simple, practical leathers, and found them almost indecently comfortable after the chain mail and heavy armour he often had to wear for weeks in a row when out on border skirmishes. Though he was always careful to wear the correct ceremonial armour, burnished to within an inch of its life, when he had to make an official appearance at Court as King's Champion. Unlike Catherine, he understood the need for proper clothes at proper occasions. He wore the same sword all the time, and there was nothing ceremonial about it; it was a broad butcher's blade in a much-used scabbard. Because it didn't hurt to remind certain courtiers and politicians and hangers-on that he was always capable of sudden violence, in the King's name.

But not today. He didn't need his sword because he wasn't the Champion today. He was just a young man in love.

The happy laughter of two young people rang joyously through the widespread gardens. Flower beds had been placed in colourful clock faces, with particular flowers carefully laid out so they would bloom only at the correct hour of the day, to spell out the correct time. Fat fuzzy bees hummed loudly, doing their bit.

Extended rows of trees had been carefully pruned and arranged and forced to form long, shadowy tunnels and graceful arches and bowers, their curving branches intertwined in intricate patterns. The whole glorious retreat was full of rich colours and richer scents.

A man-made stream ran lazily through the gardens, cool and bubbling and endlessly inviting, full of the most beautiful and exotic fish that money could buy, in a long, magical Möbius strip, forever refreshing itself. A delicately carved wooden bridge crossed the river at the most aesthetically appropriate point, with high side rails and a shady roof, lit here and there with permanently glowing paper lanterns. And in the very centre of the gardens, dark green hedges had been expertly sculpted into tall towers. They rose high above the gardens, shooting up forty or fifty feet into the sky. Catherine and Malcolm had often climbed these lofty hedge towers as children, even though—or perhaps because—such a thing was strictly forbidden. They scrambled up the leafy sides, plunging their small hands and feet deep into the tightly packed hedges, getting away with it only because they were children. An adult's weight would have sent them crashing right through the greenery. (Catherine was always the first to make a dare out of it, and Malcolm was always the first to start climbing. Because he would do anything for her, even then. Though no matter how often they raced to the top, he never let her win. He knew she would never have forgiven him that.) Once they reached the tops of their separate hedge towers, they would sit proudly on the very edge, swaying back and forth in the breeze, their small feet kicking out over the long drop, while they looked out across their whole world, spread out below them.

There were always twenty or thirty gardeners working at once, watering and weeding their way across the gardens, but none of them looked up from what they were doing to watch Catherine and Malcolm at play, in what the gardening staff understandably thought of as *their* gardens. Anyone else, the staff would have glared cold death looks at them for venturing into their territory and not showing the proper appreciation for all the hard work that had gone into it. But they made an exception for Princess Catherine and her young man. Because the staff knew that the young lovers cared for the gardens almost as much as they did.

The King hadn't walked through his gardens for as long as anybody could remember.

Catherine and Malcolm paused to admire the great cloud of shocking pink flamingos scattered across the artificial lake. Almost unbearably garish, with their impossibly long, curving necks and spindly legs, the flamingos had supposedly started out as Unreal things, magical creatures, like so many that had roamed Castle Midnight back in the day. But the flamingos had become increasingly real, generation by generation, and it had been a long time since they'd been any colour but pink. There wasn't much Unreal left in Castle Midnight these days, to everyone's quiet relief.

The Princess and the Champion moved on, hand in hand, and then chased each other round and round the great Standing Stone until they were breathless and giddy. Though tired as they were, neither of them leaned on the Stone. A tall outcropping of jagged black stone, lumpy and shapeless, it was old, very old. Some said older than the Castle itself. The old name for the Stone, among the peasants and farmers, was The God

Within. There were many places in Redhart where the ancient beliefs still persisted: that a forgotten pagan god or devil still stood imprisoned or asleep within the Standing Stone, waiting to reemerge in Redhart's hour of greatest need.

And whether you considered that a good or a bad thing depended on which versions of the old stories you listened to.

The Standing Stone was quite definitely Unreal, but almost everything else of that nature was gone. Ghosts no longer wandered the Castle corridors at night, the Castle's rooms stayed where they were supposed to, and the gargoyles up on the roof were just stone carvings. The Wild Magic had departed from Castle Midnight, and from most of Redhart, and nearly everyone agreed that while this might be less romantic, it was quite definitely safer for all concerned.

Catherine grabbed Malcolm's broad wrists in her tiny hands, and spun him round and round till both of them were giddy, and then she pulled him forward till they were face-to-face, eyes bright, mouths stretched in smiles that seemed like they would last forever. Catherine moved in closer, till their noses were almost touching and they could feel each other's breath on their mouths.

"I think we've been engaged long enough," said Catherine. "I think . . . it's time we got married!"

Malcolm laughed. "I thought I was supposed to ask you?"

"You were taking too long," said Catherine.

"What about your father, the King?" said Malcolm.

"He knows all about us!" said Catherine. "Always has. He knows everything that goes on. If he didn't think you were suitable, he'd have broken us up long ago."

"I meant," said Malcolm, "that it is traditional for the King to set the date for a Royal wedding."

"He's been taking too long," said Catherine. "I think a month from now will do nicely. I'll tell him."

"You do that," said Malcolm. "I'll watch. From a safe distance, and preferably while hiding behind something."

"You're not frightened of Daddy, are you? He's just an old softie, really."

"To you, maybe. To me, he is my King." Malcolm looked at her thoughtfully. "And besides, don't I get any say in any of this?"

Catherine pouted playfully. "You do want to marry me, don't you?"

"You know I do," said Malcolm.

"Love me?" said Catherine.

"Love you," said Malcolm.

"Forever?"

"Forever and a day."

They kissed, and then she squealed delightedly as he picked her up off her feet and swung her round and round. Such a happy day, and everything to live for. They had no reason at all to suspect bad news. In fact, when Malcolm finally put Catherine down, and they looked round to see an official Court herald making his way steadily through the gardens, in his official tabard of crimson and cream, obviously looking for someone . . . it never even occurred to the Princess and the Champion that the herald might be looking for them. Until he finally spotted the two of them and headed determinedly in their direction. Looking pale and unhappy, but determined.

"What could he possibly want with us?" said Catherine, frowning for the first time. "I haven't broken anything important for ages."

"Not everything is about you," Malcolm said fondly. "It could be there's been another border incursion by Forest forces and the King wants me to go out on patrol again."

"Oh, boring!" said Catherine.

"For you, maybe," said Malcolm, amused. "Just because we call these encounters skirmishes, it doesn't mean they aren't real battles. Good men die, on both sides, every day, fighting over that stupid stretch of land."

Catherine placed both her palms on his chest and gazed into his eyes, immediately contrite. "I do worry about you when you're away from me. Just because you're the Champion, it doesn't mean you can't get hurt."

"I'll try to remember that," Malcolm said solemnly.

"Take care of yourself," said Catherine. "That's an order."

"Yes, my Princess."

They both looked round, and moved just a little apart, as the herald finally arrived and lurched to a halt before them, more than a little out of breath. He'd been searching for them for some time, they could tell. The herald saluted them both and launched quickly into his memorised message, because he really didn't want to be stopped or interrupted, as he knew they were going to want to do.

"Princess Catherine, sir Champion, King William commands that you both attend him at the current session of Court. Immediately. As in right now, no excuses, no stopping off along the way. The King has an important announcement to make, affecting both of you. That's it—thank you. I really must be going now—goodbye."

And he was off and running, back through the gardens at full pelt, before they could even think to try to question him. Which was not a good sign. Catherine and Malcolm looked at each other.

"What the hell was that all about?" said Malcolm.

"An official announcement, in front of the whole Court, that affects both of us?" said Catherine. "It can't be . . . I haven't even talked to him about the marriage yet!"

"If this was a happy thing," Malcolm said slowly, "the herald wouldn't have bolted like that. I've never seen anyone run so fast who didn't have someone on horseback chasing him. No. I think . . . this is something to do with the worsening military situation between Redhart and the Forest. Maybe the negotiations have broken down, at last. Maybe, just maybe, this is war."

"No," said Catherine immediately. "It can't be. I'd have heard . . . something . . ."

They looked at each other for a long moment, with wide, frightened eyes, and then they both started back across the gardens, heading for Castle Midnight. And the terrible decision that lay waiting for them.

It didn't take them long to reach the massive stone Keep that provided the only main access to the Castle, a great looming structure with arrow-slit windows and a heavy portcullis—a blunt stone edifice designed solely to keep out the enemy. But that was long ago, and it had been centuries since the Keep had seen a sword drawn in anger, so now the huge stone walls were covered from top to bottom with endless intricate carvings, etched deep into the old, discoloured stone. Saints and sinners, heroes and villains, dragons and unicorns and mermaids. After so long a time at peace, the Keep had become a work of art. But the old arrow-slit windows still remained, the great iron portcullis stood ready to slam down at a moment's notice, and the Keep was always, always, guarded. By men in armour who looked like they knew how to use the swords and axes at their sides. Malcolm stopped briefly to talk with the guards, but none of them had heard anything of war, or even recent Forest incursions into the disputed territories.

Catherine and Malcolm passed through the Keep and on into the Castle proper, each of them holding the other's hand tightly now, for mutual reassurance. They moved quickly through the entrance halls and chambers, and hurried along the wide stone corridors, heading for the Court by the most direct route. They passed through oversized halls and galleries, built long ago on a larger than human scale, since Castle Midnight had been designed to impress, rather than for the comfort of its inhabitants. But down the long years, most of the heavy stone walls had been covered and decorated with all kinds of portraits and paintings. To take the edge off. There were passable portraits of important people, great scenes of important events and battles, and marvellous views from locations all across Redhart. Statues stood proudly in every nook and cranny, some painted and some not, depending on which era they were from. Representing great personages, Romantic ideals, and forgotten gods and goddesses from pagan times, who might actually have been visitors to Castle Midnight, back in those days when the Unreal was strong. There were glorious hanging tapestries, thick rugs and carpets of quite marvellous design and workmanship, some of them in urgent need of repair. Because while no comfort was too great or too expensive for King William's Castle, money was short. The border skirmishes had been going on for years, increasingly expensive in funds as well as lives.

The very latest innovation was the yellow-flamed gas lighting that was absolutely everywhere now, inside the Castle. Marsh gas, from the massive swamps to the south of the Castle. An almost inexhaustible supply, apparently, though most people tended to pick up on the word *almost*. The gas was mostly pumped through hollowed-out candelabra, bright butter-yellow flames popping out where the wicks should have been. The flickering lights also hissed and glowed through stylised face masks, or gargoyle heads, the flames jutting from eyes and mouths. Catherine had been genuinely scared by them when she was a child. Though she would rather have died than admit that to anyone, even then. She didn't much care for the gaping faces now, and made a point of ignoring the things as she stalked past them.

Malcolm knew. He'd always known, but never said anything. Because sometimes love is keeping other people's secrets as privately as your own.

Some of the statues lurking in the Castle's inner corridors were stranger and more outlandish than others. There were those who said these statues had been alive, back when Castle Midnight had been more Unreal, and that they'd been known to stomp loudly up and down the corridors. Given the monstrous shapes and attributes of some of the statues, everyone fervently hoped that they would remain just statues. There had been a serious movement, a few years back, to have all the more worrying statues smashed and destroyed, just in case, but King William put a stop to that. Because, he said, they were part of Castle Midnight's heritage. And because they might be needed someday. The courtiers and politicians had looked at one another and chosen to say nothing. Most people preferred not to remember when the Castle had been home to so many manifestations of the Unreal, with ghosts and monsters and abominations walking openly abroad. Rooms that devoured their inhabitants, and doors that suddenly led to strange new worlds. That was all part of the past now, thanks to King William's legendary grandparents, Good King Viktor and Queen Catriona, who together put down a rebellion by the Unreal, took away its power, and put the Wild Magic to sleep. For the good of all.

As Catherine and Malcolm finally drew near to the Court, they couldn't help noticing that virtually all the corridors and passageways they passed through were packed with people—from servants to aristocrats and everyone in between, all of them chattering animatedly with one another. And all of them fell suddenly silent as the Princess and the Champion bore down on them. The conversation would of course start up again the moment the two of them were safely past and out of earshot. These people knew what was going on, even if Catherine and Malcolm didn't. But no one would talk to them. In fact, people would look innocently at the two of them as they approached, and then back quickly away if they seemed to be getting too near. Some actually turned and ran rather than be pressed for information. Catherine was honestly baffled by such behaviour, being so universally beloved, but Malcolm thought he was beginning to understand. The Princess could throw a really quite remarkable temper tantrum, on the rare occasions when she couldn't get her own way, with a tendency to smash anything she could get her hands on, and even assault people who didn't back away fast enough.

He tried to slow down, so he could think things through in his usual slow and methodical way and work out what the hell was going on, but Catherine would have none of that. She was just too impatient, too desperate to know, and she hurried him ruthlessly on. That had always been her way, to meet her problems head-on.

W hen the Princess and the Champion finally reached the Court, they were both astonished to discover that the huge double doors were firmly closed. The two of them had been hurrying along hand in hand, but Malcolm now made a point of quietly but firmly separating their hands as they approached the doors . . . and the guards standing at attention before the doors. The King knew all about the closeness of their relationship—everybody did—but it wouldn't do to flaunt it in public. Some things just weren't done. Catherine didn't give a damn, but Malcolm understood propriety. He had tried to explain it to Catherine once, and she had called him a very rude word.

They stopped before the closed double doors. They weren't usually closed when Court was in session. In fact, neither Catherine nor Malcolm could ever recall seeing such a thing before. And now, instead of the two usual ceremonial guards, there were a dozen heavily armed guards, all of whom looked like experienced fighting men. Malcolm recognised a few of them from past border skirmishes. He addressed them by name, but they just stared coldly back at him. The man in charge ignored him completely, addressing himself solely to Catherine.

"Princess, it is regrettably necessary that you remain here, outside the Court, while I send in a message to inform the King that you have arrived."

"We were summoned here by the King," Malcolm said quickly, as storm clouds gathered in Catherine's face. "What is going on here?"

"I have my orders," said the guard, still looking only at Catherine. And from the way he said it, Malcolm could tell there was absolutely nothing to be gained by pressing the point. Catherine opened her mouth to say something that would undoubtedly only have made matters worse, but Malcolm grabbed her upper arm and squeezed it hard enough to make her wince, then led her a suitable distance away from the doors. Which then opened just long enough to allow a single guard to enter, before quickly closing again. Catherine yanked her arm out of Malcolm's grasp, glared at him, and then strode, scowling, up and down in front of the closed doors, rehearsing all the terrible things she was going to say to her father once she got inside.

Malcolm looked thoughtfully at the two huge statues, set on either side of the doors, of Good King Viktor and Queen Catriona. The facial likenesses were clear and detailed, but so idealised there was no way of knowing how accurate they were. Good people and wise rulers, everyone said, and a hard act to follow. Malcolm doubted they'd ever been kept waiting outside a closed door. They'd have just kicked the doors in and then walked all over anyone who got in their way. Catherine stopped pacing, to see what Malcolm was paying so much attention to.

"My great-grandparents," she said. "You think they'll ever put up statues to you and me? Doesn't seem likely, does it? How can you hope to prove yourself when you're brought up in the shadow of legends like those two? Makes me sick."

"They were just people," said Malcolm. "Doing their best in difficult times, no doubt. Read the real histories if you get a chance, not the official ones. And ignore the legends."

"In this spooky old dump, history and legend are often the same thing," said Catherine. "See that long couch over there? Do you think it would make a decent battering ram?"

Perhaps fortunately, the great double doors finally opened, falling soundlessly back on concealed counterweights. Catherine plunged straight forward into the Court, with Malcolm right behind and hurrying to catch up. As they entered the vast hall of the Court of Redhart, they discovered immediately that it was packed full of Lords and Ladies, courtiers and politicians, all of them dressed in their most formal attire. And every single one of them had been talking, loudly and animatedly, when the doors opened . . . only to fall silent the moment Catherine and Malcolm made their delayed entrance. The only sound in the Court now was the soft slapping of two sets of boots on the waxed and polished floor as the Princess and the Champion headed straight for King William on his throne.

He was looking right at them, and not in a good way. Malcolm felt sudden chills run up and down his spine. In all the years he'd served his King, he'd never known William to look at him in such a way. The courtiers and the politicians fell back, to the left and to the right, opening up a broad empty aisle for Catherine and Malcolm to walk down, funnelling them straight to the throne—just in case they'd been thinking of going somewhere else. Malcolm tried to read the expressions on the faces around him but couldn't. Whatever had happened at Court, or was about to happen, it was important enough to have stamped the same fixed expression on all their faces. Most of those present wouldn't even meet his eyes. Malcolm looked back at the King. His face was cold and set and determined, and completely unreadable. King William was wearing his most ornate and ceremonial robes, but badly, with little or no style. He was a large and blocky man, well into middle age, with iron grey hair, and his crown always looked subtly too big for him. The years of strain and endless responsibilities had taken a toll on him, but he was still a vigorous and overpowering presence. He'd always been the brute force type: everything forward and trust in Fate. But he could be subtle, and even crafty, when the occasion demanded.

He was still mostly remembered for beating a traitor to death with his bare hands, right there in the Court, in front of everyone. Because the man had been his friend . . . for so many years.

Malcolm could feel his own frown deepening, until it was actually painful. The more he saw, the less sense things made. What the hell were all these people doing here? Nothing of note had been planned for today's session. As far as he knew. It finally occurred to Malcolm that he must have been quite deliberately kept in the dark about all this. Because whatever it was that had been decided, everyone knew he wasn't going to approve of it. His unarmoured back began to crawl in anticipation of arrows from hidden archers. He hadn't done anything wrong that he was aware of, nothing to justify sudden execution without trial . . . No, that wasn't it. The looks around him were fascinated, not accusing. He glared about him and a great many people fell back, to give him even more room. Malcolm might not have the Princess' fiery temper, but he was, after all, the King's Champion and a decorated border fighter, and no one present doubted that he could be extremely dangerous if provoked.

Even if he didn't have his sword with him. It had never occurred to him that he'd need it today.

The more he studied the packed Court, the more it baffled him. Everyone was dressed up in their very best, in a riot of blazing, glorious colours, like so many parrots and peacocks. Long, swinging robes and elegant gowns, even some highly decorated sets of ceremonial armour that must surely have been pulled out from the back of some very old and neglected closets. Set faces and staring eyes everywhere he looked, as if the crowd was waiting for a Tourney to begin and first blood to be spilled. Malcolm slowed as he finally approached the King on his throne, and he slowed Catherine too, with a hidden subtle pressure on her arm. Whatever was happening here, it was important. You just didn't get this many notable people gathered together in one place unless it was for something really significant. Like a coronation, or a declaration of war. Malcolm's thoughts raced back over the last few days, but he hadn't heard anything. Had things really got so far out of hand with the Forest Kingdom, and he'd missed it because he was so wrapped up with Catherine? He looked at the Princess, who was still glowering angrily about her, but she was clearly just as much in the dark as he was.

They stopped before the throne, a surprisingly understated piece of furniture, given the Castle's usual overpowering style, supposedly designed personally by Good King Viktor to replace the original. Which, like everything else, had been built to impress, but Viktor liked his comfort. King William sat very still, looking down on his daughter and his Champion. In Redhart the King ruled, though he was, always, very firmly advised by the elected Parliament. The King nearly always went along, because he trusted the judgement of his Prime Minister. If either man were ever to openly defy the other, there would be civil war. So everyone was always very careful to get along. The Prime Minister himself, Gregory Pool, was standing right beside the throne, his face as cold and set as the King's. Catherine's scowl deepened. For both of them to be here, so publicly close together, it had to mean that whatever important and significant thing had been decided, they were both in complete agreement about it.

Gregory Pool was of medium height, but a very large fellow, with a round face and plump hands, whose buttons on his bulging waistcoat strained every time he took a breath. He liked to play the jolly, bluff, what-you-see-is-what-you-get type of character, but that was only for people who didn't work with the man. The Prime Minister possessed a first-class mind, but if he had a heart he never listened to it. He was the same age as the King but took pains to look a good few years younger.

He'd been Prime Minister of Redhart for twenty years, because he was still the sharpest knife in the political drawer, knew where all the bodies were buried or at least concealed, and could play any number of sides off against one another.

He smiled a lot but rarely meant it. Catherine couldn't stand him. Mostly because he always took her father's side over hers. And Malcolm knew that the Prime Minister always kept a careful eye on him. Because the Prime Minister knew that if the King ever lost faith in him, it would be the Champion the King turned to, to . . . take care of matters.

Catherine and Malcolm stood together before the King on his throne. Malcolm bowed, Catherine did not, merely scowling sulkily at her father. And then, to avoid having to speak to him, she deliberately looked right past the King, at the huge stained-glass windows set into the far wall behind the throne. And the King let her. Which struck Malcolm as a really bad sign. If the King was actually willing to be patient with her on such an important occasion, it could only mean that he was sure he was going to get his own way in the end. Malcolm looked at the windows too, if only because he preferred that to looking at the King looking at his daughter. The stained glass showed even more idealised images of Good King Viktor and Queen Catriona, so ornate, delicately worked and brightly coloured, that the windows didn't actually let that much light into the Court. The vast hall was mostly illuminated by floating, glowing silver spheres that bobbed unsupported on the air, here and there, wherever they felt like, lighting their particular part of the Court bright as day. They had been created long ago by some unknown sorcerer, and now no one remained who knew how the things worked. Everyone just hoped they kept going. Because it would take a hell of a lot of gas lamps to illuminate this Court.

Catherine finally looked at the King. Their gazes met and locked. When the Princess spoke, her voice was surprisingly steady. "Father, what have you done?"

"I have an important announcement to make," said the King mildly. "And it is necessary that you be here to hear it."

"Why wasn't I told about this in advance?" said Catherine.

"Because I make the decisions here," said King William. "I will decide what you need to hear, and when you need to know it. Now be still, my daughter, and pay attention." He looked out across the packed Court, and the general air of anticipation and tension ratcheted up another notch. "Be it known, my Lords and Ladies, my good advisors, and faithful friends all . . . It is my pleasant duty to announce this day that a marriage has been arranged, between Princess Catherine of Redhart . . . and Prince Richard of the Forest Kingdom."

Catherine and Malcolm were struck speechless. They looked wildly at each other, and then back at the King. Everyone at Court applauded politely, and there were even a few encouraging cheers. A band lurking at the very rear of the hall struck up a patriotic air, with a lot of brass and cymbals. And then it all went to ratshit as Catherine exploded.

"WHAT?"

Silence fell across the Court. The band stopped playing. Everyone in front tried to back away a little farther, but the rows behind weren't having it. They wanted to see everything. Catherine stood before her father, shaking with sheer fury. Even Malcolm took a thoughtful step away from her, just to be sure she wouldn't make a grab for the emergency backup dagger she knew he kept concealed in a sheath on his arm. He was thinking quickly, trying to understand why this was happening, and how best to deal with it, while he kept his face carefully calm and collected. He folded his arms tightly across his chest, to ease the pain in his heart and hold it in, while he waited for the storm to pass. But as Catherine drew in a deep breath to really let her father have it, the King leaned abruptly forward on his Throne and fixed her with a hard stare.

"Do you want a scene, daughter, or do you want an explanation?"

Catherine glared at him, her hands held up before her, clenched into fists. There were tears burning in her eyes, but she was damned if she'd shed them in front of everyone. She met her father's gaze defiantly but said nothing.

"Redhart and the Forest Kingdom have been arguing over the same stupid stretch of borderland for decades," the King said flatly. "Ever since the Forest Land was combined with the adjoining Dutchy of Hillsdown, under King Stephen, son of King Harald, brother to the legendary hero Prince Rupert, and Queen Felicity, sister to the legendary Princess Julia and daughter of the Duke of Hillsdown. Everything was fine while these two countries remained separated and angry with each other, but once they combined into a single realm, that meant the border between our two countries became more important than ever. Down through the years there have been a great many armed skirmishes, and even open battles, over who owns exactly what in those heavily disputed territories, because that narrow strip of land includes a vital Redhart trade route."

"I know," said Catherine. "I'm not stupid. I did stay awake in history class. So many battles, so many good men dead, over a bloody trade route. Over salt, and pepper. It beggars belief."

The Prime Minister took a step forward, and everyone's eyes immediately went to him. Gregory Pool coughed modestly and addressed the Court in his usual pleasant, practiced speaking voice. "It's far more than just another trade route, Princess Catherine. That narrow strip of land is what links Redhart to the outside world. To all the marvellous goods and ideas that flow up from the Southern Kingdoms. It is a lifeline, not just for business but for a good many things that our country depends on for its survival. If the Forest Kingdom should ever gain control of that stretch of land and decide to shut us out, or barricade it, we would starve. It has taken decades of patient negotiation and very careful diplomacy, but we have finally reached an agreement. The Forest has agreed to give up all claims to a large area of the disputed territories—not all, but enough—in return for a guaranteed border. Our trade route, and our security, will be assured. Forever."

"They've given us something," said the King, "so I have to give them something. I'm giving them you, Catherine. My dearest daughter."

Catherine turned abruptly to Malcolm. "Well? Are you just going to stand there and say nothing?"

"What is there to say?" said Malcolm.

Catherine stared at him, shocked that he could give her up so easily. He looked away, unable to meet her gaze. His shoulders were hunched, his hands clenched into impotent fists at his sides. And Catherine swallowed the angry words she'd been about to hurl at him. She knew him; she could see inside him. She could see the anger, the violence, simmering just below the surface. And she knew him well enough to know that if he let his temper go, like her, there would be blood and slaughter in the Court. And he would start with her father, the King. For doing this terrible thing to her.

"Malcolm?" said Catherine uncertainly.

"What do you want me to say, Catherine? What do you want me to do? *What do you want me to do?*"

Catherine looked away from him, and back at the King and the Prime Minister, and the silently watching Court. And knew she was on her own.

"So," she said to her father, "I am to marry this Prince, and be a lifetime hostage at his Court, to make sure you don't take anymore land than was agreed."

"That too," said the King. "But it will bring our two countries closer together, and will mean peace instead of war."

"But they're not even a proper Royal family!" Catherine said desperately. "They're a constitutional monarchy these days! The whole country's a bloody democracy!"

"We all have to make sacrifices," said the King. "I'm giving up my child, my own flesh and blood. You're going to give up Malcolm." He stopped then, and turned, finally, to his Champion. He actually paused a while, searching for the right words. "I am sorry, my Champion. Bravest and most noble of my soldiers. You have done so much for me, and this is how I reward you. I know you love my daughter. Even more than I do. I am . . . sorry."

"I understand," said Malcolm. His voice was rough as he faced his King, but his eyes were dry. "It's duty. I'm a soldier, first and foremost. Always have been. I've always understood about duty, and honour. And sacrifice."

"What if I say no?" said Catherine. Everyone looked at her again.

"If we throw this agreement back in the faces of the Forest King and his Parliament," said the Prime Minister, "after struggling so hard and so long to make it work, then they will take back their offer of land. Land that we must have. If they won't give it up—and they won't—we will have no choice but to take it by strength of arms. Send our armies across the border into the Forest Land and seize it. And that will mean war. And let me be very clear, Princess." He was talking to the Court now, as much as to her. "If Redhart does go to war against the Forest, neither side could afford to back down until the other was utterly defeated and made incapable of presenting any further threat. We couldn't afford to go through this again. We would have to invade and conquer the Forest people, completely subjugate them, because nothing less would end the matter.

"Or they would have to do it to us.

"Of course, neither side wants a war. Wars are expensive; they cost a lot of money, and lives, and ruined land. So the only way we could hope to make our losses back would be to tax and loot the defeated country to within an inch of its life. It would take generations . . . before our two populations could forgive what we did to each other. No more skirmishes, Princess Catherine, no more battles. This would be armies fighting armies. Slaughter and butchery on a scale neither country has seen in ages. Cities burning in the night, fields soaked in blood, rivers choked with floating bodies . . . War is nothing like the songs, Princess."

Catherine clapped both her hands to her ears and cried out in simple despair, *"I can't do it! I won't do it!"*

The King and the Prime Minister and the Court were silent. Catherine looked slowly around at them, and saw them all looking back at her with a cold, implacable certainty. And she knew that no mere temper tantrum was going to get her out of this. Nothing she could say would mean anything, because all the decisions that mattered had already been made, by all the people who really mattered.

Catherine looked sharply at her brother, Prince Christof, standing proudly on the other side of King William's throne. A tall and slender dandy, with a pleasant enough face and flat blonde hair, he'd been noticeably silent so far. He was dressed in his usual brightly coloured flashing silks, like the clashing flags of too many nations, and still managed to hold himself with grace and poise. But for all his ostentation, he still carried a perfectly ordinary sword on his hip, in a well-worn scabbard. Christof knew how to use a sword. He'd been riding out to join border skirmishes ever since he was old enough to defy his father and get away with it. Since he was fourteen. Now in his early twenties, he'd made a name for himself apart from his title, on the border, as a warrior and a patriot. There were already popular songs and stories about him. And if he was perhaps a little more fond of duels that he should be, ready to fight absolutely anybody at the drop of an insult, or something he could take as an insult, he was usually able to stop himself at first blood.

He smiled easily at Catherine, and when she saw what was in that smile and in his eyes, all her rage came flooding back. She stepped forward and stabbed an accusing finger at her younger brother.

"You knew about this! You knew all along!"

"Of course I knew," drawled Christof, still smiling. "I've been part of the negotiating team for years. I thought you knew."

"You?" said Catherine. "A diplomat? You love fighting on the border, and going on raids into the Forest Land!"

"Yes," said Christof, "I do. But I am a Prince of Redhart, and ready to do whatever is best for my country. I'm giving up something I love, so why shouldn't you?"

"Hush, boy," growled King William, and Prince Christof immediately fell silent.

The King looked as though he wanted to say something else, but he didn't. No one was surprised. The King had always been cool to his son, ever since Christof killed his mother being born. And even if Christof had made himself into a popular warrior figure, the King had never warmed to Christof's particular brand of cold intelligence. No one was surprised that the King gave all the affection he had to Catherine. As a result, the two children had never been close, though they had occasionally combined forces against a common enemy: their father.

Catherine turned her glare on the Prime Minister. "You! Pool . . . This was never my father's idea. He's never given a damn about the border, or trade routes, before. You talked him into this! The arranged marriage was all your idea, wasn't it?"

"King and Parliament stand together on this," said the Prime Minister quite calmly. "We have always been able to make the hard decisions, to do what is necessary, to preserve the security of Redhart. Now it's your turn, Princess Catherine. But . . . the arranged marriage really wasn't my idea. I can't take the credit. The idea came from your brother, Prince Christof."

Catherine looked at Christof speechlessly. He smiled easily at her. "What can I say, Sister? Some ideas are just too obvious to be overlooked."

"I know why you made yourself part of the negotiating team," said Catherine, and her voice was quiet and ugly and vicious. "I know why you did this. With me gone from the Court, Little Brother, you'll finally have the uninterrupted access to Father that you've always wanted. Access to the throne! You've always hated it that Father preferred me as his heir!"

Christof just smiled maddeningly at her.

"Enough!" said the King. "I approved of the border skirmishes for years, because they were a good training ground for our young fighting men. But events have progressed beyond that. The situation must be settled! Before it spills over into something worse. You will leave Redhart for the Forest Kingdom first thing tomorrow morning, Catherine. And you will be married to Prince Richard before the end of the year. Is that clear?"

Catherine lost her temper completely. Yelling and screaming at the top of her voice, cursing everyone before and around her with the foulest of language, and offering to duel anyone who thought they could force her into this farce of a marriage of convenience. She called her father an old fool, playing at politics he didn't understand. Called the Prime Minister a backstabbing politician, determined to prove himself more powerful than the King. Called Christof a ball-less little turd who would sacrifice anyone to get his unworthy backside on the throne. And called Malcolm a coward, to his face, for not fighting for her.

Nobody answered. No one said anything. Half the Court were embarrassed by her outburst, and the other half were quite clearly enjoying every moment. Some of them had notepads out and were jotting down the details, so they could dine out on them afterwards. Malcolm wouldn't look at her; he merely stared at the floor before the throne with dead, defeated eyes. The King was cold, the Prime Minister was remote, and Christof was still smiling. And even as she raged and swore and shook her fist, Catherine knew it was all for nothing. The decision had been made. She only shouted and swore because . . . she had to do something.

Eventually she just ran out of energy. She broke off abruptly, staring about her with wild eyes, like a deer brought to bay at the end of a hunt. Shaking, and shuddering. Malcolm turned to her and offered her a clean handkerchief from his sleeve. Catherine looked at it for a long moment, as though she didn't recognise what it was, or what it was for. And then she put a hand to her face and felt the tears there. She took the handkerchief from him and scrubbed her face clean with a numb thoroughness. When she was done, she gave Malcolm his handkerchief back. And then, only then, she looked at the King.

"Do we even know what this Prince Richard looks like?" she said.

"Of course," said the King. "Do you really think we'd marry you to a stranger? They sent us an official portrait."

He gestured sharply, and a servant hurried forward bearing a large framed painting. He held it up before Catherine, so she could look it over. The painter had done a good enough job, but once again the image was so stylised and idealised and just plain perfect that it could have been anyone. Catherine put her fist right through the portrait and punched out the servant holding it. He hit the floor hard and didn't move again. Quite possibly because he was afraid to. The torn and broken portrait lay on top of him. The King shot bolt upright to stand before his throne and glare at his daughter.

"*That is enough!* Or I will have you dragged from this Court, put in chains, and locked in your rooms under house arrest until it's time for you to leave!"

"Quite right, Father."

"Shut up, Christof."

Catherine glared back at her father unflinchingly. "You really think you can make me go through with this farce of a marriage?"

"When you've had time to think about this," said the King, "calmly and sensibly . . . you will see where your honour and duty lie. And then you will marry Prince Richard of your own free will."

"You have no other choice," said the Prime Minister.

Catherine looked around the packed Court, like an animal seeing the bars of its cage for the first time. She said nothing.

"It's not as if you'll be going alone," said the King, after the silence had dragged on uncomfortably. "You will have friends and bodyguards to accompany and protect you. Lady Gertrude will be your companion, and the Sombre Warrior will be your protector."

Catherine looked across the Court, and sure enough there was Lady Gertrude, smiling and nodding at her. Gertrude was a calm, motherly, middle-aged Lady, with a sweet smile and an implacable iron will. She had helped raise Catherine when she was just a small child, after her mother died so unexpectedly. And Catherine had to admit that she did feel just that little bit better, knowing she wouldn't be going into exile alone but would have at least one good friend and ally she could depend on.

Lady Gertrude was wearing her usual black dress, to show she was still in mourning for her one true love, killed when they were both still teenagers. He'd gone off to fight in the border skirmishes, to make a name for himself, as so many young men had. To prove to Gertrude's parents that he was worthy. He went, and he never came back. A lot of young men went looking for fame on the border and found only death. Gertrude's sad story was the first thing most people thought of when they thought of her, because she never let anyone forget that her life had been ruined by the border skirmishes, by the senseless loss of her one true love. There'd never been anyone else.

There was even a tragic, minor, and not particularly good popular song about it.

Gertrude came forward to stand before Catherine. She smiled understandingly and put out her plump hands to take both of Catherine's and squeeze them reassuringly. Catherine barely reacted.

"Do you think I should go along with this, Lady Gertrude?"

"To go into exile, to the Court of the Land that killed my dearest love?" said Gertrude in her warm, even voice. "Yes, my sweet. Because it's necessary. It's time for you to grow up, Catherine, my dear, and take on adult duties and responsibilities. You must have known this day would come. You couldn't hope to remain a careless child forever."

Catherine nodded slowly and pulled her hands away from Gertrude. She looked at the King. "Aren't you afraid I'll run away, Father, first chance I get?"

"Not if you give me your word of honour that you won't," said the King. "And you will do that, before I let you leave this Court."

Catherine turned away from them all, to look at the Sombre Warrior, standing alone, as always. He stood at the very back of the Court, joined to no faction or party. Mainly because no one else wanted to be anywhere near him. Even standing perfectly still and silent, with his great sword safely sheathed on his hip, the Sombre Warrior was a brooding, dangerous presence.

A huge, hulking figure, in battered and much-repaired chain mail, he stood calm and impassive, his whole face covered by a chalk white porcelain mask, held firmly in place by leather straps. He had lost his face in a border battle, hacked and burned away, years before. Apparently his remaining features were so hideous now that he never let anyone see them. He wore his full face mask in public, and a full steel helm in battle. The mask had only a few deft dark brushstrokes on it to suggest features. There was no gap for mouth or nose or ears, just two small holes for his dark, unblinking eyes.

The Sombre Warrior hardly ever left his chambers, except to go out and kill the enemies of Redhart on the King's orders. He had never had a lover. There had been women, and some men, who found the Sombre Warrior an attractive, tragic Romantic figure, and would have been happy to . . . comfort him, without ever wanting to see what was behind the mask. The Sombre Warrior said no to all of them. To his annoyance, this seemed to encourage his admirers rather than put them off. There was no accounting for Romance . . .

There were a few who'd tried to rip his mask off in public, for a dare or a bet or a laugh. The Sombre Warrior killed everyone who tried, and the King never allowed him to be punished, or even brought to trial, no matter how well connected the dead young men might have been, or who their grieving parents were. Everyone had left the mask strictly alone for some time now.

No one knew his real name. He could have been any age, from any region, from any background. He was the only survivor of that fateful battle somewhere across the border. He came back more dead than alive, with a ruin of a face and most of his memory gone. The Sombre Warrior lived now only to fight the King's battles.

Catherine looked at him dubiously. The fact that the King was willing to send such an important and trusted figure with her showed how seriously he was taking this, but . . . Did this perhaps mean that the Sombre Warrior was now out of favour, and the King was sending him all the way to the Forest Land so he couldn't talk about all those things he was supposed to have done on the King's behalf?

"What's he going to protect me from?" she said sullenly to the King. "Wolves? Bears? Demons?"

It was a sort of admission that she was going. That she had accepted it. The whole Court seemed to relax a little. The King sat down on his throne again and gave her his full and earnest attention. So Catherine jumped in before he could speak, just to make it clear she hadn't in any way forgiven him.

"I mean, the few remaining Werewolves are a spent force now that their leader's run away. Everyone knows that. And none of the other brigands infesting the woods would dare attack a Royal carriage."

"Hunger and greed can make even the lowliest bandit brave," said the Sombre Warrior. "I will be leading a well-armed force, six of the most experienced soldiers from your father's army. I will not allow anything to stop you from reaching the Forest Castle, Princess. On my word and on my honour."

Catherine was quietly shocked, as were most of the Court. The Sombre Warrior didn't normally speak in public. And no one had ever heard him say so much at one time before. His voice was deep and cold as it emerged from behind the porcelain mask, and slightly distorted. Catherine had to wonder how much of his mouth was left on that wasteland of a face behind the chalk white mask.

And then everyone looked round sharply as General Staker pushed his way forward, to stand, almost but not quite defiantly, before King William. The General bowed, briefly and formally, and the King acknowledged him. As the King's most prominent and experienced general, Staker had earned the right to be heard in Court, even if most people present didn't want to hear what he had to say. Staker was an excellent strategist, a winner of battles, and was much admired by the populace. Mostly because they'd never met him. The worst that could be said (openly) about him was that he'd always been a little too ready to sacrifice his own troops to win a battle. But then, Staker had never given a damn about being popular. He just wanted to win.

He looked more like a merchant than a soldier. Stocky rather than muscular, he dressed like a nouveau riche on the few occasions when he deigned to appear at Court, but he couldn't quite carry it off. He had all of the arrogance but none of the style. He had a brilliant military mind, and had distinguished himself as a vicious and deadly fighter in the field. Staker liked to get his hands dirty and his sword bloody. He'd started off as a common foot soldier and rose rapidly through the ranks, mostly by surviving battles that so many others didn't. The fighting ranks liked to think of him as one of their own, and Staker was always ready to take advantage of that. He was barely into his thirties, with a grim, impassive face, a shaven head, and a brusque, slightly forced charisma. He rarely raised his voice, but because he had a lot of political support from the more conservative factions in Court and Parliament—rather more than some people felt comfortable with—when Staker spoke in that grim, quiet monotone, people listened.

He looked the King square in the eye. "You don't have to do this, Sire. That section of borderland is ours by right. By ancient right. We don't have to take it as a gift from the Forest, or give up our precious Royal blood to them. If they won't give us what is ours, properly ours, then we should take it. It's not too late. My army stands ready to—"

He stopped talking immediately, as the King interrupted him. "I

think you'll find it's my army, actually, General Staker. And I will deter-
mine how it is to be used. You have made your feelings on this matter very
plain, on many occasions. Including in some very high-level meetings that
I know for a fact you weren't invited to. I will not go to war as long as there
exists a better way. One that does not involve mass slaughter on both
sides."

"Once a war is started, it can be very hard to stop," said the Sombre
Warrior, and once again everyone turned to look at him. "We would have
to invade and take control of the whole Forest Kingdom. Even the Demon
Prince and his demon army couldn't manage that."

"You speak of legends!" said Staker quietly but forcefully. "I speak of
peace with honour! What purpose is there in peace if we have to spit on
our honour to get it? We can win this war!"

The Sombre Warrior regarded him thoughtfully from behind his porcelain mask. "How many dead innocents is your honour worth, General?
Or should that be, how much is your pride worth?"

The whole Court began babbling loudly, talking over one another and
arguing a hundred different positions all at once. They were having a great
time. This was turning out to be one hell of a session. Not only was the
Sombre Warrior actually having a conversation with someone, in public,
but he was going head-to-head with General Staker and had all but called
him a damned fool to his face. Some of the younger and more volatile elements were trying to nerve one another up to shout *Duel! Duel! Duel!* at
them.

"There is an old saying," the Prime Minister said loudly, "that war is
far too important to be left to the generals."

Staker looked coldly down his nose at him. "Equally old saying: never
trust a politician. They've always got their own agenda. Or somebody
else's."

"*Enough!*" roared the King. His voice cut through the babble and
silenced it in a moment, as he exploded off his throne to stand before it
again. He glared impartially around him, until everyone bowed their
head or bent their knee to him, including General Staker and the Sombre Warrior. Catherine didn't, but then, nobody expected her to. And
Prince Christof didn't bow either. The Prime Minister studied him

thoughtfully. He'd noticed Prince Christof not bowing to his father, even if no one else had.

"The decision has been made," said King William forcefully. "The marriage will take place. Catherine, you will leave here first thing in the morning, with your party. After you've signed an agreement of your own free will, vowing to abide by my will in this matter."

Almost blind with unshed tears, Catherine turned her back on him and strode out of the Court without waiting to be excused. Everyone gave her plenty of room and looked after her in silence. Many of the faces were sympathetic, but not enough to defy the King and say anything. Malcolm Barrett, King's Champion, stepped forward to address the King in a calm, empty voice.

"Do I have your permission to leave this Court and go after her, Sire? To say goodbye?"

"Of course you do," said the King. "I am sorry, Malcolm. You've always been a good right arm to me. I wish I could do more for you."

"I think you've done enough, Sire," said Malcolm.

He bowed briefly and left the Court. He too was followed by mostly sympathetic faces, but he was too preoccupied to notice. The King watched him all the way, till the doors closed behind him; there was honest regret in the King's face, for everyone to see. He hadn't had the heart to tell Malcolm that he'd known all about the unofficial engagement with his daughter, but that it could never have come to anything. He couldn't allow his daughter to marry someone who wasn't of Royal stock. No matter how loyal a Champion he was.

The Prime Minister was still watching Prince Christof unobtrusively, expecting to see him look triumphant now that he was finally getting what he wanted. One step closer to the throne. But Christof seemed honestly sad as he looked after Malcolm. The Prime Minister hadn't known they were that close. He decided he was going to have to think about that.

Malcolm didn't have to go far to find Catherine. He found her standing with her face to a wall, in a nearby empty corridor, crying like she would never stop. He went up to her, and then hesitated, not sure whether to touch her. But she turned abruptly and threw herself into his arms, burying her face in his shoulder. Holding on to him like a drowning woman. She felt surprisingly small and helpless in his arms. He held her carefully, patting her back and smoothing her long hair. He didn't say anything, because . . . what was there to say? Eventually Catherine spoke to him, her voice muffled against his shoulder.

"We could run away . . . Make a new life, somewhere else . . ."

"No, we couldn't," said Malcolm. "First, because they'd find us. Second, because . . . we both know our duty. The responsibilities that come with our positions. We always knew there'd be a bill, someday, for all the things we've enjoyed. Catherine . . . how could we hope to be happy, knowing how much death and suffering we'd be responsible for?"

Catherine raised her face to meet his. "It's not fair, Malcolm! It's not fair!"

"No, it isn't," said Malcolm. "People like us shouldn't fall in love, Catherine. We're not allowed to have happy endings. Only responsible ones."

Back in the Court, King William declared the day's session to be over, and everyone bowed and curtsied quickly, then left as fast as their feet could carry them, so they could get on with the serious business of discussing everything that had just happened and dissecting every last morsel of meaning out of it. The courtiers had enough new material to keep them going for months, and the politicians even longer. King William sat stolidly on his throne, watching them all go, keeping his thoughts to himself. The Prime Minister didn't move from his side. They had many things they needed to discuss, but not while there was anyone left in the Court to hear them. There was public business, and then there was private business.

Prince Christof would have liked to stay behind, with his father. There were a great many things he also would have liked to discuss with the King, public business and private business. But he only had to look at the expressions on the faces of his father and the Prime Minister to know which way the wind was blowing. So he just bowed courteously to his father, ignored the Prime Minister, and strode unhurriedly out of the Court. One of his closest friends and supporters, the fiercely fashionable and professionally languid Reginald Salazar, had deliberately hung back to walk with him. As always, Reginald was dressed to the very height of fashion and just a little bit beyond. He moved in close beside Prince Christof so he could murmur in his ear.

"Well!" he said. "I say, old thing! Really must congratulate you. Excellent idea of yours, to suggest the arranged marriage during the negotiations, and then push it through the Court, and Parliament, without anyone ever suspecting you were the moving force behind it! So amusing! And now, with one giant leap, our hero is free of his chains. His annoying older sister is gone, and nothing stands between him and the throne he so rightly deserves—"

He broke off, looking down at the knife Prince Christof had just stuck, surreptitiously, into his side. The point had pierced the padded jerkin and nicked the skin over his ribs. A small circle of blood was forming on the jerkin. Reginald Salazar made a little whimpering noise, but kept on walking as Prince Christof urged him along.

"Keep walking, old thing," said Christof. "Don't draw attention to us; there's a good chap."

Salazar nodded quickly, and kept going, staring straight ahead. Christof removed the knife from his friend's ribs and made it disappear back up his sleeve again. He leaned in close, so he could murmur in Salazar's ear.

"Even whisper that thought again, dear Reginald, and I will have you murdered in your sleep. Treason is treason, and must not even be hinted at. Daddy . . . would not approve. Go now."

His young friend all but sprinted for the doors. Other friends and supporters of the Prince were waiting there for him, but one look at Christof's face, and Reginald's, and they quickly decided this was not a good time to bother him. They gathered the tearful Reginald into their arms and led him away in search of a safe haven, to do some serious drinking and discussing of their own. Christof slowed his pace, to give them some time to get well ahead of him. He paused in the open doors, to look back at the King and the Prime Minister, already deep in discussion.

"Sorry I had to do that to you, Malcolm," said Christof. "But she had to go. And now maybe you'll pay more attention to me. My love."

He finally allowed himself a real smile, then left the Court.

• • •

King William and Gregory Pool were left alone at last, in a quiet and deserted Court. The vast hall seemed so much larger now that there was no one to fill it, and the smallest sound seemed to echo on and on, like ghosts whispering in the corners. King William settled back on his throne, silently blessing Good King Viktor for having the good sense to install a comfortable seat of power. William would have liked to install a pillow for his lower back, but it would have sent all the wrong signals to his Court. Couldn't have them thinking he was getting old and decrepit, even if it felt like that some days. No, they'd take advantage, the bastards. He patted one arm of his throne fondly, like a pet that had done well. It was good to have something he could depend on.

Gregory Pool allowed himself to relax, as much as he ever did, and let out a deep sigh of contentment as he undid several of his waistcoat buttons. He would have liked to invest in a corset, for the long standing-around periods on public occasions, but he couldn't. Someone would talk. Someone always did. Fat men were allowed to be jolly, but they weren't allowed to try to hide their state. People would point, and laugh. It was important that the Prime Minister should appear statesmanlike and yet humble when in the public eye, but he found it more of an effort every year. He produced a small silver snuffbox from his sleeve, flipped the lid open with a practiced gesture, and then tipped just the right amount of finely ground cocaine onto his wrist. He sniffed it, delicately, and then offered the box to the King, who shook his head sternly. Pool shrugged, closed the lid, and made the box disappear back up his sleeve.

"Try not to look so openly disapproving, William," said Pool. "We all need a little something to lean on."

"And some days . . . seem so much longer than others," said the King.

"I thought it all went rather well," said Pool. "Or at least, as well as could be expected."

"She didn't actually throw anything," said the King. "Or try to stab anyone. I was impressed. Maybe she's finally learning self-control."

"I wouldn't put money on it," said Pool. He grinned suddenly. "It's Prince Richard I feel sorry for."

The two men shared a knowing smile, but it didn't last long.

In front of the Court, and Parliament, King William and Gregory

Pool were always careful to maintain a professional distance; it wouldn't do for anyone to know just how close they really were. How closely they worked together. Politics was supposed to be all about checks and balances, with Parliament and Court debating both sides of an issue in order to arrive at a consensus. In fact, William and Gregory had been close friends since they were teenagers. It was William who'd first encouraged Gregory to get into politics, so he could have someone he could talk to honestly about things that mattered. They did argue, from time to time, but they got things done. And if that meant pulling the wool over the people's eyes, and deliberately ignoring or even suppressing the occasional dissenting voice, they could live with that.

King William looked out over his empty, echoing Court and slumped back on his throne. He felt tired. He felt tired a lot these days.

"I'm sending my only daughter away," he said. "I'll never see her again."

"Of course you will!" Pool said immediately. "Bound to be lots of Royal visits, back and forth, once the Peace Treaty has been signed and settled, and the marriage has taken place. Good thing too. Lots of money in tourists. And the people do so love a Royal marriage; it helps take their minds off things they're probably better off not thinking about anyway. And you've always known she'd have to leave home eventually. Catherine could only marry another Royal, and that was always going to mean moving to another country."

"Not necessarily," said the King. "Viktor married his own Steward."

"Yes, but that was then, and this is now," Pool said firmly. "Your grandfather could get away with something like that, because he and she had just saved the whole Castle from the threat of the Unreal. Anyone who might have objected was almost certainly drowned out by the roar of popular acclaim. And though I hate to put it so bluntly, William, you're no Viktor. Everyone loved him. They respect you, but that's not the same. These days Royals must marry Royals. Preserve the Blood. That's what they're for. We all do what we must."

"My daughter hates me," said King William. "After everything I've done for her."

"Children never appreciate what you do for them," said Pool. "It's one of those unwritten rules, in the secret book about rearing children that no one ever lets you read before you have them. Because if you knew exactly what you were letting yourself in for, you wouldn't do it. My two boys are just the same."

"Of course, you and I were paragons of virtue, who never gave our parents a single sleepless night," the King said solemnly.

"Quite!" said Pool. "Catherine . . . will get over it. All part of growing up." He stopped there, and looked thoughtfully at the King. "I hate to bring this up, William, but I do have to ask. There are certain . . . requirements in an arranged Royal marriage. Catherine and Malcolm have been . . . really very close, for some time now. Are you absolutely sure she's still . . ."

"Anyone else, I'd have them gelded just for asking," growled the King. "But since it's you . . . Yes, of course I know all about the *requirements* . . . You really think I'd let things get this far if I wasn't completely sure? Catherine is quite definitely still a virgin. I had some very subtle, and very expensive, spells cast over all my children right after they were born, as my father did with me. Not strong enough to compel, or even influence behaviour; they'd have noticed. But strong enough that if anything . . . significant did start to happen, it would have set off all kinds of alarms. Up to and including loud bells and fireworks in the sky. Certainly enough to embarrass everyone involved, and attract the attention of everyone within a five-mile radius. Don't worry; I'll have it all taken off before she leaves the Castle."

"But do the children know this?" said Pool.

"Of course they know! I sat them down and had a fatherly talk with each one of them the moment they hit puberty." King William winced, remembering. "Not one of my easiest duties. Catherine hit me over the head with a ceremonial vase. Dented the crown. But . . . they all understood. She is quite definitely chaste."

"Not quite the word I would have used to describe Christof," said Pool.

"Christof is a good boy," the King said gruffly. "And he'll make a good man. Eventually."

"But will he, can he, make a good King?" said Pool.

"Rumours," said King William. "Gossip."

"I know you don't want to talk about this, William . . ."

"Then we won't."

The King looked sternly at the Prime Minister, who sighed quietly and let the matter drop, accepting that this was one of the few things he and William couldn't talk about. Even though someday they would have to.

"They'd better take good care of my little girl at the Forest Court!" the King said abruptly. "Or there will be no agreement, no Treaty, and to hell with the border! I mean it, Gregory!"

"Of course she'll be well treated," the Prime Minister said soothingly. "They love their Royals in the Forest Land, particularly now they're constitutional monarchs, with no real power. It's all pomp and ceremony over there, with cheering crowds every time they show their faces in public, and everyone lining up to bow their heads and bend the knee just for the thrill of it. And everyone who is everyone, or thinks they ought to be, jostles for position at the Forest Court in the hope that some of the Royal glamour might rub off on them. Catherine will be very popular. They love a strong character . . ."

"She's got that, all right," growled King William. "Gets it from her mother. I thought it was charming when I was courting my Lizzie, but I soon found out . . . Anyway, I'm still concerned about why the Forest Court didn't send us a proper image of Prince Richard. I mean, there are any number of magical devices they could have employed to give us a proper look at him. Do you suppose he's . . . ugly? One does hear rumours, that the Forest Line is just a little bit inbred . . ."

"Of course he isn't ugly!" snapped Pool. "Give me strength . . . I met Richard when he was just a lad, when I was visiting the Forest Court with my father, back when we were still doing trade deals, before everything fell apart. Richard was a handsome little devil. And according to my expert intelligence people, who I admit are only utterly competent, he's grown up into a fine young man."

"Hold it," said King William. "You have spies in the Forest Court?"

"Yes, I have spies in the Forest Court! I have spies everywhere. That's the point of having spies. To tell you what you need to know, when you need to know it, and preferably before they tell anyone else."

"But . . . do they have spies in my Court?"

"Of course! That's why we do some things in public and others in private. Look, leave all this to me, William. You've never worried about such things before, and it's a bit late to start now. All you need to know is that I am on top of everything. Now, Prince Richard . . . He has an excellent reputation as a fighter. Seems our Christof isn't the only Prince who likes to get involved in the border skirmishes when he knows he's not supposed to. Very popular with his own people. Something of a hero, in fact. You must have read some of the reports I gave you, William."

"Some," said the King. "I trust you, Gregory. You say he's good material, that's all I need to hear. You don't think I'd marry my daughter off to a monster, whatever the price, do you?"

The Prime Minister changed the subject. "I'm still trying to find us a half-decent magic-user. Someone with real talent and power, who might be able to bring back some of the Unreal. Just enough to be useful. That marsh gas we found in the swamps isn't going to last forever, you know. And the more real Castle Midnight becomes, the harder it is to heat and light and maintain the place."

"I had noticed, thank you," said the King. "Place is getting old, and grumpy. Like me."

"Oh, stop it, or I'll have one of the servants bring you a shawl," said Pool. "The point is, none of my contacts have turned up anyone useful yet. It's hard to find anyone of any real magical talent these days."

The King sniffed loudly. "That's because most of them go rushing off to that damned Hawk and Fisher Memorial Academy, down in Lancre, and we never see them again. I don't think they should be allowed to do that, depriving the country of a natural resource . . . We should do something about that place. All it does is turn out troublemakers."

"You leave the Hero Academy alone," the Prime Minister said sternly. "They're protected."

"Really?" said the King. "Who by?"

"I don't know! That's what's so worrying . . . Might I remind you that there is always my brother, the sorcerer Van Fleet?"

"Yes, yes," the King said testily. "I know, you keep telling me: he's very proficient, a very useful fellow. Very talented. Done a lot of useful things on our behalf. But when all is said and done, you know as well as I do that he's High Magic. The Unreal has always had its roots in Wild Magic. Last I heard, Van Fleet had been all over Castle Midnight and hadn't been able to detect anything he could get his hands on. Let alone try to call back and place under our control. Can't say I'm that disappointed, really. The Wild Magic was always a harsh mistress, and an unreliable servant. By all accounts, Castle Midnight could be a really scary place to live, back in the day."

"It'll be a scary world if we don't make this agreement work, William," Gregory Pool said soberly. "So much depends on Catherine . . . If this should go wrong, we're going to need all the help we can get."

THREE

ALL ABOUT THE PRINCE

On a colder than usual evening in early autumn, somewhere in the Forest Kingdom, a Prince and his friends went riding in search of adventure. Even though at least one of them knew he wasn't supposed to.

Prince Richard led the way, on his fine white horse, accompanied by his good friends Clarence Lancaster, who fancied himself a minstrel, and Peter Foster, who had never fancied himself as anything other than a soldier. Their horses weren't white, or purebred, or even worth a second look, but they did their job just as well. Evening was sliding slowly into night, and the last of the light was going out of the day. The trees blazed bronze and brass all around them, and just the passing of three young men on horses was enough to shake the last leaves from the trees. The wide trail was already covered with a thick mulch of fallen leaves, muffling the beat of the horses' hooves. Autumn had come early this year, as well as colder, and Prince Richard was quietly disputing with himself as to whether he might have left it just a bit late in the year to go out adventuring. Not that he'd ever admit that in front of his friends, of course. The Prince kept an ear out for wolves, who always appeared with the autumn, but there was hardly a sound anywhere. Just a few birds singing, some stubborn buzz of insects . . . In fact, the woods seemed almost unnaturally quiet.

"Are you sure we can't take some time out for a break, for a bite to eat and a drop of something warming?" said Clarence, shifting uncomfortably in his saddle. He wasn't really built for long rides, and he'd never been noted for his patience where creature comforts were concerned.

"We stopped for a hearty tea just a few hours back," Richard said ruthlessly. "Where, I might add, you managed to consume more smoked meat, travel biscuits, and brandy than Peter and I put together. It's a wonder to me that horse hasn't collapsed under you. You do know the stable master keeps the other horses in line by threatening to give them to you?"

"I am not fat! I've just got big bones."

"You've got a big stomach and a bigger appetite," said Peter, entirely unsympathetically, not taking his eyes off the trail ahead. "I've seen meat pies go running out of the kitchen when you walk in."

"I just have a great appetite for life," said Clarence loftily.

"Then stop complaining," said Richard. "We're on our way to adventure! This is what you said you wanted."

"That was what he wanted when we were all safe back at the Castle," said Peter. "Anyone with any real experience knows that adventure is someone else going through hell, a comfortable distance from wherever you are, sitting and reading about it."

"We are on a mission of mercy, on our way to rescue poor downtrodden mining folk from an unnatural menace," Prince Richard said firmly.

"On our way to an early death, more like," said Peter. "I'm only here because someone's got to watch your back and keep you out of trouble."

"Thank you, Captain Grumpy," said the Prince. "Do let us know if you spot something really depressing, so we can all have a good brood over the unfairness of life."

"Don't give him ideas," said Clarence.

"History will vindicate me," said Peter.

"I'm only here to get firsthand experience for a new song," said Clarence. "I'm quite happy to leave the actual adventuring to those more suited to it. You two get stuck in, and I'll hold the horses. I'm good at holding horses." He broke off and shivered suddenly. "How can it be this cold, this early in the season? We're only just into the fall . . . Maybe I should get my calendar overhauled."

"It is cold," said Peter. "More than properly cold. I'm wearing my long underwear and I can still feel the nip of autumn in some very private places."

"Far too much information," said Richard.

"I hate it when the seasons change, at the end of the year," said Clarence. "Always looks to me like the whole world's dying . . ."

"Stop being such a gloomy bugger," said Peter. "That's my job."

"He's just being minstrely," said Richard.

"That's not even a word," said Peter. "You made that up."

"Is it just me," said Clarence slowly, "or has all the sound gone out of the woods?"

They all listened carefully. The birds had stopped their singing, the insects had disappeared, and there wasn't even a whisper of movement in the tightly packed trees on either side of the beaten trail. The only sound left was the clear, steady progress of their mounts. It was as though the horses and their riders were the only living things left in a dying world. Richard stood up in his stirrups to look around, but the darkening shadows threw back his gaze. He slumped down again.

"Everyone keep their ears open," Peter said steadily. "We're a long way from anywhere halfway civilised, and heading into dangerous territory. There are still monsters in some of the darker parts of the Forest."

"What?" Clarence said immediately. "Dangerous territory? No one said anything to me about going into dangerous territory! I thought we were just going to check out a small mining village. Are we lost again? Do you want me to check the compass?"

"We're well on our way to Cooper's Mill," said Richard. "And you leave that compass alone. You can break delicate mechanisms just by breathing on them."

"Still," said Peter, "it does seem to me that we should have reached Cooper's Mill by now. If we'd been going by the direct route. Like we agreed."

"All right, so we're taking a little detour," said Richard. "Since we were going in the general direction anyway . . . I thought we might take the opportunity to stop off and take a look at the Darkwood."

Peter and Clarence both reined in harshly, bringing their horses to a sudden halt, and Richard had no choice but to stop too. They all looked at one another for a long moment. Clarence's normally flushed features had gone suddenly pale, while Peter studied the Prince with narrowed, thoughtful eyes.

"No wonder it feels so cold," Clarence said finally.

"You didn't say anything about going anywhere near the Darkwood," said Peter.

"Because I knew if I did, you'd both wimp out on me!" said Richard. "It's just a name! You can't let it get to you like this. The Darkwood isn't nearly as big, or as much of a threat, as it used to be. Hasn't been for years. Don't look at me like that! The whole area's barely a mile in diameter these days, and there aren't any demons left in it."

"Some people say that," said Peter. "Other people say otherwise, because they've got more sense. Just because you can't see the demons, it doesn't mean there aren't any there."

"Yes it does!" said Richard.

"There are still demons," said Clarence, looking mournfully around. "All the songs and stories say so."

"Not real demons," said Richard. "Not like back in the Demon War."

"There are still creatures that linger near the Darkwood," said Peter, glaring about him into the darkening shadows between the trees. "Lurking in the deepest, most troubled parts of the Forest. Watching from the gloom at the side of the trail, lying in wait for some poor young fools to come wandering by."

"You're getting as bad as Clarence," said Richard. "Those are just stories! It's been a hundred years now since my illustrious ancestor stamped out all the monsters during the Demon War! I just thought, since we were going to pass by the Darkwood anyway, we might as well stop and take a look. Just to see what it's really like. You said you wanted some decent new material for a song, Clarence. We could be the first men to step inside the Darkwood since . . ."

"We?" said Clarence immediately. "What's all this *we* shit? I'm not going anywhere near it!"

"Neither am I, and neither are you, your highness," Peter said firmly.

"Riding out for a little adventure is one thing; risking your soul and your sanity, quite another."

Richard just laughed at both of them, and Peter and Clarence knew the situation was hopeless. You only had to hear that bright and carefree laughter to know that the Prince had made up his mind and would do what he intended to do, and that he was determined to get his friends into trouble too, for their own good. It was, admittedly, one of the reasons why they stuck with him. Life with Prince Richard might be dangerous, but it was never dull.

Prince Richard of the Forest Kingdom was tall, dark, dashing, and far too handsome for his own good. Now in his mid-twenties, he was brave and charming and loudly cheerful, and would have been unbearable if he hadn't known all that and refused to take himself seriously. He didn't value any of his better qualities because he didn't feel he'd earned them. Which was why he was always so ready to rush off and do something unwise, in search of derring-do.

He'd done some fighting in the border skirmishes, but he hadn't found anything heroic there. Just killing. He did his duty, riding alongside his father's soldiers to drive out the invading Redhart forces, but he took no pleasure in it. He was still looking for the honour and glory promised him by the legends he'd grown up with, of his legendary ancestor, his great-granduncle, Prince Rupert. Who rode on dragons and bore the Rainbow Sword, who saved the Forest Land and all its people from utter destruction by fighting off a whole army of demons, and defeating their leader, the dreaded Demon Prince, Lord of the Darkwood. So whenever chances of action or adventure presented themselves, you could always rely on Richard to be out at the front, smiling and laughing. And nearly always the first to be dragged away by his friends when it all went horribly wrong.

Clarence Lancaster was a man of medium height and far more than medium weight, with an endless appetite for all the good things life had to offer. He and Richard had been close friends since childhood school days, when they were universally judged a bad influence on everyone else. He was determined to be a minstrel and have his songs admired and venerated across the world. He sought out heroic situations so he could observe them, from a safe distance, and then write about them in an authentic manner. Clarence was a sheltered, middle-class merchant's son, with an assured comfortable future, and he couldn't wait to throw it all away, in the name of Romance and Adventure.

He always dressed in the most colourful and radical fashions, none of which ever suited him. He had long red hair, and an equally fiery goatee. He was smart and earnest and thoughtful, and not nearly as observant as he liked to think. He and Richard had bonded early on through their shared enthusiasm for old songs and legends and their mutual distrust of all forms of authority. They were soon inseparable, and their fathers left them together in the vain hope that one might turn out to be a good influence on the other. Richard and Clarence both firmly believed that things had been much better back in the days when there were real dangers to be faced and heroic deeds could still be performed by young men who thought they needed to prove themselves to their fathers.

Clarence accompanied Richard to the border skirmishes and fought bravely enough at Richard's side when he had no other choice. But he had been horrified by the senseless, never-ending blood and slaughter and the complete lack of honour or glory. Just blood-soaked killing grounds and sad, anonymous deaths. A soldier's life turned out to be nothing like the songs. Clarence turned his back on the border the moment Richard was ready to leave, and he never went back.

Richard's only other close friend was an entirely different sort. Peter Foster was a soldier from a long line of soldiers, trained since early childhood to bear arms in the service of those who claimed to be his betters. He was in his late twenties, and liked to think of himself as the mature and steady member of the group. He'd been brought in as a teenager to train the young Prince Richard in how to fight. They'd taken to each other, and Peter never left. A large and stocky man, Peter wore hard-used leather armour instead of the more usual chain mail, because he liked to be able to move quickly and freely at all times. He carried a sword on his hip, an ugly and nameless butcher's blade, a shield on his back, and all kinds of useful, vicious, and quite appallingly nasty secrets tucked away about his person. Peter liked to feel he was prepared for anything an unfriendly world might throw at him.

He went to the border skirmishes, alongside Richard and Clarence. To look out for them, and guard their backs. A lot of his family were already there. He didn't expect anything heroic, so he wasn't disappointed by what he found. He had never believed in honour or duty, just a soldier's wage.

Peter was pleasantly ugly, with a scarred face and cool grey eyes, and he had more successes with women than Clarence and Richard put together. (Although Richard lied about his experiences. The others knew, but didn't say anything. It wasn't easy, being a Prince.)

They approached the Darkwood slowly, and very carefully. They'd left the trail behind some time back, and now they wound their way in and out of sparsely set trees in the growing gloom of late evening. There were warning signs everywhere—great wooden boards with blunt and even harsh words on them. Some so old the lettering had all but faded away, some so recent it looked like the paint was still wet. The woods were completely, unnaturally, still and silent. No bird sang; not a single insect buzzed or fluttered. No sound or sign of wildlife anywhere. The trees and vegetation had become increasingly stunted and sickly, even twisted, as the three riders drew near the Darkwood boundary. Fruiting fungi burst out of cracked tree trunks in pallid, unhealthy colours, while gnarled branches clutched at the lowering skies.

The horses didn't like where they were going. They snorted loudly, tossing their great heads and fighting the reins, and only the firm hands of their riders kept them moving in the right direction. The horses could feel that something wasn't right. And although he wouldn't admit it in front of his companions, so could Prince Richard.

They rounded a sudden corner and there it was, right in front of them. The horses lurched to a halt, digging their hooves in hard, almost throwing their riders. Night filled the forest ahead. It seemed to rise up forever, while stretching endlessly away in both directions, an impenetrable wall of shadows that marked the outer boundary of the Darkwood. The one place in the Forest where it was always dark, where night ruled and always would. The horses reared up and shrieked horribly, their eyes rolling hysterically. Richard swung quickly down out of the saddle and slapped a heavy cloth over his horse's eyes, holding it in place with both hands. The horse quietened some as Richard spoke soothingly to it and then turned the animal around and walked it back round the corner in the trail. He tied the horse's reins to a sturdy branch and wrapped the cloth firmly around its head. By the time he'd finished, Peter and Clarence had their horses tied up beside his. The three young men looked at one another. They didn't say anything. What was there to say? The Darkwood wasn't what they'd expected, but now that they'd seen it for themselves they all knew that nothing anyone could have said could have prepared them for the reality of that dark and silent wall. Richard was the first to move. He didn't discuss it with his friends. He just walked back round the corner in the trail, and stood before the Darkwood boundary, staring into the darkness. Peter and Clarence looked at each other, shrugged pretty much in unison, and went back round the corner to join him.

They stood together, shoulder to shoulder, as close as they could get, unconsciously seeking support from one another. They all shuddered pretty much in unison, and not from the cold autumn air, or even from the terrible cold wind that came gusting out of the Darkwood. There was more inside the Darkwood than just the night, and they could feel it in their souls.

"We shouldn't be here," said Peter.

"Hush," said Richard, not looking at him.

"What is that smell, coming out of the dark?" said Clarence. "Oh God, that stinks. Like everything that ever died in there has been left piled up in heaps . . . *What is that?*"

"Death," said Peter. "Rot and corruption. A warning."

"Where is that wind blowing from?" said Clarence. "Why doesn't it stop?"

"Let's get out of here," said Peter. "This is nothing like what we expected, and God knows we expected bad enough."

"No," said Richard.

"You're not seriously thinking of going in there, are you?" said Clarence.

Prince Richard smiled at his friends; if the smile seemed a bit forced, neither of them was in any state to notice.

"Seems silly not to," said Richard, "after we came all this way to see it. We've all read the stories and histories, listened to the songs, wondered what it's like in there, in the night that never ends. But have you ever spoken with anyone who's experienced it for themselves? I want to know. I want to encounter it firsthand. To know what my ancestor Prince Rupert knew. The experience turned him into a hero. I want . . . I need to test myself against the Darkwood. To see if I'm made of the same stuff as my ancestor."

"You've lost your mind," Peter said flatly. "No one would go in there of his own free will."

Richard flashed that brave, careless smile at his two friends. "I'm going in. You can stay here."

"Hell with that," Peter said immediately. "You go in there on your own, you'll never come out again." He glared at the wall of darkness before them and then looked at Clarence. "We won't be long. You look after the horses."

"Hell with that," said Clarence, thrusting his hands deep into his pockets so his friends wouldn't see how badly they were shaking. "You think I'd let you two hog all the fun? They'll write songs about us for this. And my song will be the best of all, because I was there."

The three of them looked into the Darkwood. None of them moved. Because just looking at the boundary was enough to put a chill in their hearts and slow their thoughts to a crawl. It was like looking down from a mountaintop and nerving themselves to jump. The darkness gave away nothing at all. And for all their brave words, each one of them was quietly hoping that one of the others would find the words that would let them turn away with honour. Or, failing that, each of them wanted one of the others to go first. In the end, of course, it was Richard. He stepped smoothly forward and the wall swallowed him up like silent dark waters, without even a ripple to mark his passing. Peter and Clarence plunged in after him.

They all cried out as they entered the Darkwood, stumbling to a halt just a few feet inside the boundary. Horror, and a kind of spiritual revulsion, held them where they were. The cold hit them hard, cutting into them like a knife, leaching all the heat and life and energy out of them. They didn't belong here. Nothing human did.

Richard made himself look around, his head making slow, jerky, reluctant movements. Dead trees were everywhere, rotting and slumped together. Trees that had been dying for centuries but were still standing. Still suffering. Their leafless, interlocking branches thrust up into the starless night sky and then bowed forward to form an overheard canopy, like the bars of a cage. There was some light, a shimmering silver glow from phosphorescent fungi, that clung to the trunks of those trees nearest the boundary. Just a touch of light, to make the darkness seem even darker, and more cruel. The close, still air was thick with the sick, sweet stench of death and dying things, and never-ending corruption.

Clarence stood shaking and swaying, panting for breath and sobbing like a small child. He'd never felt so alone in his life, or so close to his own death. The darkness seemed to sink into him, like a stain on his soul that he would never be free of. It occurred to him that this was the darkness you saw inside your own coffin, forever. He turned abruptly and ran, back through the boundary and out into the light, into the sane and sensible world of the living. Unable to face a spiritual darkness that was so much more than just the absence of light.

Peter tried to stay, for Richard's sake, but he couldn't. He'd been a soldier all his life, never wanted to be anything else, and walked with Lady Death for his companion in many a dark place. He'd known fear and loss and horror, but never anything like this. A darkness that didn't care how brave he'd been, or all the great things he'd done or might do. He'd never been afraid of the dark before, but he was now. He retreated, step by step, refusing to turn his back on the Darkwood. He backed right through the boundary, leaving his dearest friend behind, on his own, because even that betrayal was more bearable than staying one moment more in the Darkwood.

Prince Richard stood alone in the dark, his heart heaving painfully in his chest, his breathing coming fast and short as his lungs strained for air. He felt cold, so cold he wondered how he could ever feel warm again. Death wasn't an end here; it was a process. He could feel it. He could sense the dead trees around him, dying by inches but never quite reaching their end. Rotting forever. The silence had a force to it, like a slow, overwhelming tide, smothering even the small living sounds he'd brought with him.

The songs were wrong. This wasn't where nightmares were born; this was where dreams came to die. The darkness closed in around him, sinking into him, like a slow poison of the soul.

And . . . something was out there, in the deepest part of the dark, watching him. Perhaps even creeping up on him, to kill him horribly. Richard cried out, a miserable, almost brutal sound of simple dread. He drew his sword and swept it jerkily back and forth before him. He stepped sideways to set his back against a tree trunk, and then cried out again in revulsion as he felt the solid-looking trunk collapse under his weight, so that he almost fell backwards into the seething mess of corruption within. Because all the trees here had rotten hearts. Richard turned and ran, out of the Darkwood, while he could still remember the way. It seemed to take a lot longer to get out than it had to get in.

He broke out of the dark and into the sane and comfortable light of evening, back in the Forest again. He stumbled to a halt, made a series of quick, ugly, almost animal noises of relief, and sank to his knees in the thick mulch of compacted leaves that covered the ground. He dropped his sword and hugged himself tightly, half afraid he might just fall apart if he didn't. He could feel cold sweat dripping off his face. But he could also feel his heartbeat dropping back to normal, and at least he could breathe again.

He slowly realised his friends were there with him, talking to him, but it was just sounds. He shook his head, hard, and their words started to make sense again. He let them help him to his feet and hand him the sword he'd dropped. He sheathed the sword with an unsteady hand and then hugged both his friends fiercely. They all stood together for a long moment, holding one another close, as though they would never let go. For friendship, for understanding, and to drive the Darkwood cold out of their bodies with human warmth.

After a while, a long while, the three young men let go of each other. They looked back at the dark boundary wall, still separating the sane world from the dark world, and then they looked at one another.

"Damn," said Peter. "That was bad. I mean, that was really bad. Nothing like what I was expecting."

"It was awful," Clarence said simply. "Not just night, not just darkness. More like the complete absence of . . . everything."

"I'm sorry," said Richard, and he had never meant it more. "I should never have done that to you."

"You didn't know," said Peter. "No one could have known."

"No!" Richard said sharply. "We all knew the stories, and the songs. We just didn't believe them. In one of them, Prince Rupert said about the Darkwood, *It's dark enough in there to break anyone.*"

"It's hard to believe Prince Rupert and Princess Julia passed all the way through a much larger Darkwood back in the day, and more than once," said Peter wonderingly. "Hell, they led armies in there, and fought battles with armies of demons! How did they stand it?"

"They were greater people, then," said Clarence.

Peter produced a flask of cider brandy, popped the cork, and took a long drink. He sighed deeply, as the warmth of the rough liquor moved slowly through him, and then he passed the flask around. Clarence and Richard took long drinks too, and made appropriate noises. But it didn't really help. They had all been touched by the dark, marked by the Darkwood. In ways they weren't ready to understand, or admit to, just yet. They turned their backs on the Darkwood boundary, and walked to their horses, which whickered uncertainly as they approached, as though the animals could tell there was something . . . different about their riders now. The three young men swung into their saddles and set off for their original destination, the small mining village of Cooper's Mill. They said nothing more to one another. They were all busy with their own thoughts. Not one of them was as full of derring-do as they had all been before.

By the time they arrived at Cooper's Mill, night had fallen. None of them liked the dark now, though none of them was ready to acknowledge it. They just lit their sturdy travel lanterns and tied them firmly to their saddles. The half-moon shed a silvery light across the Forest, but it didn't help much. The three young men steered their horses close together and rode side by side. To their credit, it didn't occur to any of them to just turn around and go back. To return home, to the comfort of warmth and light. There was a thing they had sworn to do, so they would do it.

They didn't stop along the way. None of them felt like resting, let alone sleeping, in the Forest at night.

Cooper's Mill turned out to be a small gathering of single-storey rough stone houses with slate tile roofs, home to perhaps a hundred souls in all. Prince Richard led the way past the great mill on the outskirts that gave the village its name; it was still working, still grinding its flour even at this late hour, because its work would never end as long as the stream could turn the huge wheel. The small houses stood in straight rows on either side of the only main street. There wasn't a light showing, in any window or open doorway, because the whole village population had turned out to meet them. They stood together in a silent, tightly packed crowd at the far end of the village, in a small pool of light provided by paper lanterns and flaring torches. The shadows around them still seemed very dark.

Prince Richard led the way down the empty main street, his horse's hooves sounding loudly on the stone cobbles. Peter and Clarence stuck close behind, trying to sit bold and upright in their saddles, as heroes should. They'd come a long way to reach Cooper's Mill, and they felt they had a right to be appreciated. This never occurred to Richard, of course. He finally brought his horse to a halt before the crowd, and then sat there, looking at them as they looked at him. Peter and Clarence moved in carefully on either side of the Prince. They both kept their hands near their swords. Neither of them trusted crowds. Finally, the village's Mayor stepped forward, identified by the basic chain of office round his neck. Albert Mason— the man who'd first written to Prince Richard, asking for help.

He looked at Richard and his friends, and then looked past them, as though he couldn't quite believe they were all there was. When he had finally satisfied himself that there wasn't going to be any troop of armed and armoured guards, no army come to rescue his village from the threat it faced, he looked back at Richard and Peter and Clarence. He recognised the Prince, of course, from the official portraits that were always doing the rounds, and he bowed formally, if a bit jerkily. He was under a lot of strain, and it showed.

"Greetings, Mayor Mason," said Richard, raising his voice so the whole crowd could hear it. "I am Prince Richard, and these are my friends. We're here to help."

The Mayor nodded. He was squat and muscular, from long years of hard work, and he was dressed in what he probably considered his best, the formal clothes he would wear to a wedding or a funeral.

"Prince Richard," he said. "An honour, of course, your highness, but . . . where are the rest of your followers?"

"It's just us," said Richard. "Here to see what the problem is, and what needs doing to put it right. If you need more men, you shall have them. If you need public funds and resources, to repair whatever damage has been done here, I'll see you get those too."

And just like that, the Mayor and the villagers were his. Richard always knew the right thing to say to people. In public, he was always easy and charming and honourable, without even having to think about it. It was one of the things that made the young Prince so popular wherever he went. The crowd were nodding now, and making general noises of approval, but there was no cheering or applause. Things were too serious for that. Richard looked past the Mayor, at the villagers.

The entire population, gathered in one place. Men and women in rough peasant clothing, hard-wearing, like the villagers themselves.

Children too, of all ages, some so young they had to be carried. All of them watching with wide, fascinated eyes. The whole village together in one place, because no one wanted to miss this. It was probably the most important thing that had ever happened to them, or ever would. They'd be talking about this night, whatever finally happened, for the rest of their lives and passing the story down through the generations for as long as the village endured. Until finally those who were there wouldn't even recognise what the story had turned into. Peter looked across at Clarence, who nodded quickly.

"Don't worry," he murmured. "The song I shall make of this will outlast any other. I'll do us proud."

"What if we all die here?" said Peter.

"Then you won't care, will you?" said Clarence.

The Mayor looked at Peter approvingly. He knew a professional soldier when he saw one. He looked at Clarence and his colourful clothing, and seemed less certain. He looked back at Richard.

"I see you've brought your jester, your highness," said the Mayor.

"Can't see what use he'll be, save maybe as bait, but no doubt you know your own business best."

Clarence sat up straight in his saddle. "I am not a jester! Richard, tell him I'm not your jester!"

"He's not my jester," Richard said kindly. "He's a minstrel."

"Even worse," said a voice from the crowd. Peter rocked silently in his saddle, holding in his laughter.

Richard felt a little embarrassed at the clear admiration and confidence in the open faces of the villagers before him. They obviously expected him to Do Something about their problem, whatever it turned out to be. And he hadn't actually done anything yet, except say what he knew they needed him to say. He concentrated on what he remembered from the Mayor's original letter. Under normal circumstances, it wouldn't have got anywhere near him. The Prince, being popular like he was, got a lot of mail on all sorts of matters, and he had several secretaries whose job it was to sift through the piles and sort out the few things that actually mattered. Which they would then deal with. He didn't even sign his own autographs these days. But he'd been bored, looking for something to do, so he'd bounced into the office that morning and just grabbed a handful of letters for himself. And one had been the plea for help from Cooper's Mill.

Richard swung down from his horse and nodded for his companions to join him. The Mayor gestured quickly for people to hold the horses' reins, while Richard looked steadily at the Mayor.

"I think we need to see this for ourselves, Mayor. If you could please lead us to the actual trouble spot and fill us in on a few details . . ."

"Of course, your highness," said the Mayor, standing just that little bit straighter at the prospect of showing off his assumed authority. And then he slumped again, as he remembered his troubles. He turned abruptly, and the whole crowd just split silently apart before him, falling back to open up a corridor for him to walk through. Because wherever the Mayor was going, they very clearly weren't prepared to go with him. The Mayor reached out a hand, and someone stuck a flaming torch in it. He looked at the torch for a long moment, as though drawing strength from the leaping flames, and then he set off at a steady if not particularly enthusiastic pace, with Richard and Peter and Clarence following after him.

. . .

The Mayor walked out of the village and up the steep slope that led to the mine entrance, set in the side of the dark grey mountains that loomed over Cooper's Mill. It was clear from his stiff back that he was going there only because someone had to show the way and no one else would do it. He held his flaring torch high, but the light shook and trembled around him, as his hand shook and trembled. Richard observed the man's very real fear, and took the situation seriously for the first time. He'd been expecting something simple and obvious, like a pack of wolves, or maybe a bear that had taken up residence in the mine; but now he had to wonder just what it was that could terrorise a whole village so completely.

They came at last to the mine entrance. Nothing special, just a dark hole in the side of the grey mountain. Richard was reminded of the old story about Prince Richard and his Champion fighting a giant Worm creature in an abandoned mine. He mentioned it to the Mayor, just for something to say, and the Mayor nodded stiffly.

"Oh, aye, your highness. We all know that story. That was up in Coppertown, some ten, twelve miles from here. We all know Coppertown. Some of us had relatives there. No one goes there anymore, mind. No one lives there anymore."

"But . . . Prince Rupert and the Champion killed the Worm!" said Clarence. "That's the one thing all the songs and stories agree on . . ."

"Oh, they killed the Worm, all right," said the Mayor, not looking back. "Burned it right up, with lamp oil. Very clever. But not until it had killed everyone who lived in Coppertown. Every last man, woman, and child. Afterwards the town was still there, the houses were still there . . . but no one wanted to move in. You couldn't blame them, really."

"Was it haunted?" said Peter.

"No, not . . . haunted, as such. Just a bad place. Wasn't somewhere people could live anymore." The Mayor stopped right before the entrance hole and held up his torch. The light didn't penetrate more than a few feet into the dark of the opening. He looked back at Richard. "You have to understand, your highness—just because you kill the monster, it doesn't mean you've won. What's been done can't be undone. We're all hoping you'll do better. None of us want to have to leave here; this is our home.

Has been for generations, back before the Demon War, even. But we're all packed and ready, just in case."

"In case?" said Richard.

"In case there's nothing you can do," said the Mayor.

"Look, what exactly are we facing?" Richard said bluntly, trying to keep the impatience out of his voice. He wanted to sound calm and composed and professional.

"No one's entirely sure," said the Mayor. "The morning shift opened up a new coal face, you see, just last week. Deep, deep down, further than we normally like to go, chasing the new seam. They'd only been working there a few days before things started to go wrong. The men . . . heard things, at first. Things moving around. Then knockings, on the other side of the new coal face, as though the men had disturbed something, woken something up. And now it was trying to break through, from the other side.

"The work stopped, as the men had a bit of a talk about what they wanted to do. If they knocked off early, they'd be docked a full day's wages, and there's not many families round here could afford to lose that. But then . . . the men saw something. Something bad, coming right at them, out of the dark. They turned and ran. And these were hard men, your highness, experienced miners, not easily frightened. You can't be a miner and be prone to panic. But they couldn't face what they saw, down there, in the deep and the dark . . ."

"Can we talk to these men?" said Peter after a while, practical as ever.

"If you want," said the Mayor. "But you won't get much out of them. They're not saying anything. Doesn't seem likely they ever will. Whatever they saw, it broke something inside them. Perhaps because there are some things men just can't stand to see."

"Demons?" said Richard.

"There are worse things than demons," said the Mayor.

"There are?" said Clarence.

"And you want us to go down into the mine and face them?" said Peter.

The Mayor looked at him impassively. "Isn't that why you came here?"

Clarence looked at Richard. "Don't you think this would be a good time to stay *exactly where we are* and call for reinforcements? I mean, this is a bit much for just the three of us. Isn't it?"

"Your jester is right, your highness," said the Mayor.

"I am not a jester!"

"No, you're not," said Richard. "You're a good man who doesn't want to let people down."

"You always did fight dirty," said Clarence. "Oh hell, we're here. Let's do it."

"Why not?" said Peter.

The three young men who'd ridden out in search of adventure stood together before the mine entrance, looking in. Just a dark hole in the side of a dark grey mountain, its outline supported by heavy wooden beams that had clearly been there a lot longer than originally intended. They didn't look to be in the best of shape, or promise much for the state of things inside the mine itself. The dark inside the entrance seemed every bit as impenetrable as that beyond the Darkwood boundary. But at least here there was no cold wind gusting out, no stench of death and dying things. The air was still, and there wasn't a sound to be heard anywhere.

"Those beams don't look too solid to me," said Clarence.

"Improvements are expensive," said the Mayor. "The mine owners don't like spending money. They wait till something's gone wrong, until there's been an accident serious enough to slow down production. And even then, they only authorise enough money to cover the bare necessities. Just enough to get everyone back to work again. We're here to make them money, not cost them money."

"I'll speak to the owners when I get back," said Prince Richard. And he meant it. You could tell.

"You can try, your highness," said the Mayor. "Perhaps they'll listen to you."

He didn't sound convinced. He handed the flaring torch to Richard and stepped back. The others looked at him.

"You're not going with us?" said Clarence. "To . . . show us the way?"

"No," said the Mayor. "You don't need me for that. And I've got more sense. There are chalk arrows on the walls, showing the way to the new coal face. Just keep going down, and you can't miss it. If . . . when you come back out again, we'll be waiting."

The Mayor walked quickly down the steep slope, back to his people, still standing silently together at the end of the village. Richard and Peter and Clarence watched him go, and then turned back to look at the mine entrance again.

"We don't have to do this," said Peter. "The jester's right. I say we wait for some serious reinforcements."

"What could be worse than demons?" said Clarence.

"The whole village make their living out of this mine," said Richard. "Either we solve their problem or they put all their worldly possessions on their backs and walk out. On the road, with children, with winter coming. I said I'd help. I won't let these people down. So I have to go in. But I've no right to ask you to come in with me. Not after what happened in the Darkwood."

"Oh hell," said Peter. "Whatever's in there can't be as bad as the Darkwood."

"Right," said Clarence. "Nothing could be that bad."

"Piece of cake," said Peter.

"Walk in the gardens," said Clarence.

"I'd run if I had any sense," said Peter.

"Me too," said Clarence.

"You think you're so funny," said Richard. He transferred the torch to his left hand so he could draw his sword. Peter took the shield off his back and put it on his left arm and drew his sword. Clarence produced the flask of cider brandy and put it to his lips, finishing it off with a few quick swallows. He breathed heavily and drew his sword. Peter chuckled briefly.

"I wondered where that flask had got to."

"Not a bloody jester," said Clarence. "Let's do this."

They all looked at one another, and once again it was Richard who led the way in. He strode forward into the mine entrance, his back straight and his head held high. Peter and Clarence hurried after him, to walk at his sides. And if any of them were in any way bothered by the darkness, none of them showed it.

The entrance quickly became a corridor, hacked out of the mountain rock, heading down. Just a rough passageway, propped up here and there with wooden beams and timber overheads of varying age and quality.

The floor was bare stone, dark and dusty, worn smooth with long use. It was completely dark once they were inside the mine, and every sound seemed to echo forever. Richard held his torch high, but its light didn't travel far, so they always seemed to be moving through the dark in their own pool of unsteady sulphur yellow light.

Clarence's face was set and grim, and almost immediately slick with a sheen of cold sweat. Peter's gaze darted from one moving shadow to another, never still, and his hand gripped the hilt of his sword so tightly that his fingers ached. Richard stared straight ahead, and the hands that held his torch and his sword were entirely steady. Because he was the Prince, their leader and their friend, and because he'd got them into this, he had a duty to be confident enough for all of them.

The only sounds in the down-bound corridor were the scuffing of their boots on the bare floor and their own harsh breathing. So Richard could tell when Clarence's breathing became quicker and unsteady. Richard made a point of looking round at Clarence, and smiling at him reassuringly. Clarence immediately straightened up and took control of himself, because he would rather die than let his friends down, or seem less of a man in front of them. Richard looked at Peter, who looked steadily back at him. Richard grinned suddenly.

"It's dark, it's cold, and it's spooky—and none of it one-tenth as bad as the Darkwood. I don't think there's anything left that can scare us properly anymore. Not after that shithole . . ."

"Speak for yourself," said Peter, smiling in spite of himself. "Being scared in dangerous situations is good. Keeps you sharp, gives you an edge."

"Then I am sharper and edgier than you will ever be," said Clarence. "How far down are we? Feels like we've been descending for ages."

"We've barely started," said Peter. "Some of these old mines go down for miles."

"I just knew you were going to say that," said Clarence.

The passageways became increasingly squat and narrow as they continued, the stone ceilings lowering in fits and starts until they all had to walk stooped to avoid banging their heads. The air smelled bad, and discoloured water ran down the walls in sudden rushes. There were more tunnels leading off, extensions that were little more than large holes, exposing new seams. But no matter how much the main corridor branched and deviated, there were always more chalk arrows to point them in the right direction. On, and down. Always down.

Richard made sure he was always a few steps ahead of the others, leading the way. Whatever was down here, he was determined to find and face it first. Because this had all been his idea, so he had to be the one who first endured whatever was coming. His thinking on that wasn't entirely clear, but he clung to it anyway. The slope of the floor grew steadily more inclined as they went deeper and deeper into the earth, into the dark. Still more chalk arrows on the walls, pointing ahead, and down. The three of them kept going, descending through tunnels and galleries, past crumbling rock faces, under low ceilings where sudden drops of dust and rubble made them jump. Richard found he was having trouble deciding just how deep they'd come, or even how long they'd been travelling. Some of the chalk arrows were starting to look very fresh. Even . . . unfinished.

"I think we're almost there," said Peter, and the other two looked round sharply. It had been a while since any of them had spoken. The dark and the silence and the claustrophobic surroundings didn't encourage chatter. Richard stopped abruptly, and the others stopped with him. The torch was still burning and its light was still steady, but Richard suddenly wasn't at all sure how much longer it would last. It would be really bad to be caught in the dark without a light. He looked around him, and made out several small oil lamps, set into niches in the stone walls. He pointed them out to Peter and Clarence, and they moved quickly to grab several and light them from the torch. Set back into their niches, the lamps shed fresh new light . . . that served only to show just how narrow a tunnel they were in.

"How do the miners stand it, working in conditions like this every day?" said Clarence.

"Because they're harder men than we are," said Peter.

"Let them be Prince for a day, and see how they like it," said Richard.

"Oh, I think they could manage," said Peter.

"I think . . . this is where we're supposed to be," said Clarence. "No more chalk arrows, those lamps still had fresh oil in them . . . and look at the floor. Signs of a struggle, fighting. Some dried blood, but no bodies."

"Make a tracker out of you yet," said Peter. "Something bad happened here, Richard, and not long ago either."

They all held themselves very still and very quiet, looking and listening. The tunnel dropped sharply away before them, heading down to the new coal face. No more side tunnels, or branchings. Nowhere else to go. And then . . . there were noises, up ahead, past the dropped floor. In the dark beyond the light. Richard found a wall holder and put his torch into it so he would have both hands free. For whatever was coming. The three men stood together, swords at the ready. The noises were getting closer. Knockings, from behind or perhaps even inside the tunnel walls. Just like the Mayor had said. As though something, or a lot of somethings, was trying to break through from the other side. What had the miners found, down here, in the dark and in the deep? What had they disturbed? More sounds now, skittering and pattering, moving lightly across the hard floor, coming up the tunnel to meet them.

Richard and Peter and Clarence strained their eyes against the gloom outside the light. At first they thought they were seeing dancing lamps or lanterns, bobbing along in the dark. It wasn't until the things were almost close enough to enter the pool of light that Richard was able to make out what they were. What they had to be. Things he'd heard described only in old songs and stories. Clarence was the one to remember their name, of course. And to whisper it aloud.

"Kobolds . . ."

It had been a long, long time since anyone had dug deep enough to disturb these creatures of the deeps, of the deep dark places. Shimmering chalk white things, with their own phosphorescence; roughly human in shape but in no way human. Shuffling and scuffling along like oversized insects, they hopped and leapt, jumping back and forth with horrid speed, moving over and around one another with brutal indifference. With hunched backs and overlong limbs, with bony faces that had sharp, jutting horns and jaws full of heavy teeth, but no eyes at all. Because they had no need for them.

Dozens, hundreds, of the things, rising up out of the deep dark, and some of them scurried along the floor, and some ran along the walls, and some clung to the low ceiling.

Richard took a single step forward and raised his sword. Even then, face-to-face with things that didn't even have faces and didn't move in any human way, he still tried to talk to them. Because he was a Prince. Because it was their territory. But even as he spoke, the kobolds threw themselves at him, clawed hands reaching for his throat and his heart. Richard's sword swung through a short, vicious arc and sheared clean through a kobold's throat and out again. Dark blood spurted on the air and the kobold fell, to kick and scrabble helplessly on the floor as the life ran out of it. The other kobolds ignored it, surging forward inhumanly quickly, and Richard and Peter and Clarence stood their ground and cut them down with their swords. Steel flashed in the unsteady light, hacking through shimmering flesh and brittle bone. And not one kobold could reach them. For a while.

The three young men stood close together, blocking the narrow passageway, so the kobolds couldn't get past them to reach the surface and the village. Their swords rose and fell, carving flesh and juddering on bone, and dark blood flew in all directions. The kobolds didn't cry out when they were hit, or when they fell, or even when they died. Richard fought with style, Peter with practiced skill, and Clarence with an almost despairing bravado. They struck down every kobold that came within reach, whether the creatures rose up before them, or launched themselves from the walls, or reached down from the ceiling. The three young men would not be moved, and nothing got past them. The kobold dead began to pile up in front of them, forming a horrid barricade so that the kobolds had to scramble over their own dead to get to the humans. It didn't seem to bother them.

Given the narrowness of the corridor, the kobolds could come at the humans only a few at time, and for a while that gave the three men the advantage; but there were just so many kobolds. No matter how many died, there were always more. Silent and stubborn, an endless army of shimmering, bony forms, spilling up out of the dark, pressing forward with vicious claws, spurred elbows, and solid, tearing teeth. And no matter how many the young men killed, it didn't seem to deter the others at all. And eventually, Richard and Clarence and even Peter began to grow tired, and slow down. Their backs ached and their arm muscles blazed with pain, the more so because they couldn't stop even for a moment to rest. They started to take wounds. A cut here and a gouge there, harsh language ringing on the air as red blood fell to the floor. Their swords seemed to grow heavier, and Peter couldn't always haul his shield into position as fast as he would have liked. But the young men fought on, hurting and bleeding, and still the kobolds pressed forward, with no end to the leaping, shimmering forms. And the young men realized that no matter how brave, or well-meaning, or just plain stubborn they were . . . there was no way they could hold off the kobolds forever.

In the end, Richard's friends broke and ran. Not from cowardice but from the sheer endless numbers of the enemy. Clarence grabbed a burning oil lamp from its niche and sprinted back the way they'd come, yelling for the others to follow him. He didn't look back. It honestly never even occurred to him that they weren't already doing the only sensible thing and running right behind him.

Peter grabbed another lamp, shouting something foul at the approaching horde of shimmering forms, and just couldn't see the point anymore. If you couldn't win, what was the point of fighting? So he ran straight after Clarence, yelling for Richard to come with them. He didn't look back either, because he too couldn't understand why anyone would stay, when all hope was gone.

But Richard wouldn't run. He stood his ground, swinging his sword with renewed energy now that he had to hold the tunnel on his own. He wouldn't run. Not because he was a Prince, or even a hero, but because he had sworn to help the Mayor and the villagers, and he'd be damned before he'd let them down. He thought of the men and women and children gathered on the surface, and what the kobolds would do to them . . . and it never even occurred to him to run. The great glowing tide of kobolds pressed forward, and he would not be moved.

Richard remembered Coppertown, where the Worm had killed everyone. The town where no one lived anymore. Prince Rupert and the Champion killed the Worm, with lamp oil. That thought filled Richard's head even as he struck viciously and desperately at the kobolds leaping and jumping all around. Richard grabbed a burning lamp from its niche in the wall beside him, and smashed it into the face of the nearest kobold. The old glass lamp shattered at once, and blazing oil spilled all over the hunched white figure, and it burst into flames. It dropped to the floor, kicking and scrabbling round and round in circles, biting and tearing at itself in its agony. Richard grabbed more oil lamps and threw them here and there, and in a moment the tunnel before him was full of burning kobolds. A terrible light jumped and fell, and the shadows seemed to go mad. The stench of burning flesh filled the air, and when one burning kobold bumped into another, the flames spread in a moment. Until finally the barricade of dead kobolds went up, and Richard flinched back from the sudden savage heat.

And that was when he realised there was no one left for him to fight. The kobolds had stopped, to watch their own kind burn and die. Richard stood firm, black blood still dripping from his sword, though it was so heavy now he could hardly hang on to it. And then the kobolds turned and left, all at once, quite silently, disappearing back into the dark, until even the last few bobbing lights were gone. They didn't take their dead with them, the butchered and the burnt.

For a long moment Prince Richard just stood there, still holding his sword out before him, not quite able to believe it was actually over. And then he laughed, briefly, and sheathed his sword. He was desperately tired, aching in every limb and every muscle, from all that he'd put himself through. He could feel his wounds now, though he'd barely noticed taking them while he was busy fighting. He checked himself over to make sure he hadn't missed anything immediately threatening. Not that he could have done much about it if he had. He smiled, shakily, and decided he was damaged but still good. He was shaking all over now, as the adrenaline ran out and the fight caught up with him. But he was still grinning broadly. Because he was alive. And not because he'd won, but because he hadn't run.

It was good to know that he had it in him, not to run. It wasn't something you could know for sure until it was tested.

He was so tired. Part of him wanted to just sit down, to put his back against a wall and close his eyes, to get his breath and his strength back. And not even think about fighting and killing for a while. But he couldn't do that. The kobolds were gone, but they might come back. And his friends would be worried about him. So Richard sheathed his sword carefully with a shaking hand, grabbed his torch from the wall holder, and stumbled tiredly back through all the long tunnels, back to the surface.

When he finally emerged from the mine entrance, holding his torch high, he found the whole crowd of villagers waiting for him. They cheered and applauded as he stood blinking in the early-morning light. They'd refused to give up on him. Some had seen his light approaching out of the dark, and everyone had gathered to wait for him so the whole village would be there when he came back. They cheered and roared and stamped their feet at the sight of Prince Richard the Triumphant, filling the early-morning air with their celebrations, like they'd never stop.

Peter and Clarence came forward to join him, and both of them tried to hug him at once, and then beat him on the back and on the shoulders, saying his name over and over again in voices choked with emotion. Richard threw aside the stub of his torch so he could hug them back.

"I thought you were right behind us!" said Clarence. "Until I got to the main entrance and looked back, and there was only Peter behind me. I wanted to go straight back down again—"

"He did," said Peter. "I wouldn't let him. Why weren't you right behind us?"

"You won't believe the song I'm going to make of this!" said Clarence. "Prince Richard, the man who would not be moved!"

Richard just smiled, and nodded, and finally pushed them quietly but firmly to one side, so he could walk over to the waiting Mayor.

"You've got kobolds," he said bluntly. "I killed a lot of them. They really don't like fire. But there's still a hell of a lot of them left. You need to shut down the new seam. Bring down the ceiling and fill as much of the tunnel as you can with rubble. They only attacked because you encroached on their territory. Leave them alone, and they'll leave you alone. Probably."

"And that's it?" said the Mayor. "That's all you can do?"

"I can talk to the mine owners," said Prince Richard. "Persuade them to pay for the necessary work, make sure they don't pressure you to dig so deep again. You should be safe enough. But will your people go back into the mine, now they know there's kobolds?"

"Of course," said the Mayor. "That's the job. Mining has always been dangerous."

Richard nodded. "Just because you've killed the monster . . . it doesn't mean you've won. I remember."

The Mayor nodded, then went back to his people to give them the good and the bad news. Leaving Richard alone with Peter and Clarence, who suddenly didn't seem able to meet his gaze. Richard laughed briefly and put his arm across their shoulders.

"Of course, you do realise that you were the ones who did the sensible thing, right? I should have been killed. Those were suicide odds."

"We should never have left you," said Peter.

"We can't all be heroes," said Richard.

"Are you really going to talk to the people who own the mine?" said Peter.

"I don't need to," said Richard. "My family owns it, through several intermediaries. Why do you think the Mayor wrote to the Castle in the first place? I'll do what I can. Now, if you'll excuse me, I need to go find some food and a lot of drink, and hopefully a village wise woman who knows which herbs will help fight off an infection. I feel like shit. And I want to take a look at those traumatised miners before we leave. Hearing how we did might help them."

He strode off down the slope, head held high. His friends watched him go.

"How can you hate a man like that?" said Peter.

"I don't know," said Clarence. "But it's probably worth the effort, if only to keep him from getting big-headed."

They laughed quietly together, and followed their friend down the slope.

Some three weeks later, they finally made it back to Forest Castle. They took the long way home from Cooper's Mill, going by the pretty route, partly because Richard felt the need for his various wounds to heal up and partly because he wanted some time on his own, away from the duties and responsibilities of Castle life. Of being . . . Prince Richard. He spent a lot of time on his own, lost in his thoughts, and Peter and Clarence mostly left him to it. They knew he had a lot to think about, including his forthcoming arranged marriage to the Princess Catherine of Redhart.

Besides, they had a lot to think about too.

It had been a hundred years since the Demon War, and the Forest Castle had changed a lot since those days. No longer bigger on the inside than it was on the outside, which had always been its best boast for fame, the Castle was now a huge, sprawling place, the size of a large town or even a small city, with thousands of rooms. But now it was more a museum of a past way of life than a working Castle. Power had passed the Forest Royal line by. The current King Rufus was a much-loved, occasionally respected constitutional monarch. Real power in the Forest Land now resided in the elected House of Parliament, a much grander and far more modern building set quite deliberately some distance away from the old seat of power, in the proud new city of Forestall. Much of Forest Castle stood empty now, abandoned and deserted. The King had to pay for the Castle's upkeep out of his own pocket. Which was almost as empty as the Castle. *Thank God for tourists and guided tours,* King Rufus had been heard to mutter when he wasn't driving them out of the more private areas with oaths and curses, yelling at them for dropping litter or trying to steal some of the smaller items of interest, or for just generally getting in his way.

The tourists didn't mind; in fact, for many years, most said it wasn't a proper tour unless you'd been yelled at by the King.

No one was at all clear what would happen once the Royal coffers officially ran dry, because King Rufus wouldn't talk about it. Presumably, when Richard finally became King, he'd have to start selling things to raise some money. He'd already started (very quietly and secretly and just a bit guiltily) making a list of things he could do without. Just because something was old and historically significant and very valuable, it didn't necessarily mean it was a thing of beauty and a joy forever. Certain particularly ugly family portraits had already made the list.

Prince Richard had to play politics, whether he wanted to or not, to keep the Royal line popular with the people so Parliament couldn't get rid of it. Richard wasn't even sure he wanted to be King, but he most definitely distrusted what some Members of Parliament might do without the checks and balances provided by the throne. He had wondered, during his travels on the road, whether certain elements within Parliament had deliberately agreed to Redhart's suggestion of an arranged marriage in the Peace Treaty just to distract him and keep him out of Parliament's collective hair. But no—as much as he hated to admit it, not everything was about him. It was much more likely that Parliament had agreed to the Royal marriage as a way of bringing in new money, from tourism and merchandising. Richard sighed. He didn't want to marry a foreign Princess he'd never even met; he'd always said he would only ever marry for love. Choose his own bride, and to hell with Royal etiquette. But deep down, he'd always known that was just a hope and a dream. He knew where his duty and his responsibilities lay.

But, on the other hand . . . if this Catherine were to break off the marriage through her own decision, and march back to Redhart in a huff . . . Well, no one could blame him then, could they? Provided he was very careful not to get found out. The marriage could still be part of the Peace Treaty, even if it was never actually enforced. Just . . . called for. In the future.

Richard could actually see the taller towers of Forest Castle rising up beyond the trees, when Peter and Clarence rode up and set themselves on either side of him and insisted that he pay attention to them through a series of loud throat-clearing noises. He looked at them amusedly, while they took it in turns to bluntly demand that he share with them whatever it was he was brooding about. Richard told them what he'd been thinking, on various matters, in some detail, until they begged him to stop. Peter sniffed loudly.

"You might see things that way, Your Princeness, but I'd take a Member of Parliament over a Lord or Lady any day. Inbred bunch of whiners. Not all Forest politicians are bad apples. In order to be allowed to stand for Parliament, you have to have done something, some great thing of outstanding merit. Be a successful warrior, or magician, or merchant. You have to have proved yourself worthy, already made your mark in service to the Land. Can't expect people to vote for you if they've never heard of you. And these days, if you want to be a soldier or a warrior or a hero, you can't just strap on a sword and march off looking for someone to fight. You have to join the Brotherhood of Steel and get properly trained."

Clarence snorted loudly. "You say that like it's a good thing. I've heard things about the Brotherhood. Mystical indoctrination, that's what I've heard! And overly harsh discipline, in their precious Sorting Houses. Even sexual predators . . ."

"Bullshit," Peter said calmly. "Every big organisation has its enemies, eager to spread lies and propaganda. Those already in power have a vested interest in not losing it to anyone else. I enjoyed my training in the Sorting House before I came to the Castle. Never saw any of the nonsense you're talking, Clarence. Made me the man I am today."

"My mind reels with sarcastic responses," said Clarence.

"One does hear things," Richard said carefully. "The Brotherhood is one of those ideas that came up from the Southern Kingdoms. It set up here to operate as a general sorting house, working out who had a talent for what and then placing them accordingly. To invest some moral back-bone in the country. But now the Brotherhood has a hundred of these schools, these Sorting Houses, spread across the Forest Land, turning out more and more warriors every year. What will we do with them, once there aren't any more border skirmishes to soak them up? And even you must admit, Peter, that not all the Sorting Houses have good reputations. There are rumours . . ."

"Yes, well, that's true of everything and everyone," said Peter. "You should study the real history of how things used to be, before the Brother-hood of Steel was established. Warriors picking fights and goading each other into duels, just to show how brave and talented they were and to show off in public. People are always happy to see blood spilled, as long as it isn't theirs. Things got out of hand really fast, by all accounts, with blood feuds eating up whole families . . . Now, thanks to the Brotherhood, that kind of thing is only allowed in the seasonal Tourneys, under strict rules and conditions."

"The Grand Tourney is due anytime now," said Richard. "That means I'll have to make an appearance, as a soon-to-be-married Royal. The crowds love all that stuff. I hate these big public appearances; good-natured smiling and waving all day really take it out of you."

Clarence brightened up. "I love Tourneys! Lots of action and heroics to observe, and make notes on from a safe distance, and sing about later.

Good-looking girls everywhere, easily impressed by a good rhyme and a noble accent. And all kinds of exotic foreign dishes at the food stalls!"

"I do like the curried sausages," Peter said solemnly. "For when I want to set my bowels a real challenge."

"Let us not forget last year's great success: the chilli-beef-and-bacon three-bean soup," said Richard. "For when you want the shit to just explode out of your arse."

"You are both so unadventurous," said Clarence.

"Will you be appearing in the lists this year?" Peter said innocently. "Showing off your fighting skills in front of these easily-taken-advantage-of girls?"

"Hell, no!" said Clarence. "I've got more sense. If I must fight, it had better be for something more than a lady's favour. Especially if she's just blown her nose on it."

"You have got to get over that," said Peter. "I'm sure it was just an oversight."

"The Tourneys do seem to serve a useful function," said Richard. "It's hard for potential heroes to make their mark these days, what with the general shortage of monsters and demons in the Land. Look how far we had to ride to find some . . . The Tourneys keep our potential warriors busy and preoccupied, and beating the crap out of each other rather than out of innocent passers-by. I don't know why these hero wannabes always fixate on monsters . . . There's never been any shortage of human villains in the Land that could do with some serious sorting out. Bankers, landlords, politicians . . . Even the occasional instance of inappropriate magic use."

"Right," said Peter, nodding vigorously. "Remember the Necromancer, last year? Got caught raising up the recently departed to make them do hard labour in the quarries?"

"The unions soon put a stop to that," said Clarence. "Skilled labour, is quarrying."

"Never any shortage of bad guys for trainee good guys to set themselves against," said Peter. "All part of the natural balance."

"Yes, but where are they when you need one?" said Richard, and they all laughed.

The woods fell away abruptly, and Prince Richard and his companions found themselves facing the huge open clearing that held the Castle. Cut out of the Forest centuries ago, by persons and means unknown, the clearing remained open despite everything the woods could do to reclaim it. And standing right before the three riders, right on the clearing boundary, was the Standing Stone. A huge, jagged outcropping of dark stone, of no particular shape or design. It loomed over them, standing alone, surrounded by a circle of dead grass. Because no matter how many seeds fell there, nothing would flourish in the shadow of the Stone. Some people said birds and insects fell dead out of the air if they flew too close. Generations of children would come out just to stare at the Stone, and dare one another to touch it. No one ever did.

Once, the Standing Stone had been worshipped. It still had a definite sense of presence, and power. There were even those who had been heard to murmur that there was something living, sleeping, inside the Stone. An old pagan god, or a devil, depending on which stories you listened to. Richard studied the Standing Stone thoughtfully.

"When I am King, I will have this ugly thing dragged down and broken up with hammers."

"Hush," Peter said immediately. "It might be listening."

"I don't like it, and I don't trust it," Prince Richard said stubbornly.

"But there are any number of old songs about how important the Standing Stone is!" said Clarence, just a bit excitedly. "Some say an ancient hero lies sleeping inside the Stone, waiting to come forth in the Land's hour of need!"

"Then where was he during the Demon War?" said Richard, and no one had an answer for that.

Richard turned his gaze to the Forest Castle, filling most of the huge clearing and casting its great shadow over the farthest boundaries. To the casual eye, the Castle's exterior wasn't actually all that impressive. The stone was everywhere cracked and pitted, and stained from long exposure to wind and rain and passing Time. Wide mats of crawling ivy and a great undulating sea of slate grey roof tiles. Many of the tall crenellated towers had a battered, lopsided look. Crumbling battlements presided over outer walls some three to four feet thick, still standing firm against wars and demons and the endless years. Guarding the Royal line as they guarded the Forest Land.

Thousands of rooms in four great wings, along with halls and galleries, libraries and armouries, servants' quarters and stables and courtyards . . . Much of it empty now, of course. Dusty, deserted rooms, full of shadows and memories. Not even any ghosts. Because what's the point of a haunting, if there's no one to haunt?

Richard sat on his horse, ignoring the quiet impatience of his friends, just . . . looking. All around him the woods were full of life and movement and birdsong. A relief and a comfort after his experience in the Darkwood. There was no way he could have known that such a brief exposure could affect him and his friends so deeply. Neither he nor Clarence nor Peter was comfortable during the night now, though none of them would admit it, let alone discuss it with the others. They all just quietly accepted that they had to have a large banked fire burning before they could go to sleep, a fire big enough to last through the whole night. So its light would still be there if they happened to wake before morning. Like they were children again.

With good reason to be afraid of the dark.

Richard urged his horse forward, out of the woods and across the clearing, and Peter and Clarence were quickly there at his sides. Forest Castle loomed before them, growing steadily larger and more impressive the closer they got. When they finally crossed the ancient moat surrounding the Castle, Richard had to admit he was a little surprised to discover that the drawbridge was already down and waiting for them. Even though no guards were visible on duty anywhere. Had someone seen them coming? Normally you had to stand on the far side of the moat and yell your head off, and wait for someone to notice you. Wise people packed lunches for the wait. It was hard to find good help these days. The horses' hooves were loud and carrying on the quiet, as they clattered across the drawbridge. Richard looked down into the dark and murky waters of the moat. It needed cleaning out again, but that was expensive. Richard's attitude was that if some enemy should happen to fall in and be poisoned before he could drown, that was fine by him.

Back in Prince Rupert's time, a terrible monster had lived in the moat and guarded it against all comers. (The moat used to contain crocodiles, until the day something arrived and ate all the crocodiles, then took up residence in the moat amid the general feeling that if it could eat a moat full of crocodiles, it could certainly guard the Castle.) There was even a popular and very vulgar song about the day the monster and its mate and its many horrible offspring suddenly up and left, some fifty years ago. A very impressive sight, and quite a spectacle, as long as you weren't standing too close to the moat when it happened.

Prince Richard rode his horse into the great open courtyard, ready to yell his head off for a groom and a dismount; and then he sat very still as he saw the Seneschal emerge from the main Castle entrance and head straight for him, accompanied by rather a lot of armed guards. Someone had seen him coming and arranged this reception for him.

"Run!" said Peter. "We'll block their way!"

"Escape while you still can!" said Clarence.

"You think you're so funny," said Prince Richard. "Where would I go?"

He swung down out of the saddle and threw the reins to Peter. The Seneschal crashed to a halt before the Prince, and the two men looked each other over in silence. They'd known each other all their lives, and the experience had not been a happy one. The Seneschal was King Rufus' most senior servant, and he liked to give himself airs. On the grounds that he did all the real work in running the Castle. To be fair, he did. The Seneschal was a tall and slender, almost spindly man in his early forties, with a long face and a high forehead, under thinning grey hair. (He liked to blame this on the stress and strain of having to deal with the Royal line, up close and personal, every day.) He wore dark, formal, slightly old-fashioned clothes of a reserved and sombre nature. Including exquisitely tailored gloves and shiny shiny hook-and-eye boots. He tried for a calm and even dour presence when dealing with the Prince, but he nearly always descended into red-faced spluttering. Richard usually felt guilty about teasing the man afterwards. But not enough to stop doing it.

The Seneschal glared at Prince Richard as though he'd been waiting to talk to him for some time and wasn't at all happy about it.

"You said you were just *popping out for a quick ride*, your highness!" the Seneschal said loudly. "That was two months ago!"

"Well, if I'd told you it was going to be that long, you wouldn't have let me go, would you?" said the Prince reasonably.

The Seneschal started to say something cutting and obviously much rehearsed, and then stopped and looked the Prince over more carefully.

"What the hell happened to you? Your clothes are torn, I can see dried bloodstains, and there's a scar down the left side of your face that definitely wasn't there when you left! You look . . . like you've had the shit kicked out of you. Tell me you haven't gone back to fighting on the border again."

"I haven't been fighting on the border again," said Prince Richard.

"Good . . ."

"I've been fighting kobolds down in a mine at Cooper's Mill."

The Seneschal looked like he wanted to spit. "God give me strength . . . You can't keep doing this, your highness! It isn't . . . Look, we really don't have time for this. Things have changed in your unauthorised absence. Suddenly and dramatically. You have to come with me right now, to discuss things with your father."

Richard looked back at Peter and Clarence, who both nodded understandingly and steered their horses towards the stables, taking Richard's horse with them. Richard looked thoughtfully at the armed guards and then back at the Seneschal.

"Why the heavily armed escort? Anyone would think you didn't trust me to come with you."

"How well we know each other," said the Seneschal.

"I'm really not going to enjoy this meeting, am I?"

"Do you ever?"

"What is this all about, Seneschal?"

"You have to discuss that with your father, your highness."

"How is he today?" said Richard.

"Average," said the Seneschal.

Richard winced. "As bad as that? Oh, very well; let's get on with it. What does my father want to see me about? Does he even know?"

"I think it's better if I wait till I've got you and your father together in the same place," said the Seneschal. "Then I won't have to explain things twice. Do I really need these soldiers to accompany us, or will you give me your word not to run off, so I can dismiss them?"

"You have my word," said Richard. "I know my duty. And I'm just too tired to go chasing up and down corridors."

"Either you're finally developing some maturity or those kobolds really did a number on you," said the Seneschal.

"Guess," said Richard.

"Maturity," said the Seneschal. "I'm looking forward to it."

The Seneschal led Prince Richard through the pleasant and even cosy corridors of Forest Castle, where a surprisingly large number of people had turned out to wave and smile and welcome the Prince home. Richard regarded them all suspiciously, and looked at the Seneschal, who reluctantly admitted that news of the Prince's heroic actions at Cooper's Mill had got back to the Castle long before the Prince did. The details were sometimes blurred, and often contradictory, about exactly what it was he'd done, but everyone agreed it had all been very heroic. Peter and Clarence didn't even get a mention. Lords and Ladies called out congratulations and compliments to Richard as he passed, and he just smiled and nodded and kept up a great pace so he wouldn't have to stop and answer questions. The Lords and Ladies of Forest Castle only ever wanted to talk to the Prince when they were after something. The Seneschal frowned darkly, until he just couldn't stand it any longer.

"You know you're not supposed to go riding off without a proper armed escort, your highness! You have no right to place your Royal life in danger!"

"It's my life, Seneschal," the Prince said mildly.

"No, it isn't! Your life belongs to the Kingdom. What if you'd been attacked by brigands? Or kidnapped? If those kobolds had killed you, how would you have married the Princess Catherine and finally brought peace to both our nations?"

"Peter would have held me up, Clarence would have managed the responses through ventriloquism, and everything would have gone ahead as planned," said Prince Richard.

"I don't know why I bother," said the Seneschal.

"I don't either," said Richard.

They finally left the crowds behind, to their mutual relief, and made their way to King Rufus' private quarters, deep in the old heart of the original Castle structure. The Seneschal looked sharply at the two ceremonial guards standing duty outside the King's door (their main duty was to go with the King whenever he went out, and then bring him safely back again), and the two guards immediately snapped to attention. The Seneschal and the Prince sighed, pretty much in unison. The Seneschal knocked loudly on the door, pushed it open, and led the way in.

The receiving room was a mess; official papers and leather-bound books were piled up everywhere, along with half-eaten meals and even a few items of dirty laundry. Bits and pieces from various eras of Castle history that the King had sent for because he had a vague feeling they might come in handy and then forgot about. Chairs were full and tables were overloaded, and a bottle of really good champagne had been opened and then just left to go flat. The air smelled close and fusty, because the King hadn't opened a window in quite a while. In fact, half the windows still had their curtains closed, blocking out the morning light and shedding a palpable gloom over the whole room.

When Richard's mother, Queen Jane, was still alive, she kept the King's private rooms spotless. A place for everything and everything in its place. She organised regular dustings and always had vases of freshly cut flowers sitting about where they could do the most good. King Rufus went along with it all happily enough, but after his wife died . . . Rufus stopped caring about a lot of things. The Seneschal kept sending servants in to clean the King's rooms, and the King kept driving them out again, because, he said, he knew where everything was and he didn't want it disturbed.

Richard always thought that the state of the King's private rooms indicated the state of the King's thoughts. Dark and gloomy and cluttered, and just a bit lost. When King Rufus was feeling relatively together, he would try to make an effort. Read some of the more important papers that came his way. And at least on those days, the mess did seem to make some kind of sense. Richard looked around the state of the receiving room, and his heart sank. It was clearly not a good day.

King Rufus came shuffling into the room from his private study next door, muttering querulously to himself, and wandered around picking things up and putting them down again. It was obvious he was looking for something, but as usual he couldn't remember what. Though he would never admit that, even to himself. Rufus was in his seventies, hard worn and worn down, and his mind had been deteriorating ever since Queen

Jane died. Some days he didn't remember she was dead, and would ask quite innocently where she was. No one ever told him. It would have been cruel. The servants knew he'd soon forget again, so they just told him she was in the next room. And Rufus would smile and nod and go about whatever he remembered of his business.

King Rufus had been a tall and sturdy man in his prime, a warrior of much renown, but now he was hunched over and half his proper weight, because he kept forgetting to eat. His still noble head thrust forward, with its great mane of snow white hair, and he sported a full white beard, because no one wanted him trying to shave. He always seemed a kindly enough soul, with a smile for everyone, particularly if he wasn't sure whether he was supposed to know them. Today he was wearing his usual threadbare and battered old robes, which he clung to fiercely because they were familiar. His feet were bare. The Seneschal always dressed the King in his ceremonial best every time Rufus had to appear in public, and he would sit quietly while the Seneschal fussed over him and put his crown on. Rufus still remembered about duty and responsibility, even if he did have to have them and what they had to do with him explained to him.

Rufus looked around furtively as he realised he had company. He pottered around for a while, clearly hoping they'd get bored and go away, but when it became clear that wasn't going to happen, the King stopped and sighed. He looked Richard and the Seneschal over with a cautious, almost defiant gaze. He wanted to be sure he knew who they were before he committed himself to saying anything. He still had clear steel grey eyes and a firm mouth; but it had to be said that he had a lost and defeated look to him most days now. Rufus had been a great King in his time, wise and brave and dignified. He did a lot to ease the transition from Royalty to Parliament, because he believed in it and considered it in the best interests of the Forest Land. But that was then, and this was now. King Rufus' mind was going, and it seemed to Richard that every day a little bit less remained of the man his father had been.

The King's head came up suddenly, as he finally put a name to his son, and the Seneschal. A great smile lit up his face, and he nodded cheerfully to them both. He seemed to be quite happy to be interrupted in whatever it was he thought he was doing. He sat down in the nearest chair, as though it were his throne, and the Seneschal moved quickly to brush a pile of important-looking papers off the seat before the King could sit on them and crush them. The King beamed at him.

"Ah, thank you, young man. Most kind. Most kind . . . Now, who are you?"

"The Seneschal!"

"Bless you!" said the King.

"No, Sire," said the Seneschal very patiently. "That is my title. I am your Seneschal, your head servant."

"Oh, good," said King Rufus. "I'm glad we've got that settled. I thought you had allergies . . . There is a lot of dust in here. So, now we've got that settled, I have another question for you."

"Yes, your majesty, what might that be?"

"Who am I?"

"You are His Most Royal Majesty, King Rufus VII, Ruler of the Forest Land, Defender of the Faith, and Monarch of All You Survey," said the Seneschal.

The King blinked a few times. "Pardon?"

"You're King Rufus!"

"Are you sure?"

"Yes!"

The King looked at him suspiciously. "Then what was all that other stuff?"

"Those are your titles!" said the Seneschal. Richard noted interestedly that the Seneschal was already dark red in the face and shading into purple. With a bit of luck, sputtering wouldn't be far behind, hopefully to be followed by shaking of fists in the air, kicking of the Royal furniture, and with any luck, an aneurysm.

"Good, good, good," said the King. "Yes . . . What are you doing here, in my private rooms? These are private, you know."

"You have some important news for your son, Prince Richard," said the Seneschal.

"Important news, eh?" the King said brightly. "That sounds important!" He nodded serenely, and then looked hopefully at the Seneschal for a bit of a clue. The Seneschal sighed and turned to Prince Richard.

"You'd better introduce yourself to him, your highness. Just to make sure he knows who you are."

"I can't believe he's got so bad so quickly," said Richard. "Why wasn't I told?"

"You weren't here," said the Seneschal. "He's not going to get any better. We've tried everything, from medicine to magic and back again. He's not under a curse, or being poisoned, so there's nothing they can do. He's just . . . old."

"I know," said Richard. He stepped right in front of the King and smiled determinedly at him. "Hello, Father! It's me—Richard!"

"Ah, hello, young Rupert!" said the King happily.

"Richard, Sire," said the Seneschal.

"Not now, Richard," said the King to the Seneschal. "I'm talking to young Rupert here."

"No, Father. I'm Richard," said Richard.

"Then who's he?" said the King.

"The Seneschal!"

"Bless you!"

Richard hung grimly onto his self-control with both hands, because if you didn't, you were lost. "You have important news to discuss with me, Father."

"Do I?" said the King. There was a long pause.

"Well?" said Richard.

"Fine, thank you for asking," said the King. "Had a good movement of the bowels first thing, that always helps. Mustn't grumble."

"Let me, your highness, or we'll be here all morning," said the Seneschal. He snapped his fingers craftily, to get the King's attention, and then plunged right in. "Prince Richard, I have to inform you that your arranged marriage with the Princess Catherine of Redhart will be taking place rather sooner than any of us had anticipated. We have received an official communication from the Redhart Court, that the Princess is already on her way to us, and should be arriving here within the next few days. Redhart also made it very clear that they expect the marriage ceremony to take place as soon as humanly possible. They didn't actually use the words *or else*, but they were quite clearly there, between the lines."

Richard stared at the Seneschal with something very like horror. "*What?* Why weren't we given any warning?"

"Don't look at me like that!" said the Seneschal bitterly. "This is all Redhart's doing. We hadn't even decided on the flower arrangements yet. It would appear that both Parliaments have been in touch with each other, behind the scenes, and are putting the pressure on to get you two married so the Peace Treaty can be signed . . . before certain vested interests on both sides can find a way to sabotage things. And both countries probably want to get the marriage moneymaking machine started as soon as possible. Lots of money to be made from a Royal marriage. We'll still be selling ceremonial plates years from now. So you must prepare yourself, Prince Richard. Which means no more running off to play hero! Perhaps now you realise how much trouble you caused for us, when all this started kicking off and you weren't here!"

"Is that it?" said Prince Richard. "Can I go now?"

"You stand right where you are, boy," said King Rufus, and Prince Richard and the Seneschal both looked round sharply. The King was sitting up straight in his chair, his gaze was steady, and his voice was deeper and far more sure than they were used to hearing these days. Richard could feel a broad grin breaking out on his face. It was like his father had been away and now was back again. The King regarded Richard steadily.

"I know you thought you'd have more time to get used to the idea, Richard. And I know you never wanted this marriage anyway. But I have been King long enough. Too long, I'm sure some would say. Soon enough you'll have to wear the crown and sit on the throne, and serve the Land and its people with all your strength and all your heart. And for that you're going to need a wife, a Queen, at your side."

"But how can she be coming here so soon?" said Richard. He could hear the plaintive, almost childish upset in his voice, but couldn't help himself. "There's months of hard travelling between Redhart and here!"

The King gave the Seneschal a hard look, and the head servant bobbed his head quickly in response. "Normally, yes, your highness, but it seems Redhart has a particularly powerful sorcerer working for them. Called Van Fleet. Powerful enough to open up a dimensional gate, a shortcut between two places. They drove the Royal carriage into it in Redhart, and it popped out just a few days' riding from here. We've already had sightings. We've sent armed troops to meet them and escort them safely here. Two days, your highness; no more."

"You've been off adventuring again, haven't you, boy?" said the King. He fixed Richard with a disapproving gaze but couldn't keep a smile off his lips. "Trying to forget your responsibilities, by running away to play hero . . . I was just the same at your age. But it has to stop. Now! I don't really have to give you the set speech on duty and honour again, do I?"

"No, Father," said Richard. "I know what's expected of me."

The King shifted uncertainly on his chair, the strength and focus fading out of his face for a moment, as his concentration slipped, but when he looked back at Richard again his eyes were clear and cold. "I know this has all come as a shock to you, Richard. We always think there'll be more time, to do the things we always planned to do, but never got around to . . . I never met your mother before our marriage day. But we made a go of it. So will you. Because that's part of the job! Of being King. Seneschal! With this marriage so close, so unexpectedly . . . there's a lot of work that needs doing. Isn't there?"

"Yes, Sire," said the Seneschal. And Richard couldn't help noting that the Seneschal was smiling despite himself, so glad to have his old King back again.

"Then lead me to it," said King Rufus. He rose from his chair with the strength and speed of a man half his age; and then he winced, and slumped, and frowned . . . as though trying to think of something that was just on the tip of his tongue. Richard's heart sank, but the King seemed to get his second mental wind, and looked directly at him. "I would have liked a chance to actually *be* King. To fight for the Land, to stand between the people and what threatened them, to live and fight and die for the Forest. Just once. But I left it too late. Don't you make the same mistake, young Rupert."

He strode out of the room, leaving the Seneschal to hurry along in his wake. Richard could hear his father amiably barking out orders, and questions, as he disappeared down the corridor. And Richard had to wonder . . . was his father like this all the time, really, trapped inside a dying body and a crumbling mind? Looking out at the world but unable to reach it except for short periods like this? Richard hoped not. That would be cruel.

He sat down on the chair his father had just vacated. He had some hard thinking to do. He'd always known the day would come when he would have to be King. Have to place the crown on his head, and the cares of the world on his shoulders. But just as his father said, he'd always thought he'd have more time. To come to terms with it, and maybe even find a way out. He hadn't just gone riding out looking for adventure for the sake of it. He'd wanted a chance to prove himself worthy. If you had to do that before you could stand for Parliament, surely you should do that before you could be King?

Rufus had been in his fifties, and on his second wife before Richard arrived. The one and only Royal child. And so Rufus was still on the throne in his seventies, long after everyone had expected he'd be gone. Richard had spent the last few years watching his father die by inches, and knowing there wasn't a damned thing he could do about it.

The Seneschal took care of most of the everyday work, all the paper-work and day-to-day decision making. Richard helped where he could, mostly by forging his father's signature. Everyone was very polite, inside the Court and out, pretending not to notice the King's increasingly con-fused condition, but it couldn't go on much longer. The moment Richard married Catherine, the pressure would be on to retire Rufus and place Richard on the throne. And that would be the end of Richard's life, as he knew it.

He looked up suddenly, his brooding interrupted by raised voices out-side in the corridor. He swore briefly and heaved himself out of the chair. No rest for the wicked, or those who might be wicked, given a chance. Typical bloody Castle . . . He slammed out the door and into the corridor and glared around. And there, heading straight for him, was the First Minister, head of the Forest Parliament. A crowd of not very civil servants surrounded him, trying desperately to get his attention, shouting in his ear, tugging at his clothes, and even trying to thrust papers into his hand. The First Minister ignored them all, his attention fixed on Prince Richard. He finally turned on his followers and drove them all away, with shouts and curses and the occasional blow when they didn't leave fast enough for his liking. The civil servants fled, but only to regroup at the end of the corridor and wait for another chance. They stared sullenly at Prince Richard, who waved happily back at them. The First Minister planted himself in front of the Prince, drew himself up to his full height, and looked Prince Richard over. The Prince smiled sweetly at him.

Peregrine de Woodville was head of the party that currently dominated Parliament, and as King Rufus' First Minister, he set general policy for the Forest Land. And used the King's annual speeches to put a good face on it. Peregrine was a tall, thin, dry, and dusty presence who cut an aristocratic figure, and was more ostentatiously regal and overly fond of himself than any member of the Royal line, truth be told. He had a sharp, pinched face, with cold eyes and a mouth like a steel trap. He was fiercely intelligent, and never let anyone forget it. He dressed formally, but still fashionably, and never appeared in public with so much as an undone button, or an inch of lace cuff out of place. He finally deigned to nod briskly to Richard.

"Might I inquire where you've been these last few months, Prince Richard?"

"Yes," said Richard.

"What?"

"Yes, you may inquire," Richard said pleasantly.

"I know very well where you've been!" said Peregrine.

"Then why are you asking me?" said the Prince, in his most reasonable and deeply irritating voice.

"It's not your job to go out and kill monsters! Your job is to look good in public, and smile and wave for the tourists! Not put your precious Royal life at risk! Leave heroic actions to all those muscular oafs from the Sorting Houses!"

"Couldn't agree more," said Richard.

"What?" said Peregrine.

"I'm the Prince. I don't have to be brave. I have all sorts of perfectly good chaps to do that sort of thing for me."

Peregrine de Woodville looked savagely at Prince Richard. It always drove him crazy when the Prince just stood there and agreed with him. Especially when Peregrine had a whole handful of unassailable arguments that proved he was right and the Prince was wrong—and then the Prince just took all the wind out of his sails by agreeing with him. So the First

Minister couldn't put the Prince down in public, the way he was entitled to. Which was, of course, why the Prince was doing it. Peregrine had a strong feeling that wasn't playing the game.

"Princess Catherine of Redhart is on her way to the Forest Castle," said the First Minister pointedly. "She'll be here in the next forty-eight hours."

"I know," said Richard. "I'm looking forward to it."

"No, you're not!"

"I'm not?"

"I mean—" Peregrine stopped himself with an effort. If he lost his temper in public with the Prince, for no good reason, that meant the Prince had won. Peregrine drew in a sharp breath and leaned in close. "I will make your life a living hell once you are King, Richard."

"Really?" murmured the Prince. "That's just what I was thinking about you, Peregrine."

The First Minister turned his back on the Prince and stalked away. The crowd of waiting civil servants immediately closed in around him again and departed along with him. Richard waved cheerfully after them. He turned to go the other way, and then stopped and sighed heavily as he saw the Seneschal heading straight for him. Without the King. Richard seriously considered taking to his heels and racing the Seneschal to the nearest side exit, but he had a feeling the Seneschal was in better shape than he was, just at the moment, and would probably win. So Richard stood his ground and waited for the Seneschal to join him, looking reproachfully at him all the while.

"You've lost him, haven't you?" said Richard, before the Seneschal could say anything. "He's seventy-six years old! How could you let him give you the slip? He was only with you for a few minutes . . ."

"Of course I haven't lost him!" snapped the Seneschal. "I've just handed him over to the protocol department, because I finally remembered what it was I was going to say to you before I got distracted by all this pain in the arse about the Royal marriage."

"Well, go on," the Prince said pointedly. "I haven't got all day."

"I've had to make the decision to close another hundred rooms in the main Castle, your highness. We just can't afford the cost of maintaining them. Which means that less than ten percent of the Castle rooms are now occupied, or properly utilised. And that includes the Armoury." The Seneschal stopped, to look meaningfully at Richard. "You do know that certain elements in Parliament are pressing us to open up the Armoury to the public? To make it a tourist attraction, like the Cathedral?"

"That is not going to happen," said Richard. "Not while I still have any say in the matter or breath in my body. There are far too many dangerous weapons, not to mention dangerous secrets, still stored in the Forest Armoury."

"I know that, your highness," said the Seneschal. "But knowledge of these things is on a strictly need-to-know basis, and the Royal line decided long ago that Parliament didn't need to know. Because if they did, they'd wet themselves. So they honestly don't understand why we won't open up an armoury no one ever uses, and make some much-needed money from it."

"You'd better keep your ear pressed firmly to the political ground," said Richard, "and see which way the political wind's blowing—and, yes, I am aware that I am mangling my metaphors. The point is, we need as much advance warning as possible, so that if necessary I can organise a complete clearing out of the more important items and put them somewhere safe." He stopped and looked hard at the Seneschal. "Do we even have an inventory of what's still in there?"

"Well, yes and no," said the Seneschal. "We have a fairly complete record of everything we're prepared to admit is in there, but as for the rest . . . I know the Armourer has been meaning to get around to a really complete list, any time now. But you know what he's like . . ."

"Unfortunately, yes," said the Prince. "He was the only suitable man for the job."

"He's crazy!"

"Isn't that what I just said?"

"He was the only one who wanted it," said the Seneschal. "Which should have put us on our guard at the time . . . I mean, yes, he's certainly qualified, as a weapons-master and an historian. He knows all the legends of Forest Castle, including which ones are worth listening to, but . . . he's crazy! He talks to fish!"

"That was just a phase! And let's be honest—given the state of the

Armoury these days, if he wasn't crazy when he started, he would be by now. Given some of the things we keep locked up and chained down in there. Is that really what you wanted to talk to me about, Seneschal? I have some important ruminating to be getting on with."

"That's what comes of eating travel bread and wild roots in the Forest."

"I am wearing a sword," the Prince pointed out.

"There is still the matter of the Cathedral, your highness," the Seneschal said quickly. "I know it's been open to the tourists for decades now, but it is still supposed to hold its own fair share of secrets. Really quite dangerous and appalling secrets, according to some of the older and more worrying stories about exactly what Hawk and Fisher and the Walking Man found in there, when they investigated the Cathedral all those years ago. When the Cathedral was still Inverted, with Space itself turned upside down, so that the Cathedral plunged deep into the earth . . . And yes, I know I'm babbling just a bit, but that place has always scared the crap out of me. Personally, I can't help thinking that we'd all have been better off if Hawk and Fisher had left it the way it was. It would be one less thing for us, and by *us* I mean *me*, to worry about!"

"You're hyperventilating again, Seneschal," said the Prince. "Do you want a paper bag to breathe into?"

"No," said the Seneschal. "It doesn't help."

"The Cathedral has been very thoroughly searched and inspected, from top to bottom, ever since we got it back again," said Richard in his best soothing voice. "It's been checked out by clerical experts, weapons experts, half a dozen sorcerers, and at least one top-rank exorcist. And not one of them turned up anything to give us a sleepless night. The Cathedral doesn't even need maintaining. It maintains itself."

"Which is also very worrying if you think about it, so I try very hard not to," said the Seneschal. "And I will admit we do make a pile of tourist money out of the Cathedral, thanks to sightseers, religious types, and any number of pilgrimages. But that wasn't what I really wanted to talk to you about either! Dear God, my head is going round and round in circles and disappearing up its own . . . Ah! Yes! I remember!"

The Seneschal took a deep breath, let it out slowly, and then looked steadily at Prince Richard. "If you're looking for something to keep you occupied, and your mind distracted, while keeping yourself well out of the First Minister's way . . . allow me to offer you something that will quite definitely take your mind off the fast-approaching Princess Catherine. My people have just discovered a new room. Or, more accurately, a very old room that no one's seen in years."

"How many years?" said Richard.

"Or, to put it another way, a room that's been there all along, but no one was able to see it. But it's there now, right in front of everybody."

"How long has this room been missing?" said Richard.

The Seneschal gave Richard his best official shrug. "A hundred years, maybe more, your highness. From around the time of the Demon War, perhaps . . ."

"I can see why you think it would interest me," said Richard. "The question has to be, why has this room suddenly turned up now, after all these years?"

"A very good question, your highness. But I haven't the time to find out, and I can't spare any of my people to make a properly thorough investigation, so if you'd like to look into this . . ."

"Thank you, Seneschal," said the Prince.

They both stopped and looked round sharply as one of the Seneschal's people came rushing up to him and thrust a paper into his hand. The Seneschal looked it over quickly, said a very bad word, and paused only to give Richard the room's location before charging off with his assistant, to do something useful and necessary to prevent the Castle from collapsing. Richard watched him go, and then went in search of the returned room.

In the end, he found it easily enough. And it did give him an excuse to go strutting purposefully through the packed crowds and hallways, clearly too busy to stop and talk with all the people who wanted to talk to him, congratulate him, and ask for things they weren't entitled to. And probably shouldn't be allowed to have, on general principles. Richard was getting just a bit tired of being hailed as the conquering hero, especially when he knew for a fact he hadn't actually solved the problem. All he'd done was buy the people of Cooper's Mill some time.

In the end, he just followed the general air of excitement. The newly discovered door was only half a dozen corridors along, and when Richard finally stopped before it, it didn't look any different from any of the other doors up and down the long corridor. Until you looked closely. Dark, heavy wood, with large brass hinges, and a really solid-looking, old-fashioned lock. The kind of door you couldn't hope to break down without a battering ram and a lot of effort. Which suggested the room beyond the door wasn't going to be just any old room.

Half a dozen of the Seneschal's people had gathered before the door, angrily disputing with one another. One was listening through the door with a stethoscope, one was trying to pick the lock and getting nowhere, and a third was being very loudly persuaded not to try out an oversized battleaxe he really shouldn't have been allowed anywhere near.

Richard immediately recognised the one with the lock picks (which he knew for a fact she wasn't supposed to have), so he sided with her against the others, and they soon got the message and fell reluctantly back. Jacqui Piper was a delightful young woman in a badly fitting set of men's overalls, and not a lot on underneath. She specialised in opening locks that didn't want to open, kicking in doors that were often left closed for a reason, and doing things to stubborn doors that the Prince wouldn't do to a dead dog. Jacqui was pretty and petite, practical, experienced, and only just out of her teens. With a hell of a lot of attitude. Richard liked her because she didn't take any shit from anyone, including him. She also always made a point of never been impressed by his Princeness, and Richard liked that because it was so very rare. Jacqui looked round as the Prince knelt beside her to study the lock.

"Finally!" she said, in her loud and somewhat squeaky voice. "Someone who might actually take this seriously! I told the Seneschal, and I told everyone else, that this door wasn't here yesterday. I know this section of the Castle like I know the birthmark on my left tit, and I am telling you that this time yesterday, there was nothing here but some blank wall!" She stopped, to sniff loudly. "No one ever listens to me. Nice timing on the arrival, Princey; I've just run out of skeleton keys. So unless you've got a better idea, it's time for the brute force and sudden violence." She stopped to glare at one of her people. "And no, Jonathon, I am not letting you anywhere near this door with that axe. You know what happened last time." She glanced at the Prince. "Given the sheer scale of magical protections I'm seeing crawling all over this door, the axe wouldn't do him any good. Not that I give a damn. Jonathon's always had shifty eyes and wandering hands."

Richard moved in closer, to look the lock over carefully. And everyone else stepped even farther back, so they wouldn't be hit by whatever he set off. Everyone except Jacqui. Who stayed right where she was, regarding the lock as though it had just said something about her mother. Richard tried the big brass door handle, and it turned easily in his grasp. Richard raised an eyebrow and looked at Jacqui, who seemed honestly shocked. They both straightened up and stood before the door. Richard turned the handle carefully, and the door opened before him, without even the sound of a lock disengaging. Jacqui make a loud disgusted noise. Richard pushed the door open a ways but made no move to enter. There was only darkness beyond the door.

"Okay, that's . . . interesting," said Jacqui, squeezing in tight beside Richard without actually pushing him to one side. "That door was quite definitely locked. We all tried it."

"I think this door must have been keyed specially to only open to a member of the Royal line," said Richard. "That kind of magic is a lost skill. Even my father's private quarters don't have a lock like that. You'd better stand back, Jacqui, while I go in and take a look."

"Yeah, right!" said Jacqui. "Like that's going to happen. Old rooms are my business! I live for mysteries . . . And for small valuable objects I can pocket and sell on the quiet."

Richard strode into the room, pushing the door wide open so light from the corridor could rush in and illuminate the space. Jacqui stuck close beside him, just far enough behind that she could use him as a shield if necessary. But the room looked like . . . just another room. Dusty and dirty, though surprisingly free of cobwebs. Heavy curtains stood pulled together over the only window, allowing just a narrow beam of morning light to fall through. Richard walked over to the curtains and pulled them open. Light spilled into the room, even as the heavy fabric in his hands all but fell apart. Richard threw the bits and pieces aside and rubbed his hands clean on his hips. He looked across at Jacqui, who had a large silver snuffbox in her hand and was clearly trying to decide whether she could fit it into any of her pockets. She caught him looking at her, and froze.

"Aren't you needed somewhere else?" the Prince said sweetly.

"Almost certainly," said Jacqui, putting the snuffbox down with an insouciant smile. She gave an *I can always come back later when less fussy people are around* shrug and headed for the door. "If you're sure you won't need me . . ."

"I can handle this," said Richard.

"Of course you can," said Jacqui. "You big strong manly Prince, you." She grinned at him briefly. "Typical aristo, always wanting the good stuff for yourself."

She was almost out the door when the Prince spoke her name, in a loud and purposeful voice. Jacqui sighed and produced half a dozen small but very expensive items from various places about her person. She slammed the door behind her as she left, hard enough to raise a cloud of dust across the room.

Left alone at last, Richard wandered slowly round the large room, taking it in. A fair-sized room, in fact, with heavy old-fashioned furniture, a room that clearly hadn't been used in some time. Could it really date back to the Demon War? The room did have a cold feeling to it, a sort of presence . . . The light seemed strong enough now, pushing back the gloom. Richard felt a little better for that; the original dark of the room had upset him on some deep and almost primal level. As though he shouldn't be here, didn't belong here. He made his way carefully round the room, looking at everything closely and occasionally bumping into things. Until finally he noticed that most of the paintings on the walls showed scenes and battles from before the Demon War. So, over a hundred years old . . .

Richard picked up a book from a side table (very carefully, after what had happened to the curtains, but it seemed solid enough in his hands). He casually flipped it open, and then almost dropped the thing as he recognised the signature on the title page. He was holding King John's personal diary. The day-to-day journal of his great-great-grandfather, written during the last days of the Demon War. *The* King John, father of the legendary Prince Rupert. Richard staggered just a bit as the truth hit him: he was standing in the long-lost private quarters of King John, from all those years ago. He was standing in the last remnant of a forgotten realm. He put the diary down carefully; best leave it to the historians and the experts, to preserve the diary properly, and then study it.

Richard felt overcome by history. This was the room in which Prince Rupert and Princess Julia, King John and Prince Harald, and even the enigmatic High Warlock himself, had gathered in the last days of the Demon War. When all seemed lost. To talk and plan, and through their actions, change the course of history.

This was where they decided to take on the demon hordes, and bring down the Demon Prince, and save all humanity from extinction. Richard knew there had to be other rooms beyond this, somewhere, a whole suite of rooms, and God alone knew what kind of historical treasures they held. No one had been able to find this suite of rooms since they disappeared, soon after King John disappeared into the wilderness, after the war. And people had looked really hard for them. This was a magical place, at the heart of songs and legends beyond counting. A place of Destiny. Richard circled the room anxiously, again and again, just trying to take it all in, but then he stopped abruptly as a large portrait on the wall caught his attention. It showed King John, and his wife, Queen Eleanor, with someone who just had to be the High Warlock. Richard stared at the image, open-mouthed. They all looked so young . . . younger even than him.

This was from that long-ago time, the golden time, when they were all good friends and in their prime. Before it all went so horribly wrong. The warrior King and his beautiful Queen, and the greatest Wild Magician of his time. Richard stared at the tall, black-robed, black-haired, darkly handsome young man, the High Warlock, standing just a little apart from the King and Queen. The man seemed to blaze with life and energy and charisma, even through an official portrait. There were no portraits of the High Warlock anywhere now, official or otherwise. King John had them all burned, after he banished the High Warlock from his Court.

Some of the songs claimed it was for failing to save the Queen's life after she fell ill. Others, because the Queen and the Warlock fell in love. And others . . . said other things. There were lots of stories, but no one knew for sure. All the legends agreed that the High Warlock left Forest Castle and went out into the wilderness to raise up the Tower With No Doors. Where he stayed for many years, until Prince Rupert called him forth to be a hero one last time, in the Demon War.

There were all kinds of songs and stories about the man, all of which should be taken with a large pinch of salt.

Richard tore his gaze away from the portrait to stare almost wildly about him, his heart racing. The room seemed suddenly . . . oppressive. There was just so much history here, the truth about what had really happened in this room, a hundred years before. It was like being immersed in History itself. And then Richard frowned, as a cold chill crept over him. Why now? Why had this room, this particular legendary room, suddenly made itself known after being lost for so long? And why had it opened so easily to him? Because the door was keyed to the Forest Royal line—or because it was waiting for him? The man who was going to be King, a hundred years after the Demon War . . . Did that mean there was something significant here that he was supposed to recognise, and make use of?

He walked round and round the room, increasingly quickly, looking at everything but unable to spot anything out of the ordinary. He had ended up standing right in the centre of the room, looking desperately back and forth . . . when Jacqui Piper rushed back in, gasping for breath.

"What is it?" said Richard, in a harsh voice he wasn't sure he recognised.

"You have to come with me now, Prince! Right now! Honest! Message from the Seneschal, vital and important and terribly urgent. There's trouble at the Cathedral!"

"It's always something," said the Prince just a bit bitterly. "Some days this Castle just won't leave you in peace!"

"Tell me about it," said Jacqui.

They ran all the way. It wasn't often that things went wrong with the Cathedral, but when they did, they tended to go very thoroughly wrong. Suddenly and violently and all over the place. And wise men rushed for cover until it was over. Once, the Cathedral had been topologically and spiritually Inverted, and that was why the Castle had been so much bigger on the inside than on the outside for so many years. (And not because of a cock-up at the architect's, as so many had claimed.) Hawk and Fisher and the even more legendary Walking Man went into that Inverted Cathedral, and found something there, and did something to put it right, though they would talk about only some of it afterwards. But suddenly the Cathedral was no longer Inverted, and the Castle had its insides and outsides in the proper order. The Cathedral rose up to Heaven, a beacon of worship, right in the middle of the restored Castle, and was very popular with the more than usually religiously inclined. Apart from the standard religious services, the Cathedral was a magnet for religious tourists, penitents and the like, and many visitors from many lands. Their financial contributions helped greatly with the depleted coffers of the Forest King.

Richard couldn't help noting that most of the corridors he and his companion were running through were suddenly very empty. Could whatever it was that was going on in the Cathedral really be that bad?

"Has the Seneschal evacuated this area?" he said, in between heavy breathing from running so hard.

"If I was any more scared, I'd be evacuating," said Jacqui, forcing the words past her own harsh breathing.

"You are a deeply disturbing person," said Richard.

"Play to your strengths, that's what I always say," said Jacqui.

"Do you suppose . . . this could be the Burning Man, back at last?" said Richard, slowing his pace despite himself. "That poor damned soul out of Hell that Hawk and Fisher and the Walking Man met inside the Inverted Cathedral?"

"Well, before he could return, first you'd have to decide whether he ever existed," said Jacqui, also slowing down. "Or if he was just added to the story afterwards, to keep the religious fanatics happy. Hawk and Fisher left a very spotty official account of what they did and saw inside the Cathedral. And the Walking Man never said anything, even after he gave up the position to become Prince Consort to Queen Felicity. I believe in the Burning Man because I like a good story, but that doesn't mean I want to meet him."

"Good point," said Richard.

"I thought so," said Jacqui.

But when they finally limped, breathless and sweaty, into the Cathedral's lobby, they both calmed down considerably as they realised it was just another showdown between the various stallholders, merchants and hucksters who made a living selling some very suspect religious items to the very religious tourists. Richard and Jacqui stopped just inside the great arched doorway and leaned on each other for a long moment while they got their breath back. No one paid them any attention. The stallholders were all busy yelling at one another at the top of their lungs, glaring right into one another's faces and threatening one another with increasingly specific consequences. The threat of violence was heavy on the air, but no one had actually nerved themselves to the hitting point yet.

There were dozens of stallholders involved, everyone from genuine religious fanatics to hardheaded merchants, connected only by a shared determination to squeeze every last penny possible out of the tourists. Who were now standing in small groups around the perimeter of the Cathedral lobby, taking it all in with fascinated eyes and wide smiles and enjoying the spectacle intensely. It would make such a great story to tell the folks back home. By listening carefully to the clashing raised voices, Richard was finally able to work out that a Holier Than Thou contest had broken out. The words *heretic* and *blasphemer* were being bandied about with more than usual venom, along with many barbed comments on the efficacy and quality of the various items being offered for sale. Richard took a quick look around, to reassure himself it was all just the usual rubbish. Mostly religious artefacts, the writings of various Saints (illustrated editions extra), blessed holy medals, and charms guaranteed to ward off witches, demons, flood, and impotence.

The usual.

There were even some apparently quite ordinary and everyday objects, made special (and therefore expensive) because they were supposed to have been handled by all sorts of characters from the Demon War period. Mostly Rupert and Julia, of course, but any number of minor and peripheral names got a good look in. Along with a dragon's claw and a unicorn's silver hoof, and an empty wine bottle supposedly emptied by the High Warlock himself. Richard had trouble believing anyone believed in this tat, especially since most of it clearly wasn't old enough. And he found the prices particularly unbelievable.

Richard finally pushed his way through the ranks of delighted tourists, with Jacqui tagging eagerly along behind him. The tourists didn't care, being mostly engaged in speculating on the chances of actual bloodletting, and then placing their bets accordingly. Free entertainment was always the best kind. By now the various stallholders had escalated to threatening one another with curses, extra years in Purgatory, and a chance to visit Hell any moment now by a very direct route.

Richard stopped it all by barging right into the middle of them, and shouting even louder than they did. They all turned on him, outraged, and then shut up the moment they saw who it was. The fact that he had a really big sword on his hip probably helped. He glared about him.

"I am Prince Richard, Defender of the Faith and protector of Castle security! Which means I outrank every single one of you here! You should all be ashamed of yourselves, behaving in such a fashion, in such a sacred setting!"

There was a certain amount of everyone involved staring at their feet, and mutters of *He started it*, before one of the better-dressed stallholders stepped forward to confront the Prince, drawing himself up to his full height and dignity.

"This is no place for you, Prince Richard! This is none of your affair! This isn't about religion, it's about business!"

Richard punched him out. A good solid shot, right to the point of the jaw, and the watching crowd applauded happily as the stallholder measured his length on the polished marble floor. Richard smiled graciously about him, and did his best to hide the fact that his right hand really hurt. Peter would have been disappointed in him for forgetting his basic training. *Never go for the jaw; it's just one big bone. Nuts and noses; that's the thing, along with all the other soft spots. And never hit a man when he's down! Far too dangerous. Put the boot in, instead.* Richard allowed his smile to fade away as he turned a stern look on the now rather subdued stallholders.

"I do not need this kind of nonsense, not when I've got so many other things on my plate to deal with! So knock it off! One more angry word out of anyone . . . and I'll have the Seneschal send in the security guards to check everyone's permits!"

The merchants all bobbed their heads quickly and went back to their stalls. The word *permits* had taken all the starch out of them. Richard smiled.

"That's it, back to work, everyone. There are still lots of tourists standing around with some of your money left in their pockets."

The usual hubbub of religious marketing resumed, as the tourists ignored Prince Richard in favor of pursuing some enthusiastic haggling. If there wasn't going to be any violence, they wanted to get back to the more important business of paying through the nose for things they didn't really need. Richard left the Cathedral lobby, and Jacqui strolled along beside him.

"Are you really going to call the guards in to check all their permits?"

Richard grinned at her. "You don't need a permit to sell goods in the Cathedral lobby. But they didn't know that . . . Funny, that."

Jacqui shook her head admiringly. "God, you're devious."

"Why, thank you," said Richard. "All part of being a Prince."

Richard and Jacqui disappeared into the Castle. Unbeknownst to them, the First Minister, Peregrine de Woodville, and the Leader of the Loyal Opposition, Henry Wallace, had been observing them all this time from a shadowy corner of the Cathedral lobby. The two men stood shoulder to shoulder, having watched the entire confrontation with cool, thoughtful eyes.

"I told you if we paid off one of the merchants to start some trouble, the Prince would have to get involved," said Henry Wallace.

"So you did," said Peregrine. "I was interested to see how far he would go when provoked. Disappointingly, he kept a firm hold on his temper and didn't even draw his sword. A nice mix of diplomacy and brute force. A King in the making."

Henry Wallace nodded unhappily. He and Peregrine took it in turns to run Parliament, as their parties swapped back and forth, roughly every five years. There were only two parties in the Forest Land, and there wasn't really that much difference between them. Democracy was a relatively new thing, imported from the Southern Kingdoms, and everyone was still working out the rules and the options. Officially, Peregrine's party stood for reform and progress, while Henry's stood for consolidation and hanging on to the old values. But really, it was all about power.

Henry Wallace was a dark, sardonic figure, with fussy clothing that tried hard to be fashionable but never quite managed it. He had a brooding, forceful presence that made people think he was a lot smarter than he really was. And nobody could match him when it came time to delivering fire-and-brimstone speeches. (Couldn't ad-lib to save his life, though, so the party saw to it that he was always surrounded by smart young things in public, to do that for him.) Henry saw his job to be . . . a safe pair of hands.

"Richard is going to be trouble," said Peregrine. "I can tell."

"We can't have him mess this marriage up," said Henry. "The Peace agreement is just too important. Took a lot of hard work to come up with something both sides hated but could just about live with. Sometimes I have nightmares where I'm still at that bloody negotiating table, arguing endlessly and getting nowhere."

"Don't," said Peregrine, shuddering delicately. "The slaughter on the border is finally over. That's all that matters. It's time for the killing to stop. Whatever it takes."

"Of course," said Henry. "You lost people in the border wars. Friends, or family?"

"Both," said Peregrine. "You?"

"Everyone lost someone," said Henry.

The two men stood quietly together, remembering their time on the border. They'd both started out as soldiers, in the same troop, more years ago than either of them cared to remember. Full of hot blood and patriotic spirit, eager for the fray. The reality of war knocked all that nonsense out of them. They both fought well, and bravely, distinguishing themselves in some of the more prestigious battles against Redhart. They'd even fought in the particular engagement that produced the infamous Sombre Warrior. Though they never saw it happen, and only heard about it years afterwards. It just went to show how easily legends could be started, legends that the people involved knew nothing of.

The two men had never really liked each other all that much, but they'd always worked well together. Whether it was cutting down the enemy on a blood-soaked field or fighting for power afterwards, on the strength of the names they'd made for themselves. They'd quickly become leaders of their parties, at least to some degree because they never let dogma stand in the way of getting things done. While being very careful that no one ever found that out.

Both of them were prepared to do pretty much anything to push the Peace process through. They both knew war was unthinkable. Because the Forest Land would lose.

"So," said Peregrine finally. "What pressure can we bring to bear on Prince Richard to make him more . . . compliant? I'm having to spend far too much time trying to bend him to my will when I should be concentrating on more important matters."

"Could we perhaps make him think we don't really want this marriage?" said Henry. "So he'd embrace it just to spite us?"

"No," said Peregrine. "We could never sell that. He knows how much the agreement means to us. We'll just have to stress Duty and Honour, and avoiding war at all costs."

"We won't have to push that one too hard," said Henry. "Because it's true."

The First Minister sniffed loudly. "Richard's problem is he's still young enough to think that something will always turn up at the last moment to solve the problem and save the day. A nice thought to keep you from actually having to do something. Damn it, he's always known he'd have to marry a foreign Princess someday. Does he have a girlfriend at present, anyone close who might complicate things? I'm a bit out of the loop on his private life, since I don't read the scandal sheets. The wife loves them . . . Who was that pretty young thing that was just with him?"

"Just one of the Seneschal's people," said Henry. "No one important. There's never been anyone serious in Richard's life that I know of. Which is odd, for a man of his age. God knows we've all pushed suitable girls in his direction, at one time or another, carefully trained and instructed, in the hopes of influencing him on certain matters. But he always dodged."

The First Minister looked at his colleague thoughtfully. "He's not . . ."

"No, he's not. We tried that," said Henry. "He didn't care for any of the handsome young men we pushed at him either. For a while there, he must have wondered why he was suddenly so very attractive to so many pretty young things."

"There's always his friends, Peter and Clarence," said Peregrine. "Either of them might prove susceptible to the right . . . pressures. Worth checking out, I suppose." He stopped and looked at Henry. "I suppose it's too much to hope that Richard and Catherine might just . . . like each other?"

"Have you met the Princess Catherine?" Henry shuddered grimly. "I met her a few times when I was negotiating in Redhart. A real hellcat. Pretty enough, I suppose, but . . . I suppose we could always slip a love philtre in their food or drink or perhaps lay an enchantment on them? I do know a few people . . ."

"No," the First Minister said immediately. "They both have major magical defences in place against any form of outside influence. And don't ask me how I know that."

"Wouldn't dream of it," said Henry.

"We'll just have to keep piling on the pressure," said Peregrine. "On father, and son."

"Business as usual," said Henry.

The two men smiled briefly at each other and spoke aloud the one thing they did both believe in. "To a Republic! As soon as humanly possible."

Much later, in the early hours of the morning, Prince Richard lay fast asleep in his very comfortable goose-feather bed, dreaming that he could hear a beautiful female voice singing. He smiled in his sleep, so happy, so content, wrapped in the loving arms of that wonderful song. And then he snapped awake, sat bolt upright in bed, and realised he could still hear the song. He looked quickly about him. The candles he'd set out before he went to sleep, scattered all over the room, still had a few good inches of light left in them. He hadn't been able to face the idea of sleeping in the dark, even in his familiar bed and room. He hadn't liked giving in to his own weakness, didn't like the idea that anything was in charge of him except him. But the Darkwood had laid its mark upon him, as it had with so many before.

He threw his blankets aside and swung out of bed, pulling his long white nightshirt about him as he yawned fiercely and then knuckled his eyes. He wasn't really a morning person. The clock on his bedside table said almost five in the morning. Richard smiled. The sun would be up. That was something. He realised he could still hear the song, and moved quickly over to the window. He pushed the curtains aside and looked out. The early-morning light was grey and uncertain, with clouds of ground fog everywhere. Birds were singing the dawn chorus, in their usual brutal and uncaring way. He couldn't see anyone about, but the song and the voice were still clear and distinct. He strained his ears, trying to make out the words, but all he could hear was . . . joy, happiness, and glory in the world.

Richard put on a long robe and went to his door. He'd locked it before he went to sleep, a thing he'd never done before. He unlocked the door carefully and stepped out into the corridor. Everything was very still, very quiet. And no sign anywhere of the two guards who should have been standing outside his door. Richard frowned, shut his door, and padded down the corridor on his bare feet. He passed from one hallway to another, and still there was no one about. As though he were walking through a dream of the Castle.

He finally came to a window in the outer wall, and looked out. Far below, he could just make out a female figure in a long blue dress dancing along the surface of the moat, tracing an elegant figure on the water, and singing a fine song. Her feet just touched the surface without sinking into the water. Ripples spread slowly out from every point of contact.

Richard watched wonderingly. Why couldn't anyone else hear her? If he could hear her singing all the way up on the top floor, the whole Castle should be able to . . .

He descended quickly through the many corridors and galleries, heading determinedly for the ground floor. Down empty curving stairways, through vaulted hallways, with lamps and candles lit everywhere, though the early-morning light seemed to hang heavily on the still air. As though it were brittle with anticipation; as though it was waiting for something . . . And still there was no one about. No guards, no servants. Where the hell was everyone? Was he perhaps still back in his bed, still asleep? Still dreaming? No. The stone floors were profoundly cold and hard under his bare feet.

He went all the way down through the Castle and never saw a single human anywhere. He wondered in a vague sort of way why he wasn't raising the alarm. Perhaps, he felt, more and more, that it was because all of this was meant just for him. He left the Castle through the main entrance and started across the open cobbled courtyard. Not even a snort or a whinny from the stables. He walked out across the drawbridge, which was lowered even though there was no one around who could have lowered it. *Magic,* he thought. *I'm moving through a magical world.* He'd dreamed of such a thing for most of his life but never expected to just wake up in it. It felt like someone had turned off the world, or plucked him out of it, or maybe even stopped Time, just for him.

And finally there she was, dancing along the moat towards him, her feet barely disturbing the surface of the water. And for the first time he realised her whole body was made up of water. That she was drawing and maintaining her form from the contents of the moat, endlessly replacing herself with every step she took. He knew who she was now, who she had to be. The very legendary Lady of the Lake. He knew all the songs and stories about her. She was almost as tall as the Prince himself, a good six feet, wild and willowy, clear as blue crystal, shining and shimmering in the grey light of the morning. A woman made entirely of water. He'd thought she was wearing a long blue dress, but as she drew nearer he could see that both it and her body were just water, totally fluid, running away and re-forming over and over, with great slow ripples moving through her, like tides. The long blue hair that fell to her shoulders was constantly running away, continually renewing itself. Beads of water ran steadily down her calm and noble face, like tears without end, dripping off her chin.

He knew the face. He'd seen it just a few hours before, in the portrait on the wall of King John's returned room.

She had an unearthly, almost timeless beauty now, as though refined to perfection by some implacable scouring force. Blue face, blue eyes, blue lips. The Lady of the Lake, who was all the water of the Forest Land. An elemental power, and a force of Nature. She finally came to a halt before

Richard and smiled warmly at him. More ripples spread across her face as she spoke to him, and her voice was like the gurgling of a rushing stream, given shape and meaning through human influence.

"Hello, Richard," she said. "I've been waiting for you, for this moment, for more years than I care to remember."

"Is this a dream?" said Richard.

"Of a sort. I live in dreams now. The dream of the Land . . . I have returned, Richard, after so many quiet years in the Forest, because I'm needed. Because the Forest needs me. Because the Demon Prince walks the Land again."

"In the Darkwood?" said Richard.

"No," said the Lady. "But you've been to the Darkwood, haven't you? I can see its mark upon you, body and soul. My dear Richard . . . beware. Destiny has you in its grip."

"Are you really everything they say you are?" said Richard. "Are you really my great-great-grandmother? The Queen Eleanor that was?"

"Don't, dear," said the Lady. "You'll make me feel old. I was her, once. But I'm so much more now. You must prepare yourself, Richard."

"For what? For war?"

"Worse than that," said the Lady of the Lake. "I have no wisdom for you, no words of warning. Not even a weapon. I just wanted to see you, to have this quiet moment with you, my dear great-great-grandson. Because there won't be time for quiet moments when it all goes wrong."

She sank silently into the moat waters and was gone, leaving nothing behind but a single slowly spreading ripple on the surface of the water. Leaving Richard standing alone, in the grim grey morning light. He shivered once, not from the cold, pulled his robe tightly about him, and went back inside the Castle.

FOUR

....

FAMILY MATTERS

Hawk and Fisher and Chappie the dog were out on the dusty grey plain that surrounded the Millennium Oak again, taking a brisk walk in the brisk morning air, with the Administrator once more stumbling very unhappily along behind them. He'd been muttering under his breath for some time now, and none of the others felt inclined to inquire as to what he was saying. On such small compromises is civilisation built. The air was clear and fresh that early morning, the sky was a perfect blue, and everything was very peaceful. Until the Administrator decided he'd been civilised long enough and let them all have it.

"What the hell am I doing out here *again*, at this ungodly early hour? What is it this time? What do you need to tell me now that is so private and important and generally upsetting that I have to be dragged all the way out here, so that when you do upset me I can't get my hands on anything heavy and sharp-edged? And why are you both wearing backpacks? Just how long is this walk going to take?" He stopped suddenly, as a thought hit him. "Are you trying to work up the courage to tell me that your replacements won't be arriving in time after all?"

The others stopped, and looked back at him. They had covered quite a distance, though the Millennium Oak stood as tall and proud and over-whelmingly large on the horizon as ever.

"I'm afraid it's just a bit worse than that," Hawk said calmly. "And definitely not something for prying ears. Isobel and I have to leave. Right now."

"That's why the backpacks," said Fisher. "We've a long way to go. We did try to strap one on Chappie, but he wasn't having it."

"Damn right," said Chappie coldly. "I am not a pack mule."

"Of course not," said Hawk. "They're useful."

And then the three of them watched interestedly as the Administrator glared wildly at them, struck speechless with shock and fury. His face turned an unhealthy shade of purple, and his eyes actually bulged.

"The last time I saw him look like that," said Fisher, "he'd accidentally walked in on a tantric sex final exam. They had to hose him down afterwards."

"He isn't going to have a coronary, is he?" growled the dog.

"Don't be silly," said Hawk. "You need to have a heart to have one of those."

"I heard that!" said the Administrator immediately. His hands had clenched into fists. "You can't just walk out on everybody! How is the Hawk and Fisher Memorial Academy supposed to function, without a Hawk and Fisher at the helm? It's the start of a new term! You can't just walk out on us before your replacements have even arrived!"

"Ah," said Hawk, sounding perhaps not quite as regretful as he might have, "that's part of the bad news. There aren't going to be any replacements."

"Strictly speaking, there never were," said Fisher.

"Sorry," said Hawk.

The Administrator looked pleadingly up at the heavens. "Give me strength! Give me strength, a battleaxe, and a sympathetic jury; they'd never convict me! What are you two talking about?"

Hawk produced a small magical charm, just a beaten metal disc, with a complicated design stamped on it. Afterwards, the Administrator was never sure whether Hawk had the thing on a chain round his neck, or took it out of his pocket, or even if the metal disc just suddenly appeared on Hawk's outstretched palm. The disc looked ordinary enough, until the

Administrator examined it closely and realised the design stamped on it was so complicated and intricate he couldn't get his head round it at all. A design so . . . deep that just looking at it made his head hurt. It was like looking into a pond and realising that underneath the surface it just fell away forever.

"What is that?" said the Administrator. He sounded and felt far away, his brow creasing in concentration and puzzlement. "I know that. Don't I? You've always had that, haven't you . . . Why didn't I remember it until you showed it to me?"

"This is the Confusulum," said Hawk. "A very useful item. It manipulates people's perception by confusing the matter on every level you can think of." He closed his hand over the charm and the Administrator jumped, just a little, as though abruptly roused from some vague but disturbing dream.

"Where did you get it?" he said, because he felt he ought to say something.

"On our travels," said Fisher. "While we were taking care of some unfinished business."

"We won it, on a bet," said Hawk. "Or perhaps it won us. It's hard to be sure about anything where the Confusulum is concerned. It's supposed to be the physical presence in our world of some other-dimensional entity. It shouldn't be messing about in the material plane at all, but I think it just likes to play. But now, Confusulum, time's up, if you please. No more illusions."

Oh sure! said a cheerful, mischievous voice inside everyone's head at once. *No more illusions it is!*

Hawk opened his hand, and it was empty. The disc was gone. The Administrator blinked a few times.

"Is it still there?"

"Maybe," said Hawk.

"Who can tell?" said Fisher.

"Look at us, Administrator," said Hawk.

The Administrator looked at Hawk and Fisher, and cried out in shock. The middle-aged pair he was used to seeing were gone, as though they had never been there; they'd been replaced by two entirely different-looking people, both of them barely into their thirties. Hawk was tall, dark, and handsome enough in a hardbitten sort of way. His face wasn't actually scarred, but there was something about it that suggested it ought to be. Hawk was lean and wiry rather than muscular, with long dark hair pulled back and fastened at his nape with a silver clasp. He wore a simple white tunic and trousers, with a heavy dark cloak and functional knee-length leather boots. He wore his axe at his side with the ease of long habit, and there was a calm, easy, dangerous air in the way he carried himself.

Fisher was perhaps a few years younger than Hawk, easily six feet tall, with long blonde hair falling down her back to her waist in a single thick plait, weighted at the tip with a solid steel ball. She was handsome rather than beautiful, the high-boned harshness of her face contrasting with her deep blue eyes and generous mouth. She wore the same basic outfit as Hawk, though her shirtsleeves were rolled up, revealing arms corded with muscle. Her boots had steel toe caps, all the better to kick people with. Fisher wore a sword at her side, and you had only to look at her to realise she knew how to use it.

The Administrator looked down at Chappie, half expecting to see him changed too. Into a wolf, perhaps. But Chappie remained just a really big dog, with lots of grey in his dark fur and silver round the muzzle. He grinned at the Administrator, showing lots of teeth, and the Administrator looked back at Hawk and Fisher.

"It's you," he said dazedly. "I mean . . . it's always been you! All the years I've been here, every Hawk and Fisher I've served under has been you! I thought you were different people, but it was always you, under a series of disguises! Why didn't I notice? Why didn't anyone else notice?"

"Remember the Confusulum?" said Fisher.

"We've always been in charge," said Hawk. "Right from the very beginning. We came here from the Forest Kingdom, founded the Academy, and decided very early on that we didn't want to draw attention to ourselves. The Academy was what mattered, not us. So after we got the place up and running, we left; and then we came back as someone else. It's all worked out rather well, I think."

"The Confusulum kept everyone from noticing," said Fisher. "Just as well; I've never been any good with wigs and makeup. You have figured this out before, Administrator, but you kept forgetting."

"We needed to disappear from the world," said Hawk. "So we hid behind ourselves."

"You're the original Hawk and Fisher?" said the Administrator, almost breathless with shock and wonder. "The founders? The ones in all the songs and stories? *The legends?* But . . . how can that be? You'd have to be over a hundred years old! And you don't even look half as old as I am!"

"We were exposed to a lot of Wild Magic, during the Demon War," said Fisher. "And we have bathed in the Rainbow itself. We stopped ageing in our thirties. Imagine our surprise."

"No, I mean, wait just a minute!" said the Administrator, hanging on to common sense and sanity with both hands. "The Rainbow? During the Demon War? That was never any part of the Hawk and Fisher legend; that was . . . oh my God." He looked at them with wide eyes, like a child. "You're *them*, aren't you? You're Prince Rupert and Princess Julia!"

"Don't worry," Hawk said kindly. "You'll forget all this once we're gone."

"I don't know what to do," the Administrator said numbly. "I feel like I should hug you, or get down on my knees. You saved all humanity from the Demon Prince."

"We're still the same people you've always known," said Fisher. "The ones you shouted at on a regular basis."

"Yeah, trust me," said Chappie. "They're no one special."

"Does anyone else know?" said the Administrator.

"I've always known," said Roland the Headless Axeman. As he appeared out of nowhere, standing quietly but very solidly beside them. In his blunt, functional armour, with nothing but fresh air above his shoulders. "It's hard to fool the eyes when you haven't got any. I never told anyone. Never thought it was any of my business."

"Are you secretly someone special, too?" said the Administrator just a bit wildly.

"I think you've had enough shocks for one day," said Roland. Which wasn't really an answer. Everyone let it go.

The Administrator looked at Chappie. "You're *that* talking dog? The original? I thought you were just a descendant."

"Rube," said Chappie, not unkindly. "There's only ever been one dog like me. I'm not sure the world's ready for another. I could have stayed with Allen Chance, Questor to Queen Felicity of the Forest Land; but after his wife, Tiffany, started pumping out kids like a steam hammer, they didn't have time for me anymore. So I made my way here and joined up with these two. They're always fun."

Hawk smiled down at the dog. "That's the nicest thing you've ever said about us."

"Don't get used to it," growled the dog.

The Administrator considered the dog thoughtfully. "All right," he said finally. "How?"

The dog shrugged. "I was raised by the High Warlock, in his Tower With No Doors. You hang around a crazy magician long enough, you soak up a load of crazy magic. I don't just talk, you know! I am wise and wonderful and death on four legs! And I can eat *anything*."

"And you do," said Fisher.

"I may not be quite as fast as I used to be," said Chappie. "Unlike the Rainbow divers over there, I have aged. Gradually. Though on me it looks good. Distinguished."

"How long are you going to be gone?" said Roland the Headless Axeman. Possibly in self-defence.

"As long as it takes," said Hawk. "We have a long way to go, and a lot to do when we get there."

"You're going back to the Forest Land?" said the Administrator. "Why? And why now?"

"Unfinished business," said Fisher.

"Right," growled Chappie.

Hawk looked steadily at Roland and the Administrator. "Guard the Academy while we're gone. Protect the students. As far as the staff are concerned . . . tell them we're on a sabbatical. And we'll be back when we can."

"Or at least somebody very like us will be back," said Fisher.

They turned away to start their long journey, and then stopped as the

Administrator cried out after them. They looked back. The Administrator tried to smile. His eyes were full of tears.

"I just wanted to say . . . Thank you, Prince Rupert, Princess Julia. For all you did, and for all you suffered, on our behalf. Thank you."

"I'll go along with that," said Roland. "Thank you, for everything."

"You're welcome," said Hawk.

"But don't believe everything you hear in the songs and stories," said Fisher.

And so Hawk and Fisher and Chappie the dog walked out of the Dutchy of Lancre, striding across the miles of featureless plain, leaving their new lives behind them. Heading back into their past, if only partway. They knew they had to return—the Demon Prince's threat to their grandchildren had seen to that—but they had already decided they were going back as Hawk and Fisher, not Rupert and Julia. The sudden reappearance of two such legendary figures would have raised far too many questions, and complicated an already dangerous situation. And besides, they'd heard most of the myths and legends that had grown up around their time in the Demon War, and they couldn't help feeling they'd be such a disappointment in the flesh.

They headed straight for the DragonsBack mountain ridges, which formed the boundary between Lancre and the Forest Land. Eventually they left the bleak plain behind them and hit the steep grey mountain slopes with youthful strength and vigour. They were enjoying being their true selves again. Hawk and Fisher chatted easily as they strode briskly up the steep slopes, jumping crevices and hauling themselves up and over rocky outcroppings, occasionally pausing to point out to each other pleasant sights and landmarks they remembered from more than seventy years ago, when they descended the DragonsBack the first time.

All too soon it became hard going, with a cold, blustering wind plucking at their clothes like a sick child, and occasionally beating at their heads and shoulders like a school bully. They clung grimly to boulders and hugged the side of the mountain with all their strength. Chappie was secretly glad of the stops and starts. He didn't have their youthful energy, though he was damned if he'd admit it. The jagged grey slopes of the

DragonsBack were utterly devoid of life—no birds or beasts, no flowers, not even a scrap of moss or lichen anywhere. Hawk and Fisher were barely halfway up the mountain when they stopped to look back. The plain stretched away for miles and miles, and even the Millennium Oak itself seemed a small and distant thing now. Chappie threw himself down at their feet, breathing hard.

"Bounding along like a pair of bloody mountain goats!" he said loudly. "It's not natural! Or safe. One missed hand- or foothold, and you'd bounce all the way back down to the plain again. And somebody had better have brought a packed lunch, or at the very least some trail food! I am getting quite dangerously peckish . . ."

"Hush, Chappie," said Hawk, stepping out onto a precarious flat ledge so he could take a good look around him.

"Hush, hell!" growled the dog. "Muscles like mine need refuelling on a regular basis."

"Our food supply is strictly limited," said Fisher. "So you'll just have to develop some self-control, won't you?"

"Self-control? I'm a dog! If I get hungry enough, I will eat you!" He slumped down flat, resting his great head on his outstretched paws. "I notice we've stopped heading for the summit. That we have in fact been going sideways for some time now. You're looking for something, aren't you? What is it? A trail? Some secret shortcut through the mountain range, and out the other side?"

"Something like that," said Fisher. Her gaze moved slowly, carefully, across the great grey sweep of mountainside, with its jagged ridges and great falls and dozens of gaping dark cave mouths. "We are looking for one particular cave, one we haven't been back to in many years . . ."

Chappie raised his great head and looked around him nervously. "DragonsBack mountains . . . Not a name to inspire confidence, or peace of mind. I really don't like this place. Some say this is where all the old dragons came to die, when they realised their kind was finally going out of the world. They each just picked a cave, curled up, and let go of life. You won't see me doing that . . . I'll go kicking and screaming all the way when my time comes. Some say it's the strength of all these dead dragons that holds these mountains up. Helps them endure. And that the dragons' ghosts are still here, haunting the DragonsBack, and that's why no one ever wants to climb them."

Hawk looked at him amusedly. "You're not scared of ghosts, are you?"

"Of course I'm scared! You can't bite a ghost! Besides, our lives have been far too full of people, and some things not even people, coming back to life after they were supposed to be safely dead!" Chappie brightened suddenly. "Though if there are dragons here, they wouldn't be much more than bones by now. I don't know any dog who's chewed on an actual dragon bone . . ."

He scrambled up onto his feet again, as he realised neither of them was listening to him. They were both staring at a particularly large and especially dark cave mouth, farther along the mountain ridge. Chappie sniffed at the air gusting his way, and scowled suddenly.

"Okay, I am picking up traces of a scent I really don't like."

"That's the one," said Hawk, pointing at the cave mouth.

"Yes," said Fisher. "It is."

"It would be," said Chappie. "No good will come of this. You mark my words."

But he still followed them along the precarious side of the mountain as they headed straight for the mouth of the cave.

The surface beneath their feet grew increasingly treacherous, with loose rocks that just gave away when stepped on and fields of shifting scree, tiny rocks that moved like water and did their best to carry Hawk and Fisher out and over the edge, while the cold wind blasted and beat at them unmercifully. But Hawk and Fisher picked their way carefully across the slope with calm, thoughtful skill, while Chappie brought up the rear, leaping and scrambling and cursing them both under his breath. He was never in any real danger, but he had no intention of being taken for granted. Finally, they all ended up before the great cave mouth, a massive hole set well back into the mountainside. They stood and stared into the darkness, and the darkness stared back at them. The entranceway on its own was big enough to drive a carriage through and not even come close to touching the sides.

"Do you think there are bats?" said Chappie. "Don't like bats."

"No bats," said Hawk. "Not where we're going."

Fisher produced a salamander ball from her backpack and shook it hard. A fierce golden light blazed between her fingers as she held the ball up, pushing back the dark, so they could all see a great cavern leading back into the depths of the mountain. Hawk and Fisher stood very still.

"It's going to be dark in there," said Hawk. "I mean, really dark."

"We'll manage," said Fisher. "We did last time."

"I wish we could have afforded more than just the one salamander ball," said Hawk.

"They're expensive," said Fisher. "But then, you only get two to a salamander."

They shared a smile. They could stand the dark when they were together.

"What is that *smell*?" said Chappie. "I'm getting sulphur, and metals and mushrooms, and something so potent it's raising all the hairs on my back. Which I am here to tell you is a very uncomfortable experience. I've never smelled anything like this . . . I don't like it."

"You could stay here till we come out, if you like," said Hawk. "But trust me on this: there is something in there you're really going to want to see."

"But, Chappie," said Fisher, "when we get where we're going and find what we're looking for . . . whatever you do, *don't run*."

"You are not making me feel any better," said Chappie.

Hawk and Fisher strode into the cavern mouth, with Chappie padding nervously along after them. Fisher held the salamander ball high, spreading the light as far as it would go. Hawk's hand hung down by his axe, but he didn't touch it. He had his pride. He made a point of leading the way into the dark. It was a hundred years since he'd first entered the Darkwood, but all the Wild Magics and all the Rainbow's blessing hadn't been enough to remove its touch. He was scared of the dark, and always would be. He just didn't let it stop him. He picked his way carefully forward, across the rubble-strewn cave floor, as the first cavern opened up into a much larger cavern, just as he remembered.

The great open space grew larger all the time, rising up and spreading out into a massive cathedral of stone, with golden veins running through the walls. They shone brightly in the salamander light. Soon enough there were wide mats of phosphorescent fungi, clinging to the walls and ceiling, glowing every colour you could think of. They could all see quite clearly now, and didn't need the salamander ball, but Fisher wouldn't put it away. She wasn't the trusting type. They pressed on, into the immense high-ceilinged cavern, heading deep into the heart of the mountain. Huge sta-lactites hung down from the ceiling, like so many jagged teeth in a stone mouth, while moss-smeared stalagmites thrust up from the cavern floor, many of them taller than Hawk and Fisher. Chappie made a point of piss-ing on several, just on general principles. Hawk and Fisher stared about them in open awe and wonder at this huge natural amphitheatre that no other human being had ever seen. It appeared even bigger than they re-membered. Their every footstep seemed to echo forever.

Chappie didn't like any of it. This was an old place. He could tell. Older than any of the human Kingdoms. And he was becoming increas-ingly sure that they weren't alone in the cavern, and that Hawk and Fisher knew that. Had always known it. That . . . was why they were here.

They finally rounded a sudden corner and found their way blocked by a huge dark green wall that rose up to fill the side tunnel from floor to ceiling. Hawk and Fisher stopped and smiled at each other. Chappie eased carefully up to the green wall, gave it a good sniff, and then retreated rap-idly with his tail tucked between his legs.

"That's it! That's what I've been smelling all along! It's alive . . . and it's big, I mean really big, so big I can't even get my head around how big it is!"

"Will you calm down?" said Hawk. "It's not that big. There's nothing here to be scared of." He knelt down beside Chappie and hugged him round the neck till the dog stopped shaking. "Do you really think I would walk you into danger, in the dark, for no good reason? This is a friend, Chappie."

"An old friend," said Fisher.

"Well," said Chappie, "if you say so."

Hawk let go of the old dog, rubbed the animal's head briskly and pulled at his ears, and then stepped forward and addressed the great green wall in a loud and carrying voice.

"Dragon! Time to wake up!"

His voice rose up and up through the great cavern, riding on the echoes, seeming to strengthen all the time, rather than fade away. And the great green wall shifted, slowly. Hawk and Fisher clasped hands, both of them grinning broadly. Chappie hid behind them. Hawk laughed aloud as the wall slowly turned and uncurled, and a great green-scaled face appeared in the side tunnel mouth. The blunt bony head moved forward on an extended neck, emerald green scales gleaming in the light, and huge golden eyes opened unhurriedly. Hawk and Fisher and Chappie backed quickly away as the dragon came out of its den. It was thirty feet and more in length, with sweeping membranous wings that wrapped around the creature like a ribbed green cloak, clasped together at the chest by wickedly clawed hands. A long spiked tail swept back and forth in the background gloom. The dragon smiled on them all, showing dozens of very sharp teeth.

"Rupert," said the dragon, in a deep, booming voice that filled the cavern and rattled everyone's bones. "And Julia. My dear, dear friends. I always knew I'd meet you again." He looked past them, at Chappie. "And you've brought me a waking-up snack! How thoughtful!"

Chappie was immediately out from behind Hawk and Fisher, glaring up at the dragon and showing his teeth. "I am not a snack! I am their companion! Hawk, tell this oversized gecko that I am not a snack!"

"He's not a snack," Hawk said solemnly. "He's with us, Dragon. Please don't eat him. No matter how irritating he gets. And these days I am called Hawk, and this is Fisher."

The dragon nodded slowly. "Names," he said. "Dragons don't need names. We know who we are. How long have I slept? How much time has passed since we faced the Demon Prince in his place of power?"

"A hundred years," said Hawk.

The dragon looked at him, and then at Fisher. "You've aged well, for humans."

"You look tremendous!" said Fisher, still grinning.

"Just shows you the benefits of a good long nap," said the dragon.

Fisher laughed aloud and ran forward to throw her arms around the dragon's neck and hug him tightly, pressing her face against his smooth green scales.

"Oh, Dragon! I've missed you so much . . ."

"Hold everything, go previous," Chappie said sternly. "Let me get this straight. *This* is the actual dragon who fought beside you in the Demon War? The one in all the myths and legends? The one who did all those amazing things? All right, none of them can agree on exactly what they might have been, but . . . *wow.* Just *wow*! An honour to meet you, sir Dragon. Please don't eat me. I'd be very bad for you."

"An honour to meet you, sir Dog," said the dragon. "You must be special too, to be in the company of Hawk and Fisher."

"So," said Chappie, looking at Hawk and Fisher, "if this dragon's still around, does that mean there are other dragons here? Sleeping in the caves of the DragonsBack ridge? Just waiting to be awakened?"

"I'm not sure," said the dragon.

"What?" said Hawk.

"You never said there were other dragons, when we brought you here!" said Fisher.

"All this time I've been sleeping, I've been dreaming, reaching out," said the dragon. "And it seems to me I felt . . . Never mind. Another matter, for another day."

Chappie looked accusingly at Hawk and Fisher. "He . . . is supposed to be dead! You said so, way back when! It's one of the few things all the songs and stories agree on!"

"Never trust a minstrel," said Hawk. "No, he never died. Came bloody close, but the Rainbow brought him back from the edge. We just said he died so no one would disturb him while he slept and healed. He knew it would take years, maybe even decades, to get all his strength back. And you are looking good, Dragon. How do you feel?"

"Young," said the dragon. "I feel young again!"

"We're heading back to the Forest Land," said Fisher. "We'd really like it if you could come with us."

"Of course," said the dragon. He paused for a moment. "It's the Demon Prince, isn't it? He's back. That's why you have awakened me."

Fisher stopped hugging his neck and stood back, staring steadily into the glowing golden eyes. "Are you really healed, Dragon? I won't take you out of here if you're not ready."

The dragon put his huge face right in front of Fisher's. "Julia, I'm ready. What is it you need from me?"

"We need you to fly us across the Forest Land," said Hawk. "We've a lot of ground to cover, and not much time to do it in. First we have to find our children, Jack and Gillian. And then their children, Mercy and Nathanial. The Demon Prince threatened them."

"Children and grandchildren," said the dragon. "I have been asleep a long time."

"*Fly?*" said Chappie ominously. "No one said anything about flying! I'm not getting on that thing. He doesn't even have safety straps!"

"I could always carry you in my mouth," said the dragon.

"Right," said Chappie. "I am leaving now. Try to keep up."

"You'll love flying on his back!" said Hawk. "I've done it lots of times. It's a life-changing experience."

"That's what I'm afraid of," growled Chappie.

Hawk looked at the dragon. "Are we going to have to travel all the way back to the cave entrance, or is there another way out of here?"

"What do you think?" said the dragon, grinning. "You don't think I chose this exact spot by chance, do you? There's a wide-open shaft not far from here that goes all the way up to the sky. An old volcanic shaft, I think. Perfectly safe, if we don't hang about inside it too long. But once we're up and out, I won't be able to fly you very far until I've had something to eat. Quite a lot of something. Nothing like sleeping for a hundred years to build up an appetite."

"I think I may have found a kindred spirit," said Chappie. "Do you also like to roll in dead things?"

"Only after I've killed them," said the dragon.

He backed away into the side cavern and showed them a great hole in the ceiling. Fisher stood under it and waved her salamander ball around, illuminating the smooth, gleaming sides of the opening. The dragon positioned himself carefully underneath the shaft and then spread out his wings. Hawk and Fisher clambered onto his back, half encouraging and half dragging Chappie on board with them. And when they were all settled, more or less comfortably, the dragon flapped his wings. Captured compressed air boomed beneath them, and the whole cavern shook to the sound. The dragon laughed joyously and launched himself into the air, blasting up the shaft on great beating wings. Hawk and Fisher hung on tight, and Chappie dug his claws into gaps between the scales, his eyes squeezed tightly shut. Fisher whooped happily as the dragon sped upwards, heading for the circle of light at the top of the shaft. Hawk laughed aloud, and clung to Fisher and Chappie. And then they burst up and out of the mountain and soared off through the bright blue skies, with DragonsBack ridge far below them. The dragon flew away from the mountains and over the Forest Land, where the great green woods stretched for miles. Hawk and Fisher leaned out, for a better look. Chappie thrust his head under Hawk's arm, so he wouldn't have to look.

"Dogs are not meant to fly!" he said in a somewhat muffled voice.

The dragon flew steadily on, across the Forest Land, over vast stretches of wild woods and cultivated land, long, winding rivers and vast lakes, and great chequerboard displays of fields and crops. Over towns and villages and scattered farm buildings . . . and miles and miles swept past in moments. Hawk stared eagerly about him, checking for familiar landmarks. And even though he didn't care to admit it, being back in the Forest did feel like coming home again. The dragon flew on . . . until finally his hunger caught up with him. He spotted a suitable clearing and spiralled down to land. At the last moment he spread his great wings full out, cupping the air beneath them, and landed right in the centre of the open grassy clearing, as delicately as a bird.

Hawk and Fisher jumped down from his back, stretching and easing their cramped muscles, while Chappie clambered down, taking his time. They'd arrived in a great expanse of green grass, surrounded by a perimeter of tightly packed trees. Probably a cultivated area at one time, and then abandoned and allowed to just fall back. Birds sang on all sides, and one could hear a pleasant lazy buzz of insects and the occasional furtive rustle of small wildlife going about its business. The dragon waited till all his passengers were well clear, and then he charged across the clearing and plunged into the surrounding woods, and was gone. Hawk was sure he'd heard the dragon mutter *Time for a little something* . . . as he rushed past.

The dragon's sudden disappearance was followed immediately by the sound of things being chased. And caught and killed and eaten. A large hunk of hot, steaming meat flew out of the trees and landed with a thud right in front of Chappie. The dog fell on it, ripping and tearing and growling happily. Another, somewhat larger haunch of meat appeared, flying through the air to land very accurately at the feet of Hawk and Fisher. Hawk set about building a fire, and a spit, while Fisher produced various useful things from her backpack, including a nice rug to sit on, some basic cutlery, and a bottle of wine.

"Wimps," said Chappie indistinctly.

By the time they'd finished all the things that needed doing, it was night. The dragon returned, and they all sat around the fire, quietly digesting as they watched the dancing flames, enjoying the quiet and one another's company. The night sky was full of stars, with a pale half-moon hanging right overhead. The birds had stopped their singing, the insects had disappeared to wherever small, irritating things go at night, and although there were various noises out among the trees from all the usual nocturnal animals humping and killing one another (often at the same time, from the sound of it), nothing emerged from the tree line to bother the camp. Having thirty feet of dragon around was enough to make even the largest predator suitably cautious. A few flappy-winged moths fluttered around, making a nuisance of themselves for no obvious reason.

Hawk and Fisher sat side by side, leaning against each other companionably. Chappie lay at their feet, worrying a bone. The dragon lay curled in a semicircle around them, like a great green protective wall, his heavy head flat on the grass. His great golden eyes were half closed, and two thin plumes of smoke rose from his nostrils in perfectly straight lines. Fisher leaned back against his ribs, easily riding his slow breathing.

"Hawk, Fisher," said the dragon, with the air of someone trying out new names just for the practice, "does the dark still bother you even after all these years?"

"Some," said Hawk, looking out at the darkness beyond the firelight without flinching. "The poison the Darkwood put in my soul is still there. I suppose it always will be. But it doesn't rule my life, like it used to."

"You never get over it," said Fisher. "But you do learn to live with it."

"I suppose that's why the Demon Prince was able to find us so easily," said Hawk. His voice was calm and relaxed, and would probably have fooled anyone else.

"How do you feel, Dragon?" said Fisher. "Are you . . . fully recovered?"

"I feel like myself again," said the dragon. "Ready to eat a whole army of demons, and then drop something very heavy on the Demon Prince from a great height. Do you want me to fly you to Forest Castle?"

"Eventually," said Hawk. "Remember, Dragon, we have to go back as Hawk and Fisher, not as Rupert and Julia."

"Is Chappie still Chappie?" said the dragon.

"Unfortunately, yes," said Fisher. "No point in giving him another name; he'd never remember it."

"I heard that!" said Chappie. "I am me, and proud of it! And if anyone else can't handle that, that's their problem." He paused and looked up from his bone, licking at the dried blood around his muzzle. "You know, there are bound to have been a lot of changes at the Castle since you left. A lot can happen in a hundred years."

The dragon chuckled heavily, making Fisher jump as the slow ripples moved along his ribs. "Only humans could think a hundred years a long time."

"Things should change," said Hawk. "Otherwise you get bored with them. I'll be very interested to see what they've done with the old place."

"You never liked Forest Castle," said Fisher.

"No," said Hawk. "But it's still the place where I grew up, where my family was, so I suppose that makes it . . . home."

"You never liked your father either," said Fisher.

"He was the King," Hawk said simply. "He had duties and responsibilities. I always knew that. Even when he sent me out to die, on a quest I was never supposed to accomplish, I always knew why he did it. And I can't think too badly of that; it's how I met you. And the dragon."

Hawk and Fisher smiled fondly at each other. "I hated my father," said Fisher. "He had too many daughters, and I wouldn't behave like he wanted . . . and he needed a sacrifice, so he sent me off to die too. To be eaten by a dragon. Funny how things turn out. Thank you for not eating me, Dragon."

"I told you," said the dragon. "Humans give me heartburn."

"It's . . . different with sons and fathers," said Hawk. "Fathers shape your life, whether you like it or not. You either want to be just like them, or nothing like them. And you never ever break free of their influence. Even when they're dead. Perhaps especially when they're dead, because you can't show them what you've made of your life, to impress them or to spite them."

"Ghosts should stay in the past," Fisher said firmly. "Concentrate on the present. We have to find our children before we can return to Forest Castle. I need to be sure they're safe."

"Jack," said Hawk. "We'll start with Jack. At least we have a location for him."

"Really?" said Chappie. "You never told me."

"It always seemed important to let our children go their own way," said Fisher. "Let them make their own lives, free from our shadows."

"Last we heard, our boy, Jack, had taken up the religious life," said Hawk. "As a contemplative monk living in seclusion in a monastery. The Abbey of Saint Augustine."

"A monk?" said Chappie. "Jack?"

"Our boy," said Fisher, frowning despite herself. "He must be in his seventies by now. Hard to think of our son being older than us."

"A contemplative monk is just one step up from a hermit," said Hawk. "Not what I wanted for my son, but no doubt he knows his own mind best. And he did lead an active life before he got religion."

"An active life?" said Fisher. "He was the Walking Man, the wrath of God in the world of men, protecting the innocent and punishing the guilty!"

"He was?" said Chappie. "Shit . . ."

"Killing people who needed killing," said Hawk. "I have no problem with that."

"He must have," said Fisher. "Or he wouldn't be in a monastery at the end of his life."

"I wouldn't disturb him," said Hawk, "but the Demon Prince threatened our grandchildren. Jack has a right to know."

"When the Demon Prince threatened Mercy and Nathanial, he threatened all of us," said Fisher. "The whole family. We're all in danger. Of course Jack has to know."

"Right," said Hawk. "Everyone in the Abbey could be in danger! Just because Jack's there . . . So we start with Saint Augustine's."

"In the morning," said the dragon. "I don't fly in the dark. You three get your sleep. I'll stand watch. I don't feel like sleeping. I think I've had enough of that for the time being."

In the early hours of the morning, with the sun up and bright light everywhere, they all clambered back aboard the dragon and set off again, being careful to fly high above the Forest Land so that no one would be able to make out exactly what the dragon was. The Land flowed by beneath the great beating wings, all the colours of field and wood and cropland smearing together in a great rainbow blur. Hawk quickly identified one of the main rivers, and they followed its curves and turns all the way to the Abbey of Saint Augustine, set deep in dense woodlands, far away from towns and villages. Once again the dragon picked out a suitable clearing, within walking distance of the Abbey, and settled down there. Everyone disembarked, and Hawk produced an old and much-used map of the territory from his backpack. He and Fisher studied it for some time. They were pretty sure they knew where they were, in general, but a hundred-year lifetime does take its toll on the memories. In the end, Chappie got fed up and said he could guide them straight to the Abbey, because it smelled entirely different from everything else.

After a short walk through the woods, they came to a rough-hewn clearing, just big enough to contain the monastery. The Abbey of Saint Augustine was just a collection of rough stone buildings with slate roofs and grilled windows, surrounded by a long stone wall with just the one entrance door. For a house of God, it didn't look the least bit inviting. Chappie sniffed the air ostentatiously.

"Told you. This is it. I'm getting wine and smoke and a vegetable garden, and a whole bunch of people who don't wash much. And look at those buildings! I've had more aesthetic bowel movements. Ugly place. What's it for?"

"It's a place for people who want to get away from it all, so they can think big, comforting thoughts," said Fisher. "A place of religious seclusion, for those who've led very active lives, one way and another, and now regret it. So they've chosen to turn their backs on their old lives and spend their last few years in seclusion, repenting. Well away from anyone or anything that might tempt them back to their old ways and their old lives."

"When we get in there," said Hawk, "let me do the talking."

"I can't say I'm any the wiser," said Chappie. "Dogs don't look back. Or forward. We live in the moment. Eating and drinking, humping and sleeping. What else is there that really matters, when you get right down to it?"

"Friendship," said Hawk.

Chappie brushed his great head against Hawk's hip. "All right, you got me there."

"So what did your son do, to make him decide to spend the last years of his life in a place like this?" said the dragon.

"Well," Hawk said carefully, "being the Walking Man, defender of the innocent and punisher of the guilty, does take its toll on a person. And the better the person, the greater the toll."

"I think I'll step back into the woods," said the dragon. "Religious fanatics make me nervous. Or is it the other way round? I can never remember . . . Anyway, I think it's best if I stay out of sight, in the trees at the edge of the clearing. No point in upsetting anyone."

"Good idea," said Hawk. "If the Demon Prince really has returned, he might well have human agents keeping an eye on Jack, just in case we turned up here. No point in letting the creepy little bastard know we're back in the game until we have to."

"It's camouflage time, then," said the dragon. He backed rapidly into the trees and disappeared completely. Chappie shook his head in amazement.

"For thirty feet of very large dragon, complete with bloody big wings and tail, he really is awfully good at blending in with his surroundings."

"If more of his kind had learned to hide, there'd be more of them around," said Fisher.

The three of them approached the wooden door set into the wall surrounding the monastery. The door turned out to be a single slab of very solid wood, held in place by heavy brass hinges, and it was quite definitely closed. A sign above the door said, *The Abbey of Saint Augustine. For Those of a Troubled Spirit. Go away. This means you. No one here wants to talk to you. Whoever you're looking for, they aren't that person anymore.* Hawk studied the door and its surroundings with great care, without actually touching anything.

"I don't see any door handle, knocker, or bellpull," he said finally.

"Hardly surprising," said Fisher. "This is where you go when you really don't want to be disturbed by anyone."

"So what do we do?" said Chappie. "Make a loud and unruly nuisance of ourselves, until they let us in? I could do that. I'm really very good at making a horrible display of myself. Everybody says so."

"I don't think that will be necessary," said Hawk. "Though thanks for the offer. They must have seen the dragon when we circled overhead to make sure we'd got the right place. And they must have seen us land in the woods, when we could have just dropped straight down into their courtyard. So they must know we're very polite and civilised, even though we don't have to be."

"Hawk," said Chappie, "why are you saying all that in such a loud and carrying voice?"

"So whoever's listening on the other side of that door can hear me," said Hawk. Loudly.

There was the sound of several heavy bolts being pulled back, followed by two very heavy keys turning in locks, and then the door swung slowly inwards. A more than usually large man, in a battered brown monk's habit, stepped forward into the gap, blocking their way. The hood was pulled well forward to hide the face within. A large hand emerged from one over-long brown sleeve, missing one finger and carrying a lot of scars. The hand rose slowly, to push the hood back, revealing a face as red as boiled ham and about as attractive. A bald head, with a heavy brow, a great beak of a nose, and the kind of scars you got only in serious battles. He had the look of someone who'd seen more than his fair share of action, but his eyes were surprisingly warm, even kind. A man finally at peace with himself. He bowed briefly.

"Hello," he said in a rough voice that suggested he didn't do much talking anymore. "Do you know who I am? Who I used to be?"

"No," said Hawk.

"Good," said the monk. "I get on so much better with people when they don't know what I used to do. Now I am Brother Ambrose. Come in. We've been expecting you. You are here to speak with Brother Jack? Of course, of course. He said you'd turn up here any day now. He's been having . . . bad dreams. Very specific bad dreams. I hope you can help him. Sorry, no dogs."

"I am not just a dog!" said Chappie.

"Oh, it's *you*!" said Brother Ambrose. "Brother Jack warned us . . . told us, about you. The talking dog who is a friend and is not in any way possessed or demonic. Come on in; we'll make an exception for you."

"Damn right you will," growled Chappie.

The monk stood well back, to let them all enter. Chappie led the way, swaggering in with his head held high, just to make a point. Brother Ambrose closed and locked the door behind them, slamming the heavy bolts home with some force. Hawk tried not to take it personally. He looked around the empty courtyard. No stables, not even a hitching rail or a watering trough for visiting horses. They really weren't expecting company. Just an open space, with carefully raked sand and gravel. The outer wall seemed even taller and more solid from the inside. Hawk let his hand rest near, but not actually on, the axe at his side. Fisher was equally polite, though her hand was a lot nearer the sword on her hip, because she was just naturally far less trusting than he was. Chappie sniffed at the air and looked down his nose at everything.

Brother Ambrose led them past the main Abbey buildings, with their grilled windows and firmly closed doors, and then past a series of small stone cells, presumably set aside for complete seclusion and meditation, and then all the way round the back, to where half a dozen other monks in rough brown robes were quietly working an extensive vegetable garden. It was all very serene, very peaceful, as the monks planted and weeded and dug without once looking up to acknowledge the visitors. Presumably lost in their own thoughts. They all seemed content enough. Brother Ambrose pointed out a single hooded figure on his knees by the far wall, planting seeds in the earth with his bare hands.

"That's Brother Jack. Don't do anything to upset him, and don't try to take him from the Abbey against his will. We are all men of peace now, but we can remember who we were, if we have to."

He strode away, with an air of someone doing something he just knows he's going to regret later. Hawk led the way through the vegetable garden, being very careful to stick to the narrow gravel paths and give the working monks plenty of room. None of them looked up. Hawk paused briefly to stop Chappie from snapping at some roses that were singing quietly, and to stop Fisher from hacking with her sword at a bush that lunged at her. Finally they reached the monk by the far wall. He pushed his last few seeds into the moist earth, settling them into place with gentle hands. The hands were old and wrinkled, with dark liver spots.

"Hello, Jack," said Hawk. "It's your mum and dad. I know it's been a long while, but . . ."

The monk stood up, taking his time. Old joints creaked loudly. He pushed back his hood to reveal a kind and gentle face, heavily wrinkled, with closely cropped grey hair. His smile was warm, and his eyes were mild. Hawk's heart sank. He didn't recognise this old man at all. And then the smile widened into a familiar grin, and when the monk spoke Hawk knew the voice at once.

"Hello, Father," said Jack. "It's good to see you and Mother again. It has been a long time, hasn't it? You're both looking . . . good."

"You got old," said Hawk. "And I wasn't around to see it. I'm so sorry, Jack."

"Then you've come to the right place," said Jack. "Forgiveness comes as standard here. For all the wrongs we've all done."

He stepped forward and embraced Hawk, who held his son as firmly as he dared. The old man felt very fragile. When Hawk let go and stepped back, Fisher hugged Jack to her like she'd never let him go. So after a while, he let go first. Jack had always been very intuitive about things like that. Fisher stepped back, and Jack smiled down at Chappie.

"Hello, boy! Good boy! You look even older than me, Chappie! Look at all that white round your muzzle! How are you, dog?"

"Better than you, by the look of things," said Chappie, butting his head against Jack hard enough to almost knock him backwards, until Jack rubbed his head and pulled at his ears. "Why did you never come to the Academy to see us, pay us a visit?"

"Because it would have raised far too many questions," said Jack, rubbing the dog's back hard while the tail wagged madly. "And because I haven't left the Abbey in twenty years. I belong here."

"You locked yourself away here because of what you did as the Walking Man?" said Fisher.

"This isn't a prison, Mother," said Jack. "I could leave anytime. I just didn't want to. You know what a poisoned chalice the whole Walking Man thing is. You knew Jericho Lament."

"He gave it up too," said Hawk. "To marry Queen Felicity."

"And I gave it up to come here," said Jack. "Gave up being the wrath of God in the world of men. Not because I was bad at it, but because I came to enjoy it too much. Punishing the guilty isn't something you're supposed to enjoy. No, I gave it all up for peace and quiet, and never regretted it once."

"So you've been happy here?" said Fisher. "That is important to us, Jack."

"I have been very happy here, Mother," said Jack, smiling. "But I'll still leave here with you when you ask me to. That is why you came, isn't it? I've been having dreams, visions . . . about the Demon Prince."

"We need to talk, Jack," said Hawk.

Brother Jack led them out of the gardens, back past the Abbey, and into the main courtyard, where a table had been set out for them. Chairs had been set in place, and platters of fresh fruit, vegetables, and dried mushrooms. And a bottle of the Abbey's own handmade wine, along with a rather varied collection of glasses. Chappie had a good sniff at everything on offer, politely declined, had a good lap at the bowl of fresh well water set out for him, and then curled up under the table with his head on his paws while the others ate and drank and talked.

"I know," said Jack, "it's all a bit basic, isn't it? But that's the point at Saint Augustine's. We don't want anything here that might tempt us back to the outside world. We're all in recovery here, from past sins and old horrors."

A few monks were eating quietly at another table, on the far side of the courtyard. Keeping themselves to themselves. Jack pointed them out, with a subtle nod of his head.

"The one on the left, that's Brother Alistair. Used to be a moneylender. And a hirer of leg-breakers on occasion. Then he became a tax-gatherer. Now he prays more than all the rest of us put together. The monk next to him is Brother David. Used to be a mercenary soldier. Fought in every war you can think of, on every side you can think of, and never gave a damn about anything as long as the money kept coming. Now he prays for all the souls of every man, woman, and child he killed. Keeping himself busy so he can never fight and kill again."

"What have you got to repent?" said Fisher almost angrily. "You're not like them! You were the Walking Man, a force for Good!"

"For my sins, yes," said Jack. "It's not what you do, Mother; it's why you do it."

"Will someone please explain to me what the Walking Man is?" said Chappie from under the table. "I don't think I ever got it explained to me properly. Or if it was, I don't remember. I'm a very old dog. I get tired. My memory isn't what it used to be. If it ever was."

"Once in every generation," said Jack, "a man can swear his life to God, to become more than a man. If that man will swear to serve the Light, all his life, forswearing all other paths, such as love or family or personal need . . . then he can become the Walking Man. The will and the wrath of God, in the world of mortal man. Made stronger and faster, to walk in straight lines to go where he needs to go, to do what needs to be done. Punish the guilty and protect the innocent, and never let anything or anyone get in the way. And as long as that man is true to his oath, nothing and no one can ever harm him. As long as he walks Heaven's way.

"Sounds like a good deal to me," said Chappie. "Of course, I'm just a dog. I do understand good and bad, mostly; it's just that mostly I don't care. I don't have to. I'm a dog. Why did you give it up?"

"First, because I started to enjoy killing people who needed killing, and then because I grew tired of killing," said Jack. "Because it didn't seem to make any difference. No matter how many guilty people I punished, there were always more innocents who needed saving. No one seemed to learn anything from what I did, except to be scared of me. I took too much enjoyment in seeing bad men suffer and die. I forgot it was God's will I was doing, not mine. So I gave it all up, because I was no longer worthy. And I came here. Twenty years ago. I like it here. It's very peaceful. No one to protect, or punish. And now, my mother and my father, you've come to take me away from all this. Haven't you?"

"Yes," said Hawk. "The monk at the door, Brother Ambrose, said you've been having very specific bad dreams? Visions?"

"Yes," said Jack quite calmly. "About the Darkwood, and war in the Forest Land, and the return of the Demon Prince. They're not dreams, are they?"

"No," said Fisher. "He's back. That bastard Lord of the Darkwood is back."

"He appeared to your mother and me, inside the Millennium Oak, past all its protection and defences," said Hawk. "He said your daughter and Gillian's son were in danger. Said they were going to die, horribly. Unless your mother and I returned to the Forest Land."

Jack frowned, for the first time. "My daughter? Mercy? I haven't heard from her in years. What danger could she be in?"

"We're going back to Forest Castle to find out," said Fisher. "You want to come along?"

Jack sighed briefly. "Of course. Won't take me long to get my few things together. The Demon Prince! I can't believe he's back, after all these years. I thought you destroyed him . . ."

"So did we," said Hawk.

"We'll just have to make a better job of it this time," said Fisher.

"This time," said Hawk, "we'll make sure. Whatever it takes."

"Maybe I'll just eat him," said Chappie. "And you can bathe whatever I crap out in holy water."

"Can't take you anywhere," said Hawk.

"My daughter was working in the Forest Castle, last I heard," said Jack. "She wrote me a letter, some three years ago. She wasn't very precise about what she was doing, but she seemed happy enough. She's not much of a one for writing letters. Gets that from her grandparents."

Hawk and Fisher avoided looking at each other. Chappie sniggered under the table, and Fisher booted him in the ribs.

Hawk and Fisher and Chappie waited in the courtyard while Jack gathered his few possessions and made his goodbyes to his fellow monks and his apologies to the Abbot. Hawk had asked if there'd be any problems with Jack's just up and leaving, but Jack only smiled briefly and shook his head. As though he was the adult and Hawk was the child. Everyone at Saint Augustine's came and left of their own free will, Jack said patiently. That was the point. Hawk nodded stiffly. He still felt it had been a fair question. And so he and Fisher and Chappie waited, more or less patiently, before the closed door in the outer wall. For what seemed like ages and ages.

"If he doesn't get a move on," Hawk said finally, and just a bit dangerously, "I am going to start carving some really rude words into that door."

"I'll help with the spelling," said Fisher.

And then they all ducked their heads and retreated rapidly, as the entire wooden door was blasted right off its hinges. The roar of the explosion deafened them for a moment, and the air filled with black smoke. The door went flying past, tumbling end over end, before it finally hit the ground and skidded to a halt some distance away. Hawk and Fisher recovered from the noise and the shock while the door was still settling, and turned to face the ragged gap in the stone wall where the door had been. Hawk held his axe at the ready, and Fisher swept her sword back and forth before her. Chappie stood between them, growling loudly. As the black smoke cleared, a small army of bandits and brigands poured through the gap. They were of a familiar sort: big and brutal, with well-worn clothes, leather armour, and the usual assortment of weapons. They spread quickly across the open courtyard, loud and arrogant, laughing at the ease of their entrance. They had scars and tattoos, and the appearance of men who'd been on the run for some time. They had swords and axes and bows, and looked like they knew how to use them.

But they still came to a sudden halt when they saw Hawk and Fisher and Chappie waiting for them.

Their leader swaggered to the front and bowed mockingly to Hawk and Fisher. He was a familiar sort too: a tall, muscular, dangerous type in his mid-twenties, with a grubby silver breastplate over his flashy clothes and a golden sash arranged neatly across his chest. The kind of man who, when he walked into an inn, you just knew there was going to be trouble. He had at least forty armed men at his back, and Hawk could hear even more taking up positions beyond the entrance hole. The leader smiled cheerfully at Hawk and Fisher.

"Isn't it an absolutely wonderful morning? Start the day with a bang, that's what I always say. Do you know who I am?"

"No," said Hawk.

"Haven't a clue," said Fisher.

"Grrr," said Chappie.

The leader's smile didn't slip at all. "I suppose it was too much to hope for, in this back of beyond . . . I am the brigand of the wild woods and the legend of the Forest! I am Gambler Gold!" He gestured at the golden sash across his chest, waiting for recognition to sink in, and then looked rather put out when it didn't. "Oh, come on; you must have heard of me! They sing songs about me everywhere! The smiling brigand, the dazzling outlaw, the unofficial tax man on the rich and prosperous! Some of this must ring a bell . . ." He glared at his army behind him. "I told you, we have got to get ourselves a minstrel! Get the word out! People don't respect you unless you've got your very own songwriter!" He turned back to Hawk and Fisher. "We are the free men of the Forest, beholden to none, answerable to none. We take from the rich and redistribute the wealth."

"Thieves," said Hawk.

"Killers from ambush," said Fisher.

"Small fry," said Chappie.

All the bandits' eyes went immediately to the dog. Chappie's lips curled back in a savage grin, showing off big, blocky teeth. His great muscles about his shoulders and breastbone bulged. He really was a very big dog. Some of the bandits began to back away.

"Stop that!" Gambler Gold said immediately, without looking round. "Don't get distracted! It's just a dog! One of these jokers is probably a ventriloquist. You've seen one of those before, haven't you?"

"Yeah," muttered one of the brigands. "He had a dummy. Creepy little thing. Gave me nightmares for months."

"Shut up!"

"What if it's possessed?" said a fascinated voice from the back. "Or a demonic familiar?"

"What would a demonic familiar be doing in a monastery, you idiot?" said Gambler Gold. "It's just a dog!"

"Or a wolf," said the voice from the back.

"Shut up! Now, everyone follow the plan! Spread out, round up all the monks from the Abbey and the gardens, and bring them here. Anyone gives you any trouble, kill a few to encourage the others. We don't need them all."

"Bad luck to kill a monk," said the voice from the back of the crowd.

"I'll be bad luck for you if you don't shut up, Maurice!" said Gambler Gold. "I only took you on because your father begged me to, and I'm starting to understand why. They're monks, and they've got a treasure here they're keeping to themselves, so that makes them fair game. Why is no one moving? Am I going to have to lose my temper? Is that what you want? You know what happens when I lose my temper!"

"Let me guess," said Hawk. "You stamp your foot, and spit, and cry for your mother?"

"You should worry about what happens when we lose our temper," said Fisher. "We've met your sort before."

"We met the Wulfshead, and what was left of his Werewolves, at the Millennium Oak," said Hawk. "You may have noticed—we're here, and he isn't."

"Yeah," said Chappie. "Tasty." He sniggered nastily.

But for once no one was listening to him.

"The Oak?" said Gambler Gold. "In Lancre? Who are you?"

"Hawk," said Hawk.

"Fisher," said Fisher.

"Chappie!" said the dog loudly.

"I think we should leave, right now," said the voice from the back.

"Shut up!" said Gambler Gold. "Anyone can claim to be Hawk and Fisher. There's been loads of them, down the years."

The brigands looked at one another, clearly shaken, and that was when the main entrance door to the Abbey itself opened and Jack came strolling out, wearing a battered old backpack and leaning heavily on a long wooden staff. He took his time walking forward to confront the brigands and their leader, just an old man in a rough monk's habit, smiling benevolently on everybody. He stopped beside Hawk and Fisher and nodded amiably to Gambler Gold.

"I see you've introduced yourselves," he said to his mother and father. "They've got that look in their eyes . . . But let's see if we can resolve this without violence. If possible." He smiled at Gambler Gold. "You really are very noisy. I could hear you all the way on the other side of the Abbey. Now, who are you, to bring such sound and fury to a place of peace?"

"I'm Gambler Gold, and I will not be distracted from my plan of action!" said the leader of the brigands. "There is a treasure in this place, and I will have it!"

"Oh, it's you," said Jack. "Yes, we've heard of you, even in this secluded place. Jumped-up footpad with delusions of grandeur, with his very own army of liers-in-wait and killers from ambush. Rob from the rich, and keep it. There's no treasure here, boy; not a single golden chalice or a silver spoon. And while we may offer forgiveness for past sins, this is a very bad way to go about asking."

Gambler Gold just stood there with his mouth hanging open. Clearly he wasn't used to being talked to in such a manner. And then he realised all his men were watching with interest to see what he would do after being so openly defied. He drew himself up and raised his voice so everyone could hear him.

"Word has reached us," he said grandly, "that this Abbey has a very old and very special book in its library. The book that contains the original contract whereby a man can make a deal with God to become the Walking Man. We want it."

"What on earth for?" said Jack. "What use would it be to such as you?" He sounded honestly curious.

"Are you saying I'm not good enough to be the Walking Man?" said Gambler Gold.

"Well, yes," said Jack.

The calm certainty in his voice stopped Gambler Gold in his tracks again. And then he shrugged and smiled. "You're probably right. Doesn't matter. The point is, we can sell that book for one hell of a lot of money. And then it's the good life for us, right, men? No more sleeping in the woods for us!"

There was a general growl of agreement from the massed bandits. They did look like they'd been sleeping rough for some time.

"The book is in the Abbey Library," said Jack. "But you can't have it. You couldn't even look at it. You're not worthy, any of you. The very words on the page would blast the eyes right out of your head. Forget this foolishness. Go now. While you still can."

And there was something about this little old man, with his grey hair and wrinkled face, leaning quietly on his staff—something cold and certain and somehow dangerous—that silenced the small army of bandits and sent a chill up their spines. Until Gambler Gold laughed suddenly, breaking the silence and the mood.

"You're good!" he said. "Nice try! But we're not leaving without the book. If it is as dangerous as you say, thanks for the warning; we'll be sure to wrap it in your bloodstained robe for safety after we've taken it off your dead body. Because no one talks to me like that and gets away with it." He glanced back at his men. "I gave you an order! Round up the monks, kill a few of the slower-moving ones to motivate the rest, and get them all out here. Brother Holier-Than-Thou here will assist me in finding the book. And afterwards I think we'll burn this whole place to the ground, and crucify all the monks along the outer wall . . . just to show what happens when someone talks back to Gambler Gold. And his men." He smiled at Jack. "See what you did?"

"Not going to happen," said Hawk, hefting his great battleaxe easily.

"Not while we're here," said Fisher.

"I am going to bite your balls off and gargle with them," growled Chappie, looking right at Gambler Gold.

"It's talking again!" said one of the bandits, cringing away and crossing himself repeatedly.

"Then kill the bloody dog, if it's bothering you so much!" said Gambler Gold. "Now move! Rip this Abbey apart! Anything you find you like the look of is yours, apart from the book!"

The bandits roared a series of battle cries and surged forward; and

Hawk and Fisher and Chappie went to meet them. Hawk swung his axe double-handed, the great blade smashing into the first bandit he met, punching through his rib cage and out again, in a flurry of blood, before flashing on to slice right through another bandit's throat. Hawk moved on without slowing, and brought the axe head swinging down to smash clean through another man's shoulder blade and lodge in his breastbone. The sheer impact drove the bandit to his knees, crying out in shock and pain and horror. Hawk jerked the axe free, kicked the dying man onto his back, and looked around for a new target. Grinning nastily all the while. Blood dripped from his face and chest, none of it his.

Fisher's sword flashed brightly as she cut throats, opened up bellies, and stabbed bandits in the lungs. And then she strode forward over the bodies, looking around for more trouble to get into. Long decades of practicing her swordsmanship had made her faster and stronger and just plain better with a blade than most people ever were. Blood ran thickly across the sand and gravel of the courtyard as Fisher went about her bloody work, and men screamed horribly as they died at her hands.

Chappie leapt on a man's chest and slammed him to the ground, pinning him there with his great weight. The bandit tried to stab him, and Chappie tore the man's throat out with his powerful jaws. He leapt this way and that, tearing out hamstrings and biting out great chunks of flesh, always moving so quickly that no one could keep up with him. He might be old, but he was still the High Warlock's dog, and the Wild Magic burned in his blood.

None of them saw Jack watching, or the sad look in his eyes.

Hawk and Fisher and Chappie raged back and forth among the brigands, cutting them up, hacking them down, and tearing out their throats. The bandits fought fiercely, swinging their swords and axes with desperate strength and speed, and none of it helped. They were outclassed and they knew it. Gambler Gold stood back by the empty hole in the wall, watching thoughtfully. He waited till it was clear his men were being wiped out; and then he called for the rest of his men, waiting outside the wall. And another fifty men came rushing in, blades at the ready, fresh and eager for the fight.

Hawk and Fisher and Chappie grouped together and backed away, all of them splashed with blood not their own. They stood together, defying the bandits to get past them, to the defenceless monks of Saint Augustine's. And that was when Jack stepped forward. And all the bandits and killers who took their orders from Gambler Gold stopped and looked at him. Because there was just something about this small, withered old man . . . They could feel it in their bones. Gambler Gold shouted and screamed at them, and reluctantly they moved forward again. Jack went smiling to meet them, his robes flying, and his long wooden staff moved with horrid, deadly speed.

He moved swiftly among the bandits, and broke arms and legs and backs with attacks so sudden no man could stop them. He broke heads with blows so powerful the skulls all but exploded under his staff's impact. Jack might be seventy years old, but he had been the Walking Man in his time, and God's strength and speed were still with him, as long as he walked Heaven's path. It probably helped that as far as he was concerned, he was fighting again only to defend his fellow monks.

Hawk and Fisher fought back-to-back, striking down anyone who came within reach, while Chappie danced back and forth, snapping at legs and slamming men clean off their feet with one great shove from his muscled shoulder. And once anyone was on the ground his throat was Chappie's. Jack seemed almost to glide through the fight, his face calm, his eyes still subtly sad. But for all their abilities, they were still hugely outnumbered. And there was no saying which way the fight might have gone, if a dozen other monks hadn't suddenly appeared from the Abbey main entrance.

Some had swords, some had axes, some had vicious mystic energies spitting and crackling around their hands. They waded into the fight, old men with horrid pasts who had not forgotten the men they once were, no matter how hard they tried. Brigands and bandits cried out as they were cut down by skilled old hands, and torn apart by terrible magics that exploded among them. Killed by quiet and secluded monks who had once been far worse than the bandits ever were.

Soon enough it was over. The few surviving brigands threw their weapons to the ground and surrendered. Hands held high, shaking with shock. Their leader had never told them it would be like this. Only Gambler Gold himself still stood defiant, his back pressed up against the inside of the outer wall. He was breathing hard, and glaring wildly about him. Hawk and Fisher lowered their weapons, and leaned tiredly on each other, getting their breath back. Chappie collapsed at their feet, panting for breath, licking blood from his muzzle and grinning broadly. And Jack leaned on his staff and looked around him, at the bloody mess of the Abbey courtyard, scattered with the dead and the dying. He wasn't even out of breath; but of them all, he seemed to take no pleasure or satisfaction in what he'd done. All around him, his fellow monks had put away their swords and their magics, to kneel beside the dying. To pray for them and do their best to comfort them in their last moments. A few were comforting one another, for giving in to old demons they'd thought banished long ago. Jack moved over to join his father and his mother.

"You did good, son," said Hawk.

"Nice moves," said Fisher.

"Badass," said Chappie.

"I read the stories and listened to the songs," said Jack. "Ever since I was a small child, I knew all the ballads about you . . . But I never saw you fight before. You really were everything the legends said you were. And still are. You were ready to stand against a hundred evil men to protect innocents you didn't even know."

"It's what we do," said Fisher.

"Some of your fellow monks did well," said Hawk.

Jack nodded regretfully. "We all came here to forget the men we were, but they're always only sleeping, not dead."

"You think you're so clever!" screamed Gambler Gold, and everyone stopped what they were doing to look at him. He was holding something in his hand. "You didn't think I'd come here unprepared, did you? Without an ace up my sleeve? I'm Gambler Gold! See this!" He thrust his hand out before him, so they could all see the glowing silver sphere he was holding. "Stand back! Nobody move, or I'll kill us all! This is what I used to blow open your precious door! This . . . is an Infernal Device!"

"No, it bloody isn't," said Fisher. "And I should know."

Jack leaned in close beside her. "It's current slang for an explosive device, Mother."

"I said I'd burn this shithole down, and I meant it!" said Gambler Gold hoarsely. "Now get me the book or I'll do it. Do you think I'm bluffing?"

"No," said Jack. And moving forward so quickly that he was just a blur, he swung his long wooden staff round and hit the side of Gambler Gold's head so hard it exploded in a flurry of splintered bone and scattered brains. The body crumpled slowly to the ground, and Jack was there to gently take the silver sphere from the opening hand. He fiddled with it briefly, and the silver light went out. Jack smiled sadly at the headless body kicking on the ground before him, and turned away. Chappie came forward to sniff at the corpse, then looked up at Jack.

"I thought you were a monk?"

"I am," said Jack. "Just not always a very good one."

Eventually, Jack was persuaded to leave the cleaning up to the other monks, and he walked out of the Abbey with his parents and the dog. Together, they headed for the woods at the end of the clearing. It was still a bright and cheerful autumn day, but Jack didn't feel like talking, so Hawk and Fisher let him be. Chappie seemed quite chipper about the whole business, however. The dragon waited till they were right at the edge of the trees before stepping out to show himself. Jack stopped dead in his tracks, and then a slow, disbelieving smile spread across his face. He bowed formally to the dragon, and Hawk introduced the two to each other.

"Where were you while all the fighting was going on?" growled Chappie.

"You didn't need me, did you?" said the dragon innocently, and the dog's pride wouldn't let him say otherwise.

"You hid yourself very well," Jack said to the dragon. "I had no idea you were there! And there isn't much I can't spot."

"Dragons have always been good at hiding in plain sight," said the dragon. "I put it down to an essentially sneaky nature."

Jack shook his head in amazement, and smiled at his parents. "You really did know a dragon! I was never sure how much to believe in the old stories you used to tell me . . . but the dragon was real after all! Will the unicorn be turning up too?"

Hawk and Fisher looked at each other, and something unsaid passed between them.

"Unlikely," said Hawk.

"Not everything lives as long as we do," said Fisher.

"And not all legends last forever," said Hawk.

"All right," said Jack, happy to change the subject. "Where now?"

"We have to find your sister, Gillian," said Fisher.

"I used to get the occasional letter from her," said Jack. "Last I heard, she was training young warriors at a Brotherhood of Steel Sorting House not that far from the Forest Castle. I can't believe she's in any danger. Surrounded by hundreds of trained fighters. And the Sorting House is nowhere near what's left of the Darkwood."

"The Demon Prince lives inside people now," said Hawk.

"We'd better get moving," said Jack.

The dragon flew them all farther into the heart of the Forest Land, following Jack's directions, towards Gillian's Sorting House. Jack had a pretty good memory for a man in his seventies, though it helped that he still had Gillian's last letter. The monks of Saint Augustine's weren't supposed to have material possessions, but they made an exception for Jack. No one had to ask why. Hawk thought quietly that if he'd known how much Jack prized letters, he would have written more.

The dragon picked up on the geological details in the letter surprisingly quickly; it appeared that dragons knew where everything was, if you just gave them enough clues. He flew over several Sorting Houses, high enough to keep out of range of nervous archers, before finally closing in on the one Jack said was right. It turned out to consist of several large barracks arranged around an even larger central house, with courtyards and stables and training grounds—once again enclosed by a tall, protective stone wall. Hawk said the place reminded him of Saint Augustine's, and Jack said something really quite rude, for a monk. The dragon circled round and round the Sorting House, so they could all look it over. He spiralled slowly lower, until a few bowmen got brave enough to send a few arrows arcing upwards. They didn't even come close.

"Kids today," said Fisher.

The dragon caught a thermal, and swept up and away from the Sorting House. Because, as he pointed out, if he should happen to lose his temper and do something big and fiery and entirely lethal to the archers, it wouldn't make a good first impression when they finally went down to ask about Gillian. Hawk said he quite understood, and the dragon found another suitable clearing to land in, within walking distance of the Sorting House. Everyone got off, after they'd prised Chappie's claws loose, and Jack walked round and round in circles for a while, easing his old joints. Hawk watched but didn't say anything. It disturbed him to see his son so old, but he didn't know what to say, so he said nothing.

"I think I'll stay here again," said the dragon.

"Probably for the best," said Fisher. "I have a horrible feeling we're going to have to be diplomatic with the Brotherhood if we're going to spring Gillian. And that's not something Hawk and I find easy at the best of times."

"Really," murmured Jack. "You do surprise me . . ."

"But given that we could end up having to face off against a small army of highly trained fighters . . ." said Hawk.

"You call me and I'll hear it," said the dragon. "And I'll be there before you know it. Ooh, look! Dodos! Crunchy!"

And he disappeared abruptly into the woods.

"How does he do that?" said Jack.

"How else can a thirty-foot dragon sneak up on things?" said Fisher.

They hurried through the woods, and soon burst out into a wide clearing, cut from the Forest with military precision and more than big enough to hold the Brotherhood of Steel's Sorting House. The perimeter wall was solid stone, rising up a good ten feet, and the one and only entrance gate was covered with all kinds of military motifs. The outside of the wall looked like it got whitewashed daily, probably by resentful young men and women on punishment duty. Hawk insisted that everyone stay back and stand their ground, while he looked the place over. He had a strong feeling that he and his companions were being observed by hidden eyes. He'd walked into enough traps in his time to feel their presence in his bones and in his water.

But since he couldn't hope to vault the wall or crash the entrance gate, he walked right up to it, smiling cheerfully, as though he didn't have a care in the world, his hand just casually resting on the axe at his side. Fisher was right there with him, smiling her usual disturbing *don't mess with me* smile, not even bothering to look diplomatic. Jack strolled along behind them, pointing out pretty birds and butterflies to Chappie, who wasn't really interested in that sort of thing. Unless you could eat them.

As they approached the blocky metal-studded gate, it suddenly swung open before them, and a dozen heavily armed and armoured young men and women came marching out, in strict file and discipline, with an old woman in ornamental silver armour at their head. They crashed to a halt before Hawk and his party, and saluted them with drawn swords, before putting the weapons away again and crashing to attention. Hawk stopped too, and smiled at the old woman in charge. He had no problem recognising Gillian.

She was also clearly in her seventies, but in rather better shape than her brother, Jack. A tall warrior woman, who wore her chased silver armour as though it were a dressing gown, something comfortable she'd just happened to throw on. Her face had a lot of what Hawk quietly decided he was going to call character lines, but she still looked hale and hearty and a good ten years younger than she should. She carried herself like the professional fighter she was, and always would be. And for all her years she still looked like she could be extremely dangerous if the mood took her. She had close-cropped iron grey hair, cool blue eyes, a pursed mouth, and an attractive if not conventionally pretty face. She looked Hawk and Fisher over carefully, and smiled briefly.

"Of course. I knew it had to be you. The first dragon anyone's seen in a century, come looking for me . . . Hello, Father, Mother."

She stepped forward and embraced each parent in turn with brisk emotion, or at least, as much as her armour would let her. And only then looked at Jack, and Chappie. Her mouth twitched in something that might have been a smile if it had hung around long enough.

"Hello, Jack. Looking old. Still busy being holy?"

"Hello, Gillian," said Jack. "Still busy being violent?"

They both laughed quietly but made no move to embrace each other.

191

"Play nicely, children," said Fisher. "Or there will be no story at bedtime."

"Damn, that takes me back," said Gillian. "I have to say, Mum and Dad, you're both looking very yourselves. Just like I remembered you."

"I know," said Hawk. "We haven't aged, and you have. It isn't fair. But what's the first thing your mother and I taught you?"

"Life isn't fair," said Jack and Gillian, pretty much in unison. "That's why people have to be."

"We need to talk, Gillian," said Hawk. "Can you come out? Or do you want to invite us in?"

Gillian turned and glared at the young warriors she'd brought with her, presumably as an honour guard. All of them still standing rigidly at attention. "See these three, and their really ugly dog?" she said loudly. "They're with me. If anyone bothers them, I will take it as a personal affront. Understood?"

Without moving a muscle, all of the young warriors did their best to give the impression that such a thought had never entered their minds. Hawk had to smile. Even as a small child Gillian had drilled her dolls mercilessly, refighting old battles with them. She even buried some of them, if only so her mother would have to buy her new ones. It seemed some things hadn't changed.

Gillian led the way back into the Sorting House. She marched along like the soldier she still was but kept the pace down as a courtesy to the rest of her family. The honour guard . . . kept their distance. Everyone in the house's courtyard stopped what they were doing to watch them pass, but no one said anything. Hawk kept a careful eye on everyone. There were young men and women paired in duels, with all kinds of weapons; more people in full armour, riding back and forth on horseback; and long rows of targets for those learning archery. They all looked very busy, very proficient. None of them seemed at all pleased to see Hawk and his companions. Gillian ignored everyone, taking her guests inside the Sorting House and straight to her private quarters by the most direct route.

Once inside the house lobby, she dismissed her honour guard, told an inquiring officer type to piss off and mind his own damned business, and led Hawk and Fisher, Jack and Chappie, down a series of narrow stone corridors to her quarters. Which turned out to be surprisingly comfortable. Nicely padded furniture, rugs and carpets from foreign lands, and lots of weapons displayed on the walls, ready for use. There weren't enough chairs, so Gillian went out and got some from the next room. There were a few raised voices, immediately cut short, and then Gillian came back with extra chairs. She got everyone settled, put food on the table from her own private supplies, some of it quite exotic, and even managed a bone for Chappie to gnaw on.

"I'll bet Jack never gave you a bone, when you visited his spartan home," Gillian said gruffly.

"No," said Chappie. "I had to bite off a bandit's leg to get something to chew on."

Gillian looked at the dog, and then at the others. "He's not kidding, is he?"

"Unfortunately, no," said Hawk. "The years have not mellowed our family dog. Or your mother either."

Fisher snorted with laughter, and elbowed Hawk in the ribs.

"And that really was a dragon, flying overhead?" said Gillian. "It's been so long since anyone's seen one in the Forest Land, we had to go look up what species it was in the *Big Book of Unnatural Flying Things*."

"He's an old friend," said Fisher.

"The one from all the legends, in the Demon War," said Gillian. She sniffed at Jack. "You never believed any of those stories, when we were kids. I always believed."

"I have been known to be wrong about things, on occasion," said Jack. "How about you, dear sister? Any sins you'd like to confess?"

"That'll be the day," said Gillian. "You couldn't handle my sins."

"Oh, I don't know," said Jack, grinning suddenly. "I've been around."

"Anyway," Hawk said loudly, "what have you been doing, Gillian? Your mother and I rather lost track of you after you left the Forest to go down to the Southern Kingdoms."

"That was the point," said Gillian. "I wanted to make my own life, without your reputation peering over my shoulder all the time. And you did make Haven sound very . . . interesting. I had a good time down there. The city port was just as big a moral cesspit as you always said, and there was no shortage of bad guys to go after. Always something to do in Haven, usually of a violent nature. I signed up for the City Guard, just like you, and had the time of my life, tracking down and smiting evildoers. Made Captain in no time. They still remember you, you know. You're legends in Haven: the only honest Guard Captains. I like to think I was honest too, in my own brutal and unforgiving way.

"When I got too old to work the streets, I came back here. And found the Brotherhood of Steel had moved in while I was away. Just what I was looking for—a whole organisation based on the idea of hitting people. I joined up to train the next generation of fighters, and found I made a much better teacher than I ever was a fighter. Imagine my surprise." She looked from Hawk to Fisher and back again. "I'm seventy-two, and in good shape for my age, but you don't look a day older than when Jack and I were children. It's a bit creepy, to be honest."

"It's still us, Gillian," said Hawk. "I'm still your dad."

"And you're still our daughter," said Fisher.

"I walked out on you," said Gillian. She couldn't look them in the eye. "Never even said goodbye, because I thought . . . if I told you what I was going to do, you'd try to stop me. And I was determined not to be stopped. So I just left. Did you miss me?"

"Of course your mum and I missed you," said Hawk. "But we of all people knew . . . that the bird has to leave the nest if she's ever going to fly."

"I'm so sorry, Dad," said Gillian, her voice just a bit unsteady. "So sorry, Mum."

"We are not an ordinary family," Hawk said kindly. "Your mother and I always knew our children were never going to lead ordinary lives."

Gillian nodded quickly. "Why are you here now?"

"Have you heard from Nathanial recently?" said Fisher.

"Not recently, no," said Gillian. "Why?"

"The Demon Prince appeared to us, inside the Millennium Oak," said Hawk. "To tell us our grandchildren were in danger. Unless your mother and I returned to the Forest Land to save them. He also had much to say about death and war and horror, all in the near future. So we're going back to Forest Castle, as Hawk and Fisher. Jack's with us. How about you?"

"Of course," Gillian said immediately. "Nathanial's currently working at the Castle. Just like Jack's daughter, Mercy."

Hawk and Fisher looked at each other.

"I sense Fate and Destiny at work, the sneaky bastards," said Hawk.

"Really?" said Fisher. "I sense the Demon Prince, plotting his dark little heart out again."

"I used to have nightmares about him," said Gillian. "When I was just a kid. Used to think he was hiding in the shadows at the foot of my bed, every night. Watching, and waiting . . ."

Jack nodded. "I never really believed he was real, but that didn't stop me being afraid of him."

"Why has he come back now?" said Gillian.

"Because it's been a hundred years since the Demon War," said Jack. "Evil does so love to commemorate anniversaries. As a Transient Being, a concept given flesh and blood and material form, the Demon Prince has no reality, as such. He is therefore bound by rules and traditions, always repeating old actions in the hope of a new and different outcome. And he bears grudges, because he is incapable of forgetting or learning from the past." He broke off and smiled at the others. "There's lots of reading to do in a monastery."

Hawk had no idea what to say to any of that, so he turned to Gillian. "Are you going to need some time, to give in your notice to the Sorting House, and the Brotherhood of Steel?"

"Hell, no," said Gillian. "Come and go as I please. In fact, they'll probably be glad to see the back of me."

Gillian gathered up her few personal possessions and equipped herself with a whole bunch of nasty and efficient weapons. But when they went back out into the courtyard, it seemed like the whole Sorting House had emptied itself out to block her way. The entire staff and student population had turned out, to stand between Gillian and the exit. They stood spread out in ranks, ready and watchful, most of them armed. Gillian glared about her, her hand dropping to the great sword at her hip, and a great many watching faces went pale. Among the staff, as well as the students. For a long, uncomfortable moment everyone just stood and stared at everyone else; and then everyone jumped, just a bit, as a loud cracking sound broke the silence. Everyone looked at Chappie, who'd just broken the bone he'd been chewing on in half, in his powerful jaws. He opened his mouth, to let the two pieces fall to the ground, and gave everyone a hard look.

"We are all going to be very civilised about this. Aren't we?" he said, loudly and meaningfully. "You are facing legends here, and don't you forget it."

Everyone looked at the talking dog, and gave every indication of being very upset. Gillian stabbed an accusing finger at one particular member of the staff, a large and muscular sort in his late forties, in full ceremonial armour. He had a scarred face and a great mane of red hair. Everything about him suggested a powerful and experienced warrior, but he still flinched under Gillian's gaze.

"Wendover!" said Gillian. "What's this all about?"

"We heard you were thinking of leaving," said Wendover, with great dignity and authority. "You must know you can't do that."

"Watch me," said Gillian.

"You can't just walk out!" said Wendover. "You're one of the best teachers and trainers we've ever had! You have a contract with the Brotherhood!"

"Show it to me," said Gillian. "So I can rip it up and throw the pieces in your face!"

"She was just the same as a child," said Fisher, to no one in particular.

Wendover stepped forward out of the crowd and faced Gillian unflinchingly. "You know the deal, Gillian. Once in, never out. You swore to serve the Brotherhood of Steel for life."

"I swore to serve God forever," said Jack. "But family comes first. Family . . . matters."

"Windy," said Gillian, "what is it, really?"

Jack blinked. "Windy? Really?"

"Shut up, Jack," said Gillian.

Wendover looked at the ground before him, and then at her. "You can't just go, Gill. What would I do without you?"

"Silly old thing," said Gillian affectionately. "I'm not abandoning you. Just taking a short leave of absence."

"Oh," said Wendover. "Well, I suppose that's all right then."

"No, it isn't!" said another member of the staff, pushing forward to glare at both Gillian and Wendover. "A contract is a contract! You break your word, and all these young fools will think they can run off too, whenever the going gets rough! You're not going anywhere. You really think you can stand against all of us?"

He was a tall, bulky fellow in heavy armour, with a flat, flushed face and cold eyes. Just looking at him, you knew he'd never backed down from a fight in his life, and he wasn't about to start now. Gillian sniffed loudly.

"You always were a horse's arse, Pendleton. And yes, I do think I can stand against all of you, because I trained all of you! And I am not alone."

Everyone looked up sharply as a great shadow fell across the entire courtyard, covering everybody. The dragon dropped out of the sky, out of nowhere, and hovered above them all, his great outspread wings barely moving as he hung some ten feet or so over their heads. He shouldn't have been able to hover like that, thirty feet of very bulky dragon; but he was, after all, a magical creature. With glowing golden eyes and a grinning mouth just jammed full of really impressive teeth. Several young warriors fainted. Others dropped their swords, and a few started crying quietly. Gillian glared at them.

"Stop that! And pick up those swords! I trained you better than this! You're part of the Brotherhood of Steel, dammit. It's only a dragon!"

"How about we provide you with maps and provisions," Wendover said carefully, "so you can get to where you're going faster, and come back to us sooner?"

"How very sensible," said Gillian. "That all right with you, Pendleton?"

But Pendleton was standing very still, staring up at the hovering dragon with wide eyes and his mouth hanging open. Wendover gave some quick orders to the nearest students, and they rushed back inside the main building. Everyone smiled politely at everyone else, while the dragon continued to hover. Hawk beamed at Fisher.

"Doesn't it make a wonderful change, to deal with reasonable people?"

"We could have taken them," said Fisher.

. . .

Later that night, in another clearing somewhat closer to the Forest Castle, they all sat around a blazing camp-fire, catching up on family life. The dragon had hoped to make the Castle before nightfall, but even though he was feeling fresh and young again, the Forest Land was a lot bigger than he remembered, and he couldn't be sure of getting there before darkness fell. So he landed in one last clearing, let everyone off, and disappeared into the surrounding woods in search of something slow and stupid. He soon was back, tossing a meaty bone to Chappie and a much larger haunch of meat to the others. After they'd all eaten as much as they could stand, they sat around talking quietly as the last of the light went out of the day. The moon seemed a lot larger in the sky overhead, and the stars shone fiercely in the night, as though they were watching. The dragon lay curled around everyone, putting his huge green body between them and the shadows beyond the firelight.

"Why did you never want to meet your grandchildren?" Jack said finally, after they'd talked through all the safer subjects.

"It seemed for the best," Hawk said carefully. "We made a decision, your mother and I, after you and Gillian wrote to us saying you had children of your own now. We decided it was better to have no contact at all, with Mercy and Nathanial. For their sake."

"We thought it advisable to maintain a safe distance," said Fisher, poking the fire with a stick so she wouldn't have to look at Jack or Gillian. "To keep from overshadowing their lives. You had it hard enough, when we were just thought of as heroes. By the time Mercy and Nathanial came along, we were myths and legends. We wanted them to have their own lives."

"I managed," said Gillian. "And Jack."

"Did you?" said Hawk. "You went all the way down to Haven, to live the lives we lived. And Jack had to become the Walking Man to make his mark."

"That's not why I did it," said Jack quietly.

"We saw what we did to you," Hawk said firmly. "And we were determined not to let anything like that happen to our grandchildren."

"So we stayed away," said Fisher.

Jack shook his head slowly. "You always were too honourable for your own good."

"Look who's talking," said Gillian.

"And," said Fisher, "as long as no one knew they were our grandchildren, no one could ever use them as weapons against us. Or vice versa."

"So," said Gillian. "All for their own good. Nothing at all to do with you needing to hide your true identities from the world?"

"Oh, that too," said Hawk. "We've always been able to be practical, when we have to. We did try to keep an eye on them, and on you, from a safe distance; but it's a lot harder to get your hands on reliable magics these days."

"And that's why I didn't hear from you for decades?" said Jack.

"There is such a thing as letters," said Gillian.

"Letters can be intercepted," said Fisher.

"We had to turn our backs on our old lives to have new lives," said Hawk. "Rupert and Julia are part of myth and legend now. Let them stay that way."

"People would only be upset and disappointed if they met the real thing," said Fisher.

"I don't know," said Gillian. "They're still talking about Captains Hawk and Fisher, in Haven."

"It's not like you needed us," said Hawk. "You've lived . . . successful lives of your own."

"Children always need their parents," said Gillian, looking into the fire.

"I don't suppose you missed me?" said Chappie.

"No," said Jack.

"Not in the least," said Gillian.

And then they both laughed, and took it in turns to make a big fuss of him.

"I can't believe you're still alive, dog," said Jack. "You were old when I was just a kid, and now look at you!"

"*Distinguished* is the word you're looking for," said Chappie. "I am older than both of you put together, and that's in dog years. The High Warlock did good work."

"Jack," Hawk said carefully, "what happened to your wife, Amelia?"

"She left me," said Jack. "After I became the Walking Man. I don't blame her. I was . . . very caught up in myself, for some time there. Afterwards, after I'd given it all up, I did try to find her . . . if only to tell her she'd been right all along. But she'd put a lot of time and effort into disappearing. She didn't want to be found. So I went to the Abbey of Saint Augustine. A lot of people who knew both of us knew where I was. She could have found me if she'd wanted to. I hope she's still out there, somewhere. I hope she's happy."

"Your daughter might know," said Fisher.

Jack shrugged. It was his turn to stare into the fire, rather than face his parents. "Mercy might know any number of things. I never asked. I didn't want her to have to choose which parent to be true to. She was always closer to her mother than I was . . ."

"And Matthew?" said Hawk.

"He died," said Jack. "Some time back."

"Oh, Jack, I'm so sorry," said Fisher.

"I'm not," said Jack.

"Don't ask me where or even who Nathanial's father might be," Gillian said briskly. "Could have been any one of a dozen men. I never cared enough to find out. I always was generous with my affections."

Hawk looked at Fisher. "She didn't get that from me."

"Don't start," said Fisher.

Chappie sniggered.

"So, is it true?" said Gillian, grinning at her mother. "Is it true what they say in some of the songs? That you slept with Uncle Harald before you got together with Dad? That is so . . . icky!"

"See what you've started," Fisher said to Hawk. "It was during the war, Gillian. We were all in a dark place . . . I thought I'd lost your father. Things happen."

"This is me, changing the subject," said Jack. "What, exactly, did the Demon Prince say to you about the threat to your grandchildren?"

"He didn't actually say much," said Hawk.

"He said our grandchildren would die if your father and I didn't return to the Forest Land," said Fisher.

Gillian shuddered suddenly. "The Demon Prince . . . the embodiment of evil in the living world. It's hard to think of such an awful thing being real . . ."

"I'm not sure that's the right word to apply to him," said Hawk. "He's both more and less than real, as we understand the word. He comes from another dimension, called Reverie, where the Blue Moon shines forever."

Gillian shuddered again, and not from the cold night.

"You went there, didn't you?" said Jack. "You left this world, to walk in a whole other reality. What was it like?"

"Strange. Horrible. Magnificent," said Hawk. "I don't think we have the right words, or even the concepts, in our language to describe it. Reverie . . . is a world where myths come as standard."

"And you were there . . . ," said Jack. "Damn. My parents really were *legends*!"

"We were only ever just people," Fisher said calmly. "Doing what was needed."

"You were a legend, Jack," said Hawk. "As the Walking Man."

"Not on your scale," said Jack. "I saved souls. You saved the world. Twice."

"It's an overrated thing, being a legend," said Chappie. "I've known more than a few heroes in my time, and most of them were a few shillings short of a pound."

Gillian turned to look at the dragon, lying on the grass opposite her. "You knew both our parents, back when they were young. What were they really like? Prince Rupert and Princess Julia?"

"Pains in the arse, mostly," said the dragon. "And brave, and honourable. Throwing themselves against evil because there was no one else, and because they would not turn away. They shone so very brightly in the dark . . . I always felt honoured, that they made me part of their adventure. Even if they did drag me out of my nice comfortable cave and away from my collection of butterflies."

"I remember . . . ," said Fisher. "You were there with us, at the end. Facing the Demon Prince in his place of power, the darkest part of the Darkwood. He struck you down, and would have beaten you to death . . .

I still remember him kicking you in the face, and your golden blood falling . . . I never felt so ashamed in my life, for leading you into that."

"Hush, Julia," said the dragon. "You never asked me to do anything I wasn't willing to do." He paused. "What did happen to my butterfly collection?"

"Locked away in the vaults of the Millennium Oak," said Hawk. "Still in the same display cases you made for them."

"Hold it," said Jack. "He's not kidding? Butterflies? He collected butterflies, not gold?"

The dragon lifted his great head a few feet off the ground to stare at Jack. *"They're just as pretty, aren't they?"*

"Try not to upset the thirty-foot dragon, son," said Hawk. "He's a bit . . . sensitive about some things."

"Yeah," said Chappie. "Don't upset him. Or he might tell you what kind of meat you've been eating tonight."

They all looked at one another, and then at what little remained of the haunch of meat the dragon had provided for their supper. They didn't say anything. The dragon lowered his head to the grass again. Chappie sniggered.

"I still don't see why the Demon Prince chose right now to interfere in our world again," said Jack. "Has anything . . . significant, happened recently? It's easy to get out of touch when you're living the secluded life in a monastery."

"There are rumours of war," said Gillian. "And I mean real rumours of actual armed conflict, between the Forest Land and the Kingdom of Redhart. Recruitment at the Sorting Houses has been going through the roof in the last few years. Young men and women desperate to train as warriors, just to be ready for when it all kicks off. But I would have said the chances of war were actually lower now, with a Peace agreement on the table and an arranged Royal marriage in the cards, between Prince Richard of the Forest and Princess Catherine of Redhart."

Hawk brightened up immediately. "Our great-great-nephew is getting married! We have to be there for the ceremony!"

"Who as?" said Fisher. "They won't let us in as Hawk and Fisher, but we can't show up at the Forest Court as Rupert and Julia. That could throw the whole line of succession into disarray."

"There can't be anyone left alive who'd recognise us as Rupert and Julia," said Hawk. "Not after all these years. So, we turn up as the Hawk and Fisher currently in charge of the Hero Academy! They'd be bound to let them in. The Confusulum will keep anyone from asking too many questions."

"Is that thing still with us?" said Fisher.

"Who can say?" said Hawk.

"Excuse me," said Jack, "but what the hell is the Confusulum? I thought I had a good grounding in strange and exotic magical devices, but . . ."

"Just something we picked up on our travels," said Fisher. "It exists to confuse the issue. Any issue. Including what it is."

"Might be a device, might be alive. Might be something beyond our limited human comprehension," said Hawk. "We've always got on fine."

"Can I see it?" said Jack.

"If it wanted you to see it, you'd be seeing it," said Fisher.

"I think it's just shy around strangers sometimes," said Hawk.

"You always were weird, even when we were kids," said Gillian.

"I always sort of liked that," said Jack.

"I am not going to the Forest Castle as anyone but myself," Gillian said firmly. "I've got nothing to hide. I'm proud of my reputation. Even if it does make some people wet themselves."

"Same here," said Jack. "We'd be expected to turn up anyway, as relatives of the groom. I suppose we'd better get some presents . . ."

"Did you get an invitation?" said Gillian. "No, neither did I. Funny, that. I say we go, just to embarrass them."

"Hear, hear!" said Chappie. "Always lots of good food and drink at a wedding! I love cake."

"If what we saw genuinely was the Demon Prince," Hawk said heavily. "And not just some sorcerer messing with our heads, for their own purposes. If it really is him, we're going to need the old weapons. The Rainbow Sword is still in the Castle Armoury."

"Hold it," said Jack. "That's real? I thought it was just a metaphor!"

"Grow up, Jack," said Gillian.

"The Rainbow is real too," said Fisher. "And if we need more weapons, the three missing Infernal Devices should still be hidden inside the no-longer-Inverted Cathedral. We'd better check to see that they're still there."

"There are three more Infernal Devices?" said Gillian. "Three more of those cursed powerful swords? That's not in any of the songs or stories."

"Hardly surprising," said Jack. He looked thoughtfully at his parents. "Is there anything else we should be concerned about?"

"They never did find the Jewel of Compulsion that used to be set in the hilt of the sword Curtana," said Hawk. "Before the Demon Prince destroyed the sword, at the end. The Crimson Pursuant could confuse any mind, bend any will, control anyone . . . and it could still be out there, somewhere . . ."

"You are really freaking me out now," said Gillian.

"The past is never really over," said Jack. "And bad things just keep turning up again, over and over."

"You had to spend twenty years in seclusion in a monastery to work that out?" said Gillian.

"Play nicely, children," said Fisher.

"Or there'll be no desserts," said Hawk.

"Desserts?" Chappie's head came up. "There's dessert? Somebody definitely mentioned dessert!"

"When we get to the Castle," said Jack, ignoring Chappie, "is there anyone in that place we can be honest with, about who we really are and why we're there? Anyone we can trust?"

"The Demon Prince said he lives inside people now," said Hawk. "Which means . . . he could be anybody. So, no, we can't trust anyone."

"Situation entirely bloody normal, then," said Fisher.

And they both stopped and looked at their children for a long moment.

"You do understand," said Fisher, "why we never took you to the Castle as children, even for just a visit? It is your family home, by right, but . . ."

"You wouldn't have liked it, anyway," said Hawk. "I never did."

"The Castle has a lot of bad memories for your father," said Fisher. "And I can't say I was ever that fond of it."

"It is your inheritance, I suppose," said Hawk. "You are attached to the Royal line. Though you'd probably have a hard time proving it."

"Trust us on this one," said Fisher. "You don't want to be Royal. It isn't nearly as much fun as the songs and stories make out."

"Right," said Hawk.

"But . . . you could still be King," said Jack. "You're the oldest member of the line, the surviving son of King John, which gives you precedence. You could take the throne, and lead the war against the Demon Prince."

"I never wanted the throne," said Hawk. "Never."

"Your father could have been King, instead of Harald," said Fisher. "There were many who would have supported such a claim. That's why we left in such a hurry. Because he chose to be with me."

They held hands. Jack and Gillian felt their hearts jump. *Their legendary love . . .*

"Besides," said Chappie, "it's a constitutional monarchy these days, which makes it all moot. Whatever a moot is. It sounds sort of chewy . . ."

Gillian looked at Jack. "Did you ever go to Forest Castle when you were the Walking Man?"

"Yes," said Jack. "How about you?"

"Yes. I wanted to see where it all began. Your old home, Dad."

"Can't say it ever felt like home to me," said Hawk. "The Castle isn't the kind of place anyone would call home. And my relationship with your grandfather, King John, was always . . . complicated."

"You never talked much about him, even when we were kids," said Jack.

"Nothing much to say. He did his best, I suppose, under difficult circumstances. We reconciled, pretty much, at the end."

"Is it true that he's still . . . out there, somewhere, in the Land?" said Gillian. "There are a few songs that say he's with the Lady of the Lake."

"Who knows?" said Hawk, and there was enough coldness in his voice to make everyone else change the subject.

"I would like to see what Nathanial is up to," said Gillian, "that keeps him too busy to write to his mother regularly."

"My thoughts exactly, concerning Mercy," said Jack.

"There are bound to be some at the Castle capable of detecting my presence," said the dragon. "So it's probably best if I drop you all off some distance away. I'll be around, keeping an eye on you, and on things, generally."

"You don't think they'd be pleased to see a real live dragon, after all these years?" said Jack.

"No one is ever pleased to see a dragon," said the dragon. "That's part of the fun of being a dragon. We'll set off first thing in the morning."

"If this is all so urgent, why can't we go now?" said Gillian.

"Because it's night," the dragon said steadily. "I don't see well in the dark. I once flew into the side of a hill I didn't see coming."

Gillian started to say something, but Hawk stopped her with a look. And it was only then that Gillian remembered that the dragon had been in the Darkwood too.

They settled down for the night. Hawk and Fisher sat close together, wrapped in the same blanket. Even after all the years, and all the things they'd done in their long lives, they still needed a banked fire before they could sleep. Jack and Gillian noticed, and glanced at each other, and said nothing. When they were small children it was their parents, not them, who had to have a light burning while they slept. Now Jack and Gillian had a better idea of what their parents had been through. And that they really had done most of the things that legend said they had.

Jack and Gillian, both in their seventies now, looked across the fire at the two young people sitting opposite them, as though they'd never seen them before. Not as Hawk and Fisher, heroes and warriors in their own right, but as Prince Rupert and Princess Julia, myths and legends. Their parents. Who'd stayed young while Jack and Gillian grew old. They'd both made good lives for themselves, accomplished great things, but nothing to match their parents. Jack and Gillian made a point of collecting more wood for the fire, banking it up to be sure it would last through the night. After a while Hawk and Fisher said they'd take the first watch, while Jack and Gillian slept. And the two old people nodded, and said they'd take over at first light. So their parents could sleep.

Chappie got up and circled round and round before settling down with a heavy thump beside the fire. "Over a hundred years old, and I'm still doing this. Does anybody know why?"

"Because you're a nuisance," said Hawk.

Chappie farted loudly and closed his eyes.

Hawk and Fisher talked quietly while their children slipped into sleep, and looked them over fondly. Chappie snored quietly. The dragon closed his great glowing eyes and dozed. Two thin plumes of smoke rose straight up from his nostrils.

"Never thought we'd ever see the Forest again," said Hawk. "Never mind the Castle. Never wanted to. When I rode out with you, I never meant to go back again. I wonder how much things will have changed . . ."

"The Castle we're going back to and the one you remember are a hundred years apart," Fisher said carefully.

Hawk sighed heavily. "I don't know if I can do this. It was hard enough going back the last time, to investigate Harald's murder. I'm afraid the Castle will still have a hold on me. That I won't be able to leave again."

"I know, love," said Fisher. "We'll just have to watch each other's backs, like always, and fight off whatever the place throws at us."

Hawk looked at her. "Do you really think we can defeat the Demon Prince a third time?"

"This time we outnumber him," said Fisher. "There's us, the children, the grandchildren, the dog, and the dragon. All the family, together again for the first time. Who'd bet against us?"

Hawk smiled. "Poor bastard won't stand a chance."

And then they both sat up straight as they heard something moving in the dark, beyond the farthest reaches of the firelight. Hawk and Fisher stood up quickly, throwing aside the blanket and drawing their weapons. More noises, of something moving, too vague to give a direction . . . Jack and Gillian struggled to their feet, blinking and looking around, still half asleep. Old bodies take longer to catch up with warrior instincts. Hawk had his axe at the ready, Fisher had her sword. Jack grasped his wooden staff firmly, and Gillian swept her sword back and forth before her. For two people in their seventies, they both looked very competent and extremely dangerous. Chappie was up on his feet as well, sniffing at the night air and growling steadily, like a long, low rumble of thunder. The dragon lifted his great head.

"Something's out there," he said. "I can't see it, but I can feel it."

"What is it?" Jack turned to Hawk. "What did you see?"

"Didn't see anything," said Fisher. "But we heard something. Out there, in the dark."

"Could it be a demon?" said Hawk.

"They're pretty rare these days," said Gillian.

"And we're a long way from what's left of the Darkwood," said Jack.

"It's not a demon," said Chappie. "It smells dead."

"It's him," said the dragon. "I know that presence."

The dark earth right at the edge of the firelight blew apart, flying through the air in all directions at once. And out of the dirt, out of the hole, out of the dark of the earth, something rose up into the light. It stood right at the edge of the firelight, so they could see it clearly. A skeleton, its bones yellowed with age and a long time in the ground. Just bones, with not even a hint of meat or gristle to hold them together. Standing erect, it moved suddenly, jerkily, as though having difficulty remembering what movement was. The skull turned slowly to look at the living with its dark, empty eye sockets and bared teeth.

"I told you," it said, in a distant whispering voice. "I live inside people now. The living or the dead. I don't discriminate. Sometimes they know I'm there, and sometimes I don't let them know. Depending on which choice will hurt them most."

"Get out of him," said Jack. His old body was trembling, but his voice was firm and steady. "In the name of the good God I serve, I command you to depart!"

The skeleton's jaw dropped as the Demon Prince laughed at him. "You gave up any authority you might have had over me when you put down the burden of being the Walking Man. Was it my voice that whispered in your ear, then, persuading you that you didn't need to be God's errand boy anymore? Or were you just not worthy . . . ?"

"Leave him alone!" said Gillian, taking a step forward. The skull turned immediately to look at her, and she stopped where she was.

"You see, little Gillian? I came back after all! Just like I said I would when I hid in the shadows at the foot of your bed, when you were so small and vulnerable. You'll always be frightened of me, little Gillian, until I finally come for you."

Hawk and Fisher stepped forward then, putting themselves between the Demon Prince and their children, sword and axe at the ready. The skull grinned at both of them.

"Come to me, Rupert, Julia. Bring your spawn, and your pets. I'm waiting for you. One last time . . . pays for all."

Hawk's hand whipped forward, and his axe flashed through the air to split the skull in two. The whole head was torn away from the skeleton body, which collapsed immediately in a tangle of bones. Everyone rushed forward, but the Demon Prince was gone, leaving only death behind. Gillian kicked the bones apart, scattering them, and then took control of herself and stood very still, breathing hard. Jack put a hand on her shoulder.

"He knows we've come back," said Hawk.

"He always did," said Fisher.

"Would any of you mind if I took one of these bones?" said Chappie. "You can never have too many bones . . . All right, why is everyone looking at me like that?"

FIVE

WHO DO YOU SERVE?

The Royal carriage of Redhart went rolling through the Forest at an almost dangerous speed, carrying Princess Catherine and her companion Lady Gertrude. Both of them sitting as comfortably as they could, on a great many cushions, while holding on desperately to the leather straps provided to keep them from being thrown about more than was absolutely necessary. The carriage was following one of the King's main highways, but it was still more of a wide, dusty trail than a well-maintained road. Not at all what Catherine was used to. The four matched white horses plunged forward, the carriage slammed back and forth, and the dust thrown up by the churning wheels seemed to get everywhere.

The Sombre Warrior rode his great black charger some way ahead of the carriage, while his six personally chosen bodyguards and outriders surrounded the carriage in a great circle. Keeping an eye out, ready for anything. The Sombre Warrior was wearing full battle armour and a great featureless steel helm that hid his face from the world. The helm had no eye or mouth slits, but the Sombre Warrior still saw and heard everything, thanks to a special enchantment provided by King William's pet sorcerer, Van Fleet. For services rendered. It had to have been hot as hell inside the armour and the helm, but Catherine had never seen the man remove his helm for a moment, even to take a drink. Sometimes she wondered if the Warrior was still just a man, after all.

The driver lashed the horses from his high seat, driving them on; he was determined to reach the Forest Castle before night fell. He really didn't want to still be travelling through the Forest when it got dark. He'd heard all the stories. Only a generous bonus and direct orders from the King had persuaded him to take the job in the first place. He had an axe set to one side of him, and a crossbow and quarrels to the other, and neither comforted him as much as he'd hoped.

Catherine and Gertrude chose an open window each, and peered out of the jolting carriage at the passing scenery as best they could. And almost despite themselves, they were impressed. The great Forest was nothing like the small and carefully tended woodland of Redhart. The trees here were huge, reaching way up into the sky, with trunks so broad it would take half a dozen men to get their arms round them. The leaves were a blaze of colours, burning gold and bronze, falling in sudden flurries upon the carriage as the vibrations of its approach shook them loose. Birds sang so loudly they could still be heard above the constant thunder of the carriage wheels, and all kinds of wildlife slipped back and forth between the trees, sometimes pausing to watch the carriage pass, eyes gleaming brightly from the darker and more concealing shadows.

And then Catherine's heart lurched as she saw shining shapes rushing between the trees ahead. Far enough away for the moment that they were just shapes, but drawing steadily closer. Ghostly, almost human, riding gleaming demonic horses. Appearing and disappearing in the gloom between the trees. Catherine and Gertrude fell back into the carriage, well away from the open windows. Catherine yelled out a warning, but the Sombre Warrior already knew. He'd already signalled to his outriders, who moved in close around the carriage, their horses plunging along so near that Catherine felt she could have reached out the window and touched them. The Sombre Warrior drew his great sword, and almost in the same moment all six riders had weapons in their hands. None of them looked worried. In fact, they gave every appearance that they were looking forward to seeing a little action, at last. The shimmering ghostly riders were really close now—twenty of them, maybe more. Shining skeletons riding spectral horses, their bones gleaming fiercely in the gloom among the woods. Catherine forced her head back out the open window to get a better look, and to call out to the Sombre Warrior.

"What are they?"

"Attackers, your highness," said the Sombre Warrior, his voice sounding clearly and calmly from under his featureless helm. "Do not concern yourself. My men and I will protect you. We've been waiting for someone to show up."

"Are they demons?" said Gertrude, from inside the carriage.

"No," said the Sombre Warrior. "Demons don't ride. They really should have waited till it got darker. They'd have looked more impressive, more convincing, set against the night. But they couldn't wait. They had to hit us now, before we got too close to the Castle and could call for reinforcements."

"You know what those things are?" said Catherine, half leaning out the carriage window, screwing up her face against the dust. Gertrude tried to pull her back inside, but Catherine elbowed her and Gertrude fell back with a squeak.

"Of course I know, your highness," said the Sombre Warrior. "They are attackers. Men, painted with stripes of white phosphorous, to look like skeletons. It's an old smugglers' trick, out on the moors of Redhart. They should have realised . . . some tricks don't travel. Sewell!"

"Aye, sir?" said the outrider nearest the Sombre Warrior.

"You're our best archer. Pick one of those fellows and stick him with an arrow. Let's see if we can't make a skeleton bleed."

Sewell grinned, put away his sword in favour of a bow, and aimed and loosed an arrow in one swift movement. One of the leading skeletons lurched suddenly backwards, punched right out of his saddle. He fell from his horse, hit the ground hard, and didn't move again. His horse just kept going.

"You see, your highness?" the Sombre Warrior said easily. "Mounted attackers in spooky outfits. Nothing more. Driver! Bring the carriage to a halt!"

The driver looked round uncertainly. "You what? Stop here, with them? Don't you think we should make a run for it and leave these spooky bastards behind?"

"No," said the Sombre Warrior. "Much easier to defend a stationary target."

"But my orders were to keep the Princess out of danger at all costs!"

"She'll be safer here with me," said the Sombre Warrior. "Now you follow my orders, and bring this carriage to a halt right now, or I'll have Sewell shoot you out of your seat and take your place."

He didn't raise his voice, but then, he didn't have to. The driver swore fiercely and hauled in on the reins, bringing the horses and the carriage to a straining, shuddering halt. The six soldiers formed a wall between the carriage and the attackers, and then looked to the Sombre Warrior for orders. And then they all looked sharply back, as the carriage's back right wheel bowed outwards, as the rear axle cracked loudly in two. The wheel fell away, and the whole carriage lurched to one side. Catherine and Gertrude cried out. The Princess fell back inside the carriage, and the two women grabbed each other for support. The Sombre Warrior just nodded.

"Sabotage. From before we left Redhart. Whoever organised these attackers was taking no chances. Imagine what might have happened if we had tried to make a run for it. Lots of people die in carriage accidents, with no one obvious to take the blame. Just what the King's enemies wanted: the Princess dead, no marriage, no Peace agreement. Somebody put a lot of thought into this."

The skeleton riders came charging in, howling and screeching and waving glowing swords, like the fiends they pretended to be. The Sombre Warrior led his men in a charge to meet them. The two sides slammed together in a wild and thrashing melee of clashing steel, thrusting weapons, and rearing horses. Swords and axes rose and fell, and blood flew on the air in sudden jets and flurries. The whole thing didn't take long. The skeleton riders were seriously motivated, and presumably very well paid, but the Sombre Warrior and every one of his men were professional soldiers, veterans of a hundred border skirmishes. They cut and hacked the skeleton riders out of their saddles with swift, brutal blows, threw them screaming to the ground, and rode on. Blood and gore soaked into the soil, and the screams of the wounded and the dying were all very human sounds. The attackers never stood a chance against such practiced warriors.

But one skeleton rider did somehow manage to break away from the battle, and he drove his horse straight at the carriage. The driver saw the attacker coming, jumped down from his post, and ran screaming into the trees. The skeleton rider laughed aloud and went for the open carriage window, brandishing a big butcher's blade of a sword.

"He left us!" Lady Gertrude screamed, clutching at Catherine. "The driver ran away and left us!"

The skeleton rider steered his horse right in beside the open window and leaned in close, drawing back his sword for a thrust at Catherine, who was staring straight at him. It felt like she had all the time in the world to study him. Up close his costume was an obvious fake, the illusion utterly unconvincing. Just a man, with shining silver painted onto a dark costume and white skull makeup on his face. She could even make out the sweat dripping off his chin, his fierce eyes and grinning mouth. He couldn't have been much older than her.

His sword all the way back, he tensed, and Catherine lunged out of the window and plunged a long dagger into his right eye. He screamed shrilly. The force of Catherine's blow shoved the blade through the eyeball and on into the brain, where it buried itself half inside the man's head. Blood and tears exploded from the ruined eye socket, and the rider slumped forward in his saddle. Catherine hung on to the dagger and jerked it back out. The attacker swayed in his saddle, then fell slowly sideways, crashing to the ground. The horse started to shy away but stopped as it realised it was dragging a body behind it, one foot still caught in the stirrup.

Catherine fell back from the window, and sat down heavily on her cushions. Her face was grim and set. She watched thick, dark blood drip from the blade of the dagger she was holding. Lady Gertrude sat very still, staring at Catherine as though she had never seen her before.

"What have you done, my precious? What have you done?"

"What needed doing," said Catherine. "It seems I am my father's daughter, after all."

The Sombre Warrior came riding back. He glanced briefly at the dead man on the ground by the carriage, swung down from his horse, and moved quickly over to the carriage window. He looked in, his featureless steel helm filling the gap.

"Is all well here, your highness? Is either of you hurt?"

"I'm fine," said Catherine. "Fine! So's she. The other attackers . . . ?"

"Dead, every one of them. My apologies, your highness. I don't know how that one got past us."

"It's all right," said Catherine. Her voice was more or less steady. "I took care of him."

"So you did, your highness," said the Sombre Warrior. If anything, he sounded a little amused.

"Where did you get that ugly dagger, my poppet?" said Gertrude, finding her voice again.

"One last present from my Malcolm," said Catherine. "He thought it might come in useful." She wiped the blade on the cushion beside her, with single-minded thoroughness, until it was clean enough to disappear back inside the tall boot under her long travelling clothes.

"Did you happen to see what happened to the driver?" said the Sombre Warrior.

"He ran away!" said Gertrude, still a bit shrilly. "He ran away and left us!"

"He won't have got far. My men will find him and bring him back," said the Sombre Warrior. "In the meantime, I'm afraid you'll both have to disembark from the carriage for a while, my Princess and my Lady. We have to work on the axle, and re-set the wheel, before we can travel any farther. Which will be difficult, without the proper tools. But we should be able to bodge together something that will last long enough to get us to the Castle."

"We can't stay here overnight!" said Gertrude. "This is the Forest, you know!"

"Yes, I know. We'll have everything ready in an hour or so, my Lady." The Sombre Warrior did his best to sound reassuring. "Take a short walk. Stretch your legs. Don't go far."

"Understood," said Catherine. She pushed open the carriage door and jumped down. She breathed in the fresh Forest air, heavy with the scents of trees and leaves, grass and flowers, and all sorts of wildlife. A rich, heady brew, full of life and a rough vitality. Catherine smiled briefly, and felt a little of the cold and the tension go out of her. She realised Gertrude wasn't with her, and turned to look back into the carriage. Gertrude was sitting as far from the open door as she could get, shaking her head firmly.

"Come on, Gertrude," said Catherine. "You've been complaining about how cramped the carriage is for ages. A stiff walk in the fresh air will do you good."

"Here?" said Gertrude. "In the Forest? *Are you crazy?* My Princess . . ."

"I'm going for a walk," said Catherine. "You can sit here on your own and sulk if you want to."

She strode away from the carriage. Somebody inside the carriage said something very bad, and entirely unladylike, and then Gertrude scrabbled out of the carriage door. The Sombre Warrior offered her his arm, to help her down, but she ignored him. She jumped down and ran after Catherine, who was already off the trail and walking among the trees. And then the Princess stopped abruptly, as she realised she was walking across the bloody earth of the recent battle. Ahead of her, the soldiers were stripping the dead attackers of anything valuable, and joking easily with one another as they looked for clues to their opponents' identities. Catherine looked at the dead men and felt just a little guilty that she didn't care they were all dead. They'd attacked her, tried to kill her; and they deserved everything they got. The man who tried to kill her . . . got what he deserved. She didn't feel guilty at all. The Sombre Warrior came to stand beside her. Catherine discovered she felt surprisingly safe and secure in his presence. Like having a really big guard dog you could depend on. She looked up at him and saw her own face reflected in the gleaming steel helm. Catherine wasn't sure she recognised the face staring back at her. It looked . . . cold.

"These weren't just brigands, or road bandits, your highness," said the Sombre Warrior quite calmly. "My men have found signs, indications, about the bodies that confirm what I suspected. These men were soldiers from Redhart. They must have followed us through the dimensional door, before it was shut down. There are those in Redhart ready to do anything to prevent your marriage, and the Peace agreement."

"They would have killed us all, wouldn't they?" said Catherine. "But if this was arranged in advance, we're talking treason!"

"So we are, your highness. Some factions want a war. At whatever the cost."

"Have you any idea . . . have your men found anything on the bodies to suggest who gave them their orders?" said Lady Gertrude. She'd come forward to stand beside Catherine, and take the Princess' hand in hers. Gertrude's hand seemed very small and cold to Catherine, so she held it tightly. Gertrude's face was pale and confused, and she couldn't look at the dead bodies directly.

"So far, nothing conclusive," said the Sombre Warrior. "Go take your walk, ladies. I'll call you when we're ready to proceed again."

"Come away, Gertrude," Catherine said kindly. "I'm sure there are flowers and birds and butterflies, and all kinds of interesting things to look at among the trees."

She paused, as she realised the soldiers were piling all the bodies into one big heap.

"Are you going to bury them, Warrior?"

"No, your highness. We'll make a cairn for them, with wood and stones. It's better than they deserve."

"Then why bother?" said Gertrude.

"Because this is the Forest," said the Sombre Warrior, "and we don't want to attract attention."

Catherine and Gertrude didn't get far into the Forest before they came upon an overgrown, disused graveyard. They picked their way carefully through the tightly packed trees, following something that might have been a trail, once upon a time, and then suddenly the trees just fell away to either side and the two women stumbled into a small clearing, facing a collection of headstones and modest monuments, and a few rows of sunken graves. Gertrude immediately wanted to turn around and go back, but Catherine stood her ground, quietly charmed. It was like a scene from one of those old gothic novels she'd always enjoyed so much as a teenager. And sure enough, when she looked through the trees at the other end of the clearing, she could just make out the ruins of an abandoned manor house.

Catherine drifted dreamily among the graves and headstones, looking from one half-erased inscription to another. Time and the elements had wiped most of the old lettering away, blurring the engravings and obliterating lines of well-meant poetry. She couldn't find a complete name or date anywhere; the names had been either smoothed away by the years or buried under sprawling moss and lichens. Catherine knelt down before one stone showing a simple bas-relief of a young woman's head in profile, but there was nothing to identify her. Nothing to say who she was, or who might have mourned her. She looked like she might have been around Catherine's age . . . The Princess shuddered briefly. *There is only one thing you can be sure of in life,* her father had told her on more than one occasion. *Nothing lasts . . .*

Catherine straightened up suddenly, as Gertrude's shadow fell over her, and the two women stood side by side for a while, looking about them.

"Some welcome to the Forest Land this is," said Gertrude. "Our carriage falls apart, we're attacked by hired killers, and when we go for a nice little walk we end up in a graveyard!"

"To be fair," said Catherine, "those are the only interesting things that have happened so far."

"We could have been killed!" said Gertrude.

"But we weren't," said Catherine.

Lady Gertrude sniffed loudly. "I haven't been able to identify a single birdsong or butterfly since we stopped, my poppet. And the trees are just so . . . big. Almost overpowering . . . It's all so different from the gentle woodlands of our own dear Redhart. It's all so . . . rural. Unplanned. Untamed. I don't like it." She looked through the far trees, at what remained of the old manor house. "I wonder what family lived there . . . and why they chose to live all the way out here, so far from anywhere civilised."

The walls of the manor house had collapsed inwards long ago, leaving the roof to fall in on top of them, and all kinds of intruding vegetation had forced its way in through the shattered windows. It didn't look strange or mysterious, like one of the sinister ruins in Catherine's books; instead, she thought, it looked sad, and lost. A great thing brought low by neglect and the passing of years.

"This must have been the family graveyard," she said. "And given how many graves there are, the family must have lived here for generations."

"Really can't see why," said Gertrude sniffily. "A most inhospitable place, my sweet. We shouldn't be here."

"Nowhere else to be," said Catherine. "And at least it is . . . interesting."

Gertrude rolled her eyes up to Heaven at the use of that word again and sank down heavily on the nearest headstone—which fortunately held up under her weight—with the air of someone washing her hands of the whole affair. Catherine wandered happily among the headstones and markers, trying to find at least one intact name. It was all very quiet, very peaceful, and she liked to think everyone there was at rest.

When she first saw the ghost, she thought it was another of the skeletal attackers. She glimpsed something white and glowing out of the corner of one eye, looked round quite casually, and then her head came up sharply as she found herself looking straight at a gently shining figure. It jumped, startled at being so suddenly picked out from its surroundings, looked frantically back and forth, and then hid behind one of the larger head-stones. Which wasn't big enough to hide most of it. Catherine could still see its glow quite clearly, and more than enough of it to tell it wasn't any man with painted-on bones. She walked right up to the headstone and glared at the white shining figure fidgeting behind it.

"You! Yes, you—who else would I be talking to? Come out from be-hind that gravestone at once! Who are you?"

There was a long pause, and then the whole figure emerged slowly into the light, shuffling his bare feet and looking bashfully at her. He was faint, almost transparent at first, just a human shape with few details. But the more Catherine looked at him, the more the ghost seemed to come into focus. As though he were clear and distinct only when someone living was there to see him. His face was soon clear enough, every detail present and correct, but the rest of him remained stubbornly unfocused. Or perhaps, undecided. The face was that of an old man, with long white hair and a full white beard, kind eyes, and an uncertain smile. There was nothing scary or threatening about him. He looked more like some long-lost uncle, unsure of his welcome. Or even his right to be there, in that graveyard. He shone with a gentle light. He smiled at Catherine, and nodded several times.

"Hello. Yes. Nice day, isn't it? I'm a ghost. Who are you?"

"Come away, Catherine!" called Gertrude, just a bit shrilly, from the far side of the cemetery. "Never talk to ghosts, my poppet! It only encourages them!"

"I always wanted to meet a ghost," said Catherine, studying the shimmering form before her with great interest. "Castle Midnight was supposed to be lousy with the things at one time, but I never saw any. And not for want of trying. What's your name?"

"Ah," said the ghost. "Starting with the hard ones first, are we? Bit of a problem there, I'm afraid. I don't remember. I've been a ghost for so long I've forgotten whose ghost I am. Who or what I was when I was alive . . ."

"How long have you been haunting this place?" said Catherine.

"I don't know," said the ghost. "I used to haunt that old manor house, until it fell apart so much I didn't feel comfortable there anymore. Too many shadows, and too many unexpected noises . . . So now I just hang around here, and talk to the stones, and the graves. Not that they ever answer back, of course. In fact, I think I'd find it rather upsetting if any of them did. I think . . . my name might be Jasper. Yes. There's a stone just over there, with that name on it . . . and the name does feel oddly familiar. Like it might mean something."

"Well, Sir Jasper," said Catherine. "I think . . ."

"Sir Jasper!" said the ghost delightedly. "Oh yes! That sounds right! Sir Jasper! Yes. I like that. Still doesn't ring any bells, though."

"Have you always haunted this part of the Forest?" said Catherine. "Were you a part of the family who lived here?"

"Perhaps," said Sir Jasper. "I suppose so. I've been dead so long it's hard for me to be sure of anything. Certainly I don't remember being anywhere else, before being here. But I think I'm going to have to leave this place soon. I don't want to, but . . . I don't feel safe here anymore. The Darkwood isn't far from here, and it's started growing again. Just a little. Just recently. I can sense it. And that makes me very nervous."

"But you're a ghost!" said Catherine. "What have you got to be nervous about?"

"I don't know!" said Sir Jasper. "That's what's so worrying!" He sighed, then bestowed his gentle smile on Catherine again. "I'm afraid that as ghosts go, I'm a bit rubbish. And more than a little chicken. I'd jump at my own shadow, if I still had one."

"Are you really frightened of the Darkwood?" said Catherine.

"Oh yes," said Sir Jasper, looking down at his bare feet poking out from under what might have been a nightgown. "In the night there are things moving, in the shadows that shouldn't be there. And I can feel the strength of the Darkwood, where it's always dark and the sun has never shone. I can feel its growing power. The Darkwood has an influence on all the things around it. I don't want to be . . . what it would make of me. So I can't stay here. But I don't know where else to go."

"Well, that's easily settled," Catherine said briskly. "You're coming along with us, to the Forest Castle."

"What?" said Lady Gertrude.

But Sir Jasper was already jumping up and down on the spot in excitement, clapping his pale hands together. "Can I? Can I really come with you?"

"Of course you can," said Catherine.

Sir Jasper looked past her, and lost some of his enthusiasm. "Ah . . . I don't think your companion agrees."

Catherine looked round to find that Gertrude had retreated to the farthest end of the graveyard. She was standing with her arms folded very tightly across her chest, shaking her head vigorously.

"What is the matter with you, Gertrude?" said Catherine. And then she stopped and turned back to the ghost. "Oh, I'm so sorry, Sir Jasper. We haven't introduced ourselves, have we? I am the Princess Catherine of Redhart, on my way to a forced marriage with Prince Richard of the Forest, and that is my companion, Lady Gertrude."

"Delighted to meet you!" said Sir Jasper. He put out a hand for Catherine to shake, but her fingers passed right through his. Sir Jasper withdrew his hand and looked at it sadly. "Old habits die hard. Even when you're dead . . ."

"Come away from him, my Princess!" said Gertrude loudly. "It's not at all proper for you to talk with strange people without your chaperone present."

"Then come over here and join us," said Catherine.

"No thank you," said Gertrude very firmly.

"Don't let appearances fool you," said Catherine.

"Trust me, they haven't," said Gertrude.

"He's quite harmless, really," said Catherine.

"I wouldn't say that," said Sir Jasper.

"I would," said Catherine. "*Come here*, Lady Gertrude."

The Lady came very slowly forward, one reluctant and highly apprehensive step at a time. The ghost smiled at her in a hopeful sort of way.

"This is Sir Jasper the ghost," said Catherine. "He's coming with us to the Forest Castle, and I don't want to hear any arguments about it. It's always possible someone there might be able to help us find out who he is. Or rather, who he used to be."

"Why doesn't he know?" said Gertrude suspiciously.

"He's a ghost!" said Catherine. "Who knows what's normal, where ghosts are concerned?"

"Why is he wearing a nightshirt?" said Gertrude.

"Why is everyone talking about him as if he wasn't here!" said Sir Jasper.

"I was hoping you'd take a hint," said Gertrude.

Catherine stopped, and turned to look at Sir Jasper. His form had become much more definite, perhaps because now there were two people looking at him. He appeared to have a perfectly normal body now, wrapped in an old-fashioned nightshirt, which covered him from the buttoned-up top collar all the way down to his bare feet. The nightshirt was so detailed that Catherine could make out every single button, and even the touch of lace at the sleeves. Sir Jasper's face was as pale and colourless as the nightshirt, and he still shone with a gentle ghostly light.

"All right," said Catherine. "Why the nightshirt?"

"It's traditional," said the ghost, with great dignity.

Catherine looked him over, trying to decide whether the new appearance was an improvement or not. "Traditional?" she said finally.

"I remember a few things, about ghosts in general," said Sir Jasper. "What's proper, and what isn't. I did try walking around with my head tucked underneath my arm, for a while. But I couldn't see where I was going, so I kept bumping into things. And once I dropped my head, and I couldn't find myself for ages . . ." The ghost shuddered delicately. "I'm pretty sure what I look like depends on who it is that's looking at me, and since there hasn't been anyone here for ages, I have to say . . . this is probably all your fault. Have you been reading those awful gothic romances?"

"The carriage must be ready by now," said Catherine. "You can ride with us. Unless you can fly?"

"No," said Sir Jasper, very firmly. "I'm not exactly substantial, you see. Not a lot to me . . . One good headwind and who knows where I'd end up." He peered at Catherine thoughtfully. "I have to ask—what will the people of Forest Castle make of me?"

Catherine grinned. "I can't wait to find out."

They made their way back through the trees to the carriage. Catherine and Gertrude stuck to the trail, such as it was, while Sir Jasper just ambled along, walking through anything that got in his way. He even drifted through some of the larger trees, because he was so busy looking eagerly around him that he genuinely didn't see them coming. Apparently he'd been in the graveyard so long he'd forgotten what everything else looked like. All the surrounding wildlife took one look at him and then ran like fury in the opposite direction. While Sir Jasper in his turn tended to jump at sudden noises, and actually hid behind Catherine when a squirrel threw its nuts at him.

Moths, on the other hand, loved Sir Jasper. They came fluttering from everywhere at once to fly round and round him. Perhaps they liked his gentle glow. Either way, Sir Jasper was charmed by them, and even tried putting out a hand for them to land on, but they just dropped right through it. Eventually they all flew away at once, and Sir Jasper watched them go, wistfully, till they were all out of sight.

When the three of them finally emerged from the trees and approached the carriage, the Sombre Warrior turned round sharply, and stopped what he was doing to take a good look at the ghost. Sir Jasper studied the huge warrior in his featureless steel helm with great interest.

"Is there anything in there?" he said.

"Yes," said the Sombre Warrior. He turned to Catherine. "Who is this, your highness? And why can I see through him?"

"Sorry," said Sir Jasper. "I go all transparent when I get nervous. At least I don't leak ectoplasm anymore . . . Hello! Yes. I'm Sir Jasper. I'm a ghost. Why haven't you got a face?"

"Lost it in a poker game," said the Sombre Warrior.

"Oh, that's terrible," said the ghost. "And very unlucky."

"I'll say," said the Sombre Warrior. "I wouldn't have minded, but he only had two pair . . ."

"If you two have quite finished trying to weird me out," said Catherine, in her best *brooking no arguments because I am after all a Princess* voice, "Sir Jasper is with me."

The Sombre Warrior nodded. "He's your pet, your highness. Keep him on a short leash. We're ready to leave when you are."

"Well, really!" said Sir Jasper, but the Sombre Warrior had already turned his back on all of them, to look the carriage over and make sure everything was as it should be. The ghost pouted, hurt. "I am not a pet. I am an aristocrat! Or at least, I'm pretty sure I used to be."

Catherine looked at Lady Gertrude. "I'm sure you have all kinds of objections as to why I can't take Sir Jasper with us to Forest Castle. Let us take it for granted that I have listened to them all carefully and then dismissed them out of hand because I'm Royal and I can do that. He's going with us. I've got to get some fun out of this situation, and Sir Jasper should shake up the Forest Court nicely!"

"Can I just ask . . . ," said Sir Jasper, diffidently. "Neither of you seem particularly bothered by the fact that I'm dead but not departed. Why is that?"

"Castle Midnight was famous for its many ghosts, back in the day," said Catherine. "But they'd all disappeared by the time I came along. I read all the stories, listened to all the songs, including the really old ones you used to sing to me when I was still small, Lady Gertrude . . . and as soon as I was old enough to get about on my own I used to go wandering through all the darker corridors, in the early hours of the morning, searching for ghosts and spirits and anything that looked like it might go bump in the night if you prodded it hard enough."

"That's right, you did, you little . . . poppet," said Gertrude. "Just a small slip of a thing, and already you knew your own mind. You never found anything, but it didn't stop you looking. We had to lock you in your bedroom at night, just to make sure you got your proper sleep. Oh, the kicking you used to give that door . . ."

"I spent a lot of time confined to my rooms, as a child," said Catherine. "For one misdemeanour or another. Until I got old enough to charm one of my guards into teaching me how to pick a lock; after that there was no stopping me. I've always had problems with authority figures. Even though I am one." She stopped, and frowned. "Or at least I used to be. If I had any real power, I wouldn't be here. On my way to an arranged marriage with a man I haven't even met. I'll bet he's short and fat and eats biscuits in bed."

"Crumbs," said Sir Jasper. It was the best he could manage at short notice.

They arrived at Forest Castle by early evening. The Royal carriage, with Princess Catherine, Lady Gertrude, and Sir Jasper inside it, and the Sombre Warrior out in front on his great black charger. The six soldiers surrounded the carriage, sticking close and keeping their eyes open. The driver was back in his place. The Sombre Warrior had tracked him down after he ran away, and drove him back with harsh language and entirely convincing threats.

They'd made good time, and arrived with almost an hour of daylight to spare. Only to find that the drawbridge wasn't down, so they had no way of crossing the moat. Everyone took a good look at the Forest Castle. Catherine and Gertrude leaned halfway out of the open windows of the carriage, while Sir Jasper just stood up and stuck his head through the carriage roof. And for a while none of them said anything.

"I didn't know . . . ," said Catherine. "I didn't realise, I had no idea . . . It's so big! Much bigger than Castle Midnight!"

"This isn't a castle," said Gertrude. "This is a town in its own right! Maybe even a city. The outer wall goes on for miles, and look at all the towers and stonework and . . . We should have been told. We should have been warned . . ."

"Buck up!" said the Sombre Warrior. "You can't afford to show weakness in the face of the enemy. Especially if you're marrying one of them.

Size isn't everything. Look at the state of the outer wall. Cracked and pitted stone, moss and ivy everywhere . . ."

"Yes," said Catherine immediately, feeling just a bit relieved. "My father would never let Castle Midnight get into such a state."

"And one day, all of this will be yours," said Gertrude. "Maybe you could have it painted a more pleasant colour . . ."

Sir Jasper sank back down into the carriage, and hovered just above the seat next to Catherine. He looked thoughtful.

Catherine pulled her head back in the window, started to say something, and then looked at the ghost. "Are you remembering something, Sir Jasper?"

"Perhaps," said the ghost. "I think . . . No, I'm sure. I have been here before. When I was still alive."

"I suppose you must have," said Gertrude, "if you really were a knight of the realm. A knight serves his King."

"Yes," said Sir Jasper. "But which King? How long have I been gone . . . ?"

The Sombre Warrior had been bellowing at the empty battlements for some time, and finally managed to attract the attention of a lone guard. Who looked down from the lofty height, recognised the Royal crest of Redhart on the side of the carriage, and immediately had a loud and very satisfying fit of the vapours. He disappeared from the crenellated battlements, shouting loudly for help and assistance.

Sir Jasper walked through the side of the carriage and strode out across the moat. His feet made no impression on the surface of the water. Not even a single ripple. He stopped abruptly, halfway across, and peered down into the dark and murky waters.

"Is there anything living in the moat, guarding the Castle?" said Catherine, popping her head out the window again. "I seem to recall reading something about crocodiles . . ."

"I don't see anything," the ghost said dubiously. "Just a few pike and carp hardly big enough to be worth getting your rod out."

While he was still speaking, the huge drawbridge came crashing down. It hit Sir Jasper right on the top of his gently glowing head without harming him in the least, passed through his body, and slammed into place across the moat. Leaving Sir Jasper standing, confused but unaffected, on top of the drawbridge. The Forest Castle Seneschal came hurrying forward, with as many people as he'd been able to gather together on such short notice, to form a guard of honour. Sir Jasper took one look at all the people running straight at him, disappeared immediately, and reappeared back at the carriage. Catherine and Gertrude were already getting out, so he went and hid behind them. The Seneschal crashed to a halt at the very edge of the drawbridge, found he was too out of breath to say anything, and bought himself some time by bowing formally to everyone in front of him.

"Profuse apologies, Princess Catherine!" he said finally. "We only received word you'd arrived in the Forest a few hours ago! We did send an honour guard to meet you and escort you safely here, but since we only had a rough idea of where you were . . . It would appear we missed each other." He smiled weakly, spread his arms in a *these things happen* sort of way, and swallowed hard. "King Rufus and Prince Richard are on their way, I'm sure . . . Do come in, please! We have been expecting you, all appearances to the contrary. Your rooms are prepared."

So they all went inside. The Seneschal led the way, with Princess Catherine and Lady Gertrude strolling regally along on either side of him. Sir Jasper brought up the rear, staring at everything with great interest. The Seneschal had shot several looks in his direction but wasn't feeling confident enough to ask any questions as yet. The Sombre Warrior swung down from his great horse and walked behind them, followed by the Royal carriage and the six soldiers. The Seneschal led the titled guests into the Castle, leaving the Sombre Warrior to see that his men were found room in the barracks, and then to ensure that the horses were properly cared for in the stables.

The Seneschal led his honoured guests into the Castle entrance hall, looked quickly about him, saw there was still no sign of the King or the Prince, and thought quickly. He bowed formally to the Princess again.

"Would you mind awfully just . . . waiting a while, in this reception chamber, just for a few moments, while I go and see what's keeping everyone?"

Catherine gave him her best regal nod, and the Seneschal practically broke in two from bowing repeatedly as he led them to a side door. The room he showed them into clearly wasn't a formal reception chamber, just a side room, but it seemed comfortable enough, so no one said anything. Catherine and Gertrude and Sir Jasper looked about them in an ostentatiously unimpressed way, and the Seneschal shut the door quickly and hurried off.

Catherine stood in the centre of the room, arms folded, not deigning to sit. The room was actually quite a bit larger than she was used to. In Castle Midnight it would have passed for a suite all on its own. It did seem comfortable enough, though all the fittings and furnishings were very old-fashioned, to her taste. The portraits on the walls were in a whole mixture of clashing styles, from the painfully realistic to the exceedingly stylized, and Catherine scowled as she was reminded of the stylised portrait of Prince Richard that she'd been shown before. She still had no idea of what the man really looked like. It occurred to her she was finally about to meet the man she'd come all this way to marry, and a cold chill settled in her stomach. She wanted to just leave, walk out, and . . . go home. But she knew she couldn't. No way back, no way out. She took a deep breath, squared her shoulders, and glared at Lady Gertrude.

"Prince Richard had better turn up soon! But I am warning you: if he's got a single wart, or is even slightly hunchbacked, this marriage is off!"

"You can be very trying sometimes, my pet," said Gertrude. "Of course he hasn't got any of those things!"

"You haven't met him," said Catherine. "He might have."

"I would have been told," said Gertrude.

Catherine gave her a hard look. "You mean, *we* would have been told."

"Of course, my poppet."

They didn't know Richard was watching them through the half-open door. Richard had had an idea. If any of his friends or advisors had been around, and had known this, they would have trampled all over one another in their rush to talk him out of it. Whatever it was. Which was why he hadn't told any of them; he was determined not to be talked out of it. Richard had dressed himself up as a servant, in particularly scruffy and even unclean clothing, and topped it off with a marvellously ratty false beard. His idea was that if Catherine was met by a rude enough servant, her pride would be outraged, and she would take umbrage and stalk out of the Castle and insist on being taken home again. And then the marriage would be off, and no one could put any blame on him. The Prince was very fond of romantic adventure novels, in which this kind of thing happened all the time. He paused a moment to practice his slouch in front of a handy mirror. He looked awful. He dropped his reflection a sly wink and then slammed the door all the way open and swaggered into the room.

"Hello!" he said aggressively. "Who might you be?"

"I am Catherine, of Redhart," said the Princess. "And this is my companion, Lady Gertrude."

"We all have our troubles," said Richard. "Who is the gentleman in the nightie?"

"Don't mind him," said Catherine. "He's a ghost."

Richard looked sharply at Sir Jasper, who smiled affably back. The ghost had lowered his glow as much as he could, but there was still no way he was going to pass for normal. Or even mortal.

"Well," said Richard, in his best practiced obnoxious tone, "I don't know about this . . . No one said anything to me. I can't let you just go wandering about the Castle; you could be anyone! Do you have any form of identification?"

"I am expected!" said Catherine crushingly.

Richard sniffed loudly. "Oh, they all say that. I'll have to see some proof you are who you claim to be. Can you show me a birthmark? Scars? How about a tattoo?" He grinned nastily and threw in a full-on leer, just for good measure.

"*This is intolerable!*" said Catherine, going straight to full volume. "I travel all this way to get here, and now they don't want to let me in? That's it! The marriage is off! I will not be talked to like this! Come, Lady Gertrude, we shall return to our carriage and show our backs to this whole sorry excuse for a Kingdom!"

"No, no, my sweet, my poppet, my Princess!" said Gertrude, placing herself bodily between Catherine and the door. "You can't judge a Castle by one rude servant! Remember how important this marriage is!"

Catherine glowered at the disguised Prince, who was now chewing at his false beard and scratching himself in an unpleasant way.

"All right," she growled. "I'll stay. For honour, and duty, and all that stuff. But no more nonsense about identification!"

"Of course, of course, my poppet," said Gertrude. She let the disguised Prince have the full force of her glare. "You! Fellow! Here is the official invitation from King Rufus, approved by your House of Parliament, calling us to the Forest Castle for the Royal wedding!"

Richard took the heavy parchment, unfolded it, glanced at all the many official phrases and the attached crimson wax seals, and tossed it casually over his shoulder. "Seems to be in order. You'll have to register, though."

He took down a large volume from the bookshelves, opened it, and blew dust all over the Princess. She coughed and sneezed loudly.

"Nasty cold you've got there," Richard observed brightly.

Catherine brushed dusty tears from her eyes. "Let me at him! I'll brain him!"

Gertrude grabbed her firmly by the arm. "Well-bred young ladies do not brain people!"

"All right," said Catherine. "You do it."

Gertrude let that one pass. She carefully released Catherine's arm, waited a moment to be sure nothing violent or diplomatically unforgivable would occur, and then glared at Richard. "Listen, fellow! I am Lady-in-Waiting to the Princess Catherine."

"Really?" said Richard. "What are you waiting for? Though I think I could probably guess. Left it a bit late, haven't you?"

"Look here!" said Gertrude.

"Where?" said Richard, peering about him excitedly.

Lady Gertrude hung on to her self-control with an heroic effort, turned her back on the disguised Prince, and glared at Sir Jasper.

"You talk to him, sir ghost! Give him the full force of your personality. He deserves it."

Sir Jasper ambled forward, happy to be of service, and he and the Prince studied each other with great interest.

"And . . . who or what might you be?" said Richard.

"I'm Sir Jasper. I'm a ghost."

"Been one long?" said Richard.

"Who knows?" said Sir Jasper.

"I thought ghosts only came out at night," said Richard, with the air of one laying down a winning card.

"I never did have much sense of time," said Sir Jasper. "I'm always late."

"Late?"

"Of course. I'm the late Sir Jasper."

"I walked right into that one, didn't I?" said Richard. "Age?"

"Uncertain."

"Occupation?"

"Unearthly."

"I think I lost that one on points," said Richard.

"Anything else you want to ask me?" said Sir Jasper.

"Is it worth it?"

"Not really."

"Then I think I'd like to speak to the Princess again, please," said Richard. "If only because your entire existence makes my head ache."

"Just doing my job," said Sir Jasper.

Catherine came reluctantly forward again, to take Sir Jasper's place. The script Richard had worked out in his head, full of fine insults and put-downs, had clearly gone right out the window, but as he couldn't see any way of retreating with honour, he carried on.

"I'll have to have your particulars, Princess," he said.

"If you like," Catherine said sweetly. "But I doubt they'll fit you."

And for a moment they actually smiled at each other.

And that was when the Seneschal came bustling in, apologising profusely for keeping the Princess and her party waiting, and declaring that her personal chambers were quite definitely ready and waiting for her, if she would just care to follow him. And all the way through this, the Seneschal kept shooting brief glances at the disguised Prince. He clearly considered saying something, and then decided against it, on the grounds that whatever question he asked, the answer was unlikely to be anything he wanted to hear. He stopped speaking before he descended into babbling, and bowed formally to Princess Catherine and Lady Gertrude.

"Welcome to the Forest Kingdom. I'm sure you'll enjoy your stay with us."

"Don't put money on it," said Catherine.

She started out the open door, and the Seneschal and Lady Gertrude had to sprint after her to keep up. Sir Jasper ambled off after them, then stopped at the door and glanced back, just in time to see Prince Richard peel off his false beard and scratch at his itchy chin.

"Now that is a good trick!" said Sir Jasper. "I used to be able to take my whole head off . . ."

"*Sir Jasper!*" said a strident Princessy voice from outside. The ghost shrugged at the Prince and walked through the door, which had swung shut while he was talking. Prince Richard considered the closed door.

"Well, that didn't go as intended, in any number of ways. So that's Catherine . . . beautiful, intelligent, doesn't take any nonsense from anyone. Not at all what I was expecting. It's not often I find someone who can keep up with me. I . . . don't dislike her. Still not going to marry her, though. Just on general principles. I did like her ghost; it seems some of the old stories about Castle Midnight are true after all." He grinned suddenly. "She must have made an impression on me. She's got me talking to myself."

The Seneschal hadn't led his distinguished guests far into the Castle before the First Minister and the Leader of the Loyal Opposition turned up, hurrying forward to greet their Royal guest with many bowed heads and formal smiles. Word had reached them of raised voices, and even a threat to leave, and they were both ready to say or do, or at the very least promise to do, whatever it took to persuade the Princess to stay. The Seneschal introduced Peregrine de Woodville and Henry Wallace to Catherine and Gertrude, but his nerve failed him when it came to Sir Jasper, so he introduced them to Catherine twice. The politicians were so intent on making a good impression on the Princess that they completely overlooked the ghost.

"Yes, I did consider leaving," Catherine said flatly, speaking right over the First Minister's flowery words. "Given the way I was treated by that . . . awful servant. But I have been persuaded that it is my duty to stay. Do not give me cause to reconsider. Because I feel it is also my duty to make it very clear that not even the whole Forest Army could stop me if I should decide to return home!"

"Of course, of course," said Peregrine, smiling till his cheeks ached, and quietly contemplating the quickest way of sneaking a powerful sedative into her food. "I assure you, the servant in question will be found and disciplined, and every effort will be made to make you welcome and comfortable in Forest Castle. And look, here comes Prince Richard himself, to bid you welcome. At last . . ."

It was a sign of how thrown the First Minister was that he actually saw Prince Richard's arrival as a good thing. Henry Wallace readied himself to jump in and if need be talk right over the Prince if he said anything unsuitable. But Richard was now dressed in his best formal attire (having used a side route to get ahead of them), and he smiled graciously as he addressed Catherine and her party. He was warm and courteous and polite, every inch the welcoming host. He bowed low to Catherine and Gertrude, and nodded cheerfully to Sir Jasper.

Catherine's scowl slowly smoothed out, as she got her first look at her intended. Richard was tall and handsome, gracious and stately, and seemed to know how to address a Princess properly. Which was . . . something. It never even occurred to Catherine to associate the polite Prince with the very rude servant. Why should it? Princes disguised themselves as the lower orders only in bad romantic novels.

Lady Gertrude wasn't so sure, but she didn't want to make a fuss and cause a scene, just when everything was seemingly going so well. So she held her peace and went along. And everyone else was just relieved that Richard and Catherine were actually talking to each other instead of throwing things. Sir Jasper recognised Richard immediately, and smiled and waved cheerfully at him. Richard pretended not to notice. Peregrine and Henry had only just realised there was a third person in the Redhart party, and considered Sir Jasper with growing alarm. Finally Peregrine put his hand up, like a child in a classroom, to get the Princess' attention.

"Excuse me, Princess Catherine, but . . ."

"Yes, he's a ghost," said Catherine. "And he's with me. Want to make something of it?"

"Oh no, no, your highness," said Peregrine. "I suppose every country has its own customs . . ."

"Even if no one thought to mention them to us," murmured Henry.

"Oh, I'm not from Redhart!" said Sir Jasper. "I'm bred and dead in the Forest Land, man and ghost. In fact, I'm almost sure I was a knight of the realm. And I have been to this Castle before . . . Yes. Very definitely. So much looks familiar . . ."

Peregrine looked at Catherine. "He's not thinking of moving in, is he?"

"He's with me," said Catherine. "Until I say otherwise."

What could have been a very awkward moment was fortunately defused by the arrival of the Sombre Warrior. He'd changed out of his armour and replaced the steel helm with the famous chalk white porcelain mask. He bowed formally, if stiffly, to Peregrine and Henry, and a little more deeply to Prince Richard.

"The ghost is part of our official retinue," he said. "Didn't you get the note?"

Peregrine and Henry gave up, and nodded formally to Sir Jasper, who didn't even notice because he'd got bored with the whole proceeding and was concentrating on turning his glow up and down. Richard offered Catherine his arm.

"May I have the honour of escorting your highness to her prepared chambers?"

And Catherine surprised everyone, including herself, by slipping her arm through his and allowing him to lead her away. The Seneschal and Lady Gertrude followed after the two young people with silent sighs of relief, and even exchanged an understanding glance as they followed their charges up the main stairway. It's never easy guiding young Royals, especially when the Royals know they don't have to be guided if they don't want to be. The Seneschal moved in beside Gertrude and murmured in her ear.

"She's going to be trouble, isn't she?"

"Oh, you have no idea," said Gertrude.

Sir Jasper and the Sombre Warrior brought up the rear, maintaining a respectful distance from the Royals and each other. Peregrine and Henry watched them all go.

"Did you see that?" said Henry. "The Prince was nice to her! Nice! What the hell is he doing?"

"I think he's trying to confuse us to death," said Peregrine bitterly.

Catherine's iron will softened even further as she took in the extended suite of rooms King Rufus had provided for her and Gertrude. The Seneschal bustled from room to room, showing them where everything was, and pointing out items of special interest, with all the enthusiasm of a hotel porter anticipating a really generous tip. Richard stayed leaning in the main doorway, watching it all with a quiet smile, saying nothing. Every single room was unusually large and luxurious, by Redhart standards, though Catherine was careful not to appear too impressed with anything. The fittings and furnishings were still decidedly old-fashioned, as far as she was concerned. Great chunky wardrobes and chests of drawers, with solid, heavy brass, and none of the delicate style Catherine was used to. Castle Midnight might be old, even ancient, but King William prided himself on keeping up with all the latest styles and fashions.

Gertrude was wild with enthusiasm over absolutely everything, and didn't care who knew it. She oohed and aahed at the size and comfort and sheer opulence of it all, and fluttered from room to room with squeals of joy and much waving of the hands, exclaiming loudly at every new item that caught her eye. She loved the heavy antique pieces of furniture, any one of which would have sold for a king's ransom in Redhart (because King William tended to throw everything out long before it had a chance to become antique). She ran her hands caressingly over the dark lacquered surfaces, and got seriously sensual with some gold fittings.

"Never mind where the carpets came from," Catherine said loudly, breaking across the Seneschal's latest speech. "Does this suite have proper plumbing?"

The Seneschal blushed, just a little, and showed her the very large bathroom, complete with its own hot water boiler and flush toilet. Richard grinned from the doorway.

"Imported all the way from the Southern Kingdoms. We may not be as . . . fashion conscious as Redhart, but we do like to keep up. Were you perhaps afraid you'd have to empty a chamber pot out of a window?"

It was Lady Gertrude's turn to go red in the face. Catherine just laughed.

"You don't have gas lighting, though, do you?"

"We prefer light sources that aren't likely to run out suddenly," said Richard. He shared a quick grin with Catherine. He was genuinely surprised at how well they were getting on. He really wasn't used to people he could talk to as an equal. And then he realised Sir Jasper was standing very still in the middle of the room, his bare feet hovering just above the heavy carpeting, his brow creased in thought.

"Is everything all right, sir ghost?" said Richard politely.

"I don't know this room, this suite," Sir Jasper said slowly. "Nothing here is familiar. I had hoped seeing the inside of the Castle might help restore my lost memories, but . . ."

"It's a big Castle," said Richard tactfully. "Lots and lots of rooms. Even if you'd been here many times before, you wouldn't have seen all of them."

"Yes . . . ," said the ghost. "I think I might go for a little walk, a little wander around, if that's all right . . ."

To everyone's surprise, the usually diffident ghost didn't wait for anyone's permission. He just walked through the nearest wall and was gone. Everyone relaxed just a little. Sir Jasper meant well, but he still wasn't an easy presence to have around.

"You might be used to ghosts as Castle Midnight," said Richard, "but I would have to say, he does take a lot of getting used to."

Catherine and Gertrude exchanged a glance but said nothing.

"Well," said Richard, "I think I'll leave you to get settled in. The Seneschal's people are bringing up your luggage. And of course you won't need to keep the Sombre Warrior outside your door; our guards are your guards now. We'll find the Warrior a room of his own. Just down the corridor. There is to be a Welcoming Banquet later this evening. In your honour. The Seneschal will see that you get plenty of warning."

"Thank you," said Catherine. "You may leave now."

Richard smiled easily. "See you there, Princess." And he left. The Seneschal bowed and bobbed quickly, and hurried after the Prince, closing the door very firmly behind him.

"Well!" said Lady Gertrude, as soon as they were alone. She managed to put quite a lot of meaning into that one word, and threw in a raised eyebrow at no extra charge.

"He seems . . . pleasant enough," said Catherine.

"You positively encouraged him!" said Gertrude.

"Handsome enough, I suppose," said Catherine.

"Handsome is as handsome does," said Gertrude.

"I'm still not marrying him."

"Princess!"

"I know, I know . . . He's no Malcolm. My lovely Malcolm. But things could have been worse. I suppose."

"Oh, they're all smiles and charm *before* the wedding. Wait till he doesn't have to be polite," said Gertrude darkly.

"You're not about to give me a lecture on secrets of the bedroom, are you?" said Catherine. "I know all about sex. Or at least I've read every book I could find on the subject. I could probably teach him a few tricks . . . Why are you looking at me like that?"

One of the small but real pleasures of having so many empty rooms in Forest Castle was that it was always possible to (very quietly) appropriate one of the unused rooms for your own personal purposes. And provided you were (very) careful about it, no one need ever notice. Prince Richard, Peter the soldier, and Clarence the would-be minstrel had set up their very own private drinking den in a room way off the main paths, and spruced it up with all the comforts and luxuries that young men desire. Basically, comfortable chairs and lots of booze. They all felt the need for somewhere private, where they could just be themselves, and say and do all the things they weren't supposed to say and do in public. Somewhere Richard could relax and get totally rat-arsed without having to worry about letting the side down. Peter and Clarence were only too happy to keep their friend company, not least because the Prince had access to some of the finest wines in the world in the Castle cellars. Some of those incredibly dusty bottles had been laid down so long ago that the very maps had changed since then.

The room was simply but comfortably furnished, with all the usual trappings, a lot of them quietly moved over from adjoining rooms. More than enough to lend the place an air of ease and smug satisfaction. None of the three young men ever dusted, or cleaned up anything, as a point of principle. They were young men together, and they had a reputation to live down to. The door was always kept very firmly locked, and since no one knew about the room, they were never bothered by the outside world. The perfect place for the three of them to avoid their duties and responsibilities, forget about all the things they should be doing, and just put their feet up. Peter hustled all kinds of good food up out of the kitchens, because one of the under-cooks fancied him, and Clarence would bring his guitar and sing rousing songs of quite extraordinary rudeness. He had a pretty good singing voice, and a masterful touch on the guitar. As long as he stuck to the traditional songs he was fine, and if he did occasionally try out one of his original compositions on Richard and Peter . . . well, that's what friends are for.

"So," said Peter, already halfway through his first bottle, slumped down in his chair with his legs stretched out. "Princess Catherine . . . What do you think, Richard?"

"She's definitely a looker," said Richard, pouring himself another glass with a steady hand. "Strong character, too. I could have done worse, I suppose."

"He likes her!" said Clarence, giggling. He was drinking a magnificent vintage straight from the bottle, in the mistaken belief that it made him appear more manly. He always sat up very straight in his chair, but with one leg flung over the arm, to show how informal he was being.

"Just as well," said Peter.

"Even so," said Richard firmly, "I am not marrying her."

"Be strong," Peter said briskly. "No way back. Got to be done. Do you like her?"

"I don't know!" said Richard. "Maybe."

"Courtly love is supposed to be one of the most refined emotions," Clarence began, and then stopped as the others hooted at him.

"Don't you start," Peter said darkly. "If war ballads are as wrong about war as love ballads are about love . . ."

"Songs about the joys of wine and carousing are usually pretty damned accurate," said Richard.

"True," said Clarence. "You can't beat a good carouse. Are there any of those little sausages left?"

"You do know they're made from horse's ring-pieces?" said Peter.

"I only met her for a short while," said Richard, oblivious. "Can't say I know her at all. For all I know she eats garlic with every meal, doesn't bathe nearly often enough, and is always bright and cheerful first thing in the morning. I can't stand people like that. The number of servants I went through, to find a few that were properly surly and gloomy first thing, like me. Breakfast is a meal that should only ever be eaten in silence. There ought to be a law; and when I become King there almost certainly will be."

"Oh, how you've suffered!" said Peter. "Servants to make your breakfast, and cut your toast into little slices. Probably follow you into the bathroom and shake the last few drops off for you."

"I can't believe you really went for the bearded-servant routine," said Clarence. "And if I've heard the story, you can bet the Princess will hear. You've been reading too many novels, Richard."

"Has she realised yet?" said Peter.

"Don't think so," said Richard.

Peter nodded approvingly. "Dumb blonde. With a title. And money of her own. Best kind . . ."

"Someone's bound to tell her," said Clarence. "You know how servants love to gossip."

"Someone change the subject," said Richard. "No? All right then, I'll change the subject. Have any of you met the dreaded Sombre Warrior yet? I have. He's big—and I mean really big. And he's the real deal, you know. Not a story or a legend; just a bloody big soldier who's killed so many people he's probably lost count."

"I bumped into him. Briefly," said Peter. "Impressive. Definitely impressive. Looks like he could punch a horse through a wall, if the mood took him. And there's something about that creepy white mask that gives me the shudders."

"You have to wonder," said Clarence, "just what there is under that mask. Or what's left, to put it more succinctly. I mean, how bad can it be? That no one ever gets to have a look at it? We've all seen soldiers back from the wars. With scars, without eyes or ears . . ."

"They say his face was cut apart, and then set fire to," said Peter. "Who would do something like that? We all saw all kinds of blood and gore out on the border, but it was all just . . . fighting. And it's supposedly men from our side that did it; but we never saw any of that kind of thing!"

"There's always someone . . . ," said Clarence darkly.

"Had to be personal," said Richard. "Some kind of revenge attack."

"The way he speaks," Peter said slowly. "There's something not quite right about it. Too flat, too certain, even to have an accent. And sometimes it sounds mushy, distorted . . . could part of his mouth be missing? Or even burned right back to the teeth?"

"Stop it!" said Clarence, very firmly. "You are getting ghoulish now, and putting me off my drink. Which is an insult to a really good vintage."

"Why send him here?" said Richard, suddenly thoughtful. "Why send one of Redhart's greatest and most honoured soldiers into permanent exile, as the Princess' escort and bodyguard? He's a soldier, not a diplomat . . . Did he do something, say something, to King William? Or did they just think his best fighting days were over, and this was some kind of reward? A cushy retirement?"

"Hardly," said Peter. "Being her bodyguard will be a full-time job. You did hear about the attack on her carriage on the way here? Can you believe that? An open attack, by Redhart forces, on Forest territory! Still, the Sombre Warrior did well enough, by all accounts. The old killing skills are still there."

"Pity he killed all of the attackers, though," said Richard slowly. "Who knows what they might have been persuaded to say about their masters?"

"Yes," said Peter. "A pity he couldn't manage even a single prisoner . . ."

Richard and Peter looked at each other.

"The Princess is going to need a really good bodyguard," said Clarence, just a bit owlishly. "And so will you, Richard. Be grateful you've got us."

"Oh, I am," said Richard. "Really. You have no idea."

"I want to know what's under that mask," said Peter. "You know, we could always . . ."

"No, we couldn't," said Richard.

"Or we could . . . ," said Clarence.

"No, we couldn't," said Richard very firmly. "You leave that man alone. One, because he'd kill you. And two, because he's suffered enough. He has a right to keep his dignity. That's an order, mind. Royal decree."

Peter and Clarence both hooted him sarcastically, but Richard knew they'd follow his orders on this. He didn't pull rank often, but when he did, his friends knew he meant it. Richard liked to be able to put aside his title in their company, but they all knew there were times when he couldn't. Not that they ever discussed it, of course. It was just understood. Some things had to remain unsaid, if they were to be friends.

They sat together, easy in one another's company, eating, drinking, thinking. And Richard wondered why he hadn't told Peter and Clarence about his encounter with the Lady of the Lake. It was odd. He usually told them everything. But not this time . . . He didn't know why. He could trust them. He'd trusted them with so many other things . . . But he hadn't even mentioned the Lady of the Lake to the Seneschal, or to his father, the King. And they had a right to know, if anyone did. But he hadn't talked about it to anyone, because . . . it was his. His moment with a story and a legend and a Power in the Land. And some secrets . . . should stay secret.

The Sombre Warrior sat in the single stiff-backed chair provided and looked about the room they'd given him. Not a suite, but still a large and reasonably comfortable room of his own. Just down the corridor from the Princess. Better accommodations than his men, who were having to bunk down in the Castle barracks, with the other guards. The Sombre Warrior hoped there wouldn't be any unpleasantness towards his men, just for coming from Redhart—because his men could be exceedingly unpleasant if provoked. He rather wished he could be there, with his men, to share the easy banter and camaraderie of soldiers together, but he knew that wasn't possible. For many reasons, of which the mask was only one.

The room he'd been given was actually a good deal larger and more comfortable than the one he was used to back at Castle Midnight. A big bed with a deep mattress, a window with a proper view, and his very own piss pot to empty out of it. Luxury. Still, if there was one thing Forest Castle had, it was room. Room to lounge around, and stretch out in.

He'd already unpacked his belongings. It hadn't taken him long. First rule of a soldier: travel light and travel fast. And there hadn't been much he wanted to bring with him. His various weapons and pieces of armour lay scattered around the room, all within easy reach. So that even at his most relaxed, he was never far from steel. He had no treasures, no mementos, because the Sombre Warrior had no past. He levered himself up out of his chair and went to stand before the single gilt-edged mirror hanging on the wall. He looked into it, and the porcelain mask looked back. Cold and unyielding, like a presentiment of death. The false face he'd worn for so very long now.

There was a sudden heaviness to the air, a feeling of something approaching, and then the chalk white mask disappeared from the mirror, as the Sombre Warrior's reflection was replaced by an entirely different face. Peregrine de Woodville, First Minister of the Forest Land, stared coldly out of the glass. The Sombre Warrior nodded, briefly. He'd been expecting his secret spy master to make contact ever since he'd arrived. They'd always talked to each other through mirrors; it meant no one else could listen in. Or so the Sombre Warrior had always been assured. He'd never cared to understand the workings of magic.

"Do it," Peregrine said bluntly. "Take it off. I need to be sure it's really you under the mask."

The Sombre Warrior raised both hands to either side of the chalk white porcelain, carefully undid the leather straps, and removed the mask. To reveal a face entirely untouched by any kind of damage. A little paler than most, perhaps, but really only another ordinary, everyday soldier's face. The Sombre Warrior was just a story, a mask to hide behind, for the First Minister's most secret spy inside Redhart. He never was a Redhart soldier, just a Forest soldier who seized an opportunity. He covered his face, claimed to be a loyal son of Redhart come back from the wars horribly disfigured . . . and everyone just took him at his word. He'd been feeding the First Minister inside information on Redhart for years. Peregrine nodded briefly.

"You're sure your identity remains unchallenged? No one suspects?"

"I had to kill a few young fools the other day who plotted to remove my mask," said the Sombre Warrior. "There's always someone . . . I wasn't even challenged over the killings. Everyone at Redhart has been very understanding. They weren't bad sorts, just young sparks acting on a dare. But I had to kill them to warn off the others. I don't know why it bothers me. I have done far worse things in your name, down the years."

"I saved you from the gallows to be my man," Peregrine said flatly. "You damned your soul long before you met me. I own you. I know your past, and your secrets, and I hold your life in my hands. Don't you ever forget that. You'll do what I tell you to do, betray who I tell you to, and kill who I tell you to. And let us not forget, you have been very well paid for your secret services."

"Of course," said the Sombre Warrior. "Maybe I'll finally get to spend some of it, now I'm home again."

"You volunteered for this!"

"So I did. I was so much more afraid of death, then. How much longer do I have to wear this mask? How long before I can put it down and leave the Sombre Warrior behind, and be myself again?"

"You're mine for as long as I need you. I didn't pull all those strings to get you attached to the Princess Catherine as her bodyguard just so you could come home. You can still be useful to me."

"Of course," said the Sombre Warrior. "Your orders, First Minister?"

"You must keep the Princess alive and unharmed, at all costs. At least until after the wedding. We only really need a marriage ceremony to get the Peace agreement signed. Catherine herself may yet prove to be an encumbrance."

"The Princess has enemies here, inside the Castle?"

"Of course. From the Forest, and from Redhart. Keep your eyes open. Trust no one."

"I wouldn't know how," said the Sombre Warrior.

The First Minister looked at him sharply, and then turned away, his face disappearing from the mirror. To be replaced, almost immediately, by a second, different face, a second spy master. King William of Redhart stared grimly out of the glass, nodding abruptly to the Sombre Warrior's bare face. And like the First Minister before him, King William showed no surprise at what he saw.

"I'll keep this short," said the King. "My sorcerer Van Fleet doesn't know how long he can keep this line of communication open. Have you made contact with the First Minister?"

"Yes," said the Sombre Warrior. "He still thinks I'm his man. He has no suspicion that I serve you, my King, and that he only knows those secrets you want him to know. He really should have understood: live in a country long enough and you learn to love it. And you have been a very generous master, Sire."

"I have other agents inside Forest Castle," said King William. "Some a lot closer than you think. I've arranged for some of them to make themselves known to you. They will identify themselves with the phrase *red meat is good meat.*"

"Just once I'd like a code phrase that might actually crop up in real conversation," said the Sombre Warrior. "Aren't you going to ask if your daughter reached the Castle safely?"

"You would have said, if there'd been any real problems," said the King. And his face vanished from the mirror.

The Sombre Warrior stood there for a while, studying his own face, and then he smiled slowly. "I didn't come back here to serve you, William. Or Peregrine de Woodville. I am only here to take care of my own unfinished business." He put the chalk white mask back on and tightened the leather straps, and then he looked at himself again. "Whose man am I? I am my own man, now and always."

Sir Jasper the ghost went wandering through the wide stone corridors of Forest Castle. Catherine and Gertrude were busy preparing for their appearance at the Welcome Banquet. He didn't need anyone to tell him that; he just knew. He supposed he could have gone along with them, if he'd wanted, but he didn't do that sort of thing anymore. He didn't eat or drink, though he sort of remembered what that was like. He couldn't smell the smoke from the flaring torches he passed, or feel the cold stones under his feet. He felt more solid, more real, than he had in a long time, but his physical presence tended to come and go according to how much he concentrated. And how much he cared.

He was the memory of a man, not the man himself, and he forgot that at his peril.

He walked up and down the corridors, studying everything with great interest. Some things pleased him, and some disturbed him; and now and again some small thing would seem to tug at a long-buried memory . . . but none of it held any real significance. Nothing meant anything; nothing mattered. So on he went, up the corridors and through the chambers, along the empty stone galleries, looking at the portraits on the walls with only vague interest. On the few occasions when he seemed about to encounter actual people, he turned invisible so he wouldn't have to talk to them. Partly because he was preoccupied with his own business, but mostly because he was shy. He hadn't been around people for such a long time . . . He didn't know what to say to them. And then he stopped, abruptly, before one particular old portrait hanging in an alcove. Very old and faded, with cracking paint, but the face was still clear and distinct. Sir Jasper looked at it for a long time.

"I know you," he said finally. "King Eduard, who loved the fearsome Night Witch. But why do I know you? Did I serve you while I was still alive? And if so, why don't I remember, now I'm back? Did I do something . . . bad? So bad, I had to make myself forget everything?"

The face in the portrait stared silently back. It had no answer for him. Sir Jasper nodded slowly and walked on, a small and lonely ghost in a large and empty Castle.

The huge ceremonial Banquet of Welcome took place in the Great Hall. Everyone who was anybody, or thought they were, or that they ought to be, had fought and bullied and spread a lot of money around to be sure they got invitations to attend the banquet. Because this was the social gathering that everyone would be talking about for years. The first appearance of Redhart Royalty for an arranged marriage! And quite possibly the last—though no one was saying that out loud. A great many people were already placing substantial wagers on how long the marriage would last, or even if it would take place at all.

The Great Hall was full of tables, standing in long rows the whole length of the space, packed from wall to wall, from the entrance doors to the dais at the far end, where the King and his family and guests would be seated. In fact, those at the doors would have to stand on their chairs and peer through a telescope just to make out who was sitting at the King's table. Every table was covered with a cloth of gleaming white samite, and set with all the best dinner services, and the most delicate cutlery, all of it cleaned and polished to within an inch of its life. Everything had to be just so, for an occasion such as this. (Although with so many people present, the Seneschal had run out of the good service and the best cutlery, and had been forced to make up the difference with whatever he could scrounge from abandoned rooms in the rest of the Castle. He dumped the poorer items on the tables by the doors and hoped no one would notice—or at least no one who mattered.) The candles had all been removed from the chandeliers overhead, to avoid the possibility of wax dripping down on the honoured guests. The chandeliers were now stuffed with foxfire moss, which produced a gentler light but was much more dependable. And less drippy.

It took more than an hour simply to get everyone seated, while whole armies of servants bustled back and forth, bearing massive platters of food, endless glasses of wine, and anything else a guest might care to ask for. And since it was all free, some of the guests were taking advantage. (Once again, the Seneschal had run out of real servants, and had press-ganged soldiers, cooks, grooms, and anyone else who didn't run away fast enough. It meant that some of the servants' manners were a bit on the rough side, but as long as they had two legs and were breathing, that was enough for the Seneschal.)

A small orchestra crammed into a far corner played rousing patriotic airs, heavier on the strings than the more usual brass, so the guests could still hear themselves talk. Flags and banners fluttered the length of the hall, hanging from the ceilings and the chandeliers and anything else that would support their weight. And armed guards, in full dress armour, with not at all ceremonial weapons at their sides, stood to attention all along the walls. Saying nothing but watching everything and everyone with cool professional eyes, ready for action at a moment's notice. After the attack on Princess Catherine's carriage, no one was taking any chances.

One guest decided it would be amusing to make the guards jump by popping a champagne cork at them. After what happened to him, everyone left the guards strictly alone.

King Rufus sat at the very centre of the head table, arrayed in his finest robes, with his crown set squarely on his head. He looked fine and wise and noble, as long as he didn't actually talk to anyone. He knew how important the banquet was, and was on his best behaviour; but his attention did tend to wander. The Seneschal hovered constantly at the King's side, standing to attention in his best ceremonial regalia, making sure Rufus ate his food in the correct order, and with the proper utensils. Mostly the King went along, but occasionally his basic stubbornness would kick in and he'd slap the Seneschal's helping hand aside.

"I am not eating my nice boiled potatoes! Hate boiled potatoes! Who the hell thought they were suitable for a banquet? Take them away and mash them up and drown them in the good gravy. And what is *that*? I am not touching that until someone can tell me what it is!"

The Seneschal gestured for the offending boiled potatoes to be taken away, and then leaned in close. "That, Sire, is bread-and-marrowbone-jelly pudding. You like it. It's good for you."

"If it's that good, you eat it," said the King cunningly.

Princess Catherine was seated at his right hand, dressed in her most opulent attire, hearing every word and pretending not to. She'd been briefed on King Rufus before she left Redhart. One of the first things Royalty learns about appearing in public is how to notice only those things that are officially approved. Prince Richard was seated on her other side, also magnificently dressed, and doing his best to keep her entertained with charming conversation. Something else Royalty are taught from an early age, till they can practically do it in their sleep. But since all Catherine would do in response was nod and smile, and address herself to the food before her, Prince Richard was finding it all rather hard going.

The Sombre Warrior was seated at the King's left hand, because he refused point-blank to be seated any farther away from the Princess. He didn't eat, or drink. Or talk much, for that matter. He just sat there, in full ceremonial armour, watching the banquet from behind his porcelain mask, perfectly still, like a cat at a mouse hole. People kept sending over various exotic dishes and tempting titbits, in the hope that they might tempt him into lifting his mask, just for a moment; but he declined them all. One wag sent over a bottle of champagne and a paper straw, and the Sombre Warrior wouldn't even look at it.

Seated beside him was Lady Gertrude, in a party dress that was as fashionable as she could manage, given that it was all in black, because she was still in mourning for her lost love. She ate and drank everything put before her with a healthy appetite. Sitting beside her was the First Minister, Peregrine de Woodville, who did his best to pry some useful information out of her concerning matters at Redhart Court. Gertrude happily fed him complete nonsense, and hoped he choked on it. She wiped her plate clean with a piece of bread, then called for a second helping. Gertrude did like her food.

Every now and again, Rufus would remember his position and try to make pleasant small talk with Catherine. But sometimes he would call her father William, and sometimes Viktor. He had moments when he seemed perfectly sharp, and would discuss the history and politics of their two Lands with insight and clarity, and not a little wit . . . and then he would drift off, in midsentence, and talk about things and people long gone, as though he'd only talked to them yesterday. He was decent, and kind, and Catherine did her best to go along. She was actually a little relieved he was nowhere near as bad as she'd been told to expect.

It helped that there was a lot of really excellent food, everything from whole roasted swan stuffed with corn and apple and walnut, to something called a telescope, in which several kinds of birds were stuffed one inside the other and then cooked together. Catherine was quietly impressed by it all, in spite of herself. In fact, though she was loath to admit it, she was having quite a good time. Banquets at her father's Court tended to be formal, solemn affairs. And some of the wines brought up from the Castle cellars were so old they actually dated from a time when the Forest Land, Hillsdown, and Redhart had all been part of the same nation. Catherine had to wonder whether that was deliberate, and even symbolic.

There were many loyal toasts as the evening progressed, and it seemed everyone present wanted to stand up and say a few encouraging words to the young Royal couple. Catherine and Richard would just smile and nod, and lift their glasses without actually drinking from them, because other-wise they would have been blotto before the desserts. Until finally one half-drunk minor aristocrat lurched to his feet, and the whole hall fell suddenly quiet. And not in a good way. People looked determinedly at their food, or at one another in a *Now what do we do?* sort of way. Catherine looked quickly about her, and turned to Richard.

"Who is that?"

"That," said Richard, "is Lord Adrian Leverett, and a pain in the arse. We invited him because we had to, but we were rather hoping he'd have the good sense and common decency not to turn up. Bit of a loose cannon, the Leverett. But he has a right to be here. He spent many years fighting in the border skirmishes, won distinctions in several major battles. There are even a few popular songs about him, if you like them fierce and brutal."

Lord Leverett was a man in his late forties who looked ten years older. He was wearing old-fashioned formal clothes, and looked hard worn and worn down. He stood tall, if a trifle unsteady, with food and wine stains down his front, and glared stubbornly about him. When no one would meet his eye, he turned his glare on King Rufus, who stared impassively back. Catherine slowly realised that though most of those present were sincerely embarrassed by the man, there were some who were quietly nodding, in anticipation of what he was about to say.

"Do I really have to remind everyone?" Leverett said loudly. "My brother Thomas died eight years ago, in a border skirmish. Died, fighting for his country, protecting the Land he loved from invading forces! Are we really going to go through with this nonsense? This *treason*? Throw away the moral high ground, give up our ancient Forest territory, for a dishonourable Peace?" He looked around him, as though genuinely expecting an answer, but no one said anything. The King looked sadly at Leverett. And then the Sombre Warrior rose unhurriedly to his feet, and all the guards turned sharply to face him, their hands at their sides. But the Sombre Warrior just stood where he was, keeping his hand well away from his sword. He turned the porcelain mask to stare calmly at Lord Leverett, and when he spoke into the strained silence, his voice was calm and dignified.

"We all lost friends, and family, in the border skirmishes. That's why it's time to put an end to it."

Lord Leverett sneered at him. "Peace, at any price? Never! If we give up, then it was all for nothing. All our brave young men died for nothing!" He glared about him. "Not all of us want this Peace! Or this marriage! To some spoilt foreign bitch, unworthy of our Prince!"

Richard stood up and let fly with the apple in his hand. It shot through the air and hit Lord Leverett so hard on the forehead it knocked him right off his feet. He fell backwards, unconscious before he hit the floor. Guards rushed forward to pick him up and carry him outside. There was a certain amount of polite applause, and a lot of laughter. The Sombre Warrior bowed to Prince Richard, who bowed back, and then both of them sat down again.

"Nicely done, son," said King Rufus. "Shut the man up without hurting him or giving his allies anything they could use to take offense. Now, Seneschal, where's my dessert?"

Sir Jasper was still walking back and forth in the Castle, wandering in and out of walls and rooms as the mood took him, mostly invisible, so as not to bother anyone. There was hardly anyone about, because of the banquet. Sir Jasper knew that. And so many of the rooms were empty, abandoned. Nothing but dust and shadows. The ghost felt strangely upset at finding Forest Castle so empty, so seemingly down on its luck. Unwanted, and uncared for. Just like him.

He finally found his way to the Castle Armoury, and stood for a while before the huge closed doors. Something about the two massive slabs of beaten metal, covered with centuries' worth of engraved glyphs and runes and magical protections, seemed to tug at his memory. He had been here before; he knew it. Somewhen . . . The whole place *meant* something to him. It meant so much that he half wanted to just turn away and leave, rather than find out why; but he raised his ectoplasm to the sticking point and walked straight forward, ghosting through the massive metal doors. All kinds of security spells flared and sputtered harmlessly on the air, unable to get a hold on him.

Sir Jasper stopped just inside the doors, and looked hopefully around. An almost overbearingly large hall stretched away into the distance, its far boundaries lost in the gloom beyond the limited foxfire lighting. Swords and axes, maces and morningstars, in all shapes and sizes and designs, filled ancient weapons racks on both walls, hung in proud display. Many of them in simple leather and metal scabbards, perfectly preserved by the still air and subtle protective magics laid down generations before. Famous blades with honourable and even legendary names, each in its own special niche, with plaques beneath them to commemorate some great battle or triumph, alongside weapons of war so powerful or brutal that no one had dared use them for years. And none of them meant anything to Sir Jasper. He sighed heavily, and his shoulders slumped, just a little. He'd been so sure he would find some answers here.

"If I was a knight, surely I would have been here, wouldn't I?" he said, his ghostly voice not echoing at all. He was used to talking to himself. "Was I a warrior when I was alive? And if so, which King did I serve? Which King did I let down so badly? What did I do, or leave undone, that I'm not allowed to rest? What terrible crime did I commit to earn a punishment like this?"

He broke off, as he heard footsteps approaching. He hesitated, ready to turn and leave, but something held him in place as a dim figure came pottering forward out of the gloom. Tall and elongated, and of indeterminate age, wearing formal clothes that were well out of date and had almost certainly never been fashionable, the stick-thin figure beamed happily at Sir Jasper as he trotted forward to join him. He wore huge owl-like spectacles perched on a hawkish nose, dominating a pinched face under an entirely unconvincing curly wig. The striking figure finally came to a halt before Sir Jasper and clasped his bony hands together over his sunken chest. His smile was bright, and his eyes were brighter.

"Oh, hello!" he said. "Come for a nice look round, have you? That's nice. Always glad to see a new face. Don't get many visitors these days, which is probably just as well. They will keep trying to touch things . . . Of course, the Forest's real weapons depository, the actual armour for the actual armoury, isn't here anymore. No, that's held somewhere else, under control of Parliament. They've got all the shiny new stuff. This is just a museum." He laughed happily. "That's what they think! Hello, I'm Bertram Pettydew, Forest Castle Armourer. Who are you, and why can I see through you?"

"I'm Sir Jasper, the ghost. I'm almost sure I know this place, from before."

"Really?" said Bertram. "Then you must have the full guided tour! You must, you must! See if we can't jog a few ectoplasmic grey cells, hmm? Follow me, and stick close to the light, there's a good dead person. The shadows can be treacherous."

He led the way deeper into the Armoury, with Sir Jasper sticking close to his side. The ghost got the feeling that this Armoury could still be dangerous, if it felt like it. And he wasn't at all sure that being dead would be any protection against some of the things he could sense lurking in the shadows.

"The Armoury is almost forgotten, these days," said Bertram again, peering happily about him, already in full lecture mode. "A last repository for all the weapons that changed history, down through the many years. And a few others that might have, if anyone had dared use them." He paused to drop Sir Jasper a conspiratorial wink. "Parliament only thinks they've got the good stuff! Hah! That's what I say. Hah! The day they came looking, all the really good stuff hid itself till they were gone. The politicians and the like just took away all the rubbish I've been trying to get rid of for years. Laugh? I thought I'd never breathe again . . . The King knows the true state of affairs, of course. When he remembers. And Prince Richard, of course. Fine young fellow. Mind out for the mantraps."

He escorted Sir Jasper from one legendary display to another, putting names to old and terrible weapons that had done good service for the Land in their day, and giving the ghost a quick précis of wars and battles long gone. He seemed quite comfortable around Sir Jasper, who thought Bertram was just glad to have someone to talk to and show off his beloved exhibits to. They stopped before an empty setting, and Sir Jasper immediately backed away a few steps. There was something about the empty space that set all his nerves on edge. Bertram Pettydew nodded solemnly.

"Oh yes . . . This is where the Infernal Devices used to stand. The most evil, cruel, and powerful blades this Armoury has ever known. Don't ask me when they were originally fashioned, or why; such knowledge is long gone, and probably best forgotten."

"Rockbreaker," Sir Jasper said slowly. "Flarebright. Wulfsbane." His whispered words seem to echo on, hanging in the still air.

"Yes! Fancy you knowing that! Not many remember those names

these days. A lot of the old songs and stories have been terribly white-washed, cleaned up and sanitised, for modern ears. Don't want anything that might upset people . . . Idiots! History is supposed to be upsetting, to make sure you don't do it again! But no one listens to me." He looked almost benevolently on the empty space. "All gone now, of course. Lost or destroyed, in the final days of the Demon War. We still get reports of their turning up, here and there . . . but it always turns out to be a false alarm. Just as well, really. We do still have some very useful items here, though—terribly powerful and quite upsetting if you think what they might do in the wrong hands. Or even the right ones . . . I suppose Parliament should be told we still have them. I'm almost certain I'll get around to telling them. One day. When they need to know."

They moved on, Bertram happily pointing out axes of mass destruction, and spears that could fly for miles to take out one target among hundreds, and even a set of arrows that were supposed to shoot through Time and take out an enemy in the past or the future. And then he stopped suddenly, so Sir Jasper stopped with him. Bertram Pettydew heaved a sigh.

"Is there anything sadder than an Armoury that's no longer useful, no longer needed?"

"Well, that's Peace, isn't it?" said the ghost vaguely.

"Oh, of course! Of course!" said Bertram. "But I do miss a good war. You only get really good deeds during a war."

"War is coming," said Sir Jasper, with a quiet, calm certainty that made the Armourer look at him closely. Sir Jasper shrugged. "I seem to feel it. And I am rarely wrong about these things."

"Who are you, exactly?" said Bertram, blinking at him through his huge glasses. "I mean, really?"

"I'm Sir Jasper. I think. It's actually quite freeing, you know . . . not to be certain who you are, or what you were. It takes all the pressure off. But . . . more and more I think I did something bad while I was alive. And that's why I'm still here. And I know I was here, before. In this place, this Armoury. I drew a great sword and I went out to fight for my country. But who did I fight, and for what cause? For what King? And why do I have this terrible, overwhelming feeling . . . that I have been brought back to Forest Castle for a reason?"

Bertram Pettydew waited patiently, but Sir Jasper had nothing more to say. After a while, the ghost nodded vaguely to the Armourer, and the two of them walked back out of the Armoury. There was a faint layer of dust on the floor, and Bertram couldn't help noticing that he was the only one leaving footsteps. They finally ended up at the closed main doors. Sir Jasper looked back into the gloom.

"How can you stand to be here, Armourer? This place is full of ghosts."

"They don't bother me," said Bertram kindly.

Back in the Great Hall, the Banquet of Welcome was still going strong. Food was still coming, drink was still flowing, and the roar of happy conversations had long since drowned out the orchestra, who had given up, and were now sitting around passing hand-rolleds back and forth. Everything seemed to be going well. The desserts had finally arrived, fabulous creations with more chocolate and cream than even the most hardened digestion could safely handle, and men and women who only a moment before had been heard to say that they couldn't manage another mouthful, stared at what had just landed on their plates and said, "Oh, go on, then, twist my arm."

Someone sent a whole raft of drinks over to the orchestra, along with requests, and they cheerfully launched into a series of riotous old folk songs of quite staggering rudeness. Richard knew the lyrics to some of them, and really hoped Catherine didn't.

Two tables down from the head table, only a dozen feet from where the King and his guests were sitting, a minor Lady stood up suddenly. People cheered her on, thinking she was about to make a toast. She stared around her with bulging eyes, tried desperately to say something, and then fell forward, crashing across the table, and lay still. At first, her neighbours just stared, or made loud remarks about minor aristocracy who couldn't handle their drink. But then someone leaned forward for a closer look, and recoiled, shouting, "She's dead! She's dead!"

The whole hall fell silent. Prince Richard was immediately on his feet, barking out orders, because the King was clearly bewildered. Richard had the guards surround the dead Lady's table with drawn swords, to make sure no one disturbed the body, and he sent more guards to block off the entrance doors. Guests were rising to their feet all around the hall and clearly getting ready to leave, until Richard's guards made it clear that wasn't an option. At sword point, if necessary. The Lords and Ladies glared angrily at Richard, and he glared right back at them until they subsided. He spoke quickly to the Seneschal, making it clear he was not to leave the King's side, and then Richard went down to take a look at the body.

The Sombre Warrior was also on his feet, standing beside the shaken Princess Catherine with his sword in his hand. The dead woman was none of his concern; he knew his duty. Lady Gertrude moved quickly to sit beside Catherine, in Richard's empty seat, and held the Princess' hand firmly in her own. The Seneschal called forward the doctor he'd kept standing by, just in case King Rufus was worse than usual and needed a little something to keep him quiet. Dr. Stein moved quickly over to join Prince Richard. A small and only slightly fussy type of person, he was entirely calm and professional as he examined the dead body, and then looked steadily at Richard.

"Undeniably poison, your highness. Blue lips, flushed face, several other unmistakable signs. As to how . . . ?"

Everyone else who'd been sitting at the table with the dead Lady immediately jumped to their feet and clutched at one another, loudly demanding to be able to leave the table. Richard sent them away with Dr. Stein, along with quiet orders to give them all a good purge, just in case. The King was on his feet now, plaintively demanding to know what was going on, while the Seneschal did his best to calm him, but finally he had to tell the King what had happened.

"It's the lady Melanie Drayson, Sire. It would appear that she's been poisoned."

King Rufus nodded vaguely a few times, and then his head came up sharply, and just like that, his mouth was firm and his eyes were clear.

"Far too minor a line to be the real target, Seneschal. So who was the poison really meant for? Hmm? Has to be the Princess."

"Poison?" Lady Gertrude said shrilly, rising to her feet and looking wildly about her. "Someone has tried to poison my poppet? That's it! Catherine, we have to get out of here! We can't stay in this terrible place a moment longer! We have to go home!"

"Hush, Gertrude! Get a hold of yourself!" Catherine said harshly, and Gertrude immediately quietened. Catherine looked at the Sombre Warrior. "You are still sure the brigands who attacked our carriage came from Redhart? Then I wouldn't be any safer there, would I? Stop snivelling, Lady Gertrude! Compose yourself. No, the only way for me to be truly safe is to be married. After that, the enemies of the Peace agreement will have no reason to kill me. And the Peace agreement is too important to be risked." She looked across the quiet hall at Prince Richard. "Do you have any objection to moving our marriage forward, Richard?"

"No," Richard said evenly. "You're quite right; the agreement must come first. Under the circumstances, I think we should be married first thing tomorrow morning. Seneschal, make the arrangements. The Princess' safety must be assured."

"Of course, your highness," said the Seneschal.

King Rufus turned to the Seneschal. "First, summon my Necromancer. I have need of his abilities. He will uncover the truth of what has happened here."

The entrance doors opened abruptly, somewhat to the surprise of the guards who'd just locked them. The doors swung wide and the guards fell back, as a young man dressed entirely in black strode into the suddenly silent hall. He advanced steadily through the massed tables, and everyone he passed shrank back from him.

"Who the hell is that?" murmured Catherine.

"That is Raven," the Seneschal said quietly. "Our most powerful sorcerer. Called Raven because he always dresses in black, like a bird of ill omen. And yes, he often does turn up before he's called for. It's actually one of the least disturbing things about him."

"Is he really . . . ?"

"A Necromancer? Oh yes. He deals in death, and the magic of murder."

Raven the Necromancer was a tall, almost unhealthily slender fellow in his early thirties, with more than a touch of the theatrical about him. His long black robes swept around like dark wings as he moved, and when he pushed back his dark cowl it revealed a sardonic, even sinister face, with a shaven head, dark, piercing eyes, and a wide smile. He grinned broadly and looked around, sparing no one; the best thing that could be said about his smile was that it wasn't deliberately unsettling. (There were those who said he cast too many shadows, and that you could hear the muttering of dead voices as he passed, but people said a lot of things about the Necromancer.) Raven finally came to the dead Lady, still lying across the table. Richard started to repeat what Dr. Stein had told him, but Raven stopped him with a look.

"I know," said the Necromancer, in a calm, pleasant voice. "Poison. I can even tell you which poison. Belladonna."

"How can he know?" said Catherine to the Seneschal.

"Because he knows everything there is to know about death, and murder, the spooky little creep," said the Seneschal.

"I heard that!" said Raven, not looking round. And then he spun, in a whirl of dark robes, and looked up and down the hall. "And I know who the poisoner is. You!"

He stabbed an unwavering finger at a minor Member of Parliament, one Silas DeGeorge, at one of the lesser tables. Silas stood up immediately, while everyone else scrambled to get well away from him. No one was particularly surprised. DeGeorge was a well-known opponent in Parliament of the Peace agreement, and the wedding. His round face was pale and sweaty, and he looked furtively about him for signs of support, or just a way out.

"That's it?" Catherine said to the Seneschal. "Raven just points the finger, and everyone accepts that the man's guilty?"

"Pretty much," said the Seneschal. "Raven's never wrong. And anyway, look at DeGeorge."

Silas DeGeorge glared defiantly at Raven. "What have we come to, when the King makes use of such as you? You'll never get anything out of me! Long live the cause!"

He slipped a pill into his mouth and washed it down with a glass of wine. And then just like the Lady he'd murdered, he fell forward and was dead before he hit the table. There was a loud gabble of protest from everyone who'd been sitting anywhere near him, to make it clear they weren't involved and knew nothing of what he'd planned. Richard had the guards move them away, and then stared coldly at the dead body of Silas DeGeorge.

"Raven?"

"Of course, your highness. I will need somewhere private to work."

Catherine threw off restraining hands from Gertrude and the Sombre Warrior, and hurried over to join Richard. She glanced at Raven, and then at the Prince.

"He's not joking, is he? He really is a Necromancer! How can you stand to have a man like that around you? In Redhart, we usually have them killed the moment they reveal themselves!"

"Well, cancel my holiday plans," murmured Raven.

"Really powerful sorcerers are somewhat thin on the ground these days," said Richard. "We feel it's better to have him here, where we can keep an eye on him, and have some measure of control over him. And you are very loyal, aren't you, Raven?"

"Of course, your highness," said Raven, inclining his shaven head just a little.

"For your own reasons, no doubt." Richard looked at Catherine. "Don't you have any sorcerers at Redhart?"

"Only the healthy kind," said Catherine.

"That's what you think," said Raven, smiling easily into Catherine's glare before turning to bow to King Rufus, who'd just arrived.

"Can't do it here," the King said bluffly. "Not at all suitable, for a public place. Necromancy should always be a private matter. Seneschal! Is there any empty room nearby we can use?"

"Just down the corridor, Sire," said the Seneschal.

The King looked at Raven, Richard, the Seneschal, and at the approaching Sombre Warrior. "Pick up the body, gentlemen. And follow me. And then we'll see what answers we can get out of this most ignoble traitor."

"I'm coming too," Catherine said immediately.

"As you wish," said the King. "But you don't get to interfere. No matter what. Will your companion be joining us?"

Catherine looked back at Gertrude, who shook her head fiercely. Richard looked at the First Minister, who was politely comforting Gertrude, and he shook his head firmly too.

They carried the dead man out of the Great Hall, and down the corridor, and into the empty room. They sat Silas DeGeorge in a chair and arranged him neatly. He looked very small, almost shrunken. Richard surreptitiously checked the man's pulse, just to assure himself the murderer really was dead. He stepped back, and for a long moment everyone just looked at one another, not knowing what to say for the best. Finally King Rufus nodded stiffly to Raven, who smiled and bowed, then moved forward to stand before the body of Silas DeGeorge. The Necromancer made no mystical gestures, spoke no magical chants; he just looked the dead man in the eye and spoke directly to him.

"Silas DeGeorge, return to us. The Outer Reaches have no hold on you while I am here. My power calls you back, for a time. Speak to me and answer truly all questions that are put to you."

And everyone in the room apart from Raven shrank back in revulsion as the corpse writhed and squirmed in the chair. Its eyes were fixed on Raven, though everyone could tell they didn't focus. The stench of rot and corruption was heavy in the room. The corpse smiled slowly and began to speak, in a low, breathy voice that had no human inflection in it at all.

"Hello, Raven. They've been waiting for you to summon me back. They know your name, the Lords of the Gulf do. There is a price for the powers you use, and they can't wait to make you pay it. Down here, in the Houses of Pain. What's waiting for me is nothing compared to what they have in store for you."

"Hush and be obedient, unquiet spirit," said Raven, apparently entirely unmoved by the dead man's words. "Speak only as you are commanded, and speak only the truth."

"But I do, little Necromancer, I do . . ."

"Why did you kill Lady Melanie?"

"It wasn't meant to be her," said the corpse. "The poison was intended for Princess Catherine, to start a war. So many people in both Lands want this war, for so many reasons . . . You'd be surprised. How can you hope to stand against them? But somehow the poison in the wineglass missed its proper target. Ended up at the wrong table. Never trust a waiter . . . And no, before you ask—I have no idea where my orders came from. Just an anonymous note, pushed under my door."

"Could he be lying?" Richard said quietly to the Necromancer. "Or holding something back from us?"

"He can't lie with this level of compulsion on him," said Raven. "But you have to ask the right questions . . . And I don't know how much longer I can hold him."

"Too late!" said the corpse, and once again everyone cried out and fell back as the body collapsed into rot and decay, falling apart before their eyes. Raven sighed and shook his head, and everyone else looked at one another and didn't know what to say.

Raven finally bowed to King Rufus. "I have done all I can, Sire. You have a serious traitor in your midst. But you already knew that."

"Did I?" said the King querulously. His eyes were vague again. He clutched at the Seneschal's arm. "Take me out of here. I don't like it here. I don't want to be here."

And while the others clustered round the King, and comforted him as best they could, Raven the Necromancer quietly left the room. Out in the corridor, he raised his eyes to the heavens.

"You'd better get here quickly, Grandfather and Grandmother. The Forest Land has great need of Prince Rupert and Princess Julia."

SIX

SECRET MEETINGS, SECRET PEOPLE

The Stalking Man went walking through the corridors of Castle Midnight, and no one saw him. A tall, broad, fleshy man, dressed in long crimson robes with a bloodred cape and hood, he strode swiftly through crowded places, and no one knew he was there. He passed by Lords and Ladies, guards and servants, and some of them even stepped back to let him by, without ever realising or remembering.

Leland Dusque, the Stalking Man. The wrath of Hell in the world of mortal men.

He descended through long passageways and pillared galleries, and came at last to the very private door of a very private room, tucked away in a deep, dark part of the Castle where no one ever went without very good reason, or very express permission from the King himself. The armed guards on duty at that door saw the Stalking Man coming. Saw him come drifting forward out of the gloom, like a ghost soaked in blood and gore, saw his wide eyes and feral smile . . . because the Stalking Man allowed them. The two guards stood paralysed with fear until he was almost upon them, and then they fell back with almost indecent speed, scrambling to get out of his way. They were the King's own guards, sworn to serve him with their lives and their deaths, but they wanted nothing to do with this. The King had told them the Stalking Man was coming, told them to expect him, but nothing could have prepared them for the awful reality of the Stalking Man, the Devil's Agent, the Emissary of the Gulfs.

The guards stayed well back as the Stalking Man strode right up to the closed and locked door. He took hold of the heavy brass handle, and the guards heard the slow, steady sounds of the lock unlocking itself. Because no door and no lock could keep him out, or block his way. Just as no one could do him any harm, as long as he walked in Hell's way.

He pushed the door open and walked through, and it closed itself behind him and locked itself again. The Stalking Man looked steadily around him, taking in all that the great open room had to offer, and he smiled slowly. The single far-reaching chamber at the base of Castle Midnight had been fashioned and decorated to resemble a great underwater grotto. A huge swimming pool, deep and wide, lay sprawled out in a great display gleaming white tiles, with a simple walkway surrounding it. Walls and ceiling had been made over to resemble a great stone cavern, the dark false stone painted with endless scenes of whales and octopi, mermaids and undines, and all kinds of water goddesses, laughing and sporting with one another.

The air was heavy with steam, rising from the waters of the swimming pool, which were heated by hidden jets of blazing marsh gas. Condensation ran down the textured walls in endless streams. The air smelled of languorous perfumes, and left the taste of salt on the lips. It was like walking through a sybaritic dream, a personal indulgence, one man's expensive and very private pleasure. The Stalking Man smiled; he did so love to see men give in to their temptations.

King William was floating on his back in the middle of the swimming pool, his great naked body rising and falling just a little in the embrace of the heated water, his face at peace, his iron grey hair floating around his head. Without his blocky ceremonial robes and his heavy crown to bear him down, he actually looked several years younger. His eyes were half open, staring dreamily up at the faux stone ceiling, painted over with a single great display of naked sea nymphs disporting themselves with one another.

A dozen naked young women, or perhaps more properly girls on the very edge of womanhood, played happily in the water around him, careful to maintain a respectful distance from the floating King. They moved lithely and easily through the steaming water, with a minimum of effort, laughing and giggling and splashing one another. They were perfect and beautiful—nobility's daughters, rich men's daughters, all of them volunteered for the King's pleasure by their ambitious parents.

The Stalking Man stepped carefully forward, to stand at the very edge of the pool, and said the King's name. Not his title or any of his honorifics, just the name. *William.* The King lifted his head out of the water just enough to see who had addressed him, and then he smiled slowly as he recognised the Stalking Man. Not many men smiled when they saw him. The King rolled slowly over in the water and swam to the far end of the pool with long, powerful strokes. The naked girls swam quickly after him, laughing and crying out like so many birds of paradise. King William grabbed the edge of the pool and hauled himself up and out, along with a great surge of steaming water. He rose majestically to his feet and then just stood there for a moment, organising his thoughts, entirely unselfconscious in his naked state. He nodded once to the Stalking Man, and then strode over to the single chair set out for him. Not sufficiently impressive to be a throne, but still richly fashioned enough to be worthy of a King. He stood before his chair and stretched slowly, his joints making loud complaining noises. Two of the naked girls hurried forward to rub him dry with thick towels. William worked his muscles slowly, enjoying the simple pleasure of being dried, and then dismissed the girls when their hands began to take liberties with his body. He took a towel from one of the girls and slapped her across the backside as she departed, giggling. William wrapped the towel around himself, sat down on his chair, and gestured for the Stalking Man to come and stand before him. The King looked fondly at the dozen naked girls, now sitting together at the edge of the pool, chattering happily.

"My little fishies," he said. "My own precious indulgences. Sometimes I think this is the one place where I can really relax and just be myself. Surely I don't need to explain sin and temptation to you, Leland? That's what got you where you are today."

"Indeed," said the Stalking Man, in a rich, rotten voice, like fruit that's spoiled but still tasty. "I know all about the pleasures of the damned. But are you sure we're really private here? I went to great pains to be sure I arrived unseen and undetected."

"Don't worry about my little fishies," said the King. "They never remember anything they see or do in this place. A simple security spell, to prevent gossip and . . . repercussions. Don't tell me you disapprove, Leland."

"You're not the first King to keep his own private seraglio," said the Stalking Man. "As long as you remember it takes a strong man not to be ruled by his own weaknesses. I'm just amazed you're not up to your knees in bastards."

"Another useful spell," said William, just a bit coldly. "The Royal line must be kept pure, to sit on the Redhart throne. We may not have access to the old Blood Magic anymore—that ended when Good King Viktor wiped this Castle clean of the Unreal—but the line must be maintained, just in case the Unreal and the Blood Magic should return. I do take my responsibilities seriously, Leland."

"Why have you summoned me here, William?" said the Stalking Man.

"You never can bring yourself to use my title," said the King. "Is it because we've been friends for so long?"

"No," said the Stalking Man. "It's because I serve a higher master."

"You're here because I have need of you," said the King. "But first, indulge me. Answer a question for me."

"If I can."

"Are you of the High Magic or the Wild Magic?"

The Stalking Man smiled briefly. "Nothing so limiting. My power comes from the Lord of Darkness."

King William frowned. "The Demon Prince?"

"Hardly. He's just a Transient Being. Much lower down on the food chain. I am the real deal, William, and don't you ever forget it. I am the wrath of Hell and the Vengeance of the Pit. Because there has to be a balance."

King William sniffed loudly. "I've never understood all that. How can you be a balance to the Walking Man when there hasn't been one since Jack Forester gave it all up to be a monk?"

The Stalking Man shrugged. "There's always a Walking Man, somewhere, so there always has to be a Stalking Man, somewhere. I don't understand the rules either, William. I just follow them. Because the Great Game is being played out at a much higher level than you and I will ever understand."

"I never understood why you wanted . . . this," said the King.

"You know my history and my tragedy," said the Stalking Man. "That's all you need to know. Now, what is it you want, William? Why call me here so urgently, to this private place, for this very secret meeting?"

"Because there's going to be a war," said the King.

"I thought you wanted peace," said the Stalking Man. "You worked hard enough to hammer out an agreement. Gave up your only daughter in marriage to the enemy. Do you fear now it was all for nothing?"

"There are more forces arrayed against the peace than anyone anticipated," the King said carefully. "I have to hope for peace, but prepare for war. There has already been an attempt on my daughter's life. If she is killed I will have vengeance, even if it soaks both our Lands in blood."

"I sold my soul for vengeance," said the Stalking Man. "For the death and destruction of those who did me wrong. I held their still beating hearts in my hands, and found it wasn't worth it. But you won't listen to me, because you're a King and you don't have to. You will go your own way and to hell with everyone else. So here I am, William, always ready to support a war."

"Even when it's for an honourable cause?" said the King.

The Stalking Man laughed softly. "When is war ever honourable? It's always about power and politics, wealth and pride. All you Kings invoke Honour and Land and Ancient Rights, but in the end it always comes back to the pride of men. I don't care about causes, except as means to an end. I only care about blood and slaughter and destruction. The piled-up dead and the burning cities, and women weeping for men they will never see again. I walk this earth to make Humanity suffer. Reasons are irrelevant."

"Then you will be a soldier in my army," said King William. "One of my secret weapons, to turn the tide in my favour."

"Only one?" said the Stalking Man. "What other secret weapons do you have, William?"

"If I told you, they wouldn't be secret, would they?" said the King. "I must have powerful secret weapons, to back up my army. Forest Castle still holds powerful, even legendary, weapons in its Armoury. Everyone knows that. But I will put my faith in powerful men, not blades. Starting with you, Leland."

"An honour, William," said the Stalking Man, bowing mockingly. "Call for me and I will be there. It's been a long time since one of my kind went to war. I wonder if a new Walking Man will appear to face me . . . That would be a glorious battle!" And then he stopped, and considered for a moment, before looking King William in the eye. "You know why I threw away my soul, William, in return for the power of retribution. You know what I did for hate's sake, and what I have done since, for Hell's sake. I have always wondered—knowing who and what I made of myself . . . why have you let me roam free?"

"Because I always knew I might need you someday," said King William.

"Ah," said the Stalking Man. "I knew it couldn't have been anything as small as friendship."

"It is the prerogative of Kings to do terrible, necessary things to preserve their Kingdoms," said the King.

The Stalking Man nodded slowly. "Because we were friends, once . . . I will push the limits of my bonds to say this: you do know it's far easier to call up the forces of Hell than to dismiss them? I will fight in your war, William, set my teeth in the throat of your enemy . . . but you will have no say in what I will do, or how I will do it. You can let loose an arrow, but once it is free of the bow you have no control over where it will fly. I will kill and I will conquer, but only in Hell's name."

"Why, Leland," said King William, "I never knew you to be so eloquent." He considered the Stalking Man thoughtfully, for a long moment. "How did we end up here, old friend? These aren't the men we intended to be . . . I remember you, in better times. It does . . . pain me, to see you like this. Do you have to be the Stalking Man all the time? Is there ever any peace for you?"

"I didn't want peace," said the Stalking Man. "And see what has become of me. A wise man would draw a moral from that."

"Leland . . ."

"I have power now! And greater men than you have knelt and sobbed before me, begging for mercy, before I killed them anyway. Don't you pity me, William. Don't you dare. You're just a King. The Lord I serve rides on the backs of dead Kings, and bathes in their tears." He leaned in close, suddenly, to whisper in the King's ear. "I know why you're doing this, William."

And then he straightened up, turned his back on the King in a swirl of bloodred robes, and left the private room. He walked unseen back through Castle Midnight, and where he went then . . . nobody knew.

The King watched him go, stone-faced, and didn't turn away until the door was shut again and the Stalking Man safely gone. The King let out his breath then, in a long, slow sigh, and allowed himself to relax. He turned to look at his precious pool, and only then saw the bodies of his little fishies, lying facedown in the water, every one of them quite dead. Because you do not summon the Stalking Man without paying the price.

Some time afterwards, King William went for a walk in his ornamental gardens. He wore his finest ceremonial robes, and his crown, and wherever he went in the gardens the gardening staff bowed low to him and hurried to get out of his way. Unlike his daughter, King William had never taken much interest in his gardens, and rarely went there. He had them only because he inherited them, because they had belonged to his father and his grandfather before him. He saw to it that they were maintained to the highest standard, because it was expected of him and because if he was going to have ornamental gardens, then by damn they were going to be the best and most magnificent ornamental gardens ever, and a rebuke to all lesser gardens in lesser Lands.

In fact, it had been such a long time since he'd walked through his gardens, that William honestly didn't remember when he was last there. Before the children were born, certainly. Much of what he saw and encountered was new and strange to him. Catherine had loved the gardens so much that he gave her control over them as soon as she was old enough to oversee things without constantly running to him for advice. She seemed to have taken to it with great enthusiasm. He wished he'd known before she'd left. He would have liked to have complimented her on what she'd achieved here.

For a moment he seemed to see Catherine running merrily across the wide lawns, a wild, free spirit in her simple boyish clothes. But it was just a thought and a wish, gone the moment he looked at it directly. The King strode along, past flower beds and hedges and goldfish ponds covered with floating lily pads, his hands clasped tightly behind his back, his head down, thinking. He wondered whether Catherine would ever forgive him when she finally found out all the things he'd done in Redhart's name. He had used her . . . because that was what Royal offspring were for. Royal children were born to be bargaining chips, weapons, even sacrifices . . . There was power in being King, but there was helplessness too, sometimes, in the things you had to do. Because the Royal line must continue . . .

And then, finally, William looked up and realised he'd reached the place he'd been heading for all this time, even if he hadn't consciously admitted it to himself.

The Standing Stone rose tall and jagged before him, a barely human shape carved out of stone that was ancient before Castle Midnight was even dreamed of. There were those who said a pagan god slept within its stony embrace, or perhaps a devil. The God Within, that was what the people called it. Sometimes his guards caught people sneaking into the grounds to worship at the Stone, or sacrifice before it, or leave presents for it. Old traditions die hard. The King looked at the Stone, and the Stone looked back. If there was a power in it, what could he do to call it forth, to help him in his war? Would he let it loose on the Land, whatever it was? And if this was, as he suspected, the last remaining fragment of the Unreal in Castle Midnight . . . might it be enough to restore the Unreal in the Castle? And make him strong enough to take on the Stalking Man, after he was no longer needed? One monster to set against another?

The King looked at the Standing Stone for a long time, thinking many thoughts, and then he turned his back on it, without saying anything, and walked quietly away.

Elias Taggert, Steward to King William in Castle Midnight, went running through the corridors, summoned most urgently by his King.

But when he finally reached the Court and the guards threw the great door open for him, and he hurried in . . . he was astonished to discover that the Court was empty. Given the almost peremptory urgency of his summons, the Steward had assumed it must be some emergency meeting of the Court. But the whole Great Hall was empty, apart from King William sitting silently on his throne, solemn and brooding, like one of his own gargoyles. The Steward noticed immediately that while the King was wearing his finest ceremonial robes, he wasn't wearing his crown. Which meant this was to be no official meeting. Whatever was decided here, whatever orders were given, no record was to be kept. The Steward strode quickly through the empty Court to approach the throne, his rapid footsteps echoing loudly in the quiet.

"Welcome, Elias Taggert," said the King, as the Steward bowed formally before him. "I have need of you, my most loyal Steward, to carry a message I dare not entrust to anyone else. I need you to leave this Castle and go into the hills and carry my word to the Broken Man."

The Steward wanted to just stand there with his eyes wide and his jaw hanging open, but he knew what was expected of him. He stood stiff-backed and solemn-faced and did his best to keep his voice steady. "Has it really come to that, Sire?"

"No," said the King. "But it might."

"The hills . . . are a long way off," said the Steward. "We're talking weeks of travel, Sire, there and back. And I do have my duties here . . ."

"It has to be you. I need someone I can trust, to do what I ask and no more, and then to keep silent about it," said the King. "You should be honoured, Taggert."

"Oh, I am, Sire," said the Steward immediately.

"Of course you are," said the King. "You never met the Broken Man, did you? No, before your time. Your father knew him, when he was Steward before you. I think perhaps the Broken Man will listen to you, because of your name, where he might not accept anyone else. Do this for me, my Steward, and there shall be rewards. Reach out to him on my behalf."

"As your majesty wishes," said the Steward.

And then he jumped, despite himself, as a man appeared out of nowhere, standing beside the throne. The Steward knew him immediately, and didn't bow to him. He knew the sorcerer Van Fleet, in person and by reputation, and regarded him as a bad influence on the King. Taggert had to wonder how long the sorcerer had been standing there, hidden from view behind his own magic, watching and listening. Given that the King hadn't reacted at all to the sorcerer's sudden appearance, he must have known Van Fleet was there all along. Why have the sorcerer hide himself, unless King William wasn't entirely sure what the Steward's response would be? Taggert felt he should be insulted by such a lack of trust, but truly, nothing could be taken for granted where the King and the Broken Man were concerned.

Van Fleet was a large, heavyset man, much like his brother, Gregory Pool, Prime Minister of Redhart. Van Fleet was dressed in his usual brightly coloured robes, gaudy enough to put a peacock off its lunch, with no mystical signs or charms to mark him for what he was: the most powerful and learned High Magician in Redhart. (Not that there was much competition these days.) Van Fleet liked to present himself as a scholar, doing research in the Royal Library, or performing alchemical experiments in his private rooms. A quiet, harmless, studious sort. Only a few people knew the kinds of things Van Fleet did for his King on the quiet. Elias Taggert knew. He had to know, because he was the Steward. But he didn't have to like it.

Taggert jumped again, just a little, as the King resumed speaking. His voice was flat, with no room in it for objections.

"We don't have time for you to reach the hills by usual means, Steward. I need my message carried to the Broken Man today and his answer brought back to me today. So Van Fleet has agreed to provide you with a door."

Van Fleet smiled again, and gestured lazily, and the Steward had to struggle to keep from crying out. He could feel a growing presence in the Court, of something from Outside pressing in, forcing its way into reality. Something that didn't belong, imposing itself on the world through the sorcerer's strength of will. A door appeared suddenly, right before him. Just an ordinary-looking wooden door, standing still and upright, and entirely unsupported. Except it wasn't just a door. The Steward could tell it was merely something that had chosen to look like a door, to serve its purpose.

He could feel it looking at him. Van Fleet gestured again, and the door swung slowly open, like a gaping mouth. Warm golden sunlight spilled through the opening and into the Court, pushing back the gloom and the shadows. Through the doorway, the Steward could see open country, a hillside, and tree lines set against a clear blue sky. Sharp, clean scents of flowers and vegetation drifted through, all the smells and savours of living things from the great outdoors. The Steward took a step forward, then hesitated and looked back at the King.

"If you could get a move on, Taggert," said Van Fleet. "This isn't easy, you know."

The Steward ignored him, still looking at the King. "What is your message, Sire? What, exactly, do you want me to say to the Broken Man?"

"Ask him if he will return if I call for him," said the King. "If there is a war, will he come back, to lead my armies and fight for his country?"

"When you've finished your little chat with the Broken Man, just call for the door and it will come for you," said Van Fleet. "Now hurry up. It's getting hungry."

"Go," said the King.

The Steward nodded quickly, took a deep breath that didn't help as much as he'd hoped, and walked through the open door. And just like that, he was somewhere else.

Elias Taggert stood very still, looking about him. There was no trace of the Court anywhere, or the door he'd just stepped through. He was out in the open, under a cloudless sky, with uncomfortably hot sunlight beating down on him. He was standing halfway up a fairly steep hillside, with rough bare stone under his feet, and a gusting wind that did its best to push him this way and that. He looked up and saw a ragged tree line at the top of the hill, most leaves already gone, leaving dark, jagged branches thrusting out against the sky. Birds circled overhead, crying out to one another in harsh, raucous voices. The Steward looked down, and immediately wished he hadn't. The long hill stretched away below him, enough of it that it would have taken him half the day to climb up this far. A waterfall tumbled down a rock face opposite him, throwing spume and spray into the air, crashing down and down into a swift-flowing river at the bottom of the valley far below. There were flowers and plants and all kinds of vegetation all around him, and the Steward, not being in any way a country person, couldn't identify any of it. All he could think of was wildlife, with the emphasis on the word *wild*. The Steward was convinced he could hear animal sounds, from somewhere far too close for his comfort.

It was all very pretty and bucolic, and the Steward hated it. He was a city mouse, or at least a Castle mouse, and he liked it that way. He thought plants and animals should know their place and not have designs of their own on people. He rarely left Castle Midnight, and when he did he couldn't wait to get back. He looked quickly about him for wolves or bears or poisonous snakes, or even poisonous vegetation, while thinking rather plaintively, *I don't want to be here*. Was he safe from animal and plant attack, halfway up a hillside? The Steward didn't know and had no intention of hanging around long enough to find out.

He wished fleetingly that he possessed the magical powers of previous Stewards, to command the forces of the Unreal. Like his great-grandmother Catriona Taggert, who married Good King Viktor. But those powers had vanished along with the Unreal, generations before. He was just the King's servant, on the King's mission, and it was time he was about it.

The cave entrance was right in front of him. He'd never been here before, didn't know anyone who had, but he had only to look at the dark, ragged opening to know Van Fleet and his damned door had got it right. This was the place. He could feel it, in his bones and in his water. This was the Broken Man's cave, home to the man who only wished to be left alone. Most people had the good sense not to bother him; he was, after all, one of the most dangerous men in Redhart. Soldier, warrior, general, the Broken Man. The Steward shuffled forward, peering cautiously into the gloom inside the cave entrance. It was just a great hole, with rather unsafe-looking edges, set into the side of the hill. The Steward raised his voice.

"Hello? Hello, inside the cave? Sorry to bother you, but . . . I am the Steward of Castle Midnight and I bear an urgent message from his majesty, King William!"

"Go away," said a voice from deep inside the cave. It sounded . . . human enough. "I don't care what message you bring. The King and I have nothing to say to each other anymore."

"He knows that," said the Steward, just a bit desperately. "Do you really think he'd send me all this way unless it was important and urgent and necessary?"

There was a pause, and then a long sigh. "Very well. Come in, Steward. And wipe your feet; there's enough mess in here as it is."

The Steward braced himself, and made his way carefully into the dark cave entrance. It soon revealed itself to be a tunnel, heading deep into the hill, with a light shining up ahead. The Steward moved forward very cautiously, a few steps at a time, one hand braced against the left-hand wall, while his feet kicked small stones out of his way, across the largely unseen tunnel floor. The light grew steadily brighter as he drew nearer, until he rounded a sudden corner and found himself looking into a large, well-lit cavern. It looked . . . surprisingly comfortable. Almost civilised.

Foxfire moss had been made into crude lamps that were set in niches in the walls, lighting the wide cavern with a gentle silver glow. Vegetation had been strewn across the floor and stamped flat, to take the edge off the hard stone. Roughly prepared animal skins served as rugs, and lay piled up at the far end to serve as a bed. A small fire burned in one corner, set under a hole in the cavern roof that apparently served as a natural chimney. It seemed to the Steward that the fire gave off more light than heat. But . . . there were books piled up everywhere, all across the cavern, and a proper writing desk, with paper and pen and ink.

And there, sitting on a comfortable chair at the back of the cavern, the Broken Man himself.

"I know you were exiled, banished," the Steward said carefully, "but . . . is this all they let you take with you?"

"It's all I wanted," said the Broken Man. "I was allowed these luxuries, because I agreed to go, and not fight it. And I could have fought, could have defied the King; I did have supporters in those days. Whether I wanted them or not. But it never even occurred to me not to go, because there was nothing in the Court to make me want to stay. I have all I need here: my books, and my writing desk, and time to think. Peace and quiet at last. Everything I need, for a hermit's life. So what are you doing here, Steward, disturbing me?"

The Broken Man was a more than usually large, broad-shouldered man, wrapped in furs from a dozen large and very dangerous animals, with a great mane of long black hair and a rough, untrimmed black beard. The Steward knew the Broken Man had to be in his late thirties, but he looked older. In fact, he looked like some barbarian warrior, some renegade chief of throat-slitters, banished from civilisation, hiding from his enemies. A massive longsword, in a gleaming metal scabbard, stood propped casually against the wall, beside his chair. Within easy reach. And yet, the Broken Man had an intelligent, thoughtful face, with sharp, piercing eyes. And his voice was even and cultured and unconcerned.

But . . . just sitting there in his chair, entirely at ease and at peace with himself, this exiled man, this hermit . . . was still the most dangerous-looking man the Steward had ever encountered.

"Well?" said the Broken Man. "Spit it out, Steward. What does my father want with his banished son?"

"Your father fears that the peace he has worked so hard to bring about will not last," said the Steward, working hard to keep his words from stumbling over one another. "He has reason to fear that there will be war with the Forest Land—and sooner, rather than later."

"Can't he stop it?" said the Broken Man.

"Not when so many people want it," said the Steward. "In defiance of all reason and common sense."

"Why do these people want a war?"

"The usual reasons: power, profit . . . perhaps even honest patriotism."

The Broken Man nodded slowly. "So, you're Steward now. From after my time. How many years has it been since I walked away from the Court?"

"Eight years, your highness," said the Steward.

The Broken Man winced. "Don't call me that. I have no right to titles. I counted eight hard winters as they passed, but it seems longer . . . You are a Taggert?"

"Of course," said the Steward. "The tradition still stands. I am Elias . . . I believe you knew my father, the previous Steward. He died two years ago, and I took on his duties. Were the two of you . . . close, Prince Cameron?"

The Broken Man made a sharp, dismissive gesture with one hand.

"No. Don't call me that. I gave up that name, and everything it represented, when I left. I prefer the name the courtiers gave me, to hurt me: the Broken Man. I embrace it, because it is accurate." He looked sharply at the Steward. "Do you know why I was banished from my father's Court and Castle Midnight?"

"I don't think anyone knows for sure," the Steward said carefully. "Your father never talks of it, and anyone who might have known is forbidden to discuss it. Of course, there are rumours . . ."

"I was the greatest warrior and general Redhart has ever known," said the Broken Man. His voice was entirely calm, with not even a hint of boasting or pride in it. "Never defeated in battle. Victor of a hundred border skirmishes. But I was never . . . popular. I never appealed to the people, for all my triumphs. They only had to meet me to know something was wrong. Wrong with me. They were ready enough to cheer my victories, my battles won, but only from a distance. It seems I lacked . . . certain human qualities. And because of that, I could never be King. So my father sent me away, and settled on Christof as his de facto heir, and everyone had to pretend I never existed. That King William only had two children." He smiled briefly. "I can't say I miss much from my old life. I was good at being a soldier; it came easily to me, but I never took much satisfaction from it. I like being a hermit. Alone with my books, and my thoughts."

"Are you . . . happy here?" said the Steward.

"You mean, do I get lonely? No. I prefer my own company. People do come here, from time to time. Not because they know who I was, or what I used to be, but because there is a tradition in these hills of venerating hermits. We're supposed to be closer to God, you see; and therefore we might know useful things. So they come here, quietly and surreptitiously, and leave things outside my cave. Food, and gifts. Just because they believe it's the right thing to do. And sometimes they leave little messages, badly written on scraps of hoarded paper. Usually concerning philosophical, or medical problems. And I look in my books, and give them what answers I have. None of them ever tries to come inside my cave. I think they can tell that would be a bad idea."

"King William has sent me with a question for you," said the Steward.

"He wishes to know if there is a war, will you return to lead his army? If he calls for you?"

"If he calls . . . then I'll come," said the Broken Man tiredly. "But I won't stay. I will do my duty, because part of me is still Prince Cameron, eldest son to the King. But there's nothing he can say or do that will make me stay. Now go, Steward. Before I kill you for disturbing my precious solitude . . . making me remember things I have fought so very hard to forget."

The Steward turned and bolted, running wildly back down the dark tunnel, out of the cave, and into the light. The door was already there, waiting for him. It opened, and the Steward ran through it as though a pack of wolves was panting at his heels; he ran back to the safety of Castle Midnight, and things he understood. The door closed quietly behind him and disappeared.

Prince Christof, youngest child of King William, had his own very private rooms, well away from the traditional Royal family quarters. The farther away he was from his father, the easier and more comfortable he felt, and he had no doubt that his Royal father felt much the same way. Christof had his own personally chosen guards, who stood at the door to his very private rooms, and no one ever got in without a written invitation, well in advance. So the courtier Reginald Salazar approached Christof's door with more than usual trepidation. He'd been inside Christof's private rooms many times before, enjoyed Christof's company on many occasions. Eaten and drunk and partied with him, along with certain similarly minded friends. But this was the first time he'd come to Christof's door without an invitation, or at least an understanding. He had no choice, however. He had to talk to Christof.

He did his best to put on a good show as he approached the armed and armoured guards, trying hard to look calm and confident, as though he had a right to be there, but it didn't come easily. Reginald was a lover, not a fighter. He might intrigue, and even conspire, but always from a safe distance. He stopped before the guards, stuck his nose in the air, and addressed them in his most aristocratic tones.

"You know who I am. You know the Prince knows me. He needs to see me now. I have urgent information that he needs to hear. If he finds out you kept this news from him, he will not be happy."

The more experienced of the two guards looked at him pityingly. "Yes, I know you, Salazar. But you know the Prince. You know what he'll say, what he'll do, if we disturb him and he decides that what you have to say isn't important, or urgent. You really want to risk that?"

Reginald nodded, struck dumb for the moment. He knew what Christof had done in the past. But he wouldn't, couldn't, back down. The guards moved away from the door, and Reginald stepped forward. He swallowed hard and said his name, very loudly. There was a pause, and then the door swung open by itself. Reginald strode in, and didn't look back as the door shut and locked itself behind him.

Reginald stayed where he was, shifting nervously from foot to foot despite himself. He could feel cold sweat on his face. Christof was his friend, had been more than a friend, but you didn't bother him. Not if you knew what was good for you. Reginald could still remember his good friend Prince Christof sticking a knife in his ribs, deep enough to draw blood, just for saying the right thing at the wrong moment.

And then a voice from deeper in the connected rooms spoke calmly on the quiet. "Oh, very well, Reggie. Come on in. But this had better be good."

Reginald moved quickly forward, passing through the antechamber and into the Prince's main room. Christof kept this large and open space full of exotic plants and flowers, in hundreds of spectacular varieties, grown and trained across all four walls and the ceiling. The floor was one great lawn, expertly trimmed and maintained. Originally, this room and its adjoining chambers had belonged to the old Prince Lewis, brother to Good King Viktor. (Lewis had not been good, or even close to becoming King.) But Christof read accounts of how Lewis had kept his rooms full of magnificent plants and extraordinary flowers . . . and decided the idea appealed to him. So he just booted out the previous occupants and moved in, because you can do that sort of thing when you're a Prince, and set about turning his new quarters into one great living garden, a new green world, all for himself.

The King could have overruled him. Could have ordered Christof to give the rooms back. But since the rooms were so very far away, and because the occupants weren't actually anyone important, and since as long as the Prince was preoccupied with his new interests he wasn't bothering the King . . . nothing was said, and nothing was done.

The room was a jungle, the air thick with the scents of huge, pulpy, hideously coloured flowers, which seemed to slowly tilt their great heads to follow Reginald as he passed. Things stirred in the shadows of the great vines and heaving vegetation that covered the walls. Reginald kept moving forward, and found Christof in the farthest of the rooms, standing thoughtfully before his easel.

Prince Christof was wearing a traditional painter's smock over his fashionable clothes, busy at work on his latest painting. He liked landscapes. But since he never went anywhere, he painted scenes from his imagination. These large and detailed landscapes were always very colourful, wild and magnificent, and positively packed with people and incident—but they were never anywhere anyone would want to go. Christof had a violent, even brutal, imagination, and the scenes he painted were always inhabited by things that had no place in the real world. Christof heard Reginald approaching and addressed him without turning around from adding one last detail to his new masterpiece.

"I need more crimson," he said. "I've run out again. There's always more blood than you expect. This had better be important, Reggie. And I mean really important."

"Your father has sent the Steward through a dimensional door, to talk with your exiled brother!" Reginald blurted. "Taggert carries a message to Prince Cameron from your father!"

Christof sighed, and put down his paintbrush and palette on a handy stool. The mood was gone; he'd have to try again later. He cleaned his hands carefully on a piece of rag, tossed it away to one side, and finally turned to meet Reginald's anxious gaze with his best reassuring smile.

"So. My dear father wishes to talk to the Broken Man. To my dear older brother. Cameron . . . It's all right to say the name, Reggie. He isn't going to suddenly appear out of nowhere, just because you said his name aloud. That's someone else entirely. Now, how do you know this? You do know this for sure, don't you, Reggie? I'd hate to think you were disturbing my quality time over some mere gossip."

"I have my sources, my contacts; you know that, Christof!" Reginald said quickly. "It's the only way to stay safe in this Castle, with hot and cold running conspiracies everywhere you look, and factions and intrigues chasing each other up and down the corridors. The King summoned the Steward to an empty Court—except it wasn't empty! The King and the sorcerer Van Fleet were there! And the King had Van Fleet open up a dimensional door, to send the Steward out to the hills, just like he did with Catherine's carriage!"

"And what message did my father have the Steward convey to my dear departed brother?" said Christof.

"Well, I don't know that, exactly," Reginald admitted. "My source wasn't close enough to hear. But what else could it be? Your father hasn't talked to Cameron, directly or indirectly, since he sent him into exile. What could the message be, but an invitation to return?"

"Hush, hush," murmured Christof. "Do try not to over-excite yourself, Reggie. It doesn't suit you. Remember, my father didn't force Cameron out. He agreed to go. That's why he was allowed to take up his new life as a hermit inside Redhart borders. I don't believe there was or is a force in this country that could make Cameron do anything he didn't want to. But I suppose you're right. I can't see my father breaking his long silence for anything less than *Come on home, my boy; all your sins are forgiven*. Because war is in the air, and my father feels the need for his greatest warrior once again. My father never lets go of anything he owns that might prove useful one day."

Christof took Reginald in his arms and hugged him warmly, and Reginald hugged him back, with as much relief as affection. Christof stepped back and kissed Reginald on the forehead. "You have done well, my dear. Now be a good fellow, and run along. I have arrangements to make. We will get together again, you and I, for a nice little sit-down and a chat. Once I've got all this sorted out."

Reginald nodded quickly and left as rapidly as dignity would allow. Christof was his friend, his very close friend, had been for years; but when Christof got that look in his eye, and that tone in his voice . . . it was time for any sane man to make himself scarce. Because Christof was never more dangerous than when he was plotting.

. . .

Some time later, Malcolm Barrett, Champion to King William, strode up to the guards at Christof's door in a way that made it very clear he wasn't in the mood to take any nonsense from them. And given how harsh and brooding the Champion had been ever since Princess Catherine left, the guards exchanged a quick look and got the hell out of his way. The door opened before Malcolm, and he strode straight in. He allowed himself a small smile as the door shut quietly behind him and the guards shuffled back into place. He had to take his amusement where he could find it these days. He walked through the antechamber and into the main room, looking interestedly at the vivid green world Christof had made for himself inside Castle Midnight. He had to admit he was impressed. Hard to believe the Prince had accomplished so much without access to High Magic. Malcolm approved of doing things for yourself, without leaning on sorcery. He looked up sharply as Christof came forward to meet him, wearing more-formal clothing than usual. The two men bowed to each other.

"If you're so fond of greenery, you should take a stroll through the ornamental gardens, my Prince," said Malcolm. "Get out in the open air. Do you some good."

"Please, call me Chris," said the Prince. "We're all friends here."

"We are?" said Malcolm. "When did that happen? Well, I suppose we can always pretend, until proved otherwise. I got your message, Chris. What is so important that we have to meet so urgently?"

"We need to talk about my father, and what he's done," said Christof.

"Catherine's gone," Malcolm said shortly. "And she won't be coming back."

"I'm afraid my father's coldheartedness doesn't stop there," said Christof.

He gestured for the Champion to sit down, and the two men settled into the very comfortable chairs set out. Malcolm noticed the third chair, which suggested another guest still to arrive, but said nothing. He leaned back in his chair and studied Christof thoughtfully.

"All right," he said. "What has the King done now?"

"Something rather surprising, for a man supposedly so dedicated to peace," said Christof, crossing his long legs elegantly. "Given that he gave up his only daughter, my sister and your beloved, to ensure the success of his Peace agreement."

"Get to the point," said Malcolm. His voice was flat and harsh, enough to make Christof stir uneasily in his chair.

"The King has sent his Steward to talk to my older brother," said Christof. "Prince Cameron, that was. Yes . . . the name that no one ever speaks anymore. It seems the Broken Man is to be brought home, and have the soldier's laurels placed on his brow again . . . Ah! Excuse me, Malcolm. That will be my other guest. A moment, if you please. Do make yourself comfortable. There's pink champagne in the ice bucket on that table, and some very special dainties I had sent up from the kitchens."

Christof rose from his chair in one easy, languid movement and went to greet his new visitor. Malcolm looked at the food and drink on offer but didn't touch any of it. He didn't have much appetite of late. He made himself eat soup and biscuits because he knew he had to eat something, but he barely tasted them. His life held little flavour with Catherine gone. He looked around as he heard footsteps approaching, crunching heavily across the grass floor, and then he stood up to bow briefly to General Staker.

The General marched into the room as though he were on parade. Stiff and unyielding, as always, he didn't even glance at the amazing plants and flowers around him. He did seem a little surprised to find the Champion there, but bowed stiffly to him anyway. Christof got them all settled in their chairs with a minimum of fuss, keeping up a stream of charming conversation in an attempt to put his guests at their ease. With little success. The General and the Champion barely acknowledged each other's existence. They'd never had anything in common before, and the way they bristled just at being in such close proximity to each other made it clear to Christof that he had his work cut out for him.

"This had better be as important as your message made out, your highness," growled the General, cutting right across one of the Prince's more amusing anecdotes. "Everyone else may be full of the joys of Peace breaking out, but I'm keeping my men at the ready. Because somebody has to."

"Well, quite," said Christof. "As I was just saying to the Champion, it appears my father may not be as committed to the cause of peace as everyone assumes. He has just sent a message to my exiled brother, Prince Cameron, inviting him to return."

Staker sat up straight in his chair. "The Broken Man? The King's really ready to bring him back?"

"So it would appear," said Christof. "I'm still awaiting confirmation on the details of the message. And, indeed, on what my dear exiled older brother's response might be."

"How can the King do this?" said the General. "He swore to all of us that he would never allow the Broken Man back inside this Castle!"

"Question is, do we want him back?" said Malcolm. "He was our greatest warrior, by all accounts, but . . ."

"Yes, but!" said Staker. "We could use him on the battleground, no question, if there is to be a war, but afterwards? His reappearance at Court could upset the balance of power, and set all the factions we've got at one another's throats. Greatest soldier Redhart ever knew, no arguing with that. I fought beside him on the border; scariest thing with a sword in his hand I ever saw. If we are going to war, we'll need him. Excellent tactician. But if your father should go back on his word, and restore Cameron as his heir . . . No. No! Put the Broken Man on the throne, and it'll be one battle, one war, after another. Because that's all Cameron knows. I fight to win, not to fight . . . He can't be King! He's . . ."

"Broken," said Christof. And they all nodded.

"I never met the man," Malcolm said slowly. "He was always off on the borders, while my training kept me here at the Castle. My father met him a few times, when he was Champion before me. I don't think he liked or disliked the man, but he did say . . . there was something *off*, about Cameron."

"They called him the Broken Man because he came out of my dear mother's womb broken," said Christof. "There was always something lacking in Cameron. To be honest, he spooked the hell out of me as a child. I was always glad when he left, to go back to the borders again."

"I don't think anyone wants to see Cameron on the throne," said Staker, "but there are forces that would put him there, as a figurehead for their faction."

"But what can we do?" said Christof in his most reasonable voice. "I found out about this too late to stop the Steward. He's already gone, through Van Fleet's damned door. And no doubt he'll be back again equally quickly, with my brother's answer."

"I could put some archers in place," said Staker. "Put an arrow through the Steward the moment he reappears. Make it clear what happens to anyone who tries to make contact with the Broken Man."

"How very basic of you, General," Malcolm said acidly. "Kill the messenger, for the message he carries. The King would only send someone else! Probably me! And such direct action would immediately let the King know he was being spied on! No, we want the Steward to return safely, so we can learn what the Broken Man said to him. He may refuse to come back, after the way he's been treated. He must have his pride."

"No," said Christof, "I'm afraid that's wishful thinking. Dear Cameron was always very big on duty, and responsibility. And he never could say no to Father. He always did what Daddy said. Even when Daddy told him to leave. And he never could resist a war . . ."

"Are we really sure there's going to be war?" said Malcolm. "I mean, after all the effort everyone's put into making the Peace agreement?"

"Your father must think it's a real possibility," said the General. "Or he wouldn't have contacted your brother in the first place."

"My banished brother, let us not forget," said Christof. "Banished before the whole Court. Not an easy thing to undo, not after what my father said at the time."

The General snorted loudly. "Nothing like an imminent war to concentrate people's minds on what really matters. As long as Cameron can lead us to victory, how could anyone deny him anything? Including his reinstatement as the Royal heir?"

"So what are we to do?" said Christof. "What can we do that isn't treason?"

The word brought the whole conversation up short, and the three men looked steadily at one another for a long moment.

"We wait," Malcolm said finally. "And see what happens. If Catherine's marriage to the Forest Prince goes ahead; if the Peace agreement goes through; if the disputed territories come back under our control after all these years . . . Then maybe there will be peace. And no reason for the

Broken Man to return. He can rot in his cave and play hermit for the rest of his life. No reason for us to do anything."

He looked meaningfully at the General, who shifted uncomfortably in his chair. "I will abide . . . by what occurs. And wait for a sign."

He rose abruptly to his feet, bowed to the Prince and nodded to the Champion, and strode swiftly out. Malcolm started to get up, but Christof gestured quickly for him to stay, before hurrying after the General to see him out and say a few last words. Servants came in with more food and drink. Malcolm sat where he was, looking at nothing. It wasn't as if he had anywhere to go, or anything to do. The King hadn't called on him for anything, hadn't even spoken to him, since Catherine left. The King might think he was being kind, but Malcolm would have preferred to be doing *something* . . . just to keep busy, so he wouldn't have to think about things.

Christof soon came back and sat down opposite Malcolm. He sat for a while, and then leaned forward, choosing his words carefully. "I haven't seen you at Court, Malcolm. What have you been doing since my sister left us?"

"The King has been kind enough not to bother me," said Malcolm. "Probably just as well. I don't think I could look him in the face just yet. I can see why he kept news of the arranged marriage from us, I can understand why he wanted to avoid raised voices and unpleasantness . . . but even so, to just spring the whole thing on me and Catherine in front of the whole Court—I don't think I could speak to him in a suitably respectful way. Not just yet."

"You still haven't come to terms with it, have you, Malcolm?" said Christof.

"You make it sound as though she's dead!"

Christof kept his face calm and his voice sympathetic. "For you, she must be. It's the only way. You'll never see her again. You must know that. She will be Prince Richard's wife, Queen to his King, and she will never leave the Forest Land again. She's dead to you, Malcolm."

"Unless there's a war," said Malcolm. "Then all bets are off, all agreements null and void. If there's a war. But I can't, I mustn't, think that way. Because Catherine wouldn't want to be saved if the price turned out to be two countries torn apart by war."

"Then you have to move on," said Christof. "As though she was dead. Grieve for her, and let her go. Move on, and make a new life for yourself. Surely a King's Champion must have . . . duties, responsibilities, that need attending to? We talk about the possibility of war because we must. That's our duty. But nothing is set in stone, nothing is certain. Our lives are what we make of them."

"I know," said Malcolm. "There are things I could be doing, should be doing; but I just can't seem to work up the enthusiasm. It's been such a short while since Catherine and I were happy. We were in love, and she'd decided to set a date for our wedding; did you know that, Chris? And then I had no choice but to give her up, let her go. Now there's just this terrible empty hole in my life where she used to be. Mostly these days . . . I just sit around in my quarters, doing nothing, thinking nothing, just waiting for the day to be over. So I can go to bed and lose myself in sleep for a while. And if I'm lucky, I won't dream. I can't seem to make myself care about anything . . ."

"Oh, Malcolm, Malcolm . . . Don't."

Christof leaned forward and took Malcolm's hands in his. The Champion held on to the Prince's hands like a drowning man. And for a while neither of them said anything.

"This isn't healthy, Malcolm," Christof said finally. "You need to get out of your rooms, out of yourself. Look, why not come hunting with me? I'm sure I could round up some hearty sorts to keep us company. And you know you're always welcome here. If you feel you just want to talk to someone . . ."

Malcolm nodded slowly and started to get to his feet. Christof immediately let go of the Champion's hands and stood up with him. And then Malcolm surprised Christof by embracing him briefly.

"You're a good friend, Chris. Probably better than I deserve."

He turned abruptly and left. Christof stared after him.

"A good friend. Yes."

The sorcerer Van Fleet had his own private room in Castle Midnight, so he could always be ready if the King felt a sudden need for his services. And the King did seem to need him more and more these days.

For all kinds of reasons. Now here was the sorcerer's brother, the Prime Minister Gregory Pool, sitting uncomfortably in one of his comfortable chairs, looking around at the room the King had so kindly provided, and not even trying to hide his disapproval. Van Fleet sighed, very quietly. He was going to have to do something about his brother.

Van Fleet had filled most of his room with glass tubing and bell jars, and flaring marsh gas jets, and all kinds of alchemical equipment. He always had some experiment or another on the go, usually involving boiling liquids and unpleasant smells. Always something bubbling in the cauldron or cooking in the small stone oven. One wall was hidden behind rows of metal cages, set one upon the other; containing animals and birds and reptiles and a few other things not so easily identified. Because you never knew when you'd need a subject to try something out on. And of course there were shelves and shelves of glass jars, holding herbs and insect parts, mandrake root and other disturbing things. Some of the things in the jars were still moving. Because alchemy's like that.

Gregory Pool sniffed loudly, and then rather wished he hadn't. The air smelled strongly of chemicals and fresh dung. Some of the animals in the cages looked out at Pool miserably, and even pushed their paws plaintively towards him through the steel mesh. Patting the air in mute entreaty. Gregory did his best not to notice. He didn't know what Van Fleet did in this room, on his own, and he felt very strongly that he didn't want to know. In fact, he was pretty damned sure he was better off not knowing. He took out his delicately chased silver snuffbox, tapped a small quantity of cocaine out onto the back of his hand, and sniffed it up. And then addressed his brother without looking up, as he put the box away.

"Yes, I know. Don't lecture me, Van. We all need a little something to keep us going. Do I lecture you on how often you need to send out for fresh animals?"

"You've seen for yourself how useful they can be," Van Fleet said equably. "You held the black cat while I slit its throat to get enough blood to make a decent scrying pool."

Gregory Pool glanced unhappily at the large pool of drying blood on the table before him. Only a few moments before, it had been a magic mirror through which he could spy on the King and his Court, and then on Prince Christof and his treacherous friends. Knowledge was necessary, and Gregory had always been willing to pay the price. He just didn't like to get blood on his hands. He had listened carefully to every word spoken at the private meetings, studied the reactions on everyone's faces. And none of it would have been possible without his brother's help. He knew that. And so did his brother. Gregory glared at Van Fleet.

"Are you sure what we just did was High Magic? Sacrifice and spilt blood were always marks of Wild Magic in all the songs and stories."

"It's all a matter of attitude," Van Fleet said easily. "I have made no pacts with demons or devils, and my soul is still my own. You worry too much, Brother. High Magic is a science, just like alchemy."

Gregory sniffed, unconvinced, but he tacitly agreed to change the subject. "I knew Christof and his little friends were plotting, but I didn't think they'd pull the Champion and General Staker in with them! This is a combination that could prove very dangerous: an unstable Prince, a heartbroken Champion, and an overambitious General! If they wanted to know what was really going on, they should have come to me!"

"And would you have told them?" said Van Fleet, genuinely interested.

"Of course not! But it would have been the proper thing to do. And I would have told them some comforting and very convincing lies, put their hearts and minds at rest, and they would have gone away perfectly happy! The current situation is complicated enough without them sticking their well-meaning noses in where they're not wanted. I'm really quite disappointed in Prince Christof. I thought he had more sense . . ."

"He's never felt secure as heir," said Van Fleet. "Not while his older brother is still alive. With Catherine sent away to the Forest Land, he must have felt his father had finally committed himself to naming Christof as his official heir. But if Cameron does return . . ."

"The Broken Man can never be King!" Gregory said flatly. "He just can't."

"Stranger things have happened," said Van Fleet. "The King really should have executed Cameron, rather than just banishing him from the Castle. Ended the problem then and there."

"It's no easy thing for a father to order his son killed," Gregory said coldly. "And anyway, who would you send to kill such a man? We didn't have the Sombre Warrior then. No, we all discussed the situation at length, and everyone agreed that banishment was the best option. If only because we might need the Broken Man's skills as a soldier at some future time. And just maybe we were right about that."

"Is war inevitable?" said Van Fleet.

"Not if I have anything to say about it," growled the Prime Minister. "All the most powerful and influential minds in Redhart and the Forest Land agree that peace is necessary. We all put our names to the wedding, and the agreement, because the endless border skirmishes were draining our treasuries dry. But all it would take is one tragic accident, one unacceptable insult to our honour, and everything we've achieved would be swept away in a moment! And there are certain factions, certain people, in both countries . . . who cannot be trusted to leave well enough alone."

"What do you want me to do?" said Van Fleet.

"Keep an eye on Christof, and his people, and everyone the Prince meets with. Let me know immediately if they start doing things, as opposed to just talking about doing things."

"What, all of them?" said the sorcerer. "The Prince, the Champion, the General, and all their people? And everyone they might talk to? You don't want much, do you, Brother? How many eyes do you think I've got?"

"I'm paying you enough, aren't I, Brother?" said the Prime Minister. He rose to his feet and made to leave, then stopped as Van Fleet was suddenly there to block his way.

"There is one more thing, Gregory. Before you arrived, I sensed the presence of some powerful force, in conversation with the King. A most secret and unnatural presence. I took it upon myself to investigate further, and I have to tell you: the King has been talking with the Stalking Man."

The Prime Minister swore loudly. "Of course William did it secretly . . . because he knew I wouldn't approve! No good can ever come of dealing with Hell's agents. What did the King want with Leland Dusque?"

"Beats the hell out of me," said Van Fleet. "I can just about detect the Stalking Man's presence, past his shields, but there's no way I can listen in on him without his knowing I was there. And I am not about to pick a fight with the Stalking Man." He broke off, frowning. "The dimensional door I made for the King has just reappeared at Court. The Steward must be back, with the Broken Man's answer."

"I need to speak to the King," said the Prime Minister.

The Steward arrived back in King William's Court, pale and shaking and somewhat out of breath. The door disappeared quietly behind him. The King waited impassively on his throne until the Steward regained his breath and his self-control, and bowed formally.

"Talk to me, Steward," said the King. "What did he say?"

"Prince Cameron requires me to tell you that if there is a war, if you need him . . . you have only to ask and he will return," said the Steward.

The King nodded slowly. "Of course. He couldn't just come back. I have to ask him . . . How would you describe his condition, Steward? Physical and mental?"

"He seemed . . . comfortable as a hermit, Sire."

The King glared at him. "Is he sane?"

"I would say so, yes, Sire."

"And how does he feel about me? About what I did to him?"

"It's hard for me to say how he feels about anything," said the Steward carefully.

"Yes," said the King, settling back on his throne. "I know. The Broken Man . . . I'm not even sure he has emotions, as we understand them. But I must know, Steward. Does he bear me any animosity for ordering his banishment from this Court?"

"I would say not, Sire," said the Steward. "He seems to be content where he is."

"My first son, my oldest child . . . and I had to send him away," said the King. "Because he could never replace me as King. And now it seems I need him. To do the one thing he does better than anyone else. Win battles."

At the sudden sound of raised voices outside the closed doors of the Court, they both looked round sharply. They recognised the Prime Minister's voice, demanding to be allowed entry. The King smiled slightly.

"Why not?"

He sent the Steward to the doors, to pass along his order to the guards, and the King watched coldly as the Prime Minister burst through the opened doors and strode down the empty Court towards him. The King smiled sardonically as the Prime Minister bowed to him as briefly as protocol would allow.

"You've been listening in again, haven't you, Prime Minister? Spying on me, through that sorcerous brother of yours. If he wasn't so useful, I'd have his head taken off right here in front of me, and then stuck on a spike over my gates as a warning to others. And then we'd see whether he's got enough magic in him to put his head back on again . . . Be warned, Prime Minister. There is a thin line between arrogance and treason."

"Is it treason to care about the safety of the realm?" Gregory Pool demanded furiously. "You cannot seriously be considering bringing Prince Cameron back, Sire! You must know there are still factions present in this Court who would place him on the throne as their figurehead!"

"And you must know I would never suffer such a thing to happen," said the King. "The Broken Man can never be King. But he can lead our armies to victory. If necessary. We do not want to go to war, Prime Minister. It is unthinkable. But unthinkable things have happened before. And so we must be prepared for all eventualities. Because that is the duty of a King. To do what is necessary."

SEVEN

THE THINGS WE DO FOR
LOVE AND HATE

Round the back of Forest Castle, where hardly anybody goes because it's just scrubby woodland and really poor hunting, there is another large and carefully maintained artificial clearing. Nowhere near as large, or as old, as the clearing made to contain Forest Castle, but still pretty important in its own right. It was hacked out of the woods by the Brotherhood of Steel, some sixty years previously, specifically so they could have somewhere to hold their annual Grand Tourney. The Brotherhood didn't do it themselves, of course, manual labour being beneath their dignity. Instead they rounded up a whole bunch of local peasants, who didn't seem to be doing anything important, paid them a pittance, and put them to work. Along with whoever happened to be on punishment detail in the Brotherhood's Sorting Houses. These people came back so determined never to be put on punishment detail again, that even after the clearing had been established the Brotherhood continued to send whatever people they had on punishment detail to keep the clearing open and stop the woodland from creeping back.

For generations afterwards, the local peasants passed down stories of the great clearing they helped make. With an added moral to the tale: if you see the Brotherhood of Steel coming, run.

Permission to open up such a large clearing so close to Forest Castle had been provided by Parliament, on the grounds that it was better to have the Brotherhood's greatest warriors fighting it out in one place rather than in the streets and bars of the towns and the cities. (Parliament and the Brotherhood agreed to split all the costs, and the merchandising revenue, between them, and that also helped to move things along.) No one even thought to inform King Rufus about any of this, until the deal was safely signed and settled. By which time it was far too late for anyone at Court to make any useful objections. This was perhaps one of the first real signs that no one outside the Court gave a damn what the King thought anymore.

And now the seasons had passed, and the time had come round again for the annual Grand Tourney to take place. People had been working out in the clearing from the moment the rising sun had provided enough light for the workmen to see what they were doing. There was a great deal to do, and not a lot of time to do it in. Tents and marquees had to be set up, and all kinds of stalls; fighting circles had to be marked out, and the single jousting lane. Several sets of raked seating had to be carefully assembled. And somebody really low down in the pecking order had to dig a whole bunch of latrines. The people in charge of all this were of course professionals, and very well paid for their services. The people who did the actual hard labour were also pretty well paid, because by this time they'd organised themselves into unions and guilds. And there were any number of unpaid volunteers, happy to labour for hours, in return for free passes and guaranteed good positions in the raked seating, with really good views of all the major events.

The Grand Tourney, so called to distinguish it from the four lesser seasonal tourneys, took place once a year, and allowed the very best fighters and warriors and magicians to show off in public. A marvellous setting, where the best of the best were allowed and even encouraged to beat the crap out of one another in front of baying crowds, and prove once and for all that they really were the greatest in their own personal field. Theoretically, the Grand Tourney was open to everyone. But it was a long way to come, to turn up, fight and lose, and walk all the way home again . . . so most people preferred to prove themselves in the seasonal tourneys first. Still, it was a point of pride, and long tradition, that nobody who turned up ready to compete would ever be turned away. Although a lot of the people in charge, most definitely including those august personages who ran the Brotherhood's Sorting House, would have very much liked to ban anyone who'd ever attended the Hawk and Fisher Memorial Academy. Partly because they didn't have the proper attitude or show the proper respect, but mostly because when they did turn up they always won everything.

And they weren't even gracious about it.

There were golden and silver cups to be won, and extravagantly worded bronze plaques, in a whole bunch of categories. And any number of bags of gold and silver coin, for those who distinguished themselves. But mostly it was all about the winning. About proving who was the very best at what they did, in front of an admiring crowd. Preferably while grinding some hated enemy's face into the mud while you did it. Nothing like settling an old score or a long-running feud in front of a crowd and the people who mattered. A lot of politicians got their start at the various tourneys, by performing deeds of an unquestionably heroic nature in public. And a lot of politicians who'd been kicked out of Parliament for being useless, or ethically or morally or financially corrupt, often turned up to fight again, in the hope of rebuilding their reputations. The Tourney organisers never tried to keep these people out; you had to provide someone for the crowds to boo and hiss at. There were always a few goodhearted stallholders selling rotten fruit to throw, too, because if the Tourney didn't provide the right kind of things to throw, the crowds would start using their own ammunition. Everything from fresh manure to large, heavy things with jagged edges. And that could get out of hand really quickly. Crowds do so love to escalate.

The organisers also provided individual tents, for the Big Names and Major Players, brightly decorated with exaggerated scenes of previous triumphs at previous Tourneys. Then there were the larger tents, where up-and-comers and promising talents could get together and exchange good-natured banter, rough camaraderie, and death threats. And, of course, there were a couple of really big marquees for everyone else. The hopefuls, and the ambitious. Finally, there were hospital tents, gathered together and placed to one side, for the injured, the seriously damaged, and those on the way out. A large number of surgeons, healers, and priests could always be relied upon to turn up every year to man these tents, to do charitable work for the good of their souls and show off their various skills. A lot of the medical schools sent their most talented interns here, to learn things the schools couldn't teach. Nothing like sawing off a smashed limb, while the patient was still very much alive and aware and screaming his head off, to teach you what battlefield medicine was all about. (The Big Names and Major Players brought their own surgeons and healers, of course. They wouldn't be caught dead in one of the common medical tents.)

Crowds of eager onlookers started queuing up very early on, watching everything with keen interest but held back at a respectful distance by a larger than usual presence of armed and armoured security guards. Regular visitors to the annual Tourney passed the time swapping well-rehearsed tales of old battles and marvellous triumphs, and all the famous faces they claimed to have seen. These were not the kind of people who could afford the expensive advance tickets for the raked seating; they were waiting to be herded into the standing-room-only enclosures surrounded by strong wooden fences. To keep the overexcited in their place.

Security guards in what they fondly assumed were plain clothes wandered back and forth, on the lookout for familiar undesired faces. Pickpockets had become increasingly rare ever since the courts started lopping off the relevant fingers of repeat offenders. And gambling was strictly forbidden at the Tourney, because it encouraged interference by outside interests. If caught, both the bettor and the bet-taker would be immediately dragged away, thrust into a fighting circle, given swords, and told to fight it out for the amusement of the watching crowd. (Lots of rotten fruit here, and heavy jaggedy things every time.)

People came from all over, to observe and participate in the Grand Tourney, the most famous celebration of skills and courage in the Known Kingdoms. Some of the crowds travelled really long distances to get there. Not just from all over the Forest Land, but from Redhart and Lancre, and even the Southern Kingdoms. The Grand Tourney was a strictly enforced neutral ground. Anyone who broke the compact, or even tried to, could expect to be sent back home in a box. Or a large number of boxes.

Or a sack.

Every year the Grand Tourney drew a bigger audience, because this was where the heroes were. The famed swordsmen and the infamous sorcerers, and everyone who'd made a name for themselves one way or another. Soldiers back from the border, warriors fresh from fighting the colourfully named pirates from off the Lancre coast, and every wandering young hero and adventurer who hoped to make a name and reputation for himself by taking on all comers at the Grand Tourney.

This particular Grand Tourney had been postponed a month so it would coincide with the Royal marriage . . . and anticipation had only heightened the fervour of everyone concerned. The crowd was expected to be the biggest yet. Everybody who was anybody intended to be there, and people were crowding in from all around to make sure they didn't miss anything at this once-in-a-lifetime affair.

Along with a few very unexpected arrivals. Though no one knew that just yet.

The dragon dropped off Hawk and Fisher, Jack and Gillian, and the dog Chappie a safe distance away from the Castle and the Tourney. He located a small clearing and dropped out of the sky like a stone, accompanied by several gasps and at least one scream from his passengers. He stretched his massive membranous wings wide at the very last moment, cupping the trapped air beneath him, and settled down to the grassy floor in a perfect landing. Hawk and Fisher climbed down one side, Jack and Gillian on the other. And then Hawk had to go back up and drag Chappie off. The huge dog still had his eyes squeezed tightly shut, and Hawk had to pry some of his claws loose from where he'd jammed them deep into gaps between the dragon's scales. Hawk hauled Chappie down from the dragon, and into the clearing, whereupon the dog immediately pulled free, opened his eyes, and shook himself thoroughly.

"Dogs are not meant to fly!" he said loudly. "Did you feel that landing? My stomach's still up in the clouds somewhere!"

"Calm down," Hawk said kindly. "Let us not forget, you are so magical that even if you did fall off and hit the ground, odds are you'd bounce."

"You try it first," growled the dog.

"The Forest Castle is about a mile off," said the dragon, indicating the direction with a nod from his massive bottle green head. "Which is about as close to the Castle as I care to get. I do not wish to have my presence detected by any of the Castle's magic-users or by security people with really good eyesight. Partly because I don't want the attention, partly so no one will make any connection between Hawk and Fisher and the very legendary Prince Rupert and Princess Julia; but mostly because . . . I don't have good memories of my time at Forest Castle."

"Not many do," Hawk said dryly.

"But we take your point," said Fisher. "There are a lot of good reasons why our turning up at the Castle with you could cause all kinds of problems. So you stay here, and keep yourself occupied, while we check out the Tourney."

"I thought we wanted to talk to the powers that be?" said Jack.

"We do," said Hawk. "And today of all days, the Tourney is where we'll find them."

"Suits me," said the dragon. "I could use some quality time alone in the Forest."

"Hunting?" said Fisher.

"No, it's time to get my butterfly collection started again!" the dragon said cheerfully. "I'm sure all sorts of marvellous new varieties will have appeared during my absence. I just can't wait! Tally-ho!"

He surged forward into the surrounding trees, seeming to somehow slip and slide between them, and just like that, his enormous bulk vanished into the shadows. For a while they could hear him crashing enthusiastically back and forth, and then even that was gone. Hawk looked at the others.

"Did any of you happen to see a really big butterfly net in his hands?"

"Definitely not," said Fisher. "And I don't even want to think where he's been hiding it all this time."

"The stories were true!" said Jack. "You really did befriend the only dragon in creation who collects butterflies rather than gold!"

"So, no treasure hoard," said Gillian. She grinned briefly. "Saves having to fight him for it."

"The Castle is that way," sad Hawk. "Pick up your feet, everyone; the sooner we get there, the sooner we can start getting into trouble."

"That's my man," said Fisher fondly. "Always thinking of me."

They set off through the trees, following a rough-beaten trail half recovered by the Forest and already choked with masses of fallen leaves. The air was tolerably warm, and full of birdsong. Mulching leaves crunched loudly under their feet, and the Forest was full of the pleasant smells of earth and plants and flowers, and living things generally. Hawk breathed it all in deeply. This was how home had always smelled in his dreams. He'd never thought to see and hear and smell the Forest again, because he'd always thought he'd have more sense than to come back. Fisher strode along at his side, keeping a watchful eye on the shadows. The Forest held few pleasant memories for her. She only remembered the Forest in nightmares.

"I have been to Forest Castle before," Jack volunteered after a while. "When I was younger."

"Same here," said Gillian, looking eagerly about her, and continually tucking strands of her straying grey hair back behind her ears.

"I sort of felt I ought to," said Jack, leaning only lightly on his wooden staff as he strolled along. "Just to see where all the stories you told us as children took place. The Castle was a bit of a disappointment, to be honest. Dank and gloomy, and very draughty . . ."

"Right," said Gillian. "And while I wasn't actually ostracised by the Court, I sure as hell wasn't made to feel welcome."

Jack was nodding even before she'd finished talking. "About as welcome as a fart in a suit of armour. My blood links to the Royal family made everyone nervous, and my direct link to two living legends basically creeped the hell out of everyone. They were happy enough to worship the memories of Prince Rupert and Princess Julia, but none of them wanted you back. Or anyone related to you. So I just smiled at everyone, gave them my blessing, and got the hell out."

"Were you the Walking Man then?" said Hawk.

"No, this was well before that," said Jack, pausing to prod suspiciously with the end of his wooden staff at something rustling in the undergrowth. "Just as well, really. If I'd started smiting the bad guys in that place, I'd probably still be doing it. I really didn't care for the feel of the place. Of course, it may have improved since. My beliefs require me to be optimistic."

"I wouldn't put money on it," said Hawk. "Chappie! *Put that down!* There are people starving to death who'd know better than to eat that!"

"You are so unadventurous," said the dog, chewing loudly.

"What about this new House of Parliament?" said Fisher. "What's that like?"

Jack and Gillian exchanged a quick smile. "Only you would see that as something new," said Gillian. "It was established over sixty years ago!"

"I didn't go there," said Jack. "It was made clear to me, in a polite but very firm way, that I would not be welcome, even as a tourist."

"Right," said Gillian. "Politicians don't like heroes, except from a distance. They get in the way of deals and compromises, and all the quiet understandings that no one talks about in public."

"This is sounding more and more like a place we should visit," Fisher said solemnly. "If only to make it clear to one and all that no one tells members of this family where they can and can't go. I might even table a motion!"

"You don't even know what that means," said Hawk. "But we should drop in, say hello, smash the place up a bit. Just to put the fear of God into everyone and teach them some manners."

Jack shook his old grey head slowly. "My parents . . . are juvenile delinquents."

"Don't expect us to make bail when they arrest you," said Gillian.

Hawk and Fisher shared a smile. "We don't do the under-arrest thing," said Hawk. "Really would like to see someone try, though."

"Down, boy," said Fisher. "We're here to stop a war, not start one. So how do you want to play it when we get to the Grand Tourney?"

"We don't want to advertise our presence," Hawk said thoughtfully. "And we definitely don't want to reveal who we really are. Everyone would get so tangled up in the implications of Rupert and Julia's return that they wouldn't pay proper attention to the message. No . . . we're just Hawk and

Fisher, one of the many who've run the Hero Academy. Impressive enough that people will listen to us, without distracting from the importance of the message."

"We need to talk to our grandchildren," said Fisher.

"What, exactly, do you plan to say to our children?" said Jack just a bit pointedly.

"We need to sit down in family conference," Fisher said firmly. "Sit down together, and talk this through. The Demon Prince only got us to come back here by threatening the grandchildren."

"He also said there was a war coming," said Hawk. "He was quite definite about it. Which is odd, given that every bit of air coming out of the Forest is full of the arranged marriage and the new Peace agreement."

"Do we tell the King?" Jack said bluntly. "Doesn't he have a right to know what's going on?"

"He probably already knows," said Hawk. "Kings tend not to last long if they don't take care to keep themselves well informed."

Gillian was shaking her head again. "I can't believe you haven't heard . . . Of course, Jack's been living in a monastery for twenty years, and you two were out of the country, but even still . . ."

"What?" said Fisher. "What have we missed?"

"King Rufus is old," Gillian said flatly. "He's not what he was. His mind wanders . . . Word is, Prince Richard does all the real work these days."

"Then he's the man we need to talk to," said Hawk.

"I still say we need to talk to our grandchildren first," said Fisher. "Work out how best to keep them safe from the Demon Prince. Then we can talk to the people in charge and tell them what they need to do."

"Oh, I'm sure they'll just love that," murmured Jack. "Chappie, *don't eat that!* You don't know where it's been."

"I know where it's going," said the dog indistinctly.

"How are we to gain access to the people in charge?" said Gillian. "Without having to reveal who you two really are? They won't talk to Hawk and Fisher, because you're generally regarded as troublemakers. They won't talk to Jack, because he isn't the Walking Man anymore."

"And they won't talk to you, because you're just another soldier from the Sorting Houses," said Jack. "No offence."

"Of course," said Gillian. "I'm just another soldier, and you're just another monk."

"Exactly!" said Jack.

"Look, it's really very simple," said Hawk. "We go to the Grand Tourney first, take part and win everything, and then we'll be invited into the Forest Castle as the day's champions! After that, we just wait for the right opportunity."

"And if one doesn't arise, we make one," said Fisher. She grinned suddenly. "We'll show the Tourney what fighting really is. They won't know what's hit them!"

"Please try very hard not to kill anyone, Fisher," said Hawk. "Not unless you absolutely have to. We really do need to make a good impression."

"Don't know what you're talking about," said Fisher. "I don't always kill them."

"Of course not," said Hawk.

"Still, you'd better be the one to make the good impression," Fisher conceded. "I never did get the hang of that."

Jack looked at Gillian. "Other people don't have parents like this."

"I guess we're just lucky," said Gillian.

"You do know they're going to embarrass us at the Tourney, right in front of everyone?" said Jack.

"Of course!" said Gillian. "That's what parents always do in front of their children. Chappie! *Don't roll in that!* It's disgusting!"

"Humans don't know how to have fun," said the dog.

Prince Richard and Princess Catherine arrived at the Grand Tourney in their most splendid ceremonial outfits, at the head of a long procession. Neither of them actually felt much like it, having a great many other things on their minds, but they didn't really have any choice in the matter. Given that the whole affair was ostensibly being held in their honour this year. Everything was pretty much set up by the time they got there, though there was still some loud hammering and occasional bursts of bad language, going on in the background. Which the Royal couple politely pretended not to notice.

Richard and Catherine strolled unhurriedly among the raised-seating stands and the many merchandising stalls, smiling and nodding to everyone. (Being Royal, they could practically do that in their sleep.) Everyone gave every indication of being very happy to see them, and eventually Richard and Catherine, still smiling till it hurt, were escorted up the steps of the main raked seating and shown to their seats. Not so much seats as thrones, of course. Richard and Catherine sat down, and the Prince nodded a brief but determined dismissal to all the people who'd been following them around. The Lords and Ladies, the courtiers and merchants and soldiers, all bowed or curtsied and then departed at great speed, fighting viciously for the good seats. Politeness and etiquette meant nothing where the best views were concerned.

Richard looked out over the scene before him. He and Catherine had the very best seats, overlooking all the best locations: the main fighting circles, the magical display arenas, and of course the single jousting lane that ran right before them. The other main raked seating, including the King's seat, or throne, was set up opposite. There were flags and pennants and gaudy flower arrangements everywhere, and a hell of a lot of people, no matter which direction Richard looked in. He couldn't see many security people, but no doubt they were all where they needed to be, presumably in plain clothes. The few armed guards he could see seemed to have their hands full, keeping the crowds under control. The general hubbub seemed good-natured enough, but as Richard's mother always liked to say, *It's always fun until someone puts their eye out.* Queen Jane had always been very preoccupied with damage to the eye, as Richard remembered. *Don't run with scissors* had been another of her cautions. *You'll have someone's eye out!* Maybe she'd seen some awful accident when she was young . . . She'd died while Richard was still young, so things like this were mostly what he had to remember her by. Richard realised his thoughts were drifting, and he made himself concentrate on what was going on around him.

There were a great many armed men hidden in the stands along with Richard and Catherine. He'd insisted on that. After the near-poisoning the evening before, he wasn't taking any chances. He glanced coldly at the portly figure standing beside him, dressed in a really tacky and only borderline fashionable outfit, eating one spiced-pork-and-beef meatball from a platter intended for Richard and Catherine and making a real meal of it. The man with no taste in clothes was the Royal food-taster.

"How long can it possibly take to eat one meatball?" Richard demanded.

"You want me to do a thorough job, don't you, your highness? Course you do," said the food-taster, one Jeremy Hopkins. "My taste buds are so thoroughly trained and disciplined, I can detect a hundred different poisons with one good chew. The subtler poisons take longer, as you'd expect, but don't you worry, your highness, I am also trained to projectile vomit at the first hint of danger!"

"Well, there's something to look forward to," said Richard. "How do you get into a job like yours? Doesn't it . . . worry you?"

"Bless you, no, your highness!" Jeremy said happily. "It's a family position, is this, food-taster to the throne. Back through eight generations, and every one of us has made it to pensionable age! It does help that I'm a philosophical sort. I say, when your time's up . . ."

"Stop talking and relinquish the bloody meatballs," growled Richard. "Or I'll personally see to it that not every part of you survives to claim a pension."

The food-taster sighed loudly and handed over the platter of meatballs. Richard quickly helped himself, bit into the first one with cheerful defiance, and then passed the platter on to Catherine. She just shook her head briefly, hardly even glancing at what was on offer. Richard supposed he couldn't really blame her. He handed the platter back to the food-taster, who smiled smugly when he was sure Richard wasn't watching.

"You've got to eat something," Richard said reasonably to Catherine. "Unless you plan to live on fresh fruit you've plucked from the trees yourself and water you've personally drawn from the well. Come on, what are the chances of anyone trying to poison you a second time now we've got an official food-taster on the job?"

"I'm not hungry," said Catherine. "I'll try something later, I promise. I'm just not in the mood."

She looked out over the bustling crowds, making more and more noise as they increased in size. People were still flooding in, taking their seats or filling up the standing enclosures. They all seemed cheerful enough. Catherine wanted to shout at them. How dare they be so happy, so unconcerned, when someone had tried to kill her? The crowds didn't even glance at her, or Richard. They were waiting for the fights to start. A little action, a little blood . . . high drama and low comedy, and always a chance to see some hated aristo make an arse of himself. But none of the Big Names or Major Players had emerged from their separate tents yet. They understood the importance of keeping the crowds waiting, to build the anticipation and make a good entrance. Treat them mean, keep them keen. When you got right down to it, the Grand Tourney was all about show business, and everyone knew it.

Richard sat back on his fake throne and considered the Princess thoughtfully. He couldn't think of a single useful thing to do or say that would cheer her up or make her feel any better, so he sensibly decided to just leave her alone. The Prince and the Princess sat side by side, looking out over the Tourney, both of them lost in their own thoughts. Nothing much was happening yet. And from the look of it, nothing was going to go on happening for some time yet. So eventually they ended up talking to each other anyway, because there was nothing else to do.

"The woman who was poisoned in my place," said Catherine. "I forget her name . . ."

"Lady Melanie Drayson," Richard said kindly. "I've arranged for her family to be looked after. She left a husband and two small children. None of what happened was Melanie's fault, or theirs. I'll see they have every support we can offer."

Catherine looked at him properly for the first time. "You didn't have to do that."

"Of course I did," said Richard. "That's my job, as Prince—to look after my subjects."

Catherine thought about that for a while. "My father wouldn't have done it. Wouldn't even have occurred to him that he should." She glanced at him, almost shyly. "You know, you're not at all what I expected."

Richard had to smile. "All right, I'll bite. What did you expect?"

"I don't know! I suppose . . . I wanted you to be someone I could hate."

"You left someone behind in Redhart, didn't you?" said Richard.

"How did you . . . ?"

"All sorts of interested parties, from both our countries, have made it a point to tell me all sorts of things that they thought I ought to know," said Richard. "For a great many reasons. Who was he?"

"Malcolm Barrett," said Catherine almost defiantly. "King William's Champion. A great warrior. We'd been in love since we were children. As soon as we were old enough to know what love was."

"I'm sorry about that," said Richard. "I do know the man by reputation. We may even have crossed swords, out in the disputed territories. We were both fighting on the border at the same time. But it's hard to be sure who you're facing, in the middle of a melee."

"Did you . . . have anyone?" said Catherine.

"No," said Richard. "There's never been anyone special, anyone who mattered . . . I kept waiting, kept looking, expecting someone would come along eventually who'd make my heart beat that little bit faster. But . . . I suppose I just never met the right Princess."

That was a step too far. Catherine withdrew back inside herself immediately, staring out across the crowds. Richard sighed inwardly and changed the subject.

"Parliament is holding an extended Sitting, right now, talking through the arrangements for the wedding. Pushing everything through in a rush. I did offer to elope—just you and me and some village priest, in a quiet little church somewhere . . . But they all went very pale and couldn't seem to get their breath, so I pretended I was just joking. Apparently, the Forest and Redhart wedding ceremonies are very different, and we have to use all the right bits from both countries or it doesn't count."

"All of this . . . haste," said Catherine. "Because I won't be properly safe, until I'm married to you." She still wasn't looking at him.

"Well . . . yes," said Richard.

She turned abruptly to face him, her face cold, holding his gaze with hers. "How do you really feel about marrying me, Richard?"

"You do know . . . I have no more choice in this than you," Richard said carefully. "Part of being a Prince is that sometimes you just have to do things, no matter how you feel about them. Duty and responsibility and honour, and all that. I have been . . . thinking about us. And the marriage. It came as a bit of a shock. I'm sure you felt the same way. I always thought

I'd have more time . . . But your safety has to come first. We can sort everything else out, afterwards."

Catherine's mouth twitched in something approaching a smile. "You really think it's going to be that easy?"

"Honestly? Hell, no!"

And they both shared a real smile for a moment.

"What will your Malcolm do, back in Redhart?" Richard said carefully.

"Nothing," said Catherine. "He knows his duty. He'll probably even try to be happy for me." She leaned over to Richard, so they could speak very quietly and not be overheard. "I've been thinking about one thing; we're going to have to have sex, aren't we?"

Richard did his best to keep a straight face. "It is rather expected of us, once we're married. Yes."

"Do you know anything about it?" Catherine said bluntly. "I mean, I understand the basics, but . . . I never actually . . . My father put this spell on me so I couldn't . . ."

"Same here," Richard said quickly. "I quite understand. All part of protecting the Royal bloodline . . . So, you and Malcolm, you never . . ."

"I couldn't even undo my blouse for him," said Catherine. "Or undo anything of his. For fear of setting off all kinds of alarms."

"I have read a number of books on the subject," said Richard. "And looked at some very detailed pictures . . ."

They both grinned at each other.

"Maybe you could show me some of these books later," said Catherine. "Particularly the ones with pictures. If we've got to do this, I want to get it right."

"My father always said marriage would be a learning experience," Richard said solemnly.

"At least I'll get something out of this," said Catherine.

They both sat back on their thrones and looked down into the jousting lane, as the Big Names and the Major Players finally deigned to come out of their tents and parade before the ecstatic crowds. The onlookers went crazy, shouting and screaming and waving at their favourites, and throwing handfuls of rose petals over them. (Rose petals were always made available at the merchandising stalls, at very reasonable prices.) Sir Russell Hardacre was out in front, as usual—a tall, dashing fellow, always ready with a brisk no-nonsense smile. The only titled Bladesmaster in the Forest Land, he'd had his chain mail dyed in his family colours of red and purple. Right behind him came the most-discussed magic-user in the Land, Dr. Strangely Weird. High Magic, of course. Then came Sir Kay, the famous young master of the joust, his true identity hidden behind a featureless steel helm. A helm Sir Kay had sworn never to remove, unless he was defeated. And since he hadn't lost a jousting match since he entered the seasonal Tourneys, his secret identity remained . . . much discussed. He was young and fashionably slender and full of nervous energy, bouncing along in the parade and waving happily at everyone. Right behind him came Hannah Hexe, a calm, serene, and very powerful witch. One of the notorious Sisters of the Moon, graduated from what most people now called the Night Academy. She was, perhaps not surprisingly, not as popular or as loudly cheered as the others. And still the Big Names and famous faces came: Roger Zell, the Wandering Hero. Tom Tom Paladin, who roamed the Land doing good deeds, in penance for his awful past. Stefan Solomon, Master of the Morningstar. And many, many more. A few hours in the main fighting circles would soon whittle them down to the few really worth seeing.

Prince Richard and Princess Catherine watched the parade pass by with practiced smiles, and then they both looked around as Lady Gertrude came bustling up the steps to join them, in a flurry of petticoats and a stream of apologies. She elbowed the food-taster out of the way and sank heavily down into the chair beside Catherine, fanning herself with a painted paper fan while she struggled to get her breath back. She'd clearly been buying all sorts of attractive and useless things from the stalls, given the full to bulging bag she'd dumped at her feet. She soon caught her breath and began to chatter happily at Catherine while completely ignoring Richard.

"The political people have been running me ragged, my sweet, making sure all the details of the marriage ceremony are correct. So many questions! I thought I'd never get away, my poppet . . ."

Catherine frowned, just a bit dangerously. "I thought that was all settled!"

"Oh it is, it is, my petal. Absolutely nothing at all for you to be worried about! It's just . . . apparently they thought they had plenty of time to work it all out. But you and the Prince bringing the marriage forward so suddenly has changed everything. Caught them on the hop, so to speak. I've left them to it. Running round in circles, waving their hands in the air, trying to do a dozen things at once and then putting the blame on one another when it all goes wrong." She stopped and smiled demurely. "I may have made up a few things, added some details that weren't strictly needed, or accurate. Just to get my own back. If they took all of my little additions seriously, my sweet, you're going to have a very interesting ceremony. And where they're going to find a black goat with one bent horn at this time of the year . . . Anyway, the wedding is set for tomorrow. Definitely. Nothing at all for you to worry yourself about, my Princess."

"I'm more worried about where Sir Jasper is," said Catherine. "And what he's getting up to. I brought him here to stick with me, not go wandering off sightseeing. Have you seen him today, Gertrude?"

Lady Gertrude sniffed loudly. "No, and I can't say I miss him. Walking through walls like that, without even knocking! He may be dead, but there's still such a thing as propriety!"

Richard leaned forward. "The ghost isn't with you? Do I understand he's just been . . . wandering around the Castle on his own, all this time?"

"Is that a problem?" said Catherine, immediately ready to be offended on her friend's behalf.

"Not as such," Richard said carefully. "But it's really not a good idea. Forest Castle is still full of . . . surprises for the unready."

"How much trouble can a ghost get into?" said Catherine.

"In this Castle?" said Richard. "I hate to think . . . I'll send some of my people to look for him if he hasn't turned up by the end of the Tourney. Perhaps I should take him to the Castle Library, see if we can find some record of who he used to be, who his family were. Or maybe still is. He might have living descendants that we could track down for him. I mean, family still matters, even if one of them is dead."

Gertrude snorted loudly. "Good luck with that introduction."

"Hush, Gertrude," said Catherine. "That's a very kind thought, Richard."

And then they all looked across at the opposite raked seating, on the other side of the jousting lane, where the Seneschal was struggling to get King Rufus settled. At first the King walked straight past the throne set out for him, and almost off the end of the stand before the Seneschal caught up with him. He brought the King back to the throne, where the King decided he didn't like the cushion provided, and threw it away. He demanded that they send back to the Castle for his favourite cushion. The Seneschal very politely pointed out that the cushion he'd just thrown away was, in fact, his favourite cushion, which was why the Seneschal had placed a servant nearby to catch it, and here it was again, so would his majesty please sit down, before the Seneschal had one of his heads? The King accepted the cushion, plumped it up himself, and set it carefully in place before finally agreeing to sit down. He fidgeted with his ceremonial robes, seeing that they fell about him just so, but at least left the crown alone. Possibly because he'd forgotten he was wearing it. He looked around him with great interest at everything that was happening, completely ignoring the Seneschal's attempts to interest him in the speech he had to make to officially open the Grand Tourney. He finally spotted Richard and Catherine, sitting right opposite him, and brightened up a little. The Prince and Princess bowed formally to the King, who smiled and waved back at them, like a child on an outing.

"Your majesty, please!" said the Seneschal. "We have to talk about your speech!"

"What speech?" said the King. "Who am I meeting?"

"You're not meeting anyone in particular, Sire," the Seneschal said patiently. "You have to address the combatants, and welcome the crowds, and declare this year's Grand Tourney officially open."

"I see. Yes. And you are . . . ?"

"The Seneschal!"

"Bless you!"

The Seneschal glared at the King. "If I ever find out you're putting that on . . . Let us please discuss the speech, your majesty. I've got the scrolls."

"Oh, I am sorry," said the King.

"Those new pills definitely aren't working . . ."

"Don't push your luck, Seneschal," said the King, fixing him with a remarkably steady eye. "The moat still needs cleaning out . . ."

"Yes, your majesty."

The King sighed heavily, in his most put-upon way. "All right, show me the speech. What does it say?"

"You wrote it last night, Sire, with my help," said the Seneschal. "It's all written down for you; just say the words, smile at the right places, *which I've marked for you,* acknowledge the cheers of the crowd with a brisk wave of the hand . . . and then you can sit back and watch the events. You always enjoy that."

"I do?"

"Yes, Sire."

"I'll take your word for it."

The King looked dubiously at the scroll the Seneschal had given him. He unrolled it slowly, being careful not to crack the parchment with his shaking hands. He read it through, carefully, and then let the scroll roll itself up again.

"Same bullshit as the year before," he said. "Only the names change. Look at them, prancing about, preening themselves, basking in the adulation of the crowds. If they were real heroes they'd be up on the border, doing something useful with these martial skills they're so proud of. I know, I know; don't rush me. I have to be in the right mood for this. It's not easy being Royal, you know. Not when your back's killing you, and you've had to get up in the night five times to take a piss! I swear my bladder's ageing twice as fast as the rest of me."

He stood up abruptly. The nearby trumpeters took this as their cue, and launched into the Royal fanfare with great verve and gusto. Everyone fell silent, crowds and contestants alike, as they all looked up to their King. The Seneschal crossed his fingers behind his back. But King Rufus stood tall and proud, and read every word from the scroll with Royal authority and dignity. He spoke clearly and fluently, pronounced all the names correctly, and declared the Grand Tourney open in ringing tones. The contestants bowed to him and the crowd applauded fiercely, cheering their King at the top of their voices. King Rufus bowed gravely to them, waved a hand, and sat down again. The Seneschal allowed himself a breath of relief. Some days he thought these public excursions took more out of him than they did out of the King. Because there would come a day when the King wouldn't pull it together at the last moment . . . The King carefully rolled up the scroll, thrust it into the Seneschal's waiting hands, and settled back on his throne for a nice doze.

The Big Names and Major Players returned to their private tents, to prepare themselves. Everyone else got the hell out of the way as the armoured knights manoeuvred their giant chargers into position at the opposite ends of the jousting lane. Jousting was always popular with the crowds. Two men in full armour, planted on oversized horses, charged straight at each other with long wooden lances, each hoping to unseat his opponent before the other's lance punched him right out of his saddle. There was nothing the crowds liked better than the chance to see some overconfident aristocrat get dumped on his arse in public.

There was a lot to see: the horses pounding up and down in their highly coloured vestments, churning the earth into mud and filling the air with the pungent smells of sweat and dung. The knights, hunched down in their saddles, trying to make themselves as small a target as possible, which given how much armour they were wearing was a lost cause in itself. Some just rocked in their saddle as the lance slammed home, while others flew through the air in an ungainly fashion, to make a hard landing in the churned-up mud. Sometimes they got up straightaway, and sometimes they didn't. Blood, broken bones, and rattled brains were commonplace among the jousting fraternity. Most of them would gather together afterwards for some competitive hard drinking, and to compare wounds and old scars. And swap as many tall stories as they could get away with. The ones who got up quickly enough would earn cheers from the crowd, while those who were carted off the field on reinforced stretchers received even more cheers, and not a few waspish comments.

But as the jousts wore on, no obvious winner emerged. The successful knight of one joust would be unhorsed in the next, and so it went . . . until Sir Kay appeared. The young knight in the featureless steel helm thundered up and down the lists, taking on all comers and throwing them this way and that. He ducked and rolled in the saddle, somehow always dodging or deflecting the oncoming lance, while his own never wavered, slamming home every time. The crowd cheered his every triumph, and Sir Kay saluted them with his lance as he cantered back to the start to do it all again. The crowd loved that. Catherine quietly asked Richard if he knew who Sir Kay really was, behind his helm, and Richard had to admit that he didn't. Sir Kay appeared only at Tourneys, under his assumed name. Everyone assumed him to be the younger son of some minor line, trying to make a name for himself. In his own way, Sir Kay was as much a mystery as the Sombre Warrior was. Though somewhat less gloomy. Catherine tried not to giggle. But this was Sir Kay's first Grand Tourney, after two years of establishing his name at the seasonal tourneys. Much was expected of him. Everyone saw great things in his future. If he didn't get himself killed.

Time passed, and Sir Kay emerged triumphant. He had only to face one more contestant, the other survivor of the many lists. The Sombre Warrior took his place at the end of the lane opposite Sir Kay, and the two masked men faced each other. The crowds went quiet, the air full of tense expectation. Just like Sir Kay, the Sombre Warrior had said that if he lost, he would unmask.

The horses snorted loudly, sensing the anticipation in the air, and slammed their hooves against the ground, impatient to be off. The two men held their places, letting the tension build. At the end of the bout, one of them would have to take off his helm and show his face, and the audience couldn't decide which they were most curious about. The Sombre Warrior was a big man, and looked even bigger in full armour. Almost twice the size of the youthful Sir Kay. The crowd had seen lances snap and shatter against the Sombre Warrior's armoured chest, while Sir Kay had never been hit once. The Sombre Warrior urged his horse slowly forward, and the crowd tensed, but the horse was heading for the raked seating. The Sombre Warrior extended his lance out across the seats, over everyone's heads, to the Princess Catherine. She rose from her throne and tied a handkerchief to the very end of the lance. Her favour, for all to see. The crowd loved that echo of old chivalry, and cheered both of them loudly. The Princess sat down again, and the Sombre Warrior moved his horse back into position, facing Sir Kay. They both started forward.

• • •

Hawk and Fisher, Jack and Gillian, and Chappie the dog made their way through the Tourney, taking a great interest in everything it had to offer. Hawk and Fisher took the lead, striding forward, and everyone else hurried to get out of their way. The crowds knew real fighters when they saw them. Jack wandered amiably along behind them, saying *Sorry, sorry about that*, and everyone nodded respectfully to the old man in monk's robes. A few disreputable types looked like they weren't of a mind to accept the insult or the apology, but Gillian just stared them down with a cold eye. Chappie bounded happily along, here, there, and everywhere, sticking his nose into everything. And because he was after all a very big dog, everyone let him. Jack moved forward, to walk beside Hawk.

"Were the Tourneys as large and magnificent as this in your day, Father?"

"No," said Hawk. "There were no Tourneys under my father, King John. He didn't approve. Saw them as frivolous. Combat was too important to be wasted on the cheers of the populace. The only real battles I saw, up close and personal, were in the political arena. You couldn't beat the Landsgraves when it came to sneak attacks and general backstabbing. It was a much colder place here in those days."

Swordsmen stamped and thrust and parried in fighting circles on every side, because anyone who could stand up straight and carry a sword was allowed to enter. All you had to do was give your name to the steward, along with the name of your next of kin, and wait for your turn. Most didn't last long. Courage and brute strength could take a raw beginner only so far. The various Sorting Houses always sent their best swordsmen, to help sort the wheat from the chaff and demonstrate how good a swordsman the Sorting Houses could make a man. Supporters from all the various houses were also there, to cheer and boo as necessary. They all served the Brotherhood of Steel, but the Brotherhood had always believed in the value of healthy rivalry between houses.

Blades slammed together, sparks flying on the air as steel clashed with steel, and hard-faced men and women stamped back and forth in the confines of the fighting circles. Simple rules: stay within the circle, and duel to first blood. As the more hapless combatants were quickly weeded out, the duels became longer, more interesting affairs. Displays of strength and speed, and swordsmanship. Nearly always stopping at first blood. Of which there was quite a bit. Stewards were constantly running back and forth, throwing buckets of water across the churned-up earth to wash the blood away between contests. Otherwise no one could be sure of their footing.

It was all supposed to be thoroughly good-natured, and mostly it was. But now and again someone would lose their temper, and the red mist would descend, and they'd insist on fighting on. As long as it wasn't too mismatched, the stewards usually let them. The crowds weren't here for displays of skill. They wanted blood and suffering and the occasional death, even if few would actually admit it.

Hawk and his family stood together at the edge of one circle, watching. Hawk had to admit there was a lot of really skilled swordsmanship on display. Men and women who knew what they were doing. He became aware that his son, Jack, was watching the fight with a certain wistfulness.

"Do you want to have a go, Jack?" said Hawk.

"No," the monk said immediately. "It wouldn't be fair, with my Walking Man abilities. Gillian, how about you?"

"Love to," said Gillian.

She shouldered her way to the front of the queue, and no one objected once they heard her give her name and status to the steward. The watching crowd elbowed one another expectantly. A trainer from a Sorting House! Now they'd see something! Gillian drew her sword and strode briskly into the circle, where she found herself facing a young soldier in his early twenties. He took one look at the seventy-year-old woman with her iron grey hair and laughed in her face.

"Oh, he shouldn't have done that," said Jack.

"Get out of the circle, Granny!" said the soldier. "I don't care what kind of reputation you might have had once. Those days are gone. The circle's all about the here and now. Go on home and tend to your knitting."

"I can't watch," said Jack. "This is going to be bad."

"I should certainly hope so," said Fisher.

Gillian advanced on the young soldier and proceeded to beat him back and forth and round and round the circle, driving him this way and that through sheer force of skill and long years of training. She couldn't keep it up for long, but the young man didn't know that. He staggered backwards, struggling to keep his guard up, his eyes wide with shock. The moment Gillian realised she was starting to slow down, she lunged forward and disarmed him with one subtle move. The man stood there numbly, watching his sword fly through the air to land in the mud. He looked at his blade, and then at Gillian, and his face went ugly.

"It's a trick! You cheated, you rotten old bitch!"

Gillian punched him in the face. The whole crowd went *ooh!* as they heard his nose break. The young soldier left the circle, crying. The crowd applauded Gillian loudly. They liked a character. Gillian nodded happily and called, "Who's next?"

She took on a dozen more opponents and beat them all. Her opponents grew increasingly more skilled, and more respectful, but it didn't help. Long experience and an extensive knowledge of dirty tricks were always enough to trump youth and enthusiasm. Even so, Gillian was clearly slowing down and fighting for breath by the time she faced her last opponent. As much as she tried to hide it. She leaned heavily, if unobtrusively, on Jack's shoulder as she stood at the edge of the circle, accepting a drink from his water flask.

"You know," she said, mopping her face with a handkerchief that Jack provided, "this all used to be a lot easier when I was younger."

"What wasn't?" said Jack. "Look, just beat this last one, and that'll be thirteen victories in a row. Enough that the stewards will declare you swordswoman champion of the day. Then you can leave the circle and have a nice sit-down, and I'll find a shawl to put around your shoulders and fetch you your slippers. Won't that be nice?"

Gillian glared at him, threw the sweaty handkerchief back in his face, and stormed back into the middle of the circle, sweeping her sword back and forth before her. Jack grinned. He'd always known how to get his sister going. The last contestant shuffled forward, very cautiously, ready for anything. Gillian had him flat on his back in the mud in under a minute, wondering what the hell had just happened. The crowd cheered as the stewards announced Gillian as that day's champion, and Gillian got the hell out of the circle while her shaking legs would still hold her up. Hawk and Fisher crowded around her, telling her how proud they were of her, and half carried her away to the nearest seat. Where she sat slumped for some time, fighting to get her breathing under control and coughing up unpleasant things.

"You're seventy-two, for God's sake," said Jack. "Woman your age should have more sense."

"I can still kick your arse, and don't you forget it," said Gillian.

When she was ready, they all went to stand before the main raked seating so Gillian could be presented to Prince Richard. (It should have been King Rufus, really, but he was asleep. No one said anything.) The Prince congratulated Gillian warmly, said nice things about her excellent reputation at the Sorting House (courtesy of a note someone had slipped into his hand at the last moment), and invited her to enter the Castle after the Tourney, to join the rest of the day's champions at a banquet in their honour.

Gillian bowed to the Prince, acknowledged the cheers of the crowd, and then moved away, still leaning heavily on Hawk and Fisher. They hadn't got far when a tall, slender figure dressed all in black appeared out of nowhere, to block their way.

"Hello, Mother," said Raven the Necromancer.

Gillian straightened up immediately, grabbed Raven firmly by the ear, and hauled him off to one side, to a relatively quiet part of the clearing where they could talk privately. The rest of the family tagged along. They wouldn't have missed this for the world. They all studied the Necromancer with great interest, and waited for the sparks to fly.

"What the hell is this *Raven* nonsense?" demanded Gillian. "I gave you a perfectly good name: Nathanial!"

"It's show business, Mother," Raven said calmly. "No one is going to take you seriously as a Necromancer and a dealer in dark forces with a name like Nathanial."

"Well . . . why a bloody Necromancer, anyway?" said Gillian.

Raven shrugged. "I suppose we all feel the need to rebel against our family background. I just went a little further than most. Speaking of family . . ."

Gillian reluctantly made the introductions, and Raven bowed to them all. He was careful to be very polite to Jack, in his monk's robes, and reached down to make a fuss of Chappie. But he was clearly most fascinated with his grandparents, even as they made it very clear to him that they were there only as a Hawk and Fisher.

"Of course," said Raven. "I quite understand. Reputations can be such a burden, even though you can't get anywhere without one. I'm so pleased I finally got to meet you, after all these years . . . Look at the two of you! You're my grandparents, but you don't look much older than me! You really must tell me your secret."

"Clean living and a vegetable diet . . . are two things I've always avoided," Fisher said solemnly. "I can't help thinking there's a connection."

"Actually, it involves lots of exposure to Wild Magic, and whole armies of really nasty things trying to kill you," said Hawk. "I don't recommend it."

"We have met before, Nephew," said Jack. "Though you were so young you probably don't remember me."

"I'm afraid not, Uncle," Raven said politely. "But your reputation does of course precede you. Not many Walking Men live long enough to retire. You did so much good, according to all the songs and stories. Why did you give it up?"

"Because I decided I was doing it for all the wrong reasons," said Jack. "And you and I are definitely going to have a few words about this *dealing with dark forces* thing."

"Of course, Uncle. Do bear in mind what I said earlier, about show business. Not everything is necessarily what it appears, in the magic game." He grinned down at Chappie. "I love your dog. Is he a pure breed? Of some kind?"

"Too bloody right," growled the dog. "One of a kind, that's me, and proud of it. And somebody had better lead me to a food stall soon or there's going to be trouble."

"Oh . . . ," said Raven. "You're *that* dog! You know, there's a lot of stories told about you in the magic community. The High Warlock's dog . . . The wise dog, who cannot die. How is it you're still alive, Chappie?"

"Because he's too mean to die," said Hawk briskly. He glared at the dog. "Business first, sausages later."

"You never did know how to enjoy yourself," said Chappie.

. . .

They all strolled along, through the Tourney, passing endless stalls and markets and attractions. People gave them even more room than before, now that the notorious Necromancer was walking with them. Chappie kept darting off to nose for fallen food among the stalls, but he always caught up with them. Nobody bothered him either.

"You know," Raven said to Hawk and Fisher, "I have to say, you don't look a bit like your official portraits, either of you. And nothing at all like the official statues set up in your honour."

Chappie sniggered loudly. "I really must find the time to piss on them."

"Do you want to buy a dog?" Fisher said to Raven. "You can have him cheap."

"Really cheap," said Hawk.

"You'd be lost without me and you know it," said the dog complacently.

They continued on, through the many attractions set up to wring as much money from the crowds as possible and keep their minds occupied during those inevitable times when nothing much was happening. A bored crowd is a dangerous crowd. They might decide to make their own excitement. Hawk found a stall selling meaty, chewy things and bought a whole bunch of them for Chappie, to shut him up. And while he was standing around, trying to pretend the dog at his side making a disgrace of himself was nothing at all to do with him, he happened to spy a sign saying *Ride the Unicorn!* Hawk drew Fisher's attention to the sign, and they both regarded it thoughtfully. Hawk drifted in the sign's general direction, and the others followed after him, keen to see what might occur. The sign led into a small enclosure, where a dwarf in a cut-down bearskin was loudly proclaiming his wares to some mildly interested onlookers.

"Ride the lovely unicorn! Isn't he magnificent? Give the children a thrill! Boys, is your sweetheart really true to you? Put her on the unicorn and find out! Fathers, is your daughter all she should be? Put her on the unicorn and set your mind at rest!"

There were some takers, and an awful lot of giggling, as the dwarf led the unicorn around the small enclosure on a long rope. Hawk looked the unicorn over carefully, waited for a quiet moment, and then approached the unicorn's owner. The dwarf looked around, and nodded easily. He seemed a cheerful enough sort.

"Excuse me," said Hawk.

"Take your place in the queue, squire; I'll get to you in a moment. Very popular, the unicorn ride."

"It's just that I can't help noticing that the white dye job is wearing off in several places," said Hawk. "And he's wearing iron shoes instead of silver. And I know for a fact that unicorns have curlicue horns, not straight. What you have there, in fact, is a shire horse painted white with a bit of old bone stuck on his forehead."

The dwarf grinned. "Keep your voice down, squire. The Tourney organisers think they're getting a bargain."

And back he went, loudly proclaiming his wares to the eager queue. Hawk nodded slowly and left him to it.

It didn't take Hawk long to search out the axe-fighting circles. One of the bigger clues was the number of large muscular men being carried off on reinforced stretchers, while healers did their best to apply pressure to gaping wounds. First blood in an axe fight was always going to tend toward the dramatic. The rest of Hawk's family stood patiently beside him, as he watched big burly men with all kinds of axes going at one another with great gusto. There was much howling of battle cries, staggering back and forth in the blood-soaked mud of the circle, and men grunting explosively with the effort of their exertions. The stewards had given up trying to wash the blood out of the circle and stood casually to one side, chatting easily and completely ignoring the fights, until a sudden heartfelt scream announced another loser, and winner. Hawk grinned.

"That'll do me," he said briskly.

"Are you sure about this, Father?" said Gillian. "Some of those contestants are so big I'm not sure they technically qualify as people. That last one looked like someone had shaved a bear and then strapped an axe to his paw."

"Trust me," said Fisher, "your father's taken down a lot bigger, in his time."

"I shall pray for you, Father," said Jack.

"Stand well back," Hawk said cheerfully. "You don't want to get blood and gore all over you."

"Give them hell, Father," said Gillian.

Hawk strode into the circle, and the supernaturally bright sheen to his axe head immediately drew everyone's attention. Hawk announced his name loudly, and there was an instant loud buzz from the watching crowd. The stewards stood up straight, conversed briefly but animatedly with one another, and then the bravest one came forward to bow very formally.

"Pardon me, sir Hawk, but . . . given your name, and that entirely disquieting axe you're carrying, might you by any chance be . . . ?"

"Yes," said Hawk. "I used to run the Hero Academy. That's my wife, Fisher, over there, looking beautiful and exceedingly dangerous, as always. You have any objections to my taking part in this Tourney?"

"Me? No!" said the steward quickly. "Honoured to have you here!" He turned away, got out of the circle as fast as he could, and addressed the crowd. "My friends, allow me to present to you a real hero! A Hawk, from the Hero Academy, has chosen to honour us with his presence today! Give the man a big hand!"

The crowd responded with a polite but frankly rather lukewarm round of applause. *Anyone could claim a big name and a big reputation,* their faces seemed to suggest. *Show us something.* Hawk smiled easily about him, sweeping his heavy axe back and forth before him as though it were nothing. The blood-soaked mud squelched loudly under his boots as he surreptitiously dug his feet in, for a better purchase. A large northern barbarian stepped into the circle to face him: easily a head taller, barrel-chested and broad-shouldered, wearing just a loincloth and furred boots, the better to show off his appallingly developed physique. Hawk nodded amiably to his opponent. The barbarian just growled back at him, from deep in his throat. And then he surged forward, horribly quickly for someone of his size and bulk, his massive axe whistling through the air, without waiting for the steward to start things. But Hawk had been expecting that. He stepped quickly forward, ducked under the wildly sweeping axe, and slammed his own axe head deep into the barbarian's exposed hip. The steel blade juddered on the bone, with a loud chunking sound the whole audience could hear. The barbarian was brought to a sudden halt, his eyes wide with pain and shock. Hawk jerked his axe out and stepped back. Blood jetted on the air, until the barbarian clapped one huge hand across it. Hawk looked steadily at his opponent.

"First blood."

The crowd cheered and applauded loudly. This was more like it. Maybe this Hawk really was who he said he was, after all. And then the crowd's applause died away, as they realised the barbarian hadn't left the circle. He was still standing his ground, blood seeping thickly through the fingers of the hand covering the great wound on his hip. He still held his axe in his other hand, and his dark, deep-set eyes blazed with bitter fury. He raised his axe suddenly and threw it at Hawk, the huge blade tumbling end over end as it flew through the air. But Hawk was no longer standing where he had been. He'd known what the barbarian was going to do before the man did it, reading the barbarian's intentions in his tensing muscles. By the time the flying axe flashed through the space where he'd been, Hawk was right there in front of the startled barbarian. He brought his axe up and down with brutal speed and strength, and buried the heavy axe head in the barbarian's shoulder, right beside the neck. It smashed through the collarbone and drove the barbarian to his knees through sheer impact. The barbarian cried out once, in shock and pain, and blood sprayed from his mouth. Hawk jerked the axe free, like a woodsman yanking his blade out of a tree trunk, and blood sprayed everywhere. The barbarian fell forward, onto all fours, his hands pressed deep into the crimson mud. Hawk brought his axe sweeping down, with all his strength behind it, and cut off the barbarian's head. It bounced and rolled across the ground like a football, ending up at the feet of the watching crowd, who shrieked happily. The headless body collapsed and lay still.

The steward loudly proclaimed Hawk's victory, while two of his fellows hurried forward to drag the body out of the circle. Getting the head back from the crowd took somewhat longer. Hawk strolled back to join his family. Fisher grinned, Gillian shook her head slowly, and Jack looked at him steadily.

"Was that really necessary, Father?"

"Yes," said Hawk. "Break the rules once, and I'll give you a second chance. Piss me off a second time and you're a dead man."

"Age has not mellowed you," said Fisher.

"And aren't you grateful?" said Hawk.

"You were right," said Gillian, still a little dazed at what she'd seen. "Only a fool turns his back on a cheat."

"Not actually the biggest man I've ever seen you kill," said Fisher. "But bloody close."

"Size isn't everything," said Hawk.

He strode back into the circle, shaking drops of blood from his axe head. He smiled at the new opponent facing him. "First blood?"

"Oh, I think so," said his new opponent quickly.

Hawk took on twelve opponents, in swift succession. Some were stronger, some were swifter, a few were even more skilled, but none of them were as strong *and* as fast *and* as skilled as Hawk. Or had his experience. Hawk had fought men and demons in his time, in duels and skirmishes, battles and wars. He wasn't unbeatable, but there was no one at the Tourney who even came close. The crowd around the circle grew steadily thicker, as he beat men up and chopped them down, and didn't even raise a decent sweat. He didn't have to kill anyone else. Some of them even walked out of the circle, glad to still be alive. As the news spread, people came running from all over the Tourney to see what was happening. They'd never seen anything like Hawk before. They cheered and applauded and stamped their feet as the steward announced Hawk champion axeman of the day.

Fisher sniffed loudly as Hawk left the circle to the roar of the madly applauding throng. She insisted on leading the family off to the next fighting circle, where she wasted no time in announcing herself as Fisher of the Hero Academy. She stepped into the circle, swept her sword before her, and loudly declared herself ready to take on all comers. A large crowd had followed her. They pressed together several ranks deep around the circle, smiling widely in anticipation. More people were hurrying forward, from all around. The news was spreading. Hawk and Fisher were here.

A hell of a lot of swordsmen came forward to challenge Fisher. Only two champion swordspeople were ever allowed on the day of Tourney, and with the first already awarded to Gillian by Prince Richard, defeating Fisher was their only chance to qualify. And they hadn't come all this way to be put off by a legendary name. There was a certain amount of scuffling in the queue, as the various swordsmen sorted out the right pecking order, and then the first man stepped into the circle to face Fisher. A tall, heavily built fellow in well-used chain mail, he looked like he knew his business. Fisher grinned, and went forward to meet him.

Clearly an ex-soldier, with many scars, he towered over Fisher. He didn't make the mistake of underestimating her. He edged forward, cautiously, ready for an extended bout of swordsmanship. Fisher just slammed right into him and drove him back with an intimidatingly fierce display of speed and savagery. She drove him this way and that, making it look easy, and then beat the sword right out of his hand. The ex-soldier just stood there for a moment, blinking, and looking at his sword lying on the ground. And then he decided to get the hell out of the circle while he still could. It wasn't, technically speaking, first blood, but he knew he was lucky to be walking away with all his fingers still attached. Several quite experienced swordsmen waiting in the queue decided they wouldn't bother after all.

There were still plenty of hard-faced swordsmen and -women who were more than ready to have a go. Fisher took them all down, quickly and efficiently, always stepping back at first blood, if only so she didn't get any on her. The crowd loved her, shouting her name over and over. They were packed so deep round the circle now that those at the back were having to stand on benches to see what was happening. Hawk beamed fondly on Fisher, always proud to see her taking on the world and winning.

The thirteenth fighter shouldered everyone else out of his way, and strode into the fighting circle. Fisher looked him over, and immediately decided this was one to take very seriously. He was only average height and weight, lithely muscular in an athletic way. But he moved with a graceful and economical style that marked him immediately for what he was. He stood poised before Fisher, studying her with cold, unblinking eyes; and he didn't bow.

"So, you're one of the trainers from the Hero Academy," he said, in a flat, cold voice. "Mongrels. Troublemakers. Too proud to show the proper obedience to your proper masters. Too arrogant to bow down to the Brotherhood of Steel. It's time you upstarts were taught a lesson in real swordsmanship, by a properly trained fighter. I am a Bladesmaster, thanks to the Brotherhood—unbeatable with a sword in my hand. Defend yourself, bitch."

"Oh, he really shouldn't have said that last bit," murmured Hawk.

The Bladesmaster advanced steadily on Fisher in a practiced swordsman's stance. Fisher smiled, and just stood there and let him come to her. And then she lifted her sword and threw it at him, with all her strength. The blade flashed through the air, incredibly fast, and the Bladesmaster didn't even have a chance to get his own sword up to block it. Fisher's sword punched right through his throat, and out the back of his neck, in a welter of blood. The Bladesmaster fell back a step, his eyes wide with horror. He opened his mouth to say something, but only blood came out. He fell to his knees. His sword dropped from his hand. His eyes slowly closed, as the blood pumped out of his throat. Fisher walked forward to stand before him, took hold of the sword hilt standing out before her, and pulled the blade out of his neck with one easy movement, stepping aside at the last moment, to avoid the last of the jetting blood. The Bladesmaster fell forward onto his face, in the crimson mud, and didn't move again. The crowd went mad, cheering and clapping and shouting her name. Fisher saluted them once with her sword and strolled back to join Hawk, who shook his head regretfully.

"You're going to be unbearable about this for days, aren't you?"

"How well you know me," said Fisher.

This time, it was Hawk and Fisher's turn to stand before Prince Richard. He recognised their names, and the implications, immediately, and went out of his way to say many fine things about the Hero Academy before naming them both champions of the Tourney and inviting them into the Castle to join the celebration banquet. And then he looked thoughtfully at Hawk and Fisher, and for a moment it seemed as though he might be about to say something. But he didn't. He bowed respectfully to Hawk and Fisher, and they bowed formally back, and went back to their family.

"I'm starting to feel a bit left out," said Jack. "I won't fight with a sword or an axe, or any other weapon. I don't do that anymore. But I have thought of something . . ."

He led his family through the excited crowds, many of them applauding loudly as they passed. A few came forward to beg favours or coins, or just to touch their clothes, but a cold look from Hawk or Fisher was all it took to put a stop to that. Jack finally brought them to the magic circles, where various sorcerous duels and contests took place for the edification, delight, and bafflement of the watching audiences. Such duels tended to be loud and flashy affairs, and not always that easy for the inexperienced or uninitiated to follow. Jack walked straight up to the nearest steward, and was just a little disappointed that the man didn't immediately recognise his name, or who he used to be.

"What's your speciality?" said the steward briskly. "Elemental magic? Transformations? Plagues and curses?"

"Invulnerability," Jack said firmly. "There's not a magic here that can touch me."

"Best of luck with that one," said the steward. "You sure about this? Things can get pretty rough inside the circle . . . All right, all right. Next of kin for the form, please."

But in the end, Jack just stood there in the middle of the magic circle and defied anyone to move him. They all came forward—the magicians and sorcerers, the hedge wizards and witches—resplendent in their brightly coloured robes and tall, pointy hats. They blasted Jack with spells, curses, and even bolts of lightning, and couldn't get anywhere near him. Jack spoke no spells, chanted no cantrips; he just stood his ground. An old monk, leaning on a wooden staff, smiling amiably into the teeth of whatever they could throw at him. One after another, dark-eyed sorcerers filled the air with blistering energies; sloe-eyed witches all but broke their brooms in half trying to turn him into things; and wild-eyed hedge wizards called down all the wilder weathers of the four seasons. To no effect. Because, although none of them knew it, nothing could touch the retired Walking Man, as long as he walked in Heaven's path. Though Jack would have been the first to admit he was stretching that just a bit. Still, as long as he was doing it in a good cause . . .

In the end, he stood alone and unhurt in the middle of a circle that had been blasted down to the bedrock and charred around the edges, and thirteen powerful magic-users had to admit they'd done their worst and not even knocked him off balance. They retired from the field, baffled, and more than a little hurt. The steward declared Jack champion magic-user of the day, and the watching audience applauded him in a respectful sort of way. Jack went on to bow deeply before an equally baffled Prince Richard, who shrugged and invited him to the Castle banquet anyway.

"I'm ashamed of you, Jack," Hawk said afterwards. "Cheating your way to a prize like that."

"I prefer to call it lateral thinking," said Jack. "I've always believed in outthinking one's enemy."

"He didn't get that from me," said Fisher.

They continued on through the Tourney to see what else it had to offer, while Chappie led them unerringly from one food stall to another, where he insisted they try a little bit of everything. While he tried a great deal of everything.

"Now I know why you've lived so long," said Raven. "It's because you never stop eating."

"Don't knock it till you've tried it," said Chappie indistinctly.

Hawk and Fisher made it a point of pride to try some of the more exotic dishes on offer. Spiced sausage, curried bean soup, and sweet crunchy things that came in a paper cone. All the family tried a bit of this and that, except Jack, who turned up his nose at everything.

"I don't know how you can eat that stuff. You must have cast-iron stomachs."

"If you can eat the kind of stuff they sell at Haven's street stalls, you can eat anything," said Fisher.

"True," said Hawk. "I do miss that something-wriggling-on-a-stick they used to sell down by the docks. Never did find out what it was."

"Probably just as well," said Fisher wisely. She looked at Gillian. "Did they still sell that when you were down there?"

"Hell, yes," said Gillian, shuddering. "I could never eat them. Couldn't stand the way they looked at me."

"Then you should have eaten them from the other end," Fisher said ruthlessly.

"My family are barbarians," said Raven. Chappie sniggered.

"I haven't seen my daughter, Mercy, anywhere," said Jack. "I was sure she'd be here."

"Oh, my cousin is quite definitely here today," said Raven. "You'd better come with me, Uncle."

He led the family through the packed crowds, to the jousting lane, where the Sombre Warrior and the masked Sir Kay were seated on their great chargers at opposite ends of the long grassy lane. Studying each other, through their featureless steel helmets. Young women pressed forward to throw showers of rose petals over both men. Raven brought his family right to the front and made sure they all had a good view. (Mostly just by smiling at people in the way in a thoughtful fashion until they decided not to be in the way any longer. No one crowds a Necromancer.)

The Sombre Warrior and Sir Kay started forward, the steward raised his voice and brought his flag sweeping down, and just like that the two knights were off, racing down the narrow lane towards each other, urging their horses on, lances standing proudly out before them. The horses pounded on for all they were worth, their hooves digging great divots out of the wet earth and throwing them aside, while Sir Kay and the Sombre Warrior hung on grimly, and the crowd went completely out of their minds with excitement. The two men rapidly closed the gap between them. Everyone was on their feet, shouting and waving, including Prince Richard and Princess Catherine, each cheering for the respective countryman. The two horses came together, both lances struck home, snapped and splintered and broken in half by the impact . . . but the Sombre Warrior stayed put in his saddle, while Sir Kay was thrown backwards off his horse and crashed to the hard ground.

The whole crowd went suddenly silent. The Sombre Warrior reined in his horse, turned it around, and looked back to see what had happened to his opponent. A steward ran out into the lane, to grab the reins of the riderless horse. Sir Kay lay flat on his back in the churned-up earth. And then, slowly and painfully, he rolled over onto his side, and forced himself up onto his knees, and then onto his feet. He saluted the Sombre Warrior at the other end, and the crowd went mad all over again, howling and screaming, stamping their feet and pounding their hands together till it hurt. Some people wanted to run forward into the lane, to congratulate both men, but there were enough armed guards on hand to make it clear that would be a really bad idea.

The Sombre Warrior respectfully dipped his lance, with the Princess' favour still wrapped around it. Sir Kay nodded his appreciation, and then walked slowly but steadily forward to stand before Prince Richard and Princess Catherine. He bowed once, just a bit jerkily, and then raised both his hands to place them on either side of his helmet. The crowd was utterly still, absolutely silent. Tension on the air was so thick you could have sliced it with a knife. Without realising it, everyone was leaning forward. Sir Kay took off his helmet with one smooth motion, and long golden hair tumbled out, to surround a young woman's face. She smiled brilliantly around her. As one, the crowd turned to look at the Sombre Warrior, to see how he would take it, that he's come so close to being unseated and unmasked by a mere slip of a girl. The Sombre Warrior sat very still for a long moment, and then he bowed to Sir Kay.

The crowd loved it. They went completely off their heads, laughing and cheering and hugging one another with joy, jumping up and down and dancing in the enclosed sections. The greatest jest of the whole Tourney, and they'd been there to see it! They'd be telling this story to their friends and neighbours, their children and their grandchildren, for the rest of their lives. Sir Kay smiled demurely up at Prince Richard and Princess Catherine, curtsied as best she could in full armour, and then turned and walked off in search of the hospital tents.

Jack looked at Raven.

"That was my Mercy!"

"Yes, Uncle. I know."

"Still better than being a Necromancer," said Gillian.

"Well, quite," said Raven.

They tracked Jack's daughter, Mercy, to the nearest hospital tent, where the unmasked knight was limping slowly forward to be greeted by a pleasant-looking young woman in simple horsewoman's clothes, waiting at the entrance to the tent. She rushed forward and threw her arms around Mercy, holding her upright when Mercy's knees buckled and almost gave out. The young woman spoke soothingly to Mercy, and helped her into the hospital tent. Jack hurried forward. The rest of the family studied him thoughtfully, curious as to how he was taking all this. He hadn't expressed a single opinion yet, remaining resolutely cold-faced and silent. He just strode along, staring straight ahead, leaning heavily on his wooden staff but still covering quite a lot of ground for a man of his age. He finally reached the hospital tent, flung the flaps aside, and strode in. Followed by everyone else, including Chappie, all of them determined not to miss out on anything.

The young horsewoman was stripping Mercy out of her armour, revealing a slender woman in her late twenties, wearing a padded undersuit. Heavy purple bruising showed all down Mercy's left side. Both women looked round sharply at the sudden entrance, Mercy's long golden hair tumbling across her shoulders, and then she winced harshly as the sudden movement hurt her. She had a pretty, strong-featured face, with clear grey eyes and a generous mouth, and another heavy bruise on her left temple. The young horsewoman moved quickly forward, to stand protectively between Mercy and the intruders.

"What the hell do you think you're doing? You can't just barge into a hospital tent . . ."

"It's all right, Allison," said Mercy. "I've been expecting them."

Allison fell back reluctantly, staying close to her friend. Mercy smiled at Jack.

"Hello, Daddy."

"Hello, Mercy," said Jack. "So this is what you've been up to, my girl. No wonder you stopped writing."

She met his gaze defiantly. "You always told me to follow my heart, and stick to what I was good at. And I was very good at jousting. Really! I was unbeaten until today. And if that bloody Sombre Warrior hadn't turned up . . . Oh, don't scowl at me like that, Daddy! I'm a grown woman now. I've carried arms and fought in tourneys. I'm allowed to say *bloody* if I feel like it." She broke off, and smiled radiantly at him. "But I am very pleased to see you again, Daddy. It's been ever such a long time. What are you doing here? And who . . . Oh. Hello, Auntie Gillian."

"Hello, Mercy," said Gillian.

Jack caught something passing between the two women and nodded slowly. "Of course. I should have known. You're the one who trained her, Gillian!"

"You were off hiding from the world in a monastery!" snapped Gillian. "Who else was she going to turn to?"

"So you knew all about this Sir Kay business?" said Jack.

"No," said Gillian. She glared at Raven. "But you knew. And you didn't tell me!"

"You're not the easiest of people to talk to, Mother," murmured the Necromancer.

"But who are all these other people, Daddy?" said Mercy, looking suspiciously at Hawk and Fisher. "I mean, I don't know them. They could be anybody. Or are they some half brothers and half sisters from the wrong side of the blanket, from before you gave all that up to be a monk?"

"Show some respect, child," said Jack. "These are your grandparents, Prince Rupert and Princess Julia. Come home at last."

Mercy's jaw dropped, and her eyes got very wide. Her mouth worked, but it was a few moments before she could come up with a response, which in the end consisted simply of . . .

"Gosh."

Hawk smiled at her. "We're going by Hawk and Fisher these days. Don't want anyone to know we're back."

"And yes, we are looking really good for our age," said Fisher. "We know."

Mercy brought herself back under control, with an effort. "It's not an easy thing, to meet a living legend. Hello, Grandpa and Grandma! You owe me a hell of a lot of birthday presents."

"Hear, hear," said Raven.

"Get in line," said Hawk. "We owe a lot of people a lot of things."

"He never remembers birthdays," Fisher announced loudly to no one in particular. "Even when I remind him."

"But . . . you've both got to be well over a hundred years old!" said Mercy. "This is something to do with the Blue Moon, right?"

"Close enough," said Hawk.

"You don't look anything like your official portraits," said Mercy, almost accusingly. "Or your official statues."

"So we've been told," said Chappie.

Mercy and her friend Allison jumped, just a little. Chappie gave them both his most ingratiating smile.

"Never mind that," Jack said shortly. "Why didn't you write, young lady, and tell me what you were up to?"

"Because I knew you wouldn't approve," Mercy said guilelessly. "And you certainly weren't going to give me your permission. And then I'd just have had to go ahead and defy you and do it anyway, and upset you . . . So it seemed easier all round not to tell you anything."

Jack surprised them all then by smiling. "Fair enough. Aren't you going to introduce me to your friend?"

They all looked at the young horsewoman, Allison, who was standing back a little and staring at them all like a mouse hypnotised by a snake. With eyes stretched so wide they looked positively painful. Mercy put an arm round Allison's waist and pulled her close. She looked squarely at her father, fully prepared to defy him again.

"This is my girlfriend, Allison DeLain. My one true love."

Everyone looked at Jack, expecting him to be shocked, or angry, but he wasn't. He just smiled at Allison and nodded easily to her.

"You can't spend as much time in a monastery as I have, and not know all about brotherly love. Are you two happy together?"

"Yes, Daddy," Mercy said firmly. "Very happy." Allison managed a small squeak and a nod, still somewhat overawed by the company, and the occasion. Mercy kissed her on the cheek and held her close.

"Then that's all that matters," said Jack. "Though God knows where my great-grandchildren are going to come from. Perhaps I should find a nice healthy girl and get married again."

"Daddy!" said Mercy, honestly shocked. Allison giggled.

Hawk looked around the hospital tent. They'd clearly caught it at a quiet moment, though blood and discarded bandages on the floor suggested that hadn't always been the case. All the camp beds were currently empty. The healers were standing in a far corner, exchanging gossip and passing round a wine bottle. Waiting for the next rush. Hawk fixed Mercy with a firm stare.

"We need to talk to you and your brother, here," he said. "Your grandmother and I run the Hero Academy these days, and . . ."

330

Allison clapped her hands together. "Oh, this is just so amazing! Mercy, I never knew your family was . . . Sorry. I'll keep quiet now."

"Don't mind her," Mercy said fondly. "She gets overexcited so easily. Go on."

"We had a visitor," said Fisher. "The Demon Prince."

Raven and Mercy looked at each other, and then at Jack and Gillian for confirmation, and then back at Hawk and Fisher again.

"The Demon Prince?" said Mercy incredulously. "Really?"

"Like, in the stories from our childhood?" said Raven. "I mean, I've read the histories, but . . ."

"He's real," said Jack. "We met him, on the way here. Or at least, one of his sendings."

"He lives inside people now," said Gillian.

"He threatened you, specifically," said Hawk, looking hard at Mercy and Raven. "Said you'd both die, if your grandmother and I didn't return to the Forest Land. So here we are."

"I never actually thought he was real," Mercy said quietly. "Just some bogeyman, from the past."

"I knew he was real," said Raven, "but I never thought he'd be back . . . not after all you did to get rid of him."

"And the Demon Prince knows my name?" said Mercy.

"Now you know why we stayed away, with different names and new lives," said Fisher. "To distance ourselves from you, keep you safe."

"Thank you," said Raven. "For coming back. For us."

Mercy nodded quickly. "You came all the way back here, to protect grandchildren you'd never even met. Gosh."

"Family is family," said Hawk. "Anyway . . . the Demon Prince also gave us a warning, or a prophecy. He said there would be war."

"Between the Forest Land and Redhart?" said Raven.

"Presumably," said Fisher. "Like most prophecies, it wasn't big on detail."

"I honestly don't see how!" said Raven. "Prince Richard and Princess Catherine are getting married tomorrow, and the Peace agreement will be signed straight afterwards. And with the border dispute finally settled . . . there's just no reason for either side to go to war!"

He stopped as he realised Mercy was shaking her head. "You've been hearing the same rumours I have, Cousin dear; you just don't want to believe them. You know very well there are some really high-up people, and all sorts of vested interests on both sides, who don't want this Peace at any price."

"There are always rumours," said Raven.

"Someone tried to poison the Princess just yesterday!"

Raven sighed, and nodded. He looked steadily at Hawk and Fisher. "There's always someone ready to profit from a war. And some people have been profiting from the border skirmishes for a really long time. You might want to look into that. But you don't need to worry about Mercy and me. We can take care of ourselves."

"Really?" said Hawk. "Against the Demon Prince? You only know the songs and the legends. He was much worse than that."

"You really did meet him," said Allison in a very small voice. "A hundred years ago, when the Darkwood exploded outwards, and demons swarmed across the Land . . . I never really believed any of that! I thought it was just another story, to make children behave. Be good or the Demon Prince will come for you. But it's all true, isn't it? It all happened, and you were there . . . And now it's all going to happen again. Oh God, oh God . . ."

"Hush, Allison," said Mercy. "Steady, girl . . . We're just talking. Everything's going to be all right."

"You don't know that!"

Allison pulled herself away from Mercy and ran out of the tent. Mercy called after her, but Allison didn't look back. Mercy glared at Hawk and Fisher.

"You frightened her!"

"Will she keep her mouth shut about who we really are?" said Hawk.

"Yes," said Mercy. "It's just all been a bit too much for her, that's all. She'll be fine when she calms down."

"As champions of the Tourney, we've been invited inside the Castle," said Fisher. "And once we're in . . ."

"We can talk to all the right people and get a better understanding of what's really going on," said Hawk.

"There's something you need to know, Uncle Jack," said Raven, almost reluctantly. "I have good reason to believe . . . that the Stalking Man has visited King William, at Castle Midnight, in Redhart."

Gillian looked at Raven sharply. "*He's* real? Hell's vengeance on Earth? I thought he was just a legend, a made-up counterpoint to the Walking Man."

"Leland Dusque is very real," said Jack slowly. "And very dangerous. I've . . . heard stories about him, of a disquieting nature. About what he is and what he does. I can't think of any good reason why he should want to visit King William, or why William of Redhart would want to receive him."

"Well, this has all been most fascinating, and more than a little worrying, but I have to get back to the Tourney and show my face," said Raven. "A reputation like mine needs a lot of maintaining, or people will think I've gone soft and try to take advantage."

"Don't worry," Gillian said cheerfully. "We'll all come along. Keep you company."

"Yes," said Raven. "I was afraid of that."

Back at the Grand Tourney, most of the fighting circles were empty, with all but a few of the day's champions already decided, but the magical contests were still in progress. Raven led his family through the thinning crowds to the magic circles, where rather smaller groups of spectators did their best to follow the intricacies of what was going on, while maintaining what they very much hoped was a safe distance. Magical duels often ended up as surprisingly bloody affairs, with blasts of unnatural energies, lightning strikes from above, and even internal explosions. Along with some quite impressive curses. Hawk watched, fascinated, as two magicians of the darker type went head-to-head, standing unnaturally still and racked with deep concentration as they cursed each other with one appalling disease after another.

They started with the simpler stuff—shakes and shivers, boils and running sores, fevers and fugues—and then quickly escalated to leprosy, cannibal tapeworms, and infestations of bloodworms. In the end the loser just melted and ran away, like so much heated candle wax. Leaving just a pool of frothy pink liquid where he'd been standing, with his eyeballs floating sadly on the top. The winner quickly cured himself of the many maledictions he'd acquired and bowed smugly to the appreciative crowd.

Next, two magicians of the lighter quality engaged in a duel of fireworks, starting with brilliant lights in the gloomy skies overhead. Colourful manifestations lit up the sky, starting with flaring colours, spitting and sparking, followed by all kinds of carefully detailed patterns, and then moving on to more ambitious attempts as the magicians' confidence increased. Everyone watching craned their heads well back, and oohed and aahed loudly in all the right places. One magician, gesturing frantically, produced an entire pirate ship overhead, made up entirely of glowing green light. Complete with sails and rigging, and silent cannon blasting out clouds of green smoke in a broadside. His opponent snapped his fingers sharply, and just like that a massive glowing purple dragon soared silently past in the sky overhead, with a great breath of purple fire billowing from its open jaws. The dragon slammed right through the pirate ship, which immediately fell apart into wisps of green smoke. The defeated magician scowled, and stabbed one hand at the heavens; and there, standing over the Tourney, were two huge human figures. A man and a woman, glowing gold, impossibly beautiful and graceful, like living gods.

"Who the hell are they supposed to be?" said Hawk.

"Ah," said Raven. "I rather think they're supposed to be those two legendary heroes, Prince Rupert and Princess Julia."

"Nothing like us," said Fisher. "I was never that pretty; and neither was he. And I certainly never had breasts that big. I'd have fallen over."

But the crowds loved it, and the other magician gracefully admitted defeat. The two men shook hands and walked out of the circle. The crowd liked that. They approved of good sportsmanship, in small doses. Up in the sky, the dragon had already fallen apart, and the two golden figures were fading away. Hawk turned his back on the images and strode off. The rest of the family hurried after him.

The most experienced magicians dealt in transformations. Two magic-users stood face-to-face in the magic circle and struggled to outdo each other, over what they could turn themselves into. They started with easy, everyday things like wolves and bears and giant lizards, quickly escalating to horrid demonic shapes that almost certainly owed more to the dark imaginings of the two competitors than to anything ever seen in the real world. Eventually one really big and nasty creature just leaned forward, opened its jaws wide, and swallowed up the other creature. And that was that.

"I thought the Land was supposed to have a shortage of magicians?" said Hawk.

"There is a shortage," said Raven. "Of really powerful ones. These are just show-offs."

In the next circle along, two magical healers were trying to outdo each other by healing more and more extreme cases as they were brought into the circle. The blind were made to see, the deaf to hear, and cripples threw away their crutches and danced joyfully. Plague and leprosy victims stumbled thankfully back to their somewhat relieved friends and family. And one gentleman just gave a great whoop of joy, ran out of the circle, grabbed his wife by the hand, and hurried off in search of somewhere private.

"Lucky that last one didn't involve a laying on of hands," Mercy murmured to Raven, who smiled despite himself.

The two healers stood together in the magic circle, wearing pure white robes and incredibly self-satisfied smiles. Hawk was prepared to forgive them much, if only because they did such excellent work, with a minimum of dramatic chanting and waving of hands. He liked to see real professionals at work. The first healer looked around at the fascinated crowd.

"More!" he said grandly. "Bring me more!"

"Hasn't anyone had a heart attack at the Tourney today?" said the second healer. "I'm very good with heart attacks!"

"You should see what I can do with a hunchback," said the first healer.

And then they both fell silent, as the crowd split apart to allow two families through, carrying two young men on stretchers; both had been severely wounded in the fighting circles. They lay very still, their gaping, bloody wounds quickly making it clear that both of them were quite dead. The families laid the two stretchers down before the healers, and then the fathers and mothers looked beseechingly to the healers for help.

"Please," said one of the fathers, his face grey with shock. "There must be something you can do."

The crowd were quiet, looking on sympathetically as the two healers knelt down by the two bodies. They did everything they could to find even the smallest trace of life, but in the end all they could do was look at each other, shake their heads, and get to their feet again.

"I'm sorry," said the first healer. "There's nothing I can do."

"Nothing anyone could do," said the second, as kindly as he could. "We can only help the living."

"And that . . . sounds like my cue," said Raven.

He strode forward into the magic circle, and low murmurs spread quickly through the onlookers, at the sight of his night-dark robes. A few of them recognised the Necromancer, and crossed themselves. The two healers stepped back as Raven approached, and then they stood their ground and glared at him. He smiled easily back at them.

"You said there was nothing you could do," he murmured. "I'm happy to say there is something I can do."

"Get out of here, Necromancer," said the first healer. "They're dead. At peace. Leave them be."

"Haven't their families suffered enough?" said the second.

"But I am here to help the families," said Raven. He turned to look at the two sets of confused parents. "I can bring your boys back from the shores of death. I can't make them live again, but . . ."

"If you can do anything, do it," said one of the women. "Give me back my son!"

"But, Mother," said her husband uncertainly.

"You let him go into the circle!" his wife said fiercely. "You let him die!"

The father looked down at the ground, unable to answer her.

"I want my boy back," said the woman, and the other parents nodded stiffly.

Raven smiled at them all and knelt down between the two bodies. He checked their pulses briefly, just to be sure. Their skin was already cooling. He leant over each young man in turn and spat into their open eyes. He muttered under his breath, in something that was not a prayer, and then stood up and stepped back.

"*Rise up,*" he said, and the two young men sat up slowly on their stretchers. Their faces were cold and empty, and their eyes did not blink, but still they moved. Slowly, clumsily, the two dead men rose to their feet to stand before the smiling Necromancer. The mothers and fathers cried out, wringing their hands together at their breasts in sudden hope. The woman who had begged Raven's help started to move forward, to reclaim her son, but her husband held her back. And when she saw the empty, soulless look on her son's face, the woman stopped fighting her husband. The two young men stood stiffly upright, not looking at their parents, not looking at anything. Their eyes were open, but anyone could see there was no one home behind the eyes, no soul present to see anything through those empty, unblinking eyes. The two sets of parents turned their faces away, sickened. Raven looked about him, but there was no applause from anyone watching. The crowd just looked coldly back at him, and the dead things he'd raised up. Raven shrugged.

"Tough crowd. All right, let's try something a little more ambitious."

He looked at the two dead men, muttering under his breath again, and immediately they stepped forward and took hold of each other, and began to dance. The crowd made a low, shocked noise, and the parents cried out miserably, as they watched two dead men waltz back and forth across the magic circle, to unheard music. Round and round they went, faster and faster, never missing a step. Their faces had nothing in them. Gillian stepped into the circle and strode up to her son.

"Stop this. Now."

"Just putting on a show, Mother," said Raven. "Give me some time to free up those muscles, and I'll have them doing dips and bends."

Gillian slapped him hard across the face. The sound was loud and harsh on the quiet, and the force of the blow was enough to snap his head round. Raven stood very still, and then slowly turned his head back to face his mother. One cheek burned bright red. He showed no emotion at all.

"Stop this now," said Gillian.

"As you wish, Mother," said Raven.

The two dead men fell to the ground, and lay still. Their mothers and fathers moved forward to claim them again. Placed them back on their stretchers, and carried them away. The two healers left with them, and the crowd broke up too, and followed them off. Raven was left alone in the circle, with his mother.

"I only gave them what they wanted," said Raven.

"People have been burned at the stake for less than that," said Gillian.

Raven smiled slightly. "I'd like to see someone try. I really would."

"You're not that powerful, boy," said Jack.

"Ah," said Raven. "Perhaps not, Uncle Jack. But I am protected, by the King and by Parliament. Because I have proven myself so very useful to both of them."

"Place no trust in the kindness of Kings," said Hawk. "Or the promises of politicians."

"Your protection will only last as long as you're needed," said Fisher. "And that can change in a heartbeat."

"And what makes a better scapegoat, than the man no one likes anyway?" said Jack.

"Find another line of work, Nathanial," said Gillian.

They all walked away and left him standing there, with nothing at all showing in his face. Like the dead men he'd just raised up.

The family gathered together again before the main raked seating, where the last few champions of the day were being presented to Prince Richard. It was well past midday, and everyone was feeling it was time for some dinner. There would be presentation displays, and duels of skill and excellence laid on later, between past and present champions, for the delectation of the crowds, all through the long afternoon—but everyone was just that little bit impatient to get the last of the day's business done, so everyone could hurry away and concentrate on stuffing their faces. Preferably with something from a food stall absolutely guaranteed to be bad for them. The last few appointed champions stepped forward, to be commended by the Prince and invited into the Castle for the ceremonial banquet. Everyone clapped loudly, to hurry things along.

The winner of the knife-throwing event was called forward, one Angelica Rawley. She stepped out of the crowd, bobbing her head nervously, a small, mousy thing, barely out of her teens, with wide eyes and a shy smile. She bowed before the Prince, whipped out her knife and threw it at Princess Catherine. The wicked little blade flashed through the air. Catherine froze on her throne, caught off guard. But Richard reacted the moment he saw the knife appear in Angelica's hand and threw himself forward in front of Catherine. The knife slammed into his chest, all the way to the hilt. The impact threw Richard backwards into Catherine's arms. She held on to him tightly, crying out his name.

It all happened so quickly, the security guards just stood where they were. Catherine hugged Richard to her, saying his name over and over. He tried to say something, but his mouth was full of blood. And down below, Angelica Rawley put back her head and laughed and laughed.

"For Redhart!" she cried. "No Peace without Honour!"

The security guards hit her from every side at once, slamming her off her feet and throwing her to the ground. She fought them fiercely, still laughing even as their great fists hit her again and again. And then her voice broke off, her back arched, and she stopped struggling. It took the guards a moment to realise she was dead. They let go of her and stood back, baffled. One of them looked round, as Hawk and his family hurried forward.

"We didn't kill her! It was all we could do to hold on to her!"

"It wasn't you," said Raven, quietly professional. "This was a prearranged death spell, to keep her from being interrogated. I've seen it before." He looked up at the two thrones in the raked seating, where Catherine was still holding Richard in her arms and weeping hot, bitter tears. "I'd better get up there. See if I can do anything."

"You leave the Prince to me, boy," Jack said sternly. "Your business is with the dead. Bring that assassin back, get some answers out of her."

"Yes, Uncle," said Raven.

Jack made his way up the raked steps as quickly as he could, leaning heavily on his wooden staff. Catherine looked up desperately as he approached, her face wet with tears.

"Can you do something? Please! He's still breathing! He took a knife for me . . . Don't let him die!"

"Not on my watch," said Jack, smiling reassuringly at the Princess. He leaned forward and placed one hand on the Prince's chest, right next to the massive bloodstain round the knife hilt. "No good man dies on my watch."

He concentrated, praying silently, and the knife jumped right out of Prince Richard's chest, falling away to clatter on the floor. The Prince's eyes snapped open, and he drew in a large and vibrant breath. His hand went hesitantly to his chest, and when he looked down there was no wound there at all. He looked at Jack.

"I heard a Voice, and then . . . Why am I not dead? Who are you?"

"Jack Forester, at your service, your highness. A humble man of God. These days. Thank Him for your salvation, not me. It's all about the prayer, not the man. Now if you'll excuse me, I mean to have a few words with your assassin."

He stomped off back down the steps, humming tunelessly to himself. Richard realised he was lying in Catherine's arms, and started to sit up. He was still so weak she had to help him, but soon enough he was back on his throne, looking about him uncertainly. Catherine was still holding on to his hand, and he squeezed hers just as tightly.

"You've been crying," he said. "Don't cry. I'm fine. Really."

"I can't believe you risked your life to save mine," said Catherine.

"Neither can I," said Richard. "I just saw the knife . . . and knew what I had to do. Are you all right?"

"Of course I'm all right! You sit still. I want you checked out by your best healers, just in case."

"But . . . there are things I should be doing . . ."

Catherine looked down to where the Necromancer was crouching over the dead knife-thrower. "They're being done," she said.

"I'm alive," Richard said wonderingly. "How about that?"

"Bravest thing I ever saw," said Catherine.

They looked into each other's eyes, and knew something had changed between them.

Richard insisted on getting to his feet, and in the end Catherine and Gertrude got on either side of him and helped him up. He swayed a little, and then forced the last weakness out of him with an effort of will. He breathed deeply. He'd never felt more alive in his life. He started steadily down the raked steps, to join the people gathered round the dead assassin, and the crowds watching cheered and applauded loudly. Catherine wanted to go with him, to see who it was who'd tried to kill her, but Lady Gertrude hung on to her, almost hysterical at the thought of her precious going anywhere near the assassin, dead or not. Richard stopped and called the security guards on the stand to come forward and surround Princess Catherine with drawn swords. And only then, when he was sure she was safe, did he continue on down the steps.

The people parted to let him through. Raven was kneeling beside the dead body, staring into the knife-thrower's open, unblinking eyes, and frowning thoughtfully.

"Can you bring her back here?" said Richard. "Or do you need some privacy? I have questions for this person."

"I'm afraid it's not as simple as that, your highness," said Raven, not looking up. "I'm having . . . difficulties. The death spell implanted inside this poor unfortunate was specially designed to keep her from being called back by people like me." He smiled, briefly. "Fortunately, there is no one like me. *By the powers I invoke, by compacts entered into, by the forces I command, come back to us.*"

The dead woman opened her eyes, looked at him, and said, "Go to hell." And then she closed her eyes and went back to being dead again. Everyone looked at Raven. He sighed slowly, like a teacher with a particularly recalcitrant pupil.

"Don't make me come down there and get you."

The dead woman's eyes snapped open. She glared at Raven, and then smiled nastily. Everyone around her fell back a few steps, except for Raven, and Prince Richard, who screwed his face up in disgust but held his ground. Angelica Rawley ignored the Prince, focusing all her attention on the Necromancer.

"Every time you do this, you damn your soul further. Is it worth it, Nathanial? Really?"

"Might as well be damned for a sheep as a lamb," Raven said easily. "Now be still, unquiet spirit, and speak only as you are bid."

"Right . . . ," said the dead woman. "That'll be the day. Even in death I am protected by my masters, who are greater than you, little necromancer. Everything I once knew about them, I have forgotten. Including the names of those who made me forget." She giggled suddenly, a horrible, disturbing sound. And then she looked past Raven, and the Prince, to Hawk and Fisher.

"He is coming. And there is nothing you can do to stop him."

She shuddered violently, and then just fell apart. Her whole body rotted and decayed away in moments, till nothing was left but a mess of seething corruption, sinking slowly into the earth. Everyone fell back even farther, crying out at the awful stench. Soon there was nothing left of Angelica Rawley save a dark stain on the ground and a foul smell, already dispersing. Raven rose unhurriedly to his feet, looked at the Prince, and shrugged apologetically. And then everyone looked round as King Rufus came forward, accompanied by his Seneschal, and surrounded by armed guards. Everyone bowed and curtsied. They had only to look at the King to see he had returned to his full faculties, for the moment at least. The King took his son in his arms and hugged him hard for a moment; then he pushed Richard away and addressed him steadily.

"Did you get any useful information out of the knife-thrower?"

"No, Father. Her masters protected themselves very thoroughly. But that in itself shows they must be men of station, and power. Names we would know."

"There is more, your majesty," said Raven. "I don't think Angelica knew she had been prepared as an assassin until someone close at hand said the magic words that activated her. And to activate the death spell the speaker must have been really close."

Everyone looked around them, to find everyone else looking back. The King just nodded, slowly.

"Then the real assassin is still here. Among us. Waiting. Laughing at us, behind a mask of concern. Find out who these people are, my Necromancer. All my security guards, all my other magic-users, are at your disposal. Get me the truth! From now on everything you do, you do in my name and with my authority. Find these people before they strike again!"

Raven bowed. The King turned to the Seneschal.

"What . . . was I going to say? Yes. Shut down the Tourney. No more events, no more competitors. Send the people home. Who knows who else might be hiding in these crowds . . . I don't want anyone in the Castle who doesn't belong there."

"Yes, Sire," said the Seneschal. "But there is still the matter of the day's champions, invited in for the celebration banquet. A matter of long and noble tradition. Am I to cancel that too?"

"No," said Richard immediately. "Let them in. They have earned that honour."

"As you wish," said the King. "Though we haven't had much luck with banquets recently." He smiled at the Prince. "You did well, son. Very brave. I couldn't be more proud of you."

He took Richard's hand and shook it firmly. There was a low murmur of approval from the watching crowd, who didn't want to intrude on the moment. Catherine came forward, still surrounded by her guards. She went straight to Richard and held both his hands in hers, while the King nodded solemnly. And then the crowd just couldn't stand it any longer; they exploded with joy, cheering and shouting and hammering their hands together till they ached.

And so the champions of the Grand Tourney attended the banquet in their honour, set once more in the Great Hall. Only this time there were far fewer tables, and the much smaller group of people seemed almost intimidated by the huge space surrounding them. After everything that had happened, most of the people who would ordinarily have turned up to honour and laud the day's champions, and bask in their reflected glory, had decided to stay at home. Prince Richard and Princess Catherine sat at the high table, without the King. His latest effort had exhausted him. The champions sat around two long tables, packed close together. They chattered loudly, complimenting one another and affecting not to notice that they had been abandoned by the very people they'd struggled so hard to entertain. There should have been toasts, and celebrations all round, compliments and laughter . . . but since there weren't, they all just talked that little bit more loudly.

No one spoke about the assassination attempt. But a lot of people glanced at the Prince and Princess when they thought no one was looking. No one actually said anything, but many of the champions thought their thunder had been stolen.

Hawk and his family had commandeered one end of one table for themselves, with Chappie curled up underneath. He wasn't officially invited, but he wasn't the sort of dog you could keep out. Everyone was impressed, and more than a little surprised, at how Jack had brought the

Prince back from the very edge of death. He smiled and nodded for a while, and then gave them all a hard stare.

"God works through me in whatever I do. Whether it's protecting the innocent, or punishing the guilty. Beating up Forest brigands, or laying on hands. I don't get to take the credit."

"Are you holy?" Mercy said bluntly.

"Not . . . as such," Jack said carefully. "Even when I was still the Walking Man, I don't think you could have called me that. I always saw myself as just a man, doing a job. Because somebody had to."

"Have you always been able to heal people?" said Raven.

"Yes," said Jack. "Just wasn't much call for it, usually, in my line of work. Another good reason why I gave up being the Walking Man."

"Seems to me it hasn't given up on you," said Hawk. "You still have all the powers that go with the title."

Jack stirred uneasily in his chair. "I am a monk now. A man of peace. I will not kill again."

"How did it feel when you saved the Prince's life?" said Gillian.

Jack smiled properly for the first time. "Like I was finally doing what I was meant to do."

"I can't believe they tried to kill the Princess so openly," said Fisher. "Somebody really wants a war."

"I want some of those meatballs," growled Chappie from down by her feet. "If you're not going to finish those, pass them down."

At the head table, Prince Richard and Princess Catherine sat side by side, ignoring the food in front of them in favour of staring into each other's eyes and smiling big, silly smiles. The more than usually heavy security presence stood well back, to give the Royal couple as much privacy as they could. Even though it was clear to all the guards that they could have been standing there stark naked except for their swords, and the Prince and Princess wouldn't have noticed a thing.

"You didn't even hesitate," said Catherine. "Just threw yourself in front of me. Took the knife, for me. Took my death for me. No one ever did anything like that for me before."

"Trust me," Richard said dryly, "I didn't plan it. Just . . . did what I had to."

"You did the right thing without even thinking about it," said Catherine. "That's even better! That is the mark of a true hero."

"I wish you'd stop saying that," said Richard. "Heroes are supposed to rescue the Princess without nearly getting themselves killed in the process." He paused, thinking. "I couldn't let you die. Just couldn't."

"Because our marriage is so important to the Peace agreement?" said Catherine.

"No. Because you're important, to me."

"Really?"

"Much to my surprise, yes," said Richard. "All those years looking for the love of my life . . . and it's an arranged marriage that brings her to me."

"Well," said Catherine, squeezing his hand firmly, "this changes everything, doesn't it?"

"It does, doesn't it?" said Richard.

Sat together in a beer tent, back at the Tourney, because they hadn't been invited to the banquet, were Richard's friends, Peter and Clarence. The soldier and the minstrel-in-training. They sat glumly at a rough wooden trestle table covered in food stains and beer spills, drinking overpriced ale from carved wooden tankards, not so much because they wanted to as because there was nothing else to do. The tent was pretty much empty. A single barmaid, in a traditional outfit that didn't suit her, was manning the bar on her own and looking pretty pissed off about it. An old married couple were drinking cheap wine in the far corner and glaring silently at each other. And a failed champion was lying facedown in his own spilt beer, snoring loudly. The Grand Tourney was over, the stalls had closed, and most people had gone home. The only ones left . . . were the people drowning their sorrows.

Peter and Clarence had been drinking for quite a while. Peter was brooding, and Clarence was flushed, but otherwise no one could have told the difference. Peter had tried his luck in the sword-fighting contests and did quite well until he found himself facing a Bladesmaster from the Sorting Houses. Clarence had walked back and forth through the Tourney, watching all the fights, looking for material. And had been delighted to be right there at the front when Sir Kay was unhorsed and unmasked by the

Sombre Warrior. He rushed off to bash out a first version of a new song while the events were still fresh in his mind . . . and as a result completely missed out on the knife-throwing assassin. He was still sulking. He just knew he was never going to live that down.

"It's not really sword-fighting, in the circles," said Peter. "The borders, that was real fighting. Not prancing about until someone gets a scratch and shouts *First blood*. Win or die! That was what it was all about on the border. I was a soldier! Fighting for my country. Not just showing off."

"Everyone thinks they're heroes, just because they can show off in a circle," said Clarence. "The girls here won't even look at you unless you've got more muscles than brains. Like to see one of those muscle-bound mo-rons describe a battle in perfect iambic pentameter."

"He's not coming," said Peter.

"What?" said Clarence, peering at him owlishly over his tankard.

"Richard!" said Peter. "He said he'd meet us here, in the beer tent. After the Tourney was over, and he wasn't needed anymore. Said we'd have some good times together. But he isn't here. No way he's coming now."

"Be fair," said Clarence. "By all accounts, he came bloody close to dying."

"That's not it," Peter said darkly. "It's her. The Princess. He's with her, now."

"Well, yes," said Clarence. "He's marrying her tomorrow. I've got a stag night set up for tonight, and everything."

"You really think he's going to attend your stupid little party?" said Peter, slamming his tankard down hard on the table. "No . . . I saw this coming. He's moved on! Left us behind. We . . . are the embarrassing friends, the bad influence of his past. He can't go riding off on adventures anymore, not once he's married. Got to settle down. Become . . . respon-sible. Respectable. She'll soon have him under her thumb."

"But . . . it looks like it's going to be a happy marriage, at least," said Clarence. "That's a good thing, isn't it? Shouldn't we be happy for him? For them?"

Peter scowled. He emptied his tankard and called for more ale. The barmaid slouched over and poured him a refill from her jug. She would have liked to tell him to keep the noise down, would have liked to have thrown the pair of them out, but they were friends of the Prince. So she couldn't. Instead, she made a point of displaying a lot of cleavage as she bent over to fill the tankard, in the hope of a generous tip later on. Barmaiding didn't pay much, so you had to make your money where you could. But the soldier didn't even look at her, and the minstrel's eyes were far away. So she gave the soldier short measure and went back to the bar.

"You'll see," said Peter, staring into his drink. "We'll be left out of things from now on. Less and less invitations to join him, for . . . anything. Until he forgets about us completely. Taken up with all his new responsibilities, as a married man."

"We've still got his stag night to finish organising," Clarence said firmly. "And not much time left to do it in. I've been negotiating with several tavern sluts, of quite appalling reputation, to come along and warm things up. At really quite reasonable prices."

Peter considered that for a moment. "How many tavern sluts?"

"Seven!"

"What? That's not a party! Go for the full dozen!"

"You want them, you pay for them," said Clarence.

Peter sniffed. "Bit short at the moment. Have to owe you."

"Seven," Clarence said firmly. "Two of them can dance, sort of, and one of them can do this amazing thing with her . . ."

"You really think the Prince is going to show up?" Peter said angrily. "After a second assassination attempt on the Princess? He won't leave her side until they're safely married."

"But . . . it's his stag!" said Clarence. "You can't get married without a stag first! There's a law . . ."

"Pretty sure there isn't," said Peter.

"I'm still going," said Clarence determinedly. "You still going?"

"Of course I'm going! Wouldn't miss a party with a dozen tavern sluts."

"Seven."

"Whatever."

"I might be able to get a conjurer," said Clarence. "Do you want a conjurer?"

"Not really, no." Peter drank steadily from his tankard. "Always knew he'd move on. Leave us behind. Because he's Royal . . . and we're not. It's the way of things. The Prince proves how responsible he is, by leaving his disreputable friends behind."

"I'm not disreputable! I'm a minstrel!"

"I am!" Peter said loudly. "I'm disreputable, I am, and proud of it!"

And then they both sat glumly together for a while, considering the way of things.

"No more invitations to the Royal table," Clarence said despondently. "What am I going to do now, for good food and company and red-hot gossip? What am I going to do, Peter?"

"Get out in the world more?" said Peter. "Meet some girls who don't want paying?"

"Oh shut up."

"How are you sleeping?" Peter said suddenly, not looking at him.

"All right," said Clarence. "You?"

"Badly," said Peter. "Really badly."

"Me too," said Clarence. "I can't stand the dark anymore. I have to have a night-light in my room every night, like a child."

"It's the Darkwood," said Peter. "Only in the bloody thing for a minute, but it put its mark on us. Only a minute, but we're never going to be free of it. We should never have followed Richard into the Darkwood."

"He went in," said Clarence. "He was our friend. What else could we do?"

"Where will you go now?" said Peter. "What will you do? Will you and I ever meet again, after the stag? I mean, what did we ever have in common? Apart from Prince Richard?"

In a room that wasn't on any of the official Castle maps, because it kept moving about for security reasons, the First Minister of the Forest Parliament, Peregrine de Woodville, was having a very tense meeting with the Leader of the Loyal Opposition, Henry Wallace, the Seneschal (as the King's representative), and Laurence Garner, head of Forest Castle security. It was his room. One of the few seriously magical rooms left over from the days when the Castle was a magical place, bigger on the inside than it was on the outside.

Like most spies and security agents, Laurence Garner was nothing much to look at. Certainly not anybody you'd look at a second time. Average height and weight, with an unmemorable face and a soft, polite voice. Most people in the Castle had no idea of his true status and function; they thought he was just another guard. Garner liked it that way. Always ready with a quiet word and a meaningless smile, there to smooth things over and move things along. Someone you could rely on to sort things out without making a fuss. Garner was part of every important event, sitting tucked away in some quiet corner, keeping a watchful eye on everyone and everything. With a dozen armed guards under his personal command, ready to spring forward and do terrible things at his slightest nod. For now, the head of security sat quietly behind his desk, its top covered with overflowing piles of papers, waiting patiently for everyone to stop shouting at one another and quiet down so he could tell them what they needed to do.

"How the hell did that assassin get so close to the Princess?" demanded Peregrine. "Bad enough the Princess was almost poisoned at her own welcoming Banquet!"

"The knife-thrower didn't know she was there to kill anyone, until she was activated!" said the Seneschal. "Do try to keep up, Peregrine . . ."

"In my opinion," said Henry Wallace, but the other two just talked right over him.

"My men are everywhere," said Garner, raising his voice just enough to cut through everyone else's. "And they are doing everything they can. I've got guards covering every occupied room and corridor in this Castle, and even more blocking off access to the unoccupied areas. Every door and gate and opening is secure; no one gets in or out that I don't know about, in advance. I've even got men with dogs working their way through the unoccupied areas, to make sure no one's hiding out in there. I've got sorcerers watching over everything else. Not particularly high-class sorcerers, admittedly, but you have to work with what you've got. And yes, the Necromancer is doing his bit too. And no, you don't get to question him. I don't want him disturbed."

"Anybody else?" said Henry Wallace, just to remind everyone he was still there.

"This is no time for humour, Henry!" said Peregrine.

"I wasn't trying to be funny," said Henry. "I was just trying to point out that if Garner needs more money, for more people, I'm sure we could get Parliament to approve it."

"It's not money—it's manpower that's the problem," said Garner. "I've sent for reinforcements, so I can send men out into the surrounding woods . . . but I can't see how they can get here before the wedding. As it is, my people are protecting the Castle from all the usual threats, but we are dealing with professional-level threats. According to the regrettably few high-level magic-users I have access to, it's really hard to identify a killer when they don't know that's what they are. We need to find whoever it is who's activating them. Someone within the Castle is a high-level Redhart agent! It's the only answer. Someone really highly placed. If that monk hadn't been as good as he was, we'd have a dead Prince on our hands."

The First Minister stopped pacing up and down before Garner's desk, so he could concentrate his best scowl on the head of security. "What do we know about this new group of champions we've let inside the Castle? Can we trust them? I mean, does anyone here think it's just a coincidence that people from the Hero Academy have turned up at the Grand Tourney today and were right there on the scene when that little bitch nearly killed the Princess?"

"My people are doing background checks, even as we speak," said Garner. "But I think we already know most of it. These people are celebrities in their own right. Hawk and Fisher used to run the Hero Academy, down in Lancre."

"Troublemakers," said Peregrine, and everybody nodded.

"And Jack Forester used to be the Walking Man, back in his younger days," said Garner.

"Oh, bloody Hell," said the Seneschal. "That's all we needed. If I'd known, I'd never have let him inside the Castle."

"Let's try not to panic just yet," said Garner. "Apparently, the man's been living the contemplative life in a monastery for the past twenty years." He looked thoughtfully at the Seneschal. "Guilty conscience, perhaps?"

"Who hasn't?" said the Seneschal.

"I wouldn't worry too much," said Garner. "These days he's just an old monk leaning on a wooden staff."

"An old monk who brought Prince Richard back to life from a wound that should have killed him!" said Peregrine. "How retired is that?"

"At least he's not killing anyone," said Garner.

"Yet," said the Seneschal darkly.

"To further complicate things, the old warrior woman from the Sorting House, Gillian Forester, is his sister," said Garner.

"Oh, this just gets better and better," said Peregrine.

"Gillian Forester has spent most of her twilight years acting as a tutor for the Brotherhood of Steel," said Garner. "Very professional, very well thought of."

The Seneschal gave him a hard look. "You do know who Jack and Gillian Forester really are? Who their parents were?"

"Of course I know," said Garner. "It's my job to know everything that matters."

"I don't know," said Peregrine. "What am I missing?"

"Jack and Gillian Forester are the son and daughter of Prince Rupert and Princess Julia," said Garner.

"Oh, bloody hell!" said Peregrine. "That's all we need!"

"They're *that* Jack and Gillian?" said Henry. "Why are they here? Could they be here to stake a claim to the throne at last? Because of the Royal wedding?"

"Calm down, Henry, before you have an aneurysm," said Peregrine. "They're no threat to the throne. You never were very good at history, were you? They both publicly renounced any claim to the Forest throne years ago. That leaves them just . . . poor relations. Probably only here to attend the wedding and see if there's any chance of a handout from the Royal coffers while everyone's in a good mood."

"I could have them thrown into a dungeon until this is all over," Garner suggested quietly.

"The Walking Man? And a head tutor from a Sorting House?" said the Seneschal. "Yeah, right. Good luck with that one. I saw them at the Tourney; those two grey-haired coffin-dodgers could run rings around anyone you have. And do I really need to remind you . . . Yes, I see from the blank faces that I do. Gillian Forester is the mother of Raven the Necromancer."

"*What?*" said Peregrine. "Why wasn't I told this?"

"Damn right!" said Henry. "The Necromancer is the grandson of Rupert and Julia? We should have been told this the moment he started becoming so . . . prominent!"

"He now speaks with the King's voice, and the King's authority," Garner said quietly.

"You mean he outranks you?" said the Seneschal.

Garner allowed himself a small smile. "In theory, perhaps. In practice . . . I think not. It's my job to protect the King. From the folly of his own decisions, if necessary. But again, there's no reason to get excited. Raven is still merely the son of someone who's already publicly given up any claim they might have had to the throne. And he's not exactly the type to allow any faction to use him as a figurehead, is he? The point is, if you even look like you're thinking of bothering his mother, I can't help feeling the Necromancer would probably become very upset. Do you really want to risk that just when we might need him most?"

"At least . . . try to keep this troublesome family away from everyone who matters," said Peregrine.

"Prince Richard invited them in, as acclaimed champions," said the Seneschal, "and since Jack Forester saved his life. Richard has already said the monk and his family can stay here as long as they like. They are Royal guests . . . with all the privileges that entails. Still, it's a big Castle. I'm sure I can find somewhere suitably distant to put them."

"Do it!" snapped Peregrine. He glared at Garner. "Find the Redhart agent. This . . . master of assassins. I don't care how you do it, but I want him dead or in chains before the wedding!"

"Is it really too late to postpone the wedding?" said the Seneschal. "Just until we've found this agent?"

The First Minister and the Leader of the Opposition were already shaking their heads.

"Already thought of that," said Henry. "We can't risk it."

"We have to get Richard and Catherine married as quickly as possible so we can sign the Peace agreement," said Peregrine. "Once they're wed and the agreement is signed, Catherine will no longer be a target. Hopefully."

There was a long pause as they all stared at one another, hoping someone else would come up with some great idea to save the day . . . but when that didn't happen, they drew themselves up and bowed briefly to one another, and left Laurence Garner's secret room. The door closed quietly but firmly behind Peregrine, Henry, and the Seneschal. Peregrine turned back and opened the door and looked inside, but Garner and his room were already gone, back on their never-ending travels around the interior of the Castle.

"You'll have to excuse me," said the Seneschal. "I have to attend the King."

"How is he?" said the Peregrine. "After the . . . strains of today?"

"Better than usual," said the Seneschal. "The sheer number of crises has actually been good for him. Keeping him . . . alert."

"Well, that's a good thing, I'm sure," said Peregrine smoothly.

"Just have to hope it lasts," growled Henry. "The sooner we can put Richard on the throne, the better."

The Seneschal regarded the two politicians coldly. He knew how they really felt about Rufus and Richard. "You've never given the Prince his due," he said. "Shame you can't manage to get anything done around here without him, isn't it?"

"Richard won't sit on the throne for long," said Peregrine. "We'll see to that."

"You mean Parliament will see to it, don't you?" said the Seneschal.

"Parliament will do what we tell it to do!" said Henry.

The Seneschal smiled. "You see? You do know how to think like Royalty."

"And what will you do then?" said Peregrine, just a bit spitefully. "When you don't have a King or a Prince to follow around?"

The Seneschal allowed his smile to widen just a little. "Maybe I'll go into politics."

He turned his back on the both of them and sauntered unhurriedly down the corridor. Peregrine and Henry watched him go with equal loathing, and then they turned and strode off in the opposite direction.

"Give me some good news, Henry," Peregrine said tiredly. "I could really use some good news."

"Well," said Henry, "at last it would seem that Richard and Catherine have . . . bonded. So we won't have to drive them to the wedding ceremony with swords at their backs after all. Which did seem a distinct possibility, for some time."

"I can't wait till they're married," said Peregrine. "William could still call the whole thing off if he sees these attacks on the Princess' life as an assault on his honour. If he decides we can't keep his daughter safe, he could demand that she be returned to Redhart, so he can protect her properly. And we couldn't allow that. The Peace agreement would collapse."

Henry looked at him thoughtfully. "Would you really hold Catherine captive? To influence William's behaviour?"

"Well," said Peregrine, "not as such . . ."

"You need to talk to your man, the Sombre Warrior," said Henry. "See what he knows."

"Where do you think we're going now?" said the First Minister.

Not all that long afterwards, the two politicians stood outside the Sombre Warrior's door, and Peregrine knocked briskly. There was a long pause, and then the Sombre Warrior jerked the door open. He was wearing his chalk white porcelain mask and a full set of leather armour, and he had his sword in his hand. He looked the two men over, glanced up and down the empty corridor, and then lowered his sword but didn't put it away. He stepped back, inviting his guests in with a brusque nod of the head. Peregrine and Henry did their best to walk in as though they owned the place, but they both jumped a little as the Sombre Warrior slammed the door shut behind them and locked it. The Warrior strode back into the middle of the room and turned to face Peregrine and Henry. He still hadn't put his sword away.

"How may I serve you, my masters?" he said. He didn't remove his mask. Peregrine knew what lay beneath it, but Henry didn't. The Sombre Warrior was pretty sure there was a lot Henry didn't know, that Peregrine knew. Even the closest of associates kept secrets from each other in politics.

"Did you know there was to be an attempt on the Princess' life this morning?" Peregrine said bluntly.

"Of course not," said the Sombre Warrior. "Do you really think I'd allow anyone to harm my Princess? And no, before you ask, I have no idea who is behind these attempts. Or I'd give you his head myself."

"Do you know of any Redhart spies hidden inside this Castle?" said Henry.

"No one here has contacted me," the Sombre Warrior said carefully. "But then, they must know I'd never stand by and allow the Princess to come to any harm. For any reason."

The two politicians studied the Sombre Warrior for a moment. They were used to dominating people, just because of who and what they were, but it was clear from the Sombre Warrior's voice and stance that while he might serve them, he really didn't give a damn who and what they were. He was a soldier, and a killer. He would do what he was told, but the reasons behind it were none of his concern. And in some things he would not be moved at all. Quite suddenly, Peregrine and Henry felt as though they were trapped in a room with a large and very dangerous wild animal. Trained to useful purpose but not in any way tamed.

Henry looked at Peregrine. "I can't believe you've had such a highly placed spy in William's Court all this time."

"Years," Peregrine said loftily. "He's been my man for years. I own him. Isn't that right, Warrior?"

"Of course," said the Sombre Warrior. His voice from behind the porcelain mask was completely calm.

"Are you happy to be so used?" said Henry.

"Happy?" said the Sombre Warrior. He left the word hanging on the air for a moment. "I am content to serve."

"Are you comfortable here?" persisted Henry.

"These words have no meaning for me," said the Sombre Warrior.

Henry looked at Peregrine and shrugged. "It does move a man to think if we have him, inside Redhart . . . who might King William have, here? Which trusted and highly placed individual might even now be plotting new crimes against us? Or the Princess?"

"Don't waste your Parliamentary mode of speech on me, Henry," said Peregrine. "And always remember the first rule of the spying game: never trust anyone."

"You trust me, don't you?" said Henry.

"Of course I trust you. Do you trust me?"

"Of course, Peregrine."

And, honours satisfied, they both bowed briefly to the Sombre Warrior, who moved over to the door and unlocked it. Henry eased quickly past the huge figure. He couldn't help noticing the Warrior still hadn't put his sword away. Peregrine made a point of taking his own sweet time leaving, but both he and Henry were relieved to be out in the corridor again, when the door slammed shut behind them.

The Sombre Warrior locked the door, and put away his sword. He took off his mask and turned to face the mirror on his wall. And using certain prearranged magic words, he forced a contact between him and his distant master, William of Redhart. His reflection disappeared abruptly, replaced by the angry, cold-eyed visage of King William.

"You damned fool," said the King. "You were told only to use this for real emergencies!"

"You don't think this qualifies?" said the Sombre Warrior just as coldly. "Two separate attempts have been made on your daughter's life! Three, if you include the attack on her carriage, on the way here. This was organised. You had to know about it. But you never told me anything!"

"Because I knew you'd react like this," said the King. He sighed heavily. "They weren't real threats; Catherine was never in any real danger. Not with all the extra magical protections I had placed on her before she left Redhart."

"You planned this all in advance," the Sombre Warrior said slowly. "This is all happening at your orders."

"Of course," said William. "The poison would just have made her sick, the knife would just have wounded her. We needed an excuse to break the Peace agreement. Who knew Prince Richard would be stupid enough to jump in front of an assassin's knife? Still, it doesn't matter. We have arranged for another attempt, through another agent. And then, whatever happens, we'll have the pretext we need to bring Catherine home again. And sink the Peace agreement once and for all."

"But . . . why?" said the Sombre Warrior. "Why break a Peace you worked so hard to bring about?"

"You are not cleared for matters of high policy," the King said sternly.

"All you need to know is that a King must do whatever is best to preserve his Kingdom."

"I cannot allow the Princess to come to harm," said the Sombre Warrior.

"Allow?" said the King. "*Allow?* You don't get to have an opinion on this! You will do as you are told! Follow your orders, or I will reveal your true identity to everyone. And then . . . where could you go, where could you run? You have served too many masters, my Warrior, and no one loves a traitor. Stay where you are. Do not leave your room until this final attack on my daughter is over. And then there will be war."

"You said I would be contacted by another of your agents, here in the Castle," said the Sombre Warrior. "I haven't heard anything, from anyone. I should have been consulted on this . . ."

"Don't sulk, Warrior," said the King. "It doesn't become you. You never did have a head for politics. I've sent one of my hidden people to talk to you. Listen to him. Follow the orders he gives you. And never presume on your position again."

His face disappeared from the mirror, and there was only the Sombre Warrior, staring at himself. He slowly replaced his porcelain mask, in anticipation of his visitor. He sat down on his only chair, suddenly tired. When did his life become so involved, so complicated? With so many conflicting responsibilities? He had thought that when he was back in the Forest Land, back home again . . . he might actually be able to put aside his mask. Give up being the Sombre Warrior and take up his old life again. Go looking for whatever remained of his family. But he couldn't. He should have known he couldn't even hope to do that, because he wasn't that man anymore. That man died out on the border.

One thing he was sure of: the Princess Catherine needed him. Needed him to protect her, now more than ever. He didn't trust King William's magical protections. The Sombre Warrior had no respect for his masters, William or Peregrine. But he had always admired the Princess. For being free and proud and ready to defy anyone who thought they had authority over her. All the things . . . he had never been.

There was a knock at his door, and the Sombre Warrior made sure his mask was firmly strapped in place before he went to answer. And there, waiting patiently outside in the corridor, was a face the Sombre Warrior knew. The minstrel, Clarence.

"The King sent me," Clarence said politely. "And I think we both know which King I mean. What was I supposed to . . . Oh yes. *Red meat is good meat.* Stupid phrase. Practically screams *I'm up to no good.* Invite me in, please. It wouldn't be good for either of us if we were seen together. Questions would be asked."

The Sombre Warrior stood back to allow Clarence to enter, and then shut and locked the door behind him. Clarence looked around the spartan room and turned up his nose.

"This is the best they could find for you? Hardly worthy of such a famous warrior."

"You're my contact?" said the Sombre Warrior. "But you're Prince Richard's closest friend!"

"He wants to be a hero," said Clarence. "And what better way to become one than in the heat of battle? So many opportunities for the Prince to show his true worth . . . And I want a war, so there will be great deeds and marvellous battles for me to write songs about."

"That's it?" said the Sombre Warrior. "That's all you want?"

"Well, the money does help," Clarence admitted.

"Never trust a minstrel," said the Sombre Warrior.

"There is to be one more attack on the Princess," Clarence said briskly. "Very soon now. You are ordered, by King William himself, to do nothing. I have been told to assure you that the Princess will never be in any real danger. In fact, if she really has got all the protections in place that she's supposed to have, no one short of the Demon Prince himself could get anywhere near her. We should all be so safe.

"There. That's the message. Stay put till you hear the shouting, and then run to the Princess' suite so you can be righteously angry in public and demand she return home immediately. What could be simpler?"

"What indeed?" said the Sombre Warrior.

Clarence waited patiently until he was sure the huge figure had nothing more to say. "Very well, then, I must be going. Unless . . . I don't suppose you'd be prepared to sit down and talk with me about all the amazing exploits you've been involved in? I'm always looking for good new material for my songs. I could write something seriously thrilling about your . . . Ah. I see. Bad timing. Perhaps another . . ."

He bowed hastily, waited for the Sombre Warrior to unlock the door, and then left as quickly as dignity would allow. The door locked itself behind him. Clarence stood for a while in the corridor, recovering his composure, considering where his life had led him, against all his expectations.

"You should never have led me into the Darkwood, Richard," he said quietly. "I could have forgiven you anything but that."

Prince Richard stood unhappily in Princess Catherine's suite, looking around him and wondering what to do for the best. He'd escorted the Princess safely back to her quarters, along with a whole bunch of heavily armed guards, and then arranged for them to stand guard outside her door, and up and down the entire length of the corridor. He'd got Catherine seated in a comfortable chair, with a glass of brandy in her hand. She'd been fine all through the banquet, but as soon as it was over all the strength seemed to just run out of her and she started shaking. Delayed shock. Richard and Gertrude quickly bustled her away from the Great Hall before anyone else could notice, but Catherine hadn't said a single word since. Richard tried again to persuade her to drink some of the brandy. It was excellent brandy, very good for shock. Or at the very least, it would take your mind off it.

He stood back to let Lady Gertrude fuss over the Princess, chatting comfortingly and making sure Catherine had everything she needed. Richard roamed around the huge suite, carefully checking everything in turn, looking for anything that didn't belong, or even just seemed out of place. Making sure everything was as it should be. He finally came back to Catherine, to let her know everything was fine, and that she was as safe as safe could be. But Catherine didn't seem to hear or see him.

She just sat there in her chair, staring straight ahead of her but clearly seeing nothing. Still holding the brandy glass in her hand but showing no interest in it, for all of Gertrude's encouragement. Lady Gertrude kept shooting annoyed glances at Richard, indicating that in her opinion the best thing he could do was get out and leave Catherine to her, but Richard was damned if he was going anywhere while Catherine was in such a state.

He was used to seeing her as strong and resilient, but three assassination attempts in under twenty-four hours had caught up with her. He crouched down before her, placing his face right in front of hers, and talked quietly and calmly to her, as reassuringly as he knew how. It took a while, but he persevered, and finally her eyes focused on him. She smiled slightly.

"You saved my life," she said quietly. "I am grateful; really. It's just . . . I'm having trouble coming to terms with the fact that my own people, in my own country, want me dead. Are ready to murder me, to bring about a war no sane person wants. And no, Richard, there's nothing anyone can do for me right now. I need time on my own. To think. I'll talk to you later."

Richard smiled as encouragingly as he could, and stood up again. "All right. You know best what you need. Get some rest. I'll make sure you're not disturbed. And drink your brandy. It's good for shock."

"I haven't got shock," said Catherine, with a hint of her old spirit.

Richard grinned. "You haven't tried the brandy yet."

Catherine tried another smile for him, but it was clear her heart wasn't in it. Richard smiled at her, nodded to Gertrude, and left the suite. All the guards in front of the door, and up and down the corridor, immediately slammed to attention. Richard nodded absently to them, and then stared thoughtfully at the closed door to Catherine's suite. He was still having trouble coming to terms with the fact that he had nearly died at the Tourney. He could still feel the knife slamming into his chest, all the way up to the hilt. He didn't remember falling. Didn't remember Catherine catching him and holding him in her arms as he bled out. He only sort of remembered Jack Forester bringing him back. He shuddered, suddenly. If Jack hadn't been there . . .

He'd been stunned to discover afterward that Jack was family. That he had in fact been saved by the son of Rupert and Julia. Richard supposed it only made sense that the son of two such legends should be able to work miracles . . . He felt seriously tired, worn out, and much in need of a quiet lie-down for a while. He looked up sharply at the sound of approaching footsteps. And there, coming towards him, was his good friend Peter. None of the guards challenged him. They all knew Peter Foster. Some had served with him out on the border, in one campaign or another. Peter crashed to a halt before Richard and nodded sternly.

"Right," he said. "I have been thinking."

"And drinking, from the smell of it," said Richard, amused. "Oh hell, I was supposed to join you in the beer tent, wasn't I? Sorry. Been one hell of a day . . ."

"Doesn't matter," said Peter. "I have permanently appointed myself your personal bodyguard. I can't believe Clarence and I weren't around when you nearly got yourself killed. Not going to let that happen again. From now on, I go where you go. In fact, I go there ahead of you, so that if they want to get to you, they have to go through me first. And there's not many can do that."

"Right . . . ," said Richard. "Where were you, exactly, when all the excitement was going on?"

"In the beer tent," said Peter.

"Of course, yes," said Richard. "Didn't Clarence volunteer to be my bodyguard as well?"

"Lot of use he'd be," said Peter. "I'm sure he would have volunteered, if he'd thought of it. But this was my idea. And be honest; what use would a minstrel be in the face of another assassin? What's he going to do, sing something satirical at them and shame them out of it?"

"Clarence can use a sword when he has to," Richard said steadily. "He did good work out on the border. Beside you and me."

"We've all changed a lot since those days," said Peter. "Anyway, last I heard, he was busy organising your stag do, for tonight."

Richard grinned despite himself. "Of course he is. I hadn't even thought about it. But he'll have to cancel; I'm really not in the mood."

"I told him that," said Peter.

The door behind them swung open suddenly, and everyone present dropped their hand to their sword. But it was just Catherine, distracted by the sound of voices outside her door. Richard quickly assured her that all was well.

"Who's this with you?" Catherine said suspiciously.

"An old friend of mine," said Richard. "Peter Foster."

"Friend and bodyguard," said Peter.

"About time," said Catherine. "Look after him, Peter. I'm not the only one in danger here."

And then they all looked round again as heavy footsteps announced the arrival of the Sombre Warrior, along with the six guards he'd brought with him from Redhart. All the Castle guards watched carefully, hands at their sword hilts. They looked to Prince Richard for their cue and he shook his head slightly. The guards relaxed just a little. The Sombre Warrior crashed to a halt before Richard and Catherine, ignoring Peter, and bowed to them both. Peter stepped forward, deliberately putting himself between Richard and the Sombre Warrior.

"Easy, Peter," Richard said quietly.

"Easy, hell," said Peter. "What are you doing here, Warrior?"

"We are here to help guard the Princess," said the Sombre Warrior. "We will be here, outside her door, until the wedding tomorrow. And then we will escort her to the ceremony, as her honour guard. I have received no orders on this. But I felt . . . this was something I had to do."

"Of course," said Richard diplomatically. "The Princess should have an honour guard."

"Anyone would think you didn't trust Castle security," Peter said to the Sombre Warrior.

The Warrior gave all his attention to Richard. "No offence intended, your highness."

"None taken," said Richard. "But after what happened today . . . Given that the knife-thrower invoked the name of Redhart . . ."

"I chose all of my men personally," the Sombre Warrior said steadily. "They have already saved her from an attack by brigands. I trust them all with my life, and that of the Princess."

"And I trust them, and you," said Catherine. "Thank you, sir Warrior. If this is acceptable to you, Richard?"

"Of course," said Richard. Peter started to say something, but Richard shut him up with a look. He then turned his glare on the watching guards. "I'm sure there won't be any problem integrating the Warrior's men with my own."

The guards up and down the corridor took their cue from the Prince and nodded formally, if not particularly enthusiastically.

Catherine looked steadily at the Sombre Warrior. "Do you think there'll be another attack before the wedding?"

"I hear many things," said the Sombre Warrior. "Some that I am free to tell you, and some that I am not. Your enemies are still out there. But I swear to you, your highness, upon my life and upon my honour, I will stand between you and all harm."

Catherine nodded, genuinely touched. It was clear to her that the Warrior had heard something but didn't want to frighten her.

"Thank you, sir Warrior," she said. "I will feel much safer, knowing you are there."

"Best to err on the side of caution," said the Sombre Warrior. "If you wish, I could stay in your room with you . . ."

"No," Catherine said immediately. "That would be an insult to Castle security. And I am quite capable of looking after myself."

"Yes," said the Sombre Warrior. "I remember."

"The very idea!" said Lady Gertrude, peering past Catherine at all the men in the corridor. "A man? Sharing the Princess' room, at night? *Before the wedding?* Most unsuitable! Come inside, my sweet, and I'll make you a nice hot posset, to help you sleep."

Catherine inclined her head to the Sombre Warrior, and to the guards, and managed a small smile just for Richard. And then she closed the door firmly in their faces.

She could hear the guards moving about in the corridor for a while, as everyone worked out where they should be, and then she heard Richard's voice as he moved off down the corridor, with his friend and bodyguard Peter. Catherine waited until his voice was gone, and then she sank down in her chair again, utterly exhausted. She struggled to get her thoughts together, while doing her best to ignore Lady Gertrude fussing over her.

"You didn't touch that nice brandy," said Gertrude. "How about some nice hot milk instead? Shall I fetch a blanket, to wrap around you, to keep out the chills? No? Well, I'm sure you know best. You really should drink something, my dear. Fluids are good for you when you've been through a trying experience. Look, I already made this steaming hot posset, just for you. The kind you used to love when you were small. Don't let it go to waste . . ."

"Lady Gertrude?" said Catherine, not looking up.

"Yes, my sweet?"

"I know you mean well, Gertrude, but if you don't shut the hell up right now, I will find something large and heavy and use it to pound your head into the floor."

"Well, really!" said Gertrude.

"Yes, really!" said Catherine. She shook her head and sighed slowly. "I'm sorry, Gertrude. I'm just . . . Look, this is me, changing the subject." She thought for a moment, and then shook her head again. "I can't seem to concentrate on anything. I miss Sir Jasper. He always knew how to cheer me up. Has anyone seen him recently?"

"Not to the best of my knowledge," said Gertrude just a bit coldly. "I'd have said we were better off without him."

"I wouldn't," Catherine said firmly. "I think he's just what I need, to take my mind off things." She raised her voice. "Sir Jasper! Come to me! I need you!"

And just like that, the ghost was there in the room, standing before her. He looked more solid than before, more like a real old man, with white hair and beard, in a long white nightie. Gertrude jumped at his sudden appearance, and let out a loud squeak. Sir Jasper jumped at Gertrude's loud squeak, and looked very much like he would have liked to make one himself. Catherine smiled, feeling better already.

"Princess! Are you all right?" Sir Jasper looked quickly about him, and then calmed down a little as he saw no obvious threat. He brushed unconsciously at the folds of his nightie, and tugged at his long beard. "I heard what happened! The whole Castle is buzzing with the news, and it's amazing how much you can overhear when you're invisible and people don't realise you're standing right behind them. But you don't need to worry anymore, Catherine. I'm here!"

"You?" said Lady Gertrude, staring down her nose at him, her arms folded tightly across her chest. "Hah! What use are you, hiding behind things and jumping at your own shadow? What would you do if an assassin did get in here? Creep up behind him and shout *Boo!* in his ears?"

Sir Jasper looked guiltily at Catherine, and gathered his dignity about him. Which wasn't easy for an old man in a floor-length nightie.

"I am a bit rubbish as a ghost, I'll admit. But I was a knight once. I'm almost sure I was."

"Don't squabble, you two," said Catherine. "I'm tired, and my head is killing me."

Lady Gertrude and Sir Jasper were both immediately contrite. The ghost drifted back and forth around the room, trying to work out what he could usefully do, while Lady Gertrude bustled off and came back almost immediately with a heavy mug containing something hot and wet, with steam coming off it. She all but forced the mug into Catherine's hands, and the Princess took it just to get her to shut up. Gertrude stood firmly before her, silently insisting that Catherine drink the stuff. Sir Jasper happened to drift by. He glanced at the mug, and then stopped, and looked at it more closely.

"What is that?" he said, and something in his voice made Catherine sit up and pay attention.

"It's a hot posset," said Gertrude. "Just the thing to help a tired soul get a little well-earned peace."

"Yes . . . ," said Sir Jasper. "But what's in it?"

"Like you'd appreciate it even if I told you," sniffed Gertrude. "It's herbs and spices and . . . all sorts of things that are good for you! That's all. It's an old family recipe . . ."

But still, something in the way Gertrude said all that made Catherine sit up straight in her chair and take notice. She looked into the mug, and then looked at Gertrude. Sir Jasper looked at Catherine steadily.

"Don't drink that. I'll be right back."

He disappeared, gone in a moment, not even leaving a disturbance in the air behind him. Gertrude started to say something, and then stopped, as Catherine looked at her.

"What is he talking about, Lady Gertrude?" said Catherine.

"I'm sure I haven't the faintest idea, my sweet," said Gertrude, flustered. "If you don't want a posset, you don't have to have one, I'm sure. I can always make you something else. Here, give it back to me and I'll empty it down the toilet. Though it's a shame to waste perfectly good ingredients, I must say . . ."

Sir Jasper reappeared, and this time he had with him Laurence Garner, head of Castle security. Who looked very startled at suddenly being somewhere else, almost certainly without his permission. He blinked about him, quickly recovered his poise, and bowed to the Princess.

"This is the security fellow," said Sir Jasper. "I found him in a room that was positively rushing about all over the place! Security measure, I suppose. Anyway, I think you should talk to him, Catherine. Really. Right now."

"How did you know I was head of security?" said Garner to the ghost. Not unreasonably, he felt.

"Oh, I know all sorts of things," said Sir Jasper. "Not terribly useful things, mostly . . . Like who I am, or . . . Never mind me! Talk to the Princess!"

"I am Laurence Garner, your highness, head of Castle security. This ghost person seems very sure you have need of my services. What can I do to be of assistance?"

Catherine looked at Sir Jasper. "I didn't know you could do that. Just . . . pop in and out, and grab people."

"Neither did I," the ghost said cheerfully. "Until I needed to. Never know what you can do till you try." He looked at Garner. "In my day, the head of Castle security always carried a sliver of unicorn horn with him, to check for poison. Do you have such a thing about you?"

"Well, yes," said Garner. "It's traditional. Though not many people are supposed to know that." He reached up and pulled a long sliver of pure white bone from his lapel. "What is it that I need to test?"

Catherine and Sir Jasper looked at Lady Gertrude, and then Catherine held out the steaming mug she was holding.

"Oh, just let me get rid of it, if it's going to upset everyone so!" said Gertrude.

She snatched the mug out of Catherine's hand to take it away, and then seemed to stumble suddenly. She might have spilt the mug's contents all over the carpet if Sir Jasper hadn't been there to snatch the mug out of her hands.

"Careful," said Sir Jasper.

Catherine looked at him, actually startled. "I didn't know you were physically present enough to hold things, Sir Jasper."

"It's the Castle," said the ghost. "The longer I stay here, the more . . . solid I feel. The more *me*."

He looked thoughtfully at Gertrude, who glared right back at him. Sir Jasper carefully handed the mug and its steaming contents over to Garner. The head of security accepted the mug equally carefully, flinching just a little as he briefly touched the ghost's cold dead hand. He sniffed the mug's contents, frowned thoughtfully, and then lowered his sliver of unicorn horn carefully into the hot liquid. And then they all watched in silence, as a dark purple stain rose slowly up the white bone.

Garner removed the sliver, and put it and the mug down on a nearby side table, careful not to let one drop of the liquid touch his hand. And then they all looked at Lady Gertrude. She drew herself up under their accusing gaze and stared silently back at them. Catherine sank into her chair, wrapping her arms around her, suddenly shuddering uncontrollably. She felt dazed, lost, betrayed, and for a long moment she couldn't say anything.

"How could you?" she said finally. "Poison in my drink? You? You practically raised me!"

"It wouldn't have killed you," said Gertrude defiantly. "Just made you really sick for a while. Enough to put off the wedding. A third assassination attempt would have been all we needed to break the Peace agreement and get us out of this filthy country once and for all!"

Catherine wouldn't let herself look away. "You didn't come up with this on your own. Who put you up to this?"

Gertrude just stared right back at Catherine, her mouth shut in a firm line. Catherine turned to Garner.

"Take her away. Get the truth out of her. Whatever it takes."

For the first time Gertrude looked shocked. "Catherine! You'd let them do that? To me?"

"Why not?" said Catherine coldly. "I don't know you anymore."

"I had every right to do this!" said Gertrude, her voice flat and ugly. "I was put in charge of all the assassination attempts by your father! By the King himself! You were never in any real danger, not after all the extra protections he had placed on you!"

"My father . . . ," said Catherine. She slumped into her chair, looking like she'd just been hit in the face. "I don't believe you."

"I do," said Garner. "The assassins had to be activated by someone who was present on both occasions, and was in close proximity to you. And kings . . . will always do what they feel to be necessary. No matter who gets hurt in the process."

"The protections could have failed!" Catherine shouted at Gertrude. "Something could have gone wrong! My father . . . my own father was prepared to put my life at risk . . . to bring about a war? Why? No one wants this stupid war!" She shook her head, trying to understand. "He took away my lovely Champion, destroyed the life I wanted, to send me here . . . After all his preaching to me, about duty and honour and responsibility . . . how I had to come here and marry a stranger to prevent the suffering and slaughter of war . . . Liar! Hypocrite! Warmongering piece of shit! I'll never forgive him for this. Never."

She threw herself out of her chair and stamped up and down the suite, all but incandescent with rage. Garner stood back and let her do it; he could see she was only a moment away from real violence. Suddenly Catherine stopped and turned on Gertrude.

"That's it! I'm done with Redhart, and my father. I'm staying here and marrying Richard. The only one who really cares about me. He was prepared to die to save me!"

"And what about your lovely Champion, Malcolm Barrett?" said Gertrude coldly.

"He was a part of this!" Catherine shouted right in Gertrude's face. "He had to be! He's the King's Champion, the man who'll lead Redhart into war! How could he not know?" Catherine turned away, shaking, her voice choked with too many emotions.

"He didn't know," said Gertrude. "He knew nothing of any of this."

"Liar," Catherine said dully. "You'd say anything, wouldn't you? Richard's the only one I can believe in now."

"You can't marry him!" said Gertrude. "And you can't stay here! You can't betray your country!"

"My country betrayed me! My country tried to have me killed!" Catherine was breathing hard now, her hands clenched into white-knuckled fists. "Talk to me, Gertrude. Tell me why."

"We all lost someone, out on the border," said Gertrude. "Isn't that what everyone says? Well, I lost my young man. My lovely young man. We were so much in love. We were going to be married the moment he came back. Instead, they gave me a letter saying he'd died. Just another name on the list of all the brave young Redhart men who never came home. Killed by those Forest bastards. There was never anyone else for me, after him . . . And they were going to give away the land he fought and died for! It would have all been for nothing! Everything I've been through! For nothing!"

"I never knew," said Catherine. "I never thought . . ."

"You never cared," said Gertrude viciously. "I wore black, in mourning, all your life . . . and all you ever did was laugh behind my back. Silly old thing; why doesn't she get over it? Raising someone else's child, because she'll never have one of her own. You never cared, you spoilt little bitch!"

And suddenly she was lunging for Catherine with a glowing dagger in her hand. Laughing like a mad thing. Catherine was too shocked to move for a moment, unable to believe her old companion was actually trying to kill her. And then she grabbed a chair and held it out before her. Gertrude stopped and tried to stab at Catherine around the chair, the dagger's blade gleaming unnaturally bright.

Sir Jasper was suddenly standing between Catherine and Gertrude. He seemed much larger, and far more terrifying. A dead thing, full of death's power. He surged forward and enveloped Gertrude, wrapping his unearthly form around her, glowing with an unbearable light. Gertrude screamed with horror and dropped the dagger. And then she stopped screaming and sat down on the floor, not moving, not breathing, staring straight ahead with bulging eyes in a contorted face.

Sir Jasper stepped away from her. His face was cold, but he looked like a man again. Garner came forward cautiously, and leaned over Gertrude. He checked her pulse, looked back at Catherine, and shook his head. The Princess realised she was still holding the chair and put it down. She moved slowly forward to stare at her old companion, and then looked back at Sir Jasper as though she'd never seen him before.

"What did you do to her?"

"I protected you," said the ghost.

"What did you do?"

"I showed her what it's like to be me," said Sir Jasper. "To be dead. Don't look at me like that, Catherine. She would have killed you. I only did it to save you!"

He held out a hand plaintively, but she turned away, refusing to look at him. Sir Jasper became suddenly transparent, more ghostly. He faded away and was gone.

"What have I brought into this Castle?" Catherine said quietly. "He's not what I thought he was. Just a funny old ghost, searching for his past. He's not that at all. And I don't think he ever was, really."

"You must excuse me, your highness," Garner said carefully. "I have to talk to my people, pass on the information that Lady Gertrude gave up. About King William's true intentions. And, of course King Rufus and Parliament must be told. This changes everything."

"No!" Catherine said sharply. "Gertrude was right about one thing. A third assassination attempt would be enough to break the marriage and the Peace agreement. I can't give them that victory. I won't give my father his war!"

"I'm sorry, your highness," said Garner, "but I must follow my orders."

And he left the room before she could say anything else.

The Sombre Warrior turned round abruptly as Garner came out of the Princess' suite.

"How the hell did you get in there without me knowing?"

"Don't ask," said Garner. "Really, you don't want to know. There's a body in there. Lady Gertrude. Have your men go in and get her."

"Gertrude?" said the Sombre Warrior. "What happened to her?"

"Have the body placed in storage," said Garner. "There's always the chance the Necromancer will be able to get something out of her." He looked steadily into the chalk white porcelain mask. "Lady Gertrude just tried to murder the Princess. On King William's direct orders."

"Dear God," said the Warrior.

"Did you suspect something?" said Garner. "Coming here, to stand guard over her personally?"

"I suspected something," said the Sombre Warrior. "But not this. Not . . . Gertrude."

He pushed past Garner and hurried into the suite, not pausing to knock. Catherine was sitting in her chair, looking down at her hands in her lap.

"Are you safe, Princess?" said the Sombre Warrior. "Are you hurt?"

"She really did try to kill me," said Catherine, looking up at the Warrior like a child. "First with poison, then with . . . that."

She nodded to the glowing dagger, still lying on the floor. The Sombre Warrior quickly went over, knelt down beside the dagger, and studied it carefully through his mask, then picked up the ugly weapon by the handle with his thumb and forefinger.

"Nasty. I can see all kinds of magics, crawling all over the blade. Powerful enough to cut through even your defences, Princess. This was no mere attempt. Lady Gertrude meant business."

He called through the open door, and his men came hurrying in. He spoke quietly with them, gave one of them the dagger, and indicated for the others to pick up Gertrude's body and carry it out. They did so, quickly and efficiently. The Sombre Warrior turned back to Catherine.

"My men will ensure that Lady Gertrude's body is treated respectfully, your highness."

"Garner said something about the Necromancer . . ."

"No, your highness," said the Warrior. "Raven already knows he'll get nothing out of her. I'll see that the body is not disturbed. Would I be correct in assuming that this is something to do with her lost love, who died out on the border? Yes. I don't think any of us took her loss seriously enough. We should have known better. Grief never goes away if it's nursed. Gertrude held her grief to her because she had nothing else, and in the end it destroyed her. What do you want me to do now, your highness?"

Catherine looked at him blankly. "What?"

"Do you want me to start the preparations for our return to Redhart?"

"No," said Catherine. "I'm not going anywhere. I'm staying here, with Richard."

"As you wish," said the Sombre Warrior. "I'll get word to him, let him know what's happened. I'm sure he'll be here soon." He looked at the two men still waiting by the door. "You. Guard her. From everyone and everything, until the Prince gets here. Understand?"

"We follow your orders, sir Warrior," one of the guards said carefully. "Yours, and no one else's."

The Sombre Warrior turned back to Catherine. "Do you want me to stay here with you until the Prince arrives?"

"No," said Catherine, so quietly the Sombre Warrior had to concentrate to understand her. "I don't want anyone with me."

The Sombre Warrior bowed and left, taking his guards with him. So he didn't hear the last thing Catherine said.

"I can't trust anyone anymore."

EIGHT

....

MANY THINGS, RETURNING

Prince Christof, putative heir to the Redhart throne, and Malcolm Barrett, Champion to the Redhart King, came running down the corridor that led to King William's Court from different directions. They both stumbled to a halt before the closed double doors, and then leaned on each other heavily, as they struggled to get their breath back. The armed guards on duty outside the doors did their best not to stare, whilst making it very clear through stern faces and body language that they had been ordered not to let anyone pass. Because they really didn't want to have to say it out loud, to the King's son and the King's Champion, if they didn't have to. Christof and Malcolm paid the guards no attention at all. They had other things on their minds. When they both finally felt they had their breathing under control again, they straightened up, stood back, and looked at each other.

"This is not good," said Christof. "In fact, I would have to say that this is so far from good that I can't even see good from where I'm standing. I have been summoned to appear before my father many times before, for many reasons, but never at this late hour of the evening, never in such a peremptory way . . . and never with such a brutal sense of urgency."

"Can't be a standard session of the Court," said Malcolm. "Not at this hour. Can't even be an emergency session, or I'd have been briefed about it. Do you have any idea what this is about?"

"Haven't a clue," said Christof. "Which is, I suppose, a clue in itself, because I always make it a point to have someone of my own among the King's people, to warn me in advance about Bad Things Happening. If only so I can get my excuses properly in order." He did his best to force the stress from his voice and his face and assume his usual languid poise. "No doubt dear Father will get around to telling me what it is, in his own good time."

Malcolm managed a small smile. "But you don't think it's likely to be anything good."

"You don't need to keep good news secret," said Christof. "No, Mal. This is going to be really bad."

"Then why were you in such a hurry to get here?"

"Because usually when it's this bad, you just want to get it over with as quickly as possible."

They both looked fiercely at the guards, on general principles. None of the guards would meet their eyes. Christof looked at Malcolm.

"Have you heard anything from Catherine since she arrived at Forest Castle?"

"No," said Malcolm. "Not a word, directly or indirectly. Not even an *Arrived safely, nothing to worry about.* Which is worrying."

Christof looked past the increasingly nervous guards, at the closed double doors. "Perhaps that . . . is what this is all about."

Malcolm scowled. "If everything was going well, the King would just have announced it, in passing, as part of regular Court business. Something like this—a private Court session in the dead of night—can only mean something somewhere has gone seriously wrong."

They both looked round sharply as the Prime Minister, Gregory Pool, came puffing down the corridor towards them. Nature had never intended anyone as large as the Prime Minister to run, but he'd clearly been doing his best. He'd been reduced by lack of breath to a ponderous shuffle, and when he finally stumbled to a halt before the Prince and the Champion, he was wheezing so hard he couldn't get a word out. His face was an alarming shade of purple, and his eyes actually bulged from their sockets, like those of a frightened horse. But he got himself back under control surprisingly quickly, then launched into an outraged speech that he'd clearly been rehearsing in his head all the way to the Court.

"Bloody King will be the death of me! Summoning me to attend him at Court, at this hour of the bloody night, without even the slightest hint of courtesy! No *If you please* or *The urgency of the situation demands* . . . Oh no. Just a soldier banging on my door and a written command to attend the King! Right now! Dear God, my heart feels like it wants to leap right out of my chest . . . It's times like this I think the Forest Land had the right idea. A constitutional monarchy, followed by a republic, as soon as possible. Bloody Royals! No offence intended, Prince Christof."

"None taken, I'm sure," murmured the Prince. "Bloody King, indeed. Though I do have to wonder"—and here he stopped, to let his eyes drift meaningfully in the direction of the guards—"whether this might have something to do with the little get-together we all had, after our audience with the King. Where we discussed matters most private and most secret . . ."

The Prime Minister looked at him warily. "Nothing was said in your rooms that I would be dismayed to hear repeated before the King!"

"Well, quite," said Christof. "I think all of us present were very careful about what we did and did not say to each other."

"But we did meet together, in private," said Malcolm. "And now we've all been called here, to meet with the King, in private."

"General Staker's not here," said Gregory Pool.

"No, he isn't," said Christof.

They broke off again, as the Steward Elias Taggert came hurrying down the corridor to join them. He wasn't running, as such, but he looked as though he might have liked to, if his dignity would have allowed it. As one of the youngest Stewards ever appointed to the post, Elias was always very much concerned with his dignity, in public. So he walked briskly forward, covering quite a lot of ground in the process, before slamming to a halt before the others. He looked coldly at the guarded doors.

"I was in there, for a while," he said. "Just the King, and me. In an empty Court. This is not good, gentlemen, not good . . . Things are happening, decisions are being made, to which I am no longer privy . . . And if he isn't talking to me about them, who is he talking to? He only called me in to convey a message to the sorcerer Van Fleet . . ."

"What does the King want with my brother?" said the Prime Minister immediately.

"I don't know!" said the Steward. "It was a written message that I was expressly forbidden to even look at! That he should say such a thing to me . . . The King has always trusted me before! Always! I am his Steward, his voice and authority . . ."

"The letter?" prompted Christof.

"Van Fleet read it, and then threw me out of his rooms," said the Steward. "He didn't look at all happy. Now here I am, back again, waiting to be called in and given new orders, like a dog at the hearth! Something new must have happened, something vital . . . but damned if I know what."

"Is the King . . . angry about anything?" said Malcolm.

"I don't know," said the Steward. "But he certainly seemed . . . very serious."

Christof gave his full attention to the guards, and several of them went pale. Whenever the Prince looked that thoughtful, it was always dangerous for someone. It meant Christof was considering some really unpleasant new punishment. "Guards," murmured Christof. "Is there anyone inside the Court at present, with the King?"

The guards looked straight ahead, hoping not to be noticed. They were all sweating. Christof picked out the most senior guard and walked steadily forward till he could place his face right in front of the guard's.

"I am Prince Christof, son of the King and heir to the throne of Redhart. This is no time to be making enemies, guard. The King may have ordered you to say nothing, but you will have noticed that he isn't here right now and I am."

"The King is within, your highness," said the guard, staring straight ahead. "There was no one else with him, when he commanded us to close the doors and seal off the Court to all entrants."

Christof smiled at the guard. "You see? That wasn't so difficult, was it?"

"No, your highness."

"Shut up." Christof turned away, to look steadily at his fellow summoned guests. "It has occurred to me, this might be something to do with my banished brother."

They all looked at the Steward, who shrugged uncomfortably.

"I haven't seen or spoken with Prince Cameron since I was sent to speak with him," the Steward said carefully.

"And how was dear Cameron?" said Christof. "Any change for the better?"

"I couldn't say, your highness," said the Steward.

"No," said Christof, "I'm sure you couldn't."

And then everyone looked round as the huge double doors swung suddenly inwards, opening on their own. The guards looked at the doors, and then at each other, and it was clear from their pale and heavily perspiring faces that this was nothing to do with them. Christof pushed past them and strode through the opening doors with his head held high. Followed quickly by Malcolm, Gregory Pool, and the Steward. The moment the last of them had passed through the doors and into the Court, the doors immediately started closing again. Still moving entirely of their own volition. Which was a new thing for everyone, and entirely without precedent, and therefore worrying. Whenever a King is responsible for something new, and unannounced, it's time for everyone to worry. It means he's been thinking, which rarely means anything good for anyone. The guards waited for the doors to close, and then took up their positions again, standing closer together for comfort.

Inside, the Court was entirely empty. Not a courtier or a politician or a celebrity anywhere to be seen. Which was also unprecedented, and therefore worrying. The ancient glowing spheres that normally lit the entire Great Hall had now come together to hover above the throne, bobbing up and down on the air and surrounding the throne with a light almost too bright to look at. While leaving the rest of the Court to darkness and shadows. The four summoned men walked a little more closely together, almost unconsciously, as they strode steadily through the great Court, the only sound the echo of their own footsteps. They were all careful to keep their backs straight and hold their heads high. They all knew better than to appear weak or uncertain before the King, or even one another; that would be dangerous. But still, the four men stuck close together, on the grounds that there was some safety to be found in numbers. The great empty space of the Court seemed to press in around them from all sides at once, silent and menacing, as though it knew something they didn't. That its cold, dead presence was more significant than theirs. As though . . . the King preferred the cold dark to their company. There was something wrong about the King. They could all feel it, even if none of them could put it into words just yet. But none of them slowed their pace, or let the respectful smiles slip from their lips, even for a moment. Such things could be dangerous. Finally, the four men came to a halt before the throne, and they all bowed low to King William. Who leaned back on his throne, smiling coldly at them, like a gore crow on a newly raised cairn.

"Welcome, my friends," said the King, in a voice that held no friendliness at all. "I have summoned you here, just you few, because I have received an important communication from the Sombre Warrior, in the Forest Land. I have to inform you that there have been three, fortunately unsuccessful, assassination attempts on the Princess Catherine since she arrived at Forest Castle. Two attempts at poison and one open attack with a knife."

For a moment Malcolm couldn't get his breath. It was like someone had punched him in the heart. All the colour dropped out of his face as his eyes fixed unblinkingly on the King.

"Who?" he said harshly. *"Who would dare . . . ?"*

"I understand your feelings, my Champion," said the King. "If you will allow me to continue . . ."

Malcolm nodded quickly, recognising the warning in the King's voice. He realised he'd taken a step forward, and now he carefully stepped back again, to rejoin the others. His hands had clenched into white-knuckled fists, and the only expression on his face was a cold and brutal need to strike out at someone. And perhaps only Prince Christof noticed that the sheer rage burning inside the Champion seemed to have left no room for any other emotion, like concern for the Princess Catherine's condition.

"Given that my daughter has only been present in the Forest Court for two days, and already her life has been endangered three times, it is clear to me that the Forest King is incapable of proper security measures. Or perhaps he just doesn't care enough to do a proper job. It doesn't matter. I have no choice but to declare the arranged marriage cancelled. The Princess Catherine must return home at once, where I can ensure her safety. The Peace agreement is no more."

"Sire, you can't!" said the Prime Minister, and just like the Champion he so forgot himself as to take a step forward, towards the King on his throne. But unlike the Champion, when Gregory Pool realised what he'd done, he didn't immediately retreat. He stood his ground, glaring at the King, and actually raised his voice. "You can't just throw away a Peace we all worked so hard to put together!"

"I think you'll find I can, Prime Minister," the King said coldly. "I have no choice. Honour dictates the necessity of my actions."

"Your honour, Father?" Christof said calmly. "Or Redhart's honour?"

The King glared at him. "In a situation like this, they are one and the same thing, boy."

"Of course they are, Father," said the Prince.

Malcolm's thoughts were far away, divided and at war with one another. At first he was simply delighted that the arranged marriage had been cancelled, at the very last moment, against all the odds . . . and that Catherine would be coming home. To him. He'd never dared let himself believe he would ever see her again. But now everything had changed in a moment. The Forest Court could never have any claim on her, not after this; she might even become his fiancée again . . . But then he made himself push such thoughts aside. He had no right to think of his own happiness when his country was about to be plunged into a huge and bloody war. He waited for the Prime Minister to break off his ranting for a moment, then quickly put in a question of his own.

"Do we know who was responsible for the attacks on the Princess, Sire?"

"Extremists," said King William. "From both countries, apparently. The Sombre Warrior is still investigating. We've always known there are factions on both sides who don't want this Peace at any price, and would oppose it to the death. To my daughter's death, as it turned out."

"It is war, then?" said Gregory Pool. The oversized man in his colourful clothes suddenly looked tired, and old, and defeated. "No way out?"

The King shrugged, still smiling his cold, implacable smile. "There is still the possibility of future negotiations . . . but my daughter's safety is not negotiable. I have put her in harm's way, and that cannot be allowed to continue. She must return home."

"The Forest Court will take her removal, and the cancellation of the marriage, as an open insult," said the Prime Minister.

"Let them," said the King. "I no longer care what they want. Once my daughter is safely back under my protection, then, perhaps . . . we will see if it is still possible for us to speak together. Now. Van Fleet!"

The moment the King raised his voice in command, the sorcerer Van Fleet appeared out of nowhere, standing stiffly beside the throne in his wizard's robes. Everyone standing before the King jumped just a little. Malcolm glared at the sorcerer. He had to wonder how long the man had been standing there, unseen and unsuspected, watching and listening in secret. The Prime Minister looked at his brother blankly, concerned that his brother had sided with the King in not warning Gregory about this meeting in advance.

"Have you arranged the summit connection, my sorcerer?" said King William.

"Of course, your majesty," said Van Fleet, bowing low to his King while ignoring everyone else, especially his brother, the Prime Minister. "I have been in contact with the Forest Land's greatest sorcerer, Raven the Necromancer. A most powerful and puissant magic-user. A strange, even disturbing sort, but exceedingly talented for one so young. But then, given his parentage and descent . . ."

"Enough," said the King. "Make contact with the Forest Court. Do it now."

"Yes, Sire," said Van Fleet.

The sorcerer gestured quickly at the far end of the Court, beyond the four men, and they all turned to see the farthest half of the Redhart Court disappear. Gone, in a moment, replaced by half the Forest Court. Not a broadcast vision, but the real thing; they could all feel it. As though one-half of each Court had been joined to the other. The intervening space folded and slammed together, by the combined wills of two very powerful men. Malcolm looked at Van Fleet, and a cold chill ran up his spine. He'd never even suspected the man could do anything like this. Christof leaned in close beside him, to murmur in his ear.

"Did you know Van Fleet could do things like this?"

"No," Malcolm said quietly. "This is really very impressive from someone who's supposed to be just studying the High Magic."

"Yes," said Christof. "Does rather make you wonder what else he might be capable of . . ."

The Forest Court was as empty as their own, with just a few significant figures standing around the Forest Throne. Almost protectively. King Rufus sat stiffly upright on his throne, his head held high, but he still looked like he'd just been dragged out of bed, dressed quickly, and had the crown jammed on his ragged head at the last moment. He was clearly doing his best to concentrate his failing faculties, to be the King the situation demanded. But it was equally clear to all present that he really wasn't up to it. His eyes were clear, but his mouth was weak, and his hands trembled in his lap.

The Seneschal stood beside him, on his left hand, while Prince Richard and Princess Catherine stood close together on the King's right hand. The Sombre Warrior stood to one side, huge and imposing in his full ceremonial armour and featureless steel helmet. Standing opposite him was the Forest's First Minister, Peregrine de Woodville, his face screwed up in desperate lines, all but wringing his hands. But all Malcolm could concentrate on was how closely Richard and Catherine were standing together. As though they still belonged together. Catherine was holding on to Richard's arm. Almost possessively. And she wasn't looking at Malcolm. She only had eyes for her father.

"All the assassins are dead, William," King Rufus said immediately. Not bothering with any of the usual courtesies. His voice was firm enough. "Your daughter is safe; I assure you. None of the killers even got close. My people saw to that. My own son, Richard, put his life on the line, to stand between your daughter and the assassin's knife."

"He looks fine to me," said King William. "Positively undamaged. Glowing with health, I would have said."

"That's not fair, Father!" said Catherine; but her father just talked right over her, drowning her out.

"I must insist that you return home immediately, Catherine," said the King. "It is clear Rufus cannot protect you."

"Oh, I'm fine, Father!" said Catherine. "No thanks to you!"

"What?" said Malcolm immediately. "What are you saying, Catherine?"

"Do you see my companion, Lady Gertrude, anywhere here?" said Catherine, still glaring fiercely at her father. "No, of course you don't. Because she's dead! She was one of the assassins! My own companion put poison in my cup, and then tried to stab me with a magic blade!"

"Dear God," said Gregory Pool, honestly shocked. "How deep are these fanatics placed? How deep does this poison go?"

"Sombre Warrior!" said Malcolm. "Is this true?"

The huge figure inclined his steel helmet slowly. "Yes."

"Doesn't change anything," said King William. "Come home, Catherine, where you can be properly protected."

"But I wouldn't feel safe with you, Father," said Catherine, and her face and voice were every bit as cold and determined as his.

"I don't understand," said Malcolm. "Why don't you want to come home, Catherine? I'll protect you; you know I will."

She looked at him properly for the first time, and her face softened into something that meant to be kind. "I can't come home, Malcolm. Because I've fallen in love with Richard, and he with me. Not something either of us expected, I'll admit, but true, nonetheless. I'm staying here and I'm marrying Richard. I'm sorry, Malcolm. Really I am."

"You can't mean that!" said Malcolm. He didn't understand anything that was happening. He felt like he was going mad. "Look, Catherine . . . you don't have to stay there any longer. Nothing holds you there. You're free to come back. To me!"

"I'm so sorry, Malcolm," said Catherine. "I never meant to hurt you."

Malcolm turned his face away from her, to King William. "That's not my Catherine speaking. They've done something to her. They must have a hold over her, forcing her to say these things!"

"I can assure you that is not the case," said the Sombre Warrior.

"Whose side are you on?" said the Champion, his voice rising and almost breaking from all the passions raging within him.

"I side with the Princess," said the Sombre Warrior. He seemed to be looking directly at King William. "I have seen things and heard things in this place . . . And I no longer have any faith in the truth or honour of King William of Redhart."

"What?" said Gregory Pool. "What is he talking about, William? What does the Sombre Warrior know that I don't? *What have you done, William?*"

"Be still, Prime Minister!" said King William, his voice like thunder. "I am your King! You will address me as Sire!"

"Of course, Sire," said Gregory, bowing quickly. He looked dazed, his eyes a little wild. "It's just . . . This is all so . . ."

King William ignored him, staring directly at his daughter in the opposite Court. "Return home immediately, daughter. That is an order."

"Go to hell, you two-faced piece of shit," said Catherine.

There was a long silence. The Princess' words seemed to hang on the air.

"This is unacceptable," King William said finally. "Rufus, if you will not give my daughter up, we will come to you in force of arms and take her. I hereby declare that from this moment on, a state of war exists between our two countries."

"No! Don't you dare use me as your excuse!" blazed Catherine. She started forward and Richard had to grab her to hold her back. Catherine immediately pulled free of him but stood her ground, glaring at her father. "Your master of assassins, Lady Gertrude, told me you were the one behind all the attacks on me, Father! You wanted this war all along!"

"The child's gone mad," said King William. "What are you talking about, girl? Lady Gertrude was a sweet old soul. Wouldn't hurt a fly. Everyone knows that."

"I told you," said Malcolm. "They've worked a spell on her! The Forest Court has always had a taste for compulsion, and the enslaving of souls. We all remember the Curtana, the legendary Sword of Compulsion!"

"Are you seriously suggesting we would use such a thing?" said Peregrine de Woodville.

"Everyone knows the Sword of Compulsion was destroyed by the Demon Prince, at the end of the Demon War!" said Prince Richard.

"Yes, well, you would say that," said King William. "Wouldn't you?" He looked at the Sombre Warrior. "Can you do nothing, my Warrior? Can you not free my daughter from this unnatural control?"

"There's nothing wrong with the Princess," said the Sombre Warrior, his voice sounding hollow but firm from within his steel helmet. "She is not controlled by any outside force. She speaks her own mind, and she speaks the truth. You are a liar, a corruptor, and a conspirator; and you are not fit to sit on the throne of Redhart. I forsake all ties to you, and to Redhart, for as long as you remain King. I choose to remain here, with the Princess, and to serve King Rufus. Reduced as he may be, he is still a better man than you, William."

There was a long silence. No one had expected such an open renunciation from the famous Sombre Warrior. Everyone looked at King William to see what he would do.

He laughed harshly. "So, they've got to you too."

"You should never have threatened the Princess, William," said the Sombre Warrior. "You should never have put your own daughter's life at risk. There are limits, even for men such as us."

The Forest Court disappeared, gone in the blink of an eye, replaced by the dark shadowy reaches of the Redhart Court. King William turned savagely on Van Fleet.

"Get them back!"

"I am afraid . . . I cannot, Sire," said the sorcerer. His face was pale, and slick with sweat. He didn't look at all well. "The connection was broken from the other end, by the Necromancer, and without his cooperation I am unable to reinstate it."

"But Raven wasn't even there!" said King William.

"Oh, he was . . . present," said Van Fleet. "He just didn't choose to show himself. Raven is a surprisingly accomplished sorcerer. I could not hope to overcome his will. Not yet . . ."

"Are you saying this Necromancer is more powerful than you?" said King William in a quiet and very dangerous voice.

"His sources of magic are very different from mine, Sire," said Van Fleet. Which everyone present could tell wasn't really an answer. The sorcerer didn't want to look at the King. "His true capabilities have yet to be determined, your majesty. Give me time to prepare myself properly, and then . . . we shall see what we shall see."

King William turned away from his sorcerer and fixed his gaze on his Prime Minister, Gregory Pool. Whose large face had set into hard and dangerous lines of its own.

"What was the Sombre Warrior talking about there, Sire?" he said. "Did you really . . . ?"

"Of course not!" snarled the King. "They've got to him! Same as they did with my daughter! You all saw, you all heard! Did that even sound like them? Leave me now, all of you. I must think on this."

"I'm not going anywhere, Sire," said Gregory Pool. "You can't just declare war on the Forest Land unilaterally! Parliament has to discuss this first!"

"Let Parliament talk all it wants," said the King, leaning back on his throne. He was smiling that cold, implacable smile again. "I will not leave my daughter in the hands of those barbarians. When the country hears what has happened, the people will rise up and demand that I go to war, to rescue her!"

"And we shall finally have an end to the border problem," murmured Prince Christof.

"Go," said King William. "I've said everything I intend to. I'm sure you all have much you want to say to each other. Leave. Now."

And they all bowed and left, because there was clearly nothing they could say to the King that would change his mind, and because there were a hell of a lot of things they needed to say to one another that they wouldn't have felt at all comfortable saying in front of the King. When the great doors finally closed behind the four men, only the sorcerer Van Fleet remained in the Court with the King.

"Open a door for me, sorcerer," said the King. "One that will deliver me directly to the Standing Stone, in my ornamental gardens."

"Sire," Van Fleet said carefully, "I have invested many hours searching through every old book and scroll and manuscript in my possession, trying to divine some spell or magic that might let me discover what, exactly, lies within the Stone, but . . ."

"It doesn't matter," said the King. "I can't wait any longer. Open the door."

Van Fleet bowed briefly, muttered under his breath, and a door appeared, standing directly before the King on his throne. Just an ordinary, everyday sort of door of old, stained wood, standing unsupported on its own. The King rose from his throne, stretched his aching back for a moment, and then stepped down to stand before the door. He looked back at Van Fleet.

"Is it always the same door? It always looks like the same door . . ."

"It isn't a door at all, Sire," said the sorcerer. "It just looks like a door, because if it didn't, no one in their right mind would agree to step through it."

The King shrugged, and stepped forward. The door opened silently before him, and he passed through. The thing that only looked like a door closed behind him, with a quiet, satisfied sound.

The great ornamental gardens stood open and empty, silent and deserted, under a full moon; and blue-white moonlight fell heavily across the wide-open lawns. King William looked slowly about him. The gardens felt even less familiar, and certainly far less friendly, at night. He was directly before the Standing Stone, that ancient thing, with its almost human shape, that might or might not have been the remains of a sculpture. Older by far than Castle Midnight itself. The basic proportions in the Stone suggested a human form, but not on any scale a living man could be comfortable with. It too seemed even more forbidding in the cold quiet of the night. Some of the peasants still referred to the Stone as The God Within, and King William hoped they were right. Nothing less could help him now. The huge stone shape certainly seemed much more than human. More powerful than any human King. William smiled briefly. He wasn't the type to feel intimidated.

"Who are you, in there?" he said, and his voice seemed a very small thing in the empty night garden. "What are you?"

A voice came to him then, in answer. Just a whisper, like a breath of air. "What am I? Older than your Castle, King William. Older than your country. Older than your human kind. I am the rock on which Redhart is based. I am the heart of Redhart. And I have been waiting for you to come to me."

"Some say you're an ancient pagan god," said the King.

"They flatter me," said the voice. It seemed clearer, nearer, now. "I am the source of the Unreal, which once powered the whole of Castle Midnight like a mighty engine. The Unreal has slept for many years, but I can awaken it for you."

"And the price?" the King said steadily. "What do you want in return? I am not a fool; I know there is always a price to be paid in bargains such as this. I am not afraid. I will do what I must, for Redhart, and the Royal line."

"I will give you power," said the voice. "And all I ask in return is that you use it. Is this agreeable to you?"

"It is necessary," said King William. "I agree."

"Then all you have to do is call me out of the Stone," said the voice. "I just need to be asked . . . You are all descendants, my children . . . I am in your Blood. And I want you all to be strong again."

"I know the real price," said King William. "And I don't care. I pay it gladly, to make my Kingdom strong again, and maintain my line. Come out, old monster, old god. Whatever you are."

The Standing Stone seemed to flex and shudder, dark shadows rippling across the ancient corroded stone surface, and King William fell back several steps despite himself. A new, or perhaps more properly, a very old presence beat suddenly on the air, something so big, so overwhelming, as to be unbearable. King William had to raise a hand to cover his eyes. The Standing Stone cracked and broke apart, jagged pieces flying to every side, and Something came out. At first it looked like some monstrous red weed that had grown up through the Stone, penetrating it from within and forcing it apart. It rose into the air in sudden spurts, growing larger all the time, writhing and crackling as it spread and showed itself before King William, twisting and turning high in the air above him. The King slowly lowered his hand to look at what he had called forth. A huge bloodred growth, sprouting crimson flowers that unfurled slowly to soak up the moonlight. Finally, it stood swaying before King William, where the Standing Stone had been: a massive scarlet organism in a roughly human shape, some twelve feet high. And King William knew its name without having to be told.

The Red Heart.

The tall, swaying shape leaned down over King William, and two great red arms reached out. Scarlet hands unfolded, with long fingers thick with thorns, and both hands slammed down on the King's shoulders. The thorns sank deep into his flesh, and he gritted his teeth against the sudden vicious pains that shot through him. No blood flowed from any of the wounds. The pain disappeared almost immediately, and in its place William felt new strength and new power racing through him, through his flesh, through his Blood, awakening an old magic buried deep within him. He felt younger, stronger, invigorated, and he laughed aloud. And the sound his laughter made in the empty gardens was only partly human.

The Red Heart withdrew its thorny hands from the King's shoulders. Still no wounds, and no blood. The King was still laughing, just a bit breathlessly, glorying almost drunkenly in his new power.

"Return to your Castle, King William," said the Red Heart. "And call forth the sleeping power of the Unreal. Not destroyed, not banished, only sleeping. Waiting to be called back to where it has always belonged."

King William turned away from the tall, swaying bloodred thing and headed steadily back across the green lawns, towards Castle Midnight. He didn't look for the door he'd arrived through, courtesy of the sorcerer Van Fleet; it never even occurred to him to look for it. There was ancient ceremony, and purpose, in his walk.

The King walked through his gardens, and though he never spoke a word or gave any command, everything in the garden changed around him. Just his presence was enough to transform his world. Where he walked, the grass blazed up in a vivid emerald glow, the individual blades of it writhing and snapping at the air with new vitality. Flowers and plants burst up and out with sudden growth, becoming huge and glorious and monstrous. Strange new growths sprang out of the rippling earth, heaving and howling, taking on shapes never seen before. Some of them called out to the King, hailing him by name and promising him all kinds of awful obedience, and he answered them calmly, though afterwards he would claim not to remember what they promised, or what he said in return.

He strode steadily towards the massive stone Keep that gave entrance to Castle Midnight, and the guards on duty saw him coming. They saw the look on his face and the light in his eyes, and they turned and ran for their lives. They didn't recognise their King. The thousands of carvings etched deep into the old stone, of heroes and villains, poets and priests, and all the old stories of the land . . . just crumbled and fell away in long, dusty streams as the King approached, leaving only a blank slate behind. The great iron portcullis, always lowered at night, rose of its own accord to let the King through.

King William went walking through his Castle, a terrible smile upon his lips, and a terrible light radiated from him, touching everything, changing everything. Statues that had stood in corners and niches for long decades, of human shape and sometimes less than human, cold and lifeless for years beyond counting, now took on flesh and warmth and new vitality, and came happily alive again, looking around with eager eyes. Old, half-forgotten gods and goddesses danced together, free at last from the embrace of stone, singing songs that no one had dared sing for years. Old paintings on shadowed walls became living vistas to other worlds. Old carpets were suddenly new again, all damages undone, blazing with new colour and detail. Cracked walls repaired themselves, and everything seemed suddenly fresh and new again, untouched by the ravages of Time. A great power beat on the air around the King, and nothing could stand against it. His every footstep slammed down with the impact of an earth tremor; and everywhere he looked, the Castle changed.

People spilled out into the corridors from their rooms, some of them still in their sleep attire, crying out in shock and surprise, at strange faces seen in mirrors, or strange shapes that came walking through the walls. All of them fell back from the King, from the power walking relentlessly through the Castle. Voices rang out everywhere, asking questions that no one could answer. Guards came running from every direction, attracted by the general outcry, only to fall back, helpless and bewildered, as the King turned his unbearable face in their direction. King William walked through his Castle, and laughed aloud to see it come alive around him.

Doors appeared that no one had seen in decades, giving access to old rooms and halls and galleries long thought lost. Ghosts appeared, blinking suddenly into sight like forgotten memories, drifting absently through walls and structures that hadn't been there when they were still alive. Some of them walked along beside the King, for a while, whispering their thanks, before drifting off on long-delayed business of their own.

Strange lights came and went in oddly shaped windows, and inhuman voices spoke deep down in the earth beneath the Castle. Things came and went that had no business bothering the waking world, many of them thought safely banished long ago. Mirrors showed reflections of the wrong people, and windows looked out onto places no one would ever want to visit. The King broke into his own Armoury, smashing through the locked doors with just a look, and all the swords and axes and weapons of war glowed supernaturally bright on the walls, and spoke to him of old dreams of power and revenge. He went into his Castle Library, and it was suddenly so much larger than it had been. And wherever he looked, new books appeared on the shelves, full of old knowledge and secrets deliberately forgotten.

The King walked on, through the upper regions, his power beating so hard on the air now that everyone could hear it, could feel it in their bones and in their souls . . . sounding like some great iron bell pealing in the depths of Hell. King William walked on, and new corridors opened up before him that no one had walked in centuries. He made his way up onto the battlements, and from all across the great grey-tiled sea of a roof the gargoyles came scurrying forward, to fawn and frolic and rub their heavy heads and shoulders affectionately against him, and pay him homage.

King William stood at the very edge of the battlements, looking out over his Land, and his eyes were full of tears.

"King Viktor!" he cried out, his voice full of a terrible joy. "Queen Catriona! I've done it! I've brought back the old magic, awakened the Unreal! Redhart shall be great again! Are you proud of me now? Have I proved myself a worthy King at last?"

There was no answer. King William looked down onto his transformed ornamental gardens, full of strange forms and thrashing shapes, illuminated by the brilliant lights blazing from every window of Castle Midnight, and he was content.

Prince Christof met the Champion Malcolm Barrett again, running through the panicked corridors towards the Court. There were crowds everywhere, clutching at one another in tears and terror, calling out desperate questions that neither Christof nor Malcolm could answer. Though they both knew the Unreal when they saw it. They quickly learned to avoid even glancing at mirrors, or looking out the windows, and gave a wide berth to anyone or anything they didn't immediately recognise. Christof thought he knew some faces he'd seen before only in ancestors' portraits, and once, Malcolm ran right through a ghost. He didn't stop to apologise. He wouldn't have known what to say anyway.

A woman ran screaming past them, pursued by the viciously grinning husband whose horrid ways she thought she'd escaped when he died. Malcolm paused to cut the man down with his sword. He was still the Champion, and he still knew his duty. He remembered the husband. He shook the blood from his sword and quickly caught up with Christof again.

"What has my father done?" said Christof.

"Given what we're seeing, I think we know what he's done," said Malcolm. "Question is how did he do it?"

"Can we stop it?" said Christof. "Put this Unreal back to sleep again?"

"I wouldn't even know where to start," said Malcolm.

They came at last to the closed double doors of the Court, and found the Steward and the Prime Minister already there, ahead of them. There were no guards this time. Elias Taggert and Gregory Pool were both pounding on the closed doors with their fists, calling out the King's name and demanding to be let in; but there was no response. Christof and Malcolm joined them, waited a moment to get their breath back, and then pounded on the doors too, adding their voices. And then they broke off as the doors swung suddenly, silently, open before them. They all looked at one another, and then Prince Christof led the way into King William's Court.

The great empty hall seemed even darker than before, only this time the throne was surrounded by a great display of unbearably bright light, almost too fierce to look at directly. They pressed forward, screwing up their eyes against the glare, until finally the four men stood before the throne. And there was their King, sitting on his throne. The unbearable presence was gone, but he was smiling his terrible smile again.

"Father!" said Christof. "What have you done?"

"The Castle's come alive again," said King William. "I have given Castle Midnight its heart back."

"You've filled it with ghosts and monsters!" said Malcolm. "All the Unreal dangers your grandparents worked so hard to rid us of!"

"I have made the Castle strong again!" said the King. "Made this country strong again!"

"How have you done this?" said Gregory Pool. "What hideous Power did you make a deal with, to be able to do this? My brother couldn't have . . . Where is he, anyway?"

"I didn't need him," said the King. "This power is mine, as King. The old power, from the old Royal line."

"Blood Magic," said Prince Christof. "You're talking about the old inherited Blood Magic . . . but none of us have had that since Good King Viktor's time."

"It's back," said the King, still smiling. "I brought it back. The power to command one of the elements. Let there be fire!"

The ancient elemental magic of the Redhart line beat on the air like the wings of some gigantic bird, and huge crimson flames burst up round the King's throne; rings of fire, floating unsupported on the air, blasted out a heat so intense that the four men standing before the throne had no choice but to back away. The sheer heat of the flames should have been enough to consume and incinerate the man sitting on the throne; but King William sat there untouched and unaffected, still smiling that troubling smile. The flames snapped off, gone in a moment, though the awful heat still hung on the air, slowly dispersing. The four men looked blankly at their King, and he laughed softly in their faces.

"Your turn, Christof," he said cheerfully. "You have the Blood. Let's see you do something with it."

Prince Christof stood there for a moment, frowning. He could feel a change working within him, now that he knew what to look for. It was like suddenly knowing how to play a piece of music he'd known all his life. He concentrated, and it began to rain inside the Court. A pounding, heavy rain, a great storm, falling down out of nowhere. The others cried out and huddled together for protection against the beating rain. Malcolm called to Christof, but he just stood there, his face turned up into the falling rain, laughing.

"Christof," said the King, "that's enough. Christof!"

Reluctantly, Christof stopped the rain. The last few heavy drops fell out of nowhere, into the great pool of water spreading across the marble floor, and then that too disappeared. The others swore and muttered quietly, as the water that had soaked their clothes disappeared as well. Christof turned his head slowly, this way and that. He could feel the presence of water, moving deep below, in underground streams and caverns, far and far below Castle Midnight. He finally looked back at his father, as he realised Malcolm had stepped forward again to address the King.

"If the Blood Magic has returned to the Redhart Royal line," Malcolm said steadily, "does this mean Catherine has it now as well? Will it help keep her safe? Or make her a more valuable treasure to our enemies?"

"All the more reason to get her safely home again," said the King. "Before they find a way to make her use that power on their behalf. But first things first. Steward, go get my son Prince Cameron. Bring him home again."

"What?" said Christof. "Father, no! You don't need him anymore! You have me, and my power. Between us, you and I, we command fire and water!"

"You need more than fire and water to win a war," said the King. "You need an army, and a general to command it. We need Cameron's experience in winning battles. You're not a soldier, Christof."

"I was enough of a soldier to fight and bleed in your border war!" said Christof.

"Yes, you were," said the King. "But that was then, and this is now. You made a fine soldier then, boy. Sometimes I think I don't say that enough. But it takes more than that to lead an army to victory." He looked at Malcolm. "Go find General Staker, my Champion. Tell him to assemble an army for my son Cameron to lead."

"So," said Christof, "he's only the Broken Man when he's not needed?"

"Don't push your luck, boy," said the King. "There's a lot to be done. We have to invade the Forest, get my daughter back safely, and place the whole Forest Land under our control. As it always should have been. We shall be one Kingdom again, under one King and one Royal line." He sat quietly for a while, looking at something that only he could see, and smiling; and then suddenly he seemed to remember that the others were still there. He gestured dismissively at them all. "Go. Busy yourselves. I have plans to make."

There was something in his voice that none of them wanted to argue with. The four men bowed, turned, and left the Court. And they all felt a sudden surge of relief when the Court doors slammed shut behind them, cutting them off from a King they'd only thought they knew.

Outside, in the corridor, Prince Christof was the first to get his voice back and address the others. "Come to my rooms. We can talk . . . privately there."

Malcolm Barrett and Gregory Pool nodded immediately, but the Steward shook his head reluctantly. "The King's orders to me were very clear. I have to go fetch Prince Cameron home. If he'll come . . ."

"Oh, dear Cameron will come running home to Daddy, like the good little puppy dog he is," said Christof. "He talks the talk well enough, but he always did so love to feel needed."

The Steward ostentatiously gave all his attention to the Prime Minister. "I'm going to need your brother's help in this. Where might I find him, do you think?"

"Since he wasn't with the King, I'd try his personal quarters," said Gregory. "No doubt just sitting there, waiting to be called on . . . And you can tell him from me, Steward, that I shall be having words with him. Soon."

The Steward nodded and hurried away. Christof led the other two off to his private rooms. None of them talked along the way, as they passed through corridors crowded with ghosts and marvels, and more wonders than any sane man could be comfortable with. The three men stuck close together, and none of them had anything to say to the many people who called out to them, for help or advice—because none of them knew what to say, for the best. When they finally reached the security, if not safety, of the Prince's chambers, Christof flung the door open . . . and was more than a little surprised to find things not at all as he'd left them. Even after all the Unreal manifestations he'd encountered along the way, it had some-how never even occurred to him that where he lived might be affected too.

The many exotic plants and flowers that he'd cultivated so carefully, that had given his rooms so much character, had been replaced by strange new growths that towered over him, banging their misshapen heads against the ceiling, nodding and hissing at him. Some of them actually giggled at the look on his face. Christof called to his guards, who were watching from a safe distance.

"I want every single plant and growing thing ripped out of my rooms. Use swords and axes, use poison and magic; burn it all back to the stone walls if that's what it takes. I don't care. I want my rooms stripped clean, till there isn't a single living organism anywhere."

The guards nodded quickly and hurried off to find useful things. Gregory Pool produced his silver box of cocaine and took a good hard sniff. He did offer the box around, but Malcolm and Christof politely declined. Gregory just shrugged and put the box away. He was past caring what other people thought of his small but necessary vices. In the end, the three men just stood together out in the corridor and talked quietly while the guards did battle inside the Prince's rooms. The corridor was relatively empty, and unbothered by the Unreal as yet, and there they stood as good a chance as anywhere of being unobserved.

"Has the King lost his mind?" said Gregory. "Has he gone the same way as Rufus, only more suddenly? We can't go to war! It isn't a war we can win. We don't have the money to fund a full campaign! That's why he and I worked so hard to negotiate that damned Peace in the first place!"

"Well, we'll have to win it now, won't we?" said Malcolm. "And then loot the Forest Land afterwards to pay for it."

"I still want to know why my brother wasn't at Court," said Gregory. "What did he do? What awful magic did he find, to make the King so powerful? To bring back the Unreal?"

"More likely," murmured Christof, "what did my father do to gain such power, that Van Fleet couldn't bring himself to be a part of? What power source is there that my father has found access to that could bring back both the Unreal and the Blood Magic after so many years?"

"Would Van Fleet know?" said Malcolm.

"Of course he knows," said Gregory. "That's why he's hiding, sulking in his room. I'll get it out of him."

"I'd wait, just a bit," said Christof. "The King has made it very clear the Steward has first call on your brother's attention. To bring dear Cameron home again. I can't believe my father is so ready to summon him back after he went to such lengths to banish the Broken Man before the whole Court."

"Whatever else you can say about him, no one doubts your brother was the greatest warrior this land has ever known," said Malcolm. "Never once defeated in battle, either as a soldier or a general. Never lost a campaign, out on the border. The Forest only started giving us a hard time after your father banished Cameron."

"War," Gregory said bitterly. "After everything we did, it's to be war after all. Blood and slaughter, towns and cities burning the night, both our Lands reduced to savagery. Enjoy this last night of civilisation, my friends; we shall not see its like again in our time. Now, I must go to Parliament and carry out my King's orders . . . to bang the drum for war."

"Are you going to have trouble raising support for the King's plans?" said Malcolm.

"I hate to admit it," said the Prime Minister, "but war is what most of them wanted all along. They never liked the compromises the King and I persuaded them to make in return for a chance at Peace. I'll probably have trouble making myself heard over the massed cheering."

He shook his head sadly, and walked away, a large man who didn't look nearly as big as he had before. Christof and Malcolm watched him go, and then looked at each other.

"I would invite you in for a drink," said Christof, "but I'm afraid my place is a bit of a mess at the moment . . ."

"Hate to think what my room looks like," said Malcolm. "Though I doubt I'll get to see it for a while. I have the King's business to be about. Find General Staker, help him raise the army and prepare it for battle . . . I can't believe this has all happened so quickly, Chris. Everything we fought for, everything we sacrificed so much for, all thrown away in a moment. And then Catherine, saying she didn't love me anymore and that she wanted to stay in the Forest Land. With him . . . Do you really think they've got her under some kind of control?"

"I don't know," said Christof. "It didn't sound like her, but . . . who knows why a woman does anything?"

"Do you think I've lost her, Chris?" Malcolm said urgently.

"If she really does mean what she says . . . then yes, Malcolm. However the war goes, whether she comes home willingly or unwillingly, it's over between you. You have to come to terms with that. You do know . . . you're not alone. You still have your friends. You still have me . . ."

But Malcolm was already turning away, not listening, unable to concentrate on anything but his own misery. He gestured briefly, meaninglessly, to Christof and walked away. Christof stood where he was and watched Malcolm until the Champion was completely out of sight.

The Steward went looking for Van Fleet at the sorcerer's private rooms. He stood outside the closed door, studying the mystical signs and uncial runes carved deeply into the wood, and called out the sorcerer's name from a safe distance. When he couldn't get a reply, the Steward stepped reluctantly forward and banged hard on the door with his fist, doing his best to avoid the more dangerous-looking carvings. Finally, a voice from inside said, "Who's there?" in the tone of voice that made it very clear the owner was not kindly prepared for visitors. When a sorcerer speaks like that, most people have the good sense to run for their lives, but the Steward didn't have that option. He was far more scared of his King—or what his King had become. So he stood his ground, announced himself in what he hoped was a calm and even commanding tone . . . and after a worryingly long moment the door unlocked itself and swung slowly open before him. The Steward walked into the sorcerer's room as confidently as he could manage, and did his best not to jump as the door slammed shut behind him.

He didn't like the look of the sorcerer's room. The Unreal had been here, and not in a good way. Every single piece of alchemical equipment, every bit of cunningly fashioned glassware, had been smashed. Shards lay everywhere, and fluids dripped from every surface, pooling on the floor. All the animal specimens were dead. Most seemed to have just exploded, leaving bloody gobbets all over the insides of their cages. Others had been altered, by some unknown force, into shapes that could not survive. And some had simply aged to death. The Steward hoped it had been quick, for all of them.

Van Fleet sat slumped on a wooden stool in the middle of the wreckage, wearing a basic alchemical smock spattered in blood and chemical stains. He seemed a small and broken thing, stripped of his usual power and mystery.

"You know what's been happening?" said the Steward after it became obvious that the sorcerer had nothing to say.

"Of course I know," said Van Fleet. "That's why I wasn't there, at Court. The King has let loose the old god, from inside the Standing Stone. The Red Heart has come among us again, and through him the King has awakened the Unreal. The poor damned fool."

"The Red Heart?" said the Steward. "What's that?"

"I don't know!" said Van Fleet, wrapping his arms tightly around him, as though trying to hold himself together. "I thought I had an idea, but . . . it's not what I thought it was. Not what anyone thought it was. The God Within . . . and now it's out."

"What kind of deal did the King make with this Red Heart?" said the Steward.

"I don't know that either," said Van Fleet. "And I don't think I want to know . . . He should have talked to me first! I could have told him no good can come of this. But, of course, that's why he didn't talk to me. He didn't want to be talked out of this. He'd already made up his mind what he was going to do, and to Hell with the consequences."

The Steward looked round the devastated laboratory. "Why . . . ?"

Van Fleet grinned crookedly. "'Thou shalt have no other God but me' . . . The Red Heart has no room in it for rivals. What are you doing here, Steward? What do you want from me?"

"The King sent me," said the Steward.

"Did he, now?" Van Fleet laughed softly. "Better late than never . . . And what can I do for him?"

"The King requires that you provide me with another dimensional door," the Steward said firmly. "To take me back into the hills, where I was before. So I can bring Prince Cameron home again."

"I wonder if the Broken Man will even recognise his old home, now the King's made so many changes," said Van Fleet. "Don't suppose it'll matter. He won't be here long . . . before the King sends him out again. Yes, yes, I know; you want a door. You wouldn't, if you knew what it really was."

He gestured briefly, tiredly, and a door appeared out of nowhere before the Steward. It looked exactly like the last one: a simple, ordinary thing, standing upright on its own. It opened smoothly before the Steward, revealing the same view of the far hillside. Only now, it was night.

"Don't take too long," Van Fleet said roughly, "or you'll end up walking home."

The Steward stepped quickly through the door, and it closed quietly behind him.

The night was dark and shadowy, under a full moon and a deep dark sky full of shimmering stars. The Steward was standing right outside the cave entrance. He hesitated, and looked quickly about him. It was cold, with a gusting wind. There were sounds in the surrounding undergrowth. And when he looked back at the closed door, standing so still and so silent . . . he couldn't be sure, but it felt like the door was watching him. And not in a good way. The Steward turned his attention back to the cave mouth, mostly so he wouldn't have to look at the hillside. He didn't like the countryside at all during the day, but he liked it even less at night. There were too many shadows, far too many dark places where anything might be hiding. Anything at all. Things were moving at the edges of his vision, and the light from the full moon wasn't nearly enough.

There was another light, flaring deep in the tunnel beyond the cave mouth. The Steward tried hard to tell himself it was merely warm and comforting firelight. A voice from deep inside the hill addressed him.

"Come in, Elias Taggert, Steward of Redhart, and be welcome. I've been expecting you."

The Steward still wasn't convinced that inside the cave was any safer than outside, but he had his mission and his orders, and whatever might have happened he was still the King's man, so he swallowed hard and strode into the cave's mouth as though it was his own idea. He hurried down the long, dark tunnel, heading determinedly toward the flaring light, and finally stumbled into the Broken Man's cave. It looked much as it had before, lit by a great fire, but the Steward had eyes only for the Broken Man. Prince Cameron was standing with his back to the fire, tall and imposing, his huge warrior's frame wrapped in full gleaming armour, with a polished steel helm under his arm. He'd combed out and braided his great mane of dark hair, and trimmed back his full beard, but he still looked every inch the barbarian fighting man he was. The leather-wrapped hilt of a great broadsword peered over the Broken Man's left shoulder, from where the long blade hung down his back. Just standing there, he looked wild and dangerous, a mythic, nightmare figure of blood and death from Redhart history and legend. The man who never lost a fight, or a battle, because he was born to stride across the killing fields like he owned them.

"The King was kind enough to let me take my sword and armour with me when he banished me," said Prince Cameron. "I didn't want them, never thought I'd need them again, but he insisted. That's how I knew, even then, that he was thinking of bringing me back one day. When his need for my talents outweighed his . . . distaste for what I am. When he needed me to kill for him again." He smiled briefly at the still awed Steward. "The King wouldn't have sent you to talk to me in the first place if he hadn't already made up his mind."

"I'm sorry," said the Steward. "I . . ."

"Does my father ask me to return?" said Prince Cameron.

The Steward nodded quickly. "Yes. We must go. Now. Things are happening. Events are already moving at a great pace . . ."

The Broken Man smiled but didn't move. "So. It's to be war, then. He wouldn't call me back for anything less. Against the Forest Land, at last?"

The Steward nodded again and started to explain what had happened, but the Broken Man silenced him with a look.

"Reasons don't matter," he said almost kindly. "The decision is made first, and reasons decided on later, to justify the decision."

"Don't you care about who you're being called back to fight?" said the Steward.

"No," said the Broken Man quite calmly. "I kill men, and I win battles. It's what I do, what I'm best at. I never cared who I was fighting, or why. Never gave a damn how many men had to die so I could win. That's part of why they called me the Broken Man. One of the public reasons, anyway. Let us go outside, Elias Taggert. So I can take one last look at the only place where I've ever been happy. I want to say my goodbyes, because I doubt I'll ever be back again. One way or another."

The Steward led the way back through the tunnel, which grew suddenly darker as the Broken Man put out the fire in the cave. The Steward hesitated, and then hurried on as he heard the heavy, clanking sounds of armour coming up behind him. He broke out of the cave mouth in a rush and then stepped quickly aside as the Broken Man emerged onto the moonlit hillside. Prince Cameron strode forward, past the Steward, right up to the edge of the cliff face, and smiled just a little as he looked out over the long drop. Little drifts of tumbling stones fell away from the hill's edge under his great weight, but the Broken Man had eyes only for the view. He gestured for the Steward to come over and join him. The Steward shuffled forward, as close as he dared.

"Look at that moon, and all those stars," the Broken Man said softly. "Aren't they magnificent? How can men do evil in the face of such beauty? I shall miss all this, Steward. I never wanted to leave here. Never wanted to go home again. I only wanted to be left alone . . . Do you know why they called me the Broken Man? The real reason I was banished? Why I can never be King, no matter how many battles I win?"

"Not really," said the Steward. "You don't have to . . ."

"I came out of the womb broken," said Prince Cameron. "Something wrong in me. It took me, took everybody, some time to discover why everyone always felt so uncomfortable around me. It turned out I'm not a complete person. Something missing in me. I can't feel pleasure, you see. I can't experience any kind of physical, sexual, emotional satisfaction." He stopped, and looked briefly back at the Steward. "You thought I was homosexual, didn't you? When they said I couldn't be King because I could never produce an heir, you thought . . . Well, it's what most people think. But no, I feel nothing for women or men. I have never felt love nor lust, passion nor contentment, in another's arms. I can see it, recognise it in others, but I have never experienced even the smallest part of it."

"But how can you be sure?" said the Steward, just a bit desperately. He didn't think he should be hearing such things, but if the Prince was ready to bare his soul so nakedly, he felt he should say . . . something. "I mean, I thought the King put protections on all his children, so they couldn't actually . . ."

"Oh, he did," said the Prince. "But I found a way to break them. As I grew older, I felt a need to be sure, to confirm what I suspected. That the pleasures everyone else spoke of so freely, that ruled the lives of all my contemporaries, were nothing but a mystery to me. Several rather embarrassing intimate encounters later, I knew the truth . . . that none of it meant anything to me. The King found out, of course, and ordered me to undergo a whole series of treatments, medical and magical, to try to cure me . . . to make me a real man, a real son . . . but none of them worked. I remained . . . broken. Rumours started to spread. That was when people in the know started calling me the Broken Man. My father sent me to fight in the border skirmishes, so I could die an honourable death, at least. Only I turned out to be an excellent soldier, and then an even greater general. Perhaps there's something about not being able to care about people that makes you a better killer. I became . . . acclaimed, if not actually popular. And my father couldn't allow that. So he banished me. Because a man who could never continue the Royal line could never be King."

"You never . . . cared, for anyone?" said the Steward.

"In my own small way," said the Prince. "There are people whose existence matters to me. In that I would miss them, if they weren't around. But I never loved anyone. Not if I understand the term correctly. My only pleasures are those of the mind. I can enjoy the sunlight in the morning and the stars at night, or a good thought in a good book. But the way of a man with a woman escapes me. There is a thing that every other man knows, that I have never known, and never will. I can see it, but I can't feel it. My mind is full, but my heart is empty. I never wanted anyone. Probably just as well. I would only have disappointed them. There's just enough humanity in me to know how much I'm missing. That's why I didn't do anything to fight my banishment.

"In fact, I would have to say I've enjoyed being a hermit. Left alone with my books, and my thoughts, and the views . . . I prefer solitude to being surrounded by people who want things from me that I can't give them. I would have happily lived out the rest of my life here, abandoned and forgotten. But I do understand duty, and honour, and responsibilities. So I will come back and be your warrior again. Lead the Redhart army to victory one last time. Because it does feel good to be needed; and I will accept rank and approval and the roar of the crowds . . . if that's all there is for me." He turned his back deliberately on the view and nodded brusquely to the Steward. "Thank you for listening, Steward. I always promised myself I'd tell the truth to someone, someday. But please understand, Steward, if you ever repeat one word of this, to anybody, I will kill you. I am a Prince, and I have to think of my dignity."

"Yes, of course," said the Steward, his heart jumping in his chest. "I understand perfectly."

He led Prince Cameron to the waiting door, which opened before him, and they both walked through it, to Castle Midnight. The door closed behind them, and then disappeared, leaving the hillside and the cave quiet and empty.

The door didn't take them back to Van Fleet's room. Instead, the Steward and the Prince emerged directly into the Royal Court of Redhart. King William was sitting on his throne, waiting, with Prince Christof standing at his right hand and the Champion, Malcolm Barrett, standing at his left. The Steward looked quickly around, but the rest of the Court was still empty, and full of very dark shadows. He straightened his back, held his head up, and led Prince Cameron forward to stand before the throne. If the Prince was at all disturbed by the state of the dark and empty Court, it didn't show in his face. He stood before the throne in his full armour, and nodded to his father, but he didn't bow to him. Christof stirred at his father's side but didn't say anything.

"Father," said Prince Cameron, "I've come home, at your request. You look well. War suits you."

"Welcome home, Cameron," said King William. His voice was cool, even cold.

The Broken Man made a point of looking around him. "You've made changes to the Castle while I was away. I don't like them."

Christof bristled at that. "Did you think the world would stand still while you were away, Brother?"

"Christof . . . ," said the Broken Man. "You're still looking very . . . yourself. Still every inch the peacock. And just as . . . civilised as ever. But I wasn't referring to the Castle's furnishings." He looked steadily at the

King. "You have brought back the Unreal, Father. I can feel it. The whole Castle is full of ancient voices, calling out to me. And I can feel the old Blood Magic, moving within me . . ."

He frowned, thoughtfully, and the great marble floor of the Court split suddenly, jaggedly, from one end to the other. The whole Court shook as a great crevice opened up, running from the Court doors to stop just before the throne. Christof and Malcolm had to grab onto the throne to keep themselves from falling. The Steward had to grab the Broken Man's arm as the floor rocked, and the Broken Man let him. King William sat on his throne, unmoved and unaffected even as his Court rocked and rumbled before him.

"Stop that," he said, and just like that the rumbling stopped. The two sides of the crevice slammed back together, leaving only a long crack in the marble floor. The Court grew still again. Christof and Malcolm let go of the throne, and the Steward quickly took his hand away from the Broken Man's arm. Christof sneered at Cameron.

"No one likes a show-off."

"Earth magic," said Prince Cameron, not listening. "A useful tool, perhaps, in battle." And only then did he look at Christof. "You mustn't worry, Brother. I'm not staying. I'm just here to fight a war." He looked at the King again. "So what's the plan, Father? A full-scale invasion of the Forest Land would take weeks, maybe even months, just to organise. And probably take years to carry out, with massive loss of life and widespread destruction on both sides. I have to assume you have something more . . . speedy in mind."

"Exactly," said the King. "I have a much better idea. It is my intention to use the power of the Unreal to open a gateway between Redhart and the Forest Castle. Rather like the door that brought you here, Cameron. We will take our army straight to Forest Castle and lay siege to King Rufus."

This was news to everyone else in the Court, and they all looked at one another for some time.

"What power, exactly, would we be using to make such a great jump through space?" said the Champion. "This isn't just another dimensional doorway we're talking about. Van Fleet couldn't do it. We'd have to transport troops, horses, weapons, supplies, siege engines . . ."

"The Unreal has only just returned, Father," Christof said carefully. "It might well be able to open such a door, but who knows how long it will take to master the Unreal? It certainly doesn't seem to be under any control at the moment . . ."

"Fortunately, we have help," said the King. "You will all remember, I am sure, the ancient Standing Stone in my ornamental gardens? The one the peasants like to call The God Within. Well, it turns out they were right, after all. There was a god sleeping within the Stone, and I have woken him and brought him forth. See!"

He gestured grandly at the far end of the hall, and they all turned to look. And there, standing at the farthest edge of the pool of light generated from the throne, was a tall, commanding presence. A good ten feet tall, supernaturally slender, handsome, and magnificent. He had moved on from his original shape in the gardens in favour of something more nearly human. Or at least, more acceptable to humans. His skin was bloodred, and so were the formal clothes he wore so splendidly. He looked like a wingless angel, dipped in fresh blood. He smiled broadly, in a very nearly human way.

"I am the Red Heart," he said, in an aristocratic and even Royal tone of voice. "Founder of this Kingdom, Lord of the Elements, Progenitor of your Royal line. Your Blood Magic was a gift from me, long and long ago. So there's a little bit of me in all of you. I was locked away, imprisoned in Stone, before your present history began, because your ancestors were afraid of me. But now I'm back, to make you all strong again."

"Oh dear God," said Christof. "Father . . . what have you done?"

"How can we hope to control . . . that?" said Malcolm.

"You can't," said King William. "But I can. Van Fleet! I know you're listening! Stop skulking about and come forward!"

They all waited for the sorcerer to appear out of nowhere, as he usually did, but instead the great doors of the Court swung open just a little, and Van Fleet squeezed through the crack, followed by two heavily armed guards. The sorcerer had put his colourful wizard's robes back on, but now they seemed too big, too good for him. Like a child who's been caught playing grown-up and now expects punishment. The guards escorted him all the way through the empty, shadowed Court, right up to the throne, as though to make sure he didn't wander off and get lost along the way. They stood behind the sorcerer as he bowed listlessly to the throne.

He barely spared a glance for the Steward and Prince Cameron. And he didn't look once at the Red Heart, even as he passed him by.

It was clear to everyone that Van Fleet was no longer a trusted ally and willing servant of the King. Events had moved on and left Van Fleet behind. He looked around for his brother, the Prime Minister, and when he realised Gregory Pool wasn't there, he seemed to shrink into himself even further, as he realised he stood alone before his King. He nodded almost sadly to Prince Cameron.

"Welcome back, your highness. Welcome home. You won't like it. I'd run, if I were you."

"That's enough," said King William. He nodded to the two guards, and waited till they had walked back through the Court and left, before giving his full attention to Van Fleet. "I have work for you, sorcerer."

Van Fleet bowed briefly to the King, like a sullen dog brought to heel. "How may I serve you, Sire? What can I do for you that your new ally cannot?"

"You know what I want from you," said the King. "You've been studying it long enough."

"There is a way," said Van Fleet, almost reluctantly. "Not a good way, but then, that's never bothered you before, has it, my King? Basically, you need to bring all of Redhart's magic-users together in one place, and then have them channel and focus the power of the Unreal to produce a teleport spell capable of transporting all your armed forces straight to Forest Castle. Of course, most of the men and women involved in this great working will almost certainly wither up, or burn up, or just die from the strain, but . . ."

"All the magic-users?" said the Champion, frowning. "I thought one of our main problems was the general shortage of such people in Redhart these days."

"They just didn't want to make themselves known," said Van Fleet. "But with the Unreal at the King's command, I'm sure he can track them all down easily enough. Of course, herding them together in one place and then getting them to work together, and do what you want . . ."

"I am their King," said William. "They will do as I command."

Van Fleet glanced at the Red Heart, standing still and silent. "Yes, I'm sure you can make them do anything you want, now. Sire."

"But is this really feasible?" insisted Malcolm. "A single dimensional gateway big enough to transport an entire army?"

Van Fleet shrugged. "Technically speaking . . . I would say so. No one's ever done it before, but then, it's been a long time since anyone had the power of the Unreal to draw on . . . Have you discussed this with my brother, and with Parliament, Sire?"

"In time of war," said King William, "I rule, and Parliament supports. That is Redhart law."

Van Fleet nodded tiredly, as though he'd expected nothing less. He looked at the Broken Man.

"Looks like you'll get your siege after all."

"Good," said Prince Cameron. "I will tear down the walls of Forest Castle and make the survivors of the Forest Royal line kneel before me. I wonder what it will feel like, to kill a King . . ."

NINE

EMOTIONAL ENCOUNTERS

K ing Rufus sat on his throne, in his Court, surrounded by people,
some of whom he thought he knew. They were all shouting at one
another and making a lot of noise, and he wished they wouldn't.
All the raised voices did was make his head ache, and make it even more
difficult for him to think. He had to concentrate; there was something
important he had to do . . . but he couldn't think what. He sat slumped on
his throne, looking at his hands trembling in his lap. He wanted to go back
to his room and lie down. He was almost sure it was time for his nap.

Peregrine de Woodville, First Minister of the Forest Land, strode up
and down before the throne, talking at the top of his voice and wringing
his hands together. His eyes were wide and wild, like a trapped animal.
"We can't go to war!" he said loudly. "We just can't! Why isn't anyone listening to me? We haven't got the troops and we haven't got the money . . .
If we do go to war, we'll lose! Why do you think we all worked so hard on
that bloody Peace agreement? Raven . . . Raven! Where are you? Get the
Redhart Court back, at once! We have to talk them out of this. Promise
them anything, buy us some time . . . Why did you break contact?"

"I didn't," said Raven. The young sorcerer in black appeared out of nowhere, right in the middle of everyone. Most of whom fell back a few steps at his sudden reappearance, despite themselves, and then tried very hard to look as though they hadn't. Raven noticed, because he noticed everything, but he didn't smile. "The connection between the two Courts was broken at their end. And without the willing cooperation of their sorcerer, Van Fleet, I can't reestablish the connection. I'm afraid it's very clear, First Minister, that they don't want to talk to us."

"And what would you say to them anyway, Peregrine?" Prince Richard said caustically. "What could we promise them? It's obvious William wants this war. That he's been planning for it all along. Whatever you offered, he'd turn it down. While laughing in our faces. Anything we might come up with now would just be seen as begging for mercy, and we can't afford to look weak. Not now."

"I can't believe he'd go to war over me," said Princess Catherine. She was hanging on to Richard's arm with both hands, as though to hold herself up. "If I'd known he'd go so far . . ."

"This was never about you, Princess," said the Sombre Warrior immediately, his cold voice flat but certain. "Your father was determined to have this war. You said it yourself; you were just his excuse. Even if you had volunteered to go back . . . he'd still have found some reason to declare war."

The Seneschal gave the huge armoured Warrior a hard look. "You were his man. How much did you know about this in advance?"

"I had my suspicions," said the Sombre Warrior, "but no proof."

"Oh, don't worry about the Warrior," Peregrine said dismissively. "He works for me. Has done for years. He's been my secret agent in Redhart all along."

Everyone looked thoughtfully at the Sombre Warrior, who stood impassively before them, not giving an inch. Catherine thought she should feel shocked, even outraged, that one of the great legends of her land should prove to be a lie; but she was just too tired. Her whole life had been turned upside down in a few days; what was one more person who wasn't who she thought they were?

"He works for us?" said Richard. "The Sombre Warrior? I never knew that."

"You didn't need to know," said Peregrine, just a bit haughtily.

"Well, that's not exactly true, is it, given how things have turned out!" said Richard, giving the First Minister glare for glare. "What other secrets have you been keeping from us, Peregrine? Anything that might prove useful in time of war? No? Then a lot of use your secrets were." He deliberately turned his back on the First Minister, to nod to his father. "If it is to be war, then we're going to need weapons. Really powerful weapons—"

And then he stopped, as he realised King Rufus was just staring at him blankly. Everyone looked at the old man sitting slumped on the oversized throne, and no one said anything. Rufus' face was tired and slack, his eyes were dazed and uncomprehending, and it was clear he hadn't been listening to anything anyone was saying. Richard sighed quietly, and turned to the Seneschal.

"We're going to have to open up the Castle Armoury, Seneschal. The old part, that no one likes to talk about. We need the ancient weapons . . ."

"Most of the legendary weapons are gone, your highness," the Seneschal said carefully. "Lost, or forgotten, long ago."

"I know some people who could help with that," said Raven. Everyone looked round, surprised to find the Necromancer now standing by the closed doors to the Court. "With your permission, Sire?"

He was talking to Richard, not Rufus. Everyone knew that. Richard nodded, stiffly. Raven gestured at the two great doors and they swung open on their own. And in walked Hawk and Fisher, Jack and Gillian. Richard made a loud, exasperated noise, not even trying to hide his annoyance.

"The day's champions, from the Tourney? Great fighters I'm sure, but . . . I don't have time for this right now!"

"Then make time," said Hawk flatly. "You need us."

"We know a lot about war," said Fisher. "We've done this before."

"I had them wait outside," Raven said smoothly. "I was sure they had a contribution to make."

Richard made an effort to be polite to the newcomers. "No doubt there'll be a place for you in the ranks, when the fighting starts, but right now we have important decisions to make, so . . ."

"Cut the crap," said Hawk, not unkindly. "You haven't a clue what to do, or what needs doing. You need us. You need our experience."

Richard just stood there and gaped. No one had ever spoken like that to him before. But even as he was struggling to find the right words to crush this rude outsider, something in Hawk's voice seemed to pierce the fog in King Rufus' mind. He sat up straight and turned abruptly on his throne, to look at Hawk and Fisher.

"I know you . . . ," he said. "I do! I've seen you before, haven't I?"

"Yes, Father," Richard said tiredly. "These are the champions from the Grand Tourney. You met them earlier—"

"No, no, no," Rufus said testily, not looking away from Hawk and Fisher. "I met both of you, long ago, when I was just a small child. You wouldn't think I could remember something like that, would you . . . when I have so much trouble remembering where I am and what I'm supposed to be doing. But all my old memories are still here, in my head, sharp as crystal. Listen to those people, Richard. They can help us. They may be the only people who can."

Richard moved in close to the Seneschal so he could murmur quietly in the man's ear. "The old man's getting confused again. Get him out of here."

"I'm not going anywhere!" snapped Rufus.

"I am Hawk, your majesty," Hawk said carefully. "And this is Fisher."

"Are you sure?" said the King. "You don't look old enough."

"Father, these aren't the original Hawk and Fisher," Richard said loudly. "That was a long time ago."

"Oh," said the King. "Pity. We could have used them, right now." He looked meaningfully at Jack and Gillian. "But I definitely know you two. Jack and Gillian Forester. Yes? Yes. Son and daughter of Rupert and Julia. Your reputations precede you. The Walking Man and the Warrior Woman. Legends in your own right. And here you are, back home where you belong, come to help in your country's hour of need. Let me look at you . . . Oh. Oh dear. You've got old, like me. Don't get old. No one takes you seriously anymore."

"We know a lot about what's in the Armoury," said Jack, as much to Richard as to the King.

411

"What's *really* in the Armoury," said Gillian.

"Well, yes," said Richard, "I suppose you would, wouldn't you?"

"Richard!" said the King. "You need to listen to me. I need to tell you something!"

"Yes, Father," said Richard. "What is it?"

"I'm sorry, son," said King Rufus, "but I think . . . you're going to have to take charge of things, for a while. See to the raising of our armies, to the defence of Forest Castle . . . all the things that need doing. There's just enough of me left to know how much I've lost. I'm not up to the job any longer. I'd hoped you'd have more time, but . . . I'm sorry, Richard. Sorry to leave you on your own. To stand on your own, against so many enemies. But I'm tired, so tired. It's all up to you now, son. And there's something I have to do. I can't quite seem to remember what, just yet, but I'm sure there was something . . ."

His voice trailed away as he mumbled to himself, sitting on his throne, looking like he didn't belong there. Lost in his own thoughts . . . The Seneschal came forward, helped Rufus down from the throne, and led him away. Everyone bowed to the King as he passed, but he didn't notice. He was still muttering querulously to himself as the Court doors closed behind him.

"I'm going to the Armoury," Hawk said bluntly. "I know what I'm looking for. Gillian, you come with me."

"Why me?" said Gillian.

"Yes, why her?" said Fisher. "Why aren't I going with you to the Armoury? I know it just as well as you do!"

"You have to go to the Cathedral," said Hawk. "Because you know what's there."

"Ah," said Fisher. "Yes. Of course."

Richard stepped forward to glare at both of them. "Where the hell do you get off, making decisions in my Court?"

Hawk looked at him—and just that look was enough to stop the Prince right in his tracks. To his surprise, Richard found he really didn't want to push this. There was something about this Hawk person . . .

"I don't mean to presume," said Hawk, in a tone of voice that made it clear he was going to anyway, "but I know what to look for in the Armoury, and where to look for it. And I'm taking Gillian, to watch my back. Still, it is your Court, and your Armoury, so I suppose you'd better come too. Your highness."

"Nice of you to include me," said the Prince.

"If he's going, then I'm going too!" Catherine said immediately. "I'm not being left out of things!"

"And if you are going," said the Sombre Warrior, "then I must go with you, Princess. I am your bodyguard."

"No," Richard said flatly. "Sorry, sir Warrior, but no. You may be the First Minister's secret agent, and you may be the protector of my beloved, but I'm not having a Redhart man in the Castle Armoury. Just not on. This is Royal family business. I'm stretching a point to let them in, though I'm not absolutely sure why . . . but there are limits. I don't know enough about you yet, sir Warrior."

The Sombre Warrior nodded slowly. "I understand, your highness. Trust must be earned. And I have served so many masters . . . I will leave the Princess to your protection, Prince Richard. I think . . . I will go speak with Laurence Garner, head of Castle security. I'm sure we could find a lot to talk about. And I'm sure he can find me something useful to do, to guard the Castle against attack, from within, as well as without."

He turned abruptly and left the Court. No one got in his way. Richard looked at Catherine. "Do you know what he was talking about, there?"

"No," said Catherine. "But then, it seems there's a lot I never knew about that man."

"Do you know what he really looks like, behind the mask?"

"No. I don't think I want to. I can't believe his face is really as bad as the stories and songs make out, but . . . no. It would only distract from the mystique. Hey, am I really your beloved?"

"What?" said Richard.

"You called me your beloved."

"It's how I think of you. Do you mind?"

"No," said Catherine. "I like it. Sweetie."

"I'll lead a force into the Cathedral," Fisher said loudly. "Been a long time since I was last there, but it's not like I've ever been able to forget some of the things I saw in that place. Prince Richard, there are things in the

Cathedral—secrets, tucked away in hidden and forgotten places—that you're going to need."

"How do you know this?" said Richard. He wanted to be angry with her for undermining his authority, but couldn't. In her own way, Fisher was just as mysterious and intimidating as Hawk.

"Best not to ask, your highness," murmured Raven. "I know something of the Cathedral's secrets, so I will accompany Fisher. There are magical weapons and items of power that you're going to need in the war that's coming."

"Yes," said Jack. "There are. I'll come with you."

"I can manage on my own, Uncle," said Raven.

"I'm sure you could," said Jack, leaning on his wooden staff and smiling at the Necromancer. "But since we will be investigating the Cathedral, I think one of us should be in God's grace, don't you?"

"Yes, Uncle," said Raven, "you're quite right, of course."

Fisher and Jack and Raven smiled at one another, while Richard looked at them in quiet bafflement. There was clearly something going on between them, to which he wasn't privy. And since he had a strong feeling that if he asked they'd just ignore him, he decided not to ask. But he was the Prince, so he couldn't just let it go.

"Who are you people?" he said bluntly. "I mean, really?"

"We are the saviours of the Forest Land," said Hawk.

If anyone else had said that, everyone else would have laughed at them. But no one challenged Hawk. There was just something about the man . . .

"Before we set off, I'll just take a moment to send out a message to all the other magic-users in the Forest," said Raven. "That they need to come gather together, here in the Castle. There's bound to be magical attacks from Redhart, so the sooner we prepare ourselves, the better. I know Forest Castle is supposed to have all kinds of ancient, built-in protections and defences, but . . ."

"Yes," said Hawk. "But. No defence lasts forever." He stopped, as a thought struck him. "What about the Night Witch? Is she still running the Night School for Witches?"

There was a long pause. Everyone looked at him, in a quietly shocked sort of way.

"What?" said Hawk.

"Do you mean the evil and murderous Night Witch of legend?" said Raven slowly. "I didn't know there was any connection between her and the Night School for Witches."

"She used to run it, back in the day," Hawk said briskly. "It was never made public, of course, but everyone knew. Or at least everyone who mattered."

"But . . . she'd have to be hundreds of years old by now!" said Prince Richard.

"Who are we talking about here?" said Princess Catherine. "I thought I knew most of the Forest songs and legends, but . . ."

"It's old Forest history, as well as legend," said Richard. "The Night Witch, tempter of men, beautiful beyond bearing—and a twisted creature of evil who murdered young girls and bathed in their blood to keep herself young."

"That's the one," said Hawk. "She fell in love with King Eduard of the Forest, long ago. Your ancestor, Richard—though don't ask me how many great-greats are involved. And he loved her, but he couldn't bear who and what she'd made of herself. In the end she ran away, to live in the endless night of the Darkwood. To grow old alone, where no one could see she wasn't beautiful anymore."

"But she came back, to run the Night School for Witches?" said Catherine. "Why would she do that?"

"Sentiment, perhaps," said Hawk.

"But still, she'd have to be two, three hundred years, or more," said Richard, just a bit desperately.

Hawk looked at him. "Who knows how long someone like that might live?"

"Right," said Fisher. "There's lots of people still around who probably shouldn't be. Really. You'd be surprised."

Raven nodded slowly. "I will send a message to the Night School for Witches. With your real names attached. That should get her attention."

"Mention Eduard as well," said Hawk. "She might come in his memory, where she wouldn't come in mine."

He smiled easily at Richard, openly defying him to dig any deeper.

Richard honestly hadn't a clue what to say. He could deal with history; living legends were something else altogether. Hawk looked around suddenly.

"Talking of things that have lived too long, has anyone seen our dog recently?"

Chappie was wandering aimlessly through the corridors of the Castle, having been thrown out of the kitchens. Again. He didn't know why they'd made such a fuss and come after him with heavy ladles and harsh language. It was really quite a small chicken, and it hadn't been like anyone was using it, as far as he could see. He grinned widely and moved on, following his nose in a vaguely hopeful way. Until he stopped abruptly and looked about him. He wasn't sure, but he seemed to recognise this particular piece of corridor. It was mostly shadows and dust, well off the beaten path, but still . . . His eyesight had never been that good, if he was honest with himself, which he usually tried very hard not to be, but his nose was still working fine. And he was sure that he had been here, in this place, before. With his first master, Allen Chance. (Though, of course, Chappie would rather have died than ever tell Chance that he thought of him that way.) Allen Chance, Queen's Questor, hero and adventurer. Dead and gone these many years. Along with the girl he married, the witch Tiffany. And probably their children too. That was the problem with being a magical dog and living so long. You went on, but you left so many good friends behind . . . It wasn't right.

Dogs were never supposed to outlive their masters.

Of all the people Chappie had known, and reluctantly cared for, only Rupert and Julia were left. Or Hawk and Fisher, as they were now known. The dog sniffed loudly. You wouldn't catch him changing his name and pretending to be someone else. He was who he was, and proud of it, even if most people around him at the time mostly weren't. He'd adopted Hawk and Fisher as his new masters, but he never really felt like he belonged to them. Not like he had with Allen Chance. Chappie sat down abruptly on the cold stone floor and let his great head droop, just a little. Dogs need to belong to someone. Even magical dogs. Dogs aren't supposed to be on their own. Sometimes Chappie thought he stayed with Hawk and Fisher only because they were the only ones who might outlive him. They'd always treated him kindly enough; it was just that he was never sure he mattered to them. They always had so much going on . . .

He scratched himself slowly. Getting old, finally. He could feel it in his bones, and what were left of his teeth. Even dogs created by the High Warlock couldn't expect to live forever, and some days that didn't seem like such a bad thing. If he'd known he was going to live this long, he would have taken better care of himself. *All dogs go to Heaven,* Chance said to him once. *Because if they weren't there, it wouldn't be Heaven.* Chappie wasn't sure he'd be allowed in, after some of the things he'd done, but it would be nice to see his old friends again.

And not feel old anymore.

He sighed heavily and lurched to his feet. Moping was bad for you. Everyone knew that. When in doubt, go look for some trouble to get into. Where were Hawk and Fisher? Wherever they were, trouble seemed to find them. That was why he'd chosen to go live with them, after all.

Hawk and his daughter, Gillian, and Richard and his love, Catherine, made their way into the depths of the Forest Castle, heading for the old Armoury. Richard made a point of leading the way, just to show who was in charge, and Hawk let him. The Prince took them through a series of side corridors and shortcuts, some known only to him. The deeper into the Castle they progressed, the fewer people they came across, running around like mad things, trying to be helpful and just getting in the way. Because there were some parts of the Castle where no one went unless they absolutely had to.

"I can remember when no one could get to the Armoury, because it was in the lost South Wing," Hawk said suddenly, out of nowhere. "Julia found the missing wing; and then she discovered the three Infernal Devices in the restored Armoury."

Richard stopped suddenly, so they all had to stop with him. The Prince gave Hawk his hardest look. "How the hell could you know that? That was wiped from official history, and only passed down through members of the Royal line. No one was ever supposed to know! Not that I ever trusted a lot of the old stories; most of them are as much legend as history."

"You never knew the Castle as it used to be," said Hawk. "Back when it was bigger on the inside than the outside, and legends came as standard."

"Of course not," said Richard. "No one still living does! I don't know what your game is, Hawk, but . . ."

"We're wasting time," said Gillian, doing her best to be diplomatic. It wasn't something that came easily to her, but it didn't look like anyone else was going to do it. "Let's find the Armoury, and worry about everything else afterwards."

Richard gave Hawk his best dark, suspicious look. Hawk smiled easily back at him. Richard gave it up as a bad job, shrugged angrily, and went back to leading the way. Catherine trotted along beside him, unusually silent, for her. But then, the day had taken a lot out of her. Gillian moved in beside Hawk.

"Stop teasing the Prince," she said, quietly but firmly.

"It's being back in the Castle," said Hawk. "It always brought out the worst in me."

They finally arrived at the great double doors that closed off the Armoury from the rest of the Castle. Two massive slabs of beaten metal, covered with centuries' accumulation of engraved runes and glyphs and magical protections, and a whole bunch of obscure but very definitely obscene graffiti. As Prince Richard drew near, the doors swung smoothly and silently open on ancient concealed counterweights. As though they'd been waiting for him. Expecting him. Richard refused to be impressed or intimidated; he just straightened his back and stuck his chin out and kept walking forward. He was damned if he was going to be spooked by a set of doors, no matter how old or horribly protected they might be. (Growing up in Forest Castle, one of the first things you learned was not to let the Castle intimidate you, or you'd never dare leave your room.) He strode straight through the widening gap into the Armoury, and then stumbled to a stop despite himself. The sheer size and scale of the place always took his breath away, but this was different. The Armoury seemed . . . bigger. Much bigger. Catherine stood beside him, holding his hand tightly and peering about her with wide, awed eyes.

"Richard . . . I had no idea! Castle Midnight has its own Armoury, of course, as old as yours, probably, but nothing like this! Look at it . . . This has got to be bigger than the Court, or the Great Hall. It looks like it goes back forever! There's enough swords and axes and God knows what else on those walls to outfit a dozen armies! How big is this place?"

"Good question," said Richard. "As big as it needs to be, apparently. The official Forest Armoury is elsewhere these days. Under Parliament's control. No doubt Peregrine has his people running around opening it up even as we speak. This is where we keep the old, magical, legendary weapons. In an old, magical, legendary place. It's supposed to be just a museum now. A lot of the weapons here don't officially exist anymore. If only because confirmation of their existence would scare the crap out of most people."

"It was ever thus," said Hawk.

He and Gillian had squeezed in past Richard and Catherine and were looking around with interest. Richard glared at Hawk. He wanted to say something really cutting, to put the young warrior in his place, but somehow he couldn't. Just looking at Hawk, and the way Hawk looked at the Armoury, Richard had no doubt that somehow Hawk really did know this place. And what it held.

Ahead of them, the dimly lit hall stretched away into the distance. The few, and far between, foxfire lamps illuminated the weapons displayed on the walls well enough, but the way ahead was still mostly gloom and shadow. And from out of the shadows came the Armourer himself, Bertram Pettydew. He stood beaming before them. Bertram clasped his bony hands together over his sunken chest, and smiled and bobbed his oversized head at everyone.

"Oh, hello there!" said Bertram Pettydew, in his thin, reedy voice. "Hello, gents and ladies! Come for a nice look at the weapons, have you? We don't get many visitors these days. Just as well, really. They will keep wanting to touch things! Though I did have that Sir Jasper in here, just a while back. Very nice gent, for a ghost. Though he did seem very certain that there was a war on the way . . . I could have told him! Hang around here long enough, and there's always a war on the way! That's what we're here for . . ."

Catherine held up her hand to get his attention. "Sir Jasper was here? What was he doing here?"

"Came for the tour, same as you . . . And looking for clues as to who he used to be, I think," said Bertram. "Poor old thing."

Hawk and Gillian looked at Catherine, who felt obliged to explain. "Sir Jasper's a ghost. I met him in the Forest on my way here. In a deserted graveyard, quite suitably. He's been a ghost so long he's forgotten whose ghost he is. Who he used to be, when he was still alive. He took the name Jasper from a headstone in the graveyard that he felt sort of attached to, but it's probably not his real name. I brought him with me to the Castle, partly to help him find out who he was, but mostly because I thought he'd annoy all the right people. And he did!"

"He is very good at that," agreed Richard.

"I've never been keen on ghosts," said Hawk. "Life is for the living."

"Right," growled Gillian. "When I kill people, I prefer them to stay dead. Tidier that way."

"Supposedly, Castle Midnight used to be lousy with ghosts," said Catherine. "Back in the day, I mean. When I was younger, I felt cheated they'd all disappeared, back before I was born. When Good King Viktor banished the Unreal . . . No, don't ask. It's a very long story, and we really don't have the time."

"Couldn't agree more," Richard said firmly. He gave his full attention to Bertram, who smiled and preened before the Prince, in a not entirely subservient way. Richard put on his most serious voice. "War has come, Armourer. We need to see the old weapons. The ones that matter."

"Of course you do, your highness," Bertram said happily. "I did sort of get that, the moment you turned up. So many important people, all at once? Quite made my day! Don't get many visitors . . . I think that's why your father put me in charge here, Prince Richard. To put people off . . . And because I was the only one who wanted the job. I'm sure that helped. What is it you were looking for, gents and ladies? Exactly?"

"I'm pretty sure it comes under the heading of We'll Know It When We See It," said Hawk.

Bertram nodded his head doubtfully. "Yes . . . Or, more probably, no . . ."

Hawk looked past the Armourer, down the long hall stretching off into an unknown distance. "From what I remember of this place, the really powerful weapons were always kept tucked safely away in hidden little niches and corners. And the weapons tended to choose their own masters, rather than the other way round. Does that sound familiar, Armourer? Good. Lead the way."

Bertram set off, back into the shadows, without waiting for Prince Richard to tell him it was all right. Like many people, he tended to react to the authority in Hawk's voice. The Prince glared at Bertram's retreating back, and then at Hawk's and Gillian's backs, as they immediately followed after Bertram. Catherine put her arm through Richard's, and pressed it firmly to her side, just to show him he wasn't alone. And then they brought up the rear.

What light there was seemed to concentrate itself around the group now, so they could always see the surrounding weapons clearly, while the shadows held dominion ahead and behind. As though they were moving forward in a travelling pool of light. Bertram Pettydew took it all for granted, just pottering along, peering this way and that, and keeping up a stream of informative but not especially useful chatter. To which he clearly didn't require an answer, or even a response. He smiled and waved cheerfully at the rows and rows of weapons on display, all the swords and axes, maces and morning stars . . . and sometimes he paused to pat or caress some old weapon kept readily to hand, as though they were old pets or companions he was fond of. Hawk looked thoughtfully this way and that, but kept his thoughts to himself, and if he was seeing things he recognised, he kept that to himself too. Gillian stared around her, openly fascinated.

"I was only ever here the once," she said. "A long time ago. Before your time, Richard."

"You had a right to be here," Richard said stiffly. "As Rupert and Julia's daughter."

He shot a pointed look at Hawk, who ignored it, following Bertram through the Armoury and encouraging him to keep up a brisk pace. The others had to hurry after them, to Richard's growing resentment. Bertram did try to slow things down, by wanting to explain all the stories and histories attached to the old weapons they were passing, but Hawk had no time for the merely interesting and historical. Until suddenly he slammed to a halt and stared coldly at an empty niche in the wall. The others stopped too and gathered around him. Richard glared into the niche. There was, quite definitely, nothing there.

"Well?" said the Prince, struggling to hold on to his temper. "What are we supposed to be looking at? What is so special or important about an empty space?"

"Hush," said Gillian. "Can't you feel it?"

"Yes . . . ," said Catherine. "It's cold here. Cold, like the early hours of the morning, when the rivers of the soul run deep. I don't like it, Richard."

Richard nodded slowly. He could feel it too, and he didn't like it either. It was as though the empty space was looking back at them, with bad intent.

"Of course," he said slowly, to Hawk. "It's been a while since I was here. I'd forgotten about . . . this. How did you know . . . ?"

"This is where the three Infernal Devices used to stand," said Hawk, his voice full of a cold distaste. "Three of the most powerful, dangerous, and evil magical swords ever fashioned. Rockbreaker. Flarebright. Wulfsbane."

They all looked around them. There was a new tension in the air, a sense of stirring, in the shadows. As though just the naming of those ancient swords had disturbed . . . something.

"Yes," said Bertram respectfully. "This is where they stood, waiting to be called forth. Fancy you knowing that, sir Hawk. Sir Jasper recognised this space right away, as well. Of course, he was dead. You can't hide much from the dead."

Hawk stared at the empty niche in the old stone wall, held by the presence of the three terrible swords that had stood there so long ago. He hadn't been here when his father, King John, had called them forth to fight in his war. The Demon War.

"Famous, these old swords were," Bertram said happily. "Or perhaps more properly, infamous. Stood there for centuries, they did. Until King John put them to use, against the Demon Prince. Prince Rupert wielded Wulfsbane, and . . ."

"No, he didn't," Hawk said sharply. "That was Julia. King John had Rockbreaker. And Harald wielded Flarebright. Rupert could have wielded one of the Infernal Devices. King John wanted him to. But he chose not to. He didn't trust them. The Infernal Devices were alive, you see, in their own way, sentient and aware. They wanted to be used, to kill and destroy, and they seduced the minds of those who carried them."

Richard stared at Hawk for a long moment. "We . . . we have to move on. We need weapons that are still here."

Hawk nodded, and turned his face away from the empty niche. He nodded to Bertram, who quickly continued on.

Richard was next to bring the party to a sudden halt. Standing before an old broadsword hanging on the wall, beneath a simple brass plaque bearing the sword's name. *Lawgiver.* A massive, ill-used blade, wielded by seven Forest Kings in succession, until the long steel blade grew too battered and notched to hold a proper edge. Everyone in the Forest Land knew its name.

"Nothing actually magical or legendary about this sword, your highness," said Bertram. "Lot of history attached, from all the important battles it saw service in; but nothing important or significant enough to make it a part of legend. Just a good working blade, an efficient killing tool. Or at least, it was. I mean, look at the state of the thing now. I wouldn't use it for cutting up fish."

"It's still Lawgiver," Richard said sternly. "A name my people know. I can have a new edge put on it. Lawgiver's reputation is just what the people need, something to rally behind, to put a fire in their bellies."

Bertram Pettydew glared at him through his huge spectacles. "You can't just come in here and take things! Your highness . . . These are exhibits from history!"

"Not anymore," said Richard. He took the sword down off the wall. He had to use both hands to move the old broadsword, and even so, the sheer weight of the long blade nearly threw him off balance. He stepped back, and swung the sword back and forth before him, till he got the hang of it. The blade's balance was still good, even after all the damage done to it. In fact, Lawgiver seemed to settle into his hands as though it belonged there.

"You know how to use a sword," said Hawk.

"I did my time, out on the border," said Richard. He nodded sharply to Bertram Pettydew, who quickly stepped forward with an extremely battered leather scabbard, decorated with raised interlocking circles in the old pagan style. It was dull and dusty, and much in need of repair. Richard sheathed Lawgiver in the scabbard, slung it over his shoulder, and then adjusted the leather straps so the heavy blade hung comfortably down his back. He stood a little straighter under the weight of the blade, heavy with so much Forest history and the deeds of seven Kings. He smiled slightly. Wouldn't be too hard to find a decent blacksmith to put an edge back. Someone he trusted to do a good job. And then . . . He realised the others were staring at him, and he nodded sharply to Bertram.

"Well, Armourer, do you have anything else like this? A weapon without magic but steeped in history?"

Bertram nodded quickly. "Of course, your highness. This way, your highness. Yes. Lots of history here. Lots and lots."

Not much farther in, the Armourer stopped them before a slender silver blade that hung on the wall all on its own, gleaming brightly. The brass plaque below said simply *Traitor*.

"Of course," said Richard. "I remember this. The sword wielded by the infamous Starlight Duke when he raised it in rebellion against the Forest, to break off his own section of the Land and call it Hillsdown."

"That's not quite how they tell the story, in those parts of the Forest that used to be Hillsdown," murmured Bertram. "Even after the great rejoining, after our King Stephen married their Queen Felicity and we all agreed to be chums again."

"Of course," said Richard. "No, you're right. We can't use this. The sword's history would make it divisive. Not a good thing during a war."

Bertram peered about him, at all the long rows of weapons hanging on the walls, and shrugged. "There are thousands and thousands of perfectly good weapons here, your highness. You name it, and we've got it somewhere. Even I don't know exactly how many . . . I keep meaning to do an inventory, but there's always something happening to distract me. And I'm sure some of them move around when I'm not looking . . ."

Richard stared down the long, shadowy hall. They'd been walking for some time, but the end didn't seem any closer. "I never knew the Armoury was this big . . ."

"Oh, it wasn't, before today," said the Armourer. "I know this place inside out, and upside down, and I am here to tell you I never saw it stretch away this far before. It's as though all the old lost and forgotten and forbidden weapons are waking up and taking their place in the world again. Space inside the Armoury has to expand, to fit in all the weapons determined to be used . . ."

"Where is the Rainbow Sword?" said Hawk.

Bertram looked at him. "And which sword might that be, sir Hawk?"

Hawk glared at the Armourer. "The Rainbow Sword! The sword Prince Rupert used to call down the Rainbow, in the sick heart of the Darkwood, to defeat and banish the Demon Prince at the end of the Demon War! *That* Rainbow Sword!"

"I'm sorry, sir Hawk," said the Armourer, and he certainly sounded like he meant it, "but I really don't recognise the sword you're talking about."

But Prince Richard did. He caught Hawk's eye, and indicated with a quick jerk of his head that he thought the two of them should talk privately. Hawk nodded, and he and Richard moved off into the shadows, out of earshot of the others. Catherine started to go after them, just on general principles, but Gillian grabbed her by an arm and held her back. Catherine immediately pulled her arm free but stayed where she was.

"The Rainbow Sword isn't part of official history," Richard said harshly to Hawk. "It's a secret part of my family's history, passed down only through the Royal line, by word of mouth. So how do you know about it? I want the truth from you now, Hawk, or whoever you really are. Who are you? How can you know things that only members of Forest Royalty are allowed to know?"

Hawk smiled at him. "Don't you know, Richard? Haven't you worked it out yet? I've given you enough clues. Think. Who would I have to be, to know the things I know, and do the things I do?"

And just like that, Richard understood. The truth hit him like a blow to the head. His face went pale and his eyes widened. It all came together at once. Richard tried to say something but couldn't get the words out. He started to kneel to Hawk, but Hawk wouldn't let him. Instead, he took Richard by the arms, pulled him forward, and hugged him. Richard hugged him back. Not just because he finally recognised a living legend, but because family is always family.

Catherine couldn't believe what she was seeing. She turned to Gillian. "Do you know what's going on there?"

"Maybe," said Gillian.

"Talk to me! I'm a Princess!" said Catherine.

"And I run a Brotherhood of Steel Sorting House," said Gillian. "I win."

"I can't believe it's really you!" said Richard, as the two men finally let go of each other and stood back. Richard didn't even try to hide the awe and shock and hero worship running through him. "Prince Rupert . . . come back to us, in the hour of our greatest need! I mean, yes, I know you came back before, to investigate Grandfather Harald's death, but . . . Oh my God! If you're Hawk, then Fisher . . . She's Princess Julia, isn't she? Oh my God! Only the Royal family know that was you two, before, and some of us never really believed it, but . . . I'm babbling, aren't I? Sorry, I can't help it. *You're back!*"

"No one else needs to know," said Hawk.

Richard studied Hawk carefully. "You don't look a bit like your official portrait."

"I know," said Hawk. "It's a travesty. I may sue."

"Hold everything," said Richard. "You must be over a hundred years old now."

"Well over," said Hawk. "And some mornings I feel every day of it. I need industrial-strength coffee just to work up the energy to cough up half a lung."

"But . . . how?"

"Wild Magic," said Hawk. "And if you're wise, you'll settle for that."

"Who else knows?" said Richard. "No! Wait a minute! Your dog . . . that's the real Chappie, isn't it? I mean, the original! Not just a descendant . . ."

"Do you need to breathe into a paper bag for a while?" said Hawk.

"No! No, I'm fine . . . It's not easy, you know, suddenly realising you're surrounded by living legends. I wish my father were well enough to meet you. He'd get such a thrill out of it. He's the one who told me all the old stories about you when I was a child."

Hawk grinned. "Never take songs and legends too seriously. That's what got me into trouble in the first place."

"Oh my God!" Richard went all wide-eyed again. "Jack and Gillian are your children! And Raven and Mercy are your grandchildren! Damn . . ." Richard shot a quick look back at Gillian, still standing with Catherine. "She looks so much older than you . . . Still, I feel a whole lot better knowing you've come home again. An entire lineage of heroes, returned to save us all!" He stopped suddenly. "Ah . . . This is going to complicate the hell out of the Royal line of succession."

"No it isn't," Hawk said firmly. "We're not interested. Now, Richard, no one else is to know who Fisher and I really are. I mean it. Even if I'm not very good at hiding it, the fact remains that no one else needs to know. Understand?"

"Frankly, no!" said Richard. "Why can't we tell everyone? Your return would mean so much to the Forest people! It would give them new heart, new confidence, knowing that Prince Rupert and Princess Julia of history and legend had returned to lead them into battle and save us all again!"

"That's why we can't reveal ourselves," Hawk said patiently. "Our arrival now would be seen as . . . significant. People would start talking about Fate, and Destiny. They'd expect us to save them. But this is your time, and your war, Richard. You have to inspire your people and lead them to victory. And sit on the throne afterwards. I didn't want the throne before and I don't want it now. That's why I ran away, all those years ago. I'll fight for the Forest, but I won't rule it. And we're not the only ones who've returned. The Demon Prince is involved in everything that's happening here."

Richard's face went pale again. "Of course . . . If you're back, then he . . . Oh my God. I never really thought of him as . . . real. He was just the monster in the stories, probably as much metaphor as flesh. But if you're real, then of course he must be too. Damn. *Damn* . . . I feel sick. I can't fight the Demon Prince, as well as Redhart's armies!"

"Keep your voice down!" Hawk said sharply. "And get ahold of yourself. Panicking doesn't help. Trust me; I've tried it, and it never got me anywhere. The Demon Prince isn't as strong as he once was, or he'd be running this war. Not King William. Though it might be a good idea to send some of your people into the Darkwood to see what's going on there. Make sure it isn't growing . . ."

"I was in the Darkwood recently," said Richard. "It was just as bad as all the stories said. I was only able to stand it for a few moments before it drove me out. But you fought whole battles in there! How did you cope?"

"Wasn't like I had much of a choice," said Hawk.

"The Darkwood is a more deserted place these days," said Richard. "No demons. This war will be an entirely human affair."

"And you're going to have to lead your people through it," said Hawk. "Rufus is in no fit state to rule. You're going to have to be King, and sooner than you thought. Is that going to be a problem? With Parliament, or other claimants?"

"No," said Richard. "I'm all there is."

"So, it's your war, and your army," said Hawk. "You lead, and they'll follow. You know the Forest today far better than I do. I think Fisher and I are better off just being your secret weapons. You'd be surprised what we can do . . . And what King William doesn't know about, he can't prepare for."

"If you say so," said Richard reluctantly.

"Now," said Hawk. "Where is my Rainbow Sword? Tell me you haven't lost the bloody thing after all these years!"

"Of course we haven't!" said Richard, shocked at the very thought. "The family decided, long ago, that the best way to hide the Rainbow Sword was for no one to know it was ever here. Follow me."

They went back and joined the others, and then Richard led the way deeper into the Armoury, with a far more confident step than he'd shown previously. Catherine moved in close beside him so they could talk quietly.

"What was that all about?"

"Family business," said Richard. "Turns out, Hawk's a relation."

"That's it? That's all you have to say?"

"For the moment, yes. Sorry."

"I will make you pay for this later," said Catherine.

"Looking forward to it," said Richard.

Catherine smiled despite herself, and slipped her arm through his again. "Tell me something, Richard."

"If I can."

"I see all sorts of weapons hanging on these walls, but not a single shield anywhere. Why is that?"

"Not really the Forest style of defence," said Richard. "Our way has always been everything forward and trust in the Lord. Put everything you've got into your attack, and don't stop till they're all dead. We don't hide behind things. Not our way."

"That's either the bravest or the stupidest thing I've ever heard," said Catherine.

Richard just shrugged. "We're still here, and our enemies mostly aren't."

He led the way past hundreds of other weapons, gleaming bright and brave on the walls to either side or shining with supernatural glamour inside display cases. Until finally he brought them to a far corner, and there it was, standing alone and unmarked. The Rainbow Sword. Hawk recognised it immediately. He stood and stared at the old sword while the others gathered around him.

"I don't understand," said Bertram Pettydew. "It's just a sword! I mean, look at it! Nothing special about it . . . In fact, it could do with a good clean."

There was no brass plaque for this sword, no name or display. Just a sword with a long blade, standing alone in its own quiet corner. Nothing to draw attention to it; just an ordinary, everyday sword with sharp edges and a good balance. Exactly as it had first appeared to Rupert, all those years ago, when he made the Rainbow Run through the long night of the Darkwood, to call down the Rainbow and win his prize. Not for him, but so he could save others. He smiled, remembering, and then reached out to take the sword.

"Careful!" Bertram said quickly. "All the weapons beyond this point are magically protected! Only those of Royal blood can touch these swords!"

And then he broke off as Hawk drew the Rainbow Sword out of its shadowed corner, handling it with casual ease and familiarity. The long steel blade shone brightly in the gloom, and Hawk grinned broadly, remembering many things.

Bertram Pettydew all but fainted when Hawk just took the sword. He looked wildly around, as though expecting Hawk to be cut down by lightning bolts, or plagues of frogs. He turned to Richard, waving both hands in an agitated fashion.

"How is this possible, your highness? The magical protections are all in place; I reset them myself just the other day! And why was the identity of this sword kept from me? I'm supposed to know everything about the weapons here! I'm the bloody Armourer! Oh no, don't you smile at me, your highness. Don't you dare! This is all my responsibility!"

"It's family business," Richard said lightly. And Bertram actually stamped his carpet-slippered foot in frustration.

"Oh!" said Catherine, smiling suddenly. "I get it!"

"You do?" said Bertram.

"Of course! Hawk is related to the Forest Royal line, but on the wrong side of the blanket! Right? Someone's little indiscretion? That's how he knows things, and how he was able to take the sword; and why you didn't want to talk about it, Richard."

"Well," said Richard, "something like that."

Catherine snorted loudly and patted him on the arm. "Don't look so concerned, Richard. I'm not shocked. Such things do happen, even in the most regulated Royal families."

Hawk strapped the Rainbow Sword in place so that it hung opposite to his axe. It felt like having an old friend at his side once again.

Gillian cleared her throat loudly, to draw everyone's attention. The grey-haired warrior woman looked at them all sternly. "All right! Prince Richard has Lawgiver, and Hawk has his Rainbow Sword. I want something."

"Me too!" said Catherine.

Hawk and Richard exchanged understanding looks. "Gillian was just the same as a child," Hawk said quietly. He looked at Bertram. "Well? What else have you got that's . . . interesting?"

"Why ask me?" Bertram said sulkily. "What do I know? I'm only the Armourer . . ."

"Then act like one!" said Hawk. "Or I'll set fire to your wig."

Bertram looked at him. "What wig?"

"Armourer . . . ," said Richard.

"Oh, all right! All right! I'm thinking . . . I suppose there's always the Cestus . . ."

"Lead me to it," said Gillian.

The Cestus turned out to be a cunningly constructed silver gauntlet, made of many small pieces moving together; shining gently in its own glass display case. The sign attached gave the name, and a straightforward message: *Break glass in case of war, sudden invasion, or imminent apocalypse.*

"It's old," said Bertram, as they all looked doubtfully at the gauntlet. "And not exactly aesthetically pleasing. Far too . . . jointy, for my taste. But very magical. Supposedly created by the High Warlock himself."

"Weren't they all," said Hawk. "Accent on the *supposedly*."

Gillian looked suspiciously at the gleaming silver gauntlet. "What does it do, and what's the catch? I was looking for something a bit more than a glorified glove."

Bertram ignored her with perfect disdain, looking only at Richard. "If you'd care to smash the glass, your highness? I'm sure I've got a hammer here somewhere. I was just using it, to deal with the rats . . . Or do I mean a mallet? I always get those two confused . . ."

Richard simply smashed in the side of the case with the expert use of an elbow, while everyone maintained a safe distance, just in case. The glass shattered immediately, as though it was only a fraction of an inch thick, and the pieces clattered musically to the floor. Bertram looked at the mess mournfully but had the sense to say nothing. The silver gauntlet stood revealed on its stand. It didn't move or react in any way. Hawk studied it thoughtfully. It seemed to him that there was a new . . . awareness about the Cestus, even an eagerness, that he didn't think he liked. Gillian just hauled the Cestus out of the wreckage of its case and held it close to her face so she could study the details of its workmanship. If she felt anything, she didn't show it.

"It's very light," she said doubtfully. "Hardly feels like there's anything to it. One good punch with this, and the silver would probably just crumple. What's so special about it? Apart from the workmanship. Which is . . . rather nice."

"Put it on," said Bertram. Who seemed to have taken several steps back when no one was looking.

Gillian shrugged and slipped the silver gauntlet over her large right hand. The silver links seemed almost to stretch as they slid smoothly in place, fitting themselves to her hand so exactly that they seemed like a second skin. Gillian held her hand up before her, turning it back and forth, admiring the way the foxfire light caught it. And then she frowned, concentrating in an unfamiliar way, and a long silver blade shot out of the silver gauntlet. Gillian grinned broadly and swept the blade back and forth before her. It made a sharp whispering sound, as though the edge was cutting through the air itself.

"Now that's more like it," said Gillian. "I could do some bloody work with this . . ."

"You can produce any kind of blade, every kind of weapon, from the Cestus," Bertram said proudly. "Sword, axe, mace . . . That material may appear to be silver, but it isn't. It's . . . magical. Any blade you make will be unbreakable, cut through anything. And even as a gauntlet, it would still let you punch your way through a stone wall. Should you ever feel the necessity . . ."

"So why didn't you show this to us before?" demanded Richard.

"Because," said Bertram, reluctantly, "there's supposed to be a curse attached. Whoever uses the Cestus dies. And no matter how many times the bloody thing leaves this Armoury, it always comes back. Squatting inside its reassembled glass case, waiting for the next sucker to come along. Sorry. Accounts of the curse are entirely anecdotal, I assure you. But . . ."

"Hell," said Gillian, pulling the long silver blade back into the Cestus until it was just a gauntlet again. "I'm seventy-two! I think I'll risk it . . ."

"All right," said Catherine, sweetly and just a bit dangerously. "Everyone else has got a nice new toy, but where's mine? I'm not being left standing in the shadows while there's a war going on, Richard. I have my own argument with King William of Redhart, and I will do my bit! So I want a weapon too, and it had better be a bloody powerful and impressive weapon, or there is going to be trouble!"

Her voice rose steadily, and everyone winced internally, anticipating one of the Princess' well-known rages. Richard looked quickly around, to make sure there was nothing immediately deadly to hand, in case she started throwing things. And then a great blast of wind shot through the

Armoury, a storm of disturbed air that roared from one end of the great hall to the other, shaking the weapons on the walls and rattling the display cases. Famous swords clattered loudly together, as though protesting, and shook in their scabbards. But not one weapon fell from the walls, and not one display case allowed itself to be overturned, despite the violence of the winds. Catherine stared about her with cold, thoughtful eyes, and then gestured sharply; and the storm fell silent. The wind dropped away to nothing, and the air was still and calm again. Everyone looked at Catherine.

"Yes," she said. "That was me. I did that. Which can only mean . . . that the old elemental Blood Magic of the Redhart Royal line is mine. After being silent for generations. Which in turn can only mean that my father has awakened the Unreal, and Castle Midnight is full of magic again." She looked at Richard almost apologetically. "I'm sorry, my love; I had no idea he could do that. If I'd known, or even suspected, I would have said something . . ."

"Of course you would," said Richard. "It's all right, Catherine. I believe you. I trust you." He smiled slightly. "You should know that by now."

"Oh, Father," said Catherine, "what have you done?"

"The Unreal," said Gillian. Her mouth twisted, as though troubled by a bad taste. "I've heard about that. Old magic, maybe even Wild Magic. This is going to make King William even stronger, isn't it?"

"You have no idea," said Catherine. "He'll have the Blood Magic now, and my brothers, Christof and Cameron."

Richard looked at her sharply. "The Broken Man? The general who has never lost a battle? I thought your father sent him into exile."

"The King can send him away, and the King can bring him back," said Catherine. "You heard the Sombre Warrior at Court. My father has been planning this war for a long time."

"He has his sons, but we have you," said Richard. "The angriest Redhart Royal that ever was, now with storm winds at your command. You don't need a weapon, Catherine. You *are* a weapon."

The Princess smiled at him. "You say the nicest things, sweetie."

At the entrance to the Forest Castle Cathedral, Fisher and Jack and Raven stood together before the wide-open lobby and looked around them. The woman who used to be a Princess, the man who used to be the Walking Man, and a sorcerer who was not what he seemed. Fisher looked coldly at the crowds of tourists milling back and forth in the lobby, clustered around stalls selling tat and junk and religious souvenirs of a dubious nature and untrustworthy provenance. If she was at all impressed by the sheer size and spectacle of the religious market before her, she did a really good job of hiding it.

"Are we to take it you disagree with honest commerce, Grandmother?" said Raven.

"It is a bit noisy," said Jack.

"Noisy?" said Fisher. "I can barely hear myself think, as I contemplate general mayhem and mass murder. But no, if you think this is bad, you should see Haven street markets on a Saturday morning. Try doing business there and you'll be lucky to walk out with all your fingers and your shadow still attached. No, it's just . . . this is all very different from the last time I was here. I did not descend all the way into the Inverted Cathedral and redeem it from all the powers of Hell just so a bunch of get-rich-quick merchants could sell fake charms and shoddy reliquaries to the gullible."

"It makes people happy," Jack said mildly. "We may believe everything on sale here is overpriced and spiritually dubious, but the crowds don't. We must all take our spiritual comfort where we can find it. Even the simplest of souls must be catered to."

"You're defending this, Uncle?" said Raven.

"Let's just say I understand the need some people have for material help, for something they can hold on to, when the night is at its darkest," said Jack.

Fisher just sniffed, looking dangerously at the handful of guards on duty. Most of whom were just standing around, chatting with the stall-holders and tourists. Until one of them turned round and found Raven looking at him. The guard quickly set his wine bottle down and alerted the other guards to the Necromancer's presence. The guards conferred, quietly but urgently, with many an uneasy glance at Raven, and then they all left the lobby at speed, by a different exit. Whatever appalling thing was about to happen, their body language suggested, they didn't want to be around when it happened. Jack looked thoughtfully at Raven.

"We need to have a little sit-down and a chat about this reputation of yours, Nathanial."

"Yes, Uncle Jack," said the Necromancer.

"At least we aren't going to have any problems getting past security," said Fisher. "On the grounds that there doesn't seem to be any, anymore. We can just stroll right in. Pity. I'm just in the mood to punch someone obnoxious in the brains." She looked at Raven. "Unless there are more levels of security? Hidden protections you haven't told us about?"

"Why should there be any hidden protections?" said Raven. "It's a Cathedral!"

Fisher snorted loudly. "Lot you know."

She strode straight across the lobby and through the crowds, heading for the entrance gallery. People in the crowd saw her coming, took one look at her face and the way her hand was resting openly on her sword hilt, and got the hell out of her way. A wide aisle opened up for her to walk through, and Jack and Raven hurried through it, to catch up with her. Jack murmured quiet apologies to one and all as he passed. Raven didn't. Fisher strode into the empty entrance gallery and looked pugnaciously around her, hands on hips. There were no stalls here, no merchants and no tourists. Outsiders were allowed to worship inside the Cathedral, but only at strictly defined times. The entire entrance gallery of the Cathedral was one huge open space, lit by brilliant streams of light falling from nowhere obvious, bounded by sheer marble walls that shot up for hundreds of feet. Rows of dark wooden pews stood silent and empty. Prayer books were piled up here and there, along with stuffed knee pads for the older worshippers. Wonderfully detailed mosaics spread across the huge floor, blazing with all the colours of the rainbow. And everywhere Fisher looked, there were intricate carvings and noble statues and magnificent hanging tapestries. Fisher nodded slowly, as Jack and Raven came forward to join her.

"Now this is more like it. Still looks a lot like I remember. Although the last time I was here everything was covered in blood."

"That was many years ago, Mother," said Jack. "They were bound to have cleared up by now."

"Don't get sharp with your mother, Jack," said Fisher.

"What are we supposed to be looking for, exactly?" said Raven. "It's a big church, after all . . ."

Jack frowned unhappily. "According to all the old stories, this Cathedral was actually Inverted for centuries. Plunging down into the earth, instead of up into the sky. Space itself had been turned upside down by an awful act of evil magic. Mystically Inverted, a celebration of Hell, not Heaven. Its presence was supposed to be responsible for the old condition of the Castle; you know, bigger on the inside than the outside. We have Rupert and Julia to thank for the saving of this Cathedral, Raven, and the reemergence of the Castle."

Raven allowed himself a small smile. "You can't believe everything you hear in the old songs and stories, Uncle. Minstrels have a dramatic license to lie like a bastard."

"True," said Fisher. "Unfortunately, everything you just heard did happen. We were here, with the Walking Man, Jericho Lament. This was a very bad place then."

Raven looked at her, clearly wanting to disagree but not able to. "And the Burning Man? The sinner who still burned with an unconsuming fire even though he was out of Hell? I suppose you bumped into him too?"

"Yes," said Fisher. "He was our guide, down into the depths of the Cathedral. He designed it. And when it was finished, he consecrated it to Hell with a mass sacrifice of the faithful. Sending it Down, instead of Up. The blood was still here . . ." She stopped and looked around, as though still seeing it, and for a moment Jack and Raven did too. Fisher nodded slowly. "He did it all for Hell, betrayed everyone who trusted in him; and he was betrayed by Hell, in turn. He was haunting the Cathedral when we found him, burning inside and out, forever and ever."

Jack crossed himself. "And Jericho Lament was a member of your party?"

"Of course," said Fisher. "He helped us return the Cathedral to a state of grace, and sent the Burning Man back to Hell. He was a hard man, the Walking Man. No mercy in Jericho Lament."

"But he gave it up," said Jack. "Just as I did."

"Only because he'd killed enough people," said Fisher. "Some with his bare hands."

"So, not quite the saint that history paints him," said Raven. He sounded honestly shocked, and looked more than a little shaken. Knowing his uncle had been the Walking Man in his time suddenly meant a lot more to him. Raven looked across the Cathedral as though half expecting demons to come swarming out of what shadows there were. "I mean . . . not all the old stories can be right. About what you all did here. Some of the details in the older versions are actually pretty unpleasant."

"The Inverted Cathedral was designed to be Hell on Earth," said Fisher. "You don't know the worst of it. Your grandfather and I cleaned up most of it so you'd never have to know. We never talked about everything that happened, or people would still be having nightmares. No one would dare come in here." She looked upwards, tilting her head back to stare into the great open space above her, rising up and up. "We went all the way to the top . . . or more properly, the bottom . . . of the Inverted Cathedral. And then we found a door to somewhere else. A gateway that led to the Land of the Blue Moon. A place outside, beyond, our reality. Called Reverie. Where the Demon Prince and all the other Transient Beings come from. Living ideas, concepts, given shape and form in our reality, to work their mischief and do their horror. We destroyed the Demon Prince in Reverie. Or so we thought. He's harder to kill than a cockroach."

Raven and Jack looked at each other. It was one thing to know all the old and terrible stories, and quite another to listen to someone who'd actually been there. They said nothing. Every now and again, realising Hawk and Fisher really were Prince Rupert and Princess Julia out of history and legend was like being punched in the heart. And, of course, if they had to accept the reality of what Rupert and Julia did, then they had to accept the reality of that old monster, the Demon Prince. That he wasn't just some bogeyman made up to frighten children. It was like discovering that the monster who lived under your bed when you were a small child had been real all along. Raven moved in close to Jack, to murmur in his ear.

"You said you saw the Demon Prince, on your way to the Castle. What was he like?"

"I didn't actually see the Demon Prince himself, as such," Jack said quietly. "Just a corpse he wore, like a rotting coat, to speak through. Apparently the Demon Prince lives inside people now."

"So that means . . . anyone could be the Demon Prince?" said Raven. "He could be staring out the eyes of anyone we meet, listening and laughing and silently plotting against us? Terrific. As though we didn't have enough problems."

"Too much talk, not enough movement," Fisher said briskly. "Follow me, try to keep up, and stay out of the way if I have to use my sword."

"This is just a Cathedral now," Raven said carefully. "Has been for decades. There's nothing here to fight."

"Lot you know," said Fisher. "There are doors here—hidden, secret openings to places and realities beyond your worst nightmares."

"I am seventy-one years old," Jack said to Raven, "and I used to be the Walking Man, the wrath of God in the world of men. So why do I still feel six years old every time she talks to me?"

"Why do you think I ran away from home, to study magic?" said Raven.

"Jack, Raven, hurry up!"

"Coming, Mother."

"Is it any wonder I turned to Necromancy, with a family background like mine?" said Raven.

"I heard that!" said Fisher, not looking back.

"Sorry, Grandmother. Coming right along."

Fisher led the way up the long marble stairway that wound around the inside wall of the Cathedral, the wide steps protruding out of the wall itself. There was no railing to protect climbers from the increasingly vertiginous drop, so they all kept their shoulders pressed firmly against the wall, all the way up. They ascended through floor after floor, rising high into the more rarefied atmosphere of the Cathedral. There were no more crowds, no more tourists, but they did pass many religious types along the way, everyone from quietly scurrying priests to those who'd come on pilgrimage and then stayed to study the many wonders of the Cathedral. Because nothing else could ever match the experiences they found there.

Religious fanatics, like the extreme Order of the Penitents, hung strapped or even nailed to their own crosses, so they could share the suffering of the Lord. Lost in the mystical ecstasy of their penance, they paid no attention to anyone. Meditating monks sat quietly in their own little niches, wearing only simple loincloths, to show their repudiation of the material world. All of them lost in their own thoughts, or visions. Some were actually levitating, sitting cross-legged in midair. A few even had halos.

Jack sniffed loudly as he passed, unimpressed, and regarded all the more extreme types with grave suspicion. "I was a contemplative monk for twenty years, but I still took time out to weed the gardens regularly. Never trust a show-off . . ."

A tall, emaciated figure came shuffling forward from a side corridor, with great rents torn in his robes to show off the blood dripping from his stigmata. He came to a halt before Jack, to ask for his blessing. Jack had to stop or walk right through him; and while he hesitated more pilgrims appeared, addressing him by his old title, the Walking Man, and begging his blessing. Some just wanted a kind word, others wanted forgiveness for sins, and some just wanted to touch him. Jack slapped the reaching hands away and gave a hard prod with his wooden staff to anyone who tried to get too close.

"I'm a monk, not a saint!" he snapped. "And stop calling me Walking Man! I gave all that up years ago!"

"It doesn't seem to have given up on you, Uncle," murmured Raven. "No one knew we were coming this way, but here they are. Let them kneel to you, if they want. Didn't you say earlier that even simple souls must find spiritual comfort where they can?"

Jack glared at him. "This is never what I did. I was never a holy man, or a great soul. I was the wrath of God in the world of men! And all the oceans in the world couldn't clean the blood off my hands."

"I thought you only killed in a good cause, in God's name?" said Fisher.

"Killing is killing," said Jack. "And blood is blood."

The religious types were already backing away, disappointed. The Walking Man had let them down by being just a man, after all. Fisher grinned suddenly.

"Now you know why I never use my real name. Never meet your heroes. They'll always disappoint you."

Raven smiled. "Maybe we should have a talk later about your reputation, Uncle Jack?"

"Shut up, Nathanial."

"Yes, Uncle."

They continued on up through the Cathedral. Past hanging galleries and sheer marble walls, marvellous sights and countless works of art. And still a brilliant light shone from nowhere and everywhere, illuminating everything. There were still shadows, though, here and there. The religious types grew scarcer as Fisher and her party ascended, and the few they saw kept a respectful distance. Some made the sign of the cross when they saw the Necromancer, and some made the sign of the seriously upset. Raven just smiled easily back. He was used to such reactions. In fact, he'd have been disappointed at anything less. The marble stairway wound ever upwards, from floor to floor, and the three climbers passed many fascinating displays and items of religious interest. Jack and Raven would have liked to stop and examine them more closely, but Fisher drove them on with iron discipline and harsh language. She strode from step to step with boundless energy, but Jack found it hard going, and leaned increasingly heavily on his wooden staff. He was in excellent shape for a man of his age, but he was still a man of his age. Raven silently offered his uncle an arm to lean on, and Jack nodded brusquely as he accepted the help.

"What are we looking for, Mother?" Jack said finally. And just a bit testily.

"Call me Fisher," she said, without looking back. "'Mother' makes me feel ancient."

"You are ancient," said Jack unfeelingly. "You're older than me, and I'm old."

"I am not getting involved in this conversation," said Raven. "Though I am starting to feel somewhat decrepit myself. I never knew there were this many stairs in the world."

"All right, all right, we'll take a quick rest," said Fisher. She stopped, and looked back at her son and grandson, who were leaning gratefully on each other and breathing harshly. Jack lowered himself to sit on the step, amid much creaking of old bones. Raven put his back against the smooth marble wall.

"I'm getting too old for this nonsense," growled Jack. "I retired from the world twenty years ago, and it's experiences like this that help me remember why."

"We have to do this," said Fisher. "There are . . . items of power that we need to get our hands on before anyone else does. They're locked away here, behind secret doors to forgotten rooms."

"After all these years, Grandmother?" said Raven. "Are you sure?"

"Did you actually see these items of power yourself?" Jack said carefully. "Or are we just chasing legends?"

"I saw them," said Fisher, and something in her voice made them look at her sharply. "In the Ossuary, the Museum of Bones."

Jack and Raven looked at each other, and shrugged pretty much simultaneously.

"Never heard of it," said Jack.

"There is certainly no mention of such a place in any of the official histories," said Raven. "Is this one of those things you chose not to talk about, Grandmother?"

"The Ossuary contained, among other things, the three lost Infernal Devices," said Fisher. "The ones no one ever talks about. Soulripper. Blackhowl. Belladonna's Kiss."

Jack scrambled back onto his feet, forgetting how tired he was. He and Raven looked hard at Fisher, not even trying to hide their shock.

"There are more of those damned swords?" said Jack. "I was always taught there were only three, and all of them lost or destroyed during the Demon War."

"Seems like you can't trust anything to stay lost anymore," said Raven. "They're really here? They've been here all this time?"

"The great and terrible Transient Being known as The Engineer forged six Infernal Devices," said Fisher. "Six swords to rule the world or break it forever. The three in the Armoury were bad enough; these were worse. Hidden, or perhaps imprisoned, in the Cathedral long ago. Because some weapons are just too dangerous to be used."

"Then why do we want them?" said Jack.

"We don't," said Fisher. "But we can't let anyone else have them. If someone has to wield the Infernal Devices in this war, I need it to be someone trustworthy."

"And that's us?" said Raven.

Fisher smiled briefly. "Best I can manage."

"Why not Father?" said Jack. "Why isn't he here?"

"Because he had a chance to wield an Infernal Blade during the Demon War," said Fisher. "He chose not to. He always was the best of us."

"Are you really ready to let these evil swords loose in the world again?" said Jack.

"I'm thinking about it," said Fisher. "None of us ever talked about these swords before, because we were afraid that someday, someone with good intentions might try to do what we're about to do. The Walking Man Jericho Lament never spoke a word about these swords. Not even after he resigned his position and married my sister Queen Felicity, to become Prince Consort of the Forest. He didn't trust what might be done with the swords in the name of duty, and defence of the realm. And now it seems I'm no better than the people we all distrusted. Well, we'll see."

"Back in my old Walking Man days," Jack said slowly, "I walked all through this Cathedral on my last visit. Up and down and back and forth. I was a lot younger then, and stairs didn't bother me so much. And I never heard of, never saw any sign of, this Ossuary. This Museum of Bones."

"Some places are only there when they choose to be," said Fisher. Her face was set and grim, her eyes lost in yesterday. "The Ossuary was constructed entirely from human bones. Taken from the burial grounds of every priest and saint and holy man in the Forest Kingdom. Supposedly brought here to raise the general level of sanctity in the Cathedral. But in reality, the architect who became the Burning Man had them brought here so he could work blasphemy with them.

"After our business here was done, Jericho swore that he would see the museum broken up, and all the bones properly interred again. I don't think that ever happened. I can . . . feel the museum's presence, like a bruise on the air, calling me on. Perhaps Jericho decided it was more important that the Ossuary remain hidden, along with what it contained. Lost from history, and public knowledge. He never did believe in taking unnecessary chances."

"But would you really use the Infernal Devices in the war that's coming?" insisted Jack.

"Oh hell, why not?" said Fisher. "I did last time."

They looked at her, shocked again by the incredible past of this woman they only thought they knew.

"In the Demon War, I wielded Wulfsbane," said Fisher.

"I didn't know that," Jack said slowly. "What was it like?"

"The sword was alive and aware, and it hated," said Fisher. "It tried to corrupt and control me. Just the touch of the sword's blade was enough to make things rot and decay. I did horrid things with it . . . Wulfsbane was lost in battle, killing a demon the size of a tower. Or perhaps I let it go so it couldn't have me . . . I did hear that Wulfsbane reappeared some years later, only to be lost again. Good riddance, I say."

"And you're still prepared to use these new Infernal Devices?" said Jack. "After everything you went through?"

"Yes!" said Fisher. "Don't you get it? The Demon Prince is back! That changes everything."

"Can we really hope to control these swords?" said Raven. "Can we trust them?"

"Of course we can't trust them!" said Fisher. "They're Infernal Devices. The clue is in the name. But we can use them. They love war. And killing, and destruction. But we're not just here for the swords. There is . . . something else, in the Ossuary. Or at least I hope it's still there. A box. A simple wooden box, supposedly made by our Lord when he was learning how to be a carpenter. And inside that box, the original spark, from when God said *Let there be Light*. The Source, of everything."

Raven shook his head. "The places you've been, and the things you've seen, Grandmother."

"But . . . you couldn't use such a thing in a war!" said Jack. "It would be sacrilege!"

"Even if we use it to put a stop to war?" said Fisher. "Your predecessor, Jericho Lament, used it. In the Land of the Blue Moon, called Reverie. We thought it would destroy that unnatural place and all the awful things that lived there. We hoped destroying Reverie would put an end to all the Wild Magic in the world . . . But we assumed too much. We should have known better. The Transient Beings are ideas, concepts, given living shape and form in the waking world. How can anyone destroy a concept or an idea? How could we ever hope to destroy a world of Thoughts and Dreams . . . But if the Demon Prince, Lord of the Darkwood, is back in our world again, can you think of a better weapon to use against him and the Darkwood than God's own Light?"

Jack and Raven looked at each other, and had nothing to say. Some things were just too big to think about. Even after everything they'd seen and done in their very active lives, they knew it was nothing, compared to what Rupert and Julia had seen and done.

"Come on," said Fisher. "Enough resting, more climbing. Think of how fit all this exercise will make you."

"Fit for nothing," growled Jack.

"Fit to drop," said Raven.

"You didn't inherit that attitude from my side of the family," said Fisher.

They ascended even farther through the Cathedral, and the higher they went, the fewer people they encountered, until finally they climbed and walked alone. Through huge empty galleries, and corridors that seemed to have no end, their footsteps echoing loudly in the quiet. And though none of them would admit it, they could all feel a definite, growing sense of drawing closer to something significant.

"We have got to reach the spire soon," said Jack, stopping for another rest. The aching muscles in his legs trembled from the strain of the long climb, and he was having trouble getting his breath. "It can't go much higher. It just can't."

"At least there aren't any gargoyles," said Raven, trying to cheer his uncle up by distracting him. "I never did like gargoyles. I always got the feeling they were turning their heads to follow me, as I passed. Just waiting for a chance to drop down and grab me and carry me off."

"Hush," Jack said shortly. "Don't give it ideas."

"What?" said Raven.

"The Cathedral," said Jack. "It's listening. Can't you tell?"

Raven looked at Jack with new respect. "It isn't just listening, Uncle. It's talking . . . So many whispering voices, coming from everywhere at once."

Jack nodded. "I've been hearing them ever since we entered the Cathedral."

"What are they saying?" said Fisher. "Because I can't hear a thing."

"They're saying we shouldn't be here," said Jack.

"That we should turn around and go back while we still can," said Raven. "I don't think they're unfriendly voices, necessarily . . ."

"It's a warning," said Jack.

"Hell with that," Fisher said briskly. She raised her voice to address the huge empty chamber before her. "You know me! I am Princess Julia and I have been here before! I demand entry to the Ossuary!"

"The voices have stopped," Raven said softly. "They know you. They remember you. I can feel it . . ."

"They're scared of you," said Jack. "Why are the dead scared of you, Mother?"

A light appeared, just a small glowing sphere hanging and bobbing on the air before them. It was warm, and somehow comforting. Fisher reached out a hand to it, and it retreated before her. They followed the light through a maze of marble corridors, until Fisher finally stopped.

"I remember this place," she said. "And I remember that door."

She strode forward, and the bobbing light disappeared like a bursting soap bubble as she walked right through it. Fisher stopped before the door, frowning hard. Jack and Raven crowded in close around her. The door in the wall was . . . door-sized and normal.

"This is it?" Jack said finally. "The door to the Museum of Bones? Are you sure?"

"Look closer," said Fisher. There was a cold anger in her voice, her face heavily lined with distaste.

Jack leaned in until his nose was almost touching the door. He made out the fine outlines of interlocking pieces, as though the entire door was one carefully constructed jigsaw. And then he realised what he was looking at, and his head snapped back.

"What?" said Raven. "What is it, Uncle?"

"It's bones! Human bones!" Jack could barely speak, as outrage choked his voice. "This whole door has been constructed out of human bones, fitted together!"

"Museum of Bones," said Raven. "Of course . . . My God."

"No," said Jack, his face as twisted as Fisher's. "God had nothing to do with this."

Raven shrugged. "I've seen worse."

"No," said Fisher. "You haven't."

She pushed the door open with one fingertip, and it swung easily back before her, as though it didn't need more than a touch to welcome them in. Fisher took a deep breath, bracing herself. She knew what was coming. Jack and Raven could see the strain of old memories and old horror in her face, in her eyes. She strode into the room, and Jack and Raven hurried in after her, because they didn't want her to be alone in the Ossuary.

The long, narrow room before them had been constructed entirely out of bones. No effort had been made to hide the true nature of the museum. Arm and leg bones had been fused together to make the walls, with finger joints packed in to fill any gaps or crevices. The ceiling was a sky of skulls, looking down on their new visitors with dark, empty eye sockets. Two rows of glass display cases took up the whole length of the room, showing off all kinds of unpleasant things. At the farthest end of the Ossuary stood a large bone altar, with grasping bony hands for candleholders and a hollowed-out skull for a drinking vessel. The floor rose and fell in bony waves beneath their feet, a frozen sea of gleaming rib bones.

Jack put his hands together and prayed quietly. Raven didn't know what to say. Fisher looked slowly around her.

"Hasn't changed a bit, in all these years," she said, her voice carefully calm and controlled. "But I suppose blasphemy never goes out of style."

"This is sick," said Raven. "This place reeks of suffering, and the unquiet dead. I deal in death every day and even I'm offended."

"Then there's hope for you yet, Nephew," said Jack. He looked at Fisher. "When we're done, this . . . Museum of Bones must be dismantled and destroyed. Even if I have to do it myself, bone by bone. I will not allow this abomination to continue."

"That's what your predecessor said," said Fisher. "But it's still here. Perhaps its existence is necessary, to contain them."

She pointed, and there the swords were. It was as though a subtle veil had been suddenly whipped from their eyes, so they could see what had been there all along. Together, in their own little niche in the bone wall were three huge swords in long chased silver scabbards. Hanging in the air, as though held in place by their own awful presence. Fully seven feet long, six inches wide at the crosspiece, with a foot-long hilt bound in dark leather. There was nothing graceful or elegant about them. They were killing tools, designed for brutality and slaughter and the ruining of lives.

Death and destruction, formed in steel. And yet there was still a base glamour to these swords, something that called out to the darkest part of the human soul. The promise of satisfaction for all the most secret dreams of revenge, against an uncaring and an unjust world. A chance to make everyone pay for what they'd done. Raven took a step forward. Jack grabbed him hard by the arm and pulled him back.

"Don't," he said quietly. "You might wake them." He took his hand away, and Raven nodded jerkily. Jack glanced at Fisher. "You shouldn't have brought us here. This is a bad place. Don't tell me you can't feel the evil in these swords!"

"Of course I can feel it," said Fisher. "I felt it before, with the first Infernal Devices. I knew what I was getting into then, when I agreed to wield Wulfsbane. But these swords can win the war that's coming, all on their own."

"What good does it do to win the war if it costs you your soul?" said Raven.

"If it saves lives, if it saves the Land, I'm ready to risk it," said Fisher. "Besides, my soul is a pretty tarnished thing after all these years. The sword would probably spit it out."

"Don't joke, Mother, please," said Jack.

"It is possible to use the swords and not be corrupted," said Fisher. "I did it before; I can do it again. And so can you, and Raven. I have faith in you."

"You think the King will agree to this?" said Raven.

"You mean Prince Richard," said Fisher. "He's got a good head on his shoulders. He'll understand."

Raven nodded slowly. "How do we do this?"

"Step forward," said Fisher. "Make yourself known to the swords. Let the sword choose its master."

"This is wrong!" insisted Jack.

"It's necessary," said Fisher. She looked at him unflinchingly. "You don't have to do this, Jack. But consider this: if you don't take a sword, someone else will. Can you honestly name anyone else that you would trust not to be corrupted? You were the Walking Man. Who better to wield one of these swords than a man who already found the strength to give up a power he didn't want?"

"I never could win an argument with you, Mother," said Jack.

"Damn right," said Fisher.

Raven stepped forward, and his hand went straight to the sword on the left. His fingertips trailed down the long hilt, almost caressingly. "Soulripper. This is Soulripper . . . It knows me. It wants me."

"You have to be in charge," said Fisher. "Take the sword and strap it on your back. Draw it only when you absolutely have to, and use it only when you absolutely need to. Don't draw it here. You're not ready; not yet."

Raven nodded stiffly, took the sword from where it hung in midair, and strapped the long silver scabbard into place. It hung down his back, all the way to the floor, with the leather-wrapped hilt standing up beside his head. He looked suddenly older, tireder, as though weighed down by some new burden.

Jack stepped forward, to stare coldly at the sword on the right. He didn't try to touch it. "I don't want you," he said. "I don't need you. I have my staff, and my faith. But I will bear your burden, Blackhowl, so no one else has to."

He took the sword and strapped it awkwardly into place. His face was cold, determined, as though he was carrying out some messy, distasteful task. Afterwards, he stood a little straighter than he had before. Perhaps remembering other times when he'd worn a sword.

Fisher took the third sword out of its niche. The hilt seemed to nestle into her hand, as though it felt comfortable there. As though it belonged there.

"Belladonna's Kiss," she said. "I wonder what you do. I just know I'm going to hate it." And then she brought the hilt right up close to her face, so she could whisper to it. "I beat Wulfsbane, and I'll beat you."

While she busied herself strapping the sword into place down her back, Jack moved restlessly up and down the two rows of display cases, peering through the glass and studying the various exhibits. Most of them were of a thoroughly unsavoury nature, but he wouldn't allow himself to look away. When he'd finally examined them all, he looked back at Fisher.

"Where is it?" he said flatly. "Where is the box, with God's Light in it?"

"You want to take it with you?" said Fisher. "Use it in the war that's coming?"

"I would like . . . to see it," said Jack. "I would like to see a truly holy thing."

"Jericho said he'd put it back here," said Fisher. "But then, he also said he'd dismantle this place. I think . . . if it is here, and it wanted you to see it, it would have revealed itself to you by now."

"I could make it show itself," said Raven.

"No, you bloody couldn't," said Fisher. "You try to mess with what's in that box, and we'll be carrying what's left of you out of here in a bucket."

Jack sighed quietly. "I am not worthy. But then, I always knew that."

"None of us are worthy," said Raven.

"You speak for yourself," said Fisher.

King Rufus was supposed to be resting, in his private chambers. The Seneschal had even placed guards outside his door so he wouldn't be disturbed. And so he wouldn't go wandering. But Rufus had expected that. He left his rooms by his secret door, which gave onto his secret tunnel, the one he'd had put in place long ago. For when he'd wanted to be able to just go out and about, unofficially. Doing things other people wouldn't have approved of, like visiting his wife before they were married. And sometimes he would put on a disguise and go walking through the Castle, to see what was really going on, and what people were really saying about him. Rufus had always understood the advantages of being well informed. And not just knowing what other people thought he should know.

Of course, that was then, and this was now. Rufus stumbled down the dimly lit stone tunnel, holding a storm lantern out before him in a shaking hand, making the shadows dance disturbingly all around him. He didn't like the shadows. He didn't like the dark at all these days. He always felt it was hiding something from him. He moved quickly through the Castle, like a mouse in its walls, sometimes forgetting where he was going, sometimes even forgetting where he was. And then he would stop, and frown till his head hurt, and beat his fist against the old stone walls, until he remembered and could move on. He had to hurry, to get to where he was going while there was still enough of him left to know why.

He emerged from Forest Castle on the opposite side of the moat, through an old sewer outlet that was actually a secret door. Still smelled a lot like a sewer. He moved cautiously away from the moat, putting the Castle at his back, and headed for the edge of the great clearing and the beginnings of the Forest. It was early evening, and he forced himself to keep to what shadows there were. He didn't want anyone to see him. They might try to stop him, and it was vital for the safety of the whole Forest Land that he wasn't stopped. He kept telling himself that, so he wouldn't forget.

He knew he wasn't as sharp as he should be. He was holding on to what remained of his faculties through a heroic act of will, and he knew he couldn't keep it up much longer. He just prayed he could hang on long enough to do what he had to do. He shuffled forward, to the very edge of the clearing, holding his lantern out before him, and there it was, waiting for him. The Standing Stone.

King Rufus put down his lantern and then pressed both hands into the middle of his back as he straightened up. He'd been complaining about his bad back for years, but no one ever listened. He looked at the Standing Stone. A tall, jagged outcropping of dark stone, of no particular shape or design, that still somehow gave the impression of a human shape or form. No face, no features. That bothered Rufus somehow, obscurely. The Stone stood alone, on the very edge of the clearing, just before where the trees began. It was surrounded by a circle of dead grass, because nothing would grow, or flourish, in the shadow of the Stone. Some said birds and insects fell dead out of the sky, if they flew too close to the Stone. Very old stories said there was an ancient pagan god sleeping, or perhaps imprisoned, within the Standing Stone.

King Rufus looked around, to make sure he was alone, and unobserved. It was important that no one know what he was about to do. Not for himself, but for his country.

"You called me," Rufus said to the Stone, as steadily as he could. "You called, and I came. I've been hearing your voice for some time now. At first, I thought it was just another sign of my . . . problems. But no. You're real. The Old Presence. The God Within. The peasants remember where Libraries forget. You have to help me! The Forest Land needs you."

And a voice came to him, quiet and calm and entirely reasonable.

"The threat is nearer than you think, Rufus. You don't have much time. The Redhart army is coming here, to Forest Castle, very soon now."

"I know how this works," said the King. He pulled open his robes, to bare his white-haired chest. "Take my heart! Take my soul! I will pay whatever price you ask, to save this Land! Please. Make me again the man I used to be. Just for the duration of this war, make me whole and sound again, in mind and in body! So I can be the King I need to be. Take all the remaining years of my life, to give me one last chance to be the kind of King I always wanted to be. Are you listening, Stone? Do we have a deal?"

"I don't want your soul," said the Stone. "I want only to help you defend the Land. I have slept here for centuries, contained and imprisoned within this Stone. All you have to do is bring me forth, and I will make you everything you need to be. For as long as you need to be."

"I don't trust you," said King Rufus. "I know better than to trust you. I know how deals like this work out. But I have no choice. How do I bring you out of the Stone?"

"Command me to come forth," whispered the voice. "By the authority vested in you as King of this Land."

"As King of the Forest Land, I order you to come forth from this Stone," said Rufus. "And God save us all."

A figure stepped lightly out of the Standing Stone, as if from a shadow. A tall and slender, very human figure. Ten feet tall and more, made from green leaves and branches and vines. It had an emerald green, entirely human face, and it smiled easily on the King as it towered over him.

"You see, Rufus? I am not so terrible, am I?"

"Who are you?" said the King. He could hardly get the words out because his heart was pounding so hard in his chest. "What are you?"

"I am the Green Man. The great green heart of the Forest, from long before Castles and cities and the gathering places of Man. I have returned, to make this Land strong again. I bring gifts—and here is the first of them."

King Rufus screamed horribly, as a terrible, unrelenting force roared through him. His old bones broke and shattered and repaired themselves, while his muscles tore themselves apart and then put themselves back together again. His heart stopped and started, and his blood boiled in his veins. He dropped to his knees, clutching at his head with both hands. And then it stopped. Rufus groaned out loud, the pitiful sound trailing away into a pained whimper.

"There, there," said the Green Man. "I know it hurt, but you did ask for so very much. All your remaining years, concentrated into the short time this war will last. How do you feel, Rufus?"

"Young," said the King. "I feel young . . ."

And he did. He rose shakily to his feet and looked unbelievingly at the hands he held up in front of his face. No wrinkles, no liver spots, and they didn't shake at all. More important, his head was clear again. It was like waking from some awful fever, where he'd been weak and confused all the time, and seeing the world clearly again. He felt like himself again. He looked up at the Green Man, who was smiling so sweetly down at him.

"How long? How long have I got, like this?"

"For as long as you need, until the war is over," said the Green Man. "You'll burn through these hoarded years quickly, King Rufus. Don't waste them."

"I know what kind of deal I've made," said the King. "I don't need to ask about the price. It is the duty of a King to do what's necessary. To sacrifice himself, for the Land."

The Sombre Warrior went walking through the Castle, still wearing his ceremonial armour and his featureless steel helmet. He could have gone back to his room and changed into his formal clothes. Put on his porcelain mask. But his current look seemed more suitable, with a war looming. He was heading for Laurence Garner's travelling room, to pay his respects and offer his services to the head of Castle security. And along the way he met the Seneschal, coming in the other direction. The Seneschal walked right up to the Warrior and planted himself in the way of the much larger man. He looked half out of his mind with worry, so the Warrior stopped and regarded him patiently.

"Have you seen the King?" the Seneschal demanded immediately, his voice strained and desperate. "He's vanished from his private rooms, and no one can find him anywhere! I had guards at his door, and they swear they never saw him leave . . . God knows what he'll get up to on his own!

If he gets hurt, or worse, on the eve of war . . . It would be a terrible blow to the Forest Land!"

"How did he get out of his room if there were guards at his door?" said the Sombre Warrior. "Do you suspect . . . kidnap? Redhart agents, inside the Castle? Magic, perhaps?"

"Oh, wonderful!" said the Seneschal. "Give me something else to worry about! But no; no, this whole Castle is lousy with secret doors and hidden panels, and tunnels inside the walls . . . I know most of them, but it wouldn't surprise me if the King kept a few to himself." He stopped, and looked defiantly at the Warrior. "You don't know. You never knew him in his prime. He was a great King, a warrior King! Everyone says so! The people love him. They still remember! If anything should happen to him . . ."

"Have you got all your people out looking for him?" said the Sombre Warrior. "If so, then you've done everything you can. It's a big Castle. He's bound to turn up somewhere. I'm on my way to talk with the head of security. I'll make sure his people are doing all they can."

The Seneschal just stood there and shook his head, refusing to be comforted. He looked hard at the Sombre Warrior, narrowing his eyes as though to peer through the steel helm to what lay beneath. "So, you're on our side now. And we're all supposed to just accept that?"

"I serve the Princess Catherine," the Sombre Warrior said calmly. "Her father has betrayed her, but I will not."

"Do you care for her?" the Seneschal said bluntly.

"I have sworn to stand between her and all danger," said the Warrior.

"That's not what I asked," said the Seneschal.

"I will protect the Princess from everything that might endanger her," said the Sombre Warrior. "Including myself."

The Seneschal nodded slowly. He seemed grateful to have something else to think about, apart from the missing King. "You were William's man. Did he speak to you of any . . . agents he might have, inside the Castle?"

"He only ever told me what he thought I needed to know," the Warrior said carefully. "But he did give me one name. One of your own, who changed his allegiance to serve William. For reasons of his own. You know him. The Prince's friend. The minstrel, Clarence."

The Seneschal gaped at him for a moment. "*Clarence?* Are you sure? No, no, of course you're sure, or you wouldn't have said . . . Oh dear God, this is going to be a mess. How could he? The Prince and he were always so close . . . Leave it with me, sir Warrior. I'll see Clarence is picked up and questioned . . . diplomatically. As though I didn't have enough to worry about . . ."

He brushed past the Sombre Warrior, and hurried off down the corridor.

Before the Warrior could set off again, someone else came striding determinedly towards him. The Princess Catherine, looking pale but determined, her gaze set firmly on the Sombre Warrior. He stood still and let her come to him. She stopped before him and looked at him thoughtfully. He nodded his steel helmet to her.

"Why?" said Catherine. "You gave up your home, your station, everything you had in Redhart for me. Why?"

"Because I swore to protect you from all dangers," said the Sombre Warrior.

"You swore many things, to many people. Including my father. Tell me the truth, sir Warrior. Why me?"

"Because you matter," said the Warrior.

Catherine nodded slowly, considering his answer. "Take off your helmet, sir Warrior. Show me your face. Show me the truth."

The Sombre Warrior slowly raised both his hands to his steel helmet and lifted it off, tucking it carefully under one arm. Catherine's eyes widened, and she couldn't hold back a gasp, as she took in his unmarked, undamaged face. He didn't smile. It wasn't the right moment for that. But he did meet her gaze squarely.

"So," she said finally. "It was all just a story. A useful legend."

"Yes," said the Sombre Warrior.

She studied his features carefully. "I don't know you."

"No one does," said the Warrior. "That's the point. I'm not anyone anymore. No name, no past, no country to call my own. I'm the Sombre Warrior. A useful myth to send into battle, to inspire others to fight harder.

Just a mask, that everyone could see themselves in. But I am your man, now, Princess. And your enemies are my enemies."

"I still want to know why!" said Catherine.

"I chose you," said the Warrior. "I have served so many masters, usually not by choice, but none of them were worthy of me. But I saw you, in the carriage, when we were attacked. You could have run, or screamed, or begged for mercy. But you didn't. You stood your ground and fought back, killing the man who would have killed you. So I chose you, Catherine. I will serve you all my days, because you are someone who matters. My life is yours, my death is yours. Because you are worthy. I don't matter. I never did, not really. But I can serve someone who does!"

"How can you say you don't matter?" said Catherine fiercely. "After all the things you've done!"

"You don't know what I've done," said the Sombre Warrior.

Catherine held herself still, hearing the things he didn't say. She could feel the passion in him—not love, or lust, but simple sincerity. This was a side of the Sombre Warrior she'd never seen before, and she didn't want to say the wrong thing.

"Then you are mine," she said. "Put your helmet back on, sir Warrior."

He carefully replaced his steel helmet and bowed to her. "We all have to serve someone, Princess. The best we can hope for is to choose wisely. Now, if you will excuse me, I have to speak with the head of castle security."

"Of course, sir Warrior," said Catherine. "And . . . thank you."

He bowed again, and then walked on. Catherine watched him go. And wondered . . . what she would do with him.

Laurence Garner, head of Castle security, was sitting at his desk, sipping a glass of the really good wine he usually reserved for special guests, because he was in a mood. He looked tiredly at the massive pile of paperwork before him, which he fully intended to do something about, any time now. And then the door before him slammed open, and in strode the Sombre Warrior. Garner put his glass down carefully and stared at the huge figure standing before him.

"How the hell did you find me? My room is always on the move, darting back and forth about the Castle, just so dramatic entrances like this can't happen!"

"It's the helmet," said the Sombre Warrior. "It has all sorts of useful magics built in. How else do you think I see out of it?"

Garner scowled at him. "What else can it do?"

"Oh, I'm just full of surprises," said the Warrior.

"So I've heard, from the Court," said Garner. He made a point of lounging back in his chair, just to show how unimpressed he was. He didn't offer the Sombre Warrior a chair, and the Warrior didn't ask for one. Garner sighed inwardly. "Peregrine de Woodville has already been here, darting agitatedly round my office like his underwear was on fire, to tell me we are now at war. I love the *we*; I wasn't consulted. He also informed me that you were his special agent in Redhart, all these years. And the Seneschal contacted me just now, to tell me you've named the Prince's special chum, Clarence Lancaster, as a traitor. Thanks a whole bunch for that! That's going to open up a whole world of trouble, once Prince Richard finds out. And you're here . . . to offer me your services."

"You're very well informed," said the Sombre Warrior.

"I am head of Castle security! I know everything!" Garner smiled briefly. "In fact, I'm pretty sure that's part of the job description. Actually, I already knew about Clarence. He wasn't nearly as careful as he should have been when he visited you. I left him alone because he is a close personal friend of the Prince, and one must tread lightly in such matters, and because he wasn't exactly a danger . . . But now we're at war, that will have to change. It would seem he's managed to disappear for the moment, but my men will find him soon enough. The Castle's locked down; there's no way he can get out. But with so much of the old place lying empty, there's a lot of unoccupied rooms to search. We'll find him; and then we'll find out what he knows." Garner looked thoughtfully at the Sombre Warrior. "Are you here to give me more names, of more Redhart agents, to make my life even more difficult?"

"I don't know any more names," said the Warrior. "William always did believe in keeping his cards close to his chest. He never told me anything until he thought I needed to know it. I didn't even know about Lady Gertrude until it was almost too late."

"Then what use are you to me?" Garner said bluntly.

"I have served many masters," said the Sombre Warrior. "From the Forest to Redhart and back again. As a result, no one can ever really trust me. So you can use me to do all those things that need doing, that your regular people might balk at. I'll kill anyone. I don't care. I never have. And during a war there will be many dirty deeds that must be done. That those in power need never know about."

"And your price, for these services, sir Warrior?"

"Money. Lots of it. And . . . Catherine must never know."

"Agreed," said Garner. "I'm running my people ragged anyway, setting up proper defences for the Castle. I've been given access to the Armoury, so I have all the weapons I could hope for, but I don't have nearly enough people." He smiled briefly. "Do you know who I've got running the Castle defences? Mercy Forester—Sir Kay, that was. And I think it's fair to say none of us saw that one coming . . . She just turned up here and volunteered her services, and she's been a godsend. Organised the guards like she was born to it. And given her lineage, she probably was . . . Though you won't hear me saying that in front of Prince Richard. So, sir Warrior, time to go to work. This helmet of yours—think it could find Clarence Lancaster for me?"

"Almost certainly," said the Sombre Warrior.

"Good," said Garner. "Track him down, arrest him, don't bring him back alive."

There was a knock at the door.

Peter Foster, who had been a soldier, and then Prince Richard's friend, and most recently his bodyguard, walked down a corridor that no one used, to a room that no one lived in, and knocked on a door that no one knew about. He didn't look around; he'd have known if he was being followed. The door opened quickly, and Clarence looked out. The minstrel's face was pale and strained, slick with sweat. His eyes were wide and wild. Like an animal brought to ground. He grabbed Peter by the arm and hauled him inside, and then quickly shut and locked the door behind him.

Peter looked around him. Not much to see. The mostly empty room was lit by a single candle. A few pieces of furniture, covered in dust sheets.

A single chair pulled up to a side table, which bore only an empty wine bottle and a half-full glass. The room stank of fear, and desperation.

"Thank God you're here, Peter," said Clarence. He hugged the soldier suddenly. Peter let him. He could smell the wine on Clarence's breath. After a while he pushed Clarence away, and the minstrel did his best to straighten up and pull himself together.

"It's not much, is it?" he said, gesturing roughly at the room, trying to smile and not quite managing it. "But traitors can't be choosers. I had to go into hiding, Peter. Everyone's looking for me! They want me dead!"

"I know," said Peter. "Your old Redhart ally, the Sombre Warrior, is now one of us. And he gave us your name. You idiot, Clarence. How could you?"

"You've got to help me!" said Clarence miserably. He was only ever a moment away from tears. "You've got to talk to Richard, on my behalf, work out some sort of deal for me. I'm not a traitor! Not really. I was just . . . so angry at Richard. For abandoning us for the Princess, for leading us into the Darkwood . . . for making me afraid of the dark again. I just wanted to get back at him! I didn't mean for anyone to get hurt. Not really. You were there in the Darkwood too, Peter. You know what it did to us! He should never have done that to us . . ."

"Yes," said Peter. "I was there too. I understand."

"I could go into exile," said Clarence. "Not to Redhart, of course, but there's always Lancre . . . I could go away and never come back . . . Oh God, Peter, this will kill my father! He always had such hopes for me . . . You've got to help me, Peter! There isn't anyone else I can turn to! I can't go to Richard myself, not after what I've done. I couldn't speak to him. Couldn't look him in the eye. I just couldn't . . . You're my friend, Peter, my oldest friend, apart from the Prince. I knew you'd come if I got word to you. Please, you've got to help me . . ."

"Of course I'll help you, Clarence," said Peter. "That's why I'm here. That's what friends are for."

There was a knock on the door of Laurence Garner's office, and he and the Sombre Warrior looked round sharply as the door swung open and Peter Foster came in, carrying a large wooden box held shut with leather straps. He nodded to the Sombre Warrior, entirely unsurprised, and put the box down on Garner's desk. Then he stood back and nodded brusquely to the head of security.

"Peter has been working for me for some time," Garner said to the Warrior. "Keeping an eye on the Prince for me, and keeping him out of trouble. As much as possible."

"How did he find your office?" said the Warrior.

"All my people have a talisman that brings them right to me," said Garner.

"I want one," said the Sombre Warrior.

"Of course you do," said Garner. He pulled open a drawer in his desk, took out a simple bone charm, and tossed it to the Sombre Warrior, who plucked it neatly out of midair. He studied the elaborate symbols carved into the wooden charm, then tucked it neatly away about his person.

"With events escalating as they have, it made sense for Peter to present himself as Richard's personal bodyguard," said Garner.

"That was my idea," said Peter. "I was Richard's friend long before I agreed to be your agent, to protect him from all the trouble he was getting into. I've always been his friend first, Garner, and don't you ever forget it."

"I have to wonder why you aren't at Richard's side right now, where you're supposed to be," said Garner, pointedly.

"I brought you a present," said Peter.

He undid the leather straps around the box and opened the lid. Reached in, and brought out the severed head of Clarence Lancaster. The man who only ever wanted to be a minstrel. His face had a sad, resigned look to it.

"You killed your friend?" the Sombre Warrior said to Peter.

"I killed him because he was my friend," said Peter. He reached out with his free hand, to brush aside a long lock of hair that had fallen across Clarence's face. "He was a traitor, so he had to die; but I couldn't let a stranger do it. Couldn't leave him to the headsman's block and a public execution. In front of his family. The Prince doesn't need to know. His family doesn't need to know. Let them all think he got away somehow, and vanished into exile. Kinder for all concerned. I've always been there, for Clarence, cleaning up his messes."

There was another knock at the door. Peter placed the severed head back in its box. Garner glowered at the closed door.

"Far too many people know where to find me. I'm going to have to do something about that. Come in!"

The door opened, and in strode the black-clad figure of Raven the Necromancer. Without quite knowing why, everyone's eyes went immediately to the new sword hilt sticking up behind his shoulder. Raven had nothing to say about that. He just smiled and nodded easily to all concerned.

"We have been summoned to attend the King, at Court," he said. "King Rufus wants us all there, right now. Everybody, no excuses. I knew you were all here together, so I said I'd come and get you."

"How did you know . . . ?" said Peter.

Raven looked at him pityingly. "The same way I know whose head is in that box. I know everything I need to know."

"Hold it," said Garner. "King Rufus summons us? Not Prince Richard, on his father's behalf?"

"No," said Raven patiently. "If I'd meant Richard, I would have said. No . . . surprisingly, I do mean King Rufus. He's . . . changed. Taken a quite remarkable turn for the better, in fact. Don't ask me how. But before we all go rushing off to obey our good King Rufus' summons, do indulge my curiosity. Why do you have a minstrel's head in a box? Is it some new kind of musical toy? I understand they can do amazing things with clockwork these days."

"Clarence Lancaster was named a traitor by the Sombre Warrior," said Garner.

"Ah yes," murmured Raven. "I did hear. Justice is swift, isn't it?"

"Richard must never know," said Peter.

"Well, quite," said Raven. "So . . . you need someone to make your late friend disappear completely, yes? Both the head and the body, removed so absolutely that not even a trace of him will ever be found. Luckily for you, I feel the need to do a good deed, to balance out a rather darker burden I've taken upon myself. I blame my uncle's influence. Anyway . . ."

He gestured almost lazily, and the head and its box just vanished, gone in a moment, without even a disturbance in the air to mark the passing.

"Where did you send him?" said Garner. "Tell me you didn't just dump him in the moat! He has to disappear completely!"

"Please," said Raven. "I am a professional. I sent him back in Time. Far, far back into the past. I have done it before, when I had . . . old projects that needed to disappear completely so as not to embarrass me. There are sometimes . . . strange side effects. But nothing you need to worry about."

He didn't offer any details, and no one asked for any.

"That is a neat trick," said Garner. "Any chance you could do that to the whole Redhart army? Just send them away, into the past?"

"Unfortunately, no," said Raven. "The bigger the object, the harder it is to move through Time. A small thing, like a body in two parts, I can send back hundreds of years. An army, consisting of thousands of bodies . . . I'd be lucky to send them back a few seconds. Magic has its rules, and its restrictions."

"Even Wild Magic?" said Peter meaningfully.

Raven smiled at him. "I couldn't say. Now, let us all get a move on, with a shake of our tails. The King is waiting."

Sir Jasper the ghost was outside Forest Castle, walking alongside the moat. He'd been everywhere inside the Castle, most definitely including all the places he wasn't supposed to go, and nothing he'd seen anywhere had brought his memory back to him. Some things looked familiar, some places stirred thoughts or feelings, and there were moments when it seemed everything was just on the tip of his tongue . . . but all he had to show for his travels was a sense of déjà vu powerful enough to give him a headache. If he'd still had a head. So he left the Castle and went for a little walk outside.

He felt the need for some fresh air, even though he didn't breathe. And just lately, he'd been feeling a strong sense of foreboding as he walked the Castle corridors, a sense of . . . something important, about to happen. He couldn't shake it off wherever he went, so that just left outside. But now that he was here, he couldn't think of anything he wanted to do.

He could have gone walking on the waters of the moat, just skipping across the surface . . . but he was trying hard to feel more human, because it helped him feel more focused. So now he tried to avoid doing things that reminded him he wasn't alive. He decided he did like being outside, because it meant nobody bothered him. The clearing was open and empty and quiet, and even the surrounding woods grew silent as the evening approached. It was all very peaceful, but Sir Jasper didn't trust it. The more he looked at the Forest, the more its blank green face seemed like some ancient mask, with a threatening face hidden behind it.

He deliberately turned away from the Forest to look back at the Castle; and then he stopped where he was, as the Lady of the Lake rose up out of the moat's waters. Blue flesh in a blue dress, and all of it formed out of water. She rose up and up, creating herself from the moat's contents, until she stood poised and elegant on the surface. She shook her head briskly, and heavy droplets flew from the ends of her long, watery hair. She looked at Sir Jasper, and smiled at him, and he felt his heart lurch in his chest. And it was a measure of how moved he was that he didn't realise how strange that was.

The Lady of the Lake strolled across the moat to stand before him, her feet merging seamlessly with the surface of the dark water. Sir Jasper moved forward to meet her, stopping at the very edge of the moat.

"Well," the Lady said briskly, "took you long enough to get here."

"Do I know you, Lady?" said the ghost. "I feel I should, but I have to tell you that my memory is not what it should be. I look at you, and it does seem to me that I know you from somewhere . . ."

The Lady looked at him, with an expression he knew but couldn't place. "You'll remember when the time comes. I am the Lady of the Lake these days. Wherever water flows through the Forest Land, I am there. I've been waiting for you to turn up here. You have a duty and a destiny to fulfil."

"Are you sure?" Sir Jasper said doubtfully. "I'm just a ghost; and not a particularly good one. Do you know me, Lady? Who I used to be? My true name? It's a sad and lonely thing, to have no name and no past."

"I'm sorry," said the Lady of the Lake. "It's not time for the truth. Not yet."

She dropped down into the moat and was gone, dissolved back into the water, leaving not a single ripple behind. Sir Jasper sniffed loudly.

"And people say I'm weird . . ."

• • •

462

Hawk knew something was wrong the moment he and Fisher entered the Court. They'd arrived first, along with Chappie the dog, intrigued by advance whispers of the sudden change in King Rufus. Hawk looked at the new sword Fisher had acquired, and knew it immediately for what it was, but he said nothing. He'd known the risk, when he sent Fisher back into the Cathedral. He trusted her judgement; even if he didn't trust the sword.

"Which one is it?" he said quietly.

"Belladonna's Kiss," said Fisher. "And no, I don't know what it does yet."

"Maybe it makes you irresistible to men," sniggered Chappie. "Though how that's going to stop a whole army . . ."

"It's not too late to take you to the vet, you know," said Hawk.

"I have fought demons and monsters, and humped some things you don't even want to think about," said the dog. "I'm not afraid of any vet. Is that the King? I don't like him. He smells wrong."

"He looks . . . younger," said Fisher.

He did. King Rufus sat up straight on his throne, wearing fresh new clothes that fit perfectly. His crown sat firmly on his head, as though it belonged there. His face was unlined, his long hair was thick and dark, and his eyes burned with a feverish intensity. He was gnawing hungrily on a chicken leg, as though he hadn't eaten properly in ages. Everything about him was full of a new and somehow upsetting vitality. He nodded easily to Hawk and Fisher, and to Chappie, but said nothing as they came forward to stand before the throne.

"I know you," said the King, smiling. "I remember you. I remember everything now."

"What's happened to you?" said Hawk bluntly.

"Not now," said the King. "Let's wait till everyone's here. I have a lot to say, and I don't feel like repeating myself."

Richard and Catherine arrived next, arm in arm. Richard actually looked shocked when he saw the change in his father. The Prince and the Princess were followed, almost immediately, by Peter Foster and the Sombre Warrior, who both moved quickly forward to stand beside Richard and Catherine, as their bodyguards. Who they were protecting their charges from wasn't immediately apparent, but they took pains to place themselves between their charges and the King. Laurence Garner strolled in on his own, and stood on his own, so he could keep an eye on everyone.

Jack and Gillian came in next, arguing loudly with each other and paying no attention to anyone else. Jack had the Infernal Device on his back, and Gillian had the glowing silver Cestus on her hand. Jack and Gillian didn't approve of each other's new weapons, and said so in loud, carrying voices.

"You have to give up the Cestus!" Jack said urgently. "It's cursed! Everyone knows that!"

"And the Infernal Device isn't?" said Gillian. "That thing'll eat your soul, given half a chance!"

"I know that," said Jack. "Don't you think I knew that before I agreed to wield it? But who else can I trust with a sword like this? Who else has a real chance to fight off its influence? Gillian, please; let someone else bear the Cestus and its curse."

"You mean give it to some brave young soldier, with all his life ahead of him?" said Gillian. "How fair would that be? I've got a lot less to lose than most."

Jack sighed. "All right; tell you what . . . you watch my back, and I'll watch yours."

"Just like when we were young," said Gillian. "Us against the world— and let the world beware."

"When we were young . . . ," said Jack. "I never really expected to get old. Thought for sure I'd die young, in battle for some good cause or other."

"Right," said Gillian. "Being old is a pain. But it beats most of the alternatives . . ."

"I take it you have seen what's happened to the King," Jack said quietly.

"Oh, I've seen him," said Gillian. "That . . . is not natural. Wild Magic?"

"Has to be," said Jack. "You don't get that kind of wish fulfilment through clean magic."

"I thought you believed in miracles," said Gillian.

"I do," said Jack. "Which is why I know when I'm not seeing one."

He broke off as his daughter, Mercy, came striding into the Court, wearing her Sir Kay chain mail and a sword strapped to her hip. She smiled dazzlingly at everyone, tossed her blonde hair, and strolled over to join her father and her aunt Gillian.

"Where have you been, girl?" said Jack. He tried hard to sound stern, but his heart wasn't in it.

"Organising the Castle defences, Father," said Mercy. "Redhart's bound to launch a direct attack at us, and almost certainly sooner rather than later. Let them come. I've got some really nasty surprises waiting for them." She stopped, to look at the tall sword hilt rising up behind Jack's head. "So. The rumours are true. Everyone's talking about it. You've brought the Infernal Devices back into the world. Weren't we in enough trouble already?"

"We'll talk about it later," said Jack.

"Damn right we will, Father," said Mercy.

Raven arrived next, with the Seneschal. The Necromancer looked more than usually smug, while the Seneschal looked more than usually worried. He broke off in mid-conversation with Raven and hurried forward to attend the King. Who just nodded amiably to him and concentrated on his chicken leg. The Seneschal shifted nervously from foot to foot, like a child too anxious to ask for the jakes, and finally settled for taking up his usual position, standing behind the throne. The King tossed aside what was left of the chicken leg, and smiled calmly out across his Court, and his audience.

"Where is Peregrine de Woodville?" he said. "Where is my First Minister?"

"He's at Parliament, your majesty," said the Seneschal. "Gathering political support for the war. As you instructed."

The King just nodded, and gestured brusquely for everyone to draw nearer to the throne. As they did, the King produced a single long-stemmed red rose from out of his sleeve and toyed with it idly. Up close, everyone could see the extent of the change in him. He looked to be no more than in his thirties, his once spare frame loaded now with bulk and muscle. His eyes were clear and his mouth was firm, and he looked every inch the King he had once been. Richard stood directly before his father, torn between conflicting emotions. He was glad to see his father looking hale and hearty again, and delighted to see the obvious clarity and wisdom in his father's eyes. But a cold feeling in the pit of his stomach made him afraid to ask what price his father had agreed to for such a miracle. The King smiled on them all, knowing what they were all thinking and determined to make them wait for their answer.

"Hawk, Fisher," he said evenly. "Show me the marvellous new weapons you have acquired from the Armoury and the Cathedral."

So Richard showed off Lawgiver, drawing the great broadsword to reveal its newly polished and sharpened blade. Everyone nodded recognition of the legendary old name. Hawk drew the Rainbow Sword, though it looked like an entirely ordinary sword. Gillian demonstrated what the Cestus could do, to impressed murmurs. And Catherine demonstrated her newly acquired Blood Magic, by generating a great wind that rushed up and down the Court, before condensing into several small whirlwinds that spun fiercely, bumping into one another, before she dismissed them with a sharp gesture. Catherine smiled briefly.

"No one will send me anywhere I don't want to go, ever again."

And if she was looking at the King when she said this, rather than anyone else, no one said anything.

"The return of the Blood Magic must mean the Unreal has been restored to Castle Midnight," said the Sombre Warrior. "Which means William and Christof must also now possess the Blood Magic. Which will make them very powerful enemies on the battlefield."

"And Cameron," said Catherine. "Don't forget my exiled older brother, the Broken Man. You can bet my father's already called him back."

"Of course," said the Sombre Warrior. "He will have the Blood Magic too."

Pretty much everyone in the Court felt cold chills run up and down their spines at the thought of the return of Redhart's greatest warrior and general. The man who never lost a battle . . .

"You've shown me some interesting new weapons," said King Rufus. "Very pretty they are, and very useful, I'm sure, when the fighting starts. But I want to see the real weapons. The ones that will win this war for us. Show me the Infernal Devices."

"No," Hawk said immediately. "You can't draw them here. Can't draw them anywhere, except when there's an enemy to unleash them on."

"No one says no to me in my own Court," said King Rufus. "Not even you . . . sir Hawk."

"Don't push your luck, Rufus," said Hawk, and the whole Court went quiet.

"When the swords are drawn they're a danger to everyone," said Fisher after a moment. "Hawk is merely concerned for your safety. Your majesty."

"Of course he is," said King Rufus.

"I carry Belladonna's Kiss," said Fisher. "Jack Forester has Blackhowl, and Raven has Soulripper. We don't know yet exactly what their particular qualities are. That will become clear once the killing starts."

"I want one," said Rufus. "I am King. I should wield the most powerful weapon."

"The Infernal Devices are alive and aware, Father," Richard said carefully. "All the legends agree that these swords corrupt the souls of those who wield them. You are too important to the Forest Land to put yourself at such a risk."

"Well said, my son," said the King. "But since the King must have a sword with legendary power, you won't mind giving up Lawgiver to me. Will you?"

"I am honoured to present it to you, Father," said Richard.

He unstrapped the old leather scabbard and laid the ancient broadsword at his father's feet.

Chappie growled suddenly, his dark lips pulling all the way back to reveal jagged yellow teeth. The harsh sound was very loud on the quiet of the Court. Everyone looked at the dog, who was glaring at the King on his throne.

"Ask him," said the dog. "Ask him what he's done, to renew himself. I can smell the stink of demons on him."

The King just smiled. "Yes . . . I suppose it is time to tell the tale. You've been very polite, and very patient, but you all want to know what I've done to regain my lost youth, and sanity. It's really very simple. I just went for a little walk outside, to talk to the Standing Stone."

Richard glared at the Seneschal. "You were supposed to keep an eye on him!"

"He slipped away!" said the Seneschal. "He is the King, after all!"

King Rufus stood up suddenly and threw his long-stemmed rose onto the floor, at everyone's feet. It snapped and writhed, coiling and uncoiling like an angry snake, before rising up suddenly and growing rapidly to take on a new form. Until at last the Green Man stood before them. Ten feet tall, a godly but still human figure, with bright green skin wrapped in bright green robes, the face almost inhumanly noble and handsome. The Green Man smiled benignly about him.

Chappie started to lunge forward, growling fiercely, and Hawk had to grab a handful of fur at the scruff of his neck to hold him back. The Sombre Warrior and Peter Foster both drew their swords and put themselves between their charges and the old god.

"Stand down!" roared the King. "Everyone, stay where you are! And put those weapons away! This is my benefactor."

"I am the spirit of the Forest," said the Green Man in a calm and most reasonable voice. "The green heart of the green Land. I am here to make you all strong again."

"I'm already strong," said Hawk. "What are you exactly?"

"I was here before this Castle," said the tall green figure. "I was here before everything, when everyone lived in the woods, because there was no one else. Think of me as an old god, if you wish. I don't mind. I am the wild spirit, and the laughter in the woods. I am the horns on the stag and the lightning in the storm. I am all the power you will ever need."

"Father?" said Richard. "What have you done? What deal did you make, with this . . . Green Man?"

"I did what I had to," said King Rufus. "To be the King I needed to be. The King this Land needs if we're to win this war. That's what it means to be King, boy. To do what's necessary for the Land you rule."

And that was when Sir Jasper appeared out of nowhere. He looked wildly around him, and then rushed toward the throne, passing right through several people on the way. "A gateway has appeared in the Forest!" he said loudly. "Redhart is here!"

"What?" said King Rufus, his calm confidence shattered. "What are you talking about, dead man?"

"The Redhart army has come to Forest Castle!" said Sir Jasper. "All of it! They're coming here, right now!"

Raven swore briefly, and conjured up a window on the air, showing a view of what was happening outside the Castle. Everyone watched in silence as Redhart's armed forces came roaring through the woods, passing through a huge, glowing dimensional doorway. More doors appeared, spread throughout the surrounding Forest, and more troops came pouring through. Forest Castle was under attack from all sides. None of the Redhart soldiers made any move to enter the great clearing, let alone approach the moat, but it was clearly only a matter of time. Some of the soldiers were already establishing fortified defence positions. Raven let the window disappear.

"It would appear William has beaten us to the punch," King Rufus said slowly, sinking back onto his throne. "By the time Parliament can raise and gather our armies and send them here . . . it will all be over."

"Then it's up to us to stop them," said Hawk. "And win the war here. Because all William has is an army. You have legends."

"Damn right," said Fisher.

TEN
....

TRUTHS REVEALED,
IN THE HEAT OF BATTLE

A slow, heavy rain fell across the Forest and pattered loudly against the exterior of a recently erected command tent. In fact, those inside could still hear grumbling soldiers outside, hammering in the last few tent pegs. The Redhart command tent had been set in place not far from the edge of the Forest, so close they could look out across the open clearing and see the Castle through the intervening trees. When the dark sky and pouring rain allowed. Inside the tent General Staker bent over the main table, studying a magical image of the Castle supplied by the sorcerer Van Fleet. Staker wore his usual hard-worn chain mail, over battered leather armour, and looked every inch the professional soldier, happy at his work. Van Fleet was wearing his usual richly coloured peacock robes, though they seemed to hang more loosely around him than previously. Recent events had taken a lot out of the sorcerer, and it showed. He looked like he wanted to be anywhere but where he was, and didn't care who knew it.

Also gathered around the table, taking in the highly detailed image of Forest Castle, were Redhart's Champion, Malcolm Barrett, in his highly polished armour, and the Broken Man, Prince Cameron. The Champion was an impressive-looking warrior in his own right, but he was still overshadowed (and just a bit intimidated, though he would never admit it) by the huge barbarian figure of the Broken Man in his hulking armour, great mane of braided black hair, and bushy beard. Malcolm had to admit that Prince Cameron was everything the battlefield legends had promised, and more.

"Just how accurate is this image of yours, Van Fleet?" demanded General Staker. "I'm not sending my men up against the Castle unless I'm sure of the details."

"I've been studying the Castle through my farseeing glass," said Van Fleet. His voice was low and dull, and he might have seemed disinterested if he hadn't been so clearly exhausted and used up. He didn't even look at the image on the table; his puffy eyes focused instead on some inner view. "What you're looking at is an exact duplicate of Forest Castle, from the crumbling battlements all the way down to the sewer outlets. Bloody thing's so old and decrepit it's a wonder to me it's still upright. I can focus in on anything you might want to see more clearly . . . right up to individual stones in the walls."

"How long has King William had you studying this Castle?" said the Champion.

Van Fleet smiled coldly. "Ask the King."

"Don't sulk," said Staker. "It's very unbecoming in a sorcerer."

"I don't want to be here!" said Van Fleet. "I shouldn't be here. I'm a sorcerer, not a fighter. It's cold and wet and I hate the outdoors."

"We're at war," said Cameron. "Which means you're whatever your King needs you to be, and you go where he sends you."

"You should know," said Van Fleet.

"What about the Castle's magical defences?" the Champion said quickly. "Can you show us those?"

"Of course," said the sorcerer. "Prepare to be thoroughly depressed."

He gestured briefly, and the image of the Castle all but disappeared, hidden behind layer upon layer of overlapping spells and curses and magical booby traps. Laid down and refined over many generations, they blazed and spat and crackled all around the Castle. It was like looking at a single stone set in the middle of a bramble bush. If the brambles were also on fire, and poisonous.

"You can't just launch an open attack on the Castle, General," said Van Fleet, with a certain gloomy satisfaction. "Impressive though your armed forces are. Those defences would just eat them up and spit them out again."

"Then do something about it," said Cameron. "You're the sorcerer."

"I'm also a man who knows his limitations," said Van Fleet. He wanted to glare at the Prince but couldn't quite raise the nerve. He settled for glowering at the Castle image. "These protections aren't just old and well established; they're positively ancient. Laid down by sorcerers far more powerful than me. There's Wild Magic in there as well as High, along with a whole bunch of things I don't even recognise. Making my head hurt just looking at them. I haven't got anything that could even touch them. Be like licking your finger during a thunderstorm, and sticking it in the air to see if the lightning was heading your way."

"Isn't there anything you can do?" said Staker. "There must be something!"

"I can work at the outer edges," Van Fleet said reluctantly. "Defuse something here, unravel something there, work my way in, layer by layer. The defence magics extend right to the edge of the clearing, in case you hadn't noticed . . . But it could take me weeks, even months, to peel away all those layers. We'd do better to wait for the magical help the King is sending."

"The Red Heart," the Champion said heavily. "Or whatever that un-natural thing really is. Am I the only one who damn near had an accident in his underwear when that thing appeared in Court?"

"If you knew what it really was . . . or what I think it might be . . . you'd run away and hide in a whole different country," said Van Fleet. "And I may, yet."

"What do you think it is?" said Staker. "Come on, man, if we're going to fight beside it, we need to know."

"It's older than Redhart, older than Humanity," said the sorcerer. "And it's not any kind of pagan god, even if some of our more gullible ancestors worshipped it in the past."

"So what does that leave?" said the Champion.

"I think it's a demon," said Van Fleet. "Something really bad, left over from the old War . . . So you have to wonder why it's helping us. If it is . . ."

"All right," said the Champion. "Someone's been drinking his own potions again . . . Do let us know when the rational parts of your brain kick back in."

"The King assured me that when the Red Heart arrives, he will bring with him powerful magical allies," said Cameron, raising his voice just enough to bring everyone's attention back to him. "Don't ask me what these forces might be; my father didn't see fit to confide in me. Even though I'm supposed to be running this campaign. Hopefully, these new magical allies will be powerful enough to do something about the Castle's protections. Otherwise, we might as well just set up the siege engines, and throw bloody rocks at it. In which case, we could be in for a really long siege, gentlemen."

"When is the Red Heart supposed to get here?" said the Champion. "And why didn't it just come through the dimensional gate with the rest of us?"

"Ask the King," said Van Fleet.

The entrance flaps to the tent burst open as Prince Christof arrived, fussily brushing raindrops from his elegant chased armour, complete with pointed greaves, spiked elbows, and a horned steel helmet. He'd had it designed specially. His sword, on the other hand, looked entirely professional, even brutal, as it hung on his hip. He smiled about him.

"I always like to look my best on important occasions. And what could be more important than this?"

"Where have you been, Brother?" said Cameron.

"Just taking a little walk in the woods, getting the lie of the land, and the feel of the place," Christof said easily. "I can't say I care much for this Forest . . . The tall trees are impressive enough, I suppose, but there are far too many of them. It's all a bit much . . . I prefer the wide-open spaces of Redhart. I do."

"When we win this war, the Forest will be part of Redhart," said Cameron.

Christof smiled. "Then perhaps Father will give it to you, Brother."

King William hadn't wanted both his sons to go to war, but Christof had insisted on going. He was damned if he was going to just hang around the Court, running errands for the King, while his elder brother was off pursuing fame and glory. And, perhaps, his way to the throne . . . No, if there was glory to be had, Christof was determined to seize his own share. Let Cameron plot his clever strategies, and run his battles; Christof would make sure to be out and about, in all the right places, being seen doing terribly heroic things. Let the King try to give his throne to a man who stayed in his tent, while his brother was out saving the day. Even a King who'd just won a war would have to bow down to public opinion over something like that. Cameron might know battles, but Christof knew people.

He sauntered over to look admiringly at the image of Forest Castle, and dabble his fingertips in the colourful protections. Van Fleet tensed but had enough sense not to say anything.

"Will Blood Magic be any use against this Wild Magic?" said Christof. "Would it perhaps be possible for Cameron and myself, working together, to punch a hole through these defences? Big enough for our army to use?"

"Always possible, I suppose," said Van Fleet. "Blood Magic is a form of Wild Magic, after all. Oh, didn't you know that? Your Blood Magic derives from the returned Unreal, which means, strictly speaking, that anyone of the Redhart Royal line is at least partly Unreal."

"Don't push your luck, sorcerer," said Christof.

"Wasn't aware I had any left," said Van Fleet.

They all looked round sharply as the tent flaps billowed open again and the Stalking Man strode in. Followed, rather less grandly, by the Prime Minister, Gregory Pool. Leland Dusque stopped at the end of the table, struck an attitude, and grinned cheerfully about him. Knowing that none of the others wanted him there, and enjoying it. A tall, fleshy man, in his bloodred robes and hood, he dominated the whole scene, just by being there. The others might be soldiers, but he was a killer, and he gloried in it. Hell's presence on Earth, the will of the Pit in the world of men. And blood and death and horror accompanied him wherever he went.

Gregory Pool stood dripping by the entrance, as though unsure of his welcome. He was soaked to the skin in his fashionable expensive clothes, and for all his impressive size, his usual poise and assurance were gone, swept away by recent events. His subtle ploys and devious strategies were no match for the fast-moving imperatives of war. He'd only ever had influence, not real power, and the King no longer listened to him. Gregory Pool had been left behind, and he knew it.

"I shouldn't be here," he said petulantly. "I'm a politician, not a soldier."

"I already tried that line," said Van Fleet. "You'll notice I'm still here."

"You're here, Prime Minister, because the King wants you here," Christof said mildly. "To represent Parliament and make a report to them afterwards. You're here to observe, not participate. So do try not to get underfoot, there's a good chap. Personally, I would have brought a minstrel, rather than a politician. You both lie, but minstrels do it with more style."

Pool brought out his silver snuffbox and fumbled the lid open with shaking fingers. Van Fleet slapped it out of his hands. The box fell to the carpeted floor, spilling cocaine everywhere. Pool looked blankly at his fallen box and then got down on his knees and scrabbled at the scattered white powder with his unsteady hands.

"Get him out of here," said Cameron. "He serves no useful purpose. Send him back."

Van Fleet nodded, muttered under his breath, and gestured briefly; and the Prime Minister vanished.

"The King will not be pleased to see the Prime Minister back again," said General Staker.

"He can always send another observer," said Christof. "Hopefully one who can hold a tune."

"We can't afford distractions," said Cameron.

"Couldn't agree more," said Staker, glaring at the Stalking Man. "I'd feel a lot happier if he weren't around!"

"How unkind," murmured Leland Dusque.

"We can win this war without your kind of help!" said Staker.

"Perhaps, General," said Dusque. "But William wants me here. He has a use for my . . . special talents. So your opposition to my being here could be seen as treason. Couldn't it?"

"You see?" Staker said loudly to the others. "Every word he speaks is full of Hell's poison!"

"And given that William wants the Stalking Man here," said Van

Fleet, "what does that tell us all about our revered monarch's current state of mind?"

"Now that does border on treason, sorcerer," said the Champion.

"It can feel like that," said Van Fleet, "when you're the only sane man left in the room. Or the tent."

"No quarrelling in the command tent!" Prince Cameron said sharply. "Either we all pull in the same direction, or I'll kick people out until we do. Have you placed your men where I instructed, General?"

"Of course, your highness," Staker said carefully. He might be in charge of the army, but he was still more than ready to follow Cameron's orders. The Broken Man was a genius when it came to tactics. Staker gestured to Van Fleet, and the sorcerer made the image of the Castle disappear, so the General could spread out his maps on the table. They were pretty basic things, but they served to show the current troop positions surrounding the Castle. Staker and Cameron then spent some time discussing the various strengths and capabilities of each troop, and the possibilities for various attacks. Christof and the Champion did their best to follow it all, but soon gave up and settled for nodding in what they hoped were the right places. Van Fleet didn't even bother. He just stood off to one side, well away from the Stalking Man, staring at nothing and feeling sorry for himself. When the discussion finally wound down, Staker was greatly impressed. The others mostly didn't give a damn. They weren't there to discuss strategy. They were there to kill people.

Cameron finally looked up from his maps and fixed his gaze on Christof. "This is all well and good, but I can't move a single man till the Red Heart gets here with his forces. The King was most insistent on that. Do you understand our father's thinking on this matter, Brother?"

"No," said Christof. "But whatever the Red Heart may or may not be, he is clearly a Being of Power. So, we wait and see . . ."

"Since we're not going anywhere, or doing anything useful," said the Champion, "can I just remind everyone that this is all supposed to be about getting the Princess Catherine back safely?" He glared at Van Fleet. "I still don't see why you can't just teleport me inside the Castle so I can find Catherine and talk some sense into her. And then you could bring us both back out."

"Well, that's probably because you haven't been paying attention, sir Champion," said Van Fleet, glaring right back at him. "Remember the Castle's defences? All those pretty colours around the image? If I try to force you through those wards, you'll appear on the other side as a collection of large meaty chunks."

"He's right, Mal," said Christof. "There's no shortcut, no easy way to do this."

"Let me go to the Castle alone, then, as an envoy," Malcolm said desperately. "Alone and unarmed. Why wouldn't they see me then? Maybe I can make some kind of deal, over Catherine. I'm sure if I could just get her alone . . . Knowing they're surrounded by our army must have put the Forest Court in a more reasonable state of mind."

"That's very honourable of you, Malcolm," said Christof. "Putting your life on the line to save lives all around . . . But you heard Catherine. Either she truly doesn't want to come back, or she's completely under their control. Either way, they'd never let you see her, and they'd never give her up. War has been declared; neither side can back down now. No, they'd just take you prisoner, to use as a bargaining chip. The only way to rescue my dear sister is to bring down the Castle."

"What if they threaten to kill Catherine if we don't retreat?" said the Champion.

"We're at war, sir Champion," Cameron said steadily. "We will all do what we must and make whatever sacrifices may prove necessary."

"You'd let her die?" said Malcolm. "She's your sister!"

"But Cameron doesn't care," said Christof. "Cameron is famous for not caring. Isn't that right, Brother?"

"They must know that if they kill the Princess Catherine, there will be terrible reprisals," said Cameron. "We must rely on their good sense to keep her safe."

Staker looked thoughtfully at Leland Dusque. "You're famous for coming and going and no one knowing . . . Could you get through the Castle's defences and reach the Princess without being noticed?"

"Of course," said the Stalking Man. "Nothing can stand in my way, while I walk Hell's path. But I can only walk alone when I walk unseen. I couldn't take anyone with me, and I couldn't bring anyone out with me.

And besides, Jack Forester is there. The Walking Man that was. He'd know I was there. Given how similar our offices are, it's hardly surprising we have an affinity for each other."

And then he stopped. His head came up, and he smiled slowly.

"Well, speak of the devout, and up he pops. Of course, they would send him. The one envoy we wouldn't kill on sight, or dare take captive. Prepare yourselves, gentlemen; we're about to be visited by a living legend."

The tent flaps opened, and two guards came in, with Jack Forester walking between them. The guards tried hard to give the impression that Jack was under arrest, but they weren't fooling anyone. It was clear to everyone that in his own quiet way Jack scared the crap out of the guards. They gave him plenty of room, and kept their hands well away from their weapons. Jack stopped, and the guards stopped with him. Jack smiled easily about him—just a grey-haired old man, in a monk's robes, leaning on a wooden staff. For a moment none of the Redhart commanders knew what to do; and then Christof gestured for the guards to leave, which they quickly did.

Nearly everyone in the tent looked at Jack Forester with respect and admiration. They knew the stories, all the incredible things he'd done, punishing evil and protecting the innocent as God's wrath in the world of men. His travels had taken him through much of Redhart, as well as the Forest. King William had actually feasted him once, at Castle Midnight. So they all smiled and bowed to him—except for Leland Dusque.

"God save all here," said Jack. "I am here as an envoy from King Rufus."

"We know you," said Christof. "The one man they could send that we would listen to. You'll pardon if we seem a little overawed. It's not every day we come face-to-face with a living legend."

Jack made a dismissive gesture. "I gave all that up long ago. I'm just a man of God now, hoping we can find a way to avoid mass slaughter."

No one said anything. They were all studying Jack Forester, and thinking pretty much the same thing. It was hard to accept that this mild-mannered old man had once been one of the most dangerous men alive. You don't expect living legends to retire and give it all up and grow old. The man before them looked small and diminished, even fragile. And yet, there was still something about him. Jack Forester had a presence; and so did the great sword hanging down his back.

Jack looked past them all, to Leland Dusque, smiling and standing alone. The two men watched each other silently for a long moment, and then Jack turned sternly to Prince Cameron.

"How can you ally yourself with the Stalking Man? With Hell's presence on Earth? Don't you know the things he's done?"

"This is war," said Cameron, entirely unmoved. "I know the stories. Everyone does. That's what makes him such a useful weapon."

"And you're in no position to cast the first stone," said Dusque. "That is an Infernal Device on your back, isn't it?"

Everyone looked at Jack sharply as they heard the old name, their faces full of shock and horror.

"I thought they were all gone!" said Christof. "All the stories agreed: the three Infernal Devices were lost or destroyed in the last part of the Demon War!"

"No," said the Champion. "There were other swords, some said, kept secret by the Forest Kings, all these years . . ."

"And you've brought them back into the world," said Cameron.

"What other choice did we have?" said Jack.

"Am I the only one who sees an opportunity here?" said Van Fleet. "He's brought us an Infernal Device. Why not just take it for ourselves?"

"What makes you think the sword would let you take it?" said Jack. "The Infernal Devices have always chosen their own wielders."

There was an uncomfortable moment, broken when Jack took a step forward, smiling easily on all present.

"There's no need for any unpleasantness. I am an envoy, with a simple message. The war can end now, before anyone gets hurt. Go home; let the diplomats talk and find a way to renew the Peace agreement that everyone worked so hard on. You must see that is in everyone's best interests."

"You're right," said the Champion. "It can all end now. Just give us the Princess Catherine. Return her to us, and then we can all go home."

"We're not holding her," said Jack. "She has chosen to stay of her own free will."

"You would say that, wouldn't you?" said the Champion.

"The Princess did volunteer to go back," said Jack. "She was ready to do that to stop a war. But look around you, sir Champion. Do you think these men would turn back if Catherine walked into this tent right now? No. They came here to fight a war, and that's what they're going to do."

The Champion looked around, at Christof and Staker, and most especially at Cameron, and he fell silent.

The Stalking Man came forward then, and everyone else fell back despite themselves. Heaven and Hell's chosen stood face-to-face, and it was as though they were the only ones in the tent.

"I know your story," said Jack. "I know your tragedy. I know why you became the Stalking Man. But can you honestly say it has made you happy, or even content?"

"Some things are more important," said Leland Dusque. "Even a harsh comfort is better than none. And revenge does have a savour all its own."

"I can help you," said Jack.

"I don't want your help," said Dusque.

Jack sighed quietly. "No. You never did." He turned away to face Prince Cameron. "Be honest, your highness. Even if I brought Catherine here myself, would you stop? William wants this war, though I don't know if anyone really understands why. He'd still order you to continue, wouldn't he?"

Cameron nodded slowly. "It's all gone too far to stop now. This war's been a long time coming. It has to run its course."

"Not necessarily," said Jack. "I have a special reason for being here. I have been authorised by King Rufus to suggest that we settle this conflict the old honourable way—through a contest of champions. One man from each side, one match; winner take all. No need for a long, drawn-out conflict and the destruction of two countries."

"No!" General Staker said immediately. "This just shows how desperate they really are! They can see they're no match for our army. We don't need to risk everything on a gamble like this . . . We can win this war!"

"You said it yourself, General," said Cameron. "Laying siege to Forest Castle could take months. By which time the Forest armies will be here. And nothing is ever certain on the battlefield . . . No, I like this suggestion. Let's get this done, here and now. So only one man has to die."

Everyone else at the table was nodding; they liked the idea, because they knew who their champion would be. Prince Cameron. The man who had never lost a fight.

Malcolm Barrett nodded too, though somewhat reluctantly. As the King's official Champion, he felt he should be the one to fight. But honour demanded that he step down in favour of the legendarily unbeaten Broken Man.

There followed a certain amount of negotiation, between Jack and Cameron, on the details of the duel, and then they both formally agreed. Malcolm said he would escort Jack back through the troops. Jack was about to say that wasn't necessary, when he saw that the Champion wanted to speak with him privately, so he just smiled and nodded to everyone, and left the tent with Malcolm.

Outside the tent, the two men walked a little away so they could talk privately. The surrounding soldiers looked on, hunched in small groups around their steaming camp-fires, but they had no desire to get involved. A little of Jack's reputation went a long way. The rain had died away to a slow drizzle, and the air was heavy with the scents of the Forest.

"Is Catherine all right? Really?" said Malcolm.

"Of course she's all right," said Jack. "She's fine. She's where she wants to be, with the man she loves."

"I can't believe that," said Malcolm.

"But you do," said Jack.

"I don't care!" said Malcolm. Heads came up, and people looked around, disturbed by the raw emotion in his voice, and Malcolm made himself calm down. No one said anything. He was, after all, the Champion. Malcolm sighed, and looked out into the trees so he wouldn't have to look at Jack's understanding face. "You're right. Catherine doesn't matter anymore. I don't matter anymore. It's all gone too far for any of us to back down. It's a matter of honour."

"You mean pride," said Jack, not unkindly.

"Send your champion here to fight," said Malcolm. "So Cameron can kill him and you can surrender."

He went back into the tent, passing the Stalking Man coming out.

Leland Dusque came over to stand with Jack. The two men nodded to each other.

"Are you really still using that Dusque name?" said Jack. "It's so contrived. I can never take it seriously."

"Better than using my real name and embarrassing my father," said Dusque.

"I was never embarrassed," said Jack. "Horrified, saddened, but . . . I do hear about the things you do. I keep hoping you'll come to your senses and give it up. Do you really think this is what your mother would have wanted?"

"Those forest brigands had her for three days," said Dusque. "And after everything they did to her, I couldn't bear to look at her body. Had to have a closed casket for the funeral. Because you weren't there, to save her."

"I was on the other side of the Forest when I heard," said Jack. "I got there as fast as I could."

"It wasn't fast enough."

"I know. I tracked down all the brigands I could find and killed them. It didn't bring your mother back. That was one of the reasons why I gave up being the Walking Man."

"And so you ran away to join the monastery, so you could hide from the world," said Dusque. "I went to an old church in Redhart, near where Mother was born, and there I found a very different book from yours. I became the Stalking Man, the wrath of Hell in the world of men. And I tracked down every brigand you let get away and killed them all."

"All of them?" said Jack.

"Every last one, Father."

"Good. Thank you, son."

"I didn't do it for you!"

"Did it make you feel any better?"

"Yes," said Dusque. But he looked away as he said it. "Why did you never marry my mother?" he said finally.

"Mercy's mother left me because I was never there," said Jack. "I did my best to avoid commitment after that."

"If you'd married her . . ."

"I still wouldn't have been there when she needed me," said Jack. "Do you think I've never thought about that? If I had been there, perhaps I could have saved her from the brigands. Perhaps I could have saved you, from this . . ."

"I don't want to be saved," Dusque said coldly. "I enjoy my role as Hell's champion."

"You don't seem particularly happy," said Jack. "Give it up, son. Lay down your burden and walk away. Like I did."

"You were never strong enough," said Dusque. "You never really embraced your role, as I have. I'll never give it up."

"I thought that, once," said Jack. "But it's the only way you'll ever know peace."

"Peace?" said the Stalking Man. "It's overrated."

He turned away and went back into the command tent. Jack looked after him for a moment, and then made his way slowly back through the enemy lines, to Forest Castle.

Jack Forester stood before King Rufus on his throne, in the great empty Court, and made his report. There were no politicians present, no courtiers. King Rufus had decided he didn't need them. The Seneschal was there, standing at the King's side. Prince Richard and Princess Catherine, Hawk and Fisher, and Chappie. They all listened carefully as Jack told them everything that had happened inside the command tent.

"I suppose it all went as well as we could have hoped," said the King. "Pretty predictable that they'd choose Cameron as their champion. But we still have to decide on our choice."

"We haven't had an official Champion since Prince Rupert's time," said Richard, not looking at Hawk and Fisher. "Queen Felicity had her Questor, Allen Chance . . . but that position was dropped as Parliament took more power for itself."

"Why are we still arguing about this?" said Hawk. "It's me. It has to be me."

"No," said the King. "I should do it. I am young and strong again. I was made strong just for things like this."

"But the King cannot place himself in danger!" insisted the Seneschal. "What if they just kidnapped you? Threatened to execute you? We'd have no choice but to surrender."

"Then I should do it," said Richard. "Cameron is a Prince of Redhart; he should be faced by a Prince of the Forest."

"Same objection," said the Seneschal.

"You can't, Richard," said Catherine. "Cameron would kill you. He's unbeatable. Everyone knows that. He'll kill whoever we send."

"That's why it has to be me," said Hawk. "Because I have a long history of winning against people everyone said couldn't be beaten. And, you'll notice, I'm still here."

"Damn right," said Fisher.

"Very well then," said King Rufus. "Let us set one unbeatable fighter against another."

He called Richard forward so he and the Seneschal could discuss what might happen after the fight. Hawk and Fisher moved a little away. Hawk carefully removed the Rainbow Sword and gave it to Fisher.

"Keep it somewhere safe," he said. "Just in case."

"No," Fisher said immediately, trying to give the sword back to him. "I don't want it. You might need it!"

"Not in this fight. I can't take it with me, Isobel. In case I don't come back."

"You can beat him!" said Fisher. "You're a living legend! He's just a cautionary tale."

"I've beaten all kinds," said Hawk. "I've been very lucky. But everyone's luck runs out sometime. So, just in case . . . keep the sword. Because the Demon Prince is still out there, somewhere . . . and the Rainbow is the only thing that might stop him."

"I'll hold on to it for you," said Fisher. "And give it back to you when you return."

"Yes," said Hawk.

"If he does kill you," said Fisher. "I will never surrender. Even if the whole Forest Kingdom bends its knee to Redhart, I will never give in. I will kill them all, one by one, even if it takes the rest of my life."

"You always were a sore loser," Hawk said fondly.

"I'm going with you," said Chappie, butting Hawk in the hip with his great head. "Just to see fair play."

"What do you know about fair play?" said Hawk, patting the dog's head and pulling at an ear.

"Absolutely nothing," said the dog. "That's the point. I know every dirty trick there is; they won't be able to sneak anything past me. You always were too honourable for your own good."

An hour or so later, Hawk and Chappie entered the trees at the edge of the clearing and moved cautiously forward into the Forest. It was raining heavily now, coming down hard, turning the ground muddy and treacherous underfoot. The Redhart soldiers huddled together around their camp-fires, protecting them with their own bodies. They barely stirred as Hawk and his dog passed, just watched them go by with cold faces and colder eyes. There were soldiers everywhere Hawk looked, filling the Forest, and he realised for the first time just how big an armed force Redhart had brought to take Forest Castle. Hawk smiled easily at all of them, radiating a cheerful confidence, because he knew that would upset them most.

It didn't take Hawk long to reach the new clearing Cameron had had hacked out of the Forest. A great open circle, surrounded by roughly cut stumps, some still oozing fresh sap. A beaten-earth circle, cleared of roots and stones; already turning to thick mud. It was an ugly place, a ragged wound in the body of the Forest. Casual emotionless destruction to make a place for someone to die. Hawk stopped at the edge of the clearing and looked it over. His disapproval must have shown in his face, because one of the soldiers came forward to sneer at him.

"This is what we'll do to the whole damned Forest once you're dead."

Hawk punched him out, and walked on. Chappie paused just long enough to piss on the unconscious man's face, and then hurried after Hawk. They both had their reputations to maintain. The soldiers let them pass. They had their orders. Hawk came to the command tent and nodded brusquely to the guards on duty. They snapped to attention despite themselves, and pulled back the tent flaps so he could enter. Hawk strode in as though the whole thing was his idea, with Chappie close by his side. One of the guards grabbed at the dog to stop him but jerked his hand back with a howl as Chappie bit off three of the guard's fingers with one snap of his great jaws.

"Don't eat those," said Hawk, not looking back. "Bad for your diet."

"Start as you mean to go on . . . ," said Chappie indistinctly.

Hawk smiled at the men waiting for him inside the tent. Cameron and Christof, the Champion and General Staker. They introduced themselves formally, and Hawk just nodded casually back.

"So," he said. "Let's get this show on the road. The sooner this nonsense is over, the sooner I can get on with something more important. You do know the Demon Prince is out there somewhere?"

Cameron came forward to look Hawk over. He did his best to loom over Hawk, but even with his size and presence, he couldn't quite bring it off.

"You're who they chose?" he said finally. "I don't even know you."

"I'm Hawk. And that's all you need to know."

Cameron nodded slowly. "You're right. It doesn't matter who you are. I never lose. You must have heard that?"

"That's what they say about everyone. Until they lose," said Hawk.

"I know you," said Malcolm. "Or at least I've heard of you. You're the latest Hawk to run the Hero Academy, right? I always wanted to go there when I was a kid. Is it true that all Hawks carry the axe the High Warlock made?"

"Yes," said Hawk. His hand went to the axe at his side, and he patted it fondly. "It's a good axe. Gets the job done."

"I've heard of the axe," said Cameron. "I'll put it to good use after your death. Who will take the news of my victory back to your people? Where is your official second?"

"That would be me," growled Chappie.

Cameron smiled at the dog. "How marvellous! A talking animal!"

He reached down to pat Chappie's head, saw the look in the dog's eye, and quickly pulled his hand back. He glared at Hawk.

"Your dog is very badly trained."

"He isn't trained at all," said Hawk. "I wouldn't dare."

"It's all part of my charm," said Chappie. And he pissed up the table leg.

Prince Cameron did his best to give the impression of being above such things. "The clearing is ready. I don't see why we should wait. Once I've killed you, I'll have my dinner, and then we'll go into the Castle to accept Rufus' surrender." He looked at Hawk. "Is your King in any condition to understand what's happening?"

"Oh, I'd say so," said Hawk. "In fact, I think his current condition would surprise you all."

"I don't do surprises," said Cameron.

"I do," said Hawk.

By the time Hawk and Cameron got to the clearing, it was surrounded by Redhart soldiers. Hundreds of them, several rows deep. They roared and cheered for their Prince, who nodded calmly to them. He entered the clearing casually, as though it was something he did every day. He was wearing his full armour, and the sheer weight of it drove his boots deep into the thick mud. The Champion handed Cameron a long rectangular shield, solid steel, with the Royal crest of Redhart emblazoned on it. Cameron drew his massive longsword and turned to face Hawk, who was just standing there, waiting for him. Hawk drew his axe and sank into his fighter's crouch. Cameron looked at him.

"That's it?" he said. "No armour, no shield?"

"Don't believe in them," said Hawk. "They get in the way."

Cameron shook his head slowly. "Sometimes, it seems to me there is a very thin line between overconfidence and a death wish."

"Poor bastard," growled Chappie, from the edge of the clearing. "He's already dead, and he doesn't know it."

Several soldiers standing near the dog found urgent and compelling reasons to go stand somewhere else.

Cameron looked Hawk over carefully. Everything in the way Hawk held himself made it clear he was a professional, experienced fighter. And his great steel axe head shone supernaturally bright in the Forest gloom. The rain had died away for the moment, and everything in the circle seemed unnaturally clear and distinct. Cameron dug his feet deep into the mud, for better purchase, and strode forward. Huge, overpowering, carried along by the weight of his own legend. Hawk smiled, and went casually forward to meet him. Because he'd spent most of his life fighting legends.

They circled each other slowly for a while, respectful of each other's obvious competence. Cameron peered over the top of his shield, every movement he made carefully calculated, giving nothing away. Hawk moved lightly through the mud, axe at the ready, holding strength and speed in reserve for when they'd be needed. Neither of them bothered with war cries, or harsh talking. They were professionals. The watching crowd was quiet now, taking in every detail, tense with anticipation. Whatever happened in this circle would decide the war, and the fate of two nations. And whether the watching soldiers would have to go out and fight and maybe die for their country. They had faith in their Prince. He was unbeatable. Everyone knew that. Everyone except Hawk, apparently, who still looked like he thought he could win . . .

The two men surged forward, and slammed together in the middle of the clearing. Sparks flew on the air as axe and sword clashed, and then the two men withdrew from each other and went back to circling. They'd taken each other's measure, both of them going for the killing stroke, and neither of them had backed down. It was going to be a real fight, after all.

Hawk swung his axe with both hands, and Cameron put his shield in place to block it. The shining axe head sheared clean through the upper part of the shield, hacking it off. The severed part fell into the mud. Cameron backed hastily away. The top third of his shield was gone. Hawk went after him, and slammed his axe against the shield again and again, carving pieces off, whittling it away. Until finally the axe head buried itself in the shield, and the impact drove Cameron to one knee. Hawk jerked his axe free, and the shield split into two pieces and fell apart. Cameron threw what was left away and rose to his feet, his sword held out before him.

Hawk grinned.

The two men circled each other. They lunged and feinted, stamping heavily in the treacherous mud, sometimes slipping and sliding, but always recovering. They darted in to attack and then leapt back again, the sound of steel slamming against steel almost painfully loud on the quiet. Their eyes met. Hawk was still grinning. Cameron was still coldly calculating. The Prince no longer thought this was going to be a quick match, or an easy win.

They threw themselves at each other again and again, cutting and parrying, forcing each other back and forth across the clearing, their breath coming hard and ragged, sweat flying from their faces. The fight went on and on, long after other fighters would have dropped from sheer exhaustion. The speed and frequency of their attacks lessened, as they duelled each other to the limits of their strength, and beyond.

The watching soldiers were crying out at every blow now, as though they could will their Prince to victory through their support. They crowded right up to the edge of the clearing. They'd never seen a fight like this before. They knew this was one of those moments when history becomes legend; and they were there. They knew they would be telling this story to their children, and grandchildren, and anyone who would listen, for the rest of their lives.

Cameron swung his sword round in a long arc, and Hawk ducked under it at the last moment. He felt a breath of air stir his hair as the blade swept past. He swung his axe in a vicious short arc, aiming for the weak spot in Cameron's armour, where the leg met the groin. Cameron pulled back at the last moment, so the axe glanced off solid steel, denting it deeply. The sheer weight of the armour was slowing Cameron down, for all his great strength, and dampening his responses. He hadn't expected the fight to go on this long.

The two men stood facing each other for a long moment, heads hanging down, sweat dripping off their flushed faces, both of them drawing in great lungfuls of air. Glaring unyieldingly into each other's eyes. Neither of them had drawn blood yet. Hawk was still grinning. Cameron raised his sword with both hands and charged forward, bringing the heavy blade down on Hawk's head with all his strength. Hawk braced himself, and brought his axe up to block the blow, putting all his strength behind it. The long sword hammered down into the axe, and the sword blade shattered. Cameron stumbled on, with half a sword in his hand, unable to stop, and Hawk's axe punched through his armour and buried itself in Cameron's chest.

The crowd noise fell away to nothing. Cameron stood looming over Hawk, looking down at the axe head in his chest. He looked more surprised than anything. Hawk jerked the axe blade out of Cameron's armour, and a great welter of blood followed it. Cameron fell to his knees, as though only the axe's presence had been holding him up. He opened his mouth to say something, but only blood came out. Cameron fell slowly backwards, into the mud, and lay still, his face entirely expressionless. He didn't move again.

Hawk watched him for a while, just to be sure, and then slowly straightened up and looked about him. He was breathing so hard he couldn't speak. He raised his left arm and wiped the sweat from his face. He still held his axe out before him. Blood dripped steadily from the axe head. The High Warlock did good work. All around him Redhart soldiers stood silently, looking grimly back at him. None of them moved, or said a word. The unbeatable Prince had been beaten. They couldn't believe it. And then General Staker stepped into the clearing, hurried forward, and knelt beside the fallen Prince. He checked for signs of life, and when he couldn't find any, he stood up to face Hawk.

"You cheated!" he said, almost hysterically. "You must have! There's no way you could have beaten the Prince otherwise!" He looked about him for support. "This result doesn't stand! It doesn't count, because he cheated! I say we hold him as a hostage!"

"Sounds good to me," said Prince Christof, stepping forward to stand beside the General. "I mean, yes, I went along with this contest, but only because I was sure we were going to win. We didn't come all this way to give up just because Cameron wasn't up to the job. We expected too much from a man who spent the last eight years living in a cave. We should never have listened to him. We came here to rescue my sister, Catherine, and conquer a country. And that's what we're going to do."

The soldiers packed together round the clearing cheered him loudly, and nodded vigorously to one another. Cameron had let them down, and they were eager to follow a new leader. Christof looked at Hawk.

"Chain him up. Maybe we can exchange him for Catherine. Before we tear their Castle down."

"We could send bits of him back to the Castle, one at a time, until they agree to surrender," said the General.

"Is that how you want to win this war?" said the Champion, stepping out of the crowd. "With such dishonourable methods?"

"That man just killed your Prince!" said the General.

"I never liked him," said Christof, not even looking at his dead brother's body, still lying in the mud. "He was arrogant and overconfident, and it got him killed."

"We agreed to abide by the outcome of this fight," the Champion said doggedly. "If we break faith, how can we hope to make any kind of deal with them?"

"You're right," said Christof. "Hawk's no use to us as a captive."

"We could still persuade him to talk," said Staker. "Make him tell us what's going on inside the Castle . . . How to get in, past the defences . . ."

Hawk chuckled suddenly, and they all looked at him, startled. It wasn't the sound of an exhausted, beaten man.

"Come on," said Hawk. "Bring me down if you can. Who dies first?"

Nobody moved. They'd all just seen him duel a legend to the death, and none of them were in any hurry to take him on. Because they all knew, deep down, that he was the most dangerous man they'd ever seen.

"A man like that would never talk, General," said Christof. "So there's no reason to keep him alive, is there? Kill the man, General Staker. Have your men drag him down. Use as many as it takes. And then cut off his head. We'll send it back to the Forest Court to tell them we won!" He smiled briefly. "Perhaps we'll strap the head to his dog, and he can carry it back."

Staker nodded stiffly, and gestured to his soldiers. Hawk brought his axe up and braced himself. The soldiers came running forward from all sides, brave enough as a crowd, eager to get their hands on the man who had killed their undefeated Prince. Hawk swung his axe and cut down three men, one after the other, before the rest ran right over him and hauled him to the ground. The impact knocked the axe out of his hands, and it fell into the mud. Half a dozen soldiers wrestled him onto his knees, and held him there, head down. Hawk still fought them with all his strength, refusing to give up, even as General Stake swaggered forward with his sword in his hands, and stood over him.

"Don't think you've changed anything," said the General. "You're just an inconvenience. Now hold still. The harder you make me work, the more I'll enjoy it."

He rested the edge of his sword on the back of Hawk's neck for a moment. Hawk could feel his skin part under the sharp edge. A little blood ran down his neck. Staker lifted up his sword, while the soldiers held Hawk in place. And then Chappie came running forward out of the crowd, crossing the distance with amazing speed. He leapt through the air and tore out the General's throat with one vicious snap of his massive jaws. Blood spurted, and the General cried out briefly. Chappie hit the muddy ground, skidded past Hawk, and then quickly recovered. He hit the guards hard, and they scattered, crying out in shock and fear. Hawk surged up off the ground and grabbed his axe out of the mud. The soldiers were running for their lives. Chappie moved quickly round to guard Hawk's back. Staker had both hands at his throat, as though trying to hold together the terrible wound the dog's jaws had made. Blood pumped thickly between his fingers. His eyes were full of horror. Not to be killed in battle, not to be struck down by an enemy's sword, but to be beaten by a dog . . . He fell to his knees, his hands dropped away from his ragged throat, and then he fell facedown into the mud and lay still.

"Nice work," Hawk said to Chappie just a bit breathlessly. "Now get out of here."

"I'm not leaving you," said Chappie.

"You have to," said Hawk. "We're facing a whole army here. We can't win. But you can get away; they'll never stop you."

"I can't leave you!"

"Someone has to tell Fisher what happened!"

"Goodbye, Hawk," said Chappie. "I was always proud to have you as my master."

The soldiers charged into the clearing, pressing forward from all sides at once. And that was when Raven appeared out of nowhere, grabbed Hawk and Chappie, and teleported them away. The soldiers cried out in thwarted anger, as they looked around a clearing with no prey. Just two dead bodies lying in the mud.

Their Prince and their General.

In the Redhart command tent, some time afterward, Prince Christof took formal command of the army, and the situation. With the Broken Man and General Staker both gone, there was no one else. The Champion supported him, and the soldiers were desperate for someone to give them orders. *It did help that Cameron had worked out his tactics and troop deployments before he got himself killed,* Christof thought, but didn't say. He and Malcolm leafed quickly through the papers their predecessor had left behind, familiarising themselves with what needed doing. It all seemed straightforward enough. The real work had already been done; all they had to do was carry out the plan. And then claim the credit afterwards. Christof couldn't stop smiling. It couldn't have worked out better if he'd planned it himself.

The Stalking Man stood at the back of the tent, keeping his own counsel. He would do what he would do, once the fighting began. All he required was that everyone else stay out of his way. The sorcerer Van Fleet stood to one side, his arms tightly crossed, openly sulking. Waiting for orders he might or might not obey. Christof glared at him.

"Did you know Raven was here, watching the fight? Did you know what he was going to do?"

Van Fleet looked away, his courage unravelling in the face of the Prince's anger.

"Obviously not, or I'd have done something," he said sullenly. "I didn't know the Necromancer was anywhere near here. In fact, it's entirely possible that he wasn't."

Christof's scowl deepened. "Talk sense, sorcerer."

"It's always possible he was watching the proceedings through a vision, back in the Castle," said Van Fleet. "Hidden from us, behind the Castle's protections. Though I don't know how he could jump so far . . . All this way into the Forest, from the Castle . . . and then back again? That would take a lot of power. And it's not the kind of magic I'd expect from a Necromancer . . . I always said there was more to Raven than met the eye."

"Is his magic stronger than yours?" said Malcolm.

"Almost certainly," said Van Fleet. "Though I'm pretty sure I could still show him a few nasty surprises."

"I say we attack the Castle immediately," said Christof, turning his back on the sorcerer. "We can't let the Forest think they've got us on the defensive. So, do we attack the Castle from all sides at once, try to force a way in? Or do we find some way to make the Forest forces come out and fight us here, in the Forest?"

"Why doesn't anyone listen to me?" said Van Fleet, desperation pushing aside his deference. "You can't get in, no matter how many soldiers you send against the Castle! They're protected! All they've got to do is sit tight behind their defences, and we can't touch them!"

"And do I really need to remind you," said the Stalking Man, "that you're supposed to wait for the Red Heart and his magical forces? Whatever they turn out to be . . ."

"We have to contact the King," said Malcolm. "Bring him up to date on what's happened here and see what he says. Not that I mean to undermine your authority, Christof, but King William needs to know his elder son is dead. And his chief general. That may change how he sees the situation."

"Of course," said Christof. "His precious unbeatable son, specially brought back from exile to save the day. He'll want to know how that worked out."

Malcolm shot Christof a warning look. "Now is not the time to revive old grievances, Chris."

"You're quite right," said Christof. "Whatever would I do without you, Mal?" He glared at the sorcerer. "Make contact with King William. And make very sure no one else can listen in."

"I know what I'm doing," snarled the sorcerer. He stabbed a finger at the air, muttered a few carefully rehearsed Words, and a window opened in midair, giving a view of King William on his throne. The King looked round sharply.

"What's happened?" he said roughly. "You weren't supposed to make contact until the Castle had fallen."

"Things have not gone according to plan, Father," said Christof. "I regret to inform you that your son Cameron is dead. And General Staker."

The King looked at him for a long moment, with a cold, unblinking gaze. "What happened?"

Malcolm stepped forward, and told the story from beginning to end. William didn't flinch once. Didn't react at all. Just sat on his throne, thinking.

"A shame," he said finally. "You were right to assume command, Christof. It was your place to do so. Go ahead; do what needs doing. I have complete confidence in you. Don't let me down. Don't let your country down."

"My country, Father?" said Christof, with just enough emphasis in his voice for his father to take notice.

"You are the last of my sons, Christof," the King said slowly. "The throne will be yours if you win this war."

"Well," said Christof, "nothing like ambition to motivate a man . . ."

But all the time he was talking to his cold-eyed, cold-voiced father, Christof had to wonder how much his father would care if he fell in battle too.

"I am sending you the help I promised," said King William. "The Red Heart is on his way with a force . . . I think you will find more than suffi- cient. If you are wise, Christof, you will stand back and let them do the heavy lifting for you."

The window snapped shut abruptly, and the King was gone. Christof and Malcolm looked at each other.

"What the hell was he talking about?" said Christof.

"He's here," said Van Fleet, raising a hand to his head as though it hurt him. "I can feel his presence in the Forest. Like a coal, burning in my mind. He's here, and he's not alone . . . Oh dear God . . ."

He swayed on his feet, and had to grab the table with both hands to hold himself up. His face had gone deathly pale, and his eyes were wild. Christof and Malcolm hurried out of the tent to see what was happening. The Red Heart was stalking through the trees, tall and magnificent and supernaturally impressive. The soldiers scattered to get out of his way, abandoning their positions. They didn't like what he'd brought with him.

All the creatures and entities and strange manifestations of the Unreal, from Castle Midnight.

An army of unnatural things, lurching and crawling and leaping through the trees. All the ghosts and gargoyles, monsters and miracles, the strangely living and the unquiet dead. Hundreds of them, maybe even thousands, a sight to appal the eye and chill the soul. Soldiers were retreat- ing everywhere now, running wildly through the trees, crying out like frightened birds. The Unreal pressed forward, shining and blazing and flickering, to the very edge of the clearing, and then they squatted down there to stare at the Forest Castle with intelligent, malignant eyes. The Red Heart stood before Christof and Malcolm, and smiled down at them.

"Do not be alarmed. These are my children, as much as you, and they are mine to command. They will break down the Castle's defences and protections for you and leave it open for you to take. With your ladders and battering rams and siege engines. I would not deprive you of your sport. Take the Castle, take the people inside, and do what you will with them."

He turned away, not caring to wait for any answer, striding off to walk among his unnatural army.

"It makes sense, I suppose," said Christof, working hard to keep his voice calm and composed. "Set magic to fight magic."

"And better that monsters should fight and die than our soldiers," said Malcolm. He swallowed hard. "It's hardly honourable, to send such abominations into the field, but there's been nothing honourable about this war from the beginning."

"Cameron's challenge was honourable enough," said Christof. "And look how that worked out."

"And we thought the Forest people were bad," said Malcolm, "for using the Infernal Devices."

"All's fair in war," said Christof. He called for a messenger, and when the man arrived, Christof spoke curtly to him. "Go tell the Red Heart that he and his forces can attack when ready. Don't look at me like that; you don't have to get too close. And then you'd better pass the word through our army to draw well back. Give the Unreal room to operate freely."

"Don't you trust them to leave our people alone?" said Malcolm, as the messenger left the tent.

"Hell, no. Those things were spooky enough inside Castle Midnight. God alone knows what they'll do now they've been allowed to run free in the world. But we'll worry about how to put the cat back in the bag afterwards. For now, let the monsters do our dirty work. Let them fight and die so real people don't have to."

Raven and Hawk and Chappie appeared suddenly inside the Forest Castle Court. Hawk collapsed, sprawling clumsily on the floor. So tired he couldn't even keep his eyes open. He lay on his side, breathing hard, while Chappie snuffled anxiously at his face. And then Fisher was there with him, holding him in her strong arms, helping him sit up and then sitting there with him so he could lean back against her.

"Hawk? What the hell happened to you?"

"I met a man . . . who was probably a better fighter than me," said Hawk. "But he didn't have the High Warlock's axe."

He opened his eyes and smiled up into her worried face, and after a moment she smiled back. She checked him over for wounds, quickly and professionally. Chappie sat down beside them, his tail thumping loudly on the marble floor.

"Who did you have to fight, in the end?" said Fisher. "Was it Prince Cameron?"

"Yes. I killed him." Hawk considered for a moment, then said, "Arrogant, and a bit of an arsehole, but brave enough, I suppose. The other side didn't take kindly to my winning. Called the whole thing off, because I cheated by not dying. The whole army jumped me, and then their General wanted to cut my head off."

"But I stopped him," said Chappie. "Ripped his throat out. And I just want to say, he tasted really bad."

Fisher looked at the dog. She could see the blood still dripping from his jaws.

"Good dog," she said.

Hawk looked at Chappie. "You said you were proud . . ."

"I know what I said!" Chappie said loudly. "It was in the heat of the moment! You're never going to let me forget it, are you?"

"You saved my life," said Hawk. "I'll never forget that."

He got to his feet, leaning heavily on Fisher, and looked at King Rufus, sitting anxiously on his throne. The Seneschal at his side, as always. Richard and Catherine, standing together. Raven the Necromancer standing to one side, looking thoughtful.

"Something just happened," he said, in an odd, dreamy voice. "Something really . . . strange has come into the Forest. And it's brought a whole army of most unnatural friends with it."

"What are you talking about?" demanded the King. "Speak sense, dammit! Has Redhart brought in reinforcements?"

"Something like that, yes," said Raven. "You need to see this."

He opened up a large dimensional window, hanging in midair, so they could see what was happening in the Forest beyond the Castle clearing. Everyone made some kind of sound as they watched the Unreal swarming through the trees, preparing to attack. Monstrous shapes and gleaming figures, shimmering apparitions ghosting through massive tree trunks, and grey stone gargoyles flexing huge membranous wings. No two shapes the same anywhere, a chaos of flesh mixed with magical extremes; a riot of things that should never have existed in the real world.

And there, standing at the very head of them, looking out across the clearing at Forest Castle as though he knew they were looking at him: the Red Heart. The colour of freshly spilled blood, all of him, from his inhumanly handsome face to his old-fashioned clothes. He smiled slowly, like a devil let loose from Hell to work mischief.

The doors to the Court banged open, and Mercy hurried in.

"Your majesty! An army of monsters has just appeared in the Forest outside and they're—oh, I see you already know."

Raven shut down the window, and they all turned to Mercy.

"Will the Castle's protections keep those things out?" said King Rufus.

"Your guess is as good as mine," said Mercy. "Most of the defences were laid down so long ago, we don't even know what they were originally designed to fend off. But according to all the old stories, they didn't keep out the demons during the Demon War."

"No," said Hawk, "they didn't."

"So that's the Red Heart," said Richard. "Impressive, in an appalling sort of way. We're talking Wild Magic here, aren't we?"

"I would have said so," said Raven. "Though I couldn't tell you what the Red Heart actually is . . . I understand King William got it out of a Standing Stone near his Castle."

Everyone looked at the newly young King Rufus, and he met their gazes steadily.

"Yes," he said, "that's where I found the Green Man. Good thing too, as it turns out. Now we have an old pagan god to set against theirs."

"You might call it a god," said Raven. "I'm . . . still looking into the matter."

Fisher brought the Rainbow Sword over to Hawk and pressed it into his hands. "Told you I'd keep it safe till you got back."

Hawk held the old familiar weight in his hand, and felt a slow refreshing strength run through him. He straightened up, stretched slowly, and then strapped the sword into place on his hip, opposite his axe.

"Just like old times," he said.

"God, I hope not," said Fisher. She looked Hawk over. "You look better. I think the sword agrees with you."

"I feel better," said Hawk. He shuddered briefly. "Prince Cameron was good. I mean, really good. If I hadn't had the High Warlock's axe . . ."

"I'd have rushed in and tripped him," said Chappie. "Or bitten him on the bum."

"That would have been dishonourable," Hawk said sternly. "You have no sense of the fitness of things."

"Of course not," said Chappie. "I'm a dog! Look, he's dead and you're alive, and that's all that matters."

"Who's in charge of their forces, now Cameron is dead?" said Catherine.

They all looked at her. She shrugged quickly.

"I never liked him. Don't think anyone did. There was always something a bit creepy about Cameron."

"I would assume Prince Christof has taken command," said Hawk. "I didn't see anyone else there with a better claim."

"Christof . . . ," said Richard. "Got a good reputation as a fighter, during the border skirmishes. Don't know how he'll do as a commander of men . . ."

"He'll manage," said Catherine. "He's spent years preparing for this. It's what he's always wanted."

"But now the Red Heart's arrived, how much real control does Christof have?" said Fisher.

"I've been expecting this," King Rufus said heavily. "Ever since I learned William had brought the Unreal back to Castle Midnight. He never could leave well enough alone. And he never did anything without a good reason. It's clear he's been planning how to win this war for a long time . . . Though I'm still damned if I can see why he wants one." He sighed heavily and gave his full attention to Mercy. "How long do you think the Castle defences will hold, Mercy?"

"Some are so old we're having trouble waking them up," said Mercy. "And the Unreal is an unknown factor. So we can't predict anything, really. The shields could go down at the first attack, and then there'd be nothing left but to guard the battlements and man the barricades, and fight them off with cold steel. I've ordered all kinds of really unpleasant weapons brought out of the Armoury, but there just aren't enough people to use them. No one's had to defend Forest Castle against an actual siege since the Demon War . . . We can only defend so many positions, but there's enough Unreal creatures out there to hit us from every direction at once."

"Assume the worst," said the King. "How long could we hold against a full siege?"

"Depends what they throw against us," said Mercy. "It's not just the Unreal; Redhart has a whole army out there. With siege engines, assault towers, and all kinds of supplies. And who knows what kind of magic they've brought to back them up? This Castle was built to be big and strong and keep people out, but there's a lot more than people coming our way. Anything will break if you hit it hard enough and often enough."

"I say go out and fight," said Hawk. "Take the battle to them."

He was looking and sounding a lot better. Fisher and Chappie stood steadily on either side of him.

"Are you serious?" said Richard.

"You heard Mercy," said Hawk. "They're going to get in anyway. Let's do the fighting where it won't make a mess of the Castle. A surprise attack might just catch them napping. Hit them hard enough, hurt them enough, and they'll scatter. Break their confidence and they'll retreat, fall back to think again. And that could buy us enough time for the Forest army to arrive."

"We don't have enough armed men for an open assault," said Richard.

"It does have the virtue of being entirely unexpected," said the King.

"No one would expect it, because it's completely, bloody insane!" said Richard. "Our forces would be slaughtered!"

"Not necessarily," said Hawk. "What if you had another army to back yours up? An army of the most highly trained warriors and magic-users of all time? Fisher and I talked about this earlier. Raven . . . could you open a dimensional door, linking Forest Castle with the Millennium Oak, home to the Hero Academy?"

Raven smiled suddenly. "You just think of the exact location, sir Hawk, and I'll do the rest."

It took only a moment for the young sorcerer to open up a window, and immediately the witch Lily Peck was there, staring out at Hawk and Fisher.

"About time!" she said firmly. "We've been monitoring the situation and waiting for you to do the sensible thing. We've organised an attack force."

"How big a force?" said Fisher.

Lily Peck smiled. "Pretty much everybody. No one wanted to be left out of this contest. Apart from the Administrator, whose back is playing up again. And the tantric sex bunch—but then they always were weird. Otherwise, the whole Academy's raring to show off what they can do. From students to tutors to most of the staff." She looked past Hawk, at Raven. "So, you're Raven. I always thought you'd be darker. Never mind; doesn't matter. Establish a gateway in the main Castle courtyard, and we'll lock on from this side. See you soon."

The window shut down. The King was already up and off his throne and heading for the doors. Everyone else followed him out of the Court.

Soon enough, everyone who mattered had assembled on the great steps outside the main entrance, looking out over the empty courtyard. And everyone else was watching from the windows overlooking the courtyard. Out on the vast cobbled space, Raven sat cross-legged in midair, muttering in obscure languages, his black robes swirling slowly around him as though bothered by unfelt aetheric breezes. His brow furrowed deeply as he concentrated, his eyes fixed on something only he could see. A growing sense of tension filled the courtyard, pressing down on everyone, a feeling of something drawing inexorably closer. There were strange lights in the sky, and great booming voices deep in the earth, and lightning dancing outside the Castle walls. And then a massive opening appeared in midair, as though shouldering Space itself apart to make way for it, and bright sunlight spilled through from another place. And through the dimensional doorway passed a whole army, the brightest and the best from the Hawk and Fisher Memorial Academy.

Fighters and magicians, warriors in training, and heroes out of legend. More and more of them, hurrying through the opening, from the newest student to the most experienced staff. No one had wanted to be left out. Roland the Headless Axeman led the warriors, while the Witch in Residence Lily Peck led the magic-users. Everyone else found somewhere to fit in. They filled the courtyard from end to end and from wall to wall, until finally the dimensional door slammed shut. Raven dropped out of midair like a stunned bird and sprawled limply on the cobbles. Mercy was quickly there at his side.

Roland and Lily came forward to greet King Rufus as he stepped down into the courtyard to meet them. The King took the Headless Axeman in his stride, and shook his hand firmly. He went to kiss Lily's hand, but she insisted on a firm handshake too. Then they both turned away from the King to look Hawk and Fisher up and down.

"So," said Lily. "It is you. I mean, really you. I always suspected, but . . ."

"If you'd wanted us to know, you'd have told us," said Roland. As always, his voice seemed to come from somewhere above his bare shoulders. "No doubt you had your reasons."

"It doesn't matter," said Lily. "You made the Academy possible. We owe you everything. Every man and woman here will fight for you."

"Technically speaking, you'll be fighting for King Rufus," Hawk said tactfully. "To defend the Forest Kingdom."

"As you wish," said Lily.

"Where's your dead cat familiar?" said Fisher. "I hardly recognise you without that appalling creature hacking and spitting on your shoulder."

"He fell apart," said Lily Peck. "I'll put him back together again once we get home."

"Thank you all for coming to our aid," said the King, in a loud enough voice to draw everyone's attention. "If you've been watching, then you know what we're up against."

"Yes," said Roland's voice. "Redhart's army, and creatures of the Unreal. Nasty."

"Still," said King Rufus, "it would seem the odds have changed in our favour. A marvellous gathering of new and old talent, sir Hawk. Your students do you proud."

"All right," said Lily. "As Kings go, this one doesn't seem too bad."

"You look a lot younger than I expected," said Roland.

King Rufus shrugged easily. "Being old was getting in the way. So I had it surgically removed."

And then everyone stopped, and looked around, disturbed by an unexpected sound. In a far corner of the courtyard an old carved stone fountain that had stood dry and silent for many years was suddenly pumping out fresh water. Great jets of pure, clear water bubbled up and fell away in long streams, out of the mouths of ancient stone faces. And as everyone looked on, the frothing waters suddenly jumped high into the air . . . and rained down to form a single female figure, made entirely out of water. Clear blue, through and through, a tall, noble lady with a smiling face, with water running forever from her eyes. Slow tides moved through her. She walked forward, and everyone fell back to give her room.

Hawk and Fisher looked at each other. They both remembered the Lady of the Lake, though it had been some eighty years since they had last seen her, during their previous visit to Forest Castle. She seemed to be deliberately not looking at them, so they didn't try to attract her attention. She walked right up to King Rufus and stopped before him.

"I am the Lady of the Lake," she said in a rich, bubbling voice. "You know who and what I am from the old stories, so let's skip the introductions. I bring you an old possession of the Forest Kings, long thought lost. I have kept it all these years, until it was needed, and now I present it to you, King Rufus. To use as you deem fit. I give you the Crimson Pursuant."

She put forward a dripping hand, and there on her blue palm was a glowing red jewel. Darker than heart's blood, bright as a star, pulsing with power. The King looked at it but made no move to take it.

"This was once set in the hilt of the sword Curtana," said the Lady of the Lake. "Also known as the Sword of Compulsion. This jewel, the Crimson Pursuant, was lost when the sword was destroyed by the Demon Prince, at the end of the Demon War."

"I didn't know that," Hawk said quietly to Fisher. "Did you know that?"

"Hush," said Fisher.

"The jewel ended up in a river, and all things lost in water end up with me, eventually," said the Lady. "I have been looking after it all this time, waiting for the right moment to reveal it. And for the one man who is destined to put it to proper use."

It felt like everyone was holding their breath. They'd all heard of the legendary Sword of Compulsion that could make anyone do anything. That could force obedience from everyone and everything. The ultimate control, the ultimate slavery. Almost no one looked at the jewel as though they thought it was a good thing. Slowly, King Rufus reached out and took the jewel from the Lady of the Lake, his heavy hand sinking clean through the Lady's watery fingers. The King held the jewel up, and turned it back and forth, and it shone like a coal straight from Hell itself. Until the King put it away, in his pocket. He looked around the packed courtyard, as though defying anyone to say something.

The Lady of the Lake turned away from the King and advanced on Hawk and Fisher. They moved forward to meet her.

"Mother?" said Hawk.

"Yes, Rupert," said the Lady. She put out a hand to touch his cheek tenderly, and a dribble of water ran down his face. "It's so good to see you again. I did say it would be a long time, didn't I? And Julia, of course. Don't worry; no one else can hear us. This moment is just for us. We can speak openly. For a while."

"Then can you tell us what's going on here?" said Hawk. "Why would you bring that cursed jewel back into the world?"

"Because it's needed," said the Lady. "I wish I could stay, my dearest boy, but I have things to do. And so do you. We will meet one more time. If everything works out as it should . . . Now you must excuse me. There's someone else I have to talk to."

She turned away, to address an apparently empty space. "Come out of there, sir ghost! This is no time to be hiding!"

Everyone nearby jumped just a little as Sir Jasper the ghost appeared out of nowhere. He was looking much more real now, more like just an old man in a nightie. Except that his feet weren't quite touching the ground. He nodded bashfully to the Lady, and she smiled sweetly on him.

"The last pieces are falling into place now, old ghost. And your reason for being here draws closer."

"Does this mean . . . there's been a plan all along?" said Sir Jasper. "I would like to think there was some reason, some purpose, to all my suffering."

"We all like to think that," said the Lady of the Lake. "But trust me, it's nearly over. One last destiny, one last act of penance, and then we can both get some sleep."

"Am I finally going to die, at last?" said Sir Jasper. "It would feel so good, to be able to lie down at last, and know peace."

Princess Catherine stepped forward, pushing her way through the crowd to join the Lady and the ghost.

"I brought Sir Jasper here, to help him find out who he really was. Do you know his true name, Lady?"

"Of course!" said the Lady, smiling sweetly on the Princess. "Thank you for looking after him, Catherine. I'm glad he had someone, when I couldn't be with him."

And then she just disappeared, falling apart into so much loose water, which splashed onto the cobbles and ran away. Catherine and Sir Jasper looked at each other, and it had to be said that neither of them looked any wiser.

Hawk cleared his throat loudly, and everyone's head snapped round to look at him. Including King Rufus'.

"The Unreal are at our gates!" said Hawk. "Monsters, from the past. So it's a war against demons, one more time. The Demon Prince is out there, somewhere. He has to be behind all this. He always did like playing both sides against each other."

"There are those who say the Demon Prince lives inside people now," said Jack, stepping forward so everyone could see him. His monk's robe and his old reputation gave weight and authority to his words.

"He does?" said King Rufus. "Then he could be anyone!"

All who were in the courtyard started looking at one another, and not in a good way. Looking to see who might be looking back, behind someone else's eyes. Some people started backing away from others.

"Stop that!" said Hawk. "That's what he wants. He loves to make us distrust each other."

"But he could be here, now," said Prince Richard. "He could be in anyone. How would we know?"

Laurence Garner, head of Castle security, pointed suddenly at Chappie. "It's him! It has to be him! The demon dog! How else could a dog live to be a hundred years old? It's not natural!"

"I will bite you," said Chappie. "And you won't like where. I was made by the High Warlock, and he did good work."

"He saved my life," said Hawk. "And he killed the Redhart General."

There was a great turning away, as more and more people looked suspiciously at the Sombre Warrior, hidden behind his featureless steel helmet.

"There could be anyone inside that armour," said Garner. "How do we know there's anything human in there?"

"You're starting to get on my tits, Garner," said Hawk.

"And I vouch for the Sombre Warrior," Catherine said loudly.

She nodded to him, and he raised both hands and removed his helmet. There were all sorts of gasps in the courtyard, as they all saw his untouched, undamaged features. Even at the Hero Academy they knew the story of the Sombre Warrior.

"Explain yourself," said King Rufus. "I do love a good story . . ."

So the Sombre Warrior ran through his complicated life one more time, leaving out only his service for King William. He didn't want to upset anyone. There was much murmuring in the crowd when he finished. A great many things had suddenly become clear.

"You spoke of unfinished business here, earlier," said Catherine. "Can you tell us what that was, now?"

"I wanted to visit my parents' graves," said the Warrior. "I wasn't here when they died. And they died thinking I was dead. The First Minister wouldn't allow me to come home. Not while he still had a use for me in Redhart."

"It is clear to me," said King Rufus, "that you have been hard used in our service, sir Warrior. But you are home now. You can tell us your real name, if you wish, that we may do you honour."

"No," said the Sombre Warrior. "That man is dead. And he wasn't anyone you would have heard of, anyway."

He put the steel helmet back on, and became his own legend again. Catherine put a hand on his arm and patted it briefly.

And then everyone's head snapped round again as another unexpected arrival made its presence known. The Green Man came walking through the far wall as though it was nothing. He advanced unhurriedly across the courtyard, and everyone fell back to give the massive figure plenty of space. Up close, his colour didn't seem at all natural. Not the bright green of living things at all. He came to a halt before King Rufus and smiled brightly.

"The Unreal is even now venturing out of the Forest and into the clearing!" the Green Man said loudly.

"Where the hell have you been?" said King Rufus. "We could have used your help before this!"

"I have my own business to be about," said the Green Man, entirely unmoved by the anger in the King's voice. "I'm here now. Be grateful. It's only right that I lead you out into battle, as my opposite the Red Heart leads the Unreal forces. Come, Rufus. It's time for you to be the King you always wanted to be."

"No, Father!" Richard said immediately. "You can't go out onto the battlefield!"

"You can't stop him," said the Green Man.

"Why does he have to go?" said the Prince, staring defiantly back at the Green Man towering over him.

"Because the King is the Land, and the Land is the King."

"Now that is bullshit," said Hawk. "And I should know."

"Why?" said the Green Man, turning his supernaturally handsome face on Hawk. "Who are you, that you should defy me?"

Hawk glared up at him. "Don't you know?"

The Green Man looked at him for a long moment, and then his smile widened into something entirely inhuman. "You . . . You're finally here. No need for games, then, anymore."

He vanished, gone in a moment, not even leaving a ripple of disturbed air behind him.

"Where are you?" said King Rufus to the empty air. "Where have you gone? Come back! You can't leave us now! We need you!"

The crowd in the courtyard looked at one another and stirred restlessly, disturbed by the naked need in the King's voice. They weren't as convinced of the Green Man's necessity as he was. When it became clear that the Green Man wasn't coming back, the King turned on Hawk.

"What have you done? You've driven away our most powerful ally!"

"I never trusted him," said Hawk. "And neither should you. Wars should be fought and won by people, or their victories don't mean anything. Where did you say you found that thing exactly?"

"Imprisoned in an ancient Standing Stone," said the King. "He said . . ."

"Oh, I'm sure he promised you all kinds of things," Fisher said briskly. "But never believe anything a demon tells you. And all supernatural creatures should be regarded as demons until proved otherwise."

"The Castle's magical defences have just gone down!" Raven said sharply. "They were never intended to stand against an army of the Unreal."

"So there's nothing to stop them crossing the clearing and attacking the Castle," said Mercy, standing close beside the black-clad sorcerer.

"You're sure?" said the King. He suddenly looked smaller, and older. "I thought we'd have more time . . ."

"I can See what's happening, quite clearly," said Raven. "They're not even trying to hide themselves. But they're hesitating . . . for the moment. Holding their positions at the very edge of the Forest. Probably can't believe it was that easy."

"They won't stay there long," said Mercy. "If we are going out to meet them, we'd better do it soon."

"What about the Red Heart?" said Hawk. "Is he there with them? Or has he done a vanishing act like the Green Man?"

"I don't know," said Raven. "I can't See him. I've never been able to See either of them."

"Well?" said Hawk, looking at King Rufus. "It's your decision. Your majesty."

"This is what I always wanted," the King said slowly. "To be a real King, leading his forces out to battle, in a struggle that really mattered . . . My dream has finally come true. And it's a nightmare."

"Father?" said Richard.

King Rufus' head came up. "Time to go," he said. "Stop the Unreal in the Forest, before they can spread out, and stamp them into the ground. Every last one of them."

"Sounds like a plan to me," said Hawk.

"Damn right," said Roland the Headless Axeman. "This is what I've spent decades training people for."

"It's been a while since I killed a monster," said Lily Peck demurely. "But I'm sure it'll come back to me. It's the kind of thing one should do now and again, just to keep one's hand in."

"These are your tutors at the Academy?" King Rufus said quietly to Hawk. "No wonder so many of your students pass with honours. They're probably afraid not to."

"You have no idea," said Hawk.

"I heard that!" said Roland.

"How?" said Hawk.

"All right!" said Prince Richard, raising his voice so it echoed across the courtyard. "Stand ready! Once the gates are open, form up on me, and I'll lead you out!"

"And I'll be right there beside you," said Catherine.

"To fight against your own people?" said Richard. "I can't ask that of you."

"This is a battle against the Unreal," Catherine said steadily. "Not my soldiers. I can do this, Richard. I have to do this. You only have to look at the things out there to know my great-grandparents got rid of the Unreal for a good reason. And I will do this, Richard, no matter what you say. This is my vengeance against my father, for starting a war and then claiming it was all because of me!"

The King stepped forward, and two young men looked steadily at each other. Both of them tall and proud, warriors in the blood, in the prime of their lives.

"I can't let you do this, Richard," said the King. "It is my place to lead this army."

Everyone looked at him silently. No one moved. The King looked about him, taking in the expressions on their faces, and something hard and brittle seemed to break inside him. No one wanted to say it, but he knew anyway.

"I'd just be in the way, wouldn't I?" he said. "I haven't led men into battle in forty years and more. And for all my new strength and youth, you couldn't concentrate on what needed doing, because you'd be too busy trying to protect me. Because if the King falls in battle, it's all over. That's why William isn't out there with his army."

"It is the duty of a King to send his people out to fight," said Richard. "And it is his responsibility to remain behind, in safety, while they do it."

King Rufus nodded slowly, bitterly. He took off the great old sword, Lawgiver, and gave it back to Richard. The Prince accepted it gracefully and strapped it quickly into place. He strode forward across the courtyard, with Catherine at his side, their two bodyguards, Peter Foster and the Sombre Warrior, right there with them.

Behind them marched the Forest's greatest heroes, from the Grand Tourney. Sir Russell Hardacre, the Blademaster; the enigmatic sorcerer Dr. Strangely Weird; Hannah Hexe, a Sister of the Moon from the witches' Night Academy; Roger Zell, the wandering hero; Tom Tom Paladin, the penitent; and Stefan Solomon, the Master of the Morningstar. All great names from Forest history, ready to fight monsters to protect their home.

Then Hawk and Fisher and all their family, and all the heroes of the Academy. Roland the Headless Axeman and the witch Lily Peck, Jonas Crane the Blademaster and even the Alchemist himself, in his stained alchemical robes, bearing a backpack full of unpleasant surprises. And many more great names, and names in the making.

Richard gestured to the guards at the gates. The portcullis rose, and the drawbridge slammed down across the moat. And Prince Richard led his army out.

No horses; they'd be no use in the tightly packed trees at the edge of the Forest. Just men and women on foot, with steel in their hands and in their hearts.

Prince Christof and the Champion, Malcolm Barrett, stood together at the edge of the Forest and watched the army charge across the clearing towards them. They couldn't believe it when they first heard; they had to come out and see for themselves. They were as close to the nearest Unreal as they chose to get. Just being this near made them feel uncomfortable.

Monstrous creatures stamped and snorted on every side, and terrible forces roiled on the still air . . . but none of them left the safety of the trees to meet the coming army. They stood, and waited.

"So much for forcing them out of the Castle," said Christof. "What is the matter with these people? They haven't done one damn thing they were supposed to."

"That's how you win battles," said the Champion.

Van Fleet laughed mirthlessly. He was standing a way off, on his own. He looked lost, like a small child who'd wandered into a big boys' game. None of them had seen the Stalking Man for some time. No doubt he was out there, somewhere, among the Unreal. Who were probably more scared of him than he was of them. That great crimson creature, the Red Heart, could just be seen in the gloom among the trees, walking up and down among the Unreal, talking and laughing with them. And then he stopped suddenly, and disappeared. He reappeared abruptly before Christof and the Champion, grinning down at them.

"It's all up to you now," he said cheerfully. "The rules of the game just changed, and I must away."

He vanished again. Christof and the Champion looked quickly about them but couldn't see him anywhere.

"What?" said Christof. "*What?* He can't just do that! We were depending on him to lead the Unreal!"

"I don't think the Unreal follow anyone," said Van Fleet. "I don't think they'd do anything as human as that . . ."

"Easy, Chris," said Malcolm. "He's the Red Heart; he can do pretty much anything he feels like. Including rushing off and leaving us in the lurch. Now calm down! We don't want to look panicked in front of the troops."

"Even though we are," said Van Fleet.

"Shut up, Van! Look, Chris, neither of us ever trusted the Red Heart anyway. We're probably better off without him."

"But what are we going to do?" said Christof. "I didn't realise how much I was depending on that overgrown monster until we didn't have him anymore."

"We send the Unreal army out to fight the army that's coming," said

Malcolm. "Let them do the hard work, and soak up the punishment. Then our troops can move in afterwards and clean up what's left."

Christof nodded quickly. "Let the Unreal go out and die. It'll save us having to destroy them afterwards."

The rain had held off for as long as it could, but now it was back. A steady, driving storm, rain slamming down hard enough to bounce back from the increasingly muddy ground. The sky was dark and brooding overhead, and lightning flared, far away but drawing closer. The Forest army crossed the clearing, and no one came out to meet them. Richard finally slowed, and raised a hand, and the charge slammed to a halt, just short of the trees at the edge of the Forest. Beyond the trees there were only shadows. Some of them were moving. Prince Richard glared through the driving rain, the Princess Catherine at his side.

"Do we go in?" said Catherine. "I don't see anything."

"We go in," said Richard. But he didn't move.

"We can't just stand here," said his bodyguard Peter. "Firstly, because we're all getting soaked. More important, because we're too clear a target out here in the open."

Hawk and Fisher came forward. Hawk had his axe in his hand, Fisher had her usual sword. She hadn't drawn the Infernal Device yet. Hawk looked up, for no reason he could put a name to, and there above him, sailing on the open night sky, was a full Blue Moon. Of course. The Demon Prince was back, the Forest was full of monsters, and Wild Magic was loose in the world again. As though Hawk had never been away. As though everything he'd done had been for nothing. He looked at Fisher, at his side as always, and smiled briefly. He'd beaten back the darkness before, and in worse situations than this. If this was the third time he'd had to put his life on the line, for those he loved and the Land he cared for—well, maybe the third time would pay for all.

Once in a Blue Moon magical things happen. For good and bad.

"We have to go in," said Hawk. "It's enemy-held territory, there's Unreal creatures and a whole Redhart army waiting for us, and it's almost certainly some kind of trap . . . but we knew all that from the start."

"I wish we had a plan," said Richard. "I'd feel so much better if we had a plan."

"Of course we have a plan!" said Hawk. "Rush in and kill everything that moves that isn't us!"

"I've always liked that plan," said Fisher.

Richard sniffed loudly. "It's a constant wonder to me you've both lived as long as you have."

"Lots of people say that," said Hawk.

Richard swept Lawgiver back and forth before him, and then strode determinedly forward into the darkness of the trees, Catherine at his side, Peter and the Sombre Warrior right behind them. And everyone else followed.

It took a moment for their eyes to adjust to the gloom. There was light, popping and flaring all around them. Shimmering glows, like phosphorescence under water, and glowing eyes that darted back and forth among the concealing trees. And shafts of blue moonlight, forcing their way in from above. The rain came down heavily. The air was almost unnaturally still, and full of an almost unbearable tension. Everyone could feel the pressure of watching eyes, and the presence of unnatural things. The natural world of the Forest had been invaded by things that were not at all natural. Things that imposed their presence on the world through sheer force of will. There were uncanny sights and sounds, as a hidden army slowly came to life. The old green dream of the Forest had become a place where nightmares lived.

Heavy boots in muddy ground. Flash of light on drawn steel. Harsh breathing, and sudden nervous movements. The rain came down in walls, cutting men off from their neighbours. Everyone's senses were sharp enough to be painful. Every sound was too loud, and the scents of earth and greenery and living things were almost overpowering. Every man could hear his own heartbeat, feel it hammering in his chest. They could feel one another's presence, pressing forward into the Forest gloom. And they could sense awful things moving, in the trees up ahead. It was like walking in a different world, every movement full of meaning and menace, feeling so alive . . . Because we only ever really value things when they're about to be taken away. The Forest army moved forward, and the Unreal surged suddenly forward out of the dark to meet them.

Monsters reared up everywhere, huge and vicious things with shapes that made men sick to look at them. Ghosts lost their human shapes as their inner natures revealed themselves. There were beasts with claws and teeth, moving impossibly fast, driven on by appalling hungers. And giant creatures, big enough to push the trees aside and make the ground tremble under their impact. Some of these things had weapons, and some had magics; and some only had to look at the living to make them scream or die or go mad.

And as quickly as that, everything went to hell. Two great forces slammed together, and in a moment it was all just a mess, men and monsters fighting separately and in small groups, all of them cut off from one another, with no idea of what was happening anywhere else. The war, like all wars, had come down to just individuals, fighting for themselves. Doing whatever it took to win, or just to stay alive.

Raven the Necromancer quickly found himself separated from everyone else. There were fighting and screaming all around, and dark shapes running everywhere. The clash of steel on steel, and the chunking of sharp edges into yielding flesh. But he was left alone, standing in a small open space, surrounded by creatures that knew his name. They circled him slowly, keeping to the shadows while he stood steadily in a spotlight of shimmering blue moonlight. The shapes called out to him mockingly. Raven concentrated, focusing his emotions into a cold and deadly fury, and then he lashed out, blasting his surroundings with crackling magical energies that shattered trees into splinters and ripped through the Unreal things that threatened him. Flesh burned and exploded, and harsh screams filled the air. But when Raven finally stopped, exhausted, they were still there. Some had rebuilt their broken bodies, some had vanished and reappeared, and some had just stood their ground and soaked it all up. Because they were of the Wild Magic and he was not. His power was, and always had been, rooted in High Magic. And Raven knew . . . that wasn't going to be enough to get the job done here.

So he wiped his mouth with the back of his hand, stared defiantly out at all the gleaming inhuman eyes, and drew the Infernal Device known as Soulripper. He cried out involuntarily as the sword's presence beat on the air, and the Unreal things cried out too. They could tell there was a new power in the night. Raven shuddered with shock and disgust as the sword's essence sank into his mind and made itself at home there. It was like holding a handful of maggots that laughed and called you by name and knew every dark thing you'd ever wanted to do. Raven stood up a little straighter, as new strength and new power moved within him. He felt like he could tear down mountains, or set the whole Forest on fire, just by thinking about it. He held the long sword out before him, and its blade glowed in the gloom, bitter yellow like poisoned fruit. It wanted to be used, and he wanted to use it.

He went forward to meet the Unreal, laughing aloud. They threw themselves at him from every side, vastly strong, inhumanly fast, and he cut them all down before they could reach him. The sword cut through everything, with hardly an effort, and monstrous bodies crashed to the muddy ground and did not move again as the Infernal Device ripped the souls right out of them and threw them into the outer dark.

Jack Forester, that old and grey-haired man who had once been the Walking Man but gave it up in his search for peace, went to war again. With sad eyes and a grim smile. He walked slowly forward into the dark between the trees, feeling his age, hearing his old bones creak even as he leaned heavily on his wooden staff. He'd been left behind as the Forest army pressed on, and he was in no hurry to catch them up. Blue moonlight fell heavily between the trees, a harsh, ghastly light that somehow only made the surrounding shadows seem even darker. Jack could feel his skin smarting where the blue moonlight touched his bare face and hands.

Tall, spindly, bony figures moved forward out of the trees and the shadows to block his way. Long skull faces with pointed horns, flaring crimson eyes, and chattering teeth. Elongated hands with vicious claws. Unreal things that had no respect at all for who and what he used to be, and what he had tried to do with his life. Jack stopped and sighed. He leaned on his staff, and looked at them, and spoke softly.

"It's not too late," he said. "You can still turn back. You don't have to do this. Please. Walk away."

The creatures giggled and tittered, like insane children, and flexed their clawed hands.

"I love it when they beg," said one.

"Want to play, little thing?" said another.

"It's been such a long time since we had a chance to play with our food," said a third.

And they all laughed together again, in a sound that had no humour or humanity in it.

"All you see is an old man," said Jack. "And sometimes, I feel it. But I am still the Walking Man, with all his strength and protections. I gave it up, because I thought I wasn't worthy of it anymore. Apparently the choice was never mine to make. But even that isn't going to be enough here, is it? This is no fight, or battle; this is war. And so I must use a weapon of war. Don't look to me for mercy. You brought this on yourself."

"Talks too much," said one of the bony creatures. "Hurt it. Kill it."

Jack threw aside his wooden staff, as though saying goodbye to an old friend. And then he reached over his shoulder, and his hand closed around the leather-wrapped hilt waiting for him. The bony things cried out in a single horrified voice as Jack drew the Infernal Device known as Black-howl. Its presence beat on the air like the wings of some trapped giant bird. The sword's essence fell upon Jack like a terrible shadow, cutting him off from the Light he'd always served. Power thundered within him, and he felt young again. The long blade was as black as its name, a length of im-penetrable shadow, like a piece cut out of the night. The Unreal creatures backed away from it, and Jack went after them.

The sword howled but made no sound. The voice of the Infernal De-vice known as Blackhowl was an inner thing. A torment to the mind, and the soul. An everlasting howl of hatred and malice. The tall and bony creatures fell to their knees, crying out and weeping, their clawed hands sinking into their own heads as they tried to block out the awful sound. The voice of the sword was terrible and unforgiving. It didn't bother Jack. He gloried in it. The bony creatures knelt helplessly before him and begged him to kill them. And he did. He swept the long blade back and forth, cutting easily through their misshapen bodies. He killed them all and walked on, with a smile on his lips that no one who knew him would have recognised.

Hawk and Fisher fought back to back, cutting and thrusting with skills and tricks and martial experience gathered the hard way, over far too long a time. They'd always been good with a blade, but their strangely extended lives had made them incredibly good. Nothing they met could stand before them. They parried swords and dodged spells, and nothing that came at them out of the dark was monstrous or powerful enough to slow or stop them for a moment. They'd seen it all before, and worse. Hawk and Fisher stamped and skidded through thick mud, only partly diluted with spilled blood and guts, and nothing could touch them. They had spent a lifetime fighting side by side, and knew each other's moves and reactions like they knew their own.

But no matter how many Unreal creatures they killed, there were always more. And a sudden rush of leaping, flailing things, like monstrous stick insects with terrible barbed flails, overran them and forced them apart . . . and before she knew it, Fisher was on her own. She called out to Hawk, even while she fought off terrible odds, and heard his voice, somewhere out in the dark, but she couldn't see him anywhere. She moved quickly to put her back against a tree, so nothing could come at her from behind. Men and monsters raged back and forth all round her, fighting and screaming and dying.

The insect things leapt and jumped before her, approaching and drawing back, wanting to kill her but warned off by inhuman instincts. Their long, empty faces had huge compound eyes and twitching antennae. Their desire to kill and rend and feast was obvious, and somehow Fisher knew that when she was dead, and they'd finished with her, the insects would lay their eggs in her, to grow and hatch out in their own time. It was the insect way. Fisher grimaced with horror, and put her sword away. It wasn't going to be enough. She knew how bad it was going to be, but she didn't hesitate; she just reached behind her shoulder and drew the Infernal Device known as Belladonna's Kiss. And showed it to the insect things.

And they fell down before her and worshipped it.

Fisher felt the sword slip in among her thoughts, insinuating itself into her soul, and it felt like some old and long-forgotten part of her woke up to embrace it. For that was always the true horror of wielding an Infernal Device. It didn't possess you; it seduced you. Fisher held the long blade out before her, and it shone in the blue moonlight like the rotten glow of corruption, of things dying slowly and horribly.

The insect things wriggled forward with a terrible eagerness, pushing their empty faces into the thick mud in supplication, bowing down to the sword and the small thing that wielded it. Their instincts told them to run, but their hearts pulled them forward. The sword made them want to die, and to love it as it killed them.

Fisher cut down all the insect things with brief, economical blows; and then she moved on, to see what else there was to kill.

There were ghosts everywhere now: shining, shimmering, insubstantial forms . . . solid enough to strike out and wound and kill at one moment and then drift away like mist the next. They could jump out on their prey through solid things, passing right through trees or men or monsters. And some of them laughed and some of them cried, and some of them, driven mad by long years of loss and loneliness, shouted things that made no sense at all. They fought because they were Unreal, and because King William had been given dominion over them. He sent them out of Castle Midnight, out to war, and so they went. They envied every man who fell, for his complete and uncomplicated death. For an end to the obligations of the living world. Sometimes they would stop, to dance and caper in the blue moonlight, in old dances and styles that no one else remembered. And sometimes they sat down in the middle of everything, put their hands to their faces, and cried, and the tears would drip through their hands.

A group of them fell on Hawk, ravenous as wolves, attracted by the vitality that blazed within him, wanting it for themselves. They made their hands hard, so they could tear it out of him. They thought his axe was just an axe. They cried out in horror as he cut them down, the gleaming steel blade shearing through their shimmering forms, destroying them and driving them from this world forever. Because the High Warlock had made that axe to cut through anything. Hawk moved on as the last of the ghosts faded away, silently screaming. He was looking for monsters to kill, calling out to Fisher and getting no reply.

Prince Richard fought his way forward, staying always at the front of his army, forcing his way slowly deeper into the trees. Cutting down everything that rose up against him, with the great old sword Lawgiver. Doing all that was necessary, but no more, conserving his strength for the battles to come. Because for every monstrous thing he killed, there were always others to take their place, more vicious and more horrible than the ones before. He fought righteously, and he did not flinch, and he did not turn away. Because he was a Prince, and it was his job to inspire those who followed him. A part of him would have liked to have been scared, but he didn't have the time.

He'd been separated from the Princess Catherine early on, but his old friend and bodyguard Peter Foster was still there at his back, stubbornly refusing to be forced away. Defending his Prince from all those threats he never saw. Richard never knew how many times Peter saved his life, or how many wounds his old friend took, putting himself between Richard and attacks intended for him. Peter was cut, and torn, and horribly wounded, and blood dripped steadily from him, but he would not fall. Not while his Prince and friend needed him. He suffered hurt after hurt, injuries small and large, and would not cry out, for fear it would distract Prince Richard from what he needed to do. Peter gritted his teeth and struck out doggedly with his sword, cutting and killing what he could. Putting his body and his life between his old friend and all the things that would kill him. He left a long, bloody trail behind him, but still he would not fall.

The Sombre Warrior strode ahead of the Princess Catherine, cutting a path through the enemy for her to follow. It was what he did best. He swung his great sword with both hands, and the force of his terrible blows sent dead things flying this way and that, dead before they even hit the ground. He sheared right through massive creatures, gutted some and beheaded others. And those that got past his blade found that their claws and fangs made no mark on his heavy armour. They came at him in waves, and they could not slow or stop him. When the press of fighting eased, the

Sombre Warrior would cut through overhanging branches, or lesser trees, to open up a trail for others to follow. The creatures of the Unreal came at him in wave after wave, and broke against him.

Catherine stuck close behind the Warrior, using him as her shield, striking out at anything that tried to come at him through his blind spots. She was doing what she could with her Blood Magic, her elemental command of the air, but in the dark and the confusion, and the constant shifting of men and monsters fighting around her, there was a limit to what she could usefully do. There was never time for her to stop and concentrate without leaving the Sombre Warrior's back unguarded. So she stuck with him, and defended him, and killed anything that got too close.

Gillian Forester found herself fighting alone very early on, but she was used to that. In fact, she preferred it. She always felt better when she had no one to worry about but herself. She grew a long silver blade from the Cestus, that ancient gauntlet from the depths of the Armoury. It glared supernaturally bright in the gloom, as though it was cutting through the dark itself. She strode steadily forward, and though the long blade felt eerily light in her hand, still it cut through anything that dared stand against her, as though it had the weight of the world behind it. Gillian cut down one awful thing after another, and laughed at how easy it was.

She was still careful to conserve her energy. First lesson she taught her students: save your strength for when you'll need it. And while she was in excellent shape for a woman of her age, she was still a woman of her age. She whirled about with vicious, controlled cuts and parries, pacing herself. Because there was still so much to be done. The Unreal felt no such reservations. They came howling out of the trees from everywhere at once, hitting her from every side at once, and the sheer pressure of numbers overwhelmed her. They ran right over her, dragging her to the ground.

Gillian rolled back and forth in the thick mud, flailing about her with her Cestus sword. The rain was pounding down harder than ever, filling her eyes and blinding her, running down her wrinkled cheeks like tears. Claws raked her flesh, and blood spurted. Teeth closed on one shoulder and shook her roughly, even as she cried out from the pain despite herself. Gillian stabbed and cut with her silver sword, but there were just too many of them. She couldn't even force herself back to her knees. And then a great jagged blade came slamming down out of nowhere and chopped clean through her wrist, above the silver gauntlet.

Her hand jumped away, bouncing and sliding across the muddy Forest floor. She could see it, on the other side of the trail. The blade sank back into the Cestus, and it was just a gauntlet again. The fingers slowly opened, and were still. Gillian looked blankly at the blood jetting furiously from the stump of her wrist. She had time to think a single word, *Cursed*, before the massive sword came driving down again, and slammed through her heart, pinning her to the earth. Her head went back, and she looked up into the night sky, through the towering trees, and cursed the Blue Moon with her last breath.

The monsters tore her to pieces.

Jack saw his sister fall but couldn't get to her in time. It seemed like every monster in the Forest was deliberately blocking his way. He hacked a path through them, Blackhowl's awful voice either scattering them or freezing them in place so he could kill them easily; but when he finally got there, and killed the last few things feeding on the torn-up body, he already knew it was too late. Jack sank to his knees beside what was left of his sister. They hadn't reached her face yet. It was all he had left to recognise her by. He thought she still looked defiant, even in death.

Not far away, he saw the shining silver gauntlet, the Cestus, lying in the mud. He wondered numbly if it had been the old curse that killed Gillian, or just the cold, hard fact that when an army goes to war, some are going to die. He doubted he'd ever know. But it still didn't seem fair. Gillian, his sister. Daughter of the legendary Prince Rupert and Princess Julia. She'd done so much to make her own legend, to be her own person. He tried to remember the last time he told her he loved her, and how proud he'd always been of her, but he couldn't. All those years in the monastery, and then . . . they'd just been so busy. He started to pray over her, and then stopped. He was in no fit state of grace, as long as he carried Blackhowl. He looked at the Infernal Device, still nestled in his hand, shoved it point first into the muddy ground, and used the length of the blade to force himself up to his feet again. His knees creaked loudly, and his back ached.

The Infernal Device might make him feel young, but that was just another of its lies.

He didn't care. He would avenge his sister, and drown the Unreal in their own blood before he let himself rest.

He looked around, slowly, as he realised that though the fighting was still going on around him, no men or monsters were coming anywhere near. And then Jack tensed, and his head came up, as Leland Dusque the Stalking Man stepped out of the shadows to face him.

Blackhowl's terrible cry had fallen away to a sulky murmur in the back of Jack's head, as he knelt beside his dead sister; but now it began to sing loudly again, anticipating a most satisfying kill. Jack deliberately forced the sword back into its scabbard, cutting off the awful sound. The sword didn't like that, but Jack didn't care. He had always been his own man.

"I knew it," said the Stalking Man. "You just don't have it in you, do you, to kill your own son. But I have no problem at all with killing you."

"Then do it," said Jack. "If that's what it takes, if that's what you need . . . to find peace at last. To be able to lay down your burden of being the Stalking Man. Go on; kill me. I'm not going to fight you. I'm an old man; I can give my last few years to you. One last gift, from father to son."

Dusque stepped forward, his sword glowing in the gloom. Someone's blood dripped thickly from the blade. His face was twisted with emotion, his eyes wild. He drew back the sword for the killing thrust. Jack stood calmly, at peace with himself.

Their eyes met.

"You think I won't kill you?" Dusque said loudly. "That Heaven's protections will keep you safe from Hell's power?"

"I don't think Heaven or Hell have any place in this," said Jack. "This isn't about the Walking Man, or the Stalking Man. This is just a moment, in the middle of a war, between father and son. Perhaps this is what we should have done long ago. It's all right, boy. Do it. And then maybe I can finally tell your mother how sorry I have always been that I wasn't there for her."

Leland Dusque thrust his sword deep into the ground, and let go. It stood upright, quivering. Dusque shook his head, his whole body shaking. Because for all he was, and all he'd done, he still couldn't kill his father.

"Give it up, son, like I did," said Jack. "Neither your office nor mine were ever meant to be for life. Just for as long as we needed them."

"You don't understand," said Dusque. "The promises I made to Hell . . . I've done things. Bad things . . ."

"You think I haven't?" said Jack. "That's what penance is for. Why do you think I spent twenty bloody years in a monastery?"

"Hell will never give me up."

"It only ever had the power over you that you gave it. Walk away. Like I did. Service can only ever be by choice."

"And then what?" said Dusque.

Jack laughed briefly, and gestured at the battles raging around them with a wave of his hand. "I think we can probably find something useful to do. Don't you?"

Dusque nodded quickly. "Never did like William. Nasty little man." He came forward and looked down at the dead body in the mud. "Is that . . . ?"

"Yes. Your aunt Gillian. She fought well."

"She was a warrior. She probably would have hated to die in bed . . ."

Jack gave a quick bark of laughter. "You really didn't know your aunt! She would have most definitely preferred to die in bed, preferably after a really big meal, a decent brandy, and a romp with some man far too young for her."

They both smiled. Jack drew his sword, and Dusque pulled his sword out of the ground. And together, side by side, they went off to find some monsters to kill.

"What the hell was that Leland Dusque nonsense for, anyway?" said Jack. "I gave you a perfectly good name: Matthew."

"You can't be a Stalking Man and a terror in the world with a name like Matthew, Father. No one would take you seriously."

"Remind me to introduce you to Gillian's son, Raven, when this is all over," said Jack.

"What? The Necromancer? You mean Raven isn't his real name?"

"Of course not. It's Nathanial."

"You see! My point exactly!"

• • •

Jack's daughter, Mercy, went dancing through the Forest in her Sir Kay armour, her long blonde hair all aglow in the night, swinging her sword with both hands, darting in to kill an Unreal thing, and then jumping back and moving quickly on. She was fast and deadly, a delightful angel with a cutting edge, and nothing could touch her. Some things tried to run from her, and she cut them down anyway, from behind. Mercy had spent most of her life training to be a warrior, much of it in secret, and now she was free to break loose at last. It felt good, so good. She laughed and sang and danced as she killed. As much a monster as the things she moved among.

The heroes of the Forest Land fought well and bravely. Sometimes that was enough. And sometimes it wasn't.

Sir Russell Hardacre, the aristocratic Blademaster, strolled casually among the Unreal, cutting them down left and right with hardly any effort, stepping over the bodies of the fallen to kill some more. Doing what he was born to do, and loving every moment of it. Until an arrow hit him in the back of the neck and he fell forward, face-first, into the mud.

Dr. Strangely Weird, in his flowing, coloured robes, walked in glory through the carnage, unnatural energies spitting and sparking on the air around him. And wherever he turned his gaze, howling creatures melted and ran away like candle wax.

Roger Zell, who had wandered so far in search of what it meant to be a hero, moved quietly from shadow to shadow, darting out to kill before disappearing again. He preferred winning to grandstanding.

Hannah Hexe, once a member in good standing at the Night Academy, walked through the trees doing loathsome things, and blood and screams and horror went with her. The Sisters of the Moon had been quite right to throw her out.

Tom Tom Paladin strode steadily forward, cutting a path through the monstrosities that tried to block his way, not even trying to defend himself. He had so much penance to do. It was almost a relief to him when the Unreal dragged him down through sheer force of numbers and put an end to his pain.

Stefan Solomon never even saw the creature that took his head off from behind.

. . .

A running battle between Forest soldiers and a pack of wolf things swept Catherine away from Richard, carrying her and the Sombre Warrior along with them. By the time the two of them had fought free, she couldn't even see Richard and Peter any longer. She cried out, but there was no answer, and a sudden rage blazed up within her as she lost her temper, one more time. She summoned up the Wild Magic in her Blood, and a great storm raced through the Forest, a massive blast of air like a battering ram, that ripped trees up by the roots and threw them every-where. Great clouds of splinters flew through the air like shrapnel, piercing every living thing in her path. The raging winds picked up monsters and tore them limb from limb, and threw the pieces away. It was her blind rage, manifested in an intangible force that could not be stopped, that destroyed everything before her. She fought back at the world that threatened her and those she loved, pounding it with her elemental magic until it broke.

The anger fell away, and Catherine stood exhausted in an empty clear-ing, breathing hard, surrounded by the broken and splintered remains of trees, and the dead and dying remains of Unreal creatures. She looked about her, and slowly realised she couldn't see the Sombre Warrior any-where. She went looking for him, and found him some distance away, where the winds of her rage had carried him. He was standing with his back against a huge, unbroken wide-trunked tree. She ran up to him, and then stopped abruptly, as she saw the blood-smeared branch protruding from his chest. Her rage had sent him flying through the air and slammed him against the tree, and a branch had punched right through his armour. It was only the branch that was holding him up. The impact had knocked his helmet off, and she could see his bare face. Horribly, he was still alive.

She moved slowly forward, trembling with shock. It wasn't until she felt the wetness on her cheeks that she realised she was crying. She stood before him, and his eyes saw her. He tried to smile. Blood came out of his mouth.

"I'm sorry," said Catherine. "Oh God, I'm so sorry."

"We all tried to warn you . . . about your temper," said the Warrior.

She grabbed one of his hands, and held it in both of hers, but it was obvious he couldn't feel it.

"You should have chosen someone better to give your service to," she said. "Can you tell me your name now, sir Warrior? Please?"

But he was dead, his eyes looking past her at whatever it is only the dead can see. Catherine let go of his hand, and it dropped back to his side. She turned away. Whoever the Sombre Warrior was, or might have been, originally, that man was gone. He was a legend, now and forever.

Catherine walked on through the trees, calling out for Richard. A coldly focused anger moved along in the air ahead of her, striking out at any Unreal thing that dared draw near.

Chappie the dog got separated from everyone almost immediately, and he chased back and forth, taking on anything that didn't have the sense to run away. He was still a huge and powerful animal, for all his age and grey fur, and blood dripped steadily from his powerful jaws. Until finally, somewhat to his surprise, he got so far ahead of everyone else that he found himself back in the recently cut clearing where Hawk had duelled with Prince Cameron, and he had killed General Staker. Chappie shrugged, and then stopped and looked around him, sniffing suspiciously at the air. He was not alone. In fact, he was surrounded.

Chappie growled menacingly, whipping his great head back and forth, but wherever he looked the Unreal looked back. All kinds of creatures stepped slowly out of the trees and into the clearing, watching him with all kinds of glowing, inhuman eyes. Chappie turned this way and that, showing off his great teeth, snarling continuously.

"Why do you fight us?" said one of the creatures, a silver-grey wolf thing, easily twice the size of the dog. "After all, you're not like them. You're one of us. An Unreal creature, fashioned from Wild Magic, that just happens to look like a dog."

"I am a dog," said Chappie. "And I'm nothing like you."

"Join us."

"Never!"

"You're not like them, and you never will be," said the wolf thing. "No matter how long you live, or how much you pretend."

"Of course I'm not like them," said Chappie. "I'm a dog! I'm better than them! That's why I have to look after them."

The Unreal creatures surged forward into the clearing, pressing forward from every side at once, and Chappie went happily forward to meet them, to tear and bite at them, one old dog with fire in his heart, fighting for those he loved.

Raven the Necromancer found himself face-to-face with the sorcerer Van Fleet. They both looked rather ragged by now, their once impressive robes tattered and torn and stained with blood. Some of it their own. They advanced slowly on each other, like two scarecrows sent out to duel as champions, and men and monsters alike took one look at them and went somewhere else to do their fighting.

Raven and Van Fleet stopped, facing each other, a respectful distance apart. Raven like a piece of the night in his black tatters, the Infernal Device Soulripper in his hand, straining to be used. Van Fleet, in the ragged remains of his wildly coloured peacock robes, barely restrained magics spitting and crackling on the air around him. Van Fleet smiled suddenly at Raven.

"I've been looking for you, Necromancer. I've got a special spell, carefully researched and designed just to put an end to you."

He jabbed a stubby finger at Raven, while mouthing a Word so powerful it shook the sorcerer like a rag doll, and a terrible force existed in the world. Just for a moment. And then it vanished, quite suddenly, unable to find anything to hang on to. Raven was still standing where he had been, entirely unmoved and unaffected. Van Fleet gaped at him.

"That's not possible. That's just not possible! That spell was specially designed to strip you of every Necromantic spell and power source you have! I spent weeks on it. It can't have failed!"

"Well, technically speaking, it didn't," said Raven. "But unfortunately for you, I'm not a Necromancer, and never have been. I know nothing of the magic of murder and death. Never even dabbled in such things. It was all just an act. A performance I put on, to build up my reputation. I'm really just a High Magic sorcerer. Like you."

"But you made the dead sit up and talk!" said Van Fleet almost hysterically. "Everyone saw you!"

"You all saw what I wanted you to see. I moved the dead bodies around with my mind, and did all the voices myself. Just said what people expected to hear, backed up by some careful research . . . A little manipulation here, some throwing of the voice there, and everyone saw what my reputation made them expect to see. People can be very gullible. Come on, Van; you didn't really think that a grandson of Prince Rupert and Princess Julia would sell his soul in return for murder magic, did you?"

"All a trick," Van Fleet said numbly. "All an act, all this time . . ." Suddenly he glared at Raven. "I have other spells! Other magics!"

"And I have an Infernal Device," said Raven.

The two men looked at each other for a long moment. And then Raven lowered his sword and leaned on it.

"Really, Van," said Raven. "You're as fed up with this as I am, aren't you? Neither of us ever intended for things to get this far out of hand. We're sorcerers, research scholars, not fighters. You didn't want the Unreal back in Castle Midnight, never mind loose in the world."

"How did you know that?"

"Because I know you're not stupid."

"All right, maybe I'm not happy with the way things have worked out," said Van Fleet. "Maybe I never wanted this. But what can I do?"

"Work with me," said Raven, "and help shut it all down."

He grinned at Van Fleet, and after a moment the sorcerer grinned back. Raven forced the Infernal Device back into its scabbard, against its will, and then the two men walked through the Forest, striking out with their magics. And wherever they looked, the Unreal creatures dropped in their tracks, disappearing back to whatever place King William had summoned them from.

Roland the Headless Axeman and Witch in Residence Lily Peck moved steadily through the trees, leading the staff and students of the Hero Academy into battle. Swords and axes and bows did their work, and all kinds of magic danced on the air, doing appalling things to appalling creatures. Some caught fire, some exploded, and some crashed to the ground so the swords and axes could chop them up like firewood.

The Alchemist walked abroad, smiling unpleasantly, throwing nasty chemical surprises this way and that, while a young man who could work miracles moved slowly and quietly among the wounded, bringing them back from the shores of death. The staff and students of the Hawk and Fisher Memorial Academy showed what they were made of, what they had been trained to do, and frightened the crap out of everything they encountered.

Roland swung his great axe with indefatigable skill, felling everything that came within reach. He cut off heads, and limbs, and hacked his way through whole packs of unnatural creatures. Blood soaked his armour, but none of it was his. Lily Peck walked calmly beside him, looking about her in a thoughtful sort of way, and the world adjusted itself according to her will, becoming a place where the Unreal could not exist. Things faded away, screaming in rage and horror.

But every time, it took a little more out of her, and moment by moment she grew steadily older and more frail. Using up the years of her life to power her magic.

Roland stopped, for a moment, to look at her. "You never told me."

"You never asked," said Lily Peck. "Just as I never asked about you."

They moved on through the trees, leading the way. Because there was more than one kind of hero in the Hero Academy.

The Unreal was thrown back, defeated and destroyed, until finally what was left turned and ran, or just disappeared back to Castle Midnight. Half scared out of their wits, runner after runner reported the bad news to Prince Christof and the Champion in the Redhart command tent. Soon enough, Christof had no choice but to order his Redhart soldiers into battle, to take the place of the Unreal and fight the Forest force head-on.

It was what the soldiers had been waiting for. They charged forward, fresh and vital, waving their swords and axes and howling Redhart battle cries. They advanced in disciplined ranks, from their carefully chosen and prepared positions, and the Forest forces had no choice but to fall back. They'd come back together to destroy the last patches of the Unreal, but weakened and exhausted, they were no match for the Redhart army. They fell back to the edge of the trees, and then out into the clearing itself, and there they regrouped and made their stand. Setting up a wall of steel and magic and simple courage between Forest Castle and the army that threatened it.

The Redhart soldiers burst out of the last trees, saw what was waiting for them, and stopped to consider. And wait for fresh orders. They hesitated, holding their position in the last few trees at the edge of the clearing. And that was when the dragon appeared in the sky overhead, flying swiftly and strongly under the Blue Moon. A magical creature, at home in the magical night. He cupped his great membranous wings to bring himself to a halt, and then he plunged down, heading straight for the Redhart positions. The soldiers cried out in shock and alarm, and some of them turned to flee, but it was already too late. The dragon opened his great jaws, and a sea of flames struck the Redhart soldiers. The flames burned them all up as the dragon flew over the massed ranks, incinerating them in a moment, washed over by flames more fierce and more terrible than any natural fire. The whole of the Redhart army went up in flames, and fell, and burned. Hundreds, thousands, of bodies, blackened and shrivelled.

The dragon soared up into the sky again, and the flames sank down and disappeared, unable to exist without his presence. The trees at the edge of the clearing were scorched and half consumed, with dark smoke rising up into the blue moonlight, but the flames did not spread, and the Forest did not burn.

The dragon banked around, and then dropped out of the sky to land softly and carefully in the clearing, not far from the Forest force. Who, to their credit, did not flinch. Hawk and Fisher went forward to meet the dragon. No one else felt like going with them. The stench of burned meat was heavy on the night air.

"What took you so long?" said Hawk.

"It's all in the timing," said the dragon. "I may have allowed myself to become . . . a little preoccupied."

"I won't ask," said Fisher,

"Best not to," agreed the dragon.

"Did you really have to . . . ?" said Hawk.

"Yes," said the dragon. "So you wouldn't have to. This war is over now. That's all that matters."

Prince Christof and the Champion Malcolm Barrett stepped out of the trees, some way farther down from all the dead bodies, and walked out across the clearing. They kept their hands carefully away from the swords at their sides. Prince Richard and Princess Catherine went forward to meet them. They were all equally grim-faced.

And that was when King Rufus appeared. He came striding across the drawbridge over the moat and into the clearing, and everyone stopped and turned to look. They knew he was there before he appeared, because they could feel the presence on the night of the great and awful thing he carried in his hand. He held it out before him, blazing bloodred in the gloom, beating on the night like some awful ancient heart. The Crimson Pursuant. The Jewel of Compulsion. Everyone there could feel its influence, the sheer naked power just waiting to be used.

King Rufus stopped, and called Prince Richard and Princess Catherine, Prince Christof and the Champion, forward to stand before him. They did so. They had no choice. Hawk and Fisher went too; not because they had to, but because they weren't going to be left out of anything. The dragon lay curled in a great circle, watching it all with marvellous disdain. Some of those watching stirred restlessly, and looked like they wanted to do . . . something. But this was an old power, power out of legend, and no one wanted to mess with it. King Rufus smiled slowly on those he had called before him.

"In the presence of the Crimson Pursuant, you can speak only truth," he said. "Catherine, do you love my son, Richard? Do you stay here by your own choice, of your own free will?"

"Yes," said Catherine, looking at Malcolm.

The Champion nodded, slowly. He looked like he'd been hit. He knew that what he was hearing had to be the truth.

"Take her," he said to Richard. "She's yours." *I don't want her anymore,* he wanted to say, but he couldn't.

King Rufus lowered his hand and put the glowing jewel into his pocket. The crimson light disappeared, and in that moment all compulsion disappeared. Everyone could feel it. The two princes stirred slowly, as though waking from a dream.

"This war should never have happened," Rufus said steadily to Christof. "No one wanted it. Except your father, for reasons none of us have ever understood. I see no reason to continue fighting just to serve an old fool's will."

Christof nodded jerkily. He didn't look back at all his Redhart dead, most of them burned beyond recognition. He didn't need to; the night was still full of the stench of burned meat. He felt sick, and shaken to his core.

"This isn't what I signed on for," he said. "To hell with it all. Let's give the Peace agreement another chance." He looked abruptly at Catherine. "Stay here, Sister. If this is what you really want."

"What about Redhart's honour?" said Malcolm Barrett.

"It isn't worth this much slaughter," said Christof.

"There are as many Forest dead in those trees as Redhart soldiers," Richard said. "Let it go. It's over."

The Champion nodded slowly, and turned away.

And then, just as Peace was breaking out, the Red Heart and the Green Man appeared out of nowhere. Huge and towering, they came striding across the clearing, side by side, smiling unpleasantly. King Rufus snatched the Crimson Pursuant out of his pocket, but before he could use it, or even say a word, the two great figures slammed to a halt and disappeared. Gone in a moment, replaced by a single dark and very familiar figure. A tall, bone white, almost human thing, wrapped in scraps of darkness, with two glowing eyes peering out from under its wide-brimmed hat. The Demon Prince, every bit as legend described him.

He resembled a man, but his features were blurred, and he was slender to the point of emaciation. He looked like a man because it amused him to do so. He had looked like other things before, and might again, but for now he moved in the world of men. He smiled horribly, and men turned their faces away. He was the Demon Prince, and he was compelled by his nature to terrify.

Hawk and Fisher moved quickly forward, to put themselves between everyone else and the Lord of the Darkwood. The full Moon above was very Blue.

"I thought you said you could only live inside people now?" said Hawk.

"I lied," said the Demon Prince, in a happy, hateful voice. "I do that. And I do like to spread a little distrust wherever I go. Appearing as the Green Man and the Red Heart allowed me to manipulate the Kings of both Courts, by giving them both what they thought they wanted. I have always been well served by traitors. And look at what I have done! Two great thrones set at each other's throat; the Unreal returned, and Wild Magic loosed in the world one more time! Look up in the sky; have you ever seen such a Blue Moon? Here I am again . . . One last chance to make Wild Magic triumphant in the world of men!" The Demon Prince grinned broadly, showing his sharp teeth. "The Darkwood shall return, men shall become demons, and the long night will never end . . ."

"You've left it a bit late," said Hawk, doing everything he could to sound calm and composed. "The war is over."

"The war was only ever a distraction," said the Demon Prince. "So I could get my hands on what I really wanted."

He gestured at King Rufus, with a clawed dead white hand, and the Crimson Pursuant tore itself out of the King's grasp and sped across the air to slap into the Demon Prince's waiting hand. And King Rufus sank to his knees, as all the strength and all the years went out of him. He cried out in shock and horror, as old age slammed down upon him again. His body shrivelled in upon itself, his hair became grey and his face wrinkled; and his eyes had just enough sense left in them to stare at the Demon Prince in betrayal.

"Oh, don't look at me like that, Rufus," said the Demon Prince. "I promised you all the strength you'd need, until the war was over. Remember? To be paid for . . . with all the remaining years of your life. Well, time's up! Time to pay the piper. The war is over; and I win. I never needed you; I only wanted this jewel. You could have used it to win the war, and have absolute control over every living thing, but you humans always did think small. I couldn't touch the Crimson Pursuant as long as the Lady of the Lake had it, with all the strength of the Land behind her. And I couldn't reach it while it was still inside the Forest Castle, behind all those layers of protection. But you brought it outside, Rufus! And now it's mine."

"How?" said Fisher. "How are you even here? We sent you back to Reverie and destroyed you there!"

"So you did," said the Demon Prince. "You destroyed the part of me that was there, and very unpleasant it was. But I had left a small part of me behind. Sent back into the past, hidden inside two Standing Stones—my anchors, so that I would always have a way back."

"Why is the jewel so important to you?" said Hawk.

"Playing for time, are we?" said the Demon Prince. "To buy you time, to come up with some desperate last plan? Well, I don't mind. I've waited long enough for this, and I want to savour it. You must remember, I was summoned into this world by King John and his Astrologer, using the power of the Crimson Pursuant. They brought me here, and so only they can ever fully expel me. And unfortunately for all of you, they're both dead!"

"Why summon Fisher and me back here?" said Hawk.

"What joy would there be in my triumph," said the Demon Prince, "if you two weren't here to see it? And now I will use the jewel to bind you all to my will. I shall rule the long night forever, under an eternal Blue Moon, and you will all live in torment for all time as my slaves, in a nightmare that will never end."

"You always did love the sound of your own voice," said the Lady of the Lake.

Everyone looked round sharply, to see her standing just to one side, dripping over everything. She strode forward, heavy tides running back and forth in her watery body. And walking beside her, Sir Jasper the ghost, looking confused but determined. He looked very focused, very solid. He managed a quick, reassuring smile for Catherine, and then glared at the Demon Prince. Who looked the Lady of the Lake and Sir Jasper over thoughtfully, as they came to a halt before him.

"A water elemental and a ghost," he said. "No, I don't see how this is going to work. You cannot hope to stop me, not while I hold the jewel."

"That's not who we are," said the Lady of the Lake.

"I remember," said Sir Jasper, staring steadily at the Demon Prince. "I remember, finally, who I was. I'm not Sir Jasper; never was. It was the letter J on the tombstone that spoke to me, that seemed familiar. And I was so desperate for a name . . . But no. I'm not Jasper; I'm John. King John of the Forest Land. Though it took the woman who was my wife, Queen Eleanor, to remind me."

Lady and ghost smiled at each other fondly for a moment.

"No," said the Demon Prince. "No. You can't be! You're dead!"

"That's right," said the ghost. "Eleanor died, to become Lady of the

Lake, protector of the Forest Land. And when I felt the need for penance, she made it possible for me to remain here, in her arms, for however long it took till I was needed. I died, but I remained. I waited all these years for you, Demon Prince."

"But I have the Jewel of Compulsion!" shrieked the Demon Prince. He thrust the blazing jewel in the ghost's face.

And Hawk stepped smartly forward and lashed out with his axe. The blade the High Warlock made, that could cut through anything. It sheared through the Demon Prince's wrist, and his hand fell away with the jewel still in it. The hand dissipated into curls of black mist, and the ghost grabbed the jewel out of midair. The Demon Prince looked on numbly as King John nodded to Hawk.

"Thank you, my boy. I can always rely on you to save the day at the very last moment."

"Anytime," said Hawk.

The ghost turned to the Demon Prince. He held up his hand, as solid as any other, and the Jewel of Compulsion blazed very brightly.

"And now, as one who summoned you here in the first place, with all the authority of a King of the Forest Land, I banish you from this world."

The Demon Prince screamed, but already the sound was fading, becoming distant, as he fell away in a direction none of them could follow and was gone. The light changed. Everyone looked up. The moon in the sky was no longer blue.

ELEVEN

....

OUT OF HISTORY AND INTO LEGEND ONE LAST TIME

King Rufus was dead. He looked like he'd been dead for some time. Lying broken and crumpled, like something thrown away because it was no longer needed. He looked old, much older than he should have. As though all his years had caught up with him at once. Richard knelt beside him. Catherine stood over him, her hand resting gently on Richard's shoulder. Just to make sure he knew he wasn't alone. *He looks at peace now,* Richard told himself. But all he could think of were all the things he'd meant to say to his father but never did, because he always thought there'd be more time. He wondered if there were things his father had meant to say to him. After a while, Richard stood up and called out for someone to come and carry his father back into the Castle.

The Seneschal was already on his way, leading half a dozen servants with a stretcher across the drawbridge over the moat. He nodded quickly to Prince Richard, unable to speak. He stood by, crying silently, as the servants placed the dead King on the stretcher with as much dignity and reverence as they could manage. Laurence Garner came over, to stand beside the Seneschal.

"Who are you, again?" said Garner.

"I'm the Seneschal!"

"Bless you," said Garner kindly.

He smiled at the Seneschal, and after a moment the Seneschal smiled back, briefly. Walking together, they followed their King back into the Castle one last time.

Richard watched them go. He would have liked to cry, but he had too much on his mind, too much still to do. He told himself he'd cry later, when he was alone, when he had time. He put an arm around Catherine's shoulders, and she slipped an arm round his waist, and they stood together as close as they could get.

"The King is dead," said Catherine. "Long live King Richard."

"No," said Richard. "I think . . . I've had enough of Kings, and all they lead to. I think perhaps . . . I'd like to put this all behind me. And put myself forward at the next election, to become the new First Minister. How would you feel about that?"

Catherine considered it. "I could live with that," she said finally. "As long as I get to be First Wife."

"Peregrine de Woodville will go absolutely mental when he hears," said Richard.

"Best reason I can think of for doing it," said Catherine.

She looked out across the crowded clearing. There were people everywhere. The Forest fighters, the force from the Hero Academy, and some people still trickling in from the Forest, from both sides, who'd been far enough away to avoid the dragon's conflagration.

"Where's Sir Jasper?" said Catherine. "Sorry, I mean King John? I don't see him anywhere, or the Lady of the Lake."

"They've gone," said Hawk, as he and Fisher moved forward to join them. "Disappeared right after the Demon Prince did."

"We saw them go," said Fisher. "I'm pretty sure it was their idea."

"Do you think they'll ever return?" said Richard.

"With my family, who can tell?" said Hawk.

Catherine looked steadily at Hawk and Fisher. "You're them, aren't you? You're Prince Rupert and Princess Julia."

"Took you long enough to work it out," said Richard. "It's not the best-kept secret I've ever encountered."

Catherine glared at him. "How long have you known?"

"Not long," Richard said quickly.

"Rupert and Julia were never here," Hawk said steadily. "This was your victory."

"I never got to say goodbye to Sir Jasper," said Catherine. "He was my friend."

"I never got to say goodbye to either of them," said Hawk. "They were my parents."

"Oh, come on!" said Fisher. "You hardly knew your mother, and you couldn't stand your father. Not surprising. He treated you appallingly."

"He was my dad," said Hawk. "Fathers and sons—it's always going to be complicated."

Raven came over to join them, along with the Redhart sorcerer, Van Fleet. Followed by Jack Forester, and the man who used to be the Stalking Man. Some rather complicated introductions followed, and then Raven took off his sheathed Infernal Device, Soulripper, and laid it deferentially but firmly at Richard's feet.

"I don't want it," he said. "Nasty thing. And far more trouble than it's worth."

"Quite right, lad," said Jack. "Couldn't agree more." And he laid down his Infernal Device, Blackhowl.

Fisher was already unbuckling the long scabbard from her back. She threw Belladonna's Kiss onto the ground with the others.

"Put them back," she said. "And let them be forgotten again."

Bertram Pettydew, the Castle Armourer, was suddenly there with them, though none of them had seen him arrive. He smiled easily about him, tall and elegant as a flamingo, peering vaguely around through his thick spectacles.

"Oh, hello! Been having a nice war then, have you? Better let me take care of these and tuck them safely away in the Armoury. Too many people saw you carry them out of the Cathedral, after all. We don't want them to go looking . . . No. I'll find some nice shadowy niche to hide them in. Until they're needed again. Because you never know, do you . . ."

He picked up the three heavy swords quite easily, hugged them to his sunken chest, and walked quite casually back into the Castle. They all watched him go.

"Strange man," said Fisher.

"Strange Armoury," said Hawk.

"He talks to fish," said Richard.

Raven took the opportunity to confront Jack. "Where is my mother, Uncle Jack? I don't see her here anywhere."

"I'm sorry, Nathanial," said Jack. He looked sadly at Hawk and Fisher too. "She didn't make it. Gillian is dead. It took a hell of a lot of those creatures to bring her down, but . . . She died honourably, fighting all the way."

"Of course she did," said Hawk.

"My little girl is dead," said Fisher. She turned away, and wouldn't allow Hawk to comfort her.

"Damn," said Raven. "I never got the chance to tell her I wasn't really a Necromancer. Just a sorcerer putting on an act."

"She would have liked that," said Jack. "She never did approve of all that dark nonsense."

Mercy arrived to join the family gathering. Her armour was a mess, soaked in barely dried blood. She limped heavily, winced when she moved, and had a great bloody wound down one side of her face, but she seemed cheerful enough, for all that. She'd already heard of Gillian's death. Jack chose that moment to introduce the man who used to be the Stalking Man.

"Mercy, this is your half brother, Matthew."

Fisher turned back, and she and Hawk both gave Jack a very hard look.

"You told us he was dead!" said Hawk.

"It was complicated," said Jack.

"So," said Fisher. "I have another grandson. That's something."

"Welcome back, Matthew," said Hawk.

He shook Matthew's hand firmly. They'd never been a touchy-feely type of family. And then Hawk and Fisher moved off to one side, for a short but intense discussion about who was related to whom, and how.

Mercy grinned easily at her new half brother, and nodded to Jack. "Will you be going back to the monastery, Father?"

"No," said Jack. "I thought my son and I might go walking through the world, and see what there is to see. We've both got a lot on our consciences, and a hell of a lot of penance to be getting on with."

"And God help the guilty," said Matthew solemnly.

Mercy turned away, quite deliberately, and smiled on Van Fleet. "Will you be going back to Redhart, sir sorcerer?"

"Not if I can help it," said Van Fleet. "There's nothing there for me now. William's lost it . . . God knows what he'd want me to do for him if I did go back. No, I always saw myself as a scholar first, and I understand Forest Castle has an excellent library."

"You're very welcome," said Richard. "We've been looking for someone to help compile a decent index."

"I think I may join you, Van," said Raven. "I've got a lot of studying to do if I'm going to make a new reputation for myself as a sorcerer."

Richard realised that Catherine had moved away from the group, and he went over to join her. She was staring coldly at the dragon, who was lying curled in a great circle. Everyone was giving him plenty of room. His eyes were shut, and two thin plumes of smoke rose up from his nostrils in perfectly straight lines. Catherine started angrily towards him. Richard took her by the arm and stopped her. She turned her glare on him, and he immediately let go of her arm.

"Don't," said Richard.

"He killed my people!"

"If he hadn't," Richard said steadily, "I would have had to do it. I would have had to order my men to kill your men. And how would you have felt about me then? The dragon stopped the war and saved a lot more men than he killed. Leave it at that."

"You think I should be grateful?" said Catherine.

"I think you should be glad we escaped something much worse," said Richard.

They both looked round sharply as Prince Christof came forward, along with the Champion Malcolm Barrett. They all bowed politely to each other. Christof and the Champion might be the only Redhart men left alive, and surrounded on all sides by those who had once been their enemies, but Christof seemed entirely calm and at ease. The Champion . . . did his best to imitate Christof.

"I was just wondering," said Prince Christof, "if you knew what had happened to the Sombre Warrior? He doesn't seem to be around . . . I did wonder if he might have taken off his helmet at last, and retired."

"I'm sorry," said Prince Richard, "but the Sombre Warrior lies among the honoured dead. Catherine saw him die."

Christof looked at her. "Did he die well, and honourably, Sister?"

"He died protecting me," said Catherine.

They could all tell there was more to it than that, but no one felt like pressing the point.

"Would you like us to send the body back to Redhart, once it's been recovered?" said Richard. "He did live most of his life in your country."

"No," said Catherine. "The Forest was his chosen home. We'll put him to rest here."

"Next to his parents?" said Richard.

"Yes," said Catherine. "He'd have liked that."

"I have no objections," said Christof. He turned his attention to Malcolm. "It's time we were going. If you have any final words to say to the Princess Catherine, you should say them now."

He looked meaningfully at Richard, who nodded stiffly in return, and the two Princes moved away, talking quietly on matters of state. Malcolm Barrett stood before Catherine and shrugged helplessly.

"I don't know what to say, Cath. Except how did everything change so quickly? Just a few days ago . . . you and I were in love and planning our marriage. We had a life and a future, and the whole world made sense. We've loved each other since we were children, Cath!"

"Children grow up," said Catherine. "I never wanted to hurt you . . . but the world moved on, and left us behind."

"I know you love Richard," said Malcolm. "But what am I supposed to do?"

"Find someone else, and move on," said Catherine. "Be happy, Malcolm."

"The world moved on, the great wheel turned, and one of us got crushed underneath it," said Malcolm. "But I'm alive, and most of my people aren't . . . Be happy, Catherine."

He turned away abruptly, and walked over to join Richard and Christof, who were talking with Raven and Van Fleet.

"Oh, hello, Mal," said Christof quite casually. "I think I've arranged a lift home for us. These two sorcerer fellows seem convinced they can open a dimensional door and drop us off right back at Castle Midnight!"

"No problem at all," said Raven, equally casually. "Right in the Court . . ."

"If that's what you want," Van Fleet said quickly.

"Oh, I think so, yes," said Christof. "I have a lot to say to Father."

"Let's do it," said Malcolm. "There's nothing to detain us here."

The two sorcerers worked quickly together, with much muttering under the breath and many grandiose gestures, and a door appeared suddenly. A real door, solid and wooden, standing alone and entirely unsupported in the middle of the clearing. Christof strolled over, deliberately unimpressed, and pushed the door open. Through the opening they could all see King William, sitting alone on his throne, in an empty Court. The King looked around, startled, as Christof and the Champion strode through the door and into Castle Midnight's Court. The door slammed shut behind them and disappeared.

The Court seemed a much darker place without the magical lighting supplied by the Green Man. Presumably that had disappeared when he did. The old magic lighting hadn't returned either. The throne was now surrounded with dozens of candles, in old-fashioned brass candelabra, dripping wax everywhere. King William stared at his newly returned son, ignoring the Champion.

"What the hell are you doing back here, boy? What's been happening? I've heard nothing from Van Fleet, or the Green Man . . ."

"It's all done, Father," said Christof, strolling easily forward to stand before the throne. "The war is over."

"Nothing's over until I say it is!" snapped the King, leaning forward on his throne to glare at his son. "My army . . ."

"Your army's dead!" said the Champion, as he moved up to stand beside Christof. "A dragon burned them all alive."

"What?" said the King. "All my soldiers . . . No. No! It doesn't change anything! I'll send another army . . ."

"I don't think so," said Christof. "There's no point. I've talked with Richard, and we've agreed to give Peace another chance."

"Do you defy me, boy?" said the King.

"Why not?" said Christof. "Who are you? Just some mad old fool who sold this country's soul to the Green Man. Who turned out, in the end, to be the Demon Prince in disguise! So much for your famous wisdom, Father."

King William sat silently for a long moment, then sank slowly back into his throne, digesting what he'd been told. He looked more angry than anything else. Finally, he shook his head.

"It doesn't matter. I don't need the Green Man. And I can always raise another army. If you don't want to lead it, Christof, I'm sure I can find someone who will."

Christof turned to the Champion. "Leave us, Malcolm. Please. My father and I need to speak privately."

"You don't go anywhere except where I send you, Malcolm Barrett!" said the King. "You're my Champion!"

"Not anymore," said Malcolm. "You gave away everything that might have kept me here."

And then they all looked round sharply, as the Court's doors opened and the Steward, Elias Taggert, looked in.

"I have been waiting outside for some time," he said. "I heard raised voices, so . . ."

Malcolm strode over to join him. "What's been happening with the Unreal, Elias?"

"Some have come running home," said the Steward. "Much diminished and a lot less threatening. Shouldn't have much trouble with them. A lot of them are going back to sleep again, by their own will. We can cope with what's left." He looked at Christof, and then back at the Champion. "Is Prince Cameron really dead?"

"Yes," said Malcolm.

The Steward nodded sadly. "He should have stayed in his cave. He was safe there."

The two men left the Court, talking quietly, and the great doors closed behind them. Christof was left alone in the empty chamber with his father. They looked at each other coldly.

"You always wanted this war," said Christof. "Why?"

"Because of you," said the King. "You, and Cameron. My two useless sons. Neither of you worthy to sit on my throne. Cameron, because he was broken. You, because you're homosexual. Yes, I know. I've always known. The Royal line would have come to an end with either of you as King. An end to our line, and the Blood Magic that goes with it! There had to be an heir! And the only child I had who could produce one was Catherine. Who was bound to marry some outsider Royal. That's why I sent her out of Redhart; otherwise it would have been some foreign King who sat on my throne.

"I couldn't allow that. Not after so many Redhart Kings, of pure Blood, had held this throne. So I used Catherine as an agent for war. So that when we won I could make her my heir and she would be Queen of both countries. As a conqueror, she could have taken a Prince Consort instead of a King when she married. And then her son would be King of both Redhart and the Forest, and the Royal line could have continued unbroken."

"That's it?" said Christof. "That's what this has all been about?"

"Blood is all that really matters," said the King. "You should have worked that out by now, boy."

"And what about me, Father?" said Christof.

"I expected you to be killed in the fighting," said the King. "You never were as good with a sword as you liked to believe. The Broken Man would have gone back to his cave quite happily. And Catherine would have done what I told her to do. I had it all worked out . . . But no, you couldn't do anything right, could you, Christof? You've ruined everything!"

"You started a war," said Christof, "just because you wanted a grandson? Why, Father? You never cared for any of your children!"

He drew his sword and lunged forward, stabbing his father through the heart. The long blade punched right through King William's chest and out the back of the throne. For a moment neither man moved: Christof extended in full lunge, William's eyes wide with surprise. And then the King died, all the breath going out of him, and he suddenly seemed so much smaller. Christof pulled his sword free, a few inches at a time, breathing heavily. He shook a few drops of blood from the blade and sheathed the sword. He took his father by one arm and pulled him steadily forward, off the throne. William's body fell heavily onto the floor.

King Christof sat on his throne, made himself comfortable, and looked around his empty Court.

"What the hell," he said. "I can always adopt."

Outside Forest Castle, Richard and Catherine talked with Hawk and Fisher. Most people were already heading back into the Castle. The night was almost over, with dawn soon on its way. Raven and Van Fleet were talking with Roland the Headless Axeman and the witch Lily Peck. What remained of the fighting force from the Hero Academy stood patiently to one side, waiting to go home.

"What will you do now?" said Richard, looking from Hawk and Fisher to the Academy people and back again. "Will you be going back with them, to run the Academy?"

"Been there, done that," Fisher said briskly. "Time for something new."

"We've been talking," said Hawk. "Neither of us can stand the thought of the Demon Prince getting away with all this, going unpunished after everything he's done, and meant to do."

"We keep putting him down, and he keeps coming back," said Fisher. "To cause misery and destruction, and the ruin of all our dreams."

"Humanity will never get anywhere," said Hawk, "as long as the Demon Prince is free to return."

"But your father banished the Demon Prince!" said Catherine.

"There's always the possibility some well-meaning fool will summon him back," said Fisher. "He has to be stopped. Permanently."

"But how can you hope to do that?" said Richard. "I mean, as I understand it—and I'm perfectly ready to be told I don't—he's one of the Transient Beings. An idea, made flesh and bone. How can you kill an idea?"

"You can't," said Hawk. "But you can go where he comes from and make his life hell."

"There is another world," said Fisher. "Called Reverie. The Land of the Blue Moon. Where all the Transient Beings come from. A place of dreams and legends."

"We've been there before," said Hawk. "I'm pretty sure we can find our way back. And then we'll find the Demon Prince and stamp him into the ground, as many times as it takes, to punish him properly for what he's done. And then we will stand guard between that world and this. And nothing will get past us."

"But the Transient Beings are immortal!" said Richard. "You'd have to fight them forever!"

Fisher shrugged. "We like to keep busy."

"Can Raven and Van Fleet open a dimensional door for you?" said Catherine.

"Probably a bit beyond them," Hawk said kindly. "Though they'd never admit it. No, I have a way to get us there."

"You do?" said Fisher.

"Trust me," said Hawk. "Reverie . . . is the land of legends. I think we belong there now, more than here."

"Yeah," said Fisher. "We gave up being Rupert and Julia, but even Hawk and Fisher are legends now. That's what happens when you live as long as we have. We belong in Reverie."

"What about me?" said Chappie. "I'm a legend too, aren't I?"

They all looked round as he came limping forward, his great hide marred by claw marks and his grey fur caked with dried blood. But he still carried his head high, and his tail wagged happily as Hawk and Fisher hugged him and made much of him. Chappie took it all as his due.

"You're not going anywhere without me," he said firmly. "You'll always need me, to watch your back."

"Of course you're coming with us," said Hawk. "How could we leave the legendary immortal dog behind?"

"Right," said Fisher.

"Damn right," said Chappie.

Fisher looked across at the dragon, who immediately opened his huge golden eyes to look back at her.

"Well?" said Fisher. "Are you coming too? The legendary last dragon?"

"No," said the dragon. "Because I don't think I am the last. Ever since you woke me up, I've had this feeling . . . that I'm not alone in the world, after all."

Fisher squealed with delight, which made everyone else jump. She ran over to hug the dragon round his great neck and press him for details.

"Girls and their ponies," Hawk said solemnly.

He left Fisher to it, and walked away to talk with Lily Peck and Roland the Headless Axeman. Hawk was honestly shocked at how old and frail Lily looked.

"Don't worry about it, dear," she said calmly. "Easy come, easy go. I can always get some more youth. Years are just currency to a witch."

"You and Fisher aren't coming back with us, are you?" said Roland.

"No," said Hawk. "You don't need us anymore. Would you like to run the Academy?"

"No," said Roland, and Lily shook her head quickly.

"I've never been one for responsibility," she said. "Witches aren't, mostly."

"We'll just find somebody else," said Roland, "to be the next Hawk and Fisher. Someone worthy. And everything will go on as before. I will make it a point to choose someone who can annoy the Administrator properly, to keep him on his toes. No one will ever know there's been any change at all."

Hawk called Raven and Van Fleet forward, and had them open up a dimensional door back to the Millennium Oak. Hawk stood before the assembled force of the Hero Academy and bowed to them all.

"You have done great work here. Always remember, Fisher and I are so proud of every one of you."

And all the men and women of the Hawk and Fisher Memorial Academy drew their swords and thrust them into the air in salute. Hawk nodded in return. He didn't trust himself to say anything more.

"You trained us well," said Roland.

Prince Richard had finally found Peter Foster among the many wounded being treated by the Castle surgeons, on the open ground of the clearing. Peter lay on his back, staring up at the night sky, swathed heavily in bandages that were already soaked in blood. For the first time, Richard realised just how badly his old friend and bodyguard had been hurt by putting himself between his Prince and all harm. Richard knelt down beside Peter and tried to thank him, but he couldn't get the words out.

"It's all right," said Peter. "I know, I look a mess. But I can't die. Not while you still need looking after."

"I still haven't been able to find out what's happened to Clarence," said Richard. "Why he wasn't with us . . . He missed it all! Probably sleeping off a drunk somewhere."

"Yes," said Peter.

"He would have written some great songs about all this."

"Well," said Peter, "he would have written some songs . . ."

They laughed quietly together.

Not far away, Roland the Headless Axeman watched Richard talking with Peter. He would have liked to go and talk with them, but knew he couldn't.

"Goodbye, Richard, Peter, my old friends," he said quietly. "You were right; I made a much better warrior than a minstrel."

He went back to join the witch Lily Peck.

"Indulge an old woman's curiosity," she said, "while I am still an old woman. Where is your head?"

"I keep it in a box, under my bed," said Roland. "Never know when it might come in handy. I have to say, being killed was the best thing that ever happened to me."

"You're weird," said Lily Peck.

Raven and Van Fleet opened their dimensional door, and Roland the Headless Axeman and Lily Peck led the Academy force back to the Millennium Oak, in the Dutchy of Lancre. The door closed behind them, and they were gone.

Some time later, when everyone else had gone into the Forest Castle, Hawk and Fisher and Chappie the dog were left alone in the clearing. Even the dragon had flown away in search of his future. It was very quiet, with a cold wind blowing and the first light of the rising sun leaving ragged crimson streaks on the night sky.

"All right," said Fisher, "I'll bite. How are we going to get to Reverie without the sorcerers' help? Make a wish?"

Hawk grinned, and drew the Rainbow Sword. "I always knew I'd use this again."

He turned the sword over and thrust its point deep into the hard earth of the clearing. He called out silently, asking for one last miracle. Not for himself, but for all those he meant to protect from the Demon Prince and all his kind. There was a long pause, and then Chappie's head came up suddenly.

"Can you feel that? We're not alone in the night anymore. Something's coming . . ."

Hawk and Fisher didn't say anything. They could feel it too. Something ancient, primeval, vast, and powerful was heading their way from out of the dark. They looked up and the Rainbow came crashing down before them like a massive waterfall of all the colours in the world. Brilliant and beautiful, the Rainbow thundered down in colours so bright, so perfect, they were almost unbearable.

Rainbow's End.

As they stood there, dazzled and awed, they heard the sound of approaching footsteps. Strangely familiar footsteps. And out of the Rainbow there came a unicorn. Blindingly white, with a proud head and a tossing mane, and a single curlicue horn jutting from his forehead. The unicorn came forward to stand before Hawk.

"You didn't think I'd let you go without me, did you, Rupert?"

"Breeze!" said Hawk. "I never thought I'd see you again! They told me you were dead!"

"Legends can't die," said the unicorn. "Now, pick up your sword and follow me, Hawk and Fisher, and Chappie the dog. We have legendary work to do."

They all walked forward into the Rainbow, and it carried them away. The light snapped off, and the night returned. They were gone, all of them—into legend, where they belonged.

One last time.